Saucy Jack

Saucy Jack

Alias Jack the Ripper

From a Contemporary Manuscript

Neil W. Macdonald
K. Scot Macdonald

Kerrera House Press

Macdonald, K. Scot and Macdonald, Neil W.
Saucy Jack: Alias Jack the Ripper/K. Scot Macdonald and Neil W.
Macdonald—1st Edition
p.   cm.
ISBN 13: 978-0-9916653-9-6

Kerrera House Press
Culver City, CA
www.KerreraHousePress.com

First Printing: 2019
Printed in the United States of America

10 9 8 7 6 5 4 3 2 1

A manuscript from the papers of Tod Lachen,
a Scottish merchant trader and 1880s resident of London.

To Dad for starting,
to Amos for modelling,
and to all the Unfortunates of the world,
past, present and, unfortunately, future.

Other Books by K. Scot Macdonald

Non-Fiction

Fictional Deceptions:
Using Deception to Baffle, Surprise and Entertain Your Audience

Deadly Dance: The Chippendales Murders
(with Patrick MontesDeOca)

Propaganda and Information Warfare in the Twenty-first Century:
Altered Images and Deception Operations

Rolling the Iron Dice: Historical Analogies, Regional Contingencies and
Anglo-American Decisions to Use Military Force

Fiction

A Plunge Into Evil

The Shakespeare Drug

In Justice Found

Mouse's Dream

The Grizzly Extinction Plot (writing as Liam Shay)

Other Books by Neil W. Macdonald

The League That Lasted

1888

Part One: White's Row

Chapter One

4:30 p.m. Saturday, 25 February

Annie Millwood hurried along White's Row through a twilight realm of shadows cast by the brick buildings lining both sides of the narrow road. She tugged her shawl higher round her neck against the chill breeze and, late for a charwoman interview, walked faster. She could not be late.

Footsteps on the paving stones in front of her startled her out of her thoughts she looked up, eyes squinting against the tear-inducing wind. A gaunt man approached her. He took a clasp knife out of his pocket and, before she could react, stabbed her in the stomach. The force of the blow doubled her over. Gasping in shock, she straightened. He stabbed her again in the crease just above her left thigh. She screamed. He stabbed her again. The strength behind the knife thrusts pushed her back again and again. She twisted away to flee, but a hand like an iron hook caught her dress just below her neck. Another stab. Still screaming, she wrenched this way and that, struggling to escape, but the hand held her fast. Another stab and another and another.

Later that evening at the Whitechapel Workhouse Infirmary, a Metropolitan Police detective in a dark suit arrived at Annie's bedside. She failed to catch his name when he introduced himself far too quickly as he took off his black felt hat. He asked the groggy, 38-year-old, "I understand you had a spot of bother, Mrs. . .ah. . .Millwood."

"A man attacked me," Annie said, her wounds now cleaned, stitched and concealed by bandages. She winced and tried to clear her head of the pain and sensation of dislocation that blurred her senses. She lay gowned in an infirmary bed. "Where's my dress?"

"Ruined, I fear," the 'tec said matter of factly.

"No," Annie cried, the pain of worry now added to the multitude of pains wracking her body. "I need it."

"I'll require it for evidence, regardless of its state."

What would she wear to her interview, assuming the lady of the house would even see her now that she had missed her appointment? She only had one other dress and it was in such a state she would never dare wear it outside, let alone to an interview.

"Know the man who assaulted you, did you?"

"A stranger to me," Annie said, looking at the patients on either side of her on the ward who appeared far more interested in her story than in their own sorry conditions. Lowering her voice, she said, "Just walked up to me, took a clasp knife out of his pocket and started stabbing me like a fury."

"Description?" The 'tec took out a pad and a fountain pen.

"Thirties, slender, well-dressed for Spitalfields—not a labourer."

"A toff?"

"Maybe a down-on-his-luck toff."

"Anyone see this…attack?"

Annie noticed the pause and disliked the 'tec immensely. "I screamed, but no one came. Did seem to scare him off, though."

"Close by Commercial Street?"

"Number 8 White's Row; too far from the main street for anyone to hear me screams."

The detective eyed Annie. "You're certain you didn't know the man? Not even, shall we say, just briefly?"

When her body tightened in anger, Annie winced as her wounds stabbed her again. Ignoring the pain, she said, "I am the widow of an English soldier, Richard Millwood. I am no whore." She levered up off the bed. "I must be off." She had to send word to the lady to let her know what had happened and, God willing, arrange another interview. She hoped the lady would allow her a second chance; she desperately needed one or she would slide further into a life she devoutly prayed to avoid.

"Don't even let yourself think such rubbish," a nurse said, bustling up to Annie's bedside. "You're going to be here for some time, love, until you're all fine and dandy."

"I'll be fine and dandy if he finds the fiend who stabbed me, ruined me dress and made me miss my appointment."

"Sorry, Mrs.," the 'tec said, "but I fear that'll be well-nigh impossible."

"You must be able to do something."

The detective shook his head. "If you don't know 'em and there's no evidence at the scene and no witnesses, then there's little I can do."

"So a woman is attacked on the street and the police do nothing?"

"Far from it, but some villains are much harder to catch than others."

Part Two: George Yard Buildings

Chapter Two

A man, similar in stature, dress and general appearance to dozens of others surging around him, strode out of the Whitechapel Station onto the gas-lit high street just down from the five-story red-brick edifice of London Hospital. A cold wet storm had passed on, leaving only the chill air behind. It was, he thought, a fine clear evening for a hunt. So far his prowling on past nights had availed him little, except to learn to silence his quarry quickly and that he required a more effective weapon. Now, having learned, all he needed was suitable prey. It was a holiday thanks to the Bank Holiday Act of 1871 and thousands had caught trains to the coast despite the foul weather. The Great Eastern Railway reported 92,000 passengers for the day, down from 107,000 in 1887 due to the unseasonable 46-degree weather. Many, especially unfortunates, had remained in Whitechapel, lacking the desire or the means to escape its brick-and-cobblestone confines.

He was, at first glance, gaunt of appearance, but upon closer observation of his fluid stride and feline pace, far more athletic than a first glance would suppose. He was small of bone but more than adequate of muscle. Of average height, he was slender and in his early thirties, but many of the men in this mass of ordinary people marching in an unwatched parade were slender, of average height and in their early thirties.

Even if he had been a misshapen monster, he was in a crowd where giving a passerby a second glance was a definite rarity. This was Whitechapel/Spitalfields, which made him an insignificant presence, unlikely to be noticed, let alone remembered. Every other member of the crowd was intent on their personal destination, usually involving drink, grub or bed. Taking in the ever-changing night sky, the cloud- and soot-filtered moonlight on the grimy tenement brick walls or the features of their fellow humans were the last things on their minds.

Individuals in this detrained detachment were beginning to spread out by ones, twos, threes and such, heading out across London's East End: some to Whitechapel, a slum favoured with a name suggestive of purity and piety; some to Spitalfields, no worse a slum than Whitechapel, but with a name suggestive of poverty and perversity that made it appear a far more sinister place.

The man quickened his step as he walked west on Whitechapel Road. It was good to be back in the East End and, once again, to be hunting.

On another street nearby, a well-fed human let a 15-pound gray Russian Blue cat out for the evening. The cat could barely see George Akin Lusk's face past the human's protruding belly, but it was a benign face, the mouth framed by a profusion of whiskers no cat could ever grow.

"Out you go, old fellow," Lusk said, giving his cat fond strokes before shutting his back door.

George Lusk

A builder and contractor, on the Metropolitan Board of Works, and a vestryman of the parish of Mile End Old Town, George Lusk of No. 1 Alderney Road, Mile End, Whitechapel, was known throughout the East End as a man of importance—not that his cat knew any of this. His cat did know that his human was recognized and treated well as a kind of pride leader by people who frequented the local pubs. When, as a kitten, Lusky had wandered from pub to pub to be petted, fed and offered saucers of milk by publicans and patrons, he had acquired his name from one of George's many friends. Lusky, who hadn't ventured a step further from where Lusk had set him down on the top stair, had taken all this adulation in stride. He was a cat and cats, like time and tides, were independent of human infringements on their doings, let alone of any human feelings. Cats knew their place at the pinnacle of the hierarchy of all things.

Lusky surveyed the scene before him: too many people stirring. They would keep the mice and rats under cover. It was too early for any serious stalking.

He ran his rough tongue along his left foreleg for a time, sprucing up for the night. You never knew whether a lady cat might be out tonight. Finally, he padded down off the stairs and leisurely made his way up Alderney Road. His choice was far from random. Lusky was as cunning an individual as ever existed. He was heading for a maze of alleys and byways that would soon be deserted. This was where dustbins over-spilling their rotting contents could be found in profusion. It was amid these rotting piles of discarded debris that rodents roamed. It was always good to be in the East End and, once again, to be hunting.

2:26 a.m. Tuesday, 7 August

It was so easy, so simple and so sweet. He did not even have to lure her, let alone force her. She led him to the perfect secluded place for what she had in mind, which was so far from what he had in mind. The dark secluded landing was perfect.

In an instant he had his left hand on her throat, choking her. She screamed, but he silenced her before more than a single word escaped her lips. As he squeezed, her eyes bulged and her tongue slipped out from between her rouged lips. Her dark eyes lost focus. He lowered her to the landing, her legs feebly kicking under her dress even as her hands clenched and unclenched in spasms of oxygen-deprived desperation.

Panting now, he turned her body so she was on her back, her legs splayed apart and her arms falling at her sides. Grabbing her ankles, he spread her legs past shoulder-width and ripped her black jacket open. He knelt between her legs, wrenching her dark green skirt and brown petticoats up above her waist. His heart beats thundered through his heaving chest as he used the larger of the two knives he had brought—uncertain which would work best—to stab her breast. The knife made a pleasing slash, but it was too long and ungainly. Sliding the long knife into a pocket of his coat, he extracted a smaller blade from another pocket. For a moment it caught on the lining; next time he must bring a bag, especially if he wished to take home a memento.

He lifted the smaller knife and plunged it into the body beneath him, again and again and again. It was hard between his legs, pushing up and out like a steel rod against the inside of his checked pants. Gawd, he groaned, closing his eyes for a second. It had never felt like this…utter ecstasy! The tingling sensation in his piece of steel rose in a crescendo of exhilaration that exploded in a surge of orgasmic wetness in his pants. Writhing in an intoxicated bliss, his concentration internalized in absolute selfness, he swayed over her.

What was that? His head whipped around.

At the base of the stairs, in the wan yellow light from a street gas lamp, the glinting eyes of a gray cat stared up at him. Their eyes met for a moment before the Russian Blue, sensing not prey but another predator, loped out of sight in search of more appropriate feline prey or female company.

Entrance to George Yard Buildings in 1938

Waterside labourer John Saunders Reeves couldn't afford to pay for the Met's knocking-up service, whereby the constable on the local beat would wake him, so at 4:45 a.m. he was late for work as he hurried down the communal stairs from his lodging at No. 37 George Yard Buildings, Whitechapel. The stairwell was dark. The gas lights were turned off at 11 p.m. and dawn was more than an hour and half off, but it was light enough for him to stop short on the first-floor landing when the predawn light revealed the body of a woman lying on her back in a pool of some dark shining liquid. He tasted the iron smell of blood in his mouth as he swallowed hard at the sight. In the second before he bolted down the stairs in search of a Peeler, he noticed that no blood flowed from her mouth, her hands were clenched, and her clothes were disarranged and torn open down the front, leaving her legs spread wide, pale white and bare.

"When I returned with Mr. Reeves," the first police officer on the scene, Police Constable (PC) 226H Thomas Barrett, told Local Inspector Edmund Reid, Head of the Criminal Investigation Division (CID) for H Division (Whitechapel), Metropolitan Police, at 5:30 that morning, "her clothes were turned up as far as the center of the body, leaving the lower part of the body exposed. The legs were open and her position was suggestive in my mind, sir, that recent intimacy had taken place."

"Not the greatest of surprises given her likely profession," Reid said with a thin smile as he looked up at the younger man standing before the brick edifice of the George Yard Buildings. When Reid joined the force in 1872, he was the shortest man on the force at 5 foot 6 inches. He was also probably one of the bravest. An aeronaut, he made many balloon ascents and in 1877 had been the first man to descend with a parachute from 1,000 feet.

Local Inspector Edmund Reid in 1888

Inspector Ernest Ellisdon joined Reid, who now led the investigation, as he walked up the stairs toward the landing and said, "No blood on the stairs leading to or from the landing."

Reid nodded, having noted the same thing. The pair reached the landing, where the body lay.

"She was killed on the landing," Ellisdon said.

Reid nodded as he peered down at the woman's body. His eyes flicked over the scene, taking in much, noting every detail. Police surgeon Dr. Timothy Robert Killeen strode up the stairs to examine the body. After a brief exchange of pleasantries, Reid left the doctor to his work.

Lighting a cigar as he stood on the street, Reid ordered detectives to conduct a door-to-door canvass of the area. He looked up at George Yard Buildings, which had been built after slums on the site were demolished in 1875. They were designed as a model lodging house and, with 48 residences, Reid thought someone must have seen or heard something last night.

Within the hour, the canvass found one Francis Hewitt, superintendent of the dwellings, who lived with his wife just 12 feet from the murder site.

"We never heard a cry," Hewitt told Reid as he spoke to them at their peeling front door.

"Except for that cry of 'murder,'" Mrs. Amy Hewitt said as she stood just behind her husband.

Reid's attention focused on the middle-aged woman; a witness?

"But that was early in the evening," she said as her eyes narrowed in concentration.

"Any sense of where it came from?" Reid asked. People often erred about times, especially in the sleep-filled hours of the night.

Mrs. Hewitt glanced at her husband, then said, "It echoed, so it was 'ard to tell, but it didn't seem to come from the landing."

A silence followed as Reid gave the couple an encouraging look and waited to hear how the Hewitts responded to cries of 'murder' in the middle of the night.

"It is a rather rough area," Mr. Hewitt said, "so cries of 'murder' are of a frequent, if not nightly, occurrence in the district."

Once back out onto George Yard, just down from Wentworth Street, Reid reviewed whether he had done everything he should do at the scene.

"Might have someone to narrow down the time of death, sir," Ellisdon said, consulting his notes as he emerged from the red-brick archway of the George Yard Buildings. "Joseph, a carman, and Elizabeth, who works at a match factory, last name Mahoney, a young married couple, live here at No. 47. At 1:40 this morning they arrived home from their Bank Holiday weekend away. They went up to their room, but Elizabeth went out to get food for a late supper. She returned at about 1:50, having got provisions from a chandler's shop on Thrawl Street. She and her husband ate and went to bed."

"So the body wasn't there at 1:50."

"She would have tripped over it, sir."

"Or at least seen something lying there, even with the gas jets off."

By mid-morning the canvass was complete and Reid had reports from a dozen detectives; not one pointing at a suspect. As Reid left the scene, sightseers were already crowding around the entrance to the stairwell, eager to see where a murder had occurred and peer at the blood-stained flagstones on the landing.

Reid took an official four-wheeler pulled by a fine pair of bays over to the workhouse infirmary in Old Montague Street. With murder rare in Whitechapel, the district lacked a dedicated mortuary of its own and most of the bodies brought to the infirmary were victims of accidents, not man. In the shed that served as a mortuary Reid found Dr. Killeen as the police surgeon was finishing his post-mortem exam. Reid ran a stubby hand over his dark beard and moustache as he took in the body of the plump, middle-aged victim on one of the infirmary's tables. She had dark hair, a dark complexion and looked a tad shorter than he was; maybe 5 foot 3 inches.

"Stabbed 39 times," Dr. Killeen said with a sigh.

"Blighter wanted to make bloody sure she was dead," Reid said. "When?"

"Dead about three hours from when I first examined her, so about 2:30 a.m."

Reid pulled a note pad from his suit jacket pocket and a sheet of paper with it. He replaced the sheet of paper; a play bill for one of the amateur theatricals for which he was locally known.

"Twenty-two stab wounds in the trunk," Killeen said as Reid took notes. "Left lung five penetrations, right lung two, heart one, liver five, spleen two, stomach six."

"God in Heaven," Reid muttered, thinking maybe he should have kept his old job as a pastry chef. The only stab wounds in the kitchen tended to be self-inflicted and far from fatal.

"Lower part of the body: one stab wound, three inches in length and one inch in depth. Found a great deal of blood between her legs. Death was due to hemorrhage and loss of blood, although I did find blood between her scalp and the bone, suggesting strangulation, especially since the head and face are swollen and disfigured."

Reid eyed the brutalized face and profusion of stab wounds on the naked body. "What did he use?"

"Two different weapons, it appears. Most of the wounds were inflicted by an ordinary knife, but one wound on the breast—here, see, this large one—looks more like some form of dagger was used."

"Was she...ah...interfered with?"

Killeen shook his head about a possible sexual assault as he started to wash the blood off his hands in a battered wood bucket.

"Might there be any marks on her killer?" Reid asked, hoping for something with which to identify the murderer.

"No evidence of a struggle. Beyond that, one wound might have been made by a left-handed person, but the rest appear to have been inflicted by a right-hander."

"Ambidextrous?"

"Possibly."

"Thank you, Doctor." Reid tried to keep the resignation out of his voice; nothing here or at the scene to indicate a motive, let alone the identity of the murderer.

"Maybe someone saw or heard something," Killeen said.

"Let us hope."

Later that morning at the Leman Street Police Station, H Division headquarters, Reid and Ellisdon reviewed the reports from the canvass, search and post-mortem. The windows to Reid's office were open, letting in the August heat as the temperature touched 80 in stark contrast to the cold previous night. The open windows did little to dispel the smoke from Reid's cigar, which swirled about the room.

"Constable Thomas Barrett, who was first on the scene," Ellisdon reported, "saw a soldier loitering near George Yard at about 2 a.m., just before Dr. Killeen's estimated time of death of 2:30. Barrett challenged the man for being out so late. The soldier said he was waiting for a chum who had gone with a girl."

"Description?"

Ellisdon read from his notes, "A private of the Grenadier Guards with one good conduct badge, no medals. Aged 22 to 26, 5 foot 9 or 10 inches, fair complexion and dark hair. Also a small dark-brown moustache turned up at the ends."

"Excellent work. A definite lead, a most definite lead."

Wasting no time, Reid took Constable Barrett to the Tower of London that afternoon. Admitted by the guard, the police officers were escorted to the guardhouse past the ravens, which strutted across Tower Green as if they owned the place—and maybe they did, since it was foretold that if they left their departure would signal the fall of the monarchy. In the stone-walled guardhouse, Reid explained the reason for their visit. The garrison's Sergeant-Major then showed them several soldiers in the guardroom held for infractions over the Bank Holiday weekend.

Reid looked at Barrett, who shook his head.

"What about men on leave or absent over the weekend?" Reid asked.

The Sergeant-Major in his scarlet jacket and black pants said, "To arrange that, sir, will take some time."

Wednesday, 8 August

To the Sergeant-Major, 'some time' was less than 24 hours.

Reid and Barrett stood just inside the sergeants' mess as the Sergeant-Major herded, yelled and cursed his men into formation on the Tower's Inner Ward before the imposing three-story magnificence of Waterloo Block.

With his theatrical background and knowledge of the power of the tiniest actions, Reid warned Barrett, "Be careful. Every man's eyes will be watching you. A great deal depends on you picking out the right man and no other."

Barrett nodded as best he could with his uniform's leather stock around his neck.

The Sergeant-Major strode in and, reporting that all the Guardsmen were mustered, led the pair out into the bright August sunlight. Deciding to give the constable as much time and space as possible, Reid stood off to one side with the Sergeant-Major. Sweat began to bead under Reid's collar, vest, suit jacket and shirt as Barrett moved along each row of scarlet-coated men, peering at each in turn, like an especially picky customer.

Reid hoped Barrett would find the man. The newspapers were trumpeting the viciousness and ferocity of the attack far and wide with demands for the culprit to be apprehended posthaste and Barrett was Reid's only lead.

Amidst the rows of red-coats, the blue swallow-coated Barrett finally stopped in front of a man in the middle of a row. Barrett placed his hand on the soldier's shoulder: a private.

Barrett marched back to Reid, the hint of a satisfied smile touching either end of his lips. "I found the man."

"Are you certain?" Reid asked, glancing over at the chosen man's chest, from which hung medals. "Make certain, Constable."

Barrett hesitated, turned and strode back down the ranks of soldiers. He stopped before a private and placed his hand on his shoulder.

Reid muttered a curse. Barrett returned to where Reid stood.

"It's a bloody different man," Reid said, furious. "How did you come to pick out two men?"

"The man I saw in George Yard had no medals and the first man I picked had medals, so it couldn't be him."

Keeping his anger in check, Reid asked the Sergeant-Major to kindly escort both suspects to the orderly room. Once inside, Reid glanced at Barrett as the policemen stood in the spartan, but blissfully cool stone room with the Sergeant-Major and the two chosen men.

"Sir," Barrett told Reid, "I think I made a mistake picking out the man with medals."

"Are you certain?"

"Certain, sir."

Fuming, Reid asked the Sergeant-Major to dismiss the be-medaled private.

The remaining suspect turned out to be Private John Leary. After hearing Barrett's story, Private Leary told Reid, "I was not the man he saw."

Leary explained that he had been on leave on the Bank Holiday weekend with a Private Law. They visited Brixton south of the Thames and drank until the pubs closed. Leary went to the rear of a pub to relieve himself and when he returned Law had disappeared, so he set off alone through Battersea before crossing the river into Chelsea. He wandered west through Westminster, past Charing Cross and finally into the Strand. There, by chance, he met Law again at 4:30 a.m. Together they walked through the City to Billingsgate between London Bridge and the new Tower Bridge, which was under construction. In Billingsgate they had another drink and returned to barracks at 6 a.m.

Reid asked the Sergeant-Major to bring in Private Law.

"Remain silent," Reid warned Leary.

The Sergeant-Major returned with Private Law, who snapped to attention, stamping his black boots on the flagstone floor.

Reid asked him, "Can you tell me about your activities on the Bank Holiday weekend?"

Law's statement corroborated Leary's in every particular.

"Release them both," Reid told the Sergeant-Major in disgust. Reid felt as if he was living in one of the farces his amateur theatrics troupe put on. He liked such things far better when he was on stage than in real life.

Fuming, Reid followed the Sergeant-Major toward the main Tower gates with a downcast Constable Barrett following along behind like a chastened child.

At the gate, the pair of sentries in their tall black bearskin hats, red coats with broad white leather belts and black trousers with a red vertical stripe on the outside of each leg, were detaining a corporal.

"Report," the Sergeant-Major ordered one of the sentries.

"Corporal Benjamin just returned to post, Sergeant-Major. Bin absent without leave since Monday."

Reid stopped, his hopes rising. The man had been missing the night of the murder and, Reid saw, a bayonet hung from his white leather belt. Reid said, "Sergeant-Major, if I may, I'd like a word with the corporal."

Back in the orderly room once again, Reid and Barrett inspected Corporal Benjamin's bayonet and uniform for blood.

Barrett concluded, "Not a spot, sir."

Reid nodded in agreement, having checked the constable's work. "Can you please explain your whereabouts on the Bank Holiday weekend?" Reid asked the corporal, who stood at attention before him.

"Spent the night of the holiday with my father, sir. He's landlord of the Canbury Arms in Kingston-upon-Thames."

At Reid's direction, and much to his chagrin, the corporal's alibi was confirmed by dinnertime.

As the list of cleared suspects lengthened, Reid sought to identify the victim. In most murder cases the victim knew their killer, so knowing the name of the victim led to the most promising suspects. But during the canvass, no one in George Yard Buildings recognized her.

That evening, exhausted from his emotional day of ups and downs as he thought he had a solid lead on the murderer, then didn't, then did, and then didn't again, Reid bought an *Illustrated Police News* on the way home from a newsagent. A headline boldly reported "A Whitechapel Horror" above six drawings and more than a column of fine print about the murder. As he walked along Leman Street past trampers trudging their way back to doss houses after another futile day looking for work, Reid read snippets of the article that described the ferociousness of the attack and the spreading unease among the local citizenry as they realized that a lunatic murderer was loose in their city.

That night seventy working men, supplemented by students from Toynbee Hall, the Commercial Street charity founded by the Reverend Samuel Barnett and his wife Henrietta, met to decry the lack of police presence in Whitechapel/Spitalfields and to form the St. Jude's Vigilance Committee. Far from satisfied with just talk, the committee appointed a dozen men to patrol the streets between 11 p.m. and 1 a.m. to keep the citizenry safe from the homicidal maniac roaming their streets. When he heard, Reid wondered how a dozen civilians were going to stop a killer when thousands of police had failed.

Thursday, 9 August

"I was with that girl who got herself killed the other night in George Yard Buildings," a tall, masculine-looking prostitute told the desk sergeant at the busy Commercial Street Police Station mid-morning.

He looked up at her alcohol-reddened face and from long and varied experience gauged her level of intoxication: low.

"Your name, Mrs.?" he asked, drawing a witness statement form toward him across his high wood desk.

"Mary Ann Connelly."

"Naught," a constable yelled from across the entry hall. "She's known from Wapping to Bethnal Green as Pearly Poll."

Inspector Reid interviewed Pearly Poll in one of the narrow interview rooms on the station's second floor. She said that for several months she had known the victim as Emma.

"Surname?" Reid asked, smoking a cigar as a constable took notes.

Pearly Poll shrugged and shook her head.

Under Reid's questioning, Pearly Poll told her story. On the night of 6 August, she and Emma had been with two soldiers drinking their way through damp, cold Whitechapel from 10 to 11:45. The soldiers were guardsmen: a corporal and a private. At 11:45, Poll took her customer, the corporal, up Angel Alley, while Emma and the private went up into George Yard. About 30 or 40 minutes later, Poll and her corporal separated at the corner of George Yard. He set off "Aldgate way" and she walked towards Whitechapel.

Reid asked, "Did you hear anything amiss?"

"There was a quarrel about money, but not with Emma. We parted all right and with no bad words; indeed, we were all good friends."

When he heard the news, Ellisdon said, "Maybe we've found our man."

Reid shook his head. "The private was with the victim near midnight. Dr. Killeen estimates the time of death at about 2:30, so the private is probably at most a witness, not the murderer."

"Might have seen her next customer—the killer."

Reid feared the killer might be several customers down Emma's roll call that night, but the private was a start. "Back to the Tower."

"When?"

"Poll said she would know both men and agreed to appear for an identity parade at the Tower tomorrow."

Coroner Wynne E. Baxter

Wynne E. Baxter, Coroner for the South Eastern District of Middlesex, was holidaying in the long August days of Scandinavia, so George Collier, the deputy coroner, was in charge of the afternoon's inquest. In the library of the Working Lad's Institute, Whitechapel Road, royal portraits looked down as Reid and Dr. Killeen sat on either side of Collier on a raised wood platform. Representatives of the press sat in the reporters' box. The general public was excluded, but given the sensational press coverage of the murder, a large number of jurymen, 20 in all, appeared early, eager and ready to serve. The possibility of inside information about a murder tended to bring out the civic-mindedness in even the most uncivic of men.

After the jury was sworn in, Reid sat through a stream of witnesses. Elizabeth Mahoney, the married match-stick worker, appeared in a simple dark dress and spoke so quietly Collier had to ask her to stand next to the jury so they could hear her. A young, beardless and intelligent looking Alfred George Crow was a licensed cab-driver who rented lodging at No. 35 George Yard Buildings. He said he got home on 7 August at 3:30 a.m.

"I saw someone lying in the dark on the first-floor landing," he testified. "Could have been alive or dead."

"You just walked past?" Collier asked.

"Many a time vagrants sleep in the stairwell," Crow said in defense of his apparent callousness. "I passed by and went up to bed." He heard nothing the rest of the night.

Next was the poor man who found the body, John Reeves. Short and with ear-rings, he wore a black overcoat and corduroy trousers. His slight dark beard and moustache made his face seem even paler than it probably was, although, Reid thought, maybe the memory of finding the body drained his face of the majority of its usual colour. Having already read Reeve's statement, Reid barely listened as the labourer went over his discovery of the body. Even so, Reid half-listened; Reeves might add something important he had forgotten to put in his statement. Reeves didn't.

Reid testified next. He had to admit he was making little headway in identifying the victim—or maybe he was making too much headway.

"Three women have identified the body," he told the jury, "all by different names."

Given the uncertainties involved, Reid requested an adjournment of two weeks to allow for further investigation, which Collier granted. Collier concluded the day's proceedings by saying, "The man must have been a perfect savage to inflict such a number of wounds on a defenseless woman in such a way. It was one of the most brutal crimes that had occurred for some years…almost beyond belief."

Friday, 10 August

Reid paced the entry hall of the three-story Commercial Street Police Station. Every time someone entered through the oak doors, he looked over and, when he saw it wasn't the woman he required, his anger increased. Where the bloody hell is she?

"Sorry, sir, we can't find Pearly Poll," Ellisdon rushed in to report. "We have her description out to every constable and detective in the district. We'll find her."

"But not today," Reid said, striding toward the stairs to return to his office. "Send a constable to give the Sergeant-Major at the Tower my regrets, but there'll be no parade today. What the hell is she playing at? This is a murder investigation, not opening night at some bloody 20-seat West County theatre."

Monday, 13 August

Pearly Poll had had something more important to do than identify murderers, at least to her; she had gone to visit a cousin in Drury Lane. When she explained her rationale, Reid showed his acting ability by keeping his anger well hidden. He needed her help, such as it was, to find his murderer.

At 11 a.m. he was back in another guard room in the Tower waiting with Pearly Poll while the Sergeant-Major paraded his Grenadier Guardsman out of sight of the public. Even though it was a weekday, many tourists from England, the Empire and what was left of beyond, were touring the Norman stronghold. Reid prayed this parade would be more productive than the last one; it could hardly be any less productive.

Reid was soon once again sweating under the sun on the Inner Ward watching the scene play out before him with the same supporting cast, but a different lead. Pearly Poll paraded before the lines of guardsmen, inspecting this or that soldier, looking as if she was selecting a future husband, not looking for a possible murderer. She wore what Reid guessed was her finest long, box-pleated skirt that hung straight with an apron drape around her waist and a tight high-necked wool sweater. She must have been swimming is sweat, Reid thought as he wiped his brow with a red handkerchief. She promenaded back and forth.

"She's enjoying this," Reid muttered. He sweated, lit a cigar and wished she would just identify the soldier she had seen with the victim and drop the curtain on the show.

On her third time through the ranks, Reid strode over, almost biting through his cigar, and caught her eye as she neared the end of a scarlet row. "Can you see either of the men you were with?"

Pearly Poll placed her hands on her broad hips, glanced at the soldiers with the air of an inspecting general, and shook her head.

"Can you identify anyone?"

"He ain't here."

Biting back his disappointment, Reid nodded and, thanking the Sergeant-Major, told him he could dismiss his men.

As the men returned to their duties, Pearly Poll peered at a soldier who strode past her. "They don't look quite right," she mused.

Reid noticed a redness begin to colour the Sergeant-Major's face above his moustache. Reid had no doubt this was a new experience for the NCO; an unfortunate expressing a lack of perfection in the appearance of his men.

"I know," Pearly Poll said, staring at the nearest passing soldier.

Reid stared up at her in anticipation. Had she finally found his man?

"The soldiers that night had white bands round their caps."

Reid frowned; they had the wrong bloody regiment.

"Coldstream Guards, sir," the Sergeant-Major of the Grenadier Guards said, joy seeping into his voice as he happily transferred the search for the killer to the oldest regiment in the regular army—and a detested rival.

Tuesday, 14 August

Reid finally got his identification—at least of the victim. Henry Samuel Tabram of 6 River Terrace, East Greenwich, a foreman packer at a furniture warehouse, saw the victim's name in a newspaper printed as Tabram—one of the many possible names that had been offered up—and identified the body as that of his wife Martha.

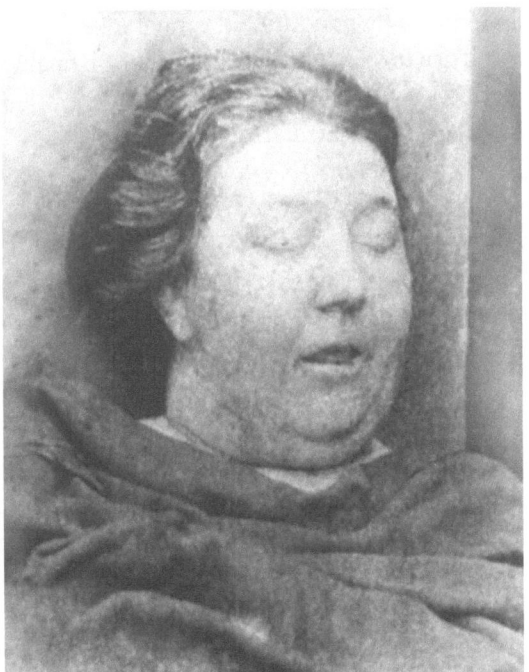

Martha Tabram

As Ellisdon brought in Henry Tabram, Reid ordered his detectives to hunt down everything they could find about Martha Tabram. His orders issued, Reid strode past rooms used by bachelor constables who lived at the station and went upstairs to an interview room where Henry Tabram awaited him.

"We married Christmas Day 1869," Martha's estranged husband said. "We'd been living together, but it felt right. We had two boys, born in '71 and '72. Fine sons, but she was a drinker. I had to leave about 13 year ago." Reid kept his face expressionless without a hint of judgement, but Tabram added, "I did support her, I did; 12 shillings a week. Least 'til she took up with another man."

"Name?" Reid asked, fountain pen poised above a witness form.

"Henry Turner, a carpenter. They was together 12 year or so, I heard."

Later that day an inspector brought Turner into one of the interview rooms just down the hall from Reid's office.

When Reid asked about Martha, the broad-shouldered Turner said, "If I gave her any money she generally spent it on drink. In fact, it was always drink. At times she stayed out all night and when she was drunk, she sometimes had fits and had to go to hospital."

While a constable took notes, Reid waited for more. Long ago he had mastered patience.

"This year I was out of work—the depression and all—so me and Martha made do as hawkers, selling trinkets and such on the streets."

A couple sliding into depravation, Reid thought.

"Her drinking," Turner said, shaking his head. "I finally had to leave her, 'bout three week ago."

"Was that the last time you saw her?"

Turner thought for a moment. "No, 'twas 4 August. I met her at her lodging house."

"Where?"

"19 George Street, Spitalfields. She didn't have a penny to her name, so I gave her 1s. 6d. to buy some stock so she could earn a few ha'pence." He rubbed his red-veined nose with a calloused hand and added, "Never saw her alive again."

Inspector Ellisdon reported to Reid the results of the investigation into Martha Tabram's life as Reid wiped a spot of soot off a tumbler and poured some apple cider from a jug. Even with all the windows open, his office was stifling in the August heat.

"She was 39 years old and a prostitute," Ellisdon said. "She told a landlady her real name was Staples or Stapleton, but we learned her real name was Martha White, born 10 May 1849, in Southwark. One of five children. When she was 16, her father died suddenly and unexpectedly at the age of 59. Her parents had separated."

"Anything more recent?" Reid asked. The cause of her murder was unlikely to be found in the 1860s.

"She left a previous lodging without paying the rent."

"Turner said she didn't have a pence to her name when he saw her on the 4th."

"She did have some goodness in her; the key to Martha's room—the one she didn't pay for—mysteriously turned up. Landlady said Martha must have secretly returned it."

"Goodness is no protection against murder," Reid said and, liking it, jotted it down in case he wanted to use it in one of his amateur theatricals.

Wednesday, 15 August

This time it was the turn of Her Majesty's Coldstream Guards to parade for Pearly Poll. Reid stood in front of the impossibly long, three-story Wellington Barracks, Westminster, in tree-lined Birdcage Walks. Reid could just see Buckingham Palace 300 yards away through the London Plane trees.

"Parade of all corporals and privates of the regiment absent or on leave on the Bank Holiday weekend last ready for inspection, sir," a corporal told the lanky captain who was escorting Reid and Pearly Poll.

"Shall we proceed?" the captain asked, as if inviting them to high tea with the colonel of the regiment.

The scene at the Tower was repeated with Pearly Poll enjoying it just as much, Reid thought. At least this time she identified two men who she said were her and "Emma's" corporal and private.

"Are you certain?" Reid asked, memories of Constable Barrett still far too fresh in his mind.

"As certain as me name."

Reid wondered how certain she was of that given he had already learned she had used multiple names throughout her life.

In the guardhouse, Reid found that the 'corporal' was actually a private.

"He has three good conduct badges," the captain told Reid and, it turned out, an alibi. Private George was with his wife at 120 Hammersmith Road from 8 p.m. 6 August to 6 the following morning.

Reid turned to the second man; the 'private' Pearly Poll had identified. At least he was a private. "Name?"

"Private Skipper, sir. I was in barracks all that night, sir. Can ask me mates; three of 'em. We played faro. . .I mean, cribbage 'til three or four, sir. No gambling in barracks, sir."

The captain soon verified Private Skipper's presence in the barracks the night of the murder. By sunset, an inspector had verified Private George's alibi. As Reid walked to the train station that evening, he lamented that Pearly Poll had drunk so much the night of the murder, making her identifications about as useful as a free ham to an orthodox Jew. He prayed his men would find the soldier witness to the final few hours of Martha Tabram's life—without him, the investigation appeared as dead as poor Martha.

Thursday, 23 August

Collier reopened the inquest. Pearly Poll testified, but her distrust of authority shone through as she refused to speak directly to the jury. Instead, she testified in her quietest voice with an officer repeating every word she said loud enough for all to hear. Reid then admitted that his investigation had made little progress. Surprising no one, the jury returned a unanimous verdict of willful murder against some person or persons unknown.

Reid sat in his front parlor that night, a fire spitting sparks to ward off the unseasonably cold night air. As he scanned *The Times*, he glanced at an article about women being given the vote in certain local elections and the recent Oaths Act, which allowed members of parliament to swear an oath to the sovereign rather than to God, allowing atheists to sit in Parliament. What next, allow the colonies to elect members to Parliament? Less than interested in such social-political news, Reid scanned the paper for his true interests: the theatre and any aerialist news. *The Mikado,* three years on, was playing at a Soho theatre, but a new play, *It's Only Around the Corner,* by a young writer, Henry Arthur Jones, caught his interest. He had heard excellent things about Jones. It was said he was destined for greatness, maybe even immortality.

As Reid skimmed the paper, his mind wandered into the labyrinth of the Tabram case. The newspapers were focused like a spotlight on the use of a bayonet in the murder and the soldier last seen with Martha. Even so, given the time when she was seen with the soldier, 11:45 p.m., and the time of death, about 2:30 a.m., there was nothing to suggest the soldier had killed her or even been a witness. It was beyond reason to suppose Martha had spent almost three hours with the soldier in the yard. Their business could not have taken more than five or ten minutes, Reid thought, even for a young virile Guardsman. The timing meant Martha had more than ample time to finish with the soldier and then go out and find one, two or even more customers before she met her demise. There was also no solid evidence at all that the murder weapon was a bayonet. In any case, if a bayonet was used, it hardly pointed an unerring finger of guilt at a soldier. Bayonets were sold in dozens of shops throughout the East End. Beyond those few clues and non-clues, Dr. Killeen thought the murderer was right handed, but that belief didn't narrow the suspects down much more than the conclusion that Martha was murdered by a man. How many right-handed men lived in Whitechapel/Spitalfields, let alone the greater East End? Reid needed a witness, a motive or a clue, but none appeared to exist. Luckily, by God's good grace, although theft and assault were common in the East End, murder was a rarity. There would probably not be another murder for months.

Part Three: Buck's Row

Chapter Three

In the streets of Whitechapel the night vapors crept into the shadowy nooks and crannies. The damp darkness cloaking the doorways and alleys hid much of the decrepit tawdriness of the tenements, the doss houses and the thousand and one structures that housed the industrial poor. The few gas lamps sputtered, casting scant illumination into the surrounding darkness. Sound, uninhibited by the coming of night, broke the visual stillness, shocking the senses with a strange out-of-nowhereness. A street tart laughed someplace in the gloom. It was the coarse garuff of the undisciplined tongue. The tinkle of glasses and the gin-stimulated talk in a dozen Crown and Anchors seeped through the solitude. Silhouetted people in the lit windows of the pubs revealed the crowded interiors, full of those staying in out of the uncommonly cold August night. It had "snowed" in July across much of England—or so the government labelled what most people called heavy sleet—and then in August London had experienced brief unseasonably hot weather, but the heat had passed and the last day of August heralded a cold September. Grotesque shadow forms were cast street-ward from the open doorways of the waterside slaughterhouses where workers toiled at their grim vocation through the night. The squeals and grunts of the dying animals, the bizarre, stretched-out shadows and sweat-stained faces of the slaughtermen blended the bloodied floors and dirty brick walls into a nightmare portrait of a deathly inferno. A pair of dock fires tinged the night sky red, adding a bloody skein to the otherworldly slaughterhouse scenes.

Mary Ann Nichols staggered along beside a grocer's wall, leaning against a latticed window for support. Her companion and fellow unfortunate, Emily Holland, who had only just met her by chance in the gloom, suggested they go to a common lodging house for the night. Mary opposed the suggestion. Emily whined, pleading with hands and voice, "I kin get you a bed at my place, Mary. Old Forgarty will let you in."

Ever independent, Mary's gray eyes sparkled as she retorted, "No. I've had me doss money three times today and I've spent it each time. Forgarty won't let me in."

"But—"

"But nuttin'. I must make me money," Mary said, walking off unsteadily.

Shrugging her shoulders in alcohol-tinged disgust, Emily turned and was about to start up Osborne Street when Mary shouted, "I'll soon get my doss money. See what a jolly bonnet I've got now."

She tipped a new bonnet she had taken from her bag and placed on her head at a ridiculously rakish angle. She strutted, laughed and disappeared into the gloom of Whitechapel Road. With her high cheekbones and youthful appearance, Emily thought Mary looked 35, not five days past her 43rd birthday, which Mary had recently divulged during a drinking bout. The clock at Whitechapel Church struck half-past two, its chimes echoing through the misty night air with a crisp clarity that seemed incongruous in the gloomy brick canyons of dark-time Whitechapel.

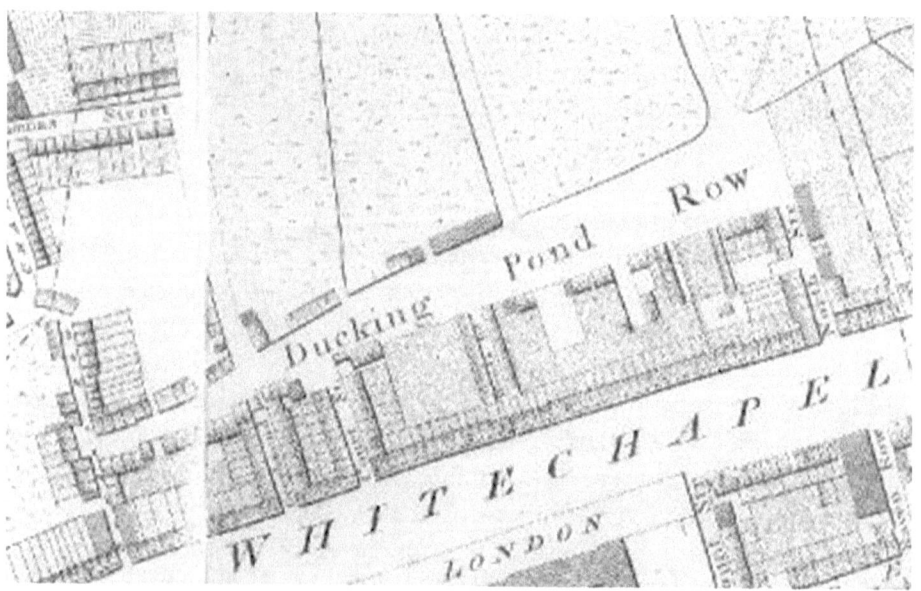

1799 map of Buck's Row, then called Ducking Pond Row

Lusky stopped mid-step to sniff the air. Prey! His muscles tightened as he lowered his hind end silently to the paving stones. He remained motionless except for his tail, which twitched in anticipation. His fur was out to catch the scents in the air, even as he closed his eyes for a moment to better hear the sound of the mouse searching for its morsels of food. Hearing the sound of prey amidst all the other noises of the night, Lusky swiveled his head and opened his eyes to scrutinize the young scavenging mouse that was witlessly working her way along the side of an overspill from a dustbin. The cat's primal instinct dominated his whole being. He checked his angle of attack to ensure nothing would impede his strike; all clear. Lusky moved ever so slowly forward, each paw-step placed in perfect position and with silent orderliness, each movement coming when the mouse's attention was turned from her stalker's direction. Slowly, slowly, slowly forward. The distance narrowed. Lusk's cat readied for his explosive charge.

At 3:15 a.m., PC 96 John Thain of the recently created J Division (Bethnal Green) patrolled his beat along Brady Street, checking every door to make certain it was secure. If a door was found unlocked, a written explanation was required from the previous constable on the beat as to why he had not found the door unlocked. Thain didn't want to get a reputation for putting other constables in the soup, so if he found an unlocked door, he would just lock it himself, assuming the door had a lock.

Thain stopped to rub his left leg. He had bruised it when he shinnied up a lamp pole to place a flask next to the gas lamp so could enjoy a warm drink later. His sergeant had shown him the trick and most of the constables he knew kept a warm drink handy in a similar fashion. A dash of warm spirit was worth a sore leg any night, but especially on such a cold night. The mercury indicated 46 degrees. Moving on, he checked another door and passed the entrance to Buck's Row; as quiet as a tomb.

County Cork-born John Neil, PC 97 of J Division, passed a slaughterhouse on Winthrop Street, where he saw horse-slaughterers Harry Tompkins, Charles Britton and James Mumford sweating, grunting and cursing at their work. Neil passed on in his blue swallow-tail coat with the high stand-up collar bearing his divisional number and tall chimney-pot hat. Tonight the heavy wool uniform kept him warm, although on many a summer night he had been awash in a sea of sweat by the end of his shift. At least now he did not have to wear the uniform off duty, as constables had been required to do until 1870 to avoid charges of appearing to be spying on civilians, although Mary and his daughters, Henrietta and Julia, had loved seeing him in his uniform.

Neil twisted his neck to adjust the leather stock which, it seemed, served only to give him a pain in the neck. As he walked into Buck's Row, he debated just not wearing the stock; few constables did. Garroting was a common means of attack, but how great were the chances of being garroted? Narrow, cobblestoned Buck's Row was ill lit, shadow-filled and gloomy. Neil knew it was a favoured spot for prostitutes, but at the moment it was devoid of unfortunates, clients or anyone else. Neil took a moment to reshape his long light-coloured mustache as he hoped his daughters were sleeping well under God's good grace. After 13 years on the force, Mary was used to his nightly absences, but he still wished he was at home nights, especially when nothing untoward was happening on his beat and the long hours of nightly boredom stretched seemingly endlessly before him.

PC John Neil

It happened almost instantaneously. At 3:30 a.m. he lunged from the black recess of the gate on Buck's Row, grabbed her from behind with his right hand, clenching her throat like a noose, thrusting her jaw up and back. As she struggled for air, he held on tight, using all the strength in his hand, impassively waiting as she struggled. A moment after she went limp, he lowered her to the pavement. Kneeling at her head, he used his new knife to slice through her throat in two quick left-to-right sweeps of his right hand. Then he got down to enjoying himself. Soon, writhing in an intoxicated bliss, his concentration internalized in absolute selfness, he swayed over her.

What was that? Something shattered his chain of delight, whipping his attention outward. Footsteps! He was on his feet in an instant and off, heading away from the oncoming thuds of shoe on stone. He hurried along the more shadowed side of 20-foot wide Buck's Row towards the Board School where the narrow tunnel of the Row turned into a three-times wider expanse of roadway. It was here when he had almost reached the corner of the school that the Bard's outrageous fortune brought him not exposure, but escape. The expanse before him was empty of police or pedestrian while behind him the footsteps that had sent him scurrying had stopped. Their owner must have come upon the desecrated body he had left behind and was giving it suitably awe-struck attention. He slipped around the corner of the darkened school and the end of the flat-iron shaped building before he turned back east into the narrow gorge called Winthrop Street that paralleled Buck's Row. His U-turn sent him doubling back a block over from the carnage he had committed in Buck's Row with a solid wall of multi-story buildings between him and discovery.

Not far away, Lusky trotted proudly along Winthrop Street. Showers the day before had left the stone and brick glistening in a silvery sheet before him, lit by the gaslight. His whiskers were tinged red. The young mouse was clamped in a merciless grip in Lusky's jaws as entrails oozed out around his surgically sharp teeth. Death had not come easily or quickly, just inevitably. If there were laws governing the actions and malicious intentions of cats, Lusky would have long ago been charged with willful, sadistic murder and sent to the gallows. But felines live in a world ruled by random chance and natural selection. He couldn't even be charged with carrying concealed weapons in his padded paws. The mouse he had caught had been tortured in that strange feline ritual of cat-and-mouse before death came from a savage snap of Lusky's saber-sharp teeth through his victim's throat. The words of Tennyson had no significance for Lusky: "I envy not the beast that takes / His license in the field of time, / Unfettered by a sense of crime, / To whom a conscience never wakes..." Lusky was poetry in motion, but his actions were without conscience or pity.

They met abruptly, coming upon each other in an instant: the man-thing from the landing a few weeks ago and the cat from the builder's home. Their startled eyes glinted red in a flicker of gaslight. The two stood transfixed for a moment in the eerie quiet—two stalkers in the demi-darkness, each merciless and inexorable in action. The man-thing almost snarled. The cat scrunched his face, poised to hiss. Each somehow knew they were of identical mold, if not of the same species. Then, neither hunter sensing the other as a clear and present danger, they parted.

As an insomniac, spiritualist and clairvoyant Robert James Lees had once again been unable to find the solace of sleep's narcotizing nature this night; but as a psychic, he had managed to mesmerize his senses into a self-induced mental abyss. Sinking slowly, ever so slowly down an enveloping tunnel of oblivion, Lees became aware of figures emerging in a kaleidoscopic blur of impressions. They turned and churned amidst swirls of steamy vapors and then a stark image burst forth: a dark-clad man, a gore-stained knife in hand, hovered over a horribly mutilated, disemboweled woman...a blood-spotted hand materialized occulting the shadowy man...and then was gone...replaced by a scarlet flood of blood that carried clots dyed the darkest crimson along its Stygian path...then followed the darkness of death...oddly a gray cat smiling in Cheshire fashion had intermittently been superimposed upon the scenes.

Startled, Lees jerked awake, terrified. He seemed apart from his body. His heart skipped beats, pounding in uncoordinated dysfunction. Then that all too familiar odd sensation invaded his throat again. He could hardly draw air into his body. His beard seemed to constrict his throat. God! He had foreseen a murder! He shook uncontrollably. A terrible urge to escape from this vision and this place seized him. Rising from bed, he hastily threw some clothes into a suitcase and with a voice trembling with anxiety woke his wife and told her he must take the next boat-train to the continent. Compulsion had conquered self-control.

His wife, Sarah, a practical person of pedestrian pursuit, shrugged. She was used to her husband's occasional rushes from reason. "Absolutely ridiculous," she muttered in a mode more motherly than contemptuous. These silly forays were a debit in their domestic life, but on the whole his "other-world" experiences paid the bills and supported their 10 living children. His credentials as a medium included holding séances for the Queen—or at least so he claimed—transmitting messages from her beloved deceased Albert; an honour, real or supposed, that not so mysteriously had catapulted him into nationwide prominence. Marriage to a medium was like any connubial union. One had to expect compromises. Sarah rolled over and went back to sleep. Even if it was the middle of the night, Lees was already on his way out the door, trying to flee the fury within.

With thirty minutes walk still before him, at 3:40 a.m. carman William Cross hurried to work at Pickfords' depot through the narrow twenty-foot wide Buck's Row toward a presently nonvisible Baker's Row hidden in the gloom ahead. Narrow side routes, Court Street and Thomas Street, led off Buck's Row, north and south, their exits only slightly lighter sections of darkness under the faint gaslight. Two-story tenements stood a mere three feet of pavement from the road on one side of Buck's Row, while warehouses formed a somber brick wall on the other.

Cross wearily scanned the dim, squalid street ahead of him with ambivalent detachment. God, he was tired.

Hallo! What was that? Something was lying in the street against the gates leading to the stables next to New Cottage. It would be damp with dew, but it might be worth somethin'; perhaps a canvas fallen off a wagon rushin' to reach market by opening time.

Cross strode across the narrow street. It was a pile of cloth. Christ, no! It was a woman. Odd bloody place to be lying, even for Whitechapel. A tall man emerged from the shadows walking southeast toward Baker's Row.

"Come, look over here," Cross called out. "There's a woman lying on the pavement."

Both men peered down at the woman. Her clothes were up almost to her stomach. Cross felt her hands; cold and limp. The newcomer, Robert Paul, a carman walking to work in Corbett's Court, pulled her clothes down to above her knees as Cross said, "I think she's dead."

Paul felt her face and, finding it warm, tried to find a heartbeat. "I think she's breathing, but it's very little if she is. Maybe try to sit her up?"

"I don't want to touch her," Cross said, shuffling away.

Both men were late for work, so, their jobs at stake, they agreed to continue on and tell the first policeman they saw.

After Paul and Cross abandoned the body, Constable Neil continued on his beat into the deserted neck of Buck's Row that stretched slightly south and west from Brady Street. It was quiet at 3:45 a.m. and a distant streetlamp cast little light this far down the dark thoroughfare. Neil swung his bullseye lantern back and forth, lighting up ever-shifting circles of paving stones and brick as he moved along on his seemingly endless circuit. The tiresome gray was occasionally interrupted by splashes of green mold or a kaleidoscope of colour where mildew, moss or other foraging fungi spread like some exorable all-enveloping thing along wood and brickwork.

Neil stopped. A body lay outside a closed stable gate. Approaching, Neil's lantern hovered over the prostate form; a woman. Probably half-rats or worse. No, wait. A dark rivulet of blood oozed from her throat, where a two-inch wide gash crossed from ear to ear. She was the worse for something far more fatal than alcohol.

PC Neil discovers the body on Buck's Row, from "Famous Crimes Past and Present," 1903

Calm and professional, Neil, who had seen knife wounds before—such a method of assault was far from uncommon in such times and such places—felt the woman's arm. No pulse. Dead. He ran the back of his hand along her arm; quite warm above the elbow. Murdered! And not long ago! Thirteen years of experience prevailed over Neil's excitement. He dispassionately noted that the woman was lying on her back, her clothes in disarray, pulled above the knees. Her eyes were wide open, set to stare forever into eternity. A new bonnet lay on the sidewalk beside her left hand. Neil had no time to dwell on the incongruity of the cheery velvet bonnet's intrusion on the macabre scene. He heard a sound up the street and could just discern another constable in the distance through the gloom.

"Thain! Thain!" Neil shouted. "Run for Llewellyn. I've a dead woman."

"Not the divisional surgeon?"

"Llewellyn's closer; get him!"

PC 56 Jonas Mizen of H division was on knocking-up duty. It would be a severe prejudice to conclude that either Whitechapel or Spitalfields were poverty stricken to the core. Although about 20 percent of Whitechapel inhabitants were poor or homeless, doctors, solicitors, policemen and gentlemen of the press called the parish home, and in a time before alarm clocks were common, many of them needed to be woken to catch trains to get to work on time, so they used the Met's knocking-up service to wake them at requested times.

Mizen was in Baker's Row at the junction of Hanbury and Old Montague Streets when Paul and Cross ran into him. In a jumbled rush, the carmen told Mizen of their discovery.

"She's either drunk or dead," Cross said. "I fear, dead."

Mizen rushed to Buck's row, where PC Neil asked him to fetch an ambulance and help from Bethnal Green Police Station.

Only 300 yards away, Medical Officer Dr. Rees Ralph Llewellyn lived at No. 152 Whitechapel Road. Just before 4 a.m., PC Thain aroused him from a dreamy, peaceful world of blue skies and bluer lakes. Damn, Llewellyn swore as he pulled on his clothes with less than the necessary inhibitions to hide his annoyance. At least Thain hadn't woken his siblings, with whom Llewelyn lived. They hated being woken on his invariably unseemly business.

Medical officers and police surgeons in the 1880s were poorly paid, rarely respected and usually considered only a slight cut above a butcher in both status and skill. Such a categorization either fostered a relationship with CID that was what could be expected or, as Llewellyn often put it, what the bastards deserved. If they woke you in the middle of the night to tell you to come and certify that some sot was dead, they could bloody well wait while your head cleared and your eyes lost that gravelly feeling. Damn these tight shoes. Where was that bloody shoe horn? Dressed, he wet his hair, which helped keep the smell of a cadaver out of it. Why hadn't they dragged the divisional surgeon out of bed instead of him?

Medical Officer Dr. Rees Ralph Llewellyn

Dr. Llewellyn arrived with PC Thain to find Neil and Mizen making notes and sketches of the murder scene as they discussed their findings.

"I talked with a woman, a Mrs. Green, in New Cottage," Neil told Thain as he gestured at a house immediately east of the gate, "but she didn't hear a thing. Also spoke with the manager of Essex Wharf, nothing." The three-story brick building with the name Essex Wharf chiseled into its facade stood across the street from the gate where the body lay.

As a crowd of horse slaughterers, grocers and market vendors on their way to work began to congregate, Dr. Llewellyn crouched on his haunches and noted the cuts to the victim's throat. In the light from Neil's lantern he saw that the cut in the throat was from left to right, probably inflicted by a left-handed murderer. He felt that the legs were warm, even though the victim's hands and wrists were cold.

"Little blood," he muttered as he peered at the gutter beside the victim. "Not more than would fill two wine glasses or half a pint at the most."

Probably killed by some disatisfied customer or some other worthless unfortunate, he thought. These women were forever fighting, or maybe her old man did her in.

Llewellyn stood, wiped his nose with the back of his hand and told the newly arrived Local Sergeant Henry Kirby, "Dead but a few minutes, maybe half an hour. It's four now. Death probably occurred at about 3:30 this morning. Nothing out of the way here: routine. I'm finished. Take the body to the Old Montague Street Workhouse Infirmary." With that, Llewellyn hurried off, destined for his warm and oft-neglected bed.

Local Sergeant Kirby—distinguished by an armband on his right sleeve; constables wore an armband on their left sleeve—with Neil and Mizen prepared to take the body to the mortuary. Several constables were holding back the crowd. "Routine! Just routine!" The crowd did not disperse, but a few melted away to appear at work, hurry back home or snuggle into some unused doorway for the last remaining hours of darkness. The majority lingered to watch the four bluecoats lift the body, drop it onto a strip of canvas-covered board and hoist it waist-high to slide it into the rear of *Old Catchall*, a name that had become attached to the district's corpse carriers. A canvas-covered wire frame hid the body from public view, but the crowd stayed all the same.

Having helped load the body into *Old Catchall*, PC Thain looked down at his bloodied hands. It looked as if he had just assisted at a surgery that had gone horribly wrong. Trying to wipe the blood off his hands with his handkerchief, Thain waited in Buck's Row for Inspector Spratling. While he waited, he watched Mrs. Green's son, one of the residents, wash the victim's blood from the paving stones and with it, the last vestiges of the murder from the scene.

Inspector John Spratling, an 18-year veteran who smoked the blackest tobacco and drank the blackest tea of anyone on the force, and Detective-Sergeant Patrick Enright, a 14-year veteran, arrived on the scene at 4:30 a.m. with several constables summoned by the network of hand rattlers and whistles, which every constable carried, as well as by shouts that linked one constable to another. A less formal network seemed to be more efficient in bringing a surge of citizenry to the scene despite the early hour.

Spratling arrived just in time to see Mrs. Green's son washing away the blood from the pavement. Pulling up his pant legs and crouching, he could still discern some blood stains between the stones. Rising, he dispatched Enright to the mortuary to ensure the body was not touched until after the post-mortem. "Get it sorted over there and then come back here with help."

As Enright hurried off, Spratling inspected the immediate area.

"No blood beyond some where the body lay," Spratling told Thain and the just-arrived PC Cartwright. "Murdered right here."

Spratling ordered Cartwright to search the surrounding area, although, he muttered, "The bugger's gone to ground by now, I'd say."

A few streets away, Lusky curled into a contented circle of grey fur. His meal was complete. He was lying in a quiet refuge beneath a set of wooden back stairs, nestled into an old piece of sacking. Satisfied with his night's prowl, he soon fell asleep.

Inspector John Spratling

At 4:45 a.m. Kirby, Neil, Mizzen and the unidentified body arrived at the shed on Eagle Place, several hundred yards from the Old Montague Street Workhouse Infirmary, which served as the mortuary for those unfortunate enough to die in East London unclaimed by kin or comrade. Kirby found the mortuary shed locked and decided to wait with the body.

Enright soon arrived. Where the hell was the morgue attendant? Enright wanted to return to help canvass the buildings around the murder site. Kirby, Neil and Mizzen stood in their blue coats and chimney-pot hats, staring blankly at him. Enright didn't dare start to examine the body. Spratling would have his arse for that.

"Spratling wants us back at the murder site," Enright told Sergeant Kirby. "I'm supposed to bring back help."

"Should keep watch on the body," Kirby said.

"No one about."

"Still. . ."

They compromised. They sent Mizzen and Neil back to the murder site and

Kirby and Enright waited with the body.

Back at the murder site, Inspector Spratling ordered a neighbourhood canvass and told Thain to help Cartwright search the area. Then Spratling rushed over to the mortuary shed and found it still locked, the body still on the ambulance, and Kirby and Enright loitering about like whores awaiting clients on a cold night.

"Go find Mann or Hatfield," Spratling ordered Enright. "Now."

Enright scurried off to the infirmary to find Robert Mann, the mortuary attendant, or James Hatfield, his assistant, both of whom were Whitechapel workhouse inmates.

Turning back the canvas covering on *Old Catchall,* Spratling, notebook in hand, began making a detailed description of the dead woman's clothes.

Between 5 and 5:20 a.m., Mann arrived from his breakfast, unlocked the mortuary and, with the help of Hatfield, who had also turned up, Kirby and Enright, shifted the body into the mortuary. Inside, Spratling continued his inspection, saying, "These women often have a pocket buried somewhere in these rough robes. Maybe we can find out who she is."

Spratling rolled up the heavy dress to the waist, stopped and stared. Was the horrendous smell strong enough to make him see things? Enright, Kirby and the morgue attendants also stared transfixed.

"Good loving Christ!" Spratling roared. "She's been disemboweled. Kirby, get that ass Llewellyn down here at once. Routine—bollocks! Why didn't he look under her damn dress? Should have got the divisional surgeon, not some know-nothing medical officer. Bloody incompetent arrogant arsehole!"

After ordering the two attendants to leave the body until the doctor returned or another detective arrived, Spratling stepped outside to cool off and to wait for the medical officer to return and complete a proper thorough post-mortem. He had a long wait. As he smoked a cigar, Inspector Joseph Henry Helson arrived.

Before going to the mortuary, Helson had been the first upper echelon member of the Met to arrive at the murder scene at about 6:45 a.m., 34 minutes after sunrise. He had been alerted by telegraph about the murder the moment he arrived at the station that morning; most of London's police stations were now linked by telegraph. Helson had only just been confirmed as lead investigator of J Division (Bethnal Green) and he was nervous. He need not have been concerned; at 43 years old, he had been on the force 19 years and looked the perfect picture of the proper 19th Century policeman. His high forehead, full beard, manly moustache and erect posture projected authority and confidence.

"I saw Godley at the scene," Helson told Spratling as they stood outside the mortuary shed in the chill morning air. Sergeant George Godley was Helson's neighbour on Rutland Road in Hackney, north of Whitechapel.

"Nice lodgings up there," Spratling commented.

"Lucky to get it." The Met provided housing for married men, while bachelors had to live in one of the police stations or in Met-owned residences called section houses.

"See the news about Lord Walsingham?"

Helson knew Spratling liked to read newspapers almost as much as he did.

"Bagged 1,070 grouse in a single day on the 30th," Spratling said, admiration in his voice.

"Is there a grouse left in England?"

"One or two, I believe."

Inspector Joseph Henry Helson

Spratling told Helson what had been done thus far with the investigation. Helson nodded and said, "I searched the immediate area."

"Anything?"

"A stain that might have been blood on Brady Street, but given the number of slaughterhouses in the area, I wouldn't wager a shilling it's even human blood."

With a nod to Spratling, Helson stepped into the mortuary to view the body. Helson introduced himself to Mann and Hatfield. The pair then started to wash and clean the body. Helson inspected the remains from a few feet away. Having taken some notes, he stepped outside and stood beside Spratling, breathing deeply to try to rid his nose of the awful smell of the dismembered body. It didn't work. He asked Spratling, "What'd the post-mortem find?"

"Not a damn thing. Llewelyn examined the body on Buck's Row, but hasn't been here yet. Bloody fool missed the fact she'd been gutted and only the devil knows what else."

"But they're cleaning the body," Helson said, confused.

At that moment Mann strode out the doorway bearing an armful of women's clothes.

"Hold there!" Spratling ordered. "Wot have you got there?"

"Clothes from the body. Not worth a pence, I'd say, and nothing in 'em besides.'"

"I ordered you not to touch the body," Spratling roared.

"Until another 'tec arrived; he did," Mann said, pointing at Helson.

"Not a bloody detective; a medical officer."

"He is an officer."

"Not a *police* officer, you fool, a *medical* officer!" Spratling cursed but it was too late, any evidence on the body was now washed away into the drains and was well on its way to the fast-flowing filthy Thames.

Detective Inspector first class Frederick George Abberline

Detective Inspector first class Frederick George Abberline woke with a searing sinus headache. Damn! Must be the weather. A thunderstorm had torn over London yesterday and his sinuses had still not recovered from their torment. His head told him it was going to be a painful day. His ears told him someone was at the door.

He tore the telegram open on his front step. The messenger boy, dressed in a bright blue coat and bowler hat, lingered for his tip, then, glancing at Abberline's expression, retreated to his bicycle as Abberline swore to himself. Damn again!

Abberline yelled after the boy, who turned to catch the coin Abberline tossed him.

"A murder in Buck's Row," Abberline told his wife, Emma, as he dressed. "It's back to Whitechapel for me."

In December 1887, Abberline had been transferred on the express orders of James Monro, Assistant Commissioner, CID, and Adolphus Williamson, Chief Constable, CID, to Scotland Yard after serving 14 years with the Met in Whitechapel.

"Monro and Williamson want me to lead the on-the-ground investigation of the Tabram murder and a woman found this morning," Abberline said, pulling on his wool suit pants. "Sorry, no time for breakfast." He grabbed his keyless gold hunting watch off the bureau, attached the chain to his vest and slid it with care into his vest pocket. As he kissed Emma goodbye he said, "May not see you for some time."

"My loss," she whispered and kissed him back.

Sergeant George Godley

When Abberline reached the murder scene, Spratling, who had returned from the mortuary, reported that between 5 and 6 a.m., Sergeant Godley had searched the area around the murder site, Buck's Row and Brady Street, as well as the adjacent railway line and embankments. Godley looked for wheel marks in the row in case the body had been dumped, but found none. Thain also investigated all the premises near where the body was found, but found no blood or weapons either.

"She was murdered here," Spratling said. "Helson agrees."

Abberline nodded. He talked to the inspectors, sergeants and constables at the scene, gathering every detail he could and offering encouragement. Two inspectors reported that the victim had five stab wounds caused by a dagger or a long, sharp knife. They had also found a broken comb and a piece of looking glass on her corpse, evidence she was living on the street with nowhere to store her possessions, however meager.

Abberline inspected the site of the murder. The investigative process had been largely well done, but it hadn't gone entirely glowingly. Particularly disturbing was PC Thain reporting that he had witnessed a young man washing the blood off the walkway.

"A mass of dry blood about six inches in diameter was precisely there," Thain told Abberline, pointing at where the body had lain. "A river of it had run towards that gutter."

"A lot of blood or a little?" Abberline asked, wishing he had arrived in time to see the corpse as the murderer had left it.

"More than I'd care to lose, sir. I helped put the body in the ambulance and got blood all over my hands. Back of her clothes were sodden with blood; must have run from her neck as far down as her waist. Also saw blood on the paving stones where the deceased's legs were."

Abberline thanked Thain as Helson, just returned from the mortuary and having gathered reports from all of the Met officers at the scene, approached and said, "No one seems to have seen a thing; not the beat constables or the fixed-point men."

Under the fixed-point system established in 1870 and continued by Chief Commissioner Sir Charles Warren, one group of constables stood guard at selected points in a grid, forbidden from leaving their post until relieved. It was a standing joke that every man at one time or other "relieved" himself at least once a night. A second group of officers patrolled the streets between these human sentries, moving from place to place in clock-like synchronized fashion with military precision. Many radical and opposition papers, such as the barely year-old *Star*, criticized the police for the fixed-point system. The system also bothered Abberline. His older brother, Edward, served in the army, but such familiarity did nothing to increase his liking for Sir Charles' application of military techniques to the police. Structured systems might have been of use when Sir Charles fought in the Kaffir War or restored order in Bechuanaland, but it was of little use in most kinds of police work.

"The people see one constable coming by on his regular rounds, another standing on a corner and they feel assured and safe," Sir Charles had repeatedly reiterated to Abberline.

Abberline thought, but did not ask the Commissioner, "Are slit-purses, cutthroats and murderers ever going to commit their crimes within sight of a watching stationary constable?"

Having ensured the area had been searched, Abberline left Helson in charge of the ongoing canvass and took a Met four-wheeler to the mortuary to inspect the body. As he entered the black carriage, a correspondent he vaguely knew—Pools or Cools or some such name—called out something about the body having been mishandled. Following police policy not to tell the press anything until a suspect was identified, Abberline ordered the constable atop the conveyance to drive on.

After a brief ride, Abberline entered the morgue shed's cool, musty confines. He walked past the rows of shell-like coffins each containing a passive piece of decaying flesh in cocoon-like convenience. The corpses appeared to be in a ghastly lifeless kind of sleep. There was no air of repose to the scene; each corpse, their eyes open, staring into the great unknown.

The attendant, his lips clenched around the stem of a clay pipe, was busying himself with a mulched and mangled cadaver. His assistant stood beside him like a nervous medical student at St. Guy's; must be new, Abberline thought.

"Poor blighter," Mann said, "mashed by a team of horses."

Abberline nodded, showed Mann his identification, and asked after the Buck's Row body. Spratling had examined the body, Mann and Hatfield attested to this.

"Angry, he was," Mann said. "Seems he made a hash of an order."

"Which order?"

"Told us not to touch the body 'til another 'tec arrived. One did, so we cleaned the body and Spratling gave us a bollocking."

Abberline cursed silently, but held his anger in check. Anger never solved a case. "Who was the other detective?"

"Kelson, Pelson," Mann struggled to recall.

"Helson," Hatfield suggested.

"That's 'im. He comes, so we washed and cleaned the body with 'im watching. We did nothing wrong, I swear."

"Had Dr. Llewellyn or the divisional police surgeon been here yet?"

"No doctor been in this place all mornin'," Mann said.

Abberline seethed with frustration. Why hadn't Helson said anything to stop the attendants from cleaning the body? Where was Dr. Llewellyn? It was doubly galling since there was so little he could do. Llewellyn was beyond his jurisdiction and, as for the offending Spratling, why had he left the body before Llewellyn arrived? In any case, what could you do with men who were continually overworked, kept on subsistence wages, and had nowhere to go if sacked and nothing to eat if docked pay? Most of the men on the force were ex-labourers with little chance of another decent job should they lose their position on the force. Abberline rubbed his throbbing forehead in frustration. The varicose vein on the back of his left leg was also beginning to develop the heavy sensation that presaged pain. He would just have to sort things before this comedy of chaos turned into a tragedy for the Metropolitan Police in general and the investigation in particular. Whatever had happened, catching the culprit would forgive all.

Abberline hobbled over to the body Mann indicated. The back of his left knee already felt tender and he put most of his weight on his right leg as he stared down at the corpse. "Where are her clothes?"

"Over there," Mann said. "Spratling made us bring 'em back in after we tipped 'em in the bin in the yard."

Abberline inventoried the pathetic jumble: a long, loose heavy overcoat, called an Ulster, probably because they were originally worn in Ireland, made of frieze, a heavy wool cloth with a shaggy, uncut nap on one side; a brown linsey-woolsey frock made from a coarse cloth of either linen and wool or cotton and wool (he was far from an expert on woman's clothing); and men's side-spring boots that would reach above the ankle. The unfortunate victim was far from the silken-clad sirens of Inspector Reid's stage productions. Abberline noticed workhouse labels on several of the garments. Helson should be able to chase those down and hopefully identify the victim, which should lead via her family, friends and companions to suspects, one of whom in most such cases was the murderer.

Abberline turned to the body of the deceased. It was not a pleasant task. The stench from the gutted abdomen assaulted his nose, making his eyes cloud and mist. He leaned in low over the corpse and inhaled deeply. It smelt God awful, but doing so lessened the impact of the smell from then on. Inspecting the corpse, he saw that her lower abdomen to her breast was cut open, with the bowels protruding. Abberline bent at the waist to inspect her hands, which appeared bruised, as if in a struggle. Her face was also bruised and her front teeth had been knocked out. She had not gone peacefully into that longest of sleeps. Good for her, although Abberline knew from long service in Whitechapel that alcohol abusers bruised easily, so her bruising could be from long before her final moments, as could the missing teeth. After some reluctant consideration, he saw no defensive wounds from a final deadly fight.

Whatever had happened to the body, if evidence had been washed away, it had been washed away. The only thing certain was that the butchered body of the unfortunate confirmed that he and the Met were dealing with a violent murderer who, Abberline feared, after Tabram and now this unfortunate would not stop until he was apprehended.

Abberline had his driver fetch a point man to stand guard at the mortuary, cautioned the constable in no uncertain terms to remain by the corpse until a police surgeon arrived, and sent the first policeman he met on the beat in search of the elusive Dr. Llewellyn.

Several hours later, a half-contrite, half-arrogant Dr. Llewellyn finally appeared at the Leman Street station having completed his post-mortem examination.

"Did the same man who murdered Martha Tabram murder this victim?"

Abberline asked as they sat at a desk in a borrowed office. His office was at Met headquarters.

"Based on Dr. Killeen's report, the wounds are not consistent with those of Tabram," Llewellyn said.

Abberline was relieved; maybe he didn't have a murderer on his hands who would continue to kill until caught. Wary of good news, he asked, "In what ways?"

"Tabram's injuries were less organized, less disciplined, almost wild in their nature. This victim's throat was cut neatly left to right, although the head was almost severed from the neck by two cuts: one four inches long and one eight inches long."

"So both assaults *were* ferocious."

"Granted. I also found a bruise from what appears to have been a thumb or a punch on the lower right jaw and also one on the cheek."

"Strangled first?" Abberline asked as he took notes with a gold-accented fountain pen; a birthday gift from Emma.

"Possibly; her face was discoloured and I found some slight lacerations on her tongue, which would be consistent with strangulation. He probably was facing her when he reached up and throttled her; then cut her throat."

"If her throat was cut while she was standing, blood would have soaked the front of her dress."

"I did not find any when I examined her in Buck's Row."

Nor had any of the constables or inspectors Abberline had interviewed at the scene. "Then it's probable she was throttled, laid down and then her throat was cut. That way the blood would be under her. Thain reported that the back of her dress was soaked with blood."

"She might have lain down of her own accord with a customer."

"It rained yesterday and the pavement was still damp. In my experience, regardless of the weather, such transactions are usually conducted against a wall, standing up."

"He probably strangled her, laid her down and kneeled by her head to slit her throat with a knife in his right hand as he held the head in his left."

"Why not the reverse?"

"That way the blood from the left carotid artery would spurt away from him."

"Keeping his clothes free of any incriminating blood; not that anyone would spare a second glance at someone with blood on their clothes given all of the slaughterhouses in the area. Type of knife?"

"Strong-bladed, moderately sharp, pointed but not an exceptionally long-bladed weapon. The murderer assaulted her with great violence. Such fury meant he didn't need an exceptionally sharp knife; maybe a sailor's jackknife or something of the sort. Her abdomen was cut open by three or four jagged, deep cuts. I also found two stab wounds in her private parts."

"Any precision to his work?"

"He may have some rough anatomical knowledge or he may just have a penchant for perusing *Gray's Anatomy*."

"In any case, he must have spent some time with the body in Buck's Row."

"Probably took four or five minutes to kill her and cut her up."

"An eternity to squat over a body on a dark street in Whitechapel when someone could happen along at any instant on their way to work."

"*De l'audace, encore de l'audace, et toujours l'audace,*" Llewellyn said with a wan smile as he quoted Napoleon's dictim about the need for audacity, more audacity, and always audacity.

After the doctor left, Abberline, with some reluctance since he preferred solving crimes to chastising his men for errors, confirmed what Kirby, Neil and Mizzen had done when they escorted the body to the mortuary. He then summoned Spratling and Helson. Helson confirmed he had been at the mortuary when the body was washed, but thought the post-mortem had already been completed. Somehow when Spratling issued his order, the mortuary keepers heard 'detective,' not 'doctor,' and Helson fit that requirement, or maybe Spratling said "medical officer" and Helson was an officer. Abberline concluded that the fiasco came down to a case of misunderstanding, but men could get away with murder due to misunderstandings.

"The next time you are charged with custody of a corpse, please take greater care in ensuring the corpse isn't touched by anyone until the police surgeon is done with it," Abberline ordered Spratling and Helson. "I know they won't walk away on their own, but we are obliged by law to keep the chain of evidence intact from the scene of the crime to the custody of the coroner. Understood?"

"Yes, sir," Helson and Spratling barked back in perfect unison.

Much as he had disliked dressing down Spratling and Helson, both of whom he thought were decent to excellent detectives, Abberline disliked even more his next meeting, which was with the Chief Commissioner of the Metropolitan Police, Sir Charles Warren.

Born in Bangor, Wales, Sir Charles was the son of a major-general. His father had served as an ensign under the Duke of Wellington. Like his father, Sir Charles was a professional soldier, far from the viewpoint, temperament and background of Abberline, who had started his working life as a clockmaker in Dorset. Sir Charles was making the rounds of the local police stations after the most recent murder. On his way to where he had been told Sir Charles waited in the station chief's office, Abberline nodded to a pair of constables he knew. A fox terrier trotted faithfully along beside them; some constables took their pet dogs on their beats. At least, Abberline thought, he didn't have to traipse over to Sir Charles' office at the Yard; traffic was worsening by the day.

Sir Charles Warren

Helson caught up with Abberline in the second-floor hall bursting with news, "Did you hear, sir? Monro's sacked."

Abberline had heard that James Monro, Assistant Commissioner, CID, had been in a dispute with Sir Charles over the appointment of a Chief Constable to serve directly under Monro. Monro wanted to appoint his friend, Melville Macnaghten, but Sir Charles disliked an incident in Macnaghten's past that had occurred in Bengal on the edge of India. Abberline had never been able to learn precisely what the Bengal incident involved, but the hiring issue became a major point of contention. Both men had offered their resignation to the Home Secretary, Henry Matthews, who had apparently accepted Monro's.

"Sorry to hear of it," Abberline said, unable to get too worked up over the matter. The exchange of one mandarin for another rarely made much difference. "Monro's sound."

"I hear Matthews just moved him to the Home Office, but that he'll retain control of Special Branch. Sounds as if Matthews wants Monro and Robert Anderson, who's been named his replacement, to keep him well informed behind Sir Charles' back."

"Anderson should be good at that." Anderson had been an operative against the Fenians in Ireland, well versed in deception, double-dealing and subterfuge.

"Aren't all the Irish?" Helson asked with a grin. "All blarney and good cheer until they stick a dirk in your back."

"A dirk is Scottish, Inspector. Best keep our weapons straight, shall we?" Abberline said with a mock look of severity.

James Monro, Assistant Commissioner, CID

Robert Anderson, Assistant Commissioner (Crime)

Helson rushed off to chase down several potential witnesses related to the Buck's Row murder. Abberline knocked at the door of Sir Charles' borrowed office. When ordered to enter, he opened the door. Sir Charles sat with a male secretary dictating an order. Abberline waited, eyeing the commissioner's erect military bearing, bronzed face and thick moustache curving down to his jaw like crossed sabers. As he peered off into the middle distance with a poetical expression that seemed at odds with his military bearing, Sir Charles said, "The

Commissioner has observed there are signs of wear, / on the Landseer lions in Trafalgar Square. / Unauthorized persons are not to climb / on the Landseer lions at any time."

Sir Charles smiled and nodded to the dark-suited secretary, who exited the room with only a disinterested glance at Abberline.

After Abberline made his report on the latest murder, Sir Charles finished a note on a pad he had made with a simple black fountain pen and said, "This latest murder catches us in transition."

"I just heard, sir."

Sir Charles eyed him, apparently gauging where Abberline's loyalties lay in the bureaucratic infighting. Abberline remained silent. Monro had been an effective head of CID, but he didn't always do what Sir Charles ordered; a firing-squad offense to Sir Charles. Then again, Abberline was the first to admit, Sir Charles *was* the senior officer.

"Even though Mr. Monro has left us, I have decided these murders require an investigation led by a single officer," Sir Charles said. "I believe you are just the officer for that command."

"Thank you, sir."

"Inspectors Helson and Spratling will assume the role of lead investigators for the Divisional force. I am also seconding Chief Inspector Henry Moore of P Division and Inspector Walter Andrews to assist."

"We can use all the men we can get, sir."

"Now, about the murders," Sir Charles said before he quietly but emotionally argued that the murderers were members of the Old Nichol Gang, who regularly blackmailed unfortunates. "They extort money and when they were rebuffed they murdered the latest victim, Tabram, and that unfortunate—what was her name?—back in April. . ."

"Emma Smith, sir?"

Sir Charles' eyes flashed, flushed full of venom. "It's those swine. No doubt about the matter. Who else would rob unfortunates? Run the gang to ground, Abberline, and we'll have this Buck's Row business solved."

"I believe the main members of the Old Nichol Gang are in gaol; have been for months, sir."

"Are you positive?"

Abberline nodded.

"Then the High Rip Gang or one of the others must be behind the murders."

Seeing Sir Charles had made up his mind, Abberline said, "We'll do our utmost to pursue the gangs, sir." He did not mention that his best efforts would not be concentrated on any gang. There was not a shred of evidence suggesting that the thugs who took their name from Old Nichol Street at the top of Brick Lane or the High Rip Gang, which had originated in Liverpool, had anything to do with the Smith, Tabram or the latest murder. More importantly, Abberline believed that the Emma Smith murder was not the work of the same villains as whoever was behind the latest two murders. He couldn't be certain, but he would have placed a sizable wager on his belief.

"Clear these cases promptly, Abberline," Sir Charles ordered. "We cannot countenance such lawlessness from these gangs, even in the East End."

News of the butchery in Buck's Row rippled across London like news of a major battle lost on India's North-West Frontier. The press, no ebbing tide in its pursuit of the latest news, swamped Victorian sensibilities by publishing every detail of every knife stroke, guaranteeing that newspaper pages attracted and repelled the prim, the proper and the prudish as well as the unwashed, uncouth and unconventional with equal revulsion and glee. The evening *Star's* coverage was equal parts about the murder—"No murder was ever more ferociously and brutally done"—and criticism of Sir Charles' administration of the Met, calling for his resignation. It would only be the slightest of exaggerations to say that the Buck's Row savagery was the topic of every conversation from the poorest public house to the poshest private club. The police from Sir Charles on down, the press and the public quickly perceived connections between the mutilation in Buck's Row and the two earlier unsolved murders of Smith and Tabram. The latest murder stirred the soul of London with a fury and fear not present in the populace in living memory.

The demise of the Buck's Row unfortunate filled the streets of Whitechapel with as many representatives of the Fourth Estate as it did policemen. Adrian Coulls, a 23-year-old transplanted Canadian just completing his first year with *The Empire,* and co-workers Roger "Old Boy" Pierce and Jason Jennings recognized reporters from the *Daily News, Daily Telegraph, Advertiser, Observer, Illustrated Police News, Pall Mall Gazette, Star,* and *The Times,* among a half dozen others at the murder scene. *The Empire* trio quickly confirmed with each other their specific assignments: Coulls – murder scene and inquest; Pierce – lead detectives; Jennings – anyone in the area who had seen or heard anything of news value. They rushed off to pursue their assignments.

As they waited for the Crow and Crown to open so they could linger over a pub lunch, George Lusk told his friends Edward, Albert and Harold, "At least they've got the most formidable force on the force heading the investigation."

"He certainly knows every villain in Whitechapel and Spitalfields," Edward agreed. "If any crime is committed in Whitechapel, Mr. Abberline knows who did it before last call."

Harold said, "I heard his old guv at H Division, Thomas, hated losing him to Whitechapel, 'a better officer there could not be,' Thomas said. God's truth."

The group's opinions were typical of the East End's inhabitants. It was no state secret that the portly, balding, 45-year-old Abberline had a genuine rapport with the East End's populace, even its poverty-pocked inhabitants. This had been verified by the citizenry presenting him with a gold keyless hunting watch when he left Spitalfields and Whitechapel for a position of importance at Scotland Yard in 1887. The murderer may have been one of the few who felt that Abberline was not the perfect policeman to lead the hunt. Then again, the killer may have felt honoured to have such an adversary pursuing him.

J Division constables continued their interviews of people living or working in the area around the murder site. This meant canvassing every home and flat, every doss house, pub and shop, searching railway embankments and wharfs, always asking the same questions of a seemingly endless supply of possible witnesses. Since it was mind-draining, boring work, Abberline, Spratling and Helson took time to see how their men were doing, passing on an encouraging word here and avoiding a discouraging word there.

Police work was not much different from newspaper work. Both policemen and reporters spent much of their time communicating in search of information. Each asked questions of Mr. X or Mrs. Y, jotted down a summary of what X or Y said, then passed these summaries on (sometimes orally, sometimes in writing) to someone higher up the pyramidal police or newspaper hierarchy.

That afternoon, while Spratling pursued a possibly promising witness, Abberline and Helson walked along Buck's Row.

"The body was on its back, hands at its sides, legs extended and slightly apart," Helson said, gesturing at where the body had been found. "Almost posed."

"Maybe our murderer has an artistic bent, although I doubt we should be searching the National Gallery for him," Abberline said. "Inspectors Moore and Andrews are organizing more foot patrols for tonight. How's the door-to-door progressing?"

"We canvassed the neighbourhood. Found a Walter Purkiss. Manager of the Essex Wharf building. Lives on the premises across the street from where the victim was found. Purkiss and his wife were sleeping in a second floor front room. They heard nothing. Neither did any of their children or a servant also sleeping in the house. Purkiss was awake between 1 and 2 a.m. Claimed,"— Helson read his notes—"'It was unusually quiet.' His wife said she didn't hear anything either. Said she was pacing the floor sometime around 3 or 4 in the morning. If she was, she was awake at the time of the murder and still didn't hear a thing. You'd think our victim would have screamed at least once when this foul monster grabbed her."

"Not if he smothered her mouth and choked her to death."

Helson nodded.

"Probably no street people in Buck's Row last night," Abberline guessed as several curious passersby paused to peer down at the paving stones, apparently looking for blood stains. "Commercial Street's a shambles with the tram construction, so unfortunates are moving into the other main streets or, given the increased competition, a few are looking for what trade they can find on dark side streets like this one."

"It was a colder morning than usual, so more people probably stayed in, if they could."

"Couple that with how warm the body was reported to be when it was found and I think we can conclude that Cross came close to stumbling upon a murder in progress."

"The killer was lucky. Henry Tomkins, a horse slaughterer, worked that night with James Mumford and Charles Brittan in the slaughterhouse opening onto Winthrop Street. Tomkins said the three of them went for a walk at midnight, not returning until 1 a.m. and neither saw nor heard anything of significance. And the slaughterhouse doors were open all night."

"Anyone passing by would hardly be noticed by the men hard at it inside." Abberline fingered his gold hunting watch in his vest pocket. It felt solid, substantial and certain of its own permanence, so unlike this case. "Any other possible witnesses from the canvass?"

"A Mrs. Green, another Buck's Row resident, was up until 4.30 a.m."

"Doesn't anyone around here sleep at night?"

"She neither heard nor saw a thing," Helson said, flipping another page in his notebook, its pages rippled from all his note-taking. "Two constables patrolling within hearing distance of the murder site heard nothing. The constable on duty in the Great Eastern Railway yard 50 feet away also heard and saw nothing."

"Seems our murderer came, saw and killed without being heard or seen—or at least not seen as being anyone out of the common-place." Abberline sighed. "I don't accept for a minute that this or the Tabram murder are the work of a gang, which leaves an individual. Certainly many villains we know we could chase down, but which one would do something like what happened here?"

Both men knew there had been a particularly vile business at the East End's Isle of Dogs recently. After a drunken quarrel, a general dealer, who was apt to sell anything, selected from his stock a 14-pound hammer and a 14-ounce razor with which to dispatch his "wife." The man slit his own throat afterwards, but had not bled enough to die before being placed in custody. He would be charged with willful homicide and attempted suicide. On the same day the Isle of Dogs murder occurred, a Glasgow man was found dead in his East London bed, his head decimated by hammer blows. The Scotsman's wife and son were arrested. These were familial murders, common and understandable, but murders like this one in Buck's Row were difficult to understand and even more difficult to solve.

"What about that villain, Benjamin Quinnell?" Helson asked. "He's a suspect in the Tabram murder."

"The one who stabbed a woman on the 22nd?" Helson nodded and Abberline ordered, "Get on to him and find out where he was last night and early this morning."

"What about this Leather Apron? For about a year unfortunates in Whitechapel have been claiming he extorts money from them and beats those who don't pay—threatened one with a big knife."

"Sergeant Thick, H Division, knows him," Abberline said, showing his years of experience in Whitechapel. "Real name's Jack Pizer. Find out from Thick what he thinks of Pizer, and circulate a description."

John Pizer

Helson nodded. He gestured to a constable who was waiting by their official four-wheeler. The constable tossed a newspaper extra into the coach, patted his chestnut horse and climbed up onto the driver's perch to take the reins. Abberline walked with Helson to the conveyance and, avoiding an aromatic pile of horse manure, climbed in.

Helson picked up the extra the driver had discarded and perused the headlines. "Press is certainly covering Buck's Row like it's the second coming," he said, settling in for the ride back to the Bethnal Green station.

"Yet they barely covered the Thames Torso Murder a few months ago."

"Harder to base a story on only a torso, I guess."

"But a face can launch a thousand news stories."

Later that day Abberline held a session with as many inspectors as could be collected at Helson's Bethnal Green station, whose jurisdiction covered Buck's

Row.

"We've had three extremely brutal murders this year," Abberline told the assembled policemen. "The first murders in Whitechapel in two years."

"Enough thieving to make up for it, though," Detective Inspector Reid muttered.

"Could you speak up some, sir?" a detective at the back of the room called out.

Assuming the detective was speaking to him and not Reid, Abberline raised his voice. "Three murders: Emma Smith, killed Easter Monday, 3 April; Martha Tabram or Turner, murdered 6 August in George Yard Buildings; and now this unfortunate in Buck's Row. The first two were prostitutes and this last one most likely was as well. The first two were alcoholics and the latest one was probably that, too. Two were killed on a holiday. Tabram was murdered on a Thursday night in August when some take holidays. All three were murdered in Whitechapel/Spitalfields. In her final days Smith lived at No. 18 George Street, while Tabram lodged at No. 19. Tabram even sometimes used the name Emma, further linking the two women. All three were murdered within 300 yards of each other; Tabram only 100 yards from where Smith was attacked."

Abberline did not need to glance down at his notes, but he paused to allow the men who were taking notes to catch up. "The murders did differ in some respects. Smith was knifed just a few times; Tabram 39 times. Tabram's throat was not cut and she was not mutilated, which makes her murder quite different from the one in Buck's Row last night. This last one had her guts split wide open and her throat slit from ear to ear. All three victims, it appears, were violated." Abberline swallowed. His throat was getting sore from talking so loud and he disliked such sordid aspects of his job as when a woman, any woman, was violated. "The Smith and Tabram murders remain unsolved and now we have another."

From a perch on the corner of a desk, Inspector Spratling said, "Chief Inspector Moore provided everyone copies of the Tabram file, but I don't think we got anything about Smith."

Inspector Andrews said, "I'm having copies made."

"Might we prevail upon Detective Inspector Reid to go over the particulars, since he was kind enough to come over from H Division at my request?" Abberline asked.

"First you make me take your job and now you make me do your work for you," Reid said as everyone laughed. Reid had succeeded Abberline as Local Inspector and Head of CID for H Division when Abberline was promoted to CO Division (Central Office) last year.

Reid stood tall to his full 5 feet 6 inches and with no notes, his rich theatre-trained voice filling the room, said "Emma Elizabeth Smith was a 5-foot-2, fair-complexioned and fair-haired 45-year-old charwoman and part-time unfortunate. She had a hard, violent life. You wouldn't wish it on your worst enemy's daughter. Emma returned to her lodging more than once with a black eye and once told her lodging house keeper that someone had thrown her out a window, although apparently not a top-floor window." Everyone chuckled. Reid knew how to entertain and, Abberline well understood, how to present a case so everyone would remember the key details.

"She was assaulted and robbed by, she said, three men in the early morning of 3 April, a Bank Holiday weekend, on a pathway opposite No.10 Brick Lane, less than 900 feet from her doss house at 18 George Street, Spitalfields," Reid said. "Her head was bruised and her right ear almost torn off. A blunt instrument, possibly a stick, had been violently thrust up her woman's passage rupturing the perineum." Reid reported that aspect of the case more quickly. In Victorian society, even reading 'begat' in the Bible aloud could raise eyebrows. "She told her lodging house keeper that several men had robbed her of all her money. She seems to have been somewhat better off financially than most of the 1,200 or so unfortunates in the area. Even so, the investigating officers, upon inspecting her clothes, found them in such a state that they couldn't tell if there were any recent tears."

"Description of her assailants?" Helson asked.

"She provided rough descriptions of the three men who attacked her before she died in London Hospital from peritonitis the next day. I recognized some gang members I know as possible suspects, but we never had sufficient evidence for an arrest."

Abberline said, "They do not appear to have intended to kill her, unlike Tabram and this latest case. Smith was also not cut up. So she probably was killed by the Old Nichol Gang, as Sir Charles believes."

"The public and press, too," Helson added, tapping a newspaper on the desk beside him.

"Depending on how high you want to set the evidence bar, she even may have identified several of her killers as members of the Old Nichol Gang," Abberline said. "I believe we can safely cross Smith's killing off as not connected with the last two, which may be related. So, first order of business: find out who this woman in Buck's Row was. We should have facsimile pictures from the artists sometime this afternoon. You all know what to do. Thank you."

It was not a speech of Gladstonian splendor. Just a few ordinary words addressed to a group of ordinary men saddled with the task of solving an extraordinary crime. Abberline saw no point in commenting on the cock-up that had left the corpse unattended or even the sloppy work of the medical officer. He had long since learned that making waves could swamp the boat in Victorian waters and meant you went nowhere but down.

Abberline knew that throughout Greater London various duty schedules now included further searches by the City of London Police, CID and the

Thames Police. Much had been done, but much had to be done. On 31 August alone, some 30 ships had arrived at London's docksides, while at least 40 more vessels made landfall in ports from Bristol to Newcastle, Liverpool to Plymouth. Hundreds of sailors and seamen had swarmed over the portside quays and out into the cities, filling the pubs and brothels, private clubs and seamen's homes with tars and salts from the far-flung corners of the Empire, as well as ports beyond and in between. Many such men were far from above a bit of violence. In many pubs, tables and chairs were bolted to the floor to prevent their use as weaponry when fights erupted, as they habitually did. Any one of these thousands of tars could easily catch a train to London even if the metropolis had not been his original port of call. Farmers and labourers, workers and trampers from countless communities ringing the metropolis could catch any one of dozens of trains and whisk in and out of Whitechapel with ease. London was the most accessible urban center on earth, a focal point for anyone seeking diversions of any kind. It was also home to five million men and women. There was no shortage of suspects from which to choose; the difficulty lay in identifying the right suspect. It was going to be a long day, Abberline knew, the first of many long days.

Chapter Four

Just back from his Scandinavian holiday, Coroner Wynne E. Baxter opened his inquiry into the death in Buck's Row in the imposing red and white Working Lads' Institute, Whitechapel Road, with its peaked roof and impressive stained-glass windows. Baxter cut a striking figure. As described by *The Observer*, he appeared in "a pair of white-and-black checked trousers, a dazzling white waist-coat, a crimson scarf, and a dark coat." Abberline, in a functional, yet worn dark suit, which *The Observer* failed to mention, slumped on a hard bench at the rear of the room between Helson and Spratling.

The trio was joined by CID Detective-sergeants Enright and Godley as observers. Helson and Godley exchanged news of wives and children before passing on various morsels of gossip about their neighbourhood. The pleasantries and news exchanged, they then joined the other policeman in scouring the considerable crowd as they tried to detect anyone exhibiting suspicious behavior. As was usual, Chief Inspector Moore had stationed other investigators to scrutinize the crowd that had accumulated outside. Everyone from the wide-eyed bloke in the fifth row fidgeting with his hair and the nervous blighter behind him drumming his fingers against his forearm to the expressionless nasty piece of goods in row eight could be exhibiting signs of guilt, innocent interest, boredom or some other emotion. Unfortunately, a person's criminality was not etched on a man's exterior, but carved deep within his soul. If the murderer was in the crowd, he was not identifiable.

Abberline knew this, but he still scanned the crowd. He remembered a bright young constable—it might have been Helson—once asking him, "Why do we do this? I couldn't pick out a villain from a vicar in an inquest crowd."

"Neither can I," Abberline had replied. "But study the faces in the crowd.

One of those faces may show up again at a murder scene, another inquest or fit a description from a witness we haven't yet interviewed. Some miscreants become anxious about how close we may be coming to identifying them so they attend an inquest to find out how much we know. Others sometimes come to reassure themselves how clever they are and a few probably get a perverse joy out of it all."

Abberline caught sight of the young reporter who had called out to him at the murder site—Coulls, that was his name—sitting with a few other reporters he recognized. From what Abberline had heard from his men, Coulls and his colleagues had been scurrying from police station to murder scene to mortuary to inquest site. Abberline knew that the police, given their standing policy not to release any information, placed the press in the difficult, if not impossible position of attempting to investigate a murder at the same time as the police, but with far fewer resources and no authority. Even so, given the public's love of seeing their name in print, detectives usually had only a shade of an advantage over the press, and sometimes not even a shade.

The inquest opened, ending any further Abberlinean speculation on police-press relations. Testimony established that marks on the deceased woman's Lambeth Workhouse clothes had led to the victim's identification as Mary Ann Nichols, who had been an inmate of the workhouse on several occasions. Abberline had already learned her name from Helson, who, like Abberline, had noted the marks on the deceased's clothes. Abberline now had inspectors out and about investigating Nichols' history and tracing her recent movements. She had most recently been bedding down at either 18 Thrawl Street or 55 Flower and Dean Street; a couple of doss houses in two of the sleaziest streets in Whitechapel's warren of poverty, depravity and disrespectability.

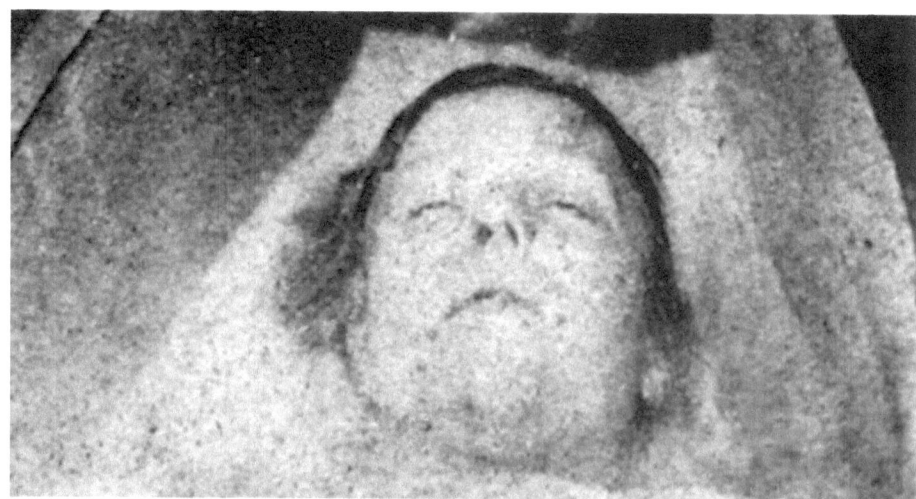

Mary Ann Nichols

The victim's father, Edward Walker, a hard-faced fossil of an ex-blacksmith, gray-bearded and gray-headed, testified that his daughter drank at times "and that was why we did not agree."

"Was she fast?" Baxter asked, although everyone in the courtroom, save possibly Walker, had already guessed she was a prostitute.

"No, I never heard anything of that sort. She used to go with some young women and men that she knew, but I never heard of anything improper."

"Did you ever turn her out for her drinking?"

"Never."

Walker had not seen her in two years and had no idea she was living in Whitechapel. He said his daughter had five children between 21 and eight or nine years of age, but had left her husband when her youngest child was a year or two old.

Constable Neil then testified about his discovery of the body. Even though he was never far from the spot of the murder that night, he had neither seen nor heard anything. Neil said he examined the road near the victim and found no wheel tracks, suggesting the body had not been transported to the site, which reinforced Abberline's conclusion that Nichols had been murdered where her body was found.

Dr. Llewelyn testified about the state of Nichols' body, which included a slight laceration on her tongue.

"Probably from strangulation," Helson whispered.

Abberline nodded, but was confused when Llewellyn said, "There were no marks of any struggle or of blood, as if the body had been dragged." The doctor then added that he found little blood at the scene.

Abberline frowned; was Llewellyn suggesting the body might have been moved? If the medical officer thought so, it went against everything Abberline had learned thus far. He needed to sort that issue out, soon.

A skin-domed man with a fringe of black hair and black eyes let a tiny twist of a grin curl across the corner of his mouth and nodded his head so slightly that the movement was hardly noticeable, except to a man as observant as Abberline. The Inspector stared for a moment at the man. Although he had not paid attention to him before, Abberline had seen something that bothered him—he wasn't sure what it was, but it was something. The man bore watching. Abberline leaned over and gave Helson a few pertinent instructions. Better find out who Baldy was.

With the last witness for the day exiting the stand, Abberline rose to ask for a lengthy adjournment, "as certain things are coming to the knowledge of the police and we wish for time to make inquiries." He said he had no guess how long he would require, but feared it would be quite some time before anything of note was discovered.

The jury foreman consulted his colleagues and announced, "The jury would like to hear more about this horrid business now, if we could."

Baxter sided with the jury, denied Abberline's request and announced the inquest would reconvene to hear eight more witnesses on the next working day, Monday, 3 September.

"Eight more witnesses to tell us what we already know," Helson muttered, "and none of it pointing at a suspect."

"Not unless we get back to work," Abberline said.

As they strode along a wood-paneled hall and out the Institute's thick oak doors, Abberline told Helson and Spratling, "It's amazing. PC Neil, that carter, Cross, who found the body a minute or two before Neil, and that other man, Paul, were all in Buck's Row at the time. PC Thain was just past the corner of Brady and Buck's Row. Mizen was also nearby. Three policemen, two citizens, all converging on the scene from different directions but no one heard or saw a damn thing. The murderer moved freely through that maze of streets, alleys and courtyards like a ghost."

Abberline and Spratling stopped for a moment as Helson sketched a map on his pad with a stub of a pencil. The detectives studied it. Abberline ran a stubby finger over the map, saying, "The blighter must have slipped round the corner here, gone up Winthrop Street and out into Brady behind Thain. Those slaughterers who were working in the yard were probably too occupied with their work to notice anyone going by unless he was banging on a Salvation Army bass drum."

"Or," Spratling said, "he could have gone straight down Court Street to Whitechapel Road and if he turned right, he'd be into Whitechapel Station and on his way to anywhere he wished in England, Scotland or Wales within minutes."

"Spratling, I want you to make certain the people living in Winthrop, Brady, Court and in that stretch of Whitechapel Road are re-interviewed. Post a few men there tonight and Sunday night through Monday morning to question anyone going to work Monday. Have them talk to everyone who passes through. We may find someone who heard or saw something early Friday morning."

Spratling nodded. The three policemen climbed into an official black four-wheeled growler and were soon bumping along over the cobblestone streets. Abberline knew that the pressure they were already feeling would increase as the implications of there being a monster loose in the streets of Whitechapel sank into the minds of the public, press and politicians. Every move he and his colleagues made would now be microscopically scrutinized by their superiors and minutely covered by the press. The *East London Advertiser* had complained about the Met's reticence toward the press concerning the Tabram murder in mid-August. Abberline didn't have to strain his memory to recall the date of the *Advertiser*'s assault: 18 August. In response, the carpet in the brass's offices at the Yard had been almost worn through by the number of constables and inspectors called to account for that day. Six weeks had passed and the pressure continued to build. The miscreant was still free and Abberline left the inquest with little hope and many worries.

The grim grisliness of the three murders, particularly the escalated horrors exhibited in Nichols' case and the police's inability to find a single clue helped accelerate the public's interest and the press's coverage into a snowballing avalanche of hysteria, even in the staid *Times*. The papers screamed "HORRIBLE MURDER IN WHITECHAPEL" in 72-point headlines and described the goriest of details with graphic realism: "Her throat cut right open from ear to ear…the blood was flowing profusely…she was discovered lying in a pool of blood." Little was left to the imagination: "the lower part of her person was completely ripped open." The killer was also given names, including the Knife and the Phantom.

The young reporter Abberline had noticed at the inquest, Adrian Coulls, arrived at *The Empire's* newsroom. The bare wood floor displayed chips, nicks and chunks out of it in a discordant pattern that lacked any discernible repetition. A worn rug here and there attempted to conceal the battered floor, but the rugs themselves looked as if they had not been cleaned since before Waterloo. Flat- and roll-top desks stood in rows, reflecting the rapid growth of the *Empire* in particular and the press in general. Every newspaper's newsroom was bursting with bodies to produce the copy to feed the high-speed presses to try to fill the public's insatiable appetite for news from near and, for the first time due to the telegraph, from afar. News from Bengal and Cape Town was now reported to Londoners by newspapers as rapidly as news from their own village was once reported by town criers. Copy boys rushed between the desks on their endless errands to and from the typesetters, copyeditors and printers on the floors below, their ink-stained fingers leaving marks on desks, blotters and plastered walls throughout the smoky, stuffy, noisy newsroom. The clatter of a couple of new-fangled typewriters with Hansen Writing Balls only added to the cacophony.

A touch of glee tinting his voice, Coulls told *The Empire's* night editor Donald Cox what he had that was new: "The police surgeon, Llewellyn, only performed a cursory examination of the corpse *in situ*. I don't think he's an 'early to bed, early to riser.'"

"Four in the morning is bloody early to any educated man," Cox said.

"Early or not, I assume he was awake when he first examined the body, but his examination was so 'cursory' he didn't even know Nichols had been disemboweled until the police summoned him back to the mortuary to make a proper examination of the body. He'd gone home to take a nap."

"He is a Medical Officer, not a Police Surgeon; far less experience. But you've got some decent copy there."

"That's the way, Cox," a veteran reporter called out from across the crowded newsroom. "Cubs—both feline and reportorial—need some reassurance before they're weaned."

Ignoring the comment, Coulls paraphrased the victim's father's testimony for Cox.

"Play up their estrangement," the editor advised. "Should make 20 inches with the information you gathered from the crime scene. Write it like you were talking to the reader down at your local, right?"

Nodding, but hardly hearing Cox's final words and doing his best to keep from showing his self-satisfaction too openly, Coulls retreated to his desk, gliding on air as he moved across the tumultuous newsroom. He was buoyed by a cub's confidence that he had a story ready to write that was of first-page importance, which would elate Cox and *The Empire's* board of editors, make his reporting peers greet him with "great story" when he came to work tomorrow, and would please *The Empire's* readers. Savoring a front-page above-the-fold story, Coulls set to a newsman's final task—actually writing the story up.

Coulls, a brash and stocky young man of 23, had been born in Antigonish, Nova Scotia of Catholic Highland parents. A desire to travel had sent Coulls several times around the globe to live the salty life of a sailor and see oceans of water from one pitching deck after another. It was while rounding Cape Horn in a gale the aged skipper of the ship described as "a light blow" that Coulls decided to return to drier, more stable footings. It was also his natural need to write that finally prevailed over all else. His father had been a news editor in Halifax. Perhaps the latent voice of his genetic inheritance finally spoke or perhaps it was pure chance, one of those things that just seem to happen that change a person's life. Marooned on the London docks, the out-of-work, debt-ridden Coulls heard of an opening on a Fleet Street paper from a sailor pal. He applied and landed the job.

As Coulls sat at his desk to start his story, Old Boy said, "As suspected, the victim was an unfortunate."

"I know." Coulls almost added, 'I didn't just get off the boat,' but remained silent; best to keep on good terms with the lean, chisel-featured reporter.

Old Boy was a true red, white and blue Englishman. Born in the City of Westminster, raised in the western fringes of the world's first city, Roger "Old Boy" Pierce knew every Nick and Nanny in London and already had helped Coulls with crucial information for a dozen stories on deadline. The "Old Boy" appellative came from his one-time tendency to call persons not of English extract "Old Boy," which had backfired and led to his studied dedication to avoid saying the two words together ever again. Some people thought it came from his being old—just over 25. Pierce never enlightened anyone about the origin of his nickname.

"Besides the workhouse marks on her clothes, I found another unfortunate,

Mary Ann Monk, who identified her," Coulls said. "She led a stream of street people down to the station. Evidently everyone in the East End has been talking about the killing, especially about the bonnet that was lying beside the victim's body. Velvet bonnets aren't common in Spitalfield."

"Spitalfields—it's plural."

"Odd name for a district; I mean, sounds like it's a glob of spit, 'Spital.'"

Old Boy laughed. "Only a transplanted colonial would come up with that. 'Aven't you noticed people 'ere drop their h's. The area used to be called Hospital Fields. The hospital and its grounds pretty well dominated the area. Over time the 'h' was dropped, taking the 'os' with it and eventually the two words became one."

"Um, interesting," Coulls said, trying to hit on a lead for his story. "You some kind of linguist?"

"Not really, but being a reporter does load one's brain with trivia. For example, the Artisans' Dwelling Act of 1875 led to redevelopment in many London slums."

"Sounds grand." A lead, my kingdom for a lead.

"It was, but it also drove more people into the remaining slums, such as Spitalfields and Whitechapel, making them even more dense. Then pogroms in Russia in 1881 and '82, which spread to Romania and Austria-Hungary, and Bismarck's expulsion of Poles from Prussia in '86 brought waves of Eastern Europeans to our shores, especially to East London, making the district about the densest neighbourhood on earth. Many native-born Englishmen say the recent immigrants depress wages, raise rents and, when they save enough to become landlords, that the Jews become rapacious. Free trade hasn't helped matters; put a lot of the middle class out of work, demoting them to the lower class and now we're in an agricultural depression caused in part by cheap grain imports from the colonies."

"Sounds like they should level the whole damn area and rebuild."

"Just be careful not to level too much," Old Boy warned as he wagged an ink-stained finger at Coulls. "Slums back onto some of the most fashionable and prosperous areas in London: St. James Square, Grosvenor Square and Covent Garden."

"At least those areas are safe."

Old Boy laughed again. "A multitude of sins can be hidden by a cloak of splendor, whereas the nakedness of poverty exposes the smallest of sins—that's good; have to use it in a novel some time. Besides, with two million people crowded into the greater East End, bound to be some villains in the lot. East London is bigger than St. Petersburg, Berlin or Philadelphia, and they all have their criminal classes, too. Granted, Spitalfields is poorer than those cities. More than 90,000 people live in extreme poverty in Spitalfields with 286 people wedged in every squalid acre. With such poverty, men and women face the eternal question of whether to sin or starve."

"Sounds like nothing good can come from such a black hole." Coulls needed a lead. How to hook the reader—and please Cox?

"Far from it; much good in the East End. Spitalfields is a major vegetable market. Aldgate is London's meat market; it's called Butchers Row or Blood Alley. True, animals are often slaughtered in the streets, but 500 men have found honest work as slaughterers, butchers and meat vendors."

"Admirable employment," Coulls said, wishing Old Boy would just shut up and let him write his story. How soon 'til deadline? Forty minutes. Didn't Old Boy have a story to write?

"Then there's Wentworth Street, where all day long uncovered wagons bring rubbish from all over London to be ground down by heavy machinery. You should go some time. The continual noise is rather appalling and the entire area is covered with grime and filth, but it is memorable; something to see."

"Maybe do it as a night out with some bonnie lass?" Coulls asked with a wry grin. Old Boy must have already finished his stories for the day.

"The London Docks are also in East London and employ a sizable number, although on an average day 20,000 men are out of work in London. Many queue at the dock gates for work; as many as 20 men for each and every job."

"Must hurt wages something awful."

"Even so, the queue starts at 3 a.m.—come one, come all."

Coulls paused in his search for a lead. "With so many men on the streets that early, not to mention market workers, the Phantom must have fit in like one of the crowd or he'd have been noticed by someone."

Coulls noticed that Old Boy paused and looked at him with a look similar to how Cox had eyed him earlier; maybe he could make it as a correspondent.

Inspector Joseph Chandler of the Commercial Street station (H Division), Spitalfields, sat in his front parlor with his wife, Martha. Chandler having checked their boys' maths homework, their gang of four was upstairs doing something for school. They attended a day school, although Chandler would have preferred a boarding school or apprenticeship. He could not afford the former and had yet to find any suitable of the latter.

"Did you remember to use bug powder?" Martha asked as she paused in her game of Patience. Martha insisted he use a plentiful amount of Keating's Bug Powder whenever he returned from work in the East End.

Chandler nodded as he sipped an after-dinner port—his third—and a rather strange case came to his mind. Larry Donovan, one of those eccentric American colonials who valued notoriety as much as life itself, had attempted one of his death-defying plunges a week ago from the foot path of the railway bridge at Charing Cross. He had bobbed to the surface of the Thames and then disappeared. So far his remains had not been found. Chandler had almost forgotten about the daredevil's most probable demise when luggage with Donovan's name on it had been found in a routine search of a thief's den. Having perfected the technique of posing as a relative of a deceased person to gain illegal entry, the thief had evidently rushed to Donovan's room as soon as he heard of the man's demise. The wily felon had fenced most of the stuff he had scoffed by the time Chandler and his men swooped, but there was still enough to put him away for a year or two. You had, Chandler thought, to give the cunning bounder a certain grudging credit for his creativity.

Chandler could understand the familiar. He knew this thief's motives and admired his means, but Donovan's daredevil antics? Risking one's life for public recognition was a strange enough activity, but to maximize the risk of leaping Thames-ward when the river was at an August low was nothing other than foolhardy. Abberline had said, "Such a man is too stupid to even know when he's committing suicide. I wonder what life was worth to a man like Donovan. Without acclaim, it must be nothing. That's the way with fools; they always value the wrong things." Still made no common sense to Chandler.

Turning to his newspaper, Chandler read in *The Times* that researchers and doctors were debating whether there might be a connection between smoking and throat disease. Middlesex Hospital researchers had found that the marked increase in malignant throat disease was not due to partaking of pipe, cigar or ordinary cigarettes, but due to the peculiar habit of Turkish and Egyptian tobacco to be mixed with an insidious poison which presumably gave these mid-Eastern tobaccos their even more peculiar taste. The researchers reported finding traces of an unclassified alkaloid and large quantities of opium in the foreign tobaccos. They also found that smoking mixtures of local manufacture were pure of such contaminants.

"Dear, they've found that foreign tobacco is mixed with all manner of poisons."

"No surprise there, Joseph," Martha said with complete confidence as she placed the seven of hearts on a long column of cards with a smile of accomplishment.

The Egyptian consular authority made counterarguments. Cope Brothers, owners of Liverpool Tobacco Works, couldn't restrain themselves from pointing out the appalling squalor, dirtiness and general degradation that surrounded the packaging of Egyptian and Turkish cigarettes. To the Copes, it was a simple choice between putting tobacco to mouth that had been handled by dirty Turks or filthy Egyptians or smoking the tidy efforts of good, clean, moral, English girls. Chandler could only agree. He smoked nothing else save John Bull's best.

"It's obvious, Chief Inspector Abberline, that the woman was murdered elsewhere and moved to the spot where she was found," Sir Charles asserted. Abberline, Helson and Spratling had been ordered to Sir Charles' wood-paneled office at the Met Central Office, 4 Whitehall Place. "Perhaps that carter who claims to have found her actually brought her there. When that other man. . .er. . ."

"Paul, sir."

"Yes, that's the chap. When he happened along, the carter pretended to have just found the body that instant. Some of those costermongers are clever as a Jew, wot?"

Abberline wondered if Sir Charles had spoken with Dr. Llewelyn, since the doctor also seemed to have suggested at the inquest that the body may have been moved, although his language had been far from clear.

Sir Charles continued, "Her clothing was placed in an appropriate fashion to cover the mutilations. It seems clear to me that the murderer was trying to hide something."

Abberline agreed. The murderer *was* trying to hide something—his identity.

Sir Charles said, "There wasn't enough blood on the ground at the scene to account for the amount lost from her body. It's right here in the examining surgeon's report. I am sure it's the Old Nichol Gang. Those thugs are a constant menace; a constant and far too abiding menace. They must be apprehended and gaoled, if not hung, the lot of them. Extorting shillings from unfortunates? Must be stopped."

Abberline nodded. The Old Nichol area had a death rate twice as high as other parts of Shoreditch and Bethnal Green, and four times that of London as a whole. One child in four in the area died before their first birthday. No wonder the gang concentrated on extorting money from unfortunates, Abberline thought. They were probably the only individuals in the area with any money, even if it was just a few shillings. Sir Charles hadn't discovered that Abberline had only ordered a superficial investigation into the gang's activities. He probably never would.

The interview was soon over. The oracle had spoken.

"Does his theory of the body being moved hold any water?" Spratling asked as the trio of policemen settled in for the long, slow ride in an official growler to the Bethnal Green Police Station. Horse-drawn traffic diverted from Commercial Street, where the North Metropolitan Tramways Company was laying track for a new line, was causing congestion that made even the shortest trips across East London an arduous and protracted adventure. "There was little blood at the scene."

"Most of the blood was absorbed by the victim's dress and ulster," Helson said. "When Thain helped shift the body onto the ambulance, the clothes soaked his hands with blood."

"Doesn't take much blood to soak your hands," Chandler said.

"We found no sign of a blood trail," Helson countered.

"When the carman, Cross, and PC Neil found the body," Abberline said, "they both said it was still warm, so I doubt the body was moved. But we need to settle the issue. I'll chat with Llewellyn and clear things up; last thing we need is the press putting it out that some madman is out and about carting corpses all over Whitechapel in the dead of night."

"Someone carrying a tarp-covered corpse on a cart wouldn't be noticed in that area with all the slaughterhouses about," Spratling said.

"No sign of a cart in the row for Cross to have used anyway," Abberline said. "Unless he lugged the body there over his shoulder, which someone would have noticed."

"Hopefully Llewellyn can clear it up," Helson said.

"Maybe ask him about the handedness of the murderer, too," Spratling said. "At first he said the killer was left-handed, but the last time I spoke with him, he had his doubts."

A half hour later Abberline was in Dr. Llewellyn's surgery asking the doctor's opinion about the murderer's handedness.

"He was probably left-handed. The throat wounds suggest it."

"Could he be right-handed?"

"Of course, almost anyone could use their non-dominant hand to slit someone's throat. It mainly depends on where he stood or crouched when he did it."

"What about Sir Charles' idea that she wasn't murdered where she was found?"

"She was killed on the spot, Inspector. Her heavy garments soaked up the blood. That is why there was so little blood on the ground."

As they talked, Abberline wondered why Llewellyn was becoming so derelict at crime scenes and often confusing on the stand at inquests. It was baffling. The man seemed keen and enthusiastic enough now, even if his advanced training had been in obstetrics.

Abberline bid Llewellyn good day and was down the street when he remembered that he wanted to ask the doctor whether the murder might have been the work of a gang. He was certain it was not, but it never hurt to ask. He turned back toward the surgery and saw the bearded and mustached physician emerge. Abberline was about to call out to him when a young lady in a dark blue dress met Llewellyn. The doctor and the lady turned and strolled down the sidewalk away from Abberline. From the smile of greeting on their faces, Abberline knew why Llewellyn had been distracted on the job. The bachelor who lived with his siblings might, just might, at last have found someone with whom to start his own family.

Chapter Five

Running roughly parallel to and just north of the Thames, Commercial Street was a crowded maze of muddled sights and a basin of pungent cistern smells. Snorting horses, nostrils flaring, strained at bit and rein; wagon, carriage and omnibus drivers cracked curses and wielded whips; vendors shrieked and yelled in a Tower of Babel's worth of foreign and domestic dialects; squeals and grunts of terrified animals shot street-ward from the slaughterhouses. Urchins clambered on hitching posts, irritating the horses as they used the reins as swings. Costermongers shouted their offers of jellied eel and other treats from their rickety carts. A guide led two toff couples on a tour of the East End: slumming, as it was called. The sun, serenely shaded by a canopy of cloud and skein of coal dust, sprayed rays of diffuse light between the buildings on a motley mix of grime-encrusted brick, moss-marked wood and mortar-missing stonework. Everything seemed in a state of decay. A moldy, miserable smell oozed from everywhere. Even the people, many presumably young and potentially robust, seemed older than they should be. Their soiled, rumpled and torn clothing fitted precisely into this living portrait of poverty, perversion and hopelessness.

A little man, Isaac Jacobs, in a simple cloth cap, frayed frock-coat and loose-fitting multi-stained trousers with sagging cuffs hurried along, stooping in a perpetual crouch, his head swiveling from side to side as if expecting to be assailed at any second from any quarter—or every quarter. He dodged past five urchins playing shove a halfpenny on the pavement. He clutched an oil-cloth-covered bundle under his right arm, holding the package in a tense grip that was augmented by occasional nervous pats and clutches from his free left hand. Now and then tiny trickles of blood seeped from the folds of the bundle and dripped down the outside of the oil cloth.

Jacobs came to the crowded five-way intersection where Commercial Street met Whitechapel Road before it continued south as Leman Street. To his left, Commercial Road intersected on a 45-degree angle. To his right, Whitechapel Road became Aldgate. The accumulation of traffic assaulted the eyes and ears, especially with navvies working night and day to lay the new tram line on Commercial Street, which created a snarl of traffic rivalling in complexity the Gordian knot of antiquity. Carriages, cabs, wagons, pushcarts, horse-buses, omnibuses, hansoms, hackneys, landaus—vehicles of all descriptions—clattered about the place in a kaleidoscope of chaos. Jacobs leapt back as a speedy two-wheeler whipped by, its whirly hubs narrowly missing him.

"Hey!" The little man had backed into a gargantuan mass of a man whose flashing blue eyes, ruddy complexion and straight black hair suggested a Celtic heritage. The big fellow glared down at the insignificant creature who had dared trod on his foot. Jacobs pulled away from the Scotsman and in so doing loosened his hold on his bundle. The movement flipped a flap of oil cloth back and sent a cascade of bloody liquid onto the street.

"What the hell?" the Celt exclaimed, doing a poor imitation of a Highland Fling as he danced back to avoid the spray.

"Blood!" someone yelled.

Jacobs scurried into the street, glancing back to see if the offended Scot was pursuing him.

"There was a murder in Buck's Row last night," someone of a suspicious bent said. The statement was enough. It united the individuals on the corner into a self-righteous crowd of avengers. The miraculous speed of human thought easily overcame its depth. The little man must be the Buck's Row murderer: the Knife.

"After 'im, men!"

The chase was on, a mindless movement of bodies surging forward, carried along by the excitement of the moment, escaping the drab everyday existence of the East End poor, unaware of the real reason for running, unaware that it was the fun and the feeling of doing something felt to be just and right that carried them forward. Jacobs ran for his life. The mass of humanity behind him avalanched into a stampede. He raced in puffing, gasping desperation down the street and burst into the Commercial Street Police Station where a sympathetic policeman helped him into a chair. The mob, most of whom having no idea who they were chasing, swept on down the street, chasing this or that phantom and anyone foolish enough to be running at their head.

Jacobs, shaking like an autumn leaf in a North Atlantic gale, accepted the policeman's kind invitation to a spot of tea; very rare and nice of a copper to make such an offer. But then Joseph Chandler was a kind man. He was also a suspicious one. He carefully noted Jacobs' name, occupation and address on an "official" complaint about Jacobs' being harassed by a mob.

"We like to keep a record of these things," Chandler said. Yes, we certainly do, he thought, smiling at the strange little man. He was a rough looking little weasel, poorly dressed and definitely of the lower class. He must have been running for some reason. He had obviously stolen a bundle of meat from his place of business to supplement his meager rations. It wasn't worth the effort trying to prove it, but it did show he was dishonest. He was a slaughterman. He was a foreigner. He was a Jew. But was he a murderer? Chandler thought that he might be. Yes, Isaac Jacobs would bear watching.

Under Abberline's instructions, Detective Sergeant Enright and Sergeant Godley interviewed more than a hundred people this cloudy September day. Other policemen including PC Thain examined all the premises in the vicinity of Buck's Row. Inspector Spratling checked the East End and District Railway lines as well as the Great Eastern line and yards, while still others scoured the entire Embankment along the grease-filmed Thames, enduring the smell of putrefying animal carcasses in the waterway that connected London with its global empire.

Lusky could only lick his fur-framed paw pads in utter indifference at the rush of blue-coated humans bustling through his hunting grounds. That man-thing he had met at the corner last night, now that was a creature of more concern. Such a man-thing was capable of cruelty to people and, worse, cats. Scavenging dogs were one thing, but it was best to keep a wary eye out for that ogre. Maybe it was the man-thing they were hunting. Humans weren't entirely devoid of intelligence.

At 7 p.m. the smoky newspaper office still bubbled with reporters, editors, copy editors and copy boys; some hard at work; a few appeared to be working, but were not; others did not appear to be working, but actually were. It was the way of the press. Smoke curled ceiling-ward from dozens of pipes, cigars and cigarettes, like so many filmy snakes under the uncertain control of some aged Indian snake charmer. Old Boy Pierce, Coulls and Jennings, all in shirt-sleeved informality, heatedly discussed the disjointed and often controversial bits of information they had gathered concerning the murder in Buck's Row. The tall one was Jason Jennings, born 6 May 1867, in Philadelphia, PA. He was raised a Protestant, educated an American, trained a printer and happy as a newsman. A year before, he had been sent to London to work as a part-time overseas correspondent for Pulitzer's *New York World*. Recently he had added a second part-time job with *The Empire* to supplement his income and was loving every miserable, poorly paid minute of his stay in the first city of the British Empire. The three men differed in religion, nationality, temperament and most other superficial things, but were bound together by a cord of comradery that was as strong as any secret society oath. They were young, they were reporters and they were on a marvelous adventure in the big city.

"Nichols left her lodging a few days ago," Pierce said. "She shared a room with an Ellen or Emily Holland for six weeks or so at 18 Thrawl Street. Where she bedded down after that is a mystery. Holland thought it was the White House in Flower and Dean Street. Nichols told a friend, 'It beats Thrawl Street. They sleep men as well as women there.'"

The trio laughed. Coulls knew one Whitechapel doss house was about the same as the next. They all had a common room with bare wood floors, a long table, a few chairs and forms against the walls for the lodgers to sit on to eat what they had managed to find; cheese and pickled red cabbage, cold bacon on bread, or maybe red herring devoured head to tail, bones and all. Lodgers, if they were lucky, were given a flickering dip wrapped around with a bit of paper to light their way up narrow spiral stairs to common sleeping rooms; if they weren't lucky, they felt their way up by hand in the dark. Some slept on a hangover bench; sitting on a bench with their arms draped over a rope to stay upright. Even the better tenements in the area saw dozens of inhabitants sleeping on straw in coffin beds in a common room, only sometimes segregated by sex, sharing a single earth closet with long lines in the morning for a privy that was as often as not full to the seat, and paying all they had for the night.

"I must have gone to every doss house in Whitechapel today," Pierce concluded, closing his eyes for a moment.

"No wonder you're tired," Coulls said. "They're as common as ships on the Thames."

As the sun set, Abberline and Helson sat on either side of Helson's desk in his office in Bethnal Green Police Station. If he sat up straight, Abberline could just see Helson's face over the uneven towers of reports, witness statements and files that had already accumulated from the investigation.

Abberline leaned back, rubbed the back of his left knee and wondered whether he shouldn't have stayed a clockmaker. He fingered the hunting watch in his vest pocket as he asked, "Any clear leads?"

"Three tentative ones, but early days," Helson said, mixing himself some Cadbury cocoa. When asked if he wanted a cocoa with a glance, Abberline declined with a shake of his head. "Suspect number one: John Pizer, alias Leather Apron, is a Polish immigrant named Severin Klosowski. He was a *feldscher* or unqualified barber-surgeon in the Russian Army and put the fear of himself into a number of women. Two: a Polish Jew, Kosminski or Kozminski, a hairdresser in Whitechapel who also practices basic medicine, has been mentioned by a witness. Three: an insane Russian doctor named Michael Ostrog."

"Chase down everything you can on these foreigners. Talk to everyone you can find who ever met them."

Michael Ostrog

"At least the public's more than eager to help."

"Unfortunately that means that things we know to be true are embellished and reported from a dozen sources as if each and every one is the original source."

"I talked to Sergeant Thick about Leather Apron." Helson dug in a pile of reports and extracted one from its depths. "He said Pizer is far from a gentleman, but he doesn't think Pizer is in any way capable of committing the Buck's Row murder."

"Just one man's opinion, but I trust Thick."

"Pizer was charged with indecent assault on 4 April."

"Still in the tombs?"

"Discharged before the murder." Helson closed the file and said, "Whatever his true capacity for violence, Thick, Moore and Andrews can't find him in any of his usual haunts. He seems to have gone to ground."

Leather Apron had become *persona non finda.*

Helson, showing the proud smile of a father, asked, "By the way, did I mention Henry got a first in rhetoric?"

"Congratulations. May have a future Prime Minister on your hands."

"More likely a Met Superintendent, given his starting point."

"If so, he better give chief inspectors a rise."

"Inspectors, too; especially inspectors with four children."

Abberline chuckled as Helson returned to his reports. "Benjamin Quinnell, the Lambeth stabber, is being held on a charge of indecently and violently assaulting a Margaret Watts in Lambeth. He tried to sexually molest her and when thwarted stabbed her in the lower abdomen. He might be a suspect in the Tabram murder, but he certainly wasn't responsible for this latest murder. He's still in goal."

A report from PC Neil noted that Mrs. Emma Green had been sleeping during the time of the Nichols murder in the bedroom of the house nearest the slaying, less than ten feet from the murder site.

"She claims to be a light sleeper and didn't hear a thing," Abberline said. "Didn't even wake up. No one else in her house woke up either. Our slayer was quiet as a mouse and efficient as a cat."

As Helson finished his cocoa, Abberline walked over to a table that was burdened with stacks of reports, but was also home to a cozy-covered teapot. "Fancy a cuppa?"

Helson nodded. Abberline lifted the tea cozy and poured Helson and himself cups of new Whittard black-leaf tea.

Helson, post-mortem report in hand, said, "Dr. Llewellyn thinks the weapon was a cork-cutter or a shoemaker's knife, not a sailor's jackknife as was first thought. He feels sure Nichols was grabbed from behind and had her throat slit before she could let out a peep."

"Our other surgeons feel she was attacked and silenced from in front. Boils down to which medical mind you wish to believe, and on which of them you believe may hang a left-handed or right-handed slayer—or maybe even an ambidextrous one."

"Still doesn't rule out Pizer."

"No, but the stealthiness of the killer does. Pizer is an argumentative, aggressive beast when he drinks. Such a man is a poor candidate to be a stealthy, silent killer."

"At least we learned a few things about Nichols."

"Even if it took all afternoon to confirm Emily Holland's identification of the body. A couple of dozen Lambeth workhouse inmates, all of whom had worked with Nichols, were paraded past the corpse before we got a positive identification, then suddenly all of them knew her, except the matron of the place, but that's nothing amazing. What workhouse matron pays attention to her charges except to yell, 'Scrub the floor,' 'Clean the windows' and 'Empty the earth closet'?"

"Nichols shared a room at 18 Thrawl Street with three other women—all streetwalkers," Helson said. "She paid 4d a night for a bed. She was a resident of Lambeth Workhouse off and on for the past year. Also worked as a servant in a house on Wandsworth Common but was dismissed for stealing £3. Married for 22 years to William Nichols."

"I was with him when he identified the body with his son this afternoon," Abberline said, wishing he could forget the searing moment. "He said, 'I forgive you, as you are, for what you have been to me.'" Abberline paused, clearing his mind of the scene with a conscious will. "William Nichols said the missing front teeth are from long ago. They separated eight years ago because of her alcoholism. He said at the inquest that the last time he saw her was at the funeral of her brother who was burnt to death in a paraffin lamp explosion in June '86."

"Some people have all the luck—all bad."

"She probably deserved better: poverty, alcoholism, prostitution. A devil of a triangle." Abberline turned his attention to his notes. "Let's see. Height: 5 foot 2 inches. Age: 43."

"Didn't look it."

"Small scar on forehead. Dress: hmmm. This woman was dirt poor, Helson. Look at the clothes list: all well-worn. Only one thing new: a black bonnet faced with black or blue velvet."

"Not likely to be a gang's extortion target."

"No. Interestingly enough, her reputation, as gathered from Thain, Godley and Enright—independently—wasn't what you'd expect. No one seemed to see her as being particularly fast with men."

"Her father agreed, but what father would disagree?"

Abberline lifted his cup of tea and stared at the curls of steam from the brew as he inhaled the aroma. "People in the East End aren't particularly protective of an unfortunate's reputation. They tend to describe people as they are, a whore's a whore to them, but perhaps they are a little more lenient when they're describing people as they were. People feel sorry for the victim or guilty because they're damn glad it wasn't them, so they cast a more-kindly eye on the deceased."

"Perhaps she was a little too fast with this." Helson held up a half-empty bottle of gin from his desk drawer. Abberline nodded and suddenly felt a tad uncomfortable. He had been about to ask if Helson had something to perk up his tea.

Sir James Fraser, Police Commissioner for the City of London for most of the past quarter century, sat solemnly before his fireplace with its supply of coke beside it, too tired to visit his club and too ill to read anything more than a few human interest stories in the evening's papers. His mind was now meandering through that strange labyrinth of idle memory and wistful musing that is so often a refuge for the depressed, the old and the infirm. The past few months had been a relatively quiet time for the City Police. Sir James was thankful. Being ill was burden enough. The usual robberies, suicides and rare homicides occurred, but nothing out of the ordinary. For no seemingly apparent reason, one particular day in mid-July came to mind. It was a few weeks past but it was as clear as an illuminated show to Sir James. George Sargent, a young railway worker and former soldier, cut his wife's throat in the presence of her mother and sister. Not bothering to dispense with the obvious witnesses, Sargent was quickly captured, tried and found guilty by a jury of people erroneously called his peers. You were never judged by your peers, Sir James thought. Who could decide such a thing? He remembered Sargent's day of execution vividly because a bull escaped custody in a food market that same day and entered the Theatre Royal by the stage door. Performers, producers and patrons of the arts had to run for life, limb and safety. The animal ignored the fleeing thespian crowd and attacked—of all things—several props of deer, goring them to shreds. Sir James' men arrived to find the enraged beast literally tearing the stuffing out of a prop stag. The bull was dispatched by firearm discharge. Sir James happened to be passing by on his way to his physician and had witnessed the final scene.

Sir James could not ascertain why he should remember such events. Sargent had killed his wife in a brainless blur of gin-generated rage and the half-crazed bull had vented his rage in a meaningless display of dominance over an artificial animal; acts that cost both assaulting parties their lives. Perhaps he remembered because it was all so absolutely futile. Maybe it was the thought that the murder of this latest unfortunate also seemed so absolutely futile. What was the point? She certainly had no money worth stealing at the risk of being hung. Her favours could be bought for far less than the cost of a decent meal at his club. It was all so baffling.

While Sir James convalesced at home, many others enjoyed the benefits of health and wealth and stepped out. As had become common in the East End, many workingmen took their families to music halls on Saturday night. Audiences participated as much as the cast in the bawdy, often vulgar shows in Drury Lane and Camden Town, at Wilton's off Wellclose Square, the Brit in Huxton High Street and The Queen's in Poplar. For the upper class, Saturday night was theatre night. Sir Charles, his wife and friends rejected taking in *That Dreadful Doctor* at the Haymarket and elected to see *The Union Jack* at the Adelphi. Their choice was enhanced by a friend's first chance to go to a theatre entirely lit by electricity. The group also discussed the new grand spectacular to which they had advance tickets—didn't everyone?—at the *Theatre Royal*. All London was waiting in anxious anticipation for Hamilton and Harris' *The Armada*, a drama bound to take its place with the giants of English plays alongside *Macbeth*, *Hamlet* and *King Lear*. Abberline declined an invitation to *The Mikado* at the Savoy and elected to check in at various station houses throughout the evening. He felt uneasy about the latest murder. Helson and Mary visited friends, playing charades and viewing lantern slides. Despite the latest murder, no extra officers were detailed for night duty. Sir Charles felt there was little need to mobilize the force to its fullest potential just because a degenerate slut or three got her throat sliced almost in two.

Sunday, 2 September

After church and an hour at home with Emma, Abberline began the Sabbath afternoon in his office. Until they caught the Phantom, work-free Sundays were a thing of the past for inspectors on the case. Abberline began by belatedly asking Helson to assign someone to follow Sir Charles' orders concerning the Old Nichol and Rip gangs.

"I'll put a couple of junior men on it."

"Good, good," Abberline said. If manpower had to be wasted, it might as well be the least in quantity and quality. He wished the commissioner would focus on new truncheons and boots for the men, rather than delving into the investigative side of the Met, especially since Sir Charles' investigatory experience rested on just one case: finding the murderers of the Palmer Expedition in the Egyptian desert; not the most analogous case to the murder of three unfortunates in London's East End. "Well, let's get on with our rounds."

They were soon bumping along the cobbled East End streets in an antiquated four-wheeler. At least the aging vehicle was stable; far better balanced than any two-person hansom. Even so, caught in traffic caused by the Commercial Street tram construction, it stopped often enough to drive even a bishop to take the Lord's name in vain.

Folding a newspaper away under his arm, Helson asked, "How do you think this Buck's Row villain got away?"

"The place is a maze of streets meandering every which way, and the area is chock-full of slaughterhouses. He could have been bathed in blood from hair to boots and not stand out in the early morning traffic of tradesmen. Come to think of it, according to Dr. Llewellyn, he probably wouldn't be covered with much, if any, blood anyway. And who's to say he didn't have a coat or cloak hanging on that gate to pull on after the job was done? At least there is one way to solve this silly controversy over the apparent lack of blood at the murder site once and for all."

"How?"

"I put Chandler and two constables to work on a little experiment earlier this morning. I hope he didn't wear his Sunday suit."

They found Inspector Chandler in a sharp check suit at the Commercial Street station with two constables in their regulation blue swallow-tail coats acting on Abberline's instructions. The trio had collected three barrels of pig's blood from nearby slaughterhouses, measured out quantities equal to that found in a human body, and in the narrow lane behind the stationhouse had diligently poured a gallon and a half of porcine blood into a gown approximating the one the victim had worn. Chandler reported, and Abberline and Helson now saw, that most of the blood was soaked up as if by a monstrous sponge. If human blood acted the same way, the mystery was solved. Abberline congratulated Chandler and his men for their efforts and then instructed them to repeat the test at different temperatures and with clothing at various degrees of wetness.

"Why, sir?" Chandler asked.

"A thunderstorm dropped rain on London the day before the Nichols murder."

"I see." Chandler frowned. "How do I make it colder?"

"Come to work tomorrow very early or just buy some ice."

Chandler nodded and returned to his bloody task.

Back in the four-wheeler, Abberline went over his latest list in his notebook of duties for various inspectors. The four-wheeler stopped.

"This traffic would have stopped even Napoleon in his tracks," Hanson said. He pulled out his newspaper, revealing within its folds the latest issue of *Punch*. "An interesting poem here, sir," he said, showing Abberline a work called, "The Nemesis of Neglect" about the East End. Abberline read: "Look at these walls; they reek with dirt and damp, / But in their shadows crouched, the homeless tramp / May huddle undisturbed the black night through. / These narrow winding courts – in thought – pursue. / No light there breaks upon the bludgeoned wife, / No flash of day arrests the lifted knife, / There shrieks arouse not, nor do groans affright. / These are but normal noises of the night. .. Must it be / That the black slum shall furnish sanctuary / To all light-shunning creatures of the slime, / Vermin of vice, carnivore of crime?"

Helson asked, "Does the author know more about the murderer than we do?"

"If he does, he doesn't know much, since at this point we don't know sod all."

Monday, 3 September

The sky gradually lightened, brightened and became a pastel gray-blue above the sprawling metropolis. Whiffs of pillow-puff clouds drifted lazily across the pale backdrop that seemed more a painter's attempt at a colour wash than a reality of nature.

Coulls struggled to read *The Times* as he bumped and bounced along in a two-wheeled hansom. He managed to read that an esteemed *Times* correspondent believed that the same murderer had probably committed the Smith, Tabram and Nichols murders, although the correspondent reported that the police had abandoned the idea that a gang was behind the murders.

The hansom went over a loose cobblestone and sent Coulls' head into the ceiling with a painful thud. Cursing Joseph Hansom and his infernal invention,

Coulls questioned his decision to take a hansom to work. He had wanted to get a jump on the day and pursue several promising leads, but walking, albeit somewhat slower, would have involved far less pain for his head and posterior.

"Nemesis of Neglect": Jack the Ripper depicted as a phantom stalking Whitechapel and as an embodiment of social neglect in a "Punch" cartoon, 1888 (John Tenniel)

Returning to *The Times*, Coulls read that Constable Neil said he passed Buck's Row 30 minutes before the body was found, yet neither saw nor heard a thing. The correspondent pointed out that Neil walked a 12-minute beat. Why had it taken more than twice that long to return to Buck's Row? Coulls decided to chase that discrepancy down.

The story ended by stating that "the mystery is most complete." Coulls wholeheartedly agreed. Whichever correspondent was the first to break the story of the identity of the Whitechapel slayer would be famous and make his career. Coulls intended to be that correspondent.

As Coulls was treated in his hansom cab like a kernel of corn in a hot popper, the business of the day brought Londoners into the streets in droves. Thousands upon thousands of scurrying citizens each bent on his or her specific tasks climbed aboard hackneys and hansoms, carriages, omnibuses, railway coaches or newly popular bicycles and flowed hither and thither in full force. The poor walked, the rich rode, all going someplace. It was as if a gigantic colony of creatures had been phototrophically stirred by the sun's early light. Each individual moved to his or her specific goal as if appointed by some unknown order that predetermined each of their places and functions. London, like all of the Victorian Empire, was strictly and systematically divided into social strata as binding as that of an insect society. How that binding might be loosened had become a topic of concern the past few years. The recent Matchgirls Strike had highlighted the abominable working conditions of the women and girls who laboured in the match factories, risking fire and disfiguring phossy jaw from handling white phosphorous. Social activist Annie Besant and several progressive MPs had helped negotiate a union and somewhat better working conditions for the women, including a separate room to eat meals away from the poisonous atmosphere of the match factory itself, and ending the many and varied deductions workers had to pay for materials and as fines for the broadest range of offenses imaginable to the management. Most forward-thinking Victorians applauded the improved working conditions—as long as they didn't own any match factories. Good works did have its limits.

In his plush office overlooking the Embankment and the Thames, James Whitehead, city alderman, unofficially Lord Mayor-elect and loyal member of London's privileged merchant class threw his arms air-ward in protest. "It's NOT that simple, Reverend. It just isn't."

"Why isn't it?" asked Reverend Samuel Barnett, Vicar of St. Jude's, Whitechapel, and founder of Toynbee Hall and the East End Dwelling Company, which built decent homes for the poor. Baron Rothschild had supplemented Barnett's efforts by founding the Four Percent Industrial Dwellings Company in 1885 to build housing for poor Jewish labourers. Barnett told Whitehead, "There should at least be adequate street lighting. Our backstreets are dark, empty canyons, inviting thievery and attacks on women."

"Please, Reverend, please," Whitehead protested. Why couldn't the man see the obvious? It might be a new idea that municipalities should be responsible for housing their working and not-working poor, but it was a new *socialist* idea and Whitehead disliked the idea intensely. No business background; that was the problem with Barnett. "It's a simple matter of there being an insufficient tax base to pay for the many things that are needed."

"There is plenty of money in the West End."

"You don't expect the citizens of the West End—good, solid, upstanding, god-fearing people—to pay higher taxes to benefit the people—some of whom pay no taxes—of the East End, do you? Next you'll be wanting Parliament to pass laws asking people in a rich, successful nation like England to pay taxes for people in some impoverished, ill-run place halfway around the globe like Greece or Siam."

"No, no, Mr. Whitehead, I just want the taxes that are collected in the East End to be spent on the East End. You know that isn't always so."

"Well, that may be a reasonable criticism."

"And if those people of West London could be encouraged to open their hearts and give a reasonable donation..."

There it was! Whitehead smiled. The fault was in the human heart, not the equitable tax system. Reverend Barnett merely wanted Whitehead to help launch another charity campaign. Barnett would have been fine had he ended his argument at this point, but like many who argue and most social activists, the Reverend didn't know when to quit. He moved on to the issue of compound leases; the subletting of property to yet another "sub-letter." Even this would have been acceptable, Whitehead thought, had Barnett not concluded with the solemn wish that "some public-spirited philanthropists can avoid the easy temptation of quick profits by way of overcrowding and prostitution."

Flare point! Spark had met black powder. Whitehead erupted with indignation. "You aren't accusing these owners—many of them titled and honourable people—of knowingly condoning prostitution in their establishments? These are all good Christian people, Reverend."

"No, no, no, sir, of course not. Nothing could be further from my mind. You misunderstand me, sir, most definitely, you misunderstand."

Calm was restored and, even though Whitehead knew the Reverend would return, soon, pushing for more of his social changes and ever more funding for the poor, the two men settled down to discuss what charity appeals might be acceptable to Whitehead and his wealthy supporters. Hand-to-mouth Whitechapel could continue to depend on a handout.

Once again Abberline settled into a hard wood seat at the Working Lads' Institute. He nodded at Helson, Enright, Spratling and Mizen who sat just down the row, all looking angelic, bathed in the sunlight streaming through a stained-glass window high on the wall of the vast room.

Coroner Baxter called Inspector Spratling first. He testified that the mortuary attendants had no authority to strip and clean the body. Spratling sounded angry as he said, "They left the victim's clothes in a heap in the yard."

Abberline already knew all about it.

Henry Tompkins, horse-slaughterer, testified next. He said the slaughter yard gates were open that night, but he heard no cry at about 2 a.m., even though the yard was quiet.

Baxter asked, "Did you see any women at that time?"

"No women about; I don't like 'em."

"Odd sort," Helson whispered.

"Slaughtering animals all day can't be good for the mind or soul," Abberline said, "let alone for attracting women."

Tompkins said there were lots of people on Whitechapel Road at the time of the murder. It was, he said, "A rough neighbourhood, I can tell you." He then added, almost as an aside, "The slaughterhouse is too far from the murder spot to hear if anyone cried anyway."

Abberline perked up. He knew that PC Neil had seen the three horse slaughterers, Tompkins, James Mumford and Charles Britton, working in the yard of Harrison, Barber & Co. on Winthrop Street at 3:20 a.m. and that the three were in the crowd when Dr. Llewelyn made his initial examination of the body. "How'd they hear about the murder if the slaughterhouse is too far to hear anything from the murder site?"

Helson flipped through his note book with a fury. Finally, he found what he was looking for. "They said PC Thain told them of the murder on his way to fetch the doctor."

"I don't recall Thain reporting that; might pay to hunt down their backgrounds."

"Neil did see them hard at work at about the time of the murder."

"Unless they murdered Nichols together, the other two would have noticed the absence of the third. Investigate them all the same, but don't squander more than the guts of a day on them."

Coroner Baxter called Helson next. Abberline surreptitiously dozed as Helson went over his arrival at the murder site and his inspection of Nichols's clothes, which were not ripped or torn. Based on analysis of the scene and the clothes, Helson found, "No indication of a struggle."

Mizen was up next and told Abberline nothing he didn't already know. Then Charles Allen Cross, the carman, testified about finding the body.

"Maybe Sir Charles is right and he did it," Helson whispered with a grin as he settled back in after his testimony. "Faked finding the body when he heard that other bloke, Paul, coming up Buck's Row."

Abberline sighed. They had already investigated Cross and found he had worked for the past twenty years delivering horse meat for Messrs. Pickford and Company without any criminal incident. "If he is the murderer, it's a sudden change in his apparently model behavior," Abberline whispered.

"Granted, he didn't have any blood on him when Paul arrived just minutes after the murder, but hard to see blood on dark clothes, and Llewellyn said there probably wasn't much blood on the killer. Might have had a knife hidden somewhere on him."

"Paul didn't see any knife, nor did any of the officers on the scene, but Cross might bear looking into." Abberline was beginning to think they should just start investigating every man between twelve and sixty in the East End. "I wish everyone who found the body was the killer; would make our job as easy as ordering a pint."

Baxter next called William Nichols, a printer's machinist and husband of the deceased. Abberline dozed, shutting out the memory of the ex-husband's identification of the body and sad words of forgiveness.

The next witness, Emily Holland, a married woman and an unfortunate, was a friend of the victim. Holland noted that the victim's Christian name was Mary Ann, but she was often called Polly, even on polite and formal occasions. As Abberline and the police had already determined, Emily had last seen Mary Ann Nichols at 2:30 a.m. in Whitechapel Road opposite the corner of Osborne Street. Abberline calculated that Mary's body had been found 500 yards away and an hour and 15 minutes later. It was anyone's guess where Mary Ann Nichols had wandered or what she had done during her last 75 minutes on earth.

Mary Ann Monk, the last witness, added little of note beyond confirming the victim's identity. Monk saw the deceased at about 7 p.m. entering a public house on New Kent Road; long before Holland's final known sighting of Nichols.

With little gained but a few precious seconds of semi-slumber, Abberline once again rose to request a lengthy adjournment to conduct further inquiries. This time Baxter agreed and ordered the inquest reconvened on 17 September.

Abberline said, "Two weeks to find a murderer who appears to be a stranger to his victims and is never seen or heard."

Helson muttered, "May need two years, not two weeks."

"You get anything else on the victim?" Cox asked in *The Empire's* newsroom after Coulls ran over the information he had gleaned from his interviews and the inquest.

"I talked to a few unfortunates," Coulls said. "Someone mentioned the velvet bonnet to Emily Holland, a friend of the victim; tweaked tears in her eyes."

Jennings bustled into *The Empire's* offices announcing to one and all, whether they wanted to hear or not, "I've got one little goodie. You know the corner of Buck's Row and Brady Street?"

Old Boy Pierce nodded, not looking up from the page proof he was scanning for errors. Cox glanced over at Jennings, as Coulls debated whether to continue his report. Many of the other reporters in the newsroom were paying attention, especially if they were struggling with a story: anything for a break from crafting the next elusive sentence.

"I found an old fellow," Jennings went on. "He's a sort of amateur historian as far as the city goes. He claims the corner of Buck's Row and Brady Street used to be the site back in Puritan times of a cucking- or ducking-stool pond for wives who committed adultery. Was even called Ducking Pond Road."

"You check to make sure the old dodger was right?" Cox yelled.

"Where do you think I've been for the past two hours? Researching the local records at the museum. I've got enough for a nice juicy story."

"Good," Cox called out. "Write it."

Coulls finished his report to Cox and ambled over to start his story. "How'd you do, Old Boy?"

"Not too good," Pierce said. "Got the latest from the Peelers, but it wasn't much. Because that Nichols woman was killed near the Jewish Cemetery some of them think the murderer is a Jew. Idea is that he wouldn't pay for her favours, she got nasty and he got nastier, so he killed her. If it'd been next to a Catholic cemetery, I guess they'd be after some bloody R.C."

"Are they looking for a live Yid or a dead ghost? Christ!" Somehow the last word didn't seem appropriate but like most newspaper people, Coulls only kept his language precise for his writing. What he said in civil or uncivil conversations was not a matter for edited surveillance. Regardless of the words, Old Boy Pierce didn't answer. He was already absorbed again in his page proof.

After dinner Inspector Chandler settled back in his cushion-covered, over-upholstered favourite chair with his feet on a padded footstool. He sipped on his evening mug of Fry's Cocoa. He had enjoyed two fine pints at his local between the station and home. The only thing about the day that bothered him was the unseasonably cold weather; nothing to be done about it, except add coal to the fire, don a cardigan and sip his cocoa. He glanced at the paper, skimming past the lists of Medical College and Schools Prizes to the sports columns. Ah! The touring Canadians beat County Antrim at Belfast 6-2. Damn Irish never were any damn good at football. In fact, Chandler reflected, the Irish weren't good at anything, save spawning kids, creating slums, and guzzling whiskey. If not a member of the Old Nichol Gang, this damned Whitechapel murderer could very well be Irish, very well, indeed. The killer was likely a Catholic or maybe even a Jew, an Irishman or other foreigner rather than an Anglo-Saxon; certainly an unemployed n'er'do-well rather than a good solid hardworking Englishman.

Ah, good. The 1887 National Challenge Cup winners, West Bromwich Albion took Sheffield Wednesday 3-1. Too bad he hadn't had time to take the train up to see the match. Good old Wolverhampton beat Notts Rangers 7-nil. The sports news read, Chandler turned to the international news. The spread of the popular press with telegraphic communication had enabled news from all over the world to reach Chandler and his middle-class ilk, making world events appear far more personal and closer than ever before. Chandler's indignation rose over African slave traders fighting British troops in Central Africa as the latter fought to end the vile slave trade. The audacity of the blighters to attack British soldiers. Such cheek!

Chapter Six

At the Buck's Row murder site Coulls found that a crowd of thirty locals had gathered. Women bent at the waist to peer at what they announced might be blood stains between the paving stones, while burly, rugged men with clay pipes stood taciturn on the fringes of the crowd, as if awaiting the start of a rugger match.

"Silly woman to be out so late," one stout man said to a mate. "Only a certain type of woman would be out alone at such an hour."

"Whatever she was," a burly labourer replied, "it was an awful cruel thing to do to her."

A middle-aged matron announced to one and all, "Thank God, I don't have to go out tonight. Most have no choice in the matter; the street or the grave it is for more than one woman in this district."

"Police said they found 'em, anyway," a broad-shouldered labourer said, as he tossed his single-use clay pipe into the gutter.

"Who?"

"Man called Leather Apron; threatens women for money, they say."

Coulls wandered away from the crowd to surreptitiously scribble notes. It would not do if the crowd thought he was a police spy, although everyone in Whitechapel appeared eager to help apprehend the killer. He had heard that L & P Walter & Son of Church Street had even written the Home Secretary requesting a reward be offered for information leading to the arrest of the Whitechapel murderer. Unfortunately, in reply the Home Office's Legal Assistant Undersecretary, Edward Leigh-Pemberton, stated that such a practice had been discontinued and that the Secretary of State was satisfied that "there is nothing in the present case to justify a departure from this rule." Nothing, Coulls thought, but an apparent absence of any firm leads, let alone promising suspects.

On his way back to *The Empire's* newsroom in a cab, Coulls glanced through the *Times'* latest on "The Whitechapel Murder." A story quoted Inspector J. Spratling as saying that he "saw two workhouse men stripping the body" of Polly Nichols as he waited for Dr. Llewellyn. Llewellyn blamed Enright for the cockup. In his turn, Detective-sergeant Enright stated that he gave instructions that the body should not be touched. Round and round the accusations went. Coulls shook his head; the police appeared more focused on squabbling with each other than apprehending the murderer.

As he neared *The Empire's* offices, Coulls glanced through one more story. While Mansfield was drawing droves of devotees to *Dr. Jekyll and Mr. Hyde* at the Lyceum, the *Times* review argued that George Grossman's burlesque treatment, *Hide and Seekyll* at the Royalty Theatre was a flop. The original, Coulls thought, was always better than any facsimile.

"George Ford," Jennings began as Coulls entered the newsroom.

"Who?" Coulls asked, wracking his mind for the name amidst the multitude of witnesses, suspects and police involved with the case.

"The Chairman of the Committee for Investigating the Abuses of Immigration."

Coulls hadn't heard of the committee, let alone the august Chair, but didn't want to admit it, let alone within earshot of a dozen trivia-addicted correspondents in the noisy, smoke-skeined newsroom.

"He supports a proposal by Master Workman Edward Powderly."

"And what does our good Master Powderly propose?" Coulls asked as he sat at his paper-strewn desk.

"Appointment of Consular Agents throughout Europe to investigate the character of all persons intending to immigrate to England to screen out murderers."

Pierce, who sat at his adjacent desk, shook his head. "Just how is the character of each person to be evaluated?"

"And how are potential murderers supposed to be screened out?" Coulls asked.

"Just ask them politely if they plan to murder anyone?" Pierce asked.

"Could cost a pretty penny," Coulls said, "but it would keep a district's worth of retired inspectors employed checking on all the potential immigrants; a pension plan of sorts for retired coppers."

"It's being called Ford's folly," Jennings said, "or Powderly's purge."

"Sounds like a laxative."

Abberline and Helson returned to the scene of the crime on Buck's Row to see if they had missed anything. Police were more prone than perpetrators to do such a thing. Neither policeman was surprised to see a few toffs in the crowd that had gathered to view the murder scene. The murder was being treated by the West Side populace with that perfectly normal curiosity exhibited toward a high-profile homicide. To them, it was like the Crystal Palace's exhibition of the Grand Ballet's fairy scenes from *A Midsummer Night's Dream*, worth watching but touching them only with its vicarious excitement. Like a stage, Buck's Row itself was neutral, save for a few darkening stains between the paving stones which showed where Mary Ann Nichols' body had once lain.

"The blighter's a phantom," Helson said. "Five men were approaching Buck's Row from different directions, all within a few minutes of the murder, and not one of them saw a single suspect."

"The closest gas lamp is up at that corner," Abberline said, pointing. "The murderer could have walked away fairly easily, probably through Brady Street or that passage through Queens Buildings into Whitechapel Road. It would have taken at least eight men, maybe more, to seal every exit. No, the culprit's not a phantom."

"He certainly knows the district."

"He also knows, or miraculously anticipates, police procedures. Neil could cover his beat in 12 to 15 minutes," Abberline began, but then stopped. "Neil said he last passed Buck's Row half an hour before discovering the body. Why'd it take him so long to complete his beat?"

Helson checked his notes, flipping pages as if a gale had hit his well-used notebook.

Seeing his increasing level of frustration, Abberline gave his junior time by saying, "A beat in the suburbs might take four hours, but not this one; and night duty is usually a couple of miles shorter than day beats in urban areas. Was he on knocking-up service?"

"No, but...."

"Probably stopped at a pub for a physic or shinnied up a lamppost to retrieve a warm flask." Abberline knew all the tricks. "In any case, we'll have to find out what kept him from his appointed rounds."

The pair walked on as Helson scribbled yet another item on his duty list. Abberline loved lists and the infatuation was rubbing off on Helson.

"Enright hasn't tracked down any of the non-goaled members of the Old Nichol or Rip Gangs yet."

"The gang members will get a lot older before he does." Abberline knew Enright was far from the best of officers. Abberline peered up and down the Row. "At night this street, particularly this narrow part of it wouldn't be well-travelled, and there wouldn't be any unfortunate standing around waiting for a customer to happen by. No, the business of prostitution is done out on the main thoroughfares. When the monetary amount for whatever service is agreed upon, the pair stroll into a quiet side street, cul-de-sac or whatever. This is an ideal place. The murderer would hear anyone coming a block away and he'd have plenty of time to escape. With the dim streets and if he wore dark clothing, it would be unlikely anyone would see blood on him, if he had any on him."

"He could even go along Court Street to Whitechapel Road and be lost amidst the throng there."

"What bothers me most is the nagging possibility that this killing is related to the Tabram murder and that we've got a madman who's going to go on killing until we catch 'im. I can understand murder caused by a surfeit of gin or a row, but this is something new—a senseless kind of murder of a stranger with no apparent motive."

Helson said, "Might help if the Habitual Drunkards Act was more severely enforced."

"What makes you think that?"

"Only 50 or 60 people are committed to retreats for chronic alcoholism each year, but if all the habitual drunks were committed, the murderer wouldn't have such easy victims to carve up."

"He'd probably just switch targets; a woman alone in a flat, a shop girl on her way home." Abberline reached down to rub the back of his knee. It felt as heavy as if it was stuck in a foot of dry mud.

"You don't think he just killed this woman because he hates harlots?"

"He may think he does, but I doubt that's the reason. He probably chose this woman because she was an easy target. Look at that one over there. You could do whatever you wished with her."

Helson nodded, although he looked to Abberline as if he couldn't think of anything he'd particularly wish to do with the old drab, save avoid her at all costs.

Having recovered a modicum of calm after his dream-induced panic attack and consequent headlong flight to the continent, medium extraordinaire Robert Lees returned to London. His vision of mutilation murder had put his nerves, never of an ordinary character, on anxiety's shaky edge somewhere between emotional exhaustion and nervous breakdown. Landing on the continent, Lees had found his quiet retreat at Pierre's comforting. He had begun to find a certain peace only to have his serenity ravaged when he foolishly picked up a copy of *The Times* and found that he *had* foreseen the savage slaughter of some woman in Buck's Row. To pre-witness a murder was a medium's worst nightmare. You knew it was coming, but you couldn't do anything to prevent it; details were always lacking. Gore and guilt were a horrendous pair of vision and emotion to live with. Several days had passed and, at last, he had been able to drag, cajole and berate himself back to London. The terror still played and strayed in subdued tones within him. Even so, all had gone as well as could be expected and now, aided by both the overt support and covert ridicule of his wife, he was half-heartedly accompanying this down-to-earth woman on her market rounds. Maybe he could return to at least some form of a normal life.

Taking a rare break, Coulls eyed St. Paul's dome down Fleet Street past the City of London and then glanced the opposite way back toward Westminster and Parliament before crossing the busy thoroughfare named for the paved-over River Fleet. The Nichols murder meant suicidal hours for the press, especially young reporters trying to make their mark in a business now rife with competition. The lifting of the 1850s tax on newspapers and the spread of cheap postal service led to an explosion in the number and circulation of newspapers as more and more people could afford such an extra as news. Journalism itself was also changing. In 1880 W.T. Stead took over the *Pall Mall Gazette* and introduced the New Journalism, which included sensational stories based on interviews and even gossip columns to appeal to a mass audience. The local pub now had competition for the latest news and gossip.

Fleet Street, 1890, looking toward St. Paul's

Safely across Fleet Street, Coulls pushed through the doors into the semi-darkness of the new Ye Olde Cock Tavern, which had just opened after a Bank of England branch was built on its former, much older site across the street. After his eyes grew accustomed to the gloom, Coulls spotted a loose gaggle of reporters at several pint-covered tables.

Pierce was telling some outlandish story as Coulls ordered at the bar before squeezing into a chair between Pierce and Jennings. Coulls settled in before his pint of bitters and slab of deep-fried fish and chips nestled in a day-old penny press newspaper. As he added malt vinegar to his fish, Catherine McLean and Lyman Gulop, who worked for one of the socialist weeklies, strode through the battered doors and joined them. Coulls had met Gulop; didn't like him. As for Catherine McLean, he only knew her by sight and reputation. She and a few other women worked for various papers; most small of circulation, all featuring social comment on the appalling living and working conditions in London's East End. It seemed that Gulop had just become editor of one of these papers. Coulls couldn't remember the name of it 10 seconds after he heard it, but then he wasn't much interested in Gulop's latest achievement.

Pierce ran through the introductions, turned to Catherine, who sat across the thickly lacquered table from Coulls, and asked, "I guess you're as busy as we are with this Buck's Row business?"

"Yes, it's on my beat."

"You're a crime reporter?" Coulls asked, surprised.

"Not exactly. I cover social conditions, the poor, the downtrodden."

It sounded to Coulls like she was writing Statue of Liberty plaques. "Who for?"

"Whoever will print my stuff; the *Commonweal, Freedom* and sometimes for the *Arbeyter Fraynd.*"

Coulls frowned.

"It's Yiddish; 'The Worker's Friend.'"

"I've heard of it. You write Yiddish?"

"No; they translate it."

"They must like your writing." He smiled. "Too bad they won't be in business long."

"Why?"

"Narrow-appeal papers are dying. High-speed presses favour general, mass circulation papers with the broadest possible appeal."

"I think there'll still be room for papers for people starving for social change," she said as she stole one of his chips. "Muckrakers in America helped bring down Tammany Hall and are attacking social injustice high and low."

Coulls nodded, but far from believed her prediction. "It can't be an easy job, sloshing around Spitalfields at all hours of the day and night. Could be dangerous."

"You slosh around Spitalfields all hours of the day and night."

"But, I'm—," Coulls caught himself short.

"A man? It's fine for a man, but too dangerous for a woman?"

"I suppose."

She thieved another chip. "You don't think women should write about such things?"

Figuring he had found a way out of a looming confrontation, Coulls replied, "I think anyone can write about anything they like, but the Phantom is cutting up women, not men."

Catherine sipped her quart of golden amber, stole another chip and said, "Someone still has to inform the wealthier classes about the plight of those at the other end of the economic spectrum."

"I doubt if many of them want to be informed. After all, it must be upsetting to have you're settled world…well, unsettled."

"You've got your Nellie Blys in America."

He wasn't sure if this was the start of an attack or a conversation. "I'm Canadian."

"Just a northern American."

"So a Scot is just a northern Englishman?" Coulls had heard of Nellie Bly, what newsman hadn't? But other than that her journalistic endeavors had aroused a certain resentment, he knew almost nothing about her.

Catherine said, "Bly had to quit writing stories about Pittsburgh factory workers."

Coulls nodded again. Pittsburgh, that was right. He'd read about some woman raising Cain about unsafe working conditions and child labour for *The Dispatch*. He asked with a grin, "Did she have to quit so she could cover something more important, like a murderer on the loose?"

"Is people dying in the hundreds from tuberculosis and cholera any less a tragedy than one or two women dying at the hands of some madman?"

"No, but it sure makes better copy," Coulls said, but even as he said it, he noticed that her eyes were a wonderful shade of hazel he had never seen before.

Wednesday, 5 September

Abberline walked over to his window at Met Headquarters and stared down into Whitehall Place, commenting, "No word from the continent concerning Klosowski or Ostrog, and not a sign of this elusive Leather Apron character either. To top it all off, it's a bright sunny morning."

"What's wrong with that?" Helson asked as he sat sipping his third tea of the morning at a desk in the corner of Abberline's third-floor office. They had decided to meet at his office to avoid the traffic caused by the construction on Commercial Street in Whitechapel. Even so, Helson had been twenty minutes late. "Been so cold, we need some sun."

"So might our Whitechapel Phantom. Crime seems to go up on clear nights. The penny dreadfuls and *The Illustrated News* always associate 'dastardly deeds' with dark foggy nights, but it doesn't seem to work out that way with real villains. If I fear any kind of weather, I fear fine clear weather."

"I guess villains don't want to stumble around in a fog or get soaked through on a rainy night any more than you or I. Maybe we should call in Sherlock Holmes."

"Who?"

"Detective character; I read about him in *Beeton's Christmas Annual* last year. Solved a crime in a story called 'A Study in Scarlet' by noticing tiny details no one else does, including two police inspectors, Lestrade and Gregson."

"Which division?"

"Fictional; pair of Cretans. Holmes even uses a magnifying glass. There's a new story about him coming out on the 18th, 'The Sign of Four.'"

"Might have heard of him if he was in *The Strand* or some real magazine. Is he supposed to be a Met inspector?"

"No; he calls himself a consulting detective."

Abberline shook his head. "So an amateur on his own solves a crime the police with all their resources have failed to solve?"

"Yes, sir."

"Sounds about as likely as us catching the Phantom before tea time."

Regardless of the weather, an intensive door-to-door interrogation of possible witnesses to the Buck's Row murder continued with grinding patience. Sergeants Thick and Godley, like their colleagues, had started the task five days past with a moderate amount of enthusiasm, but gradually lost all élan for the enterprise and now carried on with a doggedness common to any working man who needs to eat regularly. It was simple, dull, necessary work. The interviews took on a monotonous back and forth that could put the most dedicated officer into a drifting daze closer to sleep than wakefulness.

"Name?"

"Patrick Mulshaw."

"Occupation?"

"Night porter for the Whitechapel District Board of Works."

"The sewage works?"

"The Whitechapel District Board of Works, if you please."

"Where do you reside?"

"Three Rupert Street, Whitechapel."

"Where were you the night of 30 August?"

"Well, let's see, I was on duty from quarter to five in the afternoon until five to six in the morning."

"Certain of the time?"

"The church bells chime every 15 minutes."

"You work near the slaughterhouse on Winthrop Street?"

"Aye, it's maybe 70 yards away."

"Hear or see anything suspicious?"

"Didn't hear a thing, but there's a lot of noise from the slaughterhouse, you know."

Thick, Godley or one of the dozens of other policemen would shake fingers tired from writing, thank the latest non-witness and trudge on. The details seemed endless. One oft-named suspect, however, was emerging: John Pizer, better known as Leather Apron. Several witnesses swore they had seen him mistreat an unfortunate not fortunate enough to avoid him.

"Bloke carries a razor-like knife. Couple weeks ago he grabbed a woman called Widow Annie near London Hospital and threatened to slash her to pieces."

"He's got an ugly grin and a malevolent eye, that 'un."

'Malevolent?' Thick wondered. Christ. It was amazing anyone in this illiterate backwash should use such a word. How the hell did you spell it? Better just put down 'evil.'

"He's nicknamed Leather Apron alright. No, I don't know where he lives."

"Did you say Leather Apron? Hell, I know three blokes by that name."

Whitechapel was a world where men were as likely to be identified by a nickname related to their profession as by their given name. It was frustrating to realize how many tradesmen wore leather aprons and thereby had the potential to be called Leather Apron. Worse, the press had picked up on the name and was making Leather Apron a byword for danger and villainy. Commercialism, always close to the heart of the East End citizenry, didn't doddle over cashing in on this latest sensation: a Whitechapel sweetshop now featured "Leather Apron Toffee." Poverty dictated that everything, even murder, had to have its practical value.

Thursday, 6 September

The Prince of Wales was travelling in Austria, a hurricane raged off the American coast, a man tried to shoot a member of the German embassy in Paris, and a funeral was held in Brussels for a newspaperman killed in an illegal duel. Life, death, the weather, worry, and the Whitechapel Phantom went on in oblivious independence of all else.

Mix-up and mishap continued to plague Polly Ann Nichols almost a week after her death. Although the date of her funeral was public knowledge, the time when her funeral procession would begin remained a well-kept secret. This led to a large crowd assembling at the mortuary in Old Montague Street at first light on what became a dull, pale-gray day with a low pillowy canopy of cloud broken for a brief half-hour by a glint of sun through the coal-dust-tinted air. Seeing the multitude in front of the mortuary, the undertaker, driving his two-horse closed hearse, unconcernedly drove by and picked up the body in its polished elm casket at the rear entrance. Minutes later, the hearse, followed by two mourning coaches, was driving along Hanbury Street to Baker's Row and then onto Whitechapel and out to Ilford. A cordon of blue-coated constables guarded their path to keep order, as if protecting the sovereign. The long line of Bobbies weren't needed. Owners of many houses along the route had their curtains drawn, clocks stopped and mirrors covered in respect, while the crowd radiated empathy, the best part of sympathy, for the departed and her mourners. Whitechapel might seem hell's habitat to those living in more comfortable parishes of the city, but its people were not without their share of human kindness. Coulls, having collected enough tit-bits to write any number of paragraphs the day editor might want, couldn't help feeling the tragedy, but he also had to get back to the office.

As he rode in a hansom toward Fleet Street, Coulls read a story in the *Daily Telegraph* about Henry Hummerston, a Hoxton labourer, who, in a drunken rage, had tried to cut his mistress's throat. Hummerston had been sentenced on 5 September to six month's hard labour for assault. Coulls marveled at the razor-thin difference between life and death; Hummerston's drunken incompetence saved his life. If his blade had sliced through either the lady's jugular vein or carotid artery, he would have not enjoyed six month's hard labour. He would have enjoyed six seconds of hanging from a rope by the neck until dead.

As the hansom jolted along, Coulls stared out at the Borough of Stepney, which sprawled in unrelenting squalor across London's East End.

"Stop!" Coulls yelled at the driver when he spotted a man waving him down. "Please."

The cabman hauled back on the reins, bringing his chestnut steed to a snorting halt. Reggie Tompkins, a veteran reporter, and an eager-looking young man, apparently a new recruit hastily hired to augment the force now needed to cover the Nichols murder, clambered aboard the hansom. Newsboys with extras folded over their shoulders hawked the latest news on the street as fast as the presses could print new editions. Publishers were pushing their existing staffs to unprecedented efforts, even as they hurriedly hired new correspondents as fast as they could find literate scribes. The race to produce more and more editions was on: high-speed printing in pursuit of high-return profits.

"No room for three," the driver said, but his words carried little weight as Tompkins tossed him a few coins.

Jammed against one side, Coulls failed to hear the new correspondent's name as the overloaded hansom continued on its bouncing way. At least the young man was thin, not taking up too much precious space in the over-burdened two-wheeler.

"Whitechapel and Spitalfields are two of five parishes that make up London's East End," Tompkins explained, continuing what had apparently been a long oration on the geography—social, economic and otherwise—of the East End for the new reporter. "They are the most prominent and notorious. The main thoroughfares of Commercial Street, Brick Lane and Hanbury Street cut through Spitalfields, while Commercial Road and Whitechapel High Street bisect Whitechapel. Get to know them. The main arteries are connected by a higgly-piggly crisscrossing of side streets and alleys that are pockmarked by courts and squares. Mazes inside mazes, as disorganized as a bag of nails. So make certain you've got a good grasp on whatever quadrant you're working or we won't find you 'til Christmas."

"Christmas after next more likely," Coulls muttered. Even in his cramped condition, he smiled the smile of sadness that accompanied his certain knowledge that Tompkins was correct in saying a reporter needed to know every twist and turn in every section of Whitechapel and Spitalfields, but also that almost everything Tompkins said was entering the cub reporter's mind in a haze, making the entire exercise one of almost absolute waste. The area was a chaos of corridors; chaos that could neither be learned overnight, in a fortnight or in forty nights.

"Tell him about the gin pits and the pubs," Coulls said. "Something a cub reporter might actually remember. The Grave Maurice, the Blind Beggar, Ye Olde Cheshire Cheese in the City, and so many other fine establishments where you can trade your hard-earned shillings for ale, lagers and other fine and not so fine libations."

As Tompkins continued, Coulls stared out the hansom window at the streets lined with masses of people moving alongside shabby rows of dilapidated doss houses and dirty shops selling milk diluted with water, butter diluted with milk, and sugar that was more sand than sweet. A sweated tailor lumbered by burdened by a basket of fourth-hand cloth he would have to sew at home into something salable; sweating his way through a hard day to earn enough to buy a loaf of bread. Yelling, screeching, howling, swearing, squealing and laughing assaulted Coulls' ears. A pig's squeal scraped against his ear drums. It was far from uncommon to discover pigs lodging in a Whitechapel basement.

"The Rookery is full of thieves, while Butcher's Row by the Minories," Tompkins was saying, "is a city of meat. In the evenings, the gas lights illuminate a long vista of beef, mutton and veal. Legs, shoulders, loins, ribs, hearts, livers and kidneys gleam in a gaudy panoply of scarlet and white on every side."

Returning to his own ruminations, Coulls knew that overcrowding in the East End was the common condition. Coulls had heard of one establishment fronting on Flower and Dean Street which had 90 men and women living in three small rooms. The citizenry scraped out a living by means honest and dishonest. Beside the urban poor, thieves, harlots, minor villains and the indigent labourers, soldiers and sailors from the adjacent wharves frequently spent their off-duty hours and shore leave in the district. Brothels were common work places. Venereal disease was endemic and incest was said to be common. Women offered toffs their babies for a shilling, or to Slum Saviors or Salvation Lassies—Salvation Army members—for free to take to one of the Sally Ann's orphan or poor houses. The only accommodation for human waste was often a cellar pit, rarely, if ever, emptied. Night soil, slaughtered animals, horse droppings, stagnant cesspits and all manner of garbage lay on the streets, in yards and courts. This caused the entire district to exude an odour that attacked Coulls' sense of smell as much as the district's visual images assaulted his sense of sight and its cacophony of noise numbed his ears.

"God, what a hell of a place," Coulls moaned.

He was right. It was a hell of a place.

Part Four: Hanbury Street

Chapter Seven

Friday, 7 September

Coulls sat down by one of the few windows in Ye Olde Cock Tavern before a full English breakfast of two fried eggs, fried slice of bread, bangers, fried tomato and mushrooms, back bacon, baked beans, black pudding and tea. He glanced out at busy Fleet Street and then spotted a copy of *The Commonweal,* one of the papers for which Catherine McLean wrote, and, curious, picked it up as he tucked into his breakfast. The socialist paper was full of left-leaning stories on the none-too attractive aspects of slum life in the bowels of Whitechapel. The district's better-off working poor put in 15 hours a day in unsanitary, overcrowded workshops for wages that allowed them to buy just enough food to avoid death by malnutrution. The casual worker groveled subsistence from the occasional job at conditions no better than his or her full-time counterpart with the added stress of not knowing how long the present job would last and when, if ever, the next one would be found. The third tier of what seemed an English version of Dante's rings of hell was experienced by the unemployed, many of whom were migrants from the countryside desperate to escape the agricultural depression of the past few years. They found accommodations as best they could in the alleys, doorways, work houses or one of the 5,000 doss houses in East London. Although some were occasionally kipped by officialdom in gaols and debtor's prisons, which at least provided a roof and food, they were primarily people of the street. Bookish people who studied such things estimated that 40 percent of Whitechapel's population of 76,000 was impoverished—more than 30,000 people.

Coulls was about to read on when he found himself staring up at a pair of sparkling hazel eyes. Catherine McLean said in a most cheerful voice, "I saw someone with *The Commonweal*, so I thought I'd come over and enjoy the rare opportunity of talking to one of our readers."

Slowly lowering the paper while trying to look unperturbed, a perturbed Coulls said, "I just had to see what paper a lady with so much *chutzpa* worked for."

"Well, now you know," Catherine said as she sat down and stole one of his black puddings.

"Well, I, at least, now know why Sir Charles is afraid of an uprising in the East End, what with all the unemployment, poverty and injustice, the people there can't be too content."

"They're more content than you'd think," she said, finishing off the pudding and eyeing his back bacon. "Sir Charles, I gather, is afraid of an East End-West End confrontation, something along of lines of last November's riot, but he may have a bigger problem on his hands."

"What's that?"

"Religious intolerance." She took a piece of his back bacon and swallowed it in three quick bites.

"Religious intolerance?"

"I assume, then, your earlier use of the word *chutzpa* wasn't a result of your faith?"

"No, does it matter?"

"To me, no, but to a lot of West Enders, yes. About 70,000 Jews live in London and about 50,000 of them are in the East End. About 5 percent of the East End population is Jewish. Since the 1740s, Jews have been in and around Aldgate, but they've been expanding from Goulston Street into Spitalfields. Many are tailors, although the Dutch Jews are mostly cigar makers and about one in five working class Jews are street vendors with stalls, barrows or small shops. The percentage of Jews in Whitechapel is high, and Whitechapel abuts the City of London, where East meets West."

As she talked, Coulls took the opportunity to eat. "So West Enders see the Jews as a threat?"

"No; the East End gentiles object the most to the recent influx of Jews from Europe. They think the Jews take their jobs"

"How do you know all this?"

"Days spent in the census office, public and private libraries and months spent interviewing East and West Enders. We may be editorializing on the advantages of this or that reform, but we've got to back up our stories with facts."

"Do you really think the Jews are a threat?"

"No." She pinched and swallowed one of his grilled tomatoes in two bites. "To begin with, there's too few of them. I don't believe the Buck's Row murderer is a Jew, either, but if he is, it's due to his being nuttier than a squirrel's lair on

Hanukah and not his being Jewish."

"It's just his sanity—not his religion—that's at issue for me." They had agreed on something. Smiling, Coulls continued, "The workers never seem to lead revolutions anyway, the middle class does."

"So are you going to lead one?" Catherine asked with an engaging smile.

"I'd rather get a lead on the Whitechapel murderer; now that would greatly help *my* downtrodden condition."

"To improve *my* downtrodden condition, I better be off to work," she said as she rose and rushed toward the pub's door. As she exited, she called over her slender shoulder, "Thanks for breakfast."

"Almost a week gone and sod all progress," Abberline lamented that morning as he sat behind his borrowed desk at the Bethnal Green station across from Helson. "The Nichols inquest resumes in ten days and we aren't any closer to identifying the murderer than we were a week ago. Worse, looks like it'll be fine and clear tonight. Our Phantom might go on the prowl again. If he killed Smith, Tabram and Nichols, he appears to be free any night of the week. Emma Smith was attacked the night of 2/3 April – a Tuesday/Wednesday, although I think she was attacked by a gang; Tabram, the night of 6/7 August – a Monday/Tuesday, but a Bank Holiday; and Nichols, the night of 30/31 August – a Thursday/Friday, but in August, when many in the middle and upper class take holiday." Abberline's left leg ached. He was in for a pain-filled day. He wished he was home so he could put hot cloths on his leg, which often helped his varicose vein or maybe Emma would be kind enough to massage the pain away.

Helson was sorting through piles of reports, compiling duty lists, apparently oblivious to Abberline's utterings and sufferings. Helson spoke between paper piles, "There's a couple of attacks on women to be looked into. A John Allison has been charged for wounding his wife with an axe."

"Our boy isn't a wife killer," Abberline said.

"There's John Bunyan."

"The preacher who wrote *Pilgrim's Progress*? Isn't he a tad old to be a suspect for our murders?"

"The latest John Bunyan threw corrosive fluid in a woman's face. They'd been living together four years."

"That's more like our man," Abberline said, rubbing his varicose vein. "Send someone to chase down where Bunyan was Saturday morning; probably won't amount to anything."

It didn't.

"This man's not likely to have the emotional composure to hold a job," Abberline said, desperate for some way to winnow down the mass of suspects from the reams of reports arriving on his desk every hour. He kept thinking.

One of the nastier demands of Abberline's job came calling at 11 a.m. The discrepancy between the expected 12-to-15 minutes PC Neil was supposed to take to complete one round of his beat clashed with the constable's statement documented in a written report of having taken about 30 minutes to complete the circuit at the time of Polly Nichols' murder.

"I was not derelict in my duty, sir," Neil said, standing at attention before Abberline, who had shooed Helson out of the office for the confrontation.

"I know some constables feel the need to stop for a pint now and then," Abberline said, seeking more to solve the mystery, which might advance the investigation, than gain a confession of dereliction of duty to then use to punish the diligent twenty-year veteran.

"I never stop for a pint on my beat, sir, that night or any other. Besides, sir, the pubs close at 1, two-and-a-half hours before I discovered the body at 3.30."

"Maybe a pause to relieve yourself?"

"Not for 15 minutes, sir."

"Then pray explain to me the delay, constable?"

"I broke up a minor altercation between two transients at the far end of my beat from Buck's Row that night."

"Your report mentions that, but you stated it took five minutes. What happened to delay you further?"

Neil frowned. "I think now that it must have taken longer, sir."

Abberline accepted Neil's explanation. The transients could never be found to verify Neil's story and even if they could, whatever they said wouldn't be believed anyway. After pointing out that Sir Charles was cracking down on any infractions of discipline, Abberline dismissed Neil. It was not pleasant having a constable before him on the carpet. He was a detective, not a disciplinarian.

Abberline called Helson back in and turned to the latest dispatches. He opened a telegram from Warsaw first. Hopefully it would be in English. It was. A miracle!

Abberline skimmed the report and told Helson, "Klosowski did train in the Russian Army as a *feldscher* and they do perform minor surgery. No doubt he has anatomical knowledge. He came here earlier this year, which makes him and this fellow Pizer our most likely suspects."

"We also received a report on Aaron Kosminski, the Whitechapel hairdresser," Helson said. "He worked at a hospital in London at one time, although he appears to live off his sister now."

Abberline jotted down the name.

"Are we putting on extra patrols tonight?" Helson asked.

"A few, but Sir Charles doesn't think we need to. Feels the press just might blow it out of proportion and scare the populace into some rash acts."

"Like murder?"

The Reverend Barnett was revising his upcoming Sunday sermon for St. Jude's on that most serious of sins—adultery. Barnett was typical of his collared brethren. His sermons rarely subsided within an hour. They were in many ways a test of Christian faith, for to endure these lengthy harangues was an act bordering on penitence. A parishioner would be seeking at least some kind of salvation by sermon's end, even if it was only the bliss of almighty silence and a softer place to sit than a wood pew.

The Reverend checked a reference here and honed a phrase there. It did not matter that the few East Enders who attended wouldn't know if his quotes were correct or not. He wanted his Sunday assault on sin to be perfect. It was his duty to God, and besides, he expected several of his Oxford undergrads who volunteered in the East End to be there. Barnett worshipped order and preparedness. Although he did not realize it, he ate, drank, bathed, and engaged in sex according to a precise timetable. There was always the gnawing feeling within him that if he lingered too long over meal, wine or wife, the heavens would thunder in protest. Any prolonged plateau before ejaculation would leave him with feelings of guilt and disgust at his own lust. He was indeed a man of closely cut cloth.

The little man of many whiskers stared furtively through a tear in the curtain. The street seemed deserted. At least no copper had seen him come in. Christ! What luck. He'd eluded them so far even though some of them, like Thick—old Johnny Upright—could recognize him on sight. He surveyed the room. Not bad. Too bad he couldn't stay long. The Peelers were bound to recheck her place and he sure as hell didn't want to get nicked. He rubbed the stubble on his chin and wondered if he should shave. Blasted bitch! What an end of trouble that bloody Polly Nichols was causing him.

"I'll have to hole up 'ere for a time, Nell."

His sister nodded, her face grave.

"I'll need grub, 'baccy and somethin' to drink. I've been hiding out at a pal's, but I don't trust that bloke. Might turn me in for the bloody reward. I know you'd never do that, right Nell?"

It seemed more a question than a statement. The little man was tired. He'd been on the run ever since they started the Leather Apron business. He knew he should have shed that goddamn name years ago. Only luck and police stupidity had saved him thus far. He slumped onto a worse-for-wear sofa, stretching out without removing his coat, clothes or boots. He was so bloody tired. If those damn coppers did close in, he'd have to use his knife. Damn. Stupid to have threatened that tart a couple of weeks ago. Pointed the police right at him. His head sank into the lumpy pillow on the end of the worn chesterfield. He'd have to leave before dawn. He'd work his way over to the Rabbit's Warren sometime after midnight. Maybe he'd meet a tart on his way.

"Wake me 'bout midnight, Nell."

And so night came.

Lusky swept his raspy tongue down his grey ghost front, making certain all was clean and sheen. It was hunting time. His pupils narrowed to thin, black slashes. The darkness was a shaded series of sleek silhouettes before him, a canopy of gray on black. He headed south. The hunter's moon lit the city from a star-sprinkled sky. Lusky quickened his pace and disappeared into the utter blackness of an alley.

The Londoner kept his top hat, cane, white scarf and overcoat, declining an offer from a big-bosomed girl at the door to tend his things. If the place was raided, he didn't want to leave anything behind. He hoped the young girl Margaret or, perhaps, the well-rounded Isabelle was available. He decided to ask for Isabelle. He had thought the risks over since coming here last month. A young girl might easily be fooled and not recognize a case of clap, but an old saddle horse like Isabelle would keep her knees crossed if anything suspicious came dangling her way. Even so, he was willing to run the risk, for her.

"Is Isabelle free?" he enquired.

"Yes, I think so," the fat female before him said, smiling coyly up at him over a multilayer of chins.

God, he thought, she had once been almost as popular as some of those actresses. How these women let themselves go. He watched her waddle away, thinking that it'd be almost impossible to penetrate such a mass of fat. The image deflated his ardor and he was wondering if perhaps this was not the best night to come, when Isabelle floated into the salon. She was dressed in a dazzling black outfit, her dark eyes flashing in anticipation. She stopped before him.

"A little drink before we go upstairs?"

"Certainly, my dear, certainly," he answered, his eyes following along the upper hem of her gown that crossed somewhere close above her brown nipples, revealing two soft, lush mounds of super-stimulating breast. He could feel the urge already to rip the dress from her and sink his face into those luscious apple-round, white breasts. They sat on the divan, sipped their drinks and made small talk. Across the room a slender stick of a man sat fondling the ample breasts of a laughing redhead. Several couples were dancing. The orchestra played muted, soft music. Nothing racy. The number ended. He wondered how many men were ending right now upstairs, extracting their limp organs, sodden, soft and impotent. Women always had that effect on men. His face hardened as he thought of it. They made fools of men in a way.

"Let me taste your drink?" he asked.

"Why?" Isabelle asked, looking coquettish.

"Can't I?"

"You can sip it out of me, if you wish."

It was a tantalizing idea. He knew what she referred to as "me." He sipped from her glass. It was as he suspected; little gin, more water. Yet he paid for two drinks. He stared at the fat madam who was chatting up another customer. The profit was hers. How he hated these bitches. Well, he'd get his money's worth out of Isabelle's body. He'd fill her up with good Scotch, sip it out, then ram his tool right up through her uterus. Bitch! He smiled at her as she sipped coyly from her glass.

The increased police presence on the streets near the murder sites at night had been a bit of a nuisance for Lusky. It was no problem when regular citizens began to use the main byways, leaving the narrowest and darkest of side streets, alleys, courts and squares relatively empty, but their place was taken by patrolling policemen, swinging their bullseye lamps from side to side, poking into every cranny, niche and nook. They were becoming a real threat to Lusky's livelihood. The clip-clop of their heavy boots, whine of their whistles, calling back and forth to each other at all hours did nothing but drive the rats and mice into deep cover. They blundered along through the alleys like a herd of cattle on their way to the slaughterhouse. Even the ones who were stationary were badly in need of hunting acumen. They stood on well-lit street corners, fully exposed at great distance to any creature of the dark. Being a cat, however, Lusky took much of this in stride, putting it down to the stupidity and general bad manners of the average police constable.

But now, after a week, the constables were already returning to more evenly distributed patrol patterns to keep the peace in the rest of Whitechapel/ Spitalfields. Man, Lusky thought, had never learned patience, true patience, like a cat. It was odd, Lusky mused as he bathed, for all their ingenuity, they didn't seem to have learned a darn thing about stalking or hiding in wait for their prey except for that one he'd met a few nights ago. Now that one, he knew how to stalk, he knew how to hide and wait, and he seemed to know how to collect what he needed. Lusky concluded that there might be hope for man yet, but he truly didn't expect much of them. They were an evolutionary dead end. Lusky finished grooming himself for his evening jaunt.

Two blocks away, a man carrying a black leather bag stepped briskly down onto the train platform, smiled and began walking along the crowded street before him. He mused on how good—how exciting—it felt to be back in the East End. The lion was back among the lambs; the cat back among the rodents.

Saturday, 8 September

Inside a third-floor front attic flat at 29 Hanbury Street, Spitalfields, John Davis, an elderly elf of a man with a stoop who worked as a porter at Leadenhall Market, sat up in his sad sack bed. He had been awake most of the night, his mind troubled by a thousand and two little tribulations that affect any older man concerned with supporting a woman and three unwanted children on an income more suitable for the frugal, single and young. Sometime around 5 a.m. sleep had finally overcome Davis' depressing reflections and he had slept for 30 or 40 minutes. Now he was awake again. He could hear the Spitalfields' clock striking a quarter to six. He sat for a moment staring blankly at the enormously fat round bottom of the woman still asleep beside him. He could toss and turn half the night long and she still would be undisturbed. Marveling rather ill-naturedly at his bedmate's nocturnal oblivion, Davis pulled on his pants, yawned, picked a well-worn shirt from a wood packing-crate nightstand at his bedside and made his way into a partitioned-off section of the room that served as a kitchen.

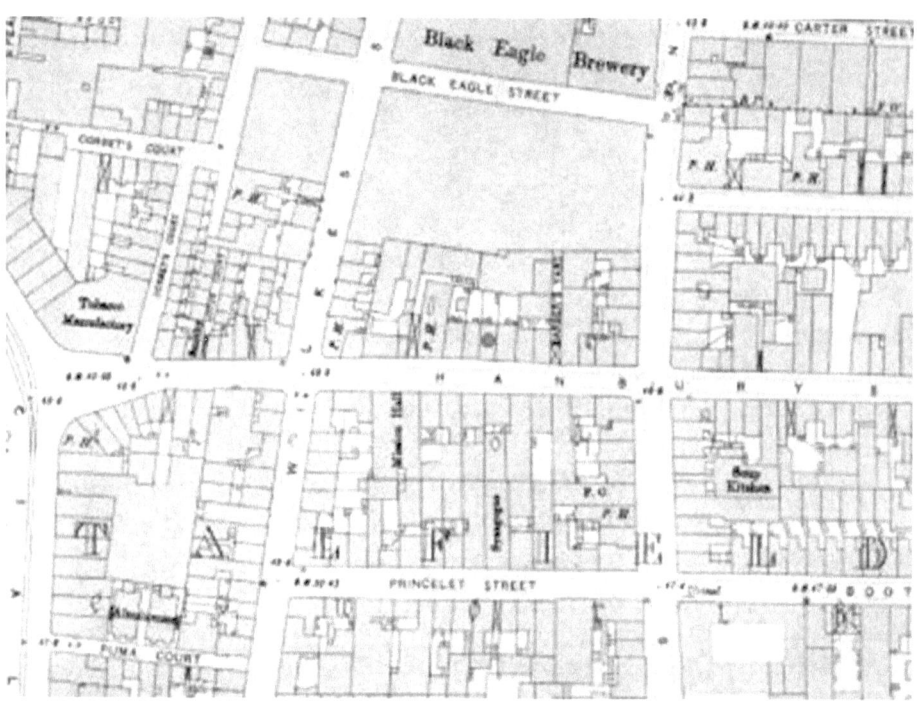

1894 map of Hanbury Street, which runs left to right in middle of image

He took a cracked tea pot from a shelf and sprinkled some leaves from a jar into the vessel. It seemed incongruous that a sleek clipper ship or a new steam-generating iron bottom had made its way halfway round the world so that these tiny pieces of leaves could be thrown so unceremoniously into Davis' marred pot; such a mundane ending for a commodity from the exotica of Ceylong. The contrast didn't enter any portion of Davis' mentality, however. He simply busied himself with filling a kettle with water from a bucket by the door. Placidly setting the vessel on the cast-iron stove, he stood for a brief moment before realizing the contrivance was cold. He removed several round sections off the top and placed pieces of wood and scraps of penny newspaper in the charred bowels of the rust-flaked firebox. He soon had a roaring flame to warm his hands and heat his tea. Life at 29 Hanbury was simple and unsullied by the complications of wealth, overt ambition or any of the hundred and one stresses that tormented middle- and upper-class folk. Its tensions were related to poverty, unemployment and the tribulations that the poor perennially dealt with.

Feeling the most primitive of urges, Davis yawned, pulled on a multiple-stained jacket and went downstairs and out the back door toward the backyard. He hurried because he wanted to get back before the water began to boil. Originally designed for the weaving trade, 29 Hanbury became a lodging house when steam power replaced hand- and foot-driven looms, and weaving moved from homes into factories. A five-foot wood fence walled the backyard on all three sides. The rear gate was closed. The usual rubble, rubbish and debris cluttered the space of dirt in between, which appeared the same as hundreds of other backyards in the area. But there was a difference this morning, a difference that would make 29 Hanbury the most talked about plot of property in London for some time to come.

Davis had no more than stepped onto the porch and into the early morning light when he saw the lifeless death-thing lying at the foot of the wood steps. The last bodily remains of a short, stout, middle-aged woman sprawled in gruesome gargoylism before him. The woman's clothes had been pulled up almost to her armpits. Her stomach was torn open in a gigantic cut. From within the bloody cavern of her opened body, her internal organs streamed out, up and over her right shoulder. Two large flaps of skin lay in pools of blood above her left shoulder. Slow wisps of steaming vapor curled into the cold morning air from the still warm gaping wound. After his first breath the smell of the disemboweled body clung to Davis' nostrils with a stubbornness he had never before known. He swallowed and grimaced, trying to force the awful odour from his nostrils, but it clung there, as if the dead never wished to be forgotten.

"Oh migawd! Oh migawd!"

An instant reflexive urge to vomit almost overwhelmed him. A rush of acidic foul-tasting mulch rushed into his mouth, but he swallowed it back down, burning his throat. Filled with horror, he ran down the exterior pathway between 29 Hanbury and its ancient neighbour. He swung open the front gate and burst into the street in time to see two workmen arriving at John Bailey's packing case factory three doors down. Davis hailed them, the acidic reflex of vomit still searing his throat. Curious, they looked as if they half wondered whether Davis had lost his senses, but followed him into the backyard. A boxcutter on his way to work, Henry John Holland, followed along behind them into the yard, where all three experienced total revulsion. One of the workmen turned and retched but, having lacked the shillings for breakfast, nothing came up. Holland ventured closest to the victim, before one of the workmen tore down the passage yelling, "Get a Bobby! Get a Bobby!" Davis and Holland followed, feet a-pounding. The remaining workman, still shaking and not desiring to be left alone with the horrid gashed-up thing on the ground, raced after them as if pursued by hellhounds.

Yard at 29 Hanbury where body was discovered

At 29 Hanbury, the fat-bottomed woman was roused by the fierce bubbling of the kettle. Dammit, John! Where had that man got to? She'd give him what for when he got back. Left for work and left the bloody kettle on. Could've burnt the place down. And her and the kids asleep. Damn him!

Detective Inspector Chandler was just exiting the Commercial Street Police Station when he saw three men sprinting toward him. He hailed them, wondering what was afoot. Soon the three agitated men were excitedly explaining their grisly discovery. Stepping back into the station, Chandler ordered several constables to join him and then rushed to the scene. When he arrived, he found a crowd in the passage and around the back door, with the whole house aroused. Even the veteran Chandler swallowed hard at the sight of the mutilated corpse.

"Constable," he called to one of his men, "Fetch Dr. Phillips, 2 Spital Square. Be quick about it!"

Chandler detailed two more constables to clear the passage of onlookers while he used a piece of old sacking from the yard to cover the remains; no one should see such a sight, no one.

It was almost 6:30 a.m. when Police Surgeon (H Division) Dr. George Bagster Phillips, MBBS, MRCS, strode into the yard bright and alert, even if his face always reminded Chandler of a sad bulldog. After bidding Chandler and several constables he knew a cheery good morning, Phillips quickly inspected the corpse.

Dr. George Bagster Phillips, MBBS, MRCS

"The body is cold, except for a certain remaining heat under the intestines," he announced. "The limbs are starting to stiffen. Looks like he tried to cut her head off."

The latest murder fell within the jurisdiction of the Met's H Division (Whitechapel). The divisional head of CID was Inspector Reid, but Reid was on his annual leave, so the investigation fell to Inspector Chandler and Detective Sergeants William Thick and Leach. As soon as he heard of the latest murder, John West, who was Acting Superintendent while Superintendent Thomas Arnold was on leave, suggested that Inspector Abberline lead the investigation since he was already engaged with the Tabram and Buck's Row murders, which appeared to have all been committed by the same villain. In fact, word had already come down assigning Abberline the new case.

In a police carriage, Abberline unconsciously clenched his teeth on the stubby stem of his pipe. Another hideous nightmare of a slaying and just a day after Nichols was buried.

"Hurry," Abberline urged the coachman.

The carriage's chestnut horse snorted and pranced as the driver maneuvered through the dense traffic. Soon no one would be able to get anywhere in London in under an hour, Abberline thought, even if it was just across Whitechapel.

The vehicle finally reached Hanbury Street. Abberline scanned the block. Good. The uniformed constables had already cordoned off the place. It might be early in the morning for most of respectable London, but for Spitalfields' inhabitants, sun-up meant get-up. A crowd was already gathering. Such a mob could destroy any number of clues if the proper precautions weren't taken. Already correspondents had arrived from the major papers. He spotted Oswald Allen of the *Pall Mall Gazette* at the front of the gawkers, pestering his officers and civilians in the crowd with questions, as well as that young reporter, Coulls. How did they get here so fast?

"She's down here, sir. We haven't moved her yet," DI Chandler said as he led the way to the corpse. "You can see she's been used in a most improper way."

"Was she covered?" Abberline asked, frowning; that differed from the other victims.

"No, sir, I covered her." With the greatest of care Chandler removed the sacking.

Improper was an understatement. A portion of the intestine stretched out from a gaping mid-body wound. It snaked out over the corpse's right shoulder almost as if it were trying to slither away from the innate ugliness surrounding it.

"It's obvious what she was expecting," Chandler said. "She's definitely in the missionary position."

"Only her slayer was expecting something else," Abberline said. His leg was throbbing with a heavy pain that refused to lessen with walking, as it usually had in the past.

The victim looked to be about 5 feet tall with what had been a fair complexion, dark brown wavy hair and a large thick nose.

"There may be some organs missing. We don't know yet."

Abberline turned at the sound of a new voice. "Ah, Dr. Phillips, you're doing the wet work, are you?"

Dr. Phillips nodded gravely. Phillips had a sad, yet serious face framed by mutton-chops. He was old fashioned in dress and appearance. Abberline thought he always looked as if he had stepped out of a century old painting. In his mid-fifties, Phillips was highly skilled and immensely popular with the beat coppers and the Met detectives.

Dr. Phillips had been dictating notes to an assistant. "As I told Chandler, the head is almost severed from the body. The miscreant either put his handkerchief around her neck to hide the slashes to her throat or to keep her head from simply rolling away."

The assistant swallowed hard and wrote hurriedly.

Chandler handed Abberline the torn half of an envelope. "We found this on the ground right there. There are marks, looks like blood, on it."

Abberline studied the envelope. "Crest of the Royal Sussex Regiment. Postmarked—London, 20 August. Two weeks ago, a Monday. Only the first letter of the address, an 'M.' Could merely stand for Mr. or the first letter of a name. An important clue or it could be irrelevant."

"I also found this near that tap in the corner of the yard," Chandler said, holding up a leather apron. Chandler's voice rose as he said, "There are faint initials on the back, J.P. Could be for John Pizer—Leather Apron."

Abberline studied the apron. "Perhaps; awfully hard to read. Could be T. P. or. . .God only knows. We'll have to look at it more closely later."

"Maybe the fiend washed his hands off at the tap."

"Possibly." Abberline's gaze scoured the yard. He chuckled to himself; how could he possibly spot something significant a dozen constables already on site had missed?

Abberline looked back down at the victim. The corpse had a gentle, even serene look on her face. It was the look of someone who had been strangled. "You know, this job is neat, not a sloppy mess. Yes, there's blood and guts everywhere, but look at the corpse. Not much blood splattered around, but again those heavy garments probably soaked up most of it. Chandler, when they move the body, go to the mortuary and inspect her clothes for anything of significance."

An inspector, Walter Dew, having gathered seven constables about him, launched his squad into the crowd watching the police work. Abberline frowned. "What the devil is Dew doing?"

Chandler shook his head, frowning.

Abberline detailed a constable to find out. "This street and even this spot are often used by prostitutes," Abberline said, based on his many years' service in the area. "She may have led the killer here herself."

"We found no blood in the passage, street or the other backyards," Chandler reported.

Abberline nodded and stared down at where he believed the victim had been murdered. He turned away from the death spot and placed a hand in his vest pocket, fingering his hunting watch while he fell silent for a century of seconds. Then he burst out with orders. "I want every shop, common lodging house and home canvassed within a half-mile radius of this point. Put every available man on the job. Find out if anyone saw any person with blood on his person, hands or cuffs, anywhere around here. Find out who this poor carved-up wretch was. Find out who last saw her alive and if they saw her with anyone; man, woman or beast. Must be 500 people live within the sound of a woman's voice from here; someone must have heard or seen something."

Chandler reported that a door-to-door investigation was already under way by the men of H Division. He unfolded a map and showed Abberline how the grid had been laid out. Abberline nodded approval and said, "Just extend the search out here, here and here, and bloody well hope we find something. There's no longer any doubt; we've got a multiple murderer on our hands."

Four constables placed the Hanbury cadaver on *Old Catchall*, the three-wheeled, one-man propelled, canvas-covered wonder of 19th Century technology. To enable the ambulance to depart, a cordon of constables created a pathway through the crowd that clogged Hanbury Street from kerb to kerb. Dozens of people died every day in Spitalfields, but heart attack, colic, pneumonia and TB did not make death a spectator sport. Murder by mutilation did.

Inspector Walter Dew

Inspector Walter Dew's rush into the crowd was triggered when he spotted the short, broad, tattooed figure of a local villain, George Squibby, in the crowd. Squibby was wanted for hurling bricks at a police officer, one of which hit a child, apparently by mistake. From personal experience, Dew knew it usually took at least six constables to arrest the combative miscreant, so he had quietly gathered seven officers to assist him.

Dew and his chosen constables forced their way through the dense crowd after Squibby, who, the moment he spotted Dew, ran like a wing breaking free in an all-square football match. Hundreds of people, thinking Squibby was the Phantom, took up the chase alongside Dew and his men, yelling, "He's one of the gang! Lynch him!"

Dew and his constables finally cornered Squibby in a house in Flower and Dean Street. A riotous crowd flowed around them, filling the street before the decrepit house. Angry yells were hurled at the house and its Phantom-suspect occupant.

"Be prepared, men," Dew advised. "He's a tough villain. He won't go quietly without a brawl."

When they broke into the house, they found, instead of a battler, a quivering, terrified young man. The screaming mob had done what the police had never been able to accomplish; the peaceful apprehension of Squibby.

Eyeing the growing angry crowd outside, Dew sent a constable for reinforcements. When they arrived, Dew and his men escorted Squibby out of the house. The crowd charged and the police only narrowly prevented them from seizing their prisoner. Dew and three constables managed to get Squibby and themselves into a four-wheeled police van. The mob surged around the vehicle, bouncing and jolting it on its springs.

"It's going over," Dew yelled as the mob shoved the four-wheeler over far enough so two wheels were off the ground. "This way!" Dew yelled, throwing his weight against the rising side of the van. The other constables and even Squibby joined him as ballast. The vehicle slammed back onto all four of its metal-rimmed wheels.

They had no sooner settled than the vehicle started to rise precariously on the other side. The constables and Squibby threw themselves the other way to prevent the four-wheeler from toppling over the opposite way.

Dew realized that sooner or later the mob would flip the four-wheeler onto its side. "Move!" Dew ordered the constable at the reins. "Now!"

Dew heard a whip crack, a horse neigh and shy, but the carriage did no more than jolt forward a foot and stop.

Looking out the window, Dew saw that the vehicle wasn't going anywhere surrounded by such a dense mob. Its wheels might as well have been set in rock.

"We'll have to take him on foot," Dew ordered, even as the vehicle titled again dangerously to the right side. "Out! Now!"

As they escaped from the seesawing four-wheeler, a cordon of constables formed a box with Squibby in the middle. As the mob fought to reach the man they thought was the Whitechapel killer, the constables and Dew pushed along, protecting the cowering Squibby and themselves as best they could from the crowds' blows. After what seemed an eternity and with bruises aplenty from punches, kicks and raining debris, they reached the relative safety of the

Commercial Street station.

"Safe at last," Dew said, hustling a gasping Squibby up to the desk sergeant to be processed into the cells in the basement.

"Sir," a constable at the door yelled. "They're surrounding the station."

Dew peered out one of the narrow windows beside the station's double oak front doors. A mob of labourers, trinket sellers, slaughtermen, tradesmen, trampers and women attracted from a nearby market filled his vision. The vanguard of the crowd thumped their fists against the station's doors.

Leaving two of his largest constables at the door to keep the mob out, Dew ran up to the first floor, flung up a window and yelled out, "The prisoner has nothing to do with the murders! Not a blasted thing!"

Another inspector joined him to yell out a window at the back of the station. Even so, the station remained under siege for hours until the disappointed mob finally, reluctantly dispersed.

Lusky lay in serene ecstasy. It had been a good meal. His stomach bulged with contentment and his whole body felt like velvet. He tucked his paws under his chest, lowered his head to the softness of the warm chesterfield and slid off to sleep. His night out had been a complete success. He slept soundly. Cats do not have a conscience.

As the story of the Hanbury Street murder spread, there was a run on newspapers like never before. Newsboys sold out the papers hanging by the fold over their shoulders in minutes and when they did, crowds clustered in front of stores awaiting new shipments of the latest extras. Like many others, one bespectacled young man found himself faced with the choice of either reading the latest news from the paper he had managed to obtain out loud or risk losing his paper and, possibly, his life to the news-desperate crowd jostling around him in an ever-tightening noose. He made just enough room to hold the paper far enough from his face to read from *The Star* to the assembled crowd, some of whom were illiterate or read no English, "'London lies today under the spell of a great terror. A nameless reprobate—half beast, half man—is at large, who is daily gratifying his murderous instincts on the most miserable and defenseless classes of our community. There can be no shadow of a doubt now that our original theory was correct, and that the Whitechapel murderer, who has now four. . .victims to his knife, is one man, and that man a murderous maniac. . .The ghoul-like creature who stalks through the streets of London, stalking down his victim like a Pawnee Indian, is simply drunk with blood, and he will have more.'"

Police and press interviewing continued throughout East London. The search for John Pizer, presently the prime prospect for Phantomhood—or was it Knifehood?—heightened. The leather apron found at the scene of the latest murder excited the investigators and gave the police hope.

Sergeant Thick, a dense, light-brown mustache curling down either side of his mouth to his jawline, consulted his notebook and asked a broad-shouldered man, "You're a porter at Spitalfields' market and it's your mother who lives and has a packing case business at 29 Hanbury and your name is John Richardson?" He had asked so many questions recently that they ran together like the days of the week.

"That's right."

"I understand you were in the backyard of 29 Hanbury this morning?"

"Yes, Inspector, sir, at about a quarter to or ten to five."

"Certain of the time?"

"Yessir. I went by Spitalfields' clock only a couple of minutes before I got to Mum's and checked me watch with it. Had to; can't be tardy for work or it's the sack I'll be having."

"Why did you go into the backyard?"

It was a friendly sort of question, but Richardson hesitated. Thick wondered if the man was naturally nervous or if it was the East-End paranoid suspicion of all authority with which he had more than enough familiarity.

Sergeant William Thick

"I wanted to see if Mum's cellar was shipshape. Coupl' a months back some bloke broke in, stole two saws and a coupl' a hammers."

"Was the front gate open or shut?" Thick asked as he scribbled notes, trying to write fast enough to keep up but neat enough so he could actually read his notes later at the station to write his report.

"Shut. I didn't go into the backyard, just opened the back door."

"What did you do then?"

"I sat on the stoop and cut a piece of loose leather off me boot so as I wouldn't trip over the bloody thing."

"What did you cut the leather off with?"

"This."

Richardson whipped a long, serrated knife up towards Thick's face. The point quivered a quarter inch from the end of the Sergeant's nose. "It's an old table knife I brought from home. Wanted somethin' with me if I bumped into that bloke wot broke into the cellar."

Thick reached out and said, "We'll look it over if you don't mind; just to clear you of any suspicion."

Richardson slowly lowered the still quivering blade and turned the handle toward Thick, who took the knife and went on as if the nose-to-knife encounter had never occurred. Although born in Salisbury in the bucolic Wiltshires, since being assigned to Whitechapel in 1868, both Thick and his nose had become more than accustomed to the ways of the East End. "How long were you in the backyard?"

"No more than a minute or two."

"The yard was empty?"

"Aye. It was just light enough to see. I could look right across the yard. I would have seen the dead woman if she'd been there. I was sitting on the second step with me feet on the flags at the foot of the steps. I understand the body was found at the foot of the stairs."

Thick nodded and thanked Richardson. He made a note to talk to Abberline about Richardson's nervousness. There seemed to be something there. What it was, Thick didn't know. He didn't suspect Richardson of killing the woman, but felt Richardson was lying about something. Thick sighed as he reviewed his notes; he could read them, but only with difficulty. If Davis found the poor woman's body at 6:15 or 6:20 and Richardson entered the yard to check for a basement break-in at 4:50 or 4:55, it left 90 minutes for the murder to have occurred. That window of time needed to be squeezed down to 10 or 15 minutes to make it easier to clear suspects and find the killer. Someone must have been by the yard at some moment during those crucial 90 minutes. People wandered about Spitalfields all night long. Several dozen could have passed 29 Hanbury in 90 minutes. The problem was to locate them before memories faded or were distorted by hearing any of the hundreds of stories already circulating the talk vines of Spitalfields.

"The Met Police seem more reluctant than usual to share anything about these murders with us or the coroner's office," Pierce noted.

"Maybe it's cuz they have nothing to share," Coulls replied as they worked on their stories in *The Empire's* newsroom. Coulls rose to open the window beside him to relieve the room's smoky stuffiness. Warped by the dampness of the nearby Thames, he struggled to make it budge, until the window finally gave way with an angry squeal of protest.

"They're after a murderer who has no apparent motive and could in all probability be a stranger to his victims," Pierce said. He dug the old tobacco out of his pipe and began to fill it from his leather tobacco pouch. "Their usual policy has been to cooperate with us when the identity of a culprit is clear. They gave us some good stuff on Leather Apron."

"I wonder if the Peelers will ever find him," Coulls said, sitting back down after his victorious window battle.

"Every reporter in the city has been after him and no one's found a bloody thing, so I wouldn't be too down on the police."

"Many are. At times the Met seems more like an occupying army than a police force intent on finding criminals. They march out of their stations at the change of shift in single file like soldiers. Sir Charles certainly didn't leave his love of army organization behind with his change of profession."

"That organization helped him keep the peace at the Queen's Jubilee, handle the February '86 troubles with the unemployed march in Piccadilly, and Bloody Sunday," Pierce said, referring lastly to a pitched battle fought on 13 November 1887 in Trafalgar Square.

"I don't think calling out the Life and Grenadier Guards to kill and maim 150 people is what the public expect of their police force."

"What else do you do when confronted by 100,000 socialists, radicals, unemployed and Irish spoiling for a brawl?" Pierce asked. "You been jawing with that socialist McLean lass, haven't you?"

Coulls didn't speak his favoured response. In the crowded newsroom, his desk was far too close to Jennings' to risk a falling out.

"Militaristic or not," Pierce continued, "even though he managed to get rid of Monro, I've heard Sir Charles no longer has Home Secretary Matthews' support. Sir Charles is also at war with the Receiver, Pennefather; a real bloody cock-up at the top."

"What happened between Monro and Sir Charles?"

"The Commissioner is a liberal, so Monro's undercover activities against the Fenians forged a wedge of mutual distaste between him and Sir Charles."

"Wish they'd all just focus on finding the killer."

"At the core of their disagreement was the debate over whether to have a battalion of constables on the beat to deter crime or a regiment of detectives in plainclothes to solve it once a crime has been committed. Sir Charles favours the former; Monro the latter. And Monro resisted Sir Charles' attempts to bring CID under his control. CID with its 'political advisor,' Dr. Robert Anderson, whose real role is to work against Irish Nationalists, caused many to worry about the rise of a political CID. Sir Charles opposed such a politicization of the police."

"Now Anderson and Monro have changed jobs just as we face a string of brutal murders," Coulls said.

"Monro just moved over to the Home Office with the title of Head of Detective Service, whatever that means. I'm sure he still talks with his old friends in CID. What it really comes down to is that Sir Charles thought he would have total control of the police, but all police orders and regulations require the approval of the Secretary of State in the Home Office, Matthews. The Minister has to answer for the police in Parliament, so he does need to be closely involved in the management of the police. For a hundred years the Secretaries of State and Commissioners have worked closely and well together."

"But not now, of all times."

"Sir Charles' appointment as Commissioner dropped him into a wizard's brew of bureaucratic bitterness. Matthews has grown increasingly hostile toward Sir Charles, especially since Bloody Sunday. Matthews didn't like being seen as the trodder of the downtrodden."

"That should be the least of his concerns. If he doesn't support Sir Charles, he's going to be viewed as the man who couldn't catch the Whitechapel Phantom."

The fact murder could be as exciting as it was macabre failed to impress one Londoner. A young boy told his employer he was riding on a cart with a delivery past 29 Hanbury that morning when he was drawn by the newsboys' screams of "'Orrible murder here." He jumped down off the cart and wiggled his wee self through the crowd and a cordon of blue-panted police.

"There she were, sir, lying on the ground. Her insides were all pulled out and they was all steamin' hot, like puddin'. She had red and white stockings on."

The employer's eyes opened to their fullest. The boy's enthusiastic revelations didn't faze him. He roared, "You're sacked."

Thus, in a way, another victim could be attributed to the Whitechapel Phantom: an 11-year-old boy was out of work.

Abberline had barely started on the stack of new reports on his desk at Scotland Yard when a PC appeared at his door to insist that Albert Cadosch, a carpenter living at 27 Hanbury, had something of significance for the Chief of Detectives. The constable brought the man into Abberline's office. Stooped and anxious, Cadosch smiled sheepishly and, following the constable's urging, started his story, "I got up this morn' 'bout quarter past five and went into me backyard."

"What time was that?" Abberline asked in a pleasant tone. Cadosch was nervous and nervous witnesses made mistakes.

"Quarter past five—oh—you mean what time I went into the yard. Oh, 'bout twenty past five."

Abberline did not bother to ask why Cadosch went into his backyard at such an hour. The obvious call of nature must have peopled half the yards in East End London in those early morning hours.

"When I was going back into the kitchen I hears a voice say, 'No!' It were a woman's voice. It wasn't in me yard, but it could have come from Number 29."

Abberline nodded.

"I came back out into the yard three or four minutes later."

Again Cadosch didn't volunteer his reasons for re-entering his backyard. Cadosch was probably one of those who forgot to take his under-the-bed-chamber pot out on his first foray to his backyard privy. In any case, Abberline concluded that it didn't really matter. Only the identity of the monster who had been in the backyard of 29 Hanbury mattered.

"When I was comin' back this time I heard a kinda knock or something fall against a fence. I didn't look to see who it was, just figured a cat had jumped off a shed and plunked down on a piece of wood or one of the neighbours was going out to the convenience; can be a rush at that hour. Glad I have one mostly to meself."

"This was about what time, again? 5:25? 5:30?"

"I don't know exactly, but it wasn't much later that I went to work. When I passed Spitalfields Church it was about two minutes after half past five."

Abberline made a notation in his notebook and thanked Cadosch for his help.

As Abberline worked to get the coal heater in his office lit to take off the morning chill, a constable entered his lair and handed him a note. Secretary Matthews requested that he attend a meeting the next morning at the Home Office to discuss the investigation into the Whitechapel murders. Abberline sighed; more time on meetings, less time trying to find the killer, but the Home Secretary was his lord and master with only Prime Minister Robert Gascoyne-Cecil, the Third Marquis of Salisbury, above him, and, of course, above the PM, the Sovereign herself.

Pierce sketched the scene before him at 29 Hanbury, rapidly charring in the main elements as if he feared the shabby site would disintegrate into a heap of dirty sawdust before he could finish. The grime- and sludge-filled gutter in the center of the street trailed off into the distance. Pierce felt the ugliness before him as he drew. He charred in the pools of filth that floated in the muddy, liquid hollows where the disjointed segments of pavement had been tossed helter-skelter by frost during past winters and then fragmented by horses' hooves and carriage wheels. He added in a few of the idling unemployed who occupied doorways, arches and assorted recesses that made up the background so unobtrusively that at times it was difficult to distinguish foreground from background. This scene was Whitechapel; the pure picture of poverty, although if he moved a block over, middle-class merchants and even physicians, solicitors and barristers called Whitechapel home. To the press, however, the only aspects of Whitechapel worth illuminating were the obscene, the grotesque and the unique—the commonplace of any community never makes news.

It was a long day for the police. Anyone who had anything to report about the 29 Hanbury murder had to be interviewed. People were questioned in lodging houses, factories, pubs and businesses throughout Whitechapel, Spitalfields and beyond. It was tiring, tedious work, but it was amazing how helpful most people tried to be. Some tried too hard. The human need to feel helpful and be seen to be on the side of righteousness was as prevalent among the people of the East End as it was among the premier citizenry of the West End. Murder is as detestable to the poor as it is to the rich.

One constable took down the statement of a woman who saw a message written on the door of 29 Hanbury.

"It said," she said, gesturing in a grandiose manner, "'This is the fourth, I will murder sixteen more and then give myself up.'"

The constable consoled her that it was unfortunate no one else had seen the message and thanked her for her sharp eyesight. He didn't ask, "What happened to the message?" or even, "Why sixteen more?" Few policemen, except perhaps the super-efficient Thick or the ultra-inefficient Enright, would have bothered.

Just outside a pub, another constable listened to pub patron Joseph Taylor who had followed a suspicious-looking citizen leaving Mrs. Muriel Fiddymont's drinking establishment, the Prince Albert, around the time of the murder. Taylor explained, "He had blood on his hands and someone said he had a knife. He was rather thin. About five-eight. Round 40 years old, maybe 50. He had a ginger moustache and short sandy hair. He warn't no workman like me, but he warn't no toff either. Sort of a poor gentleman, if you know wot I mean. The kinds you sees who's not done well in the world. He had a bad-fittin' pair of pepper'un'salt trousers, and a dark coat. And his eyes. His eyes."

The constable stopped his speed writing and looked up. "Eyes?"

"His eyes, they was like a wild one's; simply wild. I lost sight of 'im at Dirty Dicks in Half Moon Street."

Another constable, Douglas Davis, just five weeks on the force, eagerly took a statement from Thomas Ede at his place of employ. Ede said, "I work as a signalman for the East London Railway. I sees this suspicious-looking cutpurse just outside the Forester's Arms in Cambridge Heath Road. He had a long-bladed knife sticking out of his trouser pocket."

"What time was this?"

"'bout six this morning."

"Can you describe him?"

"Let's see. He were about five foot eight, dark moustache and whiskers. He were wearing a double-peak cap, dark-brown jacket, clean overalls, dark trousers. You could see them stickin' out at the bottom of his overalls."

And so it went, statement after statement, most full of unsound fury, most signifying nothing. Abberline, Helson, Chandler, Dew and dozens of other inspectors, plainclothes detectives and constables gathered information that required reams of forms to report on up the chain of command forming a tidal wave of information that threatened to engulf the investigation until it was impossible to determine what was important and what wasn't.

It was mid-afternoon when the tenacious Sergeant Thick found the residence of one Elizabeth Long, rumoured to have information of importance. She was out, but a neighbour directed him to the Rose and Anchor where after several inquiries he was able to find his potential witness. Luckily, Liz Long was still on her first gin, talking being her primary tonic.

"Well, I was passing along Hanbury Street on my way to Spitalfields Market," she told Thick. "It was about 5:30—"

"Are you certain it was 5:30?" Thick asked, hiding the anxiety that surged deep within him. Here finally was someone who had been on Hanbury Street during those 90 minutes that the police were desperate to fill in.

"I'm positive. The brewer's clock had just struck when I passed 29 Hanbury. I was in a hurry to get to the market before it opened. Wanted to get there before the crowd. Some good buys there if you beat the crowds."

Thick nodded, urging her to continue with an encouraging look. He knew even without any personal experience that it would be a foolish man who would debate Elizabeth Long about her shopping strategy.

"Good corn this time of year. And beets. I love beets."

Thick nodded. It was no use debating her vegetable preferences either. After a discourse on several other edible members of the plant kingdom, Thick was able to ask if she had seen anyone or anything in Hanbury Street.

"Oh yes. I was on the same side of the street as Number 29. I sees a man and a woman standing on the pavement talking."

Thick's heart went from a slow-paced canter to a down-the-stretch gallop. He strained to keep from looking too eager. Years of police work had taught him that appearing too enthusiastic could only lead a woman like Liz Long to adorn her story beyond belief and, more importantly, beyond usefulness. Fortunately, she stayed on topic and continued when he nodded encouragement.

"The man's back was towards Brick Lane; the woman's towards Spitalfields Market. They were talking while leaning against the shutters of Number 29."

"You were walking towards Spitalfields Market," Thick said, imaging the scene in his mind, "so you were facing the woman?"

"Yes, I saw her face clearly."

"And?"

"An inspector, a very nice man, so polite, took me to the mortuary to view the body. It was her alright."

God, Thick thought, he had chased her trail halfway across East London and some inspector had already taken her story. Oh well, he couldn't very well shut her up now and whoever talked to her might have missed something. There was also the possibility she was interviewed by a reporter, not a policeman. Most reporters wouldn't pose as a policeman to get a story, but most of them wouldn't contradict a witness who mistakenly thought they were a plainclothes detective either. After twenty years on the force, the worldly Thick had come to accept such reportorial tactics with stoic calm. He asked, "What about the man?"

"I didn't notice him so much. As I passed, his back was to me, you see. But I did notice he was a dark-complexioned chap. Had a brown deerstalker hat on and, I think, a dark coat, but I can't be sure."

"How old would you say he was?"

"I couldn't really say, but I'd guess he was over forty. I do remember he was a little taller than the woman."

The victim was short and stout, hardly over five foot, which would mean the man was maybe five foot two or three.

"He could be a foreigner."

Thick wondered what a foreigner looked like, but more importantly what a foreigner looked like to Liz Long. "What kind of foreigner?"

"Oh, just a foreigner. I don't know. He had a shabby genteel appearance."

Thick nodded. The description was familiar, but he was too tired to remember clearly. Like his colleagues, he had taken down so many descriptions, so many brown hair, black hair, blonde hair, blue eyes, brown eyes, green eyes, thin nose, long nose, fat nose, thick lips, thin lips, big ears, small ears. Everything was a humble jumble. And there was always the chance that Liz Long might have heard the man's description from someone else. A hundred different descriptions of suspects were passing through Whitechapel/Spitalfields chat lines daily.

"Perhaps a gentleman down on his luck?" Thick asked, summarizing a possible interpretation of Liz Long's description.

She nodded. "Oh yes, I remember, they were talking quite loudly. Not whispering. He said to her, 'Will you?'"

"And?"

"She said, 'Yes,' and that was all I heard."

Thick nodded solemnly as he thought that might be all the victim heard too.

It was mid-afternoon when Mrs. Richardson, John Richardson and his assorted children went into business, establishing what every business seeks: a monopoly. All monopolies must end and just half an hour later Thomas Cadosch, their next door neighbour, started to compete with them.

"Only tuppence," Richardson yelled. "Only tuppence to see the actual murder scene. Walk down the actual pathway taken by the Knife and his victim. Don't push, plenty of room. Thank you, sir, thank you."

"See the murder scene, only one penny," Cadosch countered. "The Phantom was right here. Walk where he walked, see what he saw."

And so it went: the Richardsons providing several rickety chairs and a box seat as an added inducement; Cadosch offering families a cut rate. The crowd lined up a dozen deep on the pavement and spilled over into the street. A candy vendor set up shop alongside them and several streetwalkers skirted the crowd advertising their flesh-worn wares and professional expertise. The carnival had followed the carnage to 29 Hanbury.

Newspaper pressrooms buzzed with activity into the evening as their gas lights hissed and spluttered. Paraffin lamps augmented their light as correspondents bent at their desks, focused on their stories. Given the explosion in the ranks of correspondents to meet the demand for copy, desks were crammed end to end in long rows leaving aisles scarcely wide enough for copyboys, but too narrow for several of the more corpulent correspondents who had been forced to negotiate trades for desks at the end of a row.

Tomorrow's morning editions were being drawn, written, composed and made up. Some papers planned to feature artist's drawings of the victim, the murder site and the prominent policemen. Dreadful news accompanied by gory artwork was featured in the mock-ups in many city rooms. Someone said it sold papers. It was not just a cliché. It was true. Street sales and home circulation were way up. Advertising revenue streamed in. Gore sold everything from new-fangled sewing machines to stewing meat.

After finishing work, Coulls tried to track down Catherine McLean to ask her to dinner, but he failed to find her. Accepting the immense difficulty of connecting with another over-worked correspondent, he accepted an invitation to table with his learned friend, the Professor.

Whereas the psychic Lees was a man of visions, the Professor was a man of vision. While others had learned Greek and Latin, etiquette and rhetoric, the Professor had learned mathematics and physics, biology and pragmatism. Among the Professor's avocations was a profound interest in the workings of the human mind, both normal and abnormal, and the behavior that accompanied such workings.

When Coulls arrived, the Professor was in his study writing furiously. His ink-wet words swept across the page, leaving a splatter here, there and all over the side of his left hand. He muttered, "If a man is mad, is he responsible for his madness? He might not be responsible for his actions, but what about his madness? Madness probably doesn't occur overnight. Can a person prevent himself from going mad? Does it matter? Is anyone really responsible for his actions? Who's to judge? When someone used the excuse that a would-be assassin of Queen Victoria was insane, the Queen replied, 'Well, he could have killed me just the same.'"

The Professor finally noticed Coulls waiting patiently at the door where the Professor's man, Jeeves, had deposited him. Apologies made, the pair went into the dining room to eat and talk.

"Sir Charles is wrong when he talks of the dangerous classes," the Professor said as he settled in before their evening meal of pigeon with thick gravy spiced with nutmeg, pepper and salt. Alongside the pigeon nestled forcemeat balls, baked beets, browned tomatoes, and a hot potato salad, which to Coulls hungry eyes rounded out the meal most nicely.

"In his usual myopic way," the Professor lectured, "Sir Charles is focusing on the great growing mass of industrial workers. He sees them as a cancer, malignantly destroying the British Empire from within. But these people are only displaced farmers, navvies, miners and such pushed from one livelihood to another by the shifts of our economic fortune. We're living amidst changing times; only most people don't know it. The changes are so broad most people think it's just something happening to them, not to masses of their fellow citizens. They often blame themselves for being out of work, but industries change and people are let go regardless of their behavior or competence, as if it were an act of God."

Coulls started in on the gravy-covered pigeon.

The Professor set down his glass of stout and stared thoughtfully at the vessel's rim. When he spoke he was even more serious than usual. "Your Whitechapel murderer is not of the working people. He is isolated, totally apart from everyone. His type is not any danger to society precisely because his type is so dangerous to the individual. The group grows stronger when Whitechapel Phantoms abound. They unite, take positive action. The Whitechapel Phantom won't bring the British Empire to its knees, as some socialists and anarchists think."

"Who will? The Irish or the Mahdi and his army of religious fanatics? They took Khartoum."

The Professor chuckled. "Merely sparks on the fringes of the Empire, unlikely to cause any lasting damage to anything beyond Ireland or the Sudan and, possibly, Egypt."

"Then will the British Empire last a thousand years?" Coulls asked with a grin.

"I doubt it; only the Venetian and Roman empires have managed such a run of all the empires history has witnessed."

"Then what will destroy the empire?"

"The fawning core of meritless bureaucrats could. They've sold their soul for position and thereby have corrupted from within. Sir Charles' bosses are far more dangerous to England than the Whitechapel murderer." The Professor laughed. "Poor brave Sir Charles; a victim of bureaucracy. He's as pitiful as this demented Whitechapel creature. Sir Charles is caught in a bureaucracy that prevents him from doing his job just as surely as the miner with a pit boss who's below average in intelligence. The only difference is, when the pit boss makes mistakes, output drops or the mine explodes: clear indications of failure. For bureaucracies, failure is far harder to detect, let alone to assign blame. And never forget, my young news-fellow, there are far more of such bosses than there are Whitechapel Phantoms."

"A bumbling bureaucracy brings down more misery on people than a sadistic slayer?"

"Certainly brings misery down on far more people."

By evening, crowds had formed in the streets of the East End. Rumours of other murders circulated as imaginations ran to extremes. Angry, indignant crowds gathered in Buck's Row, Hanbury Street, outside the mortuary in which the victim lay, and around police stations on Commercial Street, Leman Street and Bethnal Green. Multiple times the crowd thought they had identified the killer amongst their number, leading to the police having to intervene before some hapless soul was beaten to death.

"The crowds are beginning to threaten and abuse Jews," Helson reported to Abberline late that night at the Bethnal Green station as he hung up his overcoat in the corner of his office, which he now shared more often than not with Abberline.

Abberline shook his head in disgust. "What do they expect the public to do with the press repeating in almost every story that the murderer must be a foreigner, since no pure-blooded Englishman could commit such horrendous crimes? A Jew's the next best thing to a foreigner."

"Samuel Montagu, that Jewish MP for Tower Hamlets, is offering a £100 reward for the capture of the Knife."

"Is that what they're calling the murderer now?"

"The Knife, the Phantom or some such. Isn't it Home Office policy not to offer a reward?"

"Started with Matthews' predecessor, Sir William Harcourt; feared that rewards lead to a great deal of false information."

"Speaking of false information, a reporter asked me on my way in whether it was true that a constable on fixed-point duty was told about the Hanbury murder and refused to leave his post until he was relieved."

"Sodding correspondents," Abberline muttered, adjusting the flame on the paraffin lamp on his borrowed desk. "They'd print lies about the Second Coming even if God himself gave them the facts inscribed on tablets of stone."

"I heard, well, is it true Anderson's on leave?" Helson asked of the Irish born, devoutly Evangelical ex-barrister and new Assistant Commissioner of the Met.

"Just over a week into his post, our new leader has left for a month's recuperative holiday in Switzerland for a sore throat."

"I could use a month off." Helson sat at his desk.

"It could have been worse; his physician, I heard, recommended two months' leave."

"Maybe we don't need him," Helson said as he dropped his copy of *The Star* onto his desk beside his pipe rack. "'A Whitechapel Workman' suggests using bloodhounds to track the murderer. Should be nothing to it: get the dogs ready, wait for the next murder and off we go, right down the murderer's trail to arrest him lolling in his front parlour."

"What's the bloodhound supposed to track? The killer would need to leave something of his own behind, and he hasn't obliged us yet."

"Well, it's the least he could do—at least for the dogs' sake."

Chapter Eight

Coulls arrived for a half-day at *The Empire's* offices with a pad full of story notes only to find Jennings laughing.

"Good to find you in such high spirits this Sabbath," Coulls said as he hung up his coat and hat.

"Listen to this," Jennings said, flattening out a paper called the *Referee*. "The journalist, author, playwright and criminologist, George R. Sims, writes, 'The Whitechapel murders, which have come to the relief of newspaper editors in search of a sensation, are not the kind of murders which pay best.'"

"Don't tell Cox that," Coulls said as he sat at his desk. "We're selling more extras than the regular paper."

"'The element of romance is altogether lacking, and they are crimes of the coarsest and most vulgar variety—not the sort of murders that can be discussed in the drawing-room and the nursery with any amount of pleasure.'"

"A load of someones are certainly discussing them somewhere."

"'If only the women had belonged to another class, or been in more comfortable circumstances, there might, with skillful manipulation, have been worked up an excitement equal to the Marr and Williamson sensation.'"

"Who?"

"Pierce told me: two East End families murdered in 1811—big news, big sellers."

Coulls shook his head at the stupidity of some journalists. "Murder always sells."

"How right you are. There's news just coming in on the Trans-Atlantic cable about 44 men killed in a mine explosion in Kansas in America; be lucky to get an inch on page eleven."

"Hard to make mining as interesting as murder."

"Well, we know who she was," Abberline said. Having perused the latest reports, he unceremoniously flipped them onto the table beside his post-church luncheon of boiled beef and vegetables a constable had fetched from The Drake. "Annie Chapman; also known as 'Dark Annie,' Annie Sievey or Annie Siffey. Forty-seven, once married to a Frederick Chapman. He's definitely not a suspect."

"Why not?" Helson asked, staring down with eager eyes at his pub meal of Scottish salmon in a whiskey cream sauce.

"Dead a year and a half." Abberline eyed Helson's meal. "I didn't know they did salmon."

"They do, they do so very well indeed," Helson said with a broad expectant grin.

Abberline jotted a note on his pad about what his next pub meal would entail. "A woman named Amelia Palmer or Farmer identified the body—I wish our men would write more legibly. Evidently our victim lived in the streets and common lodging houses for the past four years. An alcoholic, a prostitute, an unemployed vagrant; not one of society's most upstanding citizens." He glanced at his meal, thought better of it even as Helson started in on his salmon, and read further down the report. "Ah, here's something. Chapman had a fight with another of her kind in a pub. The other woman was a not-so-gentle man named—get this—Harry the Hawker. That can't be right. A woman named Harry? Chapman must have met Harry later or. . .God knows. The boys are looking for the woman and Harry."

"I doubt if it'll lead anywhere," Helson said as he chewed his salmon. It did not appear to Abberline to require much, if any, chewing. "These women are always brawling, but they don't hold a grudge long. And I doubt very much if Harry the Hacker—"

"Hawker."

"Whatever he calls himself—I doubt if his kind would carve up anything more exotic than an apple; definitely not the Chapman women just because she got in a tiff with the woman he calls 'his' for the week."

Abberline nodded agreement as he cut his beef. He chewed on a piece; not as bad as he feared, but far from good. He washed it down with ale from a tankard. The constable had brought a bucket of beer from the pub for Abberline and Helson's lunch. Abberline read further in the report. "Amelia Palmer/Farmer said that Chapman was a straightforward woman when she was sober. Said she was clever and industrious with a needle. Take away the gin, the grime, the poverty. . ."

"But we can't take away the gin, the grime or the poverty. "

"True. We discovered all those a long, long time ago and they aren't disappearing anytime soon." Abberline pushed his fork furtively at his meal, moving portions around his plate as if he was creating some new art form. It was a disaster. A meal that didn't appeal to a hungry man was a meal of tasteless distinction.

"It looks rather bland," Helson said with a sympathetic smile.

"Should have stayed home for lunch with Emma after church."

"Or had the salmon, or many of these French recipes they're trying at some pubs are rather fine."

Abberline didn't like the sound of such things. He had been raised on good English beef and beer and saw little reason to change—although maybe change was warranted; the salmon looked wonderful.

"There is one compensation to such a meal," Abberline said. "I eat less of it. My physician told me, 'We dig our graves with our forks.'"

"Nonsense, sir."

Abberline eyed Helson's thin frame and thought the younger man could eat a side of beef and not gain an ounce.

"Food keeps us alive and fine foods make life worth living." Helson avoided the bucket of beer and picked up his bitters. He drank down a large draught. Where had he got the bitters from? Abberline wondered. Helson said, "It's been proven, sir, a rich hearty diet keeps you healthy."

Abberline turned his attention back to his sorry meal. "We English certainly have a peculiar compulsion to boil everything. I sometimes get the delusion that when we catch this demented Whitechapel creature, we'll boil him in some gargantuan pot for the appropriate seven hours, then pull him out all mushy and miserable looking. Mrs. Beeton might even write a cookery book someday on the most economical way of stewing such sinister souls."

He pushed his plate away and reached for his tankard of ale; at least the English were fine brewers, and the Scots and Irish weren't bad either.

"I was reading Allen in the *Pall Mall Gazette*—"

"I saw old Oswald at the murder scene," Abberline said, massaging his leg's varicose vein under the table.

"Said Mary Ann Nichols wore two brass rings—a wedding and a keeper— which were at her feet when we found her. The rings looked like they had been forcibly removed, so apparently we're checking pawn shops in the East End and points far beyond."

"A keeper?"

"It's a close fitting, simple ring worn on a finger to prevent another, more valuable ring from sliding off."

Abblerine nodded and asked, "Does he say if we've found any rings yet?"

"No, but I'm sure they'll have us keep looking until we find the goods."

Helson cut a piece of salmon, which flaked off with his fork, and raised it to his smiling mouth. Abberline drank some more ale; at least it was nutritious and everyone knew it was far safer than water.

After Helson had savored and swallowed, he said, "Yesterday *The Star* said the killer cut Chapman's throat so fearfully that, thinking he had severed her head, he tied a handkerchief around her neck to stop her head from rolling away."

"Such a tidy lunatic we have on our hands."

"I wonder why the correspondents even bother to come to the murder spot. Might as well make up their stories in the cozy comfort of their own offices."

"The problem for us," Abberline said, his stomach growling at the lack of sustenance or possibly at the aroma of Scottish salmon drifting his way, "is that some of their reports are false and some are true, and we never know which is which."

Annie and John Chapman

After a long and many dead-ended search, Sergeant Thick finally found the woman with whom Annie Chapman had quarreled. She was sitting before her evening meal of a bowl of potato soup in the communal eating room of a soot-coated lodging house in Dorset Street.

"Yep, I knowed 'er. Had a spat wit 'er. Piple been sayin' we had a fight, but warn't no such thing. I loaned 'er some of me soap last Saturday to warsh up with in the lav over there." The woman paused to slurp her soup and spill a little down her chin. "Well, I sees her next on Tuesday. Right here agin in the kitchen. I simpully, politely asked her in a nice way, if you please, if she'd give me back me soap. Well. . ." Another pause consumed more soup and sent a cascade of wet matter down her chin. Some now dripped into her lap. Thick wondered if it would not have been better if he had remained a carter on quiet, calm and secluded West Chase farm near Salisbury, where he had begun his working life, then have to listen to such a sorry specimen of humanity.

The woman continued, "She tossed a ha'penny on this table right here and said, 'Go and git a ha'penny of soap.' Imagine a ha'penny for all the soap I give 'er."

Thick did not care to imagine.

"We quarreled over the soap for a time. Then we sort of got calmed down. We went to the Ringers, the public house on the corner."

"Is that where you met Harry the Hawker? I understand your quarrel began again."

"She started it agin. Slapped me face. Had the nerve to say, 'Think yurself lucky I don't do more.' I coulda killed her. Got me wind up. I struck her in the left eye and in the chest."

She wiped her chin with the sleeve of her dark dress. The soup was gone, some of it into her mouth. The interview for all police intent and purpose was over. Thick headed his report 'Evidence of Eliza Cooper' and left.

Bursting out of its offices at numbers 3, 4, 5, 21 and 22 Whitehall Place and numbers 8 and 9 Great Scotland Yard, not to mention the stables for the mounted branch across from 7 Whitehall Place, the Met's Central Office was preparing to move to new larger headquarters on the embankment. Preparations for the move weren't helping the latest investigation. For hours after an in-office dinner, Abberline had been sorting through old files to determine which had to be moved to the new location and what could be put in storage; given the age of some of the files, they should probably be placed in the tombs in the basement and forgotten forever.

"Well, enough of this mucking about, Helson," Abberline said. "Down to business; what's the latest on the Hanbury murder?"

"I've got the reports in from the constables for today," Helson said, pulling several files off the table in the corner of Abberline's office which he had been using as a desk. "That place, 29 Hanbury, is like the rest of Whitechapel: an army seems to live in every one of those places. Mrs. Amelia Richardson and her 14-year-old grandson occupy the first floor front room. An old man, a Mr.

Walker, and his imbecilic 27-year-old son share the first-floor back. I had to help interview the son." He shook his head at the memory. "A Mrs. Hardiman, a widow who sells cat meat, sleeps on the ground floor in the same room with her 16-year-old son."

Abberline stepped across the office to the cozy-covered teapot. Without tea, the English brain was only so much grey matter.

"Mr. Thomas, his 'wife' and their 'adopted' little girl occupy the second-floor front. Two Misses Huxley—they're sisters—live on the second-floor back. Old John Davis, his 'wife,' and his, her or their three sons occupy the third-floor front. And somewhere in that maze an old lady, a Mrs. Sarah Cox, stays out of charity on somebody's part. That's. . ." Helson paused to count. "Seventeen people in five small rooms, some partitioned into half-rooms. And what's more amazing, not one of those seventeen heard or saw anything of significance."

Abberline poured some black Darjeeling tea and said, "You can get into any of those houses merely by lifting a latch. No use putting a lock on half of them because the wood's so rotten; it'd be an unnecessary courtesy to the door to use a key. People wander through the passageways like they're going along a common thoroughfare."

"Young Richardson and John Davis said they often have to throw undesirables out of the backyard and off the first-floor landing," Helson said, accepting and then sipping his tea. "That backyard at 29 Hanbury was known to the local unfortunates and was used for casual pickups."

"Street prostitution is just literally that in Whitechapel. If not up against a wall, then in a backyard."

"By the way, there's a report from Thick. Johnny Upright felt young Richardson seemed 'agitated' when he was being interviewed. Thick thinks he has something to hide."

"I'll have a talk with him. Send a constable around tomorrow and ask Richardson to come in and see me."

"I looked into the carman, Cross, who found Nichols' body," Helson reported, turning to a page in his well-used notebook. "There is a Charles Cross, born 1855 in Ickworth, Suffolk who lives at 9 Walcot Square, Lambeth. Might be a tad young for the man who found the body. He has no criminal record, but we're tracking down where he was at the time of the Chapman murder anyway. He lives and works in the area and appears to start work early."

"As do ten thousand other men." Abberline sighed. "Don't spend much time on him, but investigate until you're confident he's not our murderer."

While Londoners had learned either by word of mouth or through the Sunday supplements of the latest Whitechapel mutilation, the wonderful world of make believe continued. The touring Canadians tied the Glasgow Rangers 1-1, Queen's Park won the Scottish Challenge Cup, edging Northern 3-2, and West

Bromwich Albion, Chandler's favourite, topped Stoke 2-1. In the realm of more serious things, a fire swept through the Star and Garter Hotel in Richmond, and two prostitutes and a day labourer were taken into custody in Sunderland for robbing and beating a sailor.

Rain limited Lusky that night to a simple foray into the backyard to do his business. He swiftly returned to be let in. It was not a hunter's night. The lightning flashes and thunder blasts made any potential prey skittish and their nervousness made them alert. Besides, what prey was worth a soaking when prey would be out just as much or even more so on a fine night. A realist, Lusky curled up on the sofa and slept, waiting for a finer hunter's night.

Laura's was a house of real repute; any gentleman claiming to be a man of the world knew of its charms. Since the city's elite patronized the place, the police kept a Nelsonian right eye on it. It was only natural that the Londoner should forsake the house where Isabelle worked and eventually try Laura's. The ample-breasted, green-eyed little lady on the straight-backed settee took his interest. She had a darling little dimple that punctuated a coy, Pixie smile that invited physical intimacy. A surge of excitement coursed through his body. The Londoner smiled and started across the room toward the little lady, but before he had taken three steps a stocky, belly-bloated old gentleman came between him and his desired goal. The white-haired old man bowed before the little lady and taking her hand dropped down beside her on the settee. The Londoner cursed. His expression hardened into granite lines of hate. He whirled on his heel.

"Can I be of any—?" a willowy redhead asked.

"No, just give me my cape," the Londoner said, thrusting the redhead aside and plunging straight for the checkroom. He should never have left his cape in the first place.

"But, you haven't. . .you've only just got here."

"Just give me my cape, I tell you!"

"But—"

"Is there any trouble here?" It was Laura, her dark eyes smiling appeasement, her best diplomatic voice brightening the air.

"No, no. I just have to. . .I just remembered I have a pressing engagement." The Londoner's tone, frozen in icy anger, chilled the air.

"Sure, dearie, sure," Laura consoled, gently moving the redhead away from the angry one and taking his cape from the check girl. "Here, sir, now you hurry off and don't miss your appointment, and remember to come back and visit us when you're not so rushed. You require ample time to enjoy the pleasures my girls are able and more than willing to provide."

The Londoner snarled some sort of reply and was gone. Outside, he hailed a cab, growling as he climbed into the vehicle, "Take me to Whitechapel!"

The little man made it back to Nell's. He stood dripping in the hall before a mirror. The wet weather had washed over him in waves and left him chilled and soaked. His beard was plastered down his chin and throat like a discarded newspaper against a lamppost. His hair was flattened into a greasy wet mass of string that clung mop-like to his sodden head.

"Gawd, it's terrible out there, Nell. Not fit for man or beast. The coppers are everywhere. I had a time gettin' back here. Spent the whole bloomin' day in a cold, drafty, junk-filled loft in Flower and Dean Street. Did any of 'em come snooping round 'ere?"

"A couple," Nell said, her tiredness at the whole mess showing in her voice. "They check every day. Sometimes they drop back in the evening. It's not safe for you here."

"Well, I can't use that loft no more. Maybe they've left off snooping round me place. Not likely though. I'll hole up here for a few hours, dry off, warm up and be back on the move before daybreak."

Nell nodded. Her brother was becoming more than the usual bother he'd always been. Treated her reasonably well, he did. But why was he so rough with other women?

She handed him some dry clothes. They were as threadbare as the ones he had on, but constant changes of dress helped him elude the police and since they were dry, they kept him reasonably healthy—at least so far.

Monday, 10 September

At 7:50 a.m. Abberline arrived at the Home Office on King Charles Street a block down Whitehall from Downing Street, although technically Whitehall became Parliament Street at the corner of King Charles with Parliament just down the way. He entered the part of the building that housed the Home Office. The other part, the ostentatious part built to impress visiting dignitaries, belonged to the Foreign Office, the India Office, and the Colonial Office. Foreigners, Indians and Colonials must be overawed; the English need not be— or, then again, maybe the designers realized they could never really awe their fellow citizens. The Home Office was built as an office, designed not to impress anyone, even an Inspector first class named Abberline from Blandford Forum, Dorset.

An undersecretary of something or other ushered Abberline into Secretary Matthew's functional office. It looked more like the lair of the middle-level manager of a warehousing company than the seat of power for all things domestic in Britain. Abberline shook hands with Matthews, Monro, Andrews, Moore, and a couple of other detectives involved with the case.

"I thought it might be prudent to discuss the progress of the investigation thus far," Matthews announced as they sat at a table in the corner of his office.

Matthews and Monro sat at either end of the table. "Just to keep everyone on the same page, as it were."

"Will Sir Charles be attending?" Abberline asked, already guessing the answer.

Matthews glanced down the table at Monro.

"No need to bother Sir Charles, busy man and all that," Matthews said. "We merely wanted to ensure that the Home Office is keeping tabs on all aspects of the investigation and all that can be done, is being done to the utmost of our resources."

"Shall I report to him the particulars of the meeting?" Abberline asked, again already guessing the answer.

"Monro will ensure Sir Charles is kept informed of all he needs to know," Matthews assured Abberline.

Abberline guessed that all Monro thought Sir Charles needed to know was that Sir Charles' job would soon be Monro's, if all went according to the wishes of Matthews and Monro.

The discussion began and Abberline wondered about the state of the police force if a meeting about the investigation into the murder of three unfortunates failed to include the Commissioner of the Metropolitan Police.

The Telegraph, a paper of quality, reported on the "baleful prowler" in the East End and editorialized about "beings who look like men, but are rather demons and vampires." Detective Sergeant Thick and four constables from H division walked toward Number 22 Mulberry Street on a tip to arrest one such suspected demon whom Thick had known for 18 years: John Pizer, better known and feared as Leather Apron.

The public had by now tried and convicted Pizer as the Whitechapel slayer. One thoughtless stream of logical illogic argued that since Pizer had been demonstrating phantom-like qualities for days now by avoiding the police, Pizer must be the Phantom slayer. Thick was skeptical. He knew Pizer's work and he knew the Phantom's work; they did not appear to Thick to be one and the same.

Waiting a block and a half from Mulberry Street on Commercial Road, Thick sent a constable around to the back of the building to cut off that avenue of potential escape. While he and the other constables waited, Thick glanced east and west along busy Commercial Road. Labourers, shoppers, newsboys, urchins, a few top-hatted toffs, and all manner of humanity jostled along the sidewalks. Loaded wagons were parked in wheel-to-wheel rows perpendicular to the store fronts as sweating, grunting men unloaded merchandise and produce. Another row of wagons, many burdened by beer-barrel pyramids, waited just behind the perpendicular wagons, while omnibuses, wagons, coaches, cabs, barouches and hansoms maneuvered through the morass of muck, dirt, horseshit and refuse that formed the road itself. A penny gaff had gathered a crowd of urchins eager to ogle the fat girls, acrobats and giants in the stalls within its decrepit building for a penny a peek or to watch an hour's melodrama on its tiny stage. Bits of ginger beer bottles, single-use clay pipes and nut shells littered the pavement. Curs loped along searching for anything worth a sniff or a bite. Somewhere nearby a mother beat her wayward child with what Thick guessed from long experience would most likely be a poker, eliciting screams of pain and protest. A herd of sheep wailed and bleated as they were herded toward a nearby slaughterhouse, which only added to the cacophony of neighing horses, yelling and swearing men, screaming women, squealing children and barking dogs, squeaking wagon wheels and shouted offers of sales on this or that commodity. Newsboys screamed the latest news, while navvies added to the chaos by digging up part of the street for the new tramline. Why didn't they just work at night? Thick wondered, before turning his attention back to his job.

Deciding enough time had passed for the constable to cover the rear entrance, Thick led the way up Adler Street and turned right onto Mulberry. A horse-drawn police van, often called a Black Maria, even though it was actually deepest, darkest blue, followed them at a walk. At number 22, Thick thumped on the ancient door. It shuddered, but the lock held. No one answered. He pounded harder, afraid it might give way. At least if the door collapsed it would save them the trouble of waiting any longer. Then he spotted a curtain move in a window beside the door.

"John Pizer, if you're in there," Thick began.

A crowd was gathering. They should have come plainclothes, Thick thought, although that wouldn't have kept their identity secret long. East Enders could smell out a Peeler in less time than it took them to down a shot of gin.

One idling bloke said, "He'll carve up any copper that tries to take him."

"He won't come alive," another added.

Thick was recognized by several in the crowd and the prospect of a confrontation between Johnny Upright and Leather Apron lifted emotions to a gleeful pitch. Anticipation of exciting times gripped the increasing number of onlookers.

Thick knocked again. "I know you're in there. Come out. Make it easy for yourself."

Thick didn't know whether the blur at the window had been Pizer but it didn't hurt to run a bluff. He raised his fist to strike the door again, but it opened revealing a tired, haggard John Pizer. The notorious Leather Apron and Johnny Upright stood face to face. The crowd gasped.

Surprised, Thick quickly recovered and said, "Hello, John. We'd appreciate it if you would accompany us to the Leman Street station. We'd like to ask you some questions concerning the recent murders."

"I know nothing about the murders, but I'll come with you, Mr. Thick."

The two men walked to the waiting horse-drawn Black Maria as if they were headed to their local for a friendly pint. The crowd stared. Two of the constables entered 22 Mulberry and began a search. Pizer climbed into the police wagon and sank down on the seat. Thick climbed in beside his prisoner.

"Gawd," Pizer said. "I'm so tired. I didn't kill those women, but I had to run and hide all the time. There's been lynch mobs loose every night. I knew you'd come if I got a message to you. I was getting so tired and my coming 'round here was starting to bother Nell."

One of the constables stuck his head into the Black Maria and said, "The crowd's growing. We'll be lucky to make it back to Leman Street alive, let alone with Pizer here."

Thick nodded, looking down at the short, thickset infamous Leather Apron, sweating and shaking beside him. Thick said, "We bring in villains every day; nothing different about today."

One of the constables conducting the search emerged from Nell's rooms bearing five knives.

"Found these among his things, Sergeant," the constable said, showing Thick—and the crowd—the knives.

"Into the van with 'em," Thick ordered, far from happy that everyone had now seen Leather Apron and his knives.

"They're my tools," Pizer muttered as the constable clambered into the van with the knives. "I'm a boot finisher."

Sensing the crowd moving closer as their agitation increased, Thick decided it was time to go. The search was complete. Thick and his men calmly and quietly left, leaving the crowd behind, conveying their charge along Mulberry Street.

"Don't go down to Commercial," Thick yelled to the driver. "We'll be stuck in traffic 'til quitting time. Go up to Whitechapel and then over to Leman."

It was only at most a ten-minute walk, but traffic displaced from the construction on Commercial meant it took almost an hour to reach the Leman Street station. At least, Thick thought, all the traffic meant few, if any, paid any attention to the police van. Acting as if nothing out of the ordinary was happening, they made unnoticed progress through the congested streets.

Even so, word spread quickly. The Whitechapel killer had been taken! Leather Apron was in custody! Waves of gossip swept ahead of the police van and a crowd soon congregated outside the Leman Street station. The ripples of rumour spread out in ever encompassing excitement, bringing more and more people into the gathering multitude.

As they approached the station, Thick leaned out to look at the seething crowd.

"They've got Leather Apron!"

"Hang the Phantom!"

Thick reached up, flipped the little trap door open and shouted an order to the grim-faced driver, "Ride right through them, Constable. Do not slow down! Don't give that mob a chance to grab a rein or we're done for."

The constable driving the team of two cracked his whip high over the horses, forcing the animals into an ever-faster charge. Their hooves clattered like thunderbolts as they surged down the cobblestone street, hurtling in an abandonment bordering on the reckless.

"Stop 'em! Stop 'em! Pizer's in there!"

"Get Leather Apron!"

"Stop 'em!"

The cries welled up from the mob, but the front rows watching the black van and its snorting chestnut and brown bearing down full bore on them dispersed like the Red Sea before Moses. Men and women scrambled to either side. The once solid wall of human flesh disassembled into a scrambling series of animated parts. The police van thundered through the split human sea like a shaft of lightening rending a dark cloud asunder. The driver hauled back the reins the second the van was opposite the station's front door.

Thick jumped from the van amidst shouts of "Hang 'im!"

"Run!" Thick ordered as the mob surged back toward the van and its much-prized occupant.

Neither Pizer nor Thick's men needed any urging. They bolted from the van into the five-story station, slamming the heavy wood doors behind them just in time. Thick couldn't help but smile at his subterfuge in successfully bringing in the most wanted man in London.

His smile soon vanished. Pizer said he had slept the night of the Nichols murder in a common lodging house in Holloway Road. On 8 September, he said he stayed at 22 Mulberry Street with his sister. He said he had been with her from 6 through 10 September.

"Did you go out at all during that time?" Thick asked in a narrow interview room on the station's first floor.

Pizer looked at him as if he was a lunatic. "With all the news reports about me? I'd rather spend a year in the Black Hole of Calcutta than risk being seen on any London street."

Later that day Sergeant Thick, exhausted after the day's excitement, slumped into a chair in Abberline's temporary office at Leman Street station, as he reported, "Pizer's got a score of witnesses that place him in Crossman's lodging house during the time of Nichols' murder and the unfortunates at 22 Mulberry say he was there when Chapman was killed. The women who claim to know him as Leather Apron couldn't even pick him out of an identity parade."

"Well, we've eliminated a major suspect," Abberline said. "The entire force has been wearing their legs off trying to find him. Well done. Now we can concentrate on finding the other suspects. We're holding seven suspects at various East End stations, but we have bulletins out for at least a dozen more."

Thick didn't hear him. He was asleep.

"'A very rough district. Not respectable.' They shouldn't be able to write lies like that about Whitechapel." George Lusk accented the end of his tirade by hurling *The Telegraph* to the floor of his study. Lusky scurried from the room wondering what had got the big fellow so riled.

Like many labourers and small businessmen who made up the working class of the East End, George Lusk didn't like 'his' Whitechapel or 'his' Spitalfields described as a present-day Sodom and Gomorrah.

"Well, we'll just have to do something about this murdering bastard," Lusk vowed and, grabbing his coat, headed for the corner workingmen's club. His mind was set and determined. It was time for the men of Whitechapel/ Spitalfields to unite against the Phantom.

The first day of the Chapman inquest began at the Working Lads' Institute, Whitechapel Road, with Coroner Baxter presiding. As Abberline, Chandler and everyone else waited for the jury to return from viewing the body at the mortuary, Dr. Phillips told Abberline that Chapman had been ill with lung disease. Abberline didn't know how that would help him identify her killer but, even so, he thanked the doctor; thoroughness never hurt a case.

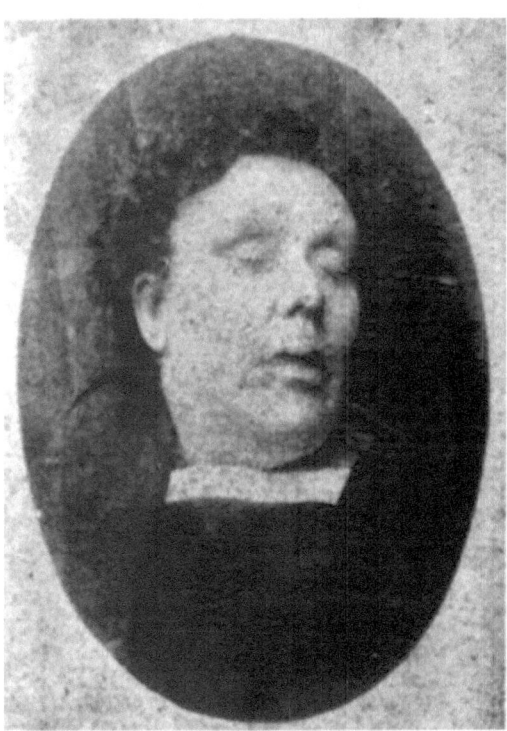

Annie Chapman

Chandler asked Dr. Phillips, "What about all this we're hearing about using bloodhounds to track the Phantom after a murder?"

Phillips rubbed his forehead with a pale, well-scrubbed hand. "I am far from an expert on the canine species, but I would think that bloodhounds would be more likely to track the victim's blood and their trail rather than the murderer, who would leave no blood himself. I doubt they would be effective."

"Plenty of blood all over the district with so many slaughterhouses in the area," Abberline said. "In any case, the papers are full of damn fool ideas. Helson said *The Star* suggested photographing the victim's eyes."

"What on earth for?" Dr. Phillips asked, frowning.

"The back of the eye—"

"The retina," Phillips provided with a smile.

"Is supposed to retain the image of the last thing the victim saw."

"The murderer," Phillips said.

"Would it work?" Chandler asked.

"Probably be useless," Dr. Phillips said, "especially in this case."

Abberline grinned and said, "Don't be so quick to dismiss it, doctor. In 1857 a Dr. Pollock of Chicago found that the eyes of the dead retained 'a clear, distinct and marked impression.'"

"Impression of the retina itself, I daresay," Phillips said.

"Helson said *The New York Tribune* even claimed that a man was convicted of murder on just such photographic evidence," Abberline said.

"Well, when Helson finds the court records for the case, I'll be more than happy to peruse them at length," Phillips said. "Probably just a fiction for papers to sell more copies."

"Funny you should say that," Abberline said. "Helson did some digging and found that one Villiers de l'Isle-Adam used just such a technique in 'Claire Lenoir.'"

"Never heard of the case."

"No reason you would, unless you enjoy reading fiction. It's a novel."

The jury finally arrived escorted by an inspector and settled into their chairs. Coroner Baxter called John Davis or Davies to recount the unforgettable morning he had found the body. Then Inspector Chandler was asked why two men at the neighbouring Bailey's packing-case company, whom Davis had called out to upon discovering the body, had not been found yet. Chandler said they were looking, but Davis had to work and had been unavailable to help identify the men.

"Your work is of no consequence compared with this inquiry," Baxter admonished Davis.

"I am giving all the information I can," Davis said.

When Chandler returned to his seat, Abberline whispered, "I'll talk to his employer."

Next Baxter called Amelia Palmer, who lived at 35 Dorset Street and had identified Annie Chapman. Amelia said Annie had been married to a veterinary surgeon. Abberline frowned. According to his reports, Annie married a coachman.

Amelia said that for the past two years Annie had lived with another man, who made wire sieves. His profession provided her with a nickname: Mrs. Sivvy. Several times Amelia had seen Annie with bruises on her face and body. Most recently, she saw Annie on Tuesday afternoon looking pale and gave her money for tea and some food, warning her not to spend it on rum.

"I have seen her the worse for drink," Amelia admitted.

Next, Timothy Donovan testified about Annie's time at the common lodging house at which he was a deputy. Like Amelia, Donovan mentioned that Annie had appeared several times with bruises on her face and body.

Baxter then called John Evans, the night watchman at 35 Dorset Street, who had helped identify the body. Evans said a pensioner who Annie kept company with, came to the lodging house at 2:30 p.m. Saturday and asked after her, but not finding her there, he left. Evans said he last saw Annie Saturday morning at 1:45 at the lodging house. Lacking the money for the night, she moved on. She was, he said, "the worse for drink, but not badly so."

The inquest adjourned for the day. Abberline and Chandler hurried outside and into a four-wheeler as Abberline checked the time on his hunting watch. He had an appointment to keep.

Forty-five minutes later, having fought horrendous traffic to reach the Met Headquarters building on the corner of Great Scotland Yard and Whitehall Place, Abberline hobbled upstairs to his office. His varicose vein felt as if it was about to burst through the back of his knee.

In his office, Abberline sat across from John Richardson, who fidgeted with his cap. Being asked to come in and talk to the Chief of Detectives investigating the Whitechapel murders was not something that happened every day, especially when there was a leather apron on the desk before you.

"There's something that puzzles us," Abberline said. "You see we have this leather apron which was soaked when we found it." He tapped the apron. "But it hadn't been raining much, if at all that night. You know where we found it?"

"No."

"Come now, John, I think you do. We found it in the backyard where you live. . .at 29 Hanbury. Now, what puzzles me—" Abberline slowly turned over a corner of the apron—"What puzzles me are these initials. They're hard to read. The apron is worn almost through, but it looks like TP or JP or—" Abberline leaned forward and, holding out the apron, said, "Take a look at it, John."

Richardson hesitated, took the apron, managed a half-smile, and said, "Yes, yes, of course, sir, always eager to help."

Abberline leaned back. Richardson's hands trembled. He looked blankly at the worn corner of the apron where the initials had been dyed into the leather.

"We thought at first," Abberline said, keeping his voice soft and even, "that the initials might be JP: the initials of a mysterious, vicious man who delights in beating up women."

"Well, it could be."

"Yes, it could. But you don't want to do what you're doing, do you, John?"

Richardson looked puzzled.

"The initials aren't JP, are they John? They're JR: John Richardson. The last stroke of the R has almost worn away. It fooled me at first, but I looked at it under a strong light and used a magnifying glass, just like that detective Conan Doyle writes about, Sherlock Holmes. Heard of him?"

"No, sir."

"Conan Doyle thinks the Knife might be a man who dresses as a woman, but never mind. I hadn't heard of him either until a colleague mentioned Holmes to me. Said he used a magnifying glass. Actually, this was the first time I ever used one on a case."

Richardson sat silent. He let the leather apron slip to the floor.

"This is your apron, isn't it, John?"

Richardson trembled.

"I don't want to make things difficult for you," Abberline said, leaning forward about to pounce. "I don't want to have to call in my assistants to question you. They have a far less amenable view of mankind than my view. Now, for the last time, this is your apron, isn't it?"

Silence.

"Isn't it?" Abberline shouted.

"Yes. Yes, guv, yes. The apron is mine."

Abberline sat back in his chair, sighed and asked, "Why didn't you tell us this earlier? Would have saved us no end of bother."

"I was scared, guv. Jesus, guv, the whole city is stirred up about the murders and Leather Apron is on everyone's lips. I thought you or Mr. Thick would think I was Leather Apron."

"Neither of us did. We didn't think anyone would be stupid or cocky enough to leave a major clue in plain sight. Such a thing only happens in penny dreadfuls, at least that's what my colleague says when he complains about them."

That night Abberline made his way along one of Whitechapel's many backstreets. A constable followed along on the inspector's unplanned and unpredictable beat. Abberline had taken to wandering Whitechapel/Spitalfields at night, hoping against logic that he might catch the murderer in the act. He also stopped at doss house kitchens and common lodging houses to chat with the residents in the sliver of a hope he would hear a vital clue to help identify the murderer.

"What's your pleasure, love?" a voice attempting to be sultry came from the darkness ahead.

The young constable raised his bullseye lantern and illuminated a tall thin redhead with a dress cut so low so as to have saved enough fabric to make a waistcoat. Abberline adjusted his bowler hat and said, "Tempting as that offer is, not tonight, love. Inspector Abberline. Might be a good time to be home, what with a murderer about."

The redhead laughed. "I ain't afraid of him. It's the Phantom or stepping off London Bridge for me. What're the odds?"

"Worse odds on a dark, deserted street like this."

"Used to work Commercial Street, but with that gawd-awful tram construction night and day, no one could do business there no more unless she was the last woman in London."

Abberline handed the redhead 6 pence, urged her to find a doss house for the night, and walked on with the young constable.

"That's the worst of it," Abberline said. "She's right, so right."

"Think we'll find him soon, sir?" the constable asked, his light playing over another pair of unfortunates loitering against a stone wall under a gaslight to better showplace their offerings.

Abberline nodded to the women, urged them to find accommodation indoors, and told the constable, "We do have suspects."

"I heard we even get leads from America, sir."

Abberline peered at the young constable with his eager, expectant expression. He wondered if he was ever so naïve, even his first day in uniform. Maybe he had been, but at least now his memory allowed him to forget such a time.

"How on earth can someone in America know who the murderer is in East London?" he asked, smiling to lessen the impact of his words. Then, seeing the look of despondency on the young constable's face, he added, "We do have clues as plentiful as pints on a Saturday night at your local, but most of them seem to lead to a man who it turns out was fingered by some woman he just threw over." Abberline shook his head. "But we'll keep looking. Diligent tracking down of every clue; that's the way to find a murderer. If the victims knew the murderer, we'll find him."

"And if they didn't?"

Abberline stopped and stared into the darkness ahead. "Then, unless we get very lucky, I fear we're going to have a lot more dead unfortunates."

Chapter Nine

Tuesday, 11 September

The George Yard Buildings, Buck's Row and Hanbury murders had sent the East End into a turmoil of terror.

"The blood of the murdered women in the East End still cries for vengeance," *The Star* reported. "So far as we can gather from the contradictory and meaningless reports of the police, the arrests already made do not promise a solution to the mystery. If the murderer is still at large, and if, as there is every reason to suppose, he is a maniac, we may look for fresh deeds of blood at his hands...The government have not taken our advice and offered a reward. . .the police are not only incompetent, but indifferent." A reward, the paper argued, would have been offered if the victims had been "ladies" instead of "the most helpless and outcast class in the community." In 1886, the paper reported, 177 inquest verdicts of murder were recorded in London, but only 72 individuals were charged with murder and a mere 35 sentences of death were passed. "We have the startling fact that 105 men and women who committed murder are at large!" Most of London was far from concerned with the 105; only one man raised concerns to a sleep-depriving level across the metropolis: the Knife.

Everyone was aware of the threat that struck with incomprehensible motive and incredible daring. Pure unadulterated fear ran through Stepney, Shoreditch, Bethnal Green, Mile End New Town, St. George in the East, and the neighbouring parishes like some silent, mystic malevolent force. Casual meetings in the street became cloaked in suspicion. The creeping cancer of public panic had been let loose. Policemen drafted from throughout the metropolis poured into Whitechapel/Spitalfields to blanket the area in protective surveillance. Uniformed and plainclothed patrols circulated through the dark and dreary world of charcoal brick and soot stone. The transferred plainclothes officers often found themselves the subject of suspicion, since the local inhabitants were now suspicious of any stranger.

Night watches were doubled but crime continued unabated. William Seaman of 11 Princes Street, Whitechapel, attempted to murder John Simkin, an 82-year-old chemist. Simkin, bloodied, battered and incredibly resilient for his age, survived being hit on the head by the hammer-wielding Seaman. John Darb, a lunatic at large, waved an empty gun at a store owner while demanding cartridges for the weapon. Suspicion ran like paranoia through every mind. Isaac Jacobs, the slaughterhouse worker who had stolen a parcel of meat from work and had recently sought refuge in Chandler's Commercial Street station, was taken into custody as a suspect in the Nichols and Chapman murders and released within an hour. Abberline never sorted out whether he had been arrested because he had blood on his clothes or because he was Jewish or some combination of both. Klosowki and Ostrog were still at large. The hard-eyed bald man Abberline had noticed at the first inquest seemed forgotten for the moment, even though his description was included in the dozens sent to every police station in the area.

It was mid-morning when Chandler burst into Abberline's office, exclaiming, "We may have Leather Apron after all. We found a witness who saw him arguing with Annie Chapman just before she was murdered."

"Who?" Abberline asked, having just returned from his daily meeting at the Home Office with the other senior detectives working the Whitechapel murders. He had been debating whether to tell Sir Charles about the meetings, but guessed the Commissioner already knew. The Home Office and Scotland Yard might be on opposite ends of Whitehall, but they were well within gossip range and the ship of state was the only ship that leaked from the top.

"Emanuel Delbast Violenia," Chandler said, "a European gentleman of good character, Spanish and Bulgarian, well dressed. He saw Pizer and Chapman quarrelling in front of 29 Hanbury and he heard Pizer quite distinctly threaten to stick her with a knife."

They still had Pizer in custody, more for his own safety than from any belief he had anything to do with the murders. "Has he identified Pizer from a show-up parade?"

"We lined Pizer up with a half dozen other Jews and Violenia picked him out first thing. All looked alike to me. We can be certain the man he saw arguing with Annie was Pizer."

"Has Violenia seen Chapman's body?"

"Not yet, but a couple of men from Leman Street are taking him to the mortuary right now. He seemed eager to please. I thought you might like to meet Violenia yourself."

Chandler, buoyed by the expectancy of wrapping up the case, rushed out the door. As he followed, Abberline feared his colleague's high hopes might well be unfounded, even though he prayed they rested on a firm foundation of fact.

Two hours later, back at Scotland Yard, Abberline told Helson, "Mr. Violenia was unable to identify Chapman as the woman he saw arguing with Pizer and I even doubt whether the confrontation occurred anywhere near 29 Hanbury. The longer we talked, the more he contradicted himself. Release Pizer."

The fearsomeness of Leather Apron began to fade into the misty recesses of memory.

His left leg propped up on the pulled-out bottom drawer of his desk to ease the pain behind his knee, Abberline read a file that had just arrived from Paris about yet another lunatic: Nicholai Vasiliev or Vassilyeff. He was born in Tiraspol in 1847, making him 41. Close enough. He was a student at Odessa University. Didn't say what he studied: medicine? He became a fanatical anarchist at school. That fit the general description of a reasonably well-to-do man down on his luck. Vasiliev was suspected of murdering several prostitutes in Paris under conditions similar to the Whitechapel murders. How similar? The report didn't provide details. At least the French had included a picture of the man. Abberline ordered a pile of facsimiles made and sent a wire to Paris asking for intimate and precise details of the murders. Did he kill and mutilate his victims in the same way as the Whitechapel monster?

Abberline scanned a Y Division (Highgate) report from north London. Two doctors, Cowan and Cobb, had come in to pass on their fears about one Joseph Isenschmid, a butcher by profession and a lunatic by mental status. The doctors said Isenschmid had left his lodgings at No. 60 Milford Road at about the times of the murders. His wife had not seen him for two months and said he regularly carried around large butcher knives. The two physicians feared he might be the murderer. The doctors were apparently far better at diagnosing a potential murderer than at describing faces. They could not provide a good enough description of Isenschmid to circulate.

Armed with pictures of Ostrog, Vasiliev and Klosowski, Abberline sent inspectors out on an all-out blitz of London's Russian clubs and societies. Kosminski remained under investigation, but appeared to stay at his sister's home most of the time. Neighbours said he hated women, but also said he was harmless for all his misogynistic talk. Abberline sent a Russian-speaking constable in plainclothes undercover into the East End. Abberline told him to attend anarchist meetings, discuss socialism in positive terms and, if possible, infiltrate any group advocating revolution. He also was to be on the lookout for a mysterious bald anarchist who had reportedly argued that the Polly Nichols murder was a good thing since it heralded the imminent end of the British Empire.

Wednesday, 12 September

"Here's another Russian suspect, courtesy of the French," Helson said as Abberline massaged the throbbing varicose vein behind his left leg in their now shared office at the Met. Sitting in the Home Secretary's meetings every morning did little for Abberline's leg pain. He needed a rest, soon, but the only way to get rest was to apprehend the murderer.

"A cane, sir?"

"Emma made me bring it. Don't need it, really."

"Course not, sir," Helson said, sitting across from Abberline. "The Paris police believe a Vasilly Konovalov, alias Alexey Pedachenko, alias Andrey Luiskovo, is a possible suspect. He's wanted for murdering a woman; mutilated her in Paris a couple of years ago. The gendarmes think he may have come here. He's described as medium height, dark blue eyes, black moustache curled and waxed at the ends, heavy black eyebrows. Wears a giant watch fob at times and spats."

"A swell," Abberline said, leaning back in his swivel chair at his desk.

"Sounds like just the suspect Dr. Lyttleton Stewart Forbes Winslow described."

"Who?"

"The alienist. Wrote *The Times* theorizing the murderer was 'not of the class of which Leather Apron belongs, but is of the upper class of society,' probably a lunatic lately discharged or escaped from some asylum, who appears sane on the surface."

"When do you find time to read so many newspapers?" Abberline asked in wonder.

"Traffic's so bad on my trip in, I could read the *Encyclopaedia Britannica* from A to Z in a fortnight. Emma likes to read, too, so we often read to each other over breakfast, once the children are sorted for school."

"Any luck with a public school?"

"Costs too much and the competition is fierce for any of the good ones. Looking for some favourable apprenticeships for Albert and Joseph, but it's a challenge. Might have found one for Albert with a carpenter, but have to speak with the man further; make certain it's a good situation."

Abberline was glad at such times he was not responsible for any children, although he knew the lack pained Emma. For a moment he wondered what his life would have been like with Martha if she hadn't died two months after they married in 1868. Emma was a fine woman, but Martha—Martha was his first love. Would she have borne him children? A son?

"Pedachenko," Helson said, "or whatever you want to call him, is also known to disguise himself as a woman, and he was a junior surgeon before going berserk."

"Add him to the files. He's as good a suspect as Vasiliev, Ostrog, Klosowski or Baldy, the political agitator. We seem to have enough mad Russians to start a working man's club."

With Helson, Chandler and his walking stick, Abberline hurried over to the Working Lads' Institute for the second day of the Chapman inquest.

Coroner Baxter called Fountain Smith, a printer's warehouseman and Annie Chapman's younger brother. Smith last saw his sister a fortnight ago, when he gave her 2s for lodging, confirming the conclusion that Annie was unfortunate in financial matters as well as in her profession.

When called, Chandler testified that he had finally found the two men Davis called out to upon finding the body. James Kent and James Green, packing-case makers for Joseph and Thomas Bayley's firm, added little, save that Kent said he covered the body with a piece of canvas.

"I thought Chandler said he covered the body," Helson whispered.

"I doubt it matters," Abberline whispered back. "Unless the killer did."

Amelia Richardson and Harriet Hardiman lived at 29 Hanbury and both testified they neither heard nor saw anything of note the night of the murder. Then John Richardson testified. When pressed, he was adamant that he had gone all the way down the stairs and was certain he would have seen the body if it had been in the yard when he first went out to check the cellar door. He also mentioned that he often found men and women in the yard and even on the landing.

Baxter asked Richardson, "Do you mean to say that they go there for immoral purpose?"

"Yes, they do."

"More so recently," Helson whispered to Abberline, "with that horrendous tram construction on Commercial Street."

"When's it due to be completed?" Abberline asked, knowing Helson's newspaper addiction would provide the answer.

"November, they claim."

Mrs. Richardson was recalled and firmly denied knowing that her yard was used for immoral purposes. Then she said her son wore a leather apron when he worked in the cellar.

Baxter asked, "It is a rather dangerous thing to wear, is it not?"

"Yes. On Thursday, 6 September, I found my son's leather apron in the cellar mildewed. He had not used it for a month. I put it under the tap in the yard and left it there. It was found there on Saturday morning by the police, who took charge of it."

Abberline already knew the apron was her son's, so he dozed, trying to will away the pain in his leg and the exhaustion he felt—far, far away.

Mrs. Richardson said there was a pan of clean water under the tap the morning of the murder, but she had also seen the pan on Friday night and it appeared undisturbed.

"The murderer didn't use the tap to wash up then," Chandler whispered.

"Probably didn't have much, if any blood on him anyway," Abberline whispered without opening his eyes.

Sergeant Thick escorted in John Pizer or Piser, as some in the press spelled his name. In a suit of loud checks, the five foot four inch Pizer described his whereabouts on the nights of the Buck's Row and Hanbury Street murders. Thick testified that Pizer's movements had been corroborated. Baxter asked why Pizer had stayed indoors.

"I will tell you why; if I went out, I would have been torn to pieces!"

After testifying, Pizer sat in the back row with Thick and they chatted amiably as if they were old pals, which in a way they were. Abberline noted no signs of lunacy in the infamous Leather Apron. Accusations against Pizer were, Abberline concluded, "groundless." He had ordered Pizer released the night before: one suspect down, a baker's dozen or more to go.

Baxter recalled John Richardson, who in the interval had fetched the knife he had used to cut the leather flap off his boot. From his seat, Abberline eyed the much-worn dessert knife and wondered whether it could cut toast, let alone a neck.

"It wasn't sharp enough," Richardson told Baxter, when the coroner expressed the same dubious belief in the knife's abilities, "so I borrowed one from the market."

"Do murderers often borrow the murder weapon?" Helson whispered and chuckled.

Lastly, Henry John Holland, a boxmaker who was passing by when Davis found the body, testified, but added nothing that caused Abberline to open his eyes from his semi-slumber.

Elsewhere life continued as usual. A man assaulted two policemen in Holloway. An arm was found floating in the Thames. A French explorer expressed the belief that Mr. Stanley was not dead, but was working secretly for the British government to secure more territory in Africa. In far-off, detached America, the Republicans nominated General Harrison for president and many Democrats pointed out that he didn't have a hope in Hell, or America, for that matter.

Joseph Helson's modest house was in a distinctly middle-class neighbourhood. The house was under-furnished in the sense that good taste was a luxury imbibed only by the wealthy. Helson's police pay allowed his wife, Mary, to stock their Met-supplied home with second-hand indulgences, the usual bric-a-brac, the antimacassar-covered sofa, the valenced mantelpiece, the shelves of china ornaments and family photographs. The carpets were worn, the screen, a little broken, the furniture, with four children, scuffed, but all was clean and in its proper place.

Perhaps the most incongruent aspect of the Helson home was not the working-class furnishings that filled the middle-class shell, but the combination itself. The brass might go with the aspidistra, but somehow both jarred beside the delicate pastels of the dominating Japanese screen. The Morris wallpaper wasn't quite in tune with the imitation tiles that had been copied from de Morgan. The chaotic cascade of shapes, forms and colours would make any artist shudder, but neither Mary nor Joseph were of such artistic temperament. If willow-pattern china was the thing, without knowing it they readily adapted their taste to fit the fashion.

After yet another long day on the job, Joseph placed the few cards remaining in his hand on the table. Game over. Dead end. The new game of Patience had its strange fascination, but it was only a time-filler or time-killer. He stretched. Their four children were already well tucked into their beds.

"Are you going up to bed now, dear?" Mary asked, peering innocently over the top of the book she was reading, Disraeli's romance *Endymion*. The look was deceptive. She knew what Joseph was thinking and he knew what she was thinking and each knew that the other knew. Helson nodded, cleared the cards away and shuffled off toward the stairs. Mary busied herself with extinguishing the downstairs gaslights. Joseph lit a paraffin lamp to carry upstairs to the bedroom, where, as was common, there was no gas light. Joseph was soon powdering his toothbrush while Mary folded down the bed sheets. It was just more of the ritual they went through fairly regularly. They would talk about what had to be done around the house or the children's grades. They would undress and get into their night attire, but almost never facing one another when they did. It was as if to see the other disrobing was a social *faux pas* or, perhaps, even a mortal sin. Mary always pulled her long flannel nighty down to her knees before removing her under-garments – a behavior that suggested the female body was not to be exposed even to a husband of thirteen years. Joseph was little different, only his pajama top wasn't long enough to cover his lower extremities, so he simply slipped off his underwear and pulled up his pajama bottoms with extreme speed and dexterity. Years of practice made for lightning-like perfection.

They then climbed beneath the covers, most times turning out the paraffin lamp; only occasionally when they felt truly daring and naughty leaving the lamp burning, but always doing it under covers and never looking closely at the parts that made their partner different. Both enjoyed what followed most when done in the dark, perhaps because the extreme blackness of their heavily draped Victorian bedroom eliminated almost all sense of sight, leaving the body to rely on the more directly carnal sense of touch. Joseph loved that delicious wet feeling that surged around his thrusting organ; the tickly, taunting touch of her pubic hair against his body and that strange tightening feeling that seemed to close in from the top of her opening. Most of all there were the times when the upper part of her sexual organ seemed to pulsate; that was when it was best of all. He loved feeling the warm flood of passion that flowed through her body, hardening the nipples of her breasts and making her hips move her magic muff and do things that would make a proper woman blush. They both swiftly removed their night attire. Tonight might bring multiple explosions deep in her before his organ erupted. He took her in his arms and felt her legs parting as his organ probed for the hot, moist gateway to paradise. The witching hour arrived.

Thursday, 13 September

The third day of the Chapman inquest found Abberline, Helson and Chandler back at the Working Lads' Institute. Abberline had politely begged off another Home Office meeting so he could attend the inquest. He would not miss much. The meetings rarely produced anything more than minutes.

Coroner Baxter called Chandler and went through the inspector's actions the morning Annie's body was discovered, including finding the torn envelope and the leather apron, as well as the perplexing lack of blood anywhere but on and under the body. Chandler said the police were still seeking the pensioner who spent time with Annie every week, but had been unable to find him as yet.

Sergeant Baugham (H Division) then testified about taking the body to the mortuary.

Baxter asked, "Are you sure you took every portion of the body away with you?"

"Yes."

Baugham testified that he stayed with the body in the mortuary shed until Chandler arrived. Chandler was recalled to testify that when he arrived at the mortuary, he replaced Baugham with another constable to watch the corpse until Dr. Phillips arrived. This time the corpse would not be undressed and washed until after a post mortem was performed.

During a pause in the questioning, the jury foreman mentioned MP Montagu's £100 reward and said, "It might help if the government offered a reward."

Baxter said, "I do not think it is government policy to offer rewards in such cases." Before the foreman could pursue the politically sensitive matter, Baxter asked Chandler, "Were you present when the doctor was making his post-mortem?"

"Yes."

"Did you see the doctor find the handkerchief?"

"It was taken off the body. I picked it up from the pile of clothing, which was in the corner of the room. I gave it to Dr. Phillips."

"Did you see the handkerchief taken off the body?"

"I did not. The nurses must have taken it off the throat."

"How do you know?"

"I don't know."

"Then you are guessing?"

Chandler said, his face as hard as a statue's, "I am guessing."

"That is all wrong, you know," Baxter said, turning to the jury. "He is really not the proper man to have been left in charge."

Baxter dismissed Chandler, who cast an angry look at the coroner as he stalked back to his seat beside Abberline.

"Don't let him goad you," Abberline whispered to Chandler. "It's not your fault Whitechapel lacks a proper mortuary with trained attendants who know how to handle a murder victim."

Baxter recalled the deputy of the lodging house, Timothy Donovan, who testified that he recognized the handkerchief as the one he saw Annie wearing.

Dr. Phillips then testified that when he first examined the body at the scene, "The face was swollen and turned on the right side, and the tongue protruded between the front teeth, but not beyond the lips; it was much swollen. The small intestines and other portions were lying on the right side of the body on the ground above the right shoulder, but attached. There was a large quantity of blood, with a part of the stomach above the left shoulder. The body was cold, except that there was a certain remaining heat, under the intestines, in the body. Stiffness of the limbs was not marked, but it was commencing. The throat was dissevered deeply. I noticed that the incision of the skin was jagged, and reached right round the neck.

"On the back wall of the house, between the steps and the palings, on the left side, about 18 inches from the ground, there were about six patches of blood, varying in size from a sixpenny piece to a small point, and on the wooden fence there were smears of blood, corresponding to where the head of the deceased laid, and immediately above the part where the blood had mainly flowed from the neck, which was well clotted.

"Having received instructions soon after 2 o'clock on Saturday afternoon, I went to the labour-yard of the Whitechapel Union for the purpose of further examining the body and making the usual post-mortem investigation. I was surprised to find that the body had been stripped and was lying ready on the table."

Surprised, Abberline stared at Phillips. Nichols' body had been scrubbed clean before the post mortem. Was Phillips mixing his murders? Abberline looked at Thick and was about to issue an order, but the sergeant was already rising to his feet.

"I'll get right on it, Chief. I didn't know a thing about this."

"What's worse, neither did I."

Thick disappeared out a side door.

Phillips continued, "It was under great disadvantage I made my examination. As on many occasions I have met with the same difficulty. I now raise my protest, as I have before, that members of my profession should be called upon to perform their duties under these inadequate circumstances."

"The mortuary is not fitted for a post-mortem examination," Baxter agreed. "It is only a shed. There is no adequate convenience, and at certain seasons of the year it is dangerous to the operator."

Then it was the jury foreman's turn, "I think we can all endorse the doctor's view of it."

Baxter said, "As a matter of fact there is no public mortuary from the City of London up to Bow. There is one at Mile End, but it belongs to the workhouse and is not used for general purposes."

Every police surgeon had the same complaint. The complaints were carefully copied down, duly recorded and, other than evoking platitudes from one public official or other, totally ineffective. Abberline had the feeling that the complaints, although legitimate, were a kind of "crying wolf"; if you bitched too often about something, the bitching lost all effect.

Returning to the victim at hand, Baxter asked about the post mortem results. Dr. Phillips said, "I noticed a bruise over the right temple. There was a bruise under the clavicle and there were two distinct bruises, each the size of a man's thumb, on the fore part of the chest. . ..There was an abrasion over the bend of the first joint of the ring finger, and there were distinct markings of a ring or rings, probably the latter."

"Those bloody rings again," Abberline muttered.

"The head being opened showed that the membranes of the brain were opaque and the veins loaded with blood of a dark character. There was a large quantity of fluid between the membranes and the substance of the brain. The brain substance was unusually firm and its cavities also contained a large amount of fluid. The throat had been severed. The incisions of the skin indicated that they had been made from the left side of the neck on a line with the angle of the jaw, carried entirely round and in front of the neck, and ending at a point about midway between the jaw and the sternum or breast bone on the right hand. There were two distinct clean cuts on the body of the vertebrae on the left side of the spine. They were parallel to each other and separated by about half an inch. The muscular structures between the side processes of bone of the vertebrae had an appearance as if an attempt had been made to separate the bones of the neck. There are various other mutilations of the body, but I am of the opinion that they occurred subsequent to the death of the woman. . ..I am entirely in your hands, sir, but is it necessary that I should describe the further mutilations? From what I have said I can state the cause of death."

"The object of the inquiry is not only to ascertain the cause of death, but the means by which it occurred," Baxter said. "Any mutilation which took place afterwards may suggest the character of the man who did it."

"You don't wish for details," Phillips warned. "I think if it is possible to escape the details it would be advisable. The cause of death is visible from the injuries I have described."

"Supposing any one is charged with the offence, they would have to come out then, and it might be a matter of comment that the same evidence was not given at the inquest."

"I am entirely in your hands," Phillips repeated, although his opposition to discussing the mutilations was clear in the set of his body.

After a moment's consideration, Baxter said, "We will postpone that for the present. You can give your opinion as to how the death was caused."

"From these appearances, I am of the opinion that the breathing was interfered with previous to death, and that death arose from syncope, or failure of the heart's action, in consequence of the loss of blood caused by the severance of the throat."

"Was the instrument used at the throat the same as that used at the abdomen?"

"Very probably. It must have been a very sharp knife, probably with a thin, narrow blade, and at least six to eight inches in length, and perhaps longer."

"Is it possible that any instrument used by a military man, such as a bayonet, would have done it?"

"No, it would not be a bayonet."

"Tabram's soldier killer again," Abberline whispered to Helson. "No bloody evidence a soldier killed her, let alone with a bayonet."

"Some stories, unlike unfortunates, are immortal," Helson whispered.

Baxter asked Phillips, "Would it have been such an instrument as a medical man uses for post-mortem examinations?"

"The ordinary post-mortem case does not contain such a weapon."

"Would any instrument that slaughterers employ have caused the injuries?"

"Yes, well ground down."

"Would the knife of a cobbler or of any person in the leather trades have done?"

"I think the knife used in those trades would not be long enough in the blade."

"Was there any anatomical knowledge displayed?"

"I think there was. There were indications of it. My own impression is that anatomical knowledge was only less displayed or indicated in consequence of haste. The person evidently was hindered from making a more complete dissection in consequence of the haste."

"Was the whole of the body there?"

The jury and audience leaned forward almost as one; the proceeding's best part had finally arrived.

"No; the absent portions being from the abdomen."

"Are those portions such as would require anatomical knowledge to extract?"

"I think the mode in which they were extracted did show some anatomical knowledge."

"A bloody doctor did it," a labourer in front of Abberline exclaimed.

Baxter asked, "Was there evidence of any struggle?"

"No; not about the body of the woman. You do not forget the smearing of blood about the palings."

"In your opinion did she enter the yard alive?"

"I am positive of it. I made a thorough search of the passage and I saw no trace of blood, which must have been visible had she been taken into the yard."

"So much for some lunatic trundling corpses hither and yon all over East London," Abberline whispered.

Baxter asked, "Was there any appearance of the deceased having taken much alcohol?"

"No, but there were signs of great privation. I am convinced she had not taken any strong alcohol for some hours before her death. She was probably drunk on beer."

"At least she was getting something nutritious," Helson whispered.

Baxter asked, "Was the bruising you mentioned recent?"

"The marks on the face were recent, especially about the chin and sides of the jaw. The bruises upon the temple and in front of the chest were of longer standing, probably of days. I am of the opinion that the person who cut the deceased's throat took hold of her by the chin and then commenced the incision from left to right."

"Could that be done so instantaneously that a person could not cry out?"

"By pressure on the throat no doubt it would be possible."

The foreman said, "There would probably be suffocation."

Baxter asked, "The thickening of the tongue would be one of the signs of suffocation?"

"Yes," Phillips said. "My impression is that she was partially strangled. The handkerchief produced was, when found amongst the clothing, saturated with blood. A similar article was round the throat of the deceased when I saw her early in the morning at Hanbury Street."

"It had not the appearance of having been tied on afterwards?"

"No. Sarah Simonds, a resident nurse at the Whitechapel Infirmary, stated that, in company of the senior nurse, she went to the mortuary on Saturday and found the body of the deceased on the ambulance in the yard. In the shed, she was directed by Inspector Chandler to undress it and she placed the clothes in a corner. She left the handkerchief round the neck. She was sure of this. They washed stains of blood from the body. It seemed to have run down from the throat. She found a pocket tied round the waist. The strings were not torn. There were no tears or cuts in the clothes."

Inspector Chandler muttered, "I instructed no bloody such thing."

Abberline sat slumped behind his desk at Met headquarters. The warm, comforting, weightless sensation of sleep seeped all around him like a soothing friendly all-encompassing fog. Even his varicose vein was easing its demands for his attention; maybe his Emma-imposed walking stick was helping. He desperately needed sleep after so many late nights touring stations, reading reports and talking with constables, inspectors, unfortunates, and all manner of East Enders. Invariably, when he finally got home and to bed with Emma, a telegram arrived at dawn announcing he was needed immediately to interview a witness or suspect. A nice nap might be just what he needed.

"H Division, Holloway station, detained the barking butcher, Isenschmid," Helson said as he strode into Abberline's office.

Abberline bolted upright, his eyes wide, but still seeing only fuzzy images.

"Sorry, sir," Helson said, staring at his slowly awakening chief.

"Go on," Abberline managed, even though the last thing he wanted was to keep his eyes open, let alone hear about mad butchers.

"They sent him to the Infirmary Fairfield Row. Certified him a dangerous lunatic."

"Might be promising," Abberline managed as he rose to stagger over to the tea pot, stretching his left leg to try to ease the heaviness from behind his knee.

"Not so promising. Thick found no evidence of blood on the man's clothes. We're making enquiries about Isenschmid's whereabouts on the nights of the murders."

"Hope springs eternal," Abberline said as he selected an orange pekoe which, he hoped, would revive his failing body and mind.

"One of our boys found a blood-stained newspaper in Cadosch's yard. Been used to carry home meat from a slaughterhouse, supposedly for a dog, but Cadosch hasn't got a dog."

"But he has got a West London appetite and an East London income. People in Whitechapel get meat anyway they can; probably has a friend in the meatpacking trade."

Friday, 14 September

In secret, the family paid for Annie Chapman to be buried; anything to avoid that greatest of Victorian indignities—a pauper's burial. To avoid a crowd of gawkers, only the family and police knew the time and place of the funeral. Almost by magic a hearse materialized out of the drifting damp morning fog and stopped before the Montague Street mortuary. A side door opened and four burly figures with long experience of such movements transferred the body swiftly from the mortuary into the hearse. The rear door of the vehicle had hardly closed when it disappeared into the fog once more. By 7 a.m. the body was on its way to the mortician on Hunt Street. At 9 the body, now in an elm coffin draped in black, was loaded onto the hearse again. The last earthly traces of Annie Chapman were on their way to their final place of decomposition. No attention was drawn to the shining black carriage of death as it moved solemnly through the streets. No mourning coaches followed. The windows were curtained, black and unrevealing.

Annie Chapman's burial ceremony at Manor Park Cemetery was as simple as it was somber. A minister who never knew Annie Chapman in life spoke over her remains in death. His aged hands sprinkled a few grains of dirt upon the coffin as he uttered the usual Christian words. The dirt trickled across the simple lettering on the casket: Annie Chapman, Died 8 September 1888, Aged 48 Years.

"Blast. The fog burned off. It's fair and clear," Abberline mused as he, Chandler and Helson waited for Sir Charles in the latter's office at Met Police headquarters, 4 Whitehall Place. Abberline looked out the window, which overlooked the six-carriage-wide thoroughfare called Great Scotland Yard. Abberline had already been to his daily Home Office meeting, which had been longer than he hoped, but not longer than he could stand. The changed weather was not a good sign. Abberline looked over at Chandler, who, contrary to Abberline's sense of foreboding, was smiling. Chandler had mentioned that Ayr had stopped the upstart Colonials from Canada 4-nil in football. All was right in his world.

Sir Charles marched in and, after they sat down at a table, he asked Abberline to summarize the extent of the investigation thus far. "We've checked more than two hundred common lodging houses, every single such dwelling within a half-mile of the murder site, and we've taken the names of all those occupants who entered or left any lodging house after two on the morning of the Chapman murder. There are still a few occupants unaccounted for, but we will track them down as rapidly as possible and investigate them thoroughly."

"Did any lodging house deputy perchance see the murderer?" Sir Charles asked.

"As far as we know, none did. No one saw anyone stained with blood entering or leaving their premises, although the murderer may not have had any blood on him. Even if he was covered in blood from hat to boots, little attention is paid to anyone inquiring for a bed in the wee hours of the morning in such places. Their money is quickly taken and he's sent up a badly lit stairway, invariably on his own."

Chandler said, "If he did get some blood on him, the murderer could clean up in any of the common wash basins in the streets before entering a dosshouse."

"If he's of middle- or upper-class origins," Abberline said, "a flat in the East End would be much safer to clean up and go to ground in than a crowded common lodging house. But he couldn't be too fancy a toff or he'd stick out like the Queen in Whitechapel. Based on our few descriptions, I think the best bet is that our murderer is a ne'er-do-well member of the upper classes who is down on his luck. Such a person would fit in with the tradesmen in Whitechapel and might have a flat in the area."

"Are you searching amongst peers, MPs, and army and naval officers then?" Sir Charles asked, his doubts clear in every word.

"We haven't got any upper-class suspect right now, but if—"

"So you are *not* investigating the upper class?"

"I didn't say that, sir. Following what evidence we have, we've investigated upper-, middle- and lower-class suspects."

And so it went, back and forth, and with every word Abberline realized how little they knew about the murderer and how far they were from identifying him.

An hour later, as they rose to leave, Abberline winced as pain shot through his left leg.

Sir Charles frowned and asked, "Are you are ailing, Chief Inspector?"

"Just one of life's aches and pains, sir," Abberline said as Chandler and Helson hurried out of the office.

Sir Charles eyed Abberline. His bushy moustache hid his mouth, but his hooded eyes carried a look of concern. "I fully realize these cases carry a field marshal's degree of responsibility," Sir Charles said, striding over to stand before Abberline. "Are you receiving all the resources you require to push the investigation forward with the greatest of alacrity from the divisions, the Yard and the *Home Office*?"

Abberline noted Sir Charles accent on the last two words. Their gazes met and in that instant Abberline knew Sir Charles knew about the daily Home Office meetings.

"I spend most of my time organizing the investigation; inspectors, constables, plainclothes and uniformed conducting door-to-door canvasses, hunting down witnesses and suspects, ensuring we pursue every potential clue."

"Capital, capital," Sir Charles said, nodding encouragement.

"If there is one area where some assistance might be welcomed, it's with the number of reports coming in from the dozens of inspectors from multiple divisions involved with the case. Enough arrive every day to keep a dozen inspectors busy reading from breakfast to last call, sir. I fear without more personnel to read them all, we may miss something of paramount importance."

Abberline, Helson and Chandler rode in an official four-wheeler pulled by two white beauties toward the Bethnal Green station, where they planned to review the night's patrol schedules.

Chandler said, "I wish we knew how this fiend lures the women to the places where he murders them; might make it easier to warn women how to avoid him."

Abberline, massaging the back of his left knee to ease the discomfort his varicose vein had caused as a result of sitting so long with Sir Charles, said, "I agree with Chief Inspector Moore. He said, 'It's not as if the murderer has to wait for his chance; the unfortunates make the chance for him. They're so miserable and hopeless, so utterly lost to all that makes a person want to live, that for the sake of four-pence, enough to get drunk on, they'll go in any man's company and run the risk that it's not him.'"

As they trundled across Trafalgar Square toward East London, Chandler reported, "I visited the Royal Sussex Regiment's first battalion at Farnborough first thing this morning about the torn part of the envelope found near Chapman's body."

"Find any suspects?" Helson asked.

"Dozens; most of the men in the regiment use the envelope, as do their families and friends, but no one admitted sending a letter to anyone in Whitechapel. I spent hours checking pay books but found no writing to match the fragment on the envelope."

"Not that there was much to compare," Abberline said.

"It may not have even been sent by a soldier, since it was mailed not from the barracks but from Lynchford Road Post Office. Worse, the Post Office stocks the envelope and sells them to the public. I bought one," he said, handing Abberline a duplicate of the envelope from which a piece was found by the body.

The carriage took them along the Strand and Fleet Street, past St. Paul's and along Mile End Road through Whitechapel. The driver avoided Commercial Street and meandered along side streets north-eastward through the heavy traffic to finally arrive at the Bethnal Green station. The trio strode upstairs to Helson's tiny office.

"Before we go over the duty assignments for tonight, let's review the timing of the Hanbury Street murder," Abberline said as he sat on a hard wood chair. He rested his left leg on a dustbin. Elevating his leg sometimes eased the pain.

After asking a constable to light the coal fire, Helson sat behind his desk in a wood swivel chair. "Dr. Phillips examined the body at 6:20 a.m. and concluded the time of death was about two hours earlier—about 4:20."

Chandler, settled into a chair beside Abberline, extracted his pipe and started filling it with black tobacco. "Liz Long said she saw the deceased at 5:30 a.m."

"She's probably wrong about the time," Helson said.

"Richardson went into the yard at 4:45 or 4:50," Abberline said, "but said he didn't see a body anywhere in the yard."

"At 6:45 that morning," Chandler said, consulting his notes, "he told me without a hint of doubt that he did not see the body in the yard. But—and it could be significant—he said that he 'did not go down the steps.'"

"From my memory," Abberline said, "if Richardson just opened the top door and looked down the steps, he could have seen the padlock on the cellar to the right, but the left side of the yard would have been hidden by the back door, which opens outward and to the left, so he probably would not have seen Chapman's body, if it was there."

"Richardson was adamant at the inquest that he walked down the stairs to check the cellar," Chandler said. "Said he sat on the lower steps with his boots on the flagstones to cut a loose piece of leather from his boot."

"But he had already told *The Telegraph* the same thing," Helson said. "He'd be unlikely to change his story after seeing it in print for all and sundry to read. Thank you, constable."

The fire lit, its heat promising to take the chill off the office, the constable exited.

"If Richardson did venture into the yard, he couldn't have failed to see the body," Chandler said.

"So did she die just after 5:30 as Richardson and Liz Long's memories suggest," Helson asked, "or 4:20 as Dr. Phillips' concluded from the medical evidence?"

"Cadosch, the neighbour, heard voices in the yard at about the same time as Liz Long," Chandler said.

Abberline said, "I tend to lean toward Dr. Phillips' medical conclusion, but I don't lean too far."

"Coroner Baxter is of the opinion that the doctor's time of death is based on feeling how warm the body was," Helson said, "but several factors could have made the body colder than expected."

"It was chilly that morning, but not that cold," Abberline said. "Annie's clothes had been thrown up to expose her legs and abdomen, so the body would cool faster."

"Phillips acknowledged those factors at the inquest, although he probably thought it was colder than it was since he had just got out of a warm bed," Helson said with a grin.

"For now let's focus on roughly 4:30 as the time of death, at least until we have clear proof that she was alive an hour later," Abberline said, deciding to rely on Dr. Phillips' more than 20 years of experience rather than witnesses, whom, he had learned after years of service, were often unreliable, especially at such an early hour.

"You'd think one of the 17 people living at 29 Hanbury, many in the five rooms overlooking the murder site, would have heard something," Helson said, shaking his head and showing his exasperation at the lack of an eye-witness to the murder.

"Some even slept with their windows open," Chandler said in disbelief. "The murderer must kill his victims as silently as a lady sips tea."

"Phillips believes she was strangled first, which would mean the murder was as silent as a snowy day on the moors," Abberline said. He rose and said, miming the actions as he described each grisly motion, "So he took her by the chin as he talked to her, which Cadosch overheard, gripped her with his right hand—thus the scratches on the left side of her neck and bruise on the right—and throttled her to keep her silent. Lowered her to the ground as she fainted, knelt above her head, knife in his right hand, and cut her throat left to right."

"If she was prone, that fits the lack of bloodstains on her front, apart from a few drops on her left arm," Helson said.

"The murderer took her uterus, parts of her vagina and bladder," Abberline said.

"Would have bloody hands from that," Helson said.

"Knows anatomy; a doctor?" Chandler asked.

"Phillips said he saw 'no meaningless cuts,'" Helson said.

"With so many people about, the murderer might have been in a hurry, so there were far fewer slashes than in the previous murders," Abberline said. "I doubt he was just lucky to cut out the uterus whole. I agree with Phillips and Baxter; it must have been someone accustomed to the post-mortem room."

"The killer tore the rings from her fingers," Chandler said. "Theft?"

"If she even had rings on that night," Abberline said. "Probably worth a shilling each, if that."

"Seemed to be whitish lines on her fingers," Chandler said.

"We haven't found any rings," Abberline said. "She had a pocket attached by strings under her dress, which the killer ripped open, dropping the contents at her feet: a piece of muslin, a small-tooth comb and a pocket comb in a paper case. No rings." He paused. The objects almost seemed arranged at the victim's feet. After creating chaos, the murderer displayed a passion for neatness. Was there a need for balance in everything, even in the disordered mind of a murderous maniac?

Helson asked, "What about the piece of envelope and pills found by her head?"

Abberline sat down and said, "The envelope led nowhere. Follow-up on the pills. Not much to go on, since everything seems to relate to Annie, not her murderer. He doesn't appear to have left a single thing with the victim."

"He would have needed a bag to take the body parts away with him; might be something at least to include as part of a description," Chandler said.

"Brash bugger," Helson said. "If Richardson, Cadosch and Long are right, Chapman was killed in daylight, unlike Tabram and Nichols. The sun rose at 5:23 and already plenty of people about. It was a market morning."

"Spitalfields Market opens at 5," Abberline recited from memory after his years of service in the area. "The western end of Hanbury Street would be clogged with wagons by that time."

Helson said, consulting his notes, "Before the murder, carmen Thompson and Richardson had just visited the yard, and while Annie was with her murderer, it appears Cadosch was in the next yard not once, but twice. Then at 5:45 as the killer finished his work, John Davis and his wife awoke and prepared for the day."

"An extraordinary risk," Abberline said. "There was a tap in the yard, but the killer didn't pause to wash up. Maybe he heard Davis and his wife stirring."

"How do we know he didn't?" Chandler asked.

"Remember from the inquest? Mrs. Richardson found a pan of clean water left from the night before still under the tap that morning."

"Might have washed up, dumped the bloody water and refilled the pan."

"Now that would take guts beyond measure," Helson said. "But no one heard the tap running that morning."

"They didn't hear a murder, either," Abberline said.

"At least we have Mrs. Long as a witness," Chandler said.

Abberline said, "If the man she saw talking to Annie was even the murderer."

"Said he was a foreigner," Chandler said.

"Whatever that means," Abberline said, letting the frustration show in his voice and instantly regretting it. His men were discouraged enough without him adding to their sense of despair. They needed something to give them hope. "She didn't see his face, so did she hear something to suggest a foreigner?"

Alderman James Whitehead sat back on a red divan at his club and sighed. "Disgusting, absolutely disgusting."

"What's that, James?" a retired army colonel asked from behind his overgrowth of mustache and billowing pipe.

"I'm reading a special early edition of *The Telegraph*. The latest atrocity in Hanbury Street; the poor woman disemboweled. Listen to this. 'The neighbourhood is described as a very rough one and respectable people are accustomed to avoid it.'" Whitehead lowered the newspaper and shook his head. "Imagine a part of London where a respectable Englishman, let alone a woman, cannot deign to walk."

He began to read aloud again, "'In these squalid parts of the city, aggravated assaults, attended by flesh wounds from knives, are frequent'—and listen to this—'men and women become accustomed to scenes of violence.' Think of it, Colonel, think of it: A place where wounding is as common as a rugger bruise, an environment where men and women are so used to blood and gore, they can totally ignore it."

"Frightful. Absolutely frightful," snorted the retired colonel. "I've never heard of such a thing. Never. It's a disgrace." He evidently hadn't ever been to a field hospital after a battle or if he had, he had totally ignored what he saw.

Chapter Ten

Saturday, 15 September

The mystery of the torn regimental envelope and pills found by Annie Chapman's body was solved when William Stevens, a painter who sometimes lived at 35 Dorset Street, appeared at the Commercial Street Police Station. Stevens said he saw Annie Chapman before she was turned out of the common lodging house just before her death. She had been to hospital and had a bottle of lotion, a bottle of medicine and a box of pills. The box fell apart. She had two pills left and found a piece of paper on the floor in which to wrap the pills: the piece of envelope.

Abberline sighed when he received the report. Another red herring; the envelope had nothing to do with the murder or the murderer. He leaned back in his office chair and closed his eyes for a moment. God, he was so tired.

"Sir...sir?"

Abberline jolted awake. A constable stood before him looking worried.

"Are you ill, sir?"

"No, no. What is it?" Abberline asked as he tried to fully wake up. How long had he been asleep?

The constable brought news that Chief Inspector Donald Swanson, a shrewd Scot with more than 20 years of experience, had been placed in charge of the investigation of the Whitechapel murders.

Even as he chased the sleep from his mind, Abberline feared he had been replaced for failing to catch the Knife, as well as for meeting with Secretary Matthews behind Sir Charles' back. Now fully awake, he hurried to Sir Charles' office upstairs and asked his secretary for a moment with the Commissioner.

Twenty minutes later, Sir Charles apologized that Abberline had heard the news from someone else. "Gossip travels even faster in the Met than it does in the Army," Sir Charles said with a rueful smile. "In any case, well, there you have it."

After plying Abberline with tea, Sir Charles reassured Abberline that he was still in charge of the on-the-ground, day-to-day investigation of the murders. Sir Charles had tasked Swanson with the sole duty of reading every report, witness statement and order related to the cases in an attempt to identify the killer.

"Is that rejigger satisfactory for you, Chief Inspector?" Sir Charles asked.

Abberline nodded, greatly relieved at the appointment. He was also not surprised. The press, especially the radical press, might have lost all faith in Sir Charles, but Abberline knew that Sir Charles had a well-earned reputation for looking after his men, including his inspectors. Abberline also liked Swanson, who never courted accolades or publicity, but always got the job done. The Scot would be a fine man with whom to work.

"Ah, Abberline, one further item," Sir Charles said as Abberline turned to leave. "Would you mind liaising with the Home Office? Matthews wants some damn fool daily meetings of all the investigators and, truth be told, I utterly lack the time to attend and you are the only man in my command who I deem even remotely suitable to stand in my stead. Would you mind terribly?"

Chief Inspector Donald Swanson

Abberline found Swanson already hard at work in his office at the Yard, which looked out across Whitehall onto the red and yellow brick Admiralty buildings. With a doughy face and thin dark hair brushed across his scalp, Swanson looked more like the teacher he had once been than the tough detective Abberline knew him to be.

"There's a report here of another stabbing in Lambeth," Swanson said after

Abberline congratulated him on his new appointment. Piles of reports already covered the top of his desk and carpeted much of the floor. "The Lambeth stabbing doesn't have anything to do with the Whitechapel mutilation murders. A hairdresser, Henry Baker or Henry Williams—Gad, how many of these blighters are named Henry? We must be long past the 10th or 20th Henry. I know, I know. They change their name every court appearance. Sometimes keeps the judges from recognizing them as a past offender. Anyway, Baker or Williams or whoever he is stabbed some woman in the breast—God! The damn stabbing was last 10 July. Henry the Hacker has been locked up since then. How do these reports get so muddled? When you first read it you think the stabbing occurred early this morning. Some fool must have got the back files mixed in here."

Abberline could only suppress a knowing smile and nod.

"With what I assumed would be your hearty agreement," Swanson said, "I've ordered all reports, files, statements and notes about the Whitechapel murder cases carted here to my desk from Bethnal Green, Leman Street, Commercial Street and every other police station investigating the murders. I also asked Moore, Andrews and Reid for all their files and notes. I'd appreciate copies of everything you've gathered, too."

"You'll need a bigger desk," Abberline said as he thought, 'There but for the grace of God and Sir Charles, go I.'

With a great paperweight lifted from his shoulders, Abberline set off for the Commercial Street station to consult Chandler about next steps in the investigation. After his hansom became ensnarled in the gridlock caused by the tram construction, he decided to walk the rest of the way. Aided by his Emma-imposed walking stick, the stroll might help his leg feel better, although the thought of not having to dig through hundreds of reports, witness statements and thousands of information-filled forms brought a lightness to his tread he had not felt since before the Nichols murder.

He found Chandler discussing a coal delivery for the station with a carman. Even with a murderer about, the station still had to function as a station and a home for the bachelor constables who lived on the premises. Winter was coming.

Coal sorted, Abberline and Chandler walked upstairs toward Chandler's office.

"George Lusk and sixteen tradesmen formed the Mile End Vigilance Committee on the 10th in the Crown public house and now are out every night," Abberline said, having run into some of their number last night. "They even asked for Home Office assistance."

"Outrageous," Chandler sputtered as they walked. "The department is—"

"Isn't adequately protecting them, so people are taking their safety into their own hands."

Chandler's face forged redder. "That is as outrageous as asking constables to contribute to a reward to catch this murderer."

"If the government's not going to do it, we might as well," Abberline said as they reached Chandler's office, almost running into a constable carrying a box of files apparently destined for Swanson's desk, if it could be found under all the reports and files already atop it. "As for a reward, I got touched for a contribution this morning."

Abberline ensured the police were out in force again that night, but he was less worried than he had been. It was foggy and the papers forecast no clearing until Sunday. He was becoming convinced the Whitechapel murderer wouldn't stumble about searching for prey in the fog or rain. The Phantom probably got his inclement-weather enjoyment elsewhere.

The girl was young; perhaps fifteen at most. She was no virgin, but she hadn't been pumped and primed too much. There was a good chance she wasn't diseased. That was the nice part. The Londoner's gaze ran over her naked figure, filling with the joy of expectation as he took in the hairy little mound at her crotch.

"Come to Daddy, girl. I won't hurt you," he said.

She came over obediently, just as she had undressed. He laughed. "I bet you got a nice juicy little tight 'un."

His hand ran down her flat stomach into the mound of hair.

"Sit down on my lap."

She sat on his lap, spreading her legs a couple of inches as she settled on him. His hand ran to the space between her legs, up the soft, smooth expanse and onto the hairy place. His index finger split the outer lips, his penis erecting hard and turgid as he felt the wetness at the end of his finger. He drove his finger into her and moved it in and out as her organ cascaded with a fiery wetness.

He flipped her over onto the sofa, pulling down his pants and undershorts in one motion. He liked to surprise the young ones this way. But this one didn't seem surprised.

"You don't like it? Look at it. Isn't it nice and big and hard?"

"Yes, sir, it's nice and big."

"I bet you haven't had one as big as this in your hole your whole life, have you? Wouldn't you like to kiss it?"

The girl hesitated.

"Kiss it!" The command was hard, vicious. A fury filled his body.

The young girl bent over and ran her lips along the throbbing phallus.

"Suck it! Take it in your mouth. Suck it! Make your nice little mouth into a cunt, you little whore. Ah..ah. . ."

She sucked on the man's penis. He was thrusting madly at her now, pushing his organ in and out of her mouth like some maddened bull. Then it quivered. He felt the sudden expansion, the bursting explosion as he released inside her mouth. Then the organ shrank away. He lay panting, staring at her.

"What would you like to do next, sir?" she asked, boredom tinging her words. He had paid for her for the night.

The Londoner scowled; should have gone with my favourite, he thought, Isabelle.

Sunday, 16 September

Sunday settled on the streets in its own particular fashion; a quiet fashion with no sign of the Phantom. The fiddler and the hurdy-gurdy grinder were gone. The playing children even seemed subdued. With little faith in religion, many of the poor attended socialist meetings to rail against free trade, which had deprived the nearby docks of hundreds of bonded warehouses and thousands of jobs. Tower Hamlets in East London was especially supportive of the four-year-old Socialist League. It was a day for Sir Charles, Abberline, Helson and Chandler to attend church and visit relatives; for the rich to do charitable works after church; for the intellectual to read; for the female to sew; for Lusky it was no different than any other day.

In a restaurant near his lodging house, Coulls said, "The latest census data disputes your conclusions about Stepney being an alien enclave, Pierce. Only twenty-five percent of the population is foreign-born or of foreign-born parents."

"I don't believe it," Pierce said as he pecked at his lunch of beef stew.

"It just seems foreigners are more prevalent. You come to a street corner and ten people are standing there talking. You hear two with a German or Russian accent, but you don't hear the eight with no accent. They blur into the background."

"Ja, mein Herr!" Pierce barked.

His lunch finished, Coulls pushed his plate with the remains of deep-fried cod away and frowned as he went over his notes. "One of the unfortunates I spoke with has a posh address in Belgravia," he said, amazed. "She must be rather gifted in certain areas to command such prices."

Pierce laughed hard and long.

"What?" Coulls asked, mystified by his colleague's reaction.

"Means no such thing, and it doesn't mean she's a duchess stooping to a spot of slumming. Many an unfortunate works as a domestic or char during the day, so she just gave her employer's address instead of her own."

Monday, 17 September

World events continued as history made its single pass through the possibilities. Brits felt the French were checked in Europe and the continental balance of power assured as the powerful German army conducted manoeuvers near Frankfurt. Female infanticide continued in the northwest provinces of India, leaving males feeling more secure as their dominance was assured on the Asian subcontinent. The hunt for the Whitechapel monster went on. The weather remained overcast.

The Nichols inquest continued. Coulls covered it, scribbling notes as another reporter kept a running transcript in shorthand. Back at *The Empire's* offices, Coulls reported to Cox that Baxter had recalled Dr. Llewellyn, who testified that no part of the viscera was missing from the corpse, unlike in the Chapman case. Emma Green, a widow who lived at New Cottage, Buck's Row, adjacent to the murder site, testified she heard nothing that night, while Thomas Ede, an East London Railway signalman, said he saw a man with a knife the morning of the eighth.

"Might be worth following up," Cox said, listening even as he edited another reporter's copy.

Coulls made a note and continued as he stood before Cox's well-ordered desk, "Purkiss, the Essex Wharf manager, his wife, the night watchman, Mulshaw, and Constable John Thail, who passed the murder spot every 30 minutes that night, all heard nothing."

"The killer must move on cat's paws." Cox stopped his editing and looked up at Coulls. "Then again, I'm never sure what the police mean when they ask if someone has seen something suspicious. It's not like the killer's going to be walking around covered with blood, carrying a uterus in one hand and a knife dripping blood in the other."

Coulls nodded, then continued, "I learned that Inspector John Spratling, J Division, wasn't happy when he arrived at the crime scene to take charge. A boy was washing away the blood. Let's see—that was at about 4.30. The body was taken to the mortuary and Robert Mann, a mortuary worker, saw the body at 5 a.m.—or may not have—locked up, and went to breakfast."

"Apparently more than armies march on their stomachs."

"Spratling left orders that the body was not to be touched, but later learned that Mann and his assistant Hatfield stripped and washed the body before Llewellyn arrived to complete his examination. Just to add to the confusion, Mann's testimony doesn't jibe with that of the police. He denied being cautioned by any policeman, including Spratling, not to touch the body. Said something about an officer—Helson—even being present when he undressed and washed the body."

"A cardinal example of a cock-up."

"Coroner Baxter said Mann is subject to fits, so his testimony is questionable."

"Still a cock-up."

"Inspector Abberline also testified. A man was seen passing by as Dr. Llewellyn was examining the body at the murder scene. The police are searching for him."

"Suspect number 437," Cox said, once again focused on his copy editing. "Is it affect or effect? Must be effect."

"The jury foreman thought that had a reward been offered by the Government after the murder in George Yard Buildings, very probably the latter two murders would not have been perpetrated. He said four horrible murders remain unsolved. The Coroner considered the first the worst, yet it attracted the least attention."

"Always better copy about a string of murders than just one."

"The foreman said he would give £25 toward a reward."

"Generous, but Mary Ann Nichols would have appreciated the money far more while she was alive."

"The foreman hoped the Government would offer a reward. He said," Coulls consulted his notes, "'These poor people had souls like anybody else.' The Coroner and Inspector Helson said no rewards are now offered in any case; haven't been for years. It matters not whether the victim was rich or poor, and there's no surety that a rich person will not be the next."

"If a rich lady is next, there'll be a reward large enough to stand every correspondent at *The Empire* dinner at the Ship and Turtle, drinks included."

Coulls grinned. "That's about what the foreman said."

Even though Swanson had assumed the task of reviewing and organizing the ever-growing mounds of paperwork related to the cases, Abberline still had his fair share of administrative paperwork. As he muttered curses at the Met bureaucracy, he wrote to request the Commissioner's approval for Inspector Chandler to travel to Farnborough to make inquiries into the regimental envelope found at the Chapman murder scene. Chandler had already gone and returned, but Abberline needed the Commissioner's authorization to ensure Chandler was reimbursed for his expenses. As he wrote, Abberline paused, looked over at the gaping maws of the shelves in his office that were sectioned into squares and which until so recently held the files, reports and statements that now resided on Swanson's well-buried desk, and smiled.

Tuesday, 18 September

Sir Charles marched the short distance down Whitehall past Horse Guards, the Scotland Office, the Cabinet Office and Downing Street. He turned right and entered the august halls of the simple, yet functional Home Office. He was precisely on time for his meeting with J. S. Sandars, assistant to E. J. Ruggles-Brise, the Private Secretary to the Home Secretary. Sir Charles would have much preferred to see Home Secretary Matthews, but repeated attempts to arrange an appointment had failed, so he had reluctantly settled for Sandars.

In Sandars' snug third-floor office overlooking King Charles Street, Sir Charles promptly got to the point. He remarked "very strongly upon the great hindrance which is caused to the efforts of the police by the activity of agents of press associations and newspapers. These 'touts' follow the detectives wherever they go in search of clues, and then having interviewed a person with whom the police have had conversation and from whom inquiries have been made, compile the paragraphs which fill the papers. This practice impedes the usefulness of detective investigation and moreover keeps alive the excitement in the district and elsewhere."

Although Sandars said Ruggles-Brise and the Home Secretary agreed wholeheartedly and fully with Sir Charles' views on the press, there was little that could be done about the vile scribblers.

"We can't very well lock up each and every correspondent from each and every newspaper," Sandars said with a wry smile.

"Well, maybe just some of the more egregious scribblers."

Sanders pursed his lips as if he had just tasted lemon. "I am afraid such a course is just not on, at least at the present time and in the current political environment, as I am certain you fully appreciate and completely understand."

Sir Charles sniffed and said, "Don't know why not. We would have shot a few as spies in Bechuanaland. Do a world of good."

The September London Court Sessions started with 129 cases, including six murders, four attempted murders and seven cases of abusing girls on the slate. A new play, *Lesbia*, was on at the Lyceum. Eighty-year-old Lord Sidney Godolphin Osborne, cleric, philanthropist and writer, was the first to advance a "Jill the Phantom" theory, arguing under the well-known initials 'S.G.O.' in one of his many letters to *The Times* that the Whitechapel murders might have been committed by a jealous woman. Pierce commented, "I'd hate to see the state of a woman jealous of an unfortunate working the back streets of Whitechapel night after night."

In the dark of the evening, City Constable John Johnson strode along his beat in the parish of the Minories Holy Trinity near the Tower.

"Murder! Murder!"

Following the sound of the screams, Johnson rushed into Three Kings' Court, an unlighted forty-square-foot yard, and discovered a man with an unfortunate.

"What are you doing here?" Johnson demanded.

"Nothing," the man said, calm as the lake in St. James park as he eyed Johnson with disdain.

The woman, who said she was Elizabeth Burns, pleaded with Johnson to escort her out of the court. Deciding it must have been a breakdown in negotiations over a tryst or a tiff over payment, Johnson sent the man on his way.

Johnson had just watched the man turn a corner out of sight when Elizabeth said, "Dear me, he frightened me very much when he pulled a big knife out."

Aghast, Johnson raced to the corner, but amidst the passing stream of humanity on the busy ill-lit street, he could not spot the man. Slapping his truncheon against his thigh in frustration, he rushed back to Burns and asked, "Why didn't you tell me about the knife before?"

Elizabeth turned demure and said, "I was much too frightened."

Alexander Freinberg, often called Finlay in an attempt at assimilation, leaned against his coffee stall in Whitechapel High Street. The aging merchant's business was like many others that occupied a corner here or a niche in a wall there, offering coffee, tea or cocoa for a penny a mug and ham sandwiches, boiled eggs, jellied eel, sausages, baked potatoes, cake, bread and butter or watercress for a few pence more. Finlay yawned and poured himself a black quantity of coffee from a dented urn as a girl with a club foot hobbled by. It was hard to stay awake. He looked up as a burly drunken sot fell against the side of his stall, shaking it to a dangerous degree. The drunk steadied himself and stared angrily at the old stall owner.

"What are you looking at?" the drunk screamed, whipping a knife out from beneath his coat.

Finlay, his gray hair turning a shade whiter, stared at the aggressor.

"What are you looking at? No one looks at Charles Ludwig like that."

The drunk lunged at Finlay, who took to his toes and bolted for the rear of his stall. Ludwig followed, cursing and waving his knife like a child with a new whirligig. Finlay, feeling even older than he had moments before, fired his coffee back toward Ludwig and circled to the front of his stall. Missed by most of the coffee projectile, Ludwig followed with a curse, stabbing wildly at the fleeing Finlay. Soon the two were pursuing a reckless and erratic course around the stall; Finlay, his ancient eyes wild with fear, his rapidly beating, aging heart threatening to pop out of his rib cage; Ludwig, his entire body flamed with alcoholic rage, his voice thundering threats horrible and vile as he brandished his blade.

It was a violent situation that presented itself to PC 211 Gallagher as he stepped out of the fog. Finlay, puffing and terrified, was about to break a precious plate over Ludwig's less precious skull, while the latter flailed the foggy atmosphere in a hopeless attempt to stab the rapidly retreating old man. Gallagher intervened.

Mutterings of "They've got the Knife" and "They caught the Phantom" swept through the Whitechapel crowd that had gathered, but more perceptive people in the crowd saw the situation as more crazed than criminal.

Ludwig was soon on his way to the tombs in the basement of the Commercial Street station. Abberline, making one of his nightly rounds of the stations, helped investigate the case. Finlay, his lease on life renewed, was gulping down great quantities of caffeine-filled coffee and wondering if his heart would ever stop pounding.

Abberline soon learned that Ludwig was a quarrelsome lout who had been tossed from the German Club earlier in the evening by the manageress and Elizabeth Burns thought he might have been the man who brandished a knife at her. He didn't seem connected to the Whitechapel murders, but Abberline had him held over as the police investigated his background and whereabouts on the nights of the murders.

As Abberline left the station, he paused for a second. There was something familiar about Ludwig, but Abberline couldn't focus his sleep-deprived mind on what it was. He shrugged and took a cab to the next station on his rotation for the night: Leman Street.

Once at 76 Leman Street, Sergeant Thick, who had lived at the station for four years as a new recruit and had a network of acquaintants, informers and gossipers stretching near and far, reported to Abberline that his sources had told him that the women in the Holloway area near Elthorne Road had given suspect Isenschmid the nickname Leather Apron.

"Not another Leather Apron," Abberline moaned.

"More commonly called the Mad Butcher. Apparently he goes early in the morning to market to get sheep's heads, kidneys and feet, takes them home, dresses them and re-sells them to restaurants and coffee houses in the West End."

"Probably the only way he can make a living."

"Living or not, he's barmy; styles himself the King of Elthorne Road."

"I'd prefer King of England myself, but to each his own."

"King or lunatic, we watched his house, caught him on the 12th and now his majesty holds court in Bow Infirmary Asylum."

Thick handed Abberline a form containing the Mad Butcher's description: early forties, 5 foot 7 inches, ginger hair on head and face, powerfully built. Abberline said, "He's probably the same man Mrs. Fiddymont and the others saw at 7 on the morning of the Chapman murder with blood on his hands in the Prince Albert Public House on Brushfield Street. Witnesses said he had two butcher knives with him."

"The doctors at the asylum said he's violent at times."

"Most promising, most promising," Abberline said. He found an unoccupied roll-top desk and, taking a piece of blank paper from one of the cubbyholes in the desk, proceeded to compose a report. He wrote, Isenschmid "appears to be the most likely person that has come under our notice to have committed the crimes…"

Wednesday, 19 September

Over his breakfast of cold roast beef and tea, Reverend Barnett smiled and said, "Ah, at last, dear, here it is in *The Times*, my letter. It took several days to get into print, but the mills of our Lord grind slowly at times. Well worth the wait, though, well worth the wait."

His wife, Henrietta, a social reformer, philanthropist and solid lump of a woman, nodded and returned an acknowledging smile.

Barnett read aloud, "'These Whitechapel horrors will not be in vain if at least the public conscience awakes to consider the life which these horrors reveal. We need efficient police supervision, adequate street lighting, removal of the slaughterhouses, and control of rental houses by responsible landlords.'"

"So true, my dear, so true. We must have reform of such practices."

"*The Times* editors have even taken up the task. Most gratifying. They write, 'London at large is responsible for Whitechapel and its dens of crime. If the luxury and wealth of the west cannot find some means of mitigating the squalor and crime of the east, we shall have to abate our faith in the resources of civilization.' That's good." Barnett smiled in deepest satisfaction. "It took us 'til this decade to beat cholera. Just two decades ago thousands died right here in London of smallpox. We've got public health under control, and the Slavery Abolition Act of 1833 ended slavery and the Royal Navy now patrols the seas to prevent the infernal trade in our fellow man. Now we shall banish poverty, idleness and crime from God's green earth." He paused, sat even straighter than usual, drawing himself up to gigantic proportions to roar, "We haven't got these things under control now, but, by God—I mean by the Grace of God—"

"I am sure He knows what you mean, dear."

The Vicar was sermonizing and didn't hear his wife, going right on, "By God's good grace we shall get them under control. It may take 'til the 20th Century, but we'll get them all under control. The future is ours, it is bright and good. God and history are on our side." His words reached out and flowed over his congregation of one. Smiling, he concluded, "In the glorious, sunlit future there won't be the crime we have today. His will will be done."

"Amen," his wife whispered in a voice full of holy gravitas.

Helson arrived at Abberline's office at Scotland Yard with *The Daily Telegraph* tucked under his arm as Abberline debated whether one or both of them needed to attend day four of the Chapman inquest later that morning.

"Any breakthroughs at the Home Office?" Helson asked with a grin.

Abberline had just returned from his daily meeting.

"None, although the walk back seems to help my leg and I get to stroll with Swanson." As Abberline played mother with the teapot, he gestured at the newspaper and asked, "Have they found the murderer yet?"

Helson chuckled and tossed the paper on the desk. "No, but they reported that two farthings were found near Annie's body, polished brightly, which, they claim, 'had been passed off as half-sovereigns upon the deceased by her murderer.' How could anyone save the murderer know that?"

"Amazing how much correspondents know about the murders even when we don't admit reporters to the scenes."

"Correspondents have been asking me about Annie's supposed rings again," Helson said, rubbing his dark-rimmed eyes.

"I don't think she even had any rings on that night," Abberline said, bringing over their morning tea.

"Apparently we missed a crucial witness, too."

Abberline was about to sip his tea when he stopped, the cup inches from his lips.

"A Mrs. Darrell saw the killer at 5 a.m."

"Who in the name of all that's holy is Mrs. Darrell?" Abberline asked, wracking his memory for the name and coming up blank.

"Probably Mrs. Long."

Abberline's frown deepened, thoroughly confused. He felt as exhausted as Helson looked.

"*The Times* reported that Mrs. Darrell saw the Whitechapel killer with Annie Chapman, but her story is almost exactly the same as Mrs. Long's."

"So they either botched the name or this Mrs. Darrell is gaining a little neighbourhood notoriety by repeating the story she read about Mrs. Long." Abberline sipped his black tea, careful not to burn his tongue; nothing worse than a burned tongue. "Anything else I should know from our esteemed investigative partners in the press?"

"They report that a man entered the passage to No. 29 Hanbury at 2 a.m. the night of the murder."

"No evidence for it, is there?" Abberline asked, not wanting to rely on his sleep-deprived memory.

"It appears they're referring to a man Mrs. Richardson saw in the passageway, not the night of the murder, but a month before."

"Swanson believes the only person who we can be reasonably certain has ever seen the murderer is Mrs. Long."

"And all she saw was a 'foreigner.'"

"Wish I could tell a foreigner on sight."

"Maybe he wore a kimono, like in *The Mikado*."

"Have to ask Reid if he knows any lunatic actors on the loose with a penchant for Japanese fashions, knives and cutting up unfortunates."

Turning to his notebook, Helson reported that inspectors had found, interviewed and cleared two of three medical students who attended London Hospital and were rumoured to be insane.

"And the third?"

"John Sanders of 20 Abercorn place, Maida Vale. He's gone abroad."

"Or so his friends and acquaintances say; probably in some comfortable discrete asylum nestled in the most bucolic part of Kent, whiling away his insane days."

"Or in Spa."

"Where?"

"Belgium."

"Why on earth would he go there? Chocolate?"

"They're holding the world's first beauty contest."

"Not counting that one with Paris as the judge and Helen as the winner, wot?"

After a briefing by Abberline and Swanson, Sir Charles Warren sat in his office at Met Police headquarters and dictated a report to the Home Office on the progress of the investigation. He outlined Abberline's suspicions about the mad butcher Jacob Isensmith or Isenschmid, and about Oswald Puckridge, a chemist, who was released from an asylum on 4 August, three days before the Tabram murder. Educated as a surgeon, Puckridge had threatened to "rip people up" with a long knife. Abberline's men were searching for Puckridge, but he had yet to be found. Beyond his coincidental release date, Abberline had told Sir Charles they had discovered nothing to tie Puckridge to the murders.

Pausing to peruse a long list of other reported dark-horse suspects, Sir Charles chose one to give the Home Office at least some sense of the difficulty of pursuing the many leads the police were receiving every hour of every day. He smiled when he spotted a good example of such leads: A brothel keeper claimed a man living in her house was seen with blood on him the morning of the Chapman murder. Although she refused to give her name, she did provide where he could be found and his description. Sir Charles happily related that, amazingly, Met detectives had found the suspect, but his happiness vanished when he read that the suspect had bolted and had not been seen since.

"Strike mention of that last suspect," Sir Charles told his secretary. "No need to lead them into the forest of suspects we are presently pursuing; they're bound to become lost."

In Fleet Street just the other side of the compact City of London from Whitechapel, Jennings and Coulls lounged over coffee before heading to the Chapman inquest. Old Boy was off interviewing the mentalist Dr. Winslow.

"I wonder why the police spend so much time looking for the murderer among the poor," Coulls said. "A middle-class killer could easily flit into his flat, store or office in the parish after a killing. Wouldn't be fifty other people occupying the place, like a common lodging house. Our phantom killer could have a room all to his lonesome to clean up in and to keep his trophies in."

"Well, my friend," Jennings replied, taking on a fatherly tone, "You certainly don't know the mentality of our English friends, and you've been in this country how long? Tut, tut, my boy. The English, you must come to see in the fullness of time, have a nice, neat order to their Victorian society: the uppers, the middles and the lowers, and ne'r the twain—or trio—shall meet. The three classes are totally different species, each living in a world apart from the others. The uppers are the good people: moral, upstanding, righteous. They're allowed the occasional indiscretion. It's expected. They're rich enough to be eccentric. If one or two of them stray, they're considered aberrations, mutations in the greater genetic scheme. The uppers just don't do such things as carve up Whitechapel whores."

"And the middles?"

"Hell, they're eternal virgins. Pure goodness. But the lowers, they're the scum of the earth, the flotsam and jetsam. But to keep everything nice and inconsistent, the lowers are allowed to have a few good, upstanding citizens. The lowers, you see, are also the guts of the army, the keel of the navy and the Salt of the Earth, whatever that means."

"Wasn't salt highly valued at one time?"

"Not anymore."

Nodding a hello to Sergeant Thick and whispering to ask with a smile if he now spelled his name with an 'e' as Helson had noticed it spelt in several newspapers, Abberline followed Helson into the police section of seats in the Working Lad's Institute for another day of the Chapman inquest. The proceedings were already well under way. Abberline scanned his notes. Annie Chapman. Age: 48. Height: five feet. Hair: light brown, wavy. Eyes: blue. Distinguishing marks: two teeth in lower jaw missing. Residence: Usually a common lodging house at 35 Dorset Street, Spitalfields.

Thick whispered that Coroner Baxter had already called Eliza Cooper, the lodger in Dorset Street who had quarreled with Annie over a bar of soap the Tuesday before Annie's murder. She added nothing new.

"Dr. Bagster Phillips," Baxter recalled the police surgeon to testify.

"Perhaps Baxter will get more from Phillips this time," Helson said.

The press had been after Dr. Phillips for refusing to provide the full gruesome details of the latest murder at the inquest on the previous day and after Baxter for not forcing the physician to do so. Nothing seemed to raise an Englishman's hackles more than the idea that something was being suppressed. The gentlemanly Phillips was now almost as vile a villain as the Whitechapel

Phantom.

"I wonder if there would be any clamor to disclose everything if our victim had been of West Side origins," Abberline pondered. "There are more double standards in our fair country than beef-steak pies."

"Will you pipe down? I want to hear what the coroner is saying."

The command interrupting Abberline came from a fierce-faced matron of high-class origins, considerable age and stately bearing. She sat directly behind Helson in a haughty pose of regal contempt and aimed her aquiline nose toward the chief of detectives. She resembled a giant sparrow, but bird-like or not, she was obeyed. Silence was instant.

CID policy was not to supply the public or press with information until a suspect was identified, which Dr. Phillips sought to follow. Baxter's job was to preserve evidence of the crime, therefore he needed all known information, including about the mutilation of the body. Conflict was inevitable.

Baxter told Phillips, "Whatever may be your opinion and objections, it appears to me necessary that all the evidence you ascertained from the post-mortem examination should be on the records of the Court for various reasons, which I need not enumerate. However, painful it may be, it is necessary in the interests of justice."

"I have not had any notice of that. I should have been glad if notice had been given me, because I should have been better prepared to give the evidence."

"Did he think he was coming to a bloody high tea?" Helson whispered.

"His appeal to impropriety failed so he's trying to wriggle out by claiming that someone slipped up and didn't tell him what questions he was going to be asked," Abberline said.

"No coroner ever does that."

"I know that, you know that and Phillips knows that, but Phillips is banking on the jury not knowing it."

"Shhhh," the nesting sparrow shushed them, anger clear on her face.

Baxter asked, "Would you like to postpone it?"

"Oh, no," Dr. Phillips said, the soul of helpfulness. "I will do my best. I still think that it is a very great pity to make this evidence public. Of course, I bow to your decision, but there are matters which have come to light now which show the wisdom of the course pursued on the last occasion, and I cannot help reiterating my regret that you have come to a different conclusion."

Phillips paused, but Baxter wanted his information and just stared at Phillips, waiting.

Finally, Phillips repeated what he had said on the last occasion about the damage to the head and throat. Then he added, "When I come to speak of the wounds on the lower part of the body I must again repeat my opinion that it is highly injudicious to make the results of my examination public. These details are fit only for yourself, sir, and the jury, but to make them public would simply be disgusting."

Abberline had to admire Dr. Phillips' perseverance and adherence to a code of manners at least 50 years out of date.

His voice rising in anger, Baxter said, "We are here in the interests of justice, and must have all the evidence before us. I see, however, that there are several ladies and boys in the room, and I think they might retire."

A constable escorted a couple of ladies outside and sent a number of newspaper messenger boys scurrying out the back door, but the other audience members stayed put. A few, however, sat debating the wisdom of remaining, their faces paling.

Dr. Phillips again raised an objection, remarking, "In giving these details to the public I believe you are thwarting the ends of justice."

"A doctor lecturing an attorney on the law," Abberline whispered as Baxter's face hardened in anger. "Next the solicitor will testify about the medical evidence."

"We are bound to take all the evidence in the case," Baxter said, "and whether it be made public or not is a matter for the press."

The papers had put Baxter on the griddle and he was leaping out of his public frying pan whilst casting Phillips full into the fire.

The foreman said, "We are of the opinion that the evidence the doctor had on the last occasion wished to keep back should be heard."

Several Jurymen cried out, "Hear, hear."

Baxter said, "I have never before heard of any evidence requested being kept back."

His feathers ruffled, Phillips stiffened. "I have not kept it back. I have only suggested whether it should be given or not."

"We have delayed taking this evidence as long as possible because you said the interests of justice might be served by keeping it back, but it is now a fortnight since this occurred and I do not see why it should be kept back from the jury any longer."

"I am of the opinion that what I am about to describe took place after death, so that it could not affect the cause of death, which you are inquiring into."

"That is only your opinion and might be repudiated by other medical opinions."

Dr. Phillips pursed his lips, concealing what Abberline guessed was his anger at his medical opinion being questioned. Phillips said, his voice as formal as a bishop's, "Very well. I will give you the results of my post-mortem examination."

"And that was. . .?"

"The uterus, its appendages, part of the bladder and. . ."

"And what, Dr. Phillips?"

"The upper part of the vagina had been removed and taken away."

"What the 'ell is the utorus, 'enry?" a man in the row ahead of Abberline asked his companion, who could only shrug.

Baxter asked after the weapon. Phillips said, "I am of the opinion that the length of the weapon with which the incisions were inflicted was at least five to six inches in length, probably more, and must have been very sharp. The manner in which the incisions were done indicated a certain amount of anatomical knowledge."

"Can you give any idea how long it would take to perform the incisions found on the body?"

"I think I can guide you by saying that I myself could not have performed all the injuries I saw on that woman, and effect them, even without a struggle, under a quarter of an hour."

"Whoever said she was struggling?" Helson whispered. "Kind of difficult with your throat cut from ear lobe to ear lobe."

The haughty bird behind him glared.

Phillips said, "If I had done it in a deliberate way, such as would fall to the duties of a surgeon, it would probably have taken me the best part of an hour. The whole inference seems to me that the operation was performed to enable the perpetrator to obtain possession of these parts of the body."

The foreman asked, "Is there anything to indicate that the crime in the case of the woman Nichols was perpetrated with the same object as this?"

Baxter said, "There is a difference in this respect; the medical expert is of the opinion that in the case of Nichols the mutilations were made first."

Helson whispered, "His testimony the other day seemed more gory than today's."

"If you withhold information, the public always thinks it will be more sensational than anything you actually tell them," Abberline whispered back.

The foreman asked about photographing the eyes of the victim and Dr. Phillips repeated what he had told Abberline; "The operation would be useless." When asked, he also said a bloodhound would be more likely to trace the blood of the victim than the murderer.

With Dr. Phillips' testimony concluded, Elizabeth Long testified about the man she saw with Annie Chapman outside 29 Hanbury on the morning of the murder.

"You say he looked foreign?" Baxter asked. "What nationality? German?"

"No, I don't think so."

"Slavic, say Russian?"

"No."

"Northern European: Norwegian? Swedish, perhaps?"

"No."

Abberline whispered, "At this rate, we'll get to Chinese by breakfast tomorrow."

Baxter continued, "What about southern Mediterranean: Italian or Spanish?"

"I can't be sure."

"What about Lascar? Or Hindi?"

"No. No. He was a white man."

"Ah, let's see. Probably not Nordic or Teutonic or Slavic or Latin. What about southeastern European; Greek, Hungarian—ah?

As the listing of nationalities continued, a man near Abberline turned to a sour-faced pal beside him and muttered, "Maybe he was Gaelic, eh, Jock?"

His fellow Scot only scowled more severely.

The finale to Baxter's examination of Liz Long was that she couldn't—or wouldn't—provide a guess as to what nationality the man might have been. He was simply "foreign-looking."

Edward Stanley, presumed to be the Pensioner, testified next. He said he saw Annie Chapman on occasion; the last time on 2 September in the early afternoon when he said she was wearing two brass rings and had bruises on her face. He denied ever hurting Annie and even refused to admit he was the Pensioner.

Baxter recalled Timothy Donovan, who said Stanley was the Pensioner. Stanley retorted that he was in Gosport from 6 August to 1 September when the murder occurred.

"Run his alibi to ground," Abberline told Helson, who nodded, adding yet another task to his long list of things to investigate.

Albert Cadosch testified next. He was the neighbour who heard voices and thumping on the fence at 29 Hanbury the morning of the murder. When asked if he looked over the fence to see who was there, he said, "I did not."

In a classic English understatement, the foreman said, "It's a pity you did not."

William Stevens, a painter, said he saw Annie with the brass rings, before he repeated the story about Annie finding the piece of regimental envelope on the lodging house kitchen floor, which she used to hold her pills.

The foreman again raised the possibility of a reward and Baxter again replied that the government did not plan to offer one. The foreman said about £300 had been raised by private means but a government reward would have "more dignity."

"More dignity, more press coverage," Helson whispered, "and more false leads."

Abberline wondered, but he was certain Swanson already had his desk thoroughly and completely buried under reports, witness statements and suggestions from the public, with or without a reward. It wasn't as if anyone living in London, let alone the East End, had not heard of the murders and why would any sane person withhold information they thought might lead to the arrest of the murderer?

With his list of witnesses exhausted, Baxter adjourned the inquest until Wednesday the 26th, at which time the jury would return a verdict.

The press reported Phillips' revelations about the parts of Annie Chapman the Phantom had removed and taken with him. No one seemed more or less upset thereafter and no wave of copycat organ-theft crimes followed. Most people had imagined that some organ had been taken. Now that nothing was left to the imagination, most people's imaginations seemed to have shorted out. The issue died for the moment.

Sergeant Thick continued to work long hours, missing his wife and four living children. After a late night, a busy morning and a rushed lunch, he entered Abberline's borrowed office at the Leman Street station to report that the Mad Butcher, Isenschmid, had been detained, as ordered, on suspicion of murder.

"Have we learned anything further about him?" Abberline asked, grimacing at the pain in his leg after a long morning at the inquest, only with the prospect of a long night ahead of him as he made the rounds of the East End stations and doss houses.

"Neighbours and his relations say he was depressed and away from home for several weeks," Thick said, standing ruler-straight before Abberline, giving credit to at least one interpretation of his nickname Johnny Upright. "He was 10 weeks in Colney Hatch Lunatic Asylum, discharged middle of December last and came home, according to the doctors, 'quite well.'"

"Wish they could cure every ailment as fast."

"Isenschmid has not slept at home for two months. His wife said"—Thick read his notes—"'I do not think he would injure anyone but me. I think he would kill me if he had the chance. He is fond of other women.'"

"At least we'll know who to arrest if we find her mutilated body in a backyard. Good work, Sergeant."

"We're still trying to arrange for Mrs. Fiddymont and the others who saw the man on the 8th in the pub to see Isenschmid. Doctor says no."

"Is he that dangerous? Thought he was cured."

"Doctor said it might be injurious to his patient."

"More likely be injurious to another unfortunate. Let me talk with the good doctor."

Abberline decided to take pity on his leg and get out from behind his desk. He needed a haircut. With his walking stick, he hobbled to the nearest barber shop in Whitechapel High Street, slipped off his coat and was about to sit in one of the chairs when the owner barked out, "Ludwig!"

The name took Abberline by surprise. Wasn't Ludwig the name of the nutter who had chased some old fellow around his stall with a knife a few days ago? He turned toward the assistant.

"Just take…," he stopped, aghast. Good God. It couldn't be. Ludwig the threatener was approaching him. No, no, it couldn't be. The man was still in custody. Abberline stared at the newcomer. The two men must be twins. Abberline could hardly sit still. This demanded further investigation. He'd have to make certain.

"Shave, sir?" the new Ludwig asked, stropping a straight razor on a belt hanging from the side of the barber's chair.

After settling for a haircut and no shave, Abberline hurried over to Scotland Yard and rummaged through his picture files. By the time he found what he was looking for, Helson had appeared with a strong lead.

That afternoon at the Bethnal Green Police station a constable had burst into Helson's office waving a telegram like a semaphore flag and said, "He was arrested last night at the Pope's Head Tavern. He could be the killer, Mr. Helson. He could be him."

"Slow down," Helson said, placing his fountain pen down on the blotter atop his desk beside the duty order he was drafting. "Who?"

"William…Henry…Piggott," the constable said, spacing out his words with the greatest of difficulty. "They're holding him at Gravesend, arrested Sunday night, 9 September."

Helson took the telegram. He read that the arrested man had been found in a filthy state. His clothes were stained, apparently with blood; his shirt torn and bloody. He also had a severe bite wound, presumably human, on his left forefinger and other suspicious marks on his body.

"I'll pick up Abberline and go see what this bloke has to say for himself," Helson said as he donned his overcoat.

It was late afternoon when Abberline and Helson reached Gravesend Police Station about 20 miles east of London on the south bank of the Thames Estuary and on the northern border of Kent.

"Piggott was quite upset when we questioned him about the murder in Hanbury Street," Chief Inspector James Gellwade explained. "He trembled something awful either from fear or drink. I'm not sure which. He's admitted he was in Whitechapel Saturday morning and not far from the death scene."

The three officers walked down to the station's basement and into a cool short corridor, which housed the gaol proper. The chilling atmosphere of the cells seemed to seep sideways across the corridor from the icy outer stone walls. God! These places never seemed real, Abberline thought. In a way gaols weren't real; not real in an ordinary person's sense of the world. No one in West London ever could conceive of the physical feeling of coldness, hardness and utter discomfort that pervaded these human cages. Nothing was soft; nothing welcoming. It was as if the place had been built without human hand or heart.

"Well, here he is," Gellwade said, stopping before a barred cubicle. An unshaven scruff of a man huddled in apathetic indifference in the cell's corner opposite the reeking metal container that served as a necessary. The man had not used it, but had gone on the floor. The sight assaulted the eyes, the stench assaulted the nose and the very air made Abberline's skin prickle.

"Mr. Piggott. Mr. Piggott," Helson addressed the derelict. "I'm Inspector Joseph Helson of the Criminal Investigation Department of Scotland Yard and this is. . .Can you hear me, Mr. Piggott?"

The creature cowering in the corner only shook. Abberline wondered if it was from the cold—the cells were unheated—or from decades of alcoholic abuse. It looked like delirium tremens to him, but he was no doctor. The man did resemble the description of the man that Mrs. Fiddymont described; the blood-stained fellow who entered the Prince Albert Public House.

The trip back to London was a nightmare. Wedged between Abberline and Helson, Piggott vacillated between bouts of nausea, screaming about insects crawling under his unbitten hand, and retreating into a sullen stupor of oblivion, refusing to speak directly to anyone. The other prisoners being transported to London gave the trio as much space as possible in the cramped police van. The sight and smell of Piggott demanded distance and dictated caution. Abberline knew he would need a bath with ample application of Keating's Bug Powder back at the station or Emma would never let him into the house. Luckily he kept spare clothes and bug powder at his office for the now common times when he did not make it home for the night.

"Well, that was a bloomin' waste of time," Helson announced hours later, tossing his coat onto a coat rack in his office at the Bethnal Green station.

Abberline, his leg pounding as if someone was driving a spike into the back of his knee, slumped into a chair. "Not completely, Joseph. We did eliminate Piggott as a suspect. That's progress of a kind, and there's another eight suspects who've been brought in just tonight; eight more possible Phantoms. Have some tea."

It was now late evening. Helson and Abberline's best hopes of having caught the Whitechapel murderer had roller-coastered up and down. First, on arriving in London their fortunes seemed to have been star-struck. Piggott was identified as having slept at a common lodging house in Whitechapel on the night before the Chapman murder. That placed him near the scene of the crime. Then a police surgeon examined the stains on Piggott's clothes and shoes, and concluded they were blood. An inspector retrieved a package which Piggott had left at a fish and pie shop. The package contained blood-stained clothes.

"But whose?" the Divisional Surgeon had puzzled. "We can be sure it's blood, but we have no way of telling whose. The blood on his clothes could be his own. After all, his finger was badly bitten, and septic, too. I'm not even completely certain the stains are human blood."

Abberline and Helson hurriedly arranged for Piggott to participate in an identity parade of 17 men before Mrs. Fiddymont, Joseph Taylor and Mary Chappell to see if they could identify him as the bloodstained man seen in the Prince Albert Public House just after Annie Chapman's murder. Only Chappell identified him, raising Abberline's hopes, but then she waffled and said she wasn't sure. Mrs. Fiddymont only shook her head and said, "That warn't the man." Liz Long, who had presumably seen Chapman talking to the murderer outside 29 Hanbury, couldn't identify Piggott either.

Lacking evidence linking Piggott to the Chapman murder, Abberline and Helson turned him over to the divisional surgeon, who, concurring with popular medical and public opinion, pronounced him a lunatic. Piggott disappeared into the dreary confines of an isolated up-country asylum.

Then a cablegram from Russia arrived with news on the background of suspect Michael Ostrog.

"He's a convict whose background carries 'the taint of criminal activity of the most vicious kind'—odd words," Abberline said, reading the cablegram. "Must be the translation. He's considered a dangerous lunatic by the Russian police and he's a medical doctor."

Helson nodded as suspicion now spun toward the mysterious Ostrog. He headed a list of dangerous foreigners on the loose in London, closely followed by Klosowski. The problem was finding them.

It was late when a hungry and tired Sergeant Thick checked back into H Division's Leman Street station. Ever since the startling revelation that Chapman's body had also been scrubbed, the thin detective had been on the move. He had scurried from station to station and morgue to morgue to unravel the latest Gordian knot of a muddle. He found the answer to the riddle at the third morgue he visited after talking to inspectors and constables at four stations. Idiots, he thought, can't even correctly record where they took a body.

"We were told to make certain we scrubbed every body ready for the police and that's what we did," a belligerent morgue attendant answered indignantly when Thick finally found the right morgue.

"Who told you that? You were supposed to leave the body alone."

"Here's the special directive." The attendant rummaged through a hash of papers on his desk and produced a printed sheet. "From Sir Charles Warrant, that's who."

"Warren, Sir Charles Warren, not Warrant." Thick took the paper from the attendant and read it.

"Good God, man, it says here to 'make certain the cadaver is looked after according to PROPER PROCEDURES.' It doesn't—"

"That's right, guv, and the proper procedure is to wash every corpse down."

Thick stared at the paper. Jesus Christ almighty! Sir Charles' bureaucratic minions had done it again. Why the hell hadn't the sodding fools written out what proper police procedures meant? Thick controlled his rising temper. It was a time for calm and a time to fix the problem. "Did this go out to every morgue?"

"You work for the police. I don't. If you don't know, how do you expect me to?"

"Well, there's been a cock-up. Here, I'll write out what has to be done if, heaven forbid, we get another mutilated corpse."

"You're going over Sir Charles' orders? I sure as hell wouldn't."

"Well, there it is, I'm going over his orders. Chief Inspector Abberline will back me and send new orders. Till then, I'll sign and date this. Now, don't clean up any battered corpse until you get official police sanction from an investigating officer."

It was hours before Thick's order reached every East End morgue and station house.

Wednesday, 19 September

A day of leads chased down, suspects found, investigated and, unfortunately for all concerned, save for the suspect, cleared.

The first chance he could get free of office duties, Abberline caught a cab from Scotland Yard to the barbershop in Whitechapel High Street. He had some information, but he would have to talk to Ludwig II to get more. The owner had a surprise for him. Not only was the Ludwig twin not at work, "The fellow who works here isn't Charles Ludwig or his twin cuz he's an only child," the owner said. "His name's Ludwig Schloski or something like that. A Pole, I think."

"When does he come to work?"

"He shoulda bin here an hour and a half ago, but no great loss if he doesn't show."

To Abberline it was a great loss. He ordered the constable on point duty near the shop to watch for Schloski and returned to the Yard.

Thursday, 20 September

Bright sunshine bathed the day. Workmen went on strike at the Eiffel Tower, a hideous iron scaffolding planned as the great attraction of the 1889 World Exhibition. Sensible Englishmen shook their heads at such architectural humbug and were relieved by telling each other that the abomination would only mar the Parisian skyline while the exhibition was underway. After the exhibition it was scheduled to be dismantled. During the night, a thick fog blotted London into oblivion. The Phantom didn't materialize.

Friday, 21 September

Sir Charles began the day griping about a play he and his wife had attended. "Claimed a woman should be able to divorce if she has a bad marriage. That's the world of art; no grounding in reality." He straightened the blotter on his desk and asked his secretary, "Well, enough of that, what's on the ledger today?"

"Well, sir, the Scots caught James M'Kill, the tunnel murderer."

"Good show for the Scots, but not so bloody good for those muttonheads we have down at CID. One of my wife's friends told me about a cartoon in *Punch* showing a blindfolded P.C. playing blind-man's bluff with a gang of ruffians. Should have drawn the whole of CID blindfolded."

"Blind Man's Bluff," Punch cartoon by John Tenniel, 22 September 1888

"CID did manage to find Pizer."

"Pizer?"

"John Pizer, the fellow who's called Leather Apron—or at least one of them."

"Ah, yes. Finally, some progress in this blasted case."

"But they let him go."

"What?!"

"No evidence, sir."

"Blast! Monro did nothing but destroy that unit. Those people down at CID lack something, I suspect it's discipline. Plain and simple discipline."

Saturday, 22 September

The radical and opposition press used the murders as an opportunity to attack the government, not that they needed much incentive.

"The radicals are just trying to get back at the government for its anti-Irish activities and its aggressive intervention against socialist and labour demonstrations," Helson said over a breakfast of cold roast beef and a tankard of ale with Mary. A pile of the newspapers to which they subscribed teetered between their plates. The children had disappeared after breakfast to pursue some highly important secret task, apparently, Helson had overheard, related to Christmas.

"It's not just the radicals now, even the Conservative papers are attacking the Met," Mary said. "Here, the *East London Advertiser* says Sir Charles is 'a martinet of apparently a somewhat inefficient type," while *The Daily Telegraph* said…here it is…that the detective service has been reduced to an 'utterly hopeless and worthless condition' by Sir Charles' militarization of the police."

Helson sipped his ale and said, "The press is just upset we don't do their work for them by giving them every snippet of information we gather about the murders."

Helson took a bite of roast beef, the tasty over-done, crispy end portion, which no one else he knew ever desired, and picked up *The Illustrated Police News*. "Listen to this brilliance from the Passing Notes section, 'The theory that the succession of murders which have lately been committed in Whitechapel are the work of a lunatic appears to us to be by no means at present well established. We can quite understand the necessity for any murderer endeavouring to obliterate, by the death of his victim, his future identification as a burglar.'"

"A burglar?" Mary asked in disbelief. "Are they mad? Not to mention the misuse of the word; don't they know a burglar steals from a residence or business, not from a person?"

"Thievery and burglary are all the same to them. There's more brilliance; 'Moreover, as far as we are aware, homicidal mania is generally characterized by the one single and fatal act, although we grant this may have been led up to by a deep-rooted series of delusions. It is most unusual for a lunatic to plan any complicated crime of this kind. Neither, as a rule, does a lunatic take precautions to escape from the consequences of his act; which data are most conspicuous in these now too celebrated cases.'"

"They don't appear to have studied any such celebrated cases," Mary said as she shook her head at the stupidity of it all.

Helson tossed the paper back on their stack. "Correspondents have no understanding of criminals."

"Nor, it seems, of the truth."

Glancing out their dining room window as he picked up another newspaper,

Helson saw that the day was fine and clear. Two ideas Abberline had raised juxtaposed themselves in Helson's mind: a clear night and a tendency for the Whitechapel murderer to strike on weekends. Helson set the paper down as he felt a sense of foreboding for the coming fine night.

A gang of ruffians hounded poor Isaac Jacobs again. The man, whose only crime was fitting the general public's idea of what the Phantom must look like, could only run for safety which he found by scaling a wall in Leadenhall Street and creeping into a cellar with an unlocked door. The toughs ran right by him three times before giving up their blood sport for the comfort of the nearest pub.

The inquest into Polly Nichols' murder continued, with Signalman Edes recalled but adding little to the proceedings. Coroner Baxter summed up the case and after a short consultation, the jury returned a verdict that Abberline could have predicted from the start: willful murder against some person or persons unknown.

Thankfully for the fears of Abberline and Helson, dusk brought a misty fog.

Chapter Eleven

Sunday, 23 September

By morning the Phantom had not been heard from. Many hoped the increased patrols had scared him off. Abberline wondered.

Literary and not so literary minded West Enders settled down this Christian Sabbath to read Anna Katharine Green's latest detective novel, *Behind Closed Doors*. Abberline, his inspectors, Sir Charles, Swanson, and their wives attended their respective churches. East Enders visited the neighbours, slept, drank, and did what people do when they lay around. The sporting crowd watched Seabreeze win the Lancashire Prize. People talked about the 13-year-old girl who had confessed to murdering a boy in Plymouth and wondered what the world was coming to. Fog closed in again at night. Abberline and his walking stick made the rounds of the East End stations, accepting cups of tea in doss house kitchens. He found the fog comforting—or at least he hoped it would be a comfort.

Monday, 24 September

By 6 a.m. Abberline returned home, changed and slipped into bed.

"Quiet?" Emma asked, not even opening her eyes in their darkened bedroom.

"Silent," Abberline said. "Fog appears to be the unfortunates' friend."

"They can certainly use a friend."

"There's nothing peculiar about this monster," Abberline addressed his detectives at Met headquarters, fresh from his walk back from the daily Home

Office meeting through ground clouds that kept temperatures in the 50s. "He hasn't flaming red hair, doesn't walk with a grotesque limp, and is neither a dwarf nor a giant. He's an ordinary looking bloke who can merge in with the other ordinary looking blokes in the East End. Keep impressing that on your men."

"We do," Helson said, "But Sir Charles tells them different."

"Yeah, we're supposed to look for socialists, anarchists and foreigners."

Abberline nodded to convey his understanding, even as he wondered what a socialist, anarchist or foreigner looked like. Most foreigners he knew only wanted to fit in with British society, and socialists and anarchists tended to look about the same as your average hard-working labourer. "Just impress upon them that we aren't looking for a monster, at least not in appearance."

That afternoon, a report arrived on Abberline's desk. On Saturday night in Birttley Fell, County Durham, in northeast England, the body of a young woman was found in a field.

"She sustained horrific injuries," Abberline told Helson. "Her throat was cut and her intestines were protruding. She was identified as 28-year-old Jane Beetmoor."

"The Phantom branching out to new locations?" Helson asked, his face the picture of consternation.

Abberline shrugged. "Have Dr. Phillips and an inspector, maybe Roots, go up and have a look at the body; see if it's the same as our boy's work."

The endless striving for copy drove Coulls to interview a chemist about blood stains. He learned that it was often impossible to determine if a stain was blood since any mixing with rust invalidated every known test. He also discovered that one person's blood couldn't be singled out from anyone else's. Perhaps the best quote came when he asked if scientists could distinguish between human and animal blood stains.

"A Frenchman, Barruel, argues that if you boil sulphuric acid with cow's blood you get a barn-like odour and if you do the same with human blood you get the smell of human sweat," the chemist explained. "I've never been able to detect any difference, but maybe we English haven't got the nose for it."

Coulls did have a nose for a story and incorporated the material into a 15-inch piece that made the third page before he hurried out to meet Catherine McLean for lunch at a Fleet Street pub. Much to his disappointment, she sent a copy boy with a note that she regrettably had to cancel. Instead, Coulls found a PC who was into his fourth pint of bitters and who, unlike almost all of his colleagues, was happy to talk. It was only after buying the rotund constable another two pints that Coulls learned the man was desk-bound and last trudged a beat in 1872 near Elephant and Castle in Southwark. He knew less about the Whitechapel murders than Coulls. Not wanting to throw any more good money after a bad source bereft of news, Coulls was attempting to say goodbye when the constable complained about having to write a 16-page report on a new truncheon Sir Charles most ardently desired. Coulls soon had a nice article prepared in his mind on Sir Charles' penchant for demanding long reports about matters that appeared far from important at a time when a mad murderer was loose in the East End.

Back in the newsroom, while Coulls was finishing his disasterpiece, as Old Boy was wont to call their efforts, Jennings and Pierce discussed the opposition.

"That guy Shaw over at *The Star* has a rather cute article on how the Phantom is affecting life in London, Old Boy."

"That socialist dramatic critic?"

Jennings nodded, waving a newspaper. "Shaw wrote, 'While we conventional Social Democrats were wasting our time on education, agitation and organization, some independent genius has taken the matter in hand, and by simply murdering and disemboweling four women, converted the proprietary press to an inept sort of communism. Maybe reform of the East End's horrid conditions is now possible.'"

"I didn't think a good son of capitalism like you would waste his time reading such radicalism."

"I have to admit he's right in a sense. The Knife has cut a swath through the upper crust's complacency. They'll have to make at least some gestures toward improving conditions."

"Too bad a few tarts had to get chopped to hell to get them to act."

"Shaw missed one reality about the East End though," Jennings said. "Those local tradesmen have set up patrols to guard the streets that their own shops are on. The backstreets where they don't have shops stay unwatched, and that's where the drabs have to go with their customers, especially with Commercial Street dug up for the new tramway. But like all bloody socialists, Shaw thinks Charlie Citizen is going to risk person and property for some other guy's domain. That just won't wash. I'll guard your store if you guard mine. But if I haven't anything to guard, damned if I'm gonna risk a hair for your goodies."

Old Boy nodded. Capitalism had spoken and its voice was that of human nature.

Tuesday, 25 September

The temperature reached 69 as London had its thirteenth day without rain. Workmen hoisted a statue of General Gordon into place in Trafalgar Square. The police arrested Dr. James Gloster in Lambeth for murdering a woman during an abortion, tracked down a couple of landlords in the Minories who had failed to cleanse and lime wash their premises, and handled an assault-suicide by a 73-year-old fishmonger.

What would prove to be the first of an avalanche of letters about the murders to the press and police arrived. The first was addressed to Sir Charles Warren at the Met. Many of the letters, like the first, were misspelled and of varying coherence. The first read:

"Dear sir, I do wish to give myself up I am in misery with nightmare I am the man who committed all these murders in the last six months my name is so [silhouette of a coffin] and so I am a horse slaughterer and work in Name [blocked out] address [blocked out] I have found the woman I wanted that is chapman and i done what I called slautered her but if any one comes I will surrender but I am not going to walk to the station myself so I am yours truly keep the Boro road clear or I might take a trip up there [silhouette of a knife] this is the knife that I done these murders with it is a small handle with a large long blade sharp both sides."

The deluge of letters began and would soon number more than 300; by some counts as many as 700. Thorough as always, Sir Charles ordered them all carefully read, even though he believed that every single one was a hoax.

Wednesday, 26 September

The sun's rays slanted through the dirty windows of the temporary Hall of Justice on an increasingly more acute angle as the morning wore on, the dusty rays of light slowly changing in pattern and perspective. Abberline couldn't help noticing the unswerving natural order of design being portrayed. He wondered if there was the same unswerving order to unnatural things, like the murders. There must be. There must be some form of logic behind these seemingly illogical slayings. Why would God allow disorder amidst his grand plan? Concluding that it was not for his mind to fathom, he was content that he was missing one of the daily Home Office meetings so he could attend the Chapman inquest. He turned his attention back to what Coroner Wynne Baxter was saying, something about rings and the uterus being missing from the body.

Continuing his summation, Baxter said, "The injuries have been made by someone who had considerable anatomical skill and knowledge. There are no meaningless cuts. It was done by one who knew where to find what he wanted, what difficulties he would have to contend against, and how he should use his knife, so as to extract the organ without injury to it. No unskilled person could have known where to find it, or have recognized it when it was found. For instance, no mere slaughterer of animals could have carried out these operations. It must have been someone accustomed to the post-mortem room. The conclusion that the desire was to possess the missing part seems overwhelming. If the object were robbery, these injuries were meaningless, for death had previously resulted from the loss of blood at the neck. Moreover, when we find an easily accomplished theft of some paltry brass rings and such an operation, after, at least, a quarter of an hour's work, and by a skilled person, we are driven to the deduction that the mutilation was the object, and the theft of the rings was only a thin-veiled blind, an attempt to prevent the real intention being discovered."

"What in blazes is he driving at?" Chandler muttered.

"Did we find any evidence the murderer took any rings?" Helson asked, frowning.

"None," Abberline said.

Baxter continued, "The difficulty in believing that this was the real purport of the murderer is natural. It is abhorrent to our feelings to conclude that a life should be taken for so slight an object; but, when rightly considered, the reasons for most murders are altogether out of proportion to the guilt. It has been suggested that the criminal is a lunatic with morbid feelings. This may or may not be the case; but the object of the murderer appears palpably shown by the facts, and it is not necessary to assume lunacy."

The statement shocked Abberline. The jury appeared equally befuddled. The public had long since concluded the murderer was as mad as a hatter. Not a lunatic? Who else but a lunatic would murder like this Whitechapel butcher?

"For it is clear there is a market for the object of the murder," Baxter said. "Within a few hours of the issue of the morning papers containing a report of the medical evidence given at the last sitting of the Court, I received a communication from an officer of one of our great medical schools, that they had information which might or might not have a distinct bearing on our inquiry. I attended at the first opportunity, and was told by the sub-curator of the Pathological Museum that some months ago an American had called on him, and asked him to procure a number of specimens of the organ that was missing in the deceased. He stated his willingness to give £20 for each, and explained that his object was to issue an actual specimen with each copy of a publication on which he was then engaged. Although he was told that his wish was impossible to be complied with, he still urged his request. He desired them preserved, not in spirits of wine, the usual medium, but in glycerin, in order to preserve them in a flaccid condition, and he wished them sent to America direct. It is known that this request was repeated to another institution of a similar character. Now, is it not possible that the knowledge of this demand may have incited some abandoned wretch to possess himself of a specimen? It seems beyond belief that such inhuman wickedness could enter into the mind of any man, but unfortunately our criminal annals prove that every crime is possible."

Abberline cursed under his breath. Why hadn't the fool told the police? Why had he gone off to play detective on his own?

"I need hardly say that I at once communicated my information to the Detective Department at Scotland Yard," Baxter said. "Of course I do not know what use has been made of it, but I believe that publicity may possibly further elucidate this fact and, therefore, I have not withheld from you my knowledge.

By means of the press some further explanation may be forthcoming from America if not from here."

"Now he expects the sodding press to solve the case?" Helson whispered.

"He doesn't," Abberline said. "He just wants to get back in their good graces."

"Surely," Baxter said, "it is not too much even yet to hope that the ingenuity of our detective force will succeed in unearthing this monster. It is not as if there were no clue to the character of the criminal or the cause of his crime. His object is clearly divulged. His anatomical skill carries him out of the category of a common criminal, for his knowledge could only have been obtained by assisting at post-mortems or by frequenting the post-mortem room. Thus the class in which search must be made, although a large one, is limited. We should know that he was a foreigner of dark complexion, over forty years of age, a little taller than the deceased, of shabby-genteel appearance, with a brown deerstalker hat on his head, and a dark coat on his back. If your views accord with mine, you will be of the opinion that we are confronted with a murder of no ordinary character, committed not from jealousy, revenge or robbery, but from motives less adequate than the many which still disgrace our civilization, mar our progress, and blot the pages of our Christianity."

Baxter's oration completed, after a brief consultation, the jury foreman rose and said, "We can only find one verdict, that of willful murder against some person or persons unknown."

"Helson," Abberline said. "Find out from which hospital and director Baxter got that letter. Talk to the people concerned. And ask Baxter who he gave the information to at the Yard. I never heard a word of it."

That afternoon six men stood in rakish stances before Chandler's desk. Their combined tenure in Her Majesty's prisons exceeded two centuries. Chandler reached for a tin of Cadbury's cocoa to make a drink, but thought better of it. He feared sharing with the six men. If he gave them mugs of tea, he would consider himself lucky to receive even one mug back.

Chandler asked, "I understand you want to see me on a matter of grave importance?"

"Yes, Guv, I mean, Inspector Chandler. We cum down to Commercial Street station here cuz we wont to 'elp catch the Phantom, we does."

"This bas—basket is puttin' heat on all of us. Look, we ain't always been on the right side, you knows that, but none of us ever do things this monster does. Me ol' lady's scared to death. Won't even go out and fetch me a bucket of beer."

"Yeah, we'll help you, Inspector Chandler. You can bet we'll track 'im down. We don't promise he'll be all alive like when we catch 'im, but we'll git 'im for you."

Chandler was flabbergasted. He looked from felon to felon as each pledged his support.

"Well, I'll have to take it to my superiors. I don't know what to say. Naturally we'll accept any help we can get, but we can't condone violence."

The Whitechapel murderer had even alienated the underworld.

Her Majesty's mails brought an increasing cascade of letters to CID headquarters concerning the Whitechapel murders. Abberline, resting his aching leg up on an overturned dustbin, and Chandler, chewing on his pipe, worked their way through the letters like miners prospecting for a paper-thin seam of gold, which may or may not exist.

"Well, about half our writers don't think he's mad," Abberline said. "I'd agree that he at least appears sane."

"Why?" Chandler asked, slitting open his tenth envelope of the morning.

"Well, with all of Whitechapel up in arms Annie Chapman went down that dark sideway into the backyard of 29 Hanbury with him quite willingly, expecting nothing, save her services rendered. He must have at least a surface veneer of sanity."

Chandler skimmed through a letter and sighed, "This writer believes our murderer is a deluded religious crusader who feels appointed by the Almighty to rid the world of streetwalkers."

"If that's true, the killings will continue in London alone until the 21st Century."

Chandler recounted what he called the "ridiculous" offer from the six villains.

"It might do no harm and might actually do some good to encourage the first suggestion of law-abiding behavior on the part of your volunteers," Abberline said. "After all, the murderer isn't likely to strike if a few of those ruffians command a city street."

"That may be, sir, but. . ." Chandler chewed his pipe stem with a fierceness Abberline had never before seen. "If we allow villains to take part in law enforcement, well, it would be the beginning of the end, the thin edge of the wedge, the—"

"We will accept their offer."

Chandler stared at Abberline and sputtered, "I don't. . .I can't. . ."

"Never fear, I'll assign Godley to coordinate the efforts of your worthies, although they did come to you out of all the inspectors they could have chosen," Abberline said, suppressing a grin as he enjoyed Chandler's increasing discomfort.

"I just happened to be on duty, sir, not a jot more to it than that, I swear."

"I have no doubt, inspector, no doubt at all."

As Abberline later rode to the Thames Magistrate's Court in an official growler, he read the file which he had just received about one of the Russian suspects: Michael Ostrog. Sergeant Thick, working with many others, learned that Ostrog, posing as Max Kaife Gosslar, a 27-year-old German student, was arrested for stealing watches, purses, coats, and all manner of portable items in Oxford in 1863, including items from the chapel, dining hall and college rooms. At least, Abberline thought, the man was thorough in his thievery.

On 11 February 1863, Abberline read, Ostrog stole an opera glass and case from Charles Leir at Oriel College. Ostrog was arrested at Cambridge on 17 February and tried at the county assize on 3 March. He pled guilty and received 10 months. A second indictment against him for stealing a dressing case, two coats, a cape, a pair of trousers, silver cufflinks and a handkerchief from the Reverend George Price at New College, also on 11 February, was dropped since he admitted the first charge. Abberline shook his head at the audacity of the man, stealing from a man of the cloth. Although, in Abberline's experience, the most religious were often the most trusting in their fellow man; a trust sadly too often misplaced.

Abberline sighed. He could guess the general outline of the rest of the report, but he continued reading.

After his release, Ostrog appeared at Bishop's Stortford in Hertfordshire posing as Count Sobieski, the son of a fallen Polish nobleman. 'Count Sobieski' claimed he had escaped from Russian-ruled Warsaw after being sentenced like his father to end his days in Siberia, where, Abberline thought, it would be fitting for Ostrog to end his days. Well-bred and with amiable manners, he reportedly won many friends. The owner of the Coach and Horses gave him a fine room and even finer food at no charge. He also stayed with a gentleman for four days, borrowed money and departed on excellent terms. At Cambridge once again he obtained money under false pretenses from many an undergraduate. The law caught up with him on 2 February 1864, when Ostrog was prosecuted as a rogue and a vagabond at Cambridge Police Court and sentenced to three months' imprisonment.

The growler stopped. Abberline looked out; snarled in traffic.

In the summer of '64 in Tunbridge Wells, money and gifts were bestowed on Ostrog as Count Sobieski, now promoted to son of the late Polish king. He played the part well. He asked the band on the Parade to play the Polish national anthem, acted gloomy, and combined with his tall frame, handsome countenance and excellent manners, was a favourite of the ladies. In December a theft in Tormoham, Devonshire, led to another four months' imprisonment, this time at hard labour.

The labour, Abberline reflected, might have been hard, but it did not change Michael Ostrog's criminal behavior. In 1865 Ostrog was in Gloucestershire masquerading as Knuth Ostin, a university educated Swede who, he claimed, had left the country to avoid the consequences of a duel. He said he was awaiting money from his mother and lived well for a time at others' expense. He was arrested 23 October 1865. At that time, he was 29, 5 foot 10 inches tall with a dark complexion and brown hair and eyes.

The growler jerked forward and began to move again.

In January 1866 Ostrog was accused of obtaining food, lodgings and money under false pretenses, but was acquitted and released. Abberline had to admire the man's abilities and audacity. He could talk his way out of goal and, the report said, even gave items he had stolen to various women friends as presents.

At the July 1866, Kent Summer Assize in Maidstone, his silver tongue failed him and he was sentenced to seven years' penal servitude for stealing some books. The judge knew of his past crimes and wanted to send a message. Thick's digging had turned up that Ostrog was shocked by the sentence, but reportedly walked out of court "with a firm step."

The file went on and on with more cons, more arrests and more prison time, followed with unvarying repetition by yet more cons. A cobbler didn't suddenly become a confidence man, Abberline thought, and a confidence man didn't suddenly become a cobbler.

Abberline frowned. In 1873, Ostrog finally varied from his recurring theme. In September he was arrested but pulled a revolver—a unique case of violence for him—which the police managed to wrest away from him. He was sentenced to 10 years for theft of a silver cup and released in 1883. He was arrested again in 1887 for the theft of a tankard at the Royal Military Academy, Woolwich. While handcuffed, he tried to throw himself under a train, nearly dragging a young constable with him.

On 26 September 1887, Ostrog was certified insane and committed to Surrey County Lunatic Asylum in Tooting. Thick's notes mentioned that the inspectors involved in the case believed that Ostrog's sudden mental illness was a ploy to avoid a long prison sentence at hard labour. He was released on 10 March 1888 as recovered. He was required to report monthly to the police under the Prevention of Crime Acts of 1871 and 1879. He had not.

As the growler stopped and the driver called down, "We'll be a bit, sir, traffic," Abberline closed the file. He did not think Ostrog's usual crimes made him an ideal suspect for multiple murders, but Ostrog might be insane and, Thick had noted, he had masqueraded as a doctor. Maybe Ostrog did have a medical background. Who knew? However, there was no record of him ever attacking women. He was also tall, at 5 foot 10 inches, so he did not fit witness descriptions of the killer as a stout man of average height. The average height of an Englishman was 5 foot 6 or 7. Ostrog would have been noticeably tall to any witness, especially when standing beside Annie Chapman, who was 5 feet, yet Mrs. Long said the killer was only a little taller than Annie. Even so, Abberline made a note to tell Helson and Chandler to distribute Ostrog's description to all police stations and post it in the *Police Gazette*. He also made a note to commend

Thick for his most thorough and exemplary report. If every report were as thorough, Abberline thought, they would have caught the Knife weeks ago.

Helson spent the afternoon looking into Coroner Baxter's story about the American seeking to buy female organs from a local hospital director. As he sat down heavily in a wood chair across from Abberline in the latter's office just after 8 p.m., he said, "Every hospital director I spoke to denied ever hearing of, let alone meeting, such a man. Baxter was unable to find the letter from the director who first put him onto the story and the director Baxter claimed wrote him denied ever sending such a letter or ever meeting such a man."

"You don't think Baxter made it all up?" Abberline had just returned from Thames Magistrate's Court, where he had asked that Ludwig be remanded for another week so the police could continue their investigation into his past behavior and possible crimes. The remand was granted.

"No, I think this American did enquire about purchasing such organs. The hospital director was afraid some orderly or less scrupulous doctor sold him what he desired. I figured someone has been making a few pounds on the side emptying the odd corpse here and there of its innards and the hospital director found out and feared a scandal. I threatened to bust-open a page-one scandal if he didn't supply me with names and details."

"Well played; we may as well use the press for a change instead of them using us to sell their newspapers."

Helson beamed.

"Did Baxter tell you who he forwarded the information to at the Yard?"

"He couldn't remember," Helson said with a look of utter exasperation. "He said an inspector took it all down or it might have been a constable."

"Or a charwoman."

"I did get the American's name from the hospital director. Godley and I chased him down. The man certainly has his peculiarities. He wanted the specimens pickled in glycerin to preserve their flaccid condition. Weird."

"The organ buyer?"

"Him, too, but we were able to eliminate him as our murderer; found several reputable witnesses who were with him at a club when the killings took place."

"Good work, Helson."

"But the journal he was going to send the specimens out with is non-existent. No record of it. What puzzles me is what did he really want the organs for?"

"Probably an aid to masturbation."

The Gordon's gin bottle was almost empty, but Coulls and Jennings were nearly full. They had been working fourteen-hour days since the Nichols murder. Their respite, in part thanks to the Phantom and in part thanks to exhaustion, had come.

"How can they hope to catch the bloody bastard?" Jennings asked. He journeyed to the bar and returned with more beer to join the gin and six pints the pair had already downed. He continued as if he'd never left, "The system doesn't recruit the right people for the job. There aren't three active brains in all of Scotland Yard, police dogs excluded, of course. That poet Matthew Arnold—"

"The old headmaster at Rugby?"

"One and the same. He used to argue that religious and moral principles were the first criteria for choosing a candidate for an academic degree. Gentlemanly conduct was the second criterion. Brains? Hell, Arnold put intellectual ability third. Bloody third. With a system like that, what can you expect? The British built an empire on brains and guts and now they throw it all away on pomp and privilege disguised as moral principle and gentlemanly conduct. I remember the first story I ever covered in this country; a speech by Gladstone. The old fart was arguing for retention of the classics in college education. Evidently 17 of 22 hours each week are given over to Latin and Greek. Gladstone said that education should never take a practical bent. You know what that got them? Sir Charles bloody Warren."

"Wasn't he trained as an engineer?" Coulls asked, trying to force his mind to think, but failing.

"A *Royal* Engineer to you. All the same, he and Anderson—more Anderson —are as pompous as they are privileged, able to quote Greek and Latin, but unable to catch a cold, let alone the Phantom of bloody Whitechapel."

"Have you seen Catherine McLean about the past couple of days?"

"Once or twice. Why?"

"Seems busier than I am."

Jennings stared at Coulls and seemed to sober up, at least a tad. "Some things are not meant to be, mate."

Both men drank deeply of their youngest pints.

"Is he the Knife or the Phantom?" Coulls asked, his mind having drunkenly meandered from Catherine's fine eyes and face to wondering what sobriquet he should use in his stories.

"Cox usually calls him 'The Sodding Bugger.'"

"Probably wouldn't let me use that in a story, but he does need a name, a good one, given all the attention he's attracted. Hard to sell papers without a good name, a good hook for the reading public to keep 'em interested, 'specially since there hasn't been a murder in more than a fortnight." Coulls wracked his mind, which still seemed to be working at the rate of an imbecilic five-year-old. A name, a name, my next byline for a name...

Thursday, 27 September

The day came in overcast and cool. Charles Carter, a cabdriver, and Alexander Brewster, a labourer, were apprehended in Battersea Park after trying to drown a woman in a fountain. Jennings quipped, "They should be charged with illegal use of a public facility."

A stack of mail arrived at the Central News Agency (CNA), a distribution service for the major metropolitan newspapers. The over-worked city editor muttered, "What the hell's this?" as he tore open the sixth missive. The first five had found their final destination in his dustbin. His fatigue vanished as he read the sixth note. He retrieved the letter's envelope from the dustbin and yelled for a reporter who had just gone to the convenience. The reporter hearing his editor's voice thundering through walls both thin and thick hurriedly dispensed with his private urinations and rushed back into the main office.

"Read this, Jenkins. Christ. Read this," the editor yelled, attracting the notice of every man in the busy agency. "Contact every newspaper in town, Lee. We've got the story of the century. Rogers, make copies of this damned thing for every bloody paper in town. Have we got something! Have we got something!"

"What's up?" a newly arrived copyeditor who had just been hired from *The Times* asked as he rubbed at the sleep that refused to be evicted from his right eye.

"We've got a letter from the Knife and every damn paper in town 'll pay a premium for it."

The sleepy copyeditor frowned and asked, "Hadn't we better check with the police before we release it?"

"Christ," the editor cursed. "William Saunders and Edward Spender founded our agency with the intent of spreading the news, far and wide, *all* the news."

"Some say news of dubious veracity," the new copyeditor muttered, used to the higher standards of the august *Times*.

"Why'd you accept a job here, then?" Tom Bulling, another editor, yelled from across the newsroom.

The copyeditor shrugged. "I let a hoax slip through and *The Times* sacked me."

"Might be a bloody hoax," a veteran reporter called out. "But it might be the most sensational story of the year; wish I'd caged it."

"Hoax or no," Bulling said, "it's news. The people have a right to know."

The editor stared down at the missive: to distribute or not to distribute? Scoop or hoax?

The Whitechapel Phantom had finally materialized, or at least partially so, and in so doing a new name appeared for the first time in the annals of infamy.

Friday, 28 September

"Dr. Phillips and Roots said the girl's body in County Durham was not the work of the Phantom," Abberline told Swanson when they met for their regular consult.

"A local affair?" Swanson asked from behind his paper-entombed desk.

"Apparently. A young labourer, William Waddell, came under suspicion. He was seen with Jane, the victim, on the night of her murder, and he fled the district. Two days after the murder, he traded his clothes, which were bloodstained, at a clothing brokers in exchange for clothes of lesser value. The police up north are looking for him."

"Wish our man was as obliging with clues."

Robert Lees had another vision. This time the victim's ears dripped blood, the victim's face was mutilated beyond recognition and, worse yet, a second cadaver floated in a sea of artery red blood. This latter corpse was rent apart. Lees shuddered at the vision. He almost ran for the continent again but there was no guarantee the demon visions wouldn't find him even if he ran to the farthest reaches of the earth. He decided to go on the offensive and offer his services to the CID tomorrow—or maybe the day after. He would have to steel his nerves to face, in all likelihood, a rude rejection of his visions and of his unique services, but what else could he do?

The weather remained dry as a trembling arch of cloud overhead gave an unsettled appearance to the sky. A man, Levi Bartlett, was charged with beating his wife to death with a hammer and slitting her throat. Another, Thomas Haberfield, was arrested for trying to murder his daughter with a razor. A chimney collapsed at a colliery in Wigan where a worker, Joseph Platt, was killed; another, Thomas Pennington, fell and hit a wire which sliced off his right leg; and a third, Charles Hope, plunged 90 feet to land unscathed. Hope had won out.

Part Five: Berner Street and Mitre Square

Chapter Twelve

Police and vigilante patrols flooded the East End and the night passed without any sign of the Whitechapel murderer, whatever his moniker. The day came in warm and clear, the temperature hovering in the 60s. The warming weather cast a terrible foreboding over Abberline. It was an excellent day for those who dabbled in the money markets. Capitalism being so cognitively satisfying, Friday's active trading was followed by Saturday smiles of profit on the seller's face and grins of expected future earnings on the buyer's face. On the football pitch, the touring Canadians stopped Lincoln City 3-1 and West Bromwich Albion edged Burnley 4-3.

The press carried a story of a Jew named Ritter who was tried for the murder and mutilation of a Christian woman in a village near Cracow in 1881. Ritter's assumed motivation was a need to obey sacred Jewish writings which advocated sacrificial slayings of the Phantom kind. Although Ritter was acquitted and despite the fact such slaughter was never advocated in any Jewish script, more than a few Londoners were convinced there was "something to the story." There was—pure nonsense, but the eyes of these beholders saw a sinister Semite behind the Whitechapel murders.

In his office, Abberline read a cover letter from the Central News Agency's (CNA) editor to Chief Constable Adolphus Williamson of the Yard; "The Editor presents his compliments to Mr. Williamson and begs to inform him the enclosed was sent to the Central News two days ago and was treated as a joke." It bore a London East Central postmark dated 27 September. A two-day delay because the editor thought it was a hoax, Abberline fumed. Since when had it become an editor's job to determine the authenticity of evidence related to three homicides?

Abberline read the enclosed, poorly punctuated letter, written in red ink:

25 Sept. 1888

Dear Boss

I keep hearing the police have caught me but they won't fix me just yet. I have laughed when they look so clever and talk about being on the right track. That joke about Leather Apron gave me real fits. I am down on whores and I shan't quit ripping them till I do get buckled. Grand work the last job was. I gave the lady no time to squeal. How can they catch me now. I love my work and want to start again. You will soon hear of me with my funny little games. I saved some of the proper red stuff in a ginger beer bottle over the last job to write with but it went thick like glue and I can't use it. Red ink is fit enough I hope <u>ha ha</u>. The next job I do I shall clip the lady's ears off and send to the police officers just for the jolly wouldnt you. Keep this letter back till I do a bit more work. then give it out straight. My knife's so nice and sharp I want to get to work right away if I get a chance. Good luck.

yours truly
Jack the Ripper

Dont mind me giving the trade name

Then, written perpendicularly in red crayon:

wasn't good enough to post this before I got all the red ink off my hands curse it. No luck yet they say I am a doctor now ha ha.

Was it a hoax? The problem was Abberline had nothing to compare it against. Even if they received further letters, he could only compare them to see if they were written by the same hand, but that would only prove that one writer was at work, not whether the writer was the murderer.

The CNA was known for sensational stories with little basis in fact but, Abberline wondered, if it was a hoax created by the CNA, why hadn't they published it? Therefore, Abberline reasoned, the letter in all likelihood had been sent to the CNA. Abberline re-read the letter. Nothing in it provided proof that the writer was the killer. The editor was probably correct; it was probably a hoax. Even so, he sent a copy to Swanson.

Coulls had been right; the murderer needed a name. The names the Knife, the Fiend and the Phantom of Whitechapel quickly faded from the public mind, replaced by just one name: Jack the Ripper.

Press and police, managing editors and publishers agonized over whether to publish or hold back the letter.

"Can you please hold up release until we can investigate its authenticity?" Abberline asked the CNA editor in the newsman's office, which appeared to be even more cluttered with paper than Swanson's lair.

"I've got five reporters and an office boy who know about it already," the editor, who wore a check suit with the vest unbuttoned, said. "It's a smashing story for us."

"I know, but it just might be the first real clue we've got."

"I can't speak for the people who already know. They may have—John, have any of the copies of this letter gone out yet?" he asked a younger man perched on the edge of a table near his office door.

"Just to. . .let's see. . .*The Times* and *The Telegraph*."

This revelation led to a historic press meeting at *The Times*. Abberline stood nervously waiting with Helson while the biggest editors, publishers and owners began to gather just before evening deadlines. No paper had published the letter, yet. Striding as confidently as he could to the front of the room through the pipe and cigar smoke, Abberline began, "As most or all of you know, the Central News Agency received a letter two days ago. You each have a facsimile of it. You can do us a great service by spreading this from one end of the country to the other—when the time is ripe. I'd like to ask you to hold back from publishing it for a short time."

"Embargo it?" an editor yelled.

"You must be daftt!"

"You're barking mad!"

"Why?"

"There were a couple of lines in the letter that would allow us to authenticate it," Abberline shouted over the uproar, which only increased.

The newsmen's opposition to delay was clear and strident. Abberline decided that if he was in for a pence, he might as well be in for a pound. He changed his approach. "I'll be perfectly frank," he yelled. "You can print it if you wish and you can quote me." The room fell silent. "To be blunt, we haven't a clue who the Whitechapel murderer is and we're convinced he'll kill again. It's a terrible thing to say, but we may not be able to stop him. This letter, if it's authentic, gives us at least a chance to stop a fifth, but unfortunately not a fourth murder."

Abberline stared in stone seriousness at the silent crowd. Damn. Would they go along with his suggestion or would they print the letter? His admissions left him at the mercy of the least ethical editor, the most circulation-conscious publisher, the sleaziest sensation-monger. He was about to go on when a distinguished looking gentleman in the second row asked, "How long do you desire us to embargo this information?"

A rakishly dressed man at the back yelled, "It's news. News sells. We can't sit on this forever. Wait long enough and it won't be news."

"He's right!"

"Yeah, he's bloody well right."

"It's already been two days, two days too long!"

The distinguished gentleman shot to his feet and turned toward the crowd in the back, saying, "Come off it, Carl. Since we all have it, it doesn't give much if any advantage to any one paper, just whoever can get an extra out quickest and I think I speak with complete accuracy when I say we can beat any of you."

Claps and laughter followed. Abberline wondered who the stately old fellow was. The old man now turned back toward Abberline and again asked the question, but this time he worded it quite differently, asking, "How long do you require?"

Abberline shrugged. "I don't really know, but he threatens to strike again soon. We have to balance the chance of someone recognizing his handwriting, which is probably disguised, against verifying that this letter has even come from the Whitechapel murderer."

The old gentleman nodded. "You are saying that if a lady gets carved up and her ears cut off, then this letter is authentic. A terrible price to pay."

"If we know the letter is authentic, we can try and see if someone can identify the handwriting. But that isn't the most important reason for holding back publication. Personally, I doubt if anyone will recognize the handwriting. I hope that by not publishing we'll bring him out into the open even more. This man longs for attention. I believe he wrote this letter to garner publicity. When he doesn't find anything about it in any of the papers, he may get careless and this may occur before he kills again. As to your question, I don't think we need more than a week."

The words went like a ricocheting bullet through the crowd, igniting a dozen cross conversations. A week in the news business was a century in any other business.

"You expect him to strike this weekend, then?" the distinguished gentlemen asked above the tumult.

"Yes, but it's just my opinion."

The crowd buzzed. The old gentleman turned back to the crowd, which fell silent. "I think Mr. Abberline's assumption makes sense on the basis of what's in this letter. I also think he has been beyond reasonable with us. He has done something few in the police force have ever done. He has been frank with us. He has admitted CID have been unable to get anywhere as of yet. When have the police ever been so open? We have asked them to be more open. Now that this gentleman has done just what we have been clamoring for, let us not be small minded. He asks that we embargo the letter until after this weekend. I say, give him two weekends."

Silence. First one, then two, then a dozen shouts of agreement greeted his proposal. Helson smiled. Abberline beamed inwardly. On the way outside, he asked, "Who was that old fellow?"

Helson grinned. "John Walter, owner of *The Times*."

The late mail brought another postcard, which quickly found its way into Abberline's hands. It was short, curt and ominous. It read:

> Beware I shall be at work on the 1st and 2nd inst. in Minories at
> 12 midnight, and I give the authorities a good chance but there
> is never a policeman near when I am at work.
>
> Yours Jack the Ripper

It had been posted from Liverpool, but Abberline could not make out the smudged date.

"Christ!" Abberline exclaimed. "Is the barmy sod so bloody confident he's sending us a schedule of his coming carnage?"

The murderer had flung down the gauntlet; a cat taunting the British bulldog. Abberline had no choice but to fill the East End with Met personnel, both uniformed and plainclothed, particularly the Minories.

"Keep your eyes open," Abberline told a room full of PCs.

"What are we looking for, sir?" a young constable asked Abberline at the Commercial Street station as they prepared for the night's patrols.

Abberline paused. It was a bloody good question. Every man with a woman? Every man with a woman in a secluded location? Every man with a knife? Every man using a knife to cut up a woman?

"Stop and question every man you see," Abberline ordered. "I don't care what he looks like or what he's doing; question every man, everywhere—and take down descriptions and times for every single man you meet."

Coulls crafted a story as Old Boy Pierce tilted back in his chair at a dangerous angle. Coulls' story was based on a copy of a copious report Sir Charles had ordered produced on the desperate need for new boots. Coulls obtained the copy from his desk sergeant pub pal. Women were dying in Whitechapel and Sir Charles was focused on footwear.

At a pause in his story, Coulls wondered how Pierce always finished his stories so fast. He didn't even use one of the new typewriters, writing his stories long-hand with a dip pen. Was it experience, did he just write faster around the inevitable gaps in his reporting or did he just make things up?

"Not much creativity there," Old Boy mused. He lit a cigar and puffed for a moment, savoring the aroma with a smile. Coulls didn't know what Pierce was talking about and he wasn't about to ask; deadline was imminent. The paper had to be put to bed in less than twenty-five minutes; the millions of pieces of metal type, one for each letter, arranged for each story to allow the printing of the paper by the mammoth high-speed presses in the basement.

"Jack is such a common name," Old Boy said. Many correspondents had heard of the CNA letter, even though no editor had dared print it yet. "It won't last long in history. The Phantom of Whitechapel might, but it's a tad long. The Knife, now there's a sobriquet to last for the ages. Yes, the Knife will live long and be on the tongue of historians for long after our bones have turned to dust and our flesh eaten away by worms."

"Common, isn't it?" Jennings asked as he handed his story off to a copy boy, barely tall enough to reach the top of the correspondent's desk. "Jack is probably the most common English name: Jack Tar, Jack Frost, Jack O' lantern, Jack of all trades—"

"Jack off," Old Boy said. "Probably modelled on Spring Heeled Jack."

"Who?" Coulls asked and regretted asking the instant he did. Fifteen minutes until deadline. He had to finish his story. Where were his notes on Sir Charles and his new truncheon?

"A burglar and prison-breaker," Old Boy replied. "He wore bizarre disguises while assaulting and terrifying women and children in London in '37 and '38. Never identified, let alone caught."

"He'd be—wot?—on the grave's side of 70 by now," Jennings said. "Maybe our Jack models himself after Jack Sheppard."

"Who?" Coulls asked.

"Notorious thief and jail-breaker."

"Maybe he's Jack the Ripper," Coulls ventured.

"Doubt it."

"Why?"

"Hung at Tyburn in 1724."

"How would our Jack have ever even heard of him?" Pierce asked.

"Popular book about him was published in 1840 and there was a play about him a few years ago; popular as free ale on a hot day," Jennings said. "His name appears destined to live on far longer than yours, even if you ever do write that novel you're forever planning that sits in your bottom desk drawer."

"Which will be securely and locked at all times henceforth. Maybe the name is from John Rann, better known as Sixteen String Jack, since he decorates his knees with silk strings; at least he does in the penny dreadfuls."

"Done," Coulls announced as he typed 30 to indicate the end of his story for the printers.

"So what did you call him in your story?" Jennings asked.

"Jack the Ripper."

"Such a common name," Jennings repeated.

Coulls smiled as he gestured for a copy boy and said, "No choice; you always have to stay up with the latest fashions in this business."

Since their questionable veracity was bound to keep him awake all night, Abberline decided to get expert advice concerning the Ripper letter and postcard in an attempt to settle the matter. He and Helson visited his old friend, the Professor, early that evening. In the Professor's drawing room, the walls, save for two high, narrow widows, were covered with bookcases from broad-plank floor to plaster ceiling. The bookcase shelves were full from side to side with bound volumes, with many more stuffed in the space between the tops of each row of books and the bottom of the shelf above. Some appeared to Abberline to be wedged tight enough that a crowbar would be required to extract them.

"Well, there are quite a few possibilities, Frederick," the Professor told the pair of policemen as he peered at a copy of the letter Abberline had brought. Helson raised an eyebrow at the Professor's informal use of Abberline's Christian name.

As Abberline moved a teetering stack of books off the end of a purple sofa to make a space for his posterior to reside and Helson shifted a wad of typescript from a ladder chair, the Professor said, "The use of the terms 'Boss,' 'fix me' and 'quit' suggest a knowledge of the American idiom. Neither is almost ever used here in England, but the Americans use them with depressing repetition."

"One for Klosowski," Abberline said as he spotted the glimmer of a promising suspect. "He's been reported as a fastidious dresser, often passing himself off as an American."

"This Klosowski," the Professor asked, "He was born in England?"

"No," Helson said. "He's a Pole. Came here late last year for a job as a barber on India Dock road."

"Then it's unlikely he wrote this."

Abberline's glimmer winked out as suddenly as it had appeared.

"The author of this message is well versed in the English language," the Professor said. "I'd say he's not an American, but a native Englishman with knowledge of Americanisms. He tried to disguise his writing, education and nationality, but it comes through. He's a well-educated man. He's got the underlying style right, the flow, nice rounded letters, the correct spellings. He tries to fool us. He leaves out the apostrophe on 'wouldnt' but spells 'straight' correctly. There aren't many uneducated people who can spell 'straight' correctly in the Queen's English."

"Is the apostrophe missing from 'wouldn't'?" Abberline asked.

The Professor looked more closely. "Ah…maybe, maybe not. In any case, there are some other interesting aspects to this letter. You tell me several doctors think this man had medical knowledge. I wonder. If he's telling the truth and if the 'proper red stuff' is blood, as I expect it is, then what he did doesn't make sense. Any man with even an elementary acquaintance with blood would have known that blood would coagulate in a ginger beer bottle. That would include anyone from a doctor to a butcher."

Helson asked, "How do we know he's telling the truth?"

"He has little reason not to. Otherwise why bring it up? He wants to shock. I think he really meant to write this in blood, not just red ink."

"This was mailed in London on the morning of the 28th and is dated the 25th," Abberline said. "Do you think that has any significance?"

The Professor asked, "The killings have been on weekends?"

"Or bank holidays, although Nichols was murdered on a Thursday night in the summer."

"Assuming the date of the 25th is correct, and again there doesn't seem any reason why it wouldn't be, it's possible the murderer doesn't live in London. The 25th was a. . .let's see. . .yes, a Tuesday. He waited until Friday to mail the letter."

"When he came to town on the weekend," Helson said.

"It's a possibility." The Professor stopped and stared at Helson. "Please forgive me, did you want some tea, wine, beer, spirits?"

Helson and Abberline shook their heads as one.

"Ah, well then, there we are," the Professor said, turning back to the letter. "He wouldn't want to mail this from his own postal district and he was free on Friday to come down to London."

"Free from what?" Helson asked. "Work?"

"Family? Although going off to London on weekends does not suggest a married man."

"So a bachelor with a job," Helson said.

"If you're right," Abberline said, wishing he did not have to say what he was thinking, "he'll most likely be loose in London tonight or tomorrow night."

After finishing his story, Coulls rushed out of the office on a new assignment. But first he had one important stop to make.

"You're writing about social conditions?" Catherine McLean asked when they met at the Admiral, a pub just off Fleet Street.

Coulls had a new assignment: interview the poor, the even poorer, and the most poor of all; talk to hags and whores who were the potential victims of the phantom psychotic; talk to shopkeepers, tradesmen, common people. He was to write a series of stories that would truly and accurately reflect East End conditions.

Catherine asked, "What next, a gossip column?"

As he reached for probably his last pint of Kilkenny's for quite some time,

Coulls said, "I'll stick to the East End and the conditions that spawned the Phantom for now, thanks."

"If the conditions spawned him, it certainly was a long gestation," Catherine said, sipping a sherry from a dainty glass, which Coulls had bought her.

"Any advice?"

"Don't get garroted or robbed."

"I'll try to avoid such fates."

"And if you meet any women in the East End, buy them a gin, not a bloody dainty sherry."

At 8:45 p.m. Constable Louis Robinson and Sergeant James Byfield completed placing an extremely drunk woman into a cell at Bishopsgate Police Station. She had been impersonating a fire engine with all the appropriate bells and clanging on Aldgate High Street. The rumpled woman refused to give them her name, address or occupation. The police easily guessed the answer to the last question.

"I found her in the gutter, propped her against a wall but she toppled over," Robinson said. "She must be pickled in whatever she's been drinking."

"She'll sober up in a few hours," Byfield predicted. Gaoler George Hutt agreed. It was a routine arrest and in a week they would all three, the drunkard probably included, in all likelihood have forgotten all about it.

It was an important evening for Alderman James Whitehead. The 54-year-old had held office for four years. Tonight was the culmination of his concentrated ambition. At shortly after 9 p.m. he was officially confirmed Lord Mayor-elect for the upcoming civic year. The long-expected victory was honey sweet. He had been referred to as Lord Mayor-elect for months, but now it was official. A manufacturer of fans, a man of the oft-despised merchant class, he had risen above his mercantile station to a position of civic prominence. Pride and power interlocked as he happily clenched hands with well-to-do well-wishers. Thoughts of the 9 November day of days and the spectacular Lord Mayor's Parade flooded his mind. He had arranged to transform the traditional unruly, circus-like Lord Mayor's Show into a far more dignified State Procession. It would be the greatest day in his life. Nothing could possibly spoil it; nothing in God's creation.

"Have we given our instructions to everyone?" Abberline asked Helson at CID headquarters. After their Professorial missive consultation, Abberline was anxious about the coming night.

Helson nodded. "I've even got some men ready with horses and a few with bicycles."

"Those clumsy contraptions. Where did you put those poor blighters?"

"At every central corner. You can move faster on a bicycle than on foot. If he strikes, we should be able to cut off every exit that way. I've smothered the Minories with men."

"What about the rest of Whitechapel and Spitalfields?"

"Blanketed. Here; I've plotted the beats."

Abberline studied the map. "Where are Chandler, Moore and Andrews?"

"Chandler is checking on H Division men, while Moore and Andrews divided Whitechapel/Spitalfields in half and are each covering half all night."

They set out to make their now nightly visits to the police stations in the area supplemented by stops at a few dozen doss houses throughout the night. Abberline now had temporary desks at most of the stations—Leman, Commercial, Arbour Square, King David Lane, and Bethnal Green—and spent far more time in the field than he did at any desk, let alone at home. At least Emma understood or tried to appear that she did. It must be over soon—or at least so she and Abberline prayed every day and with extra devotion on Sundays.

Old Jack Fraser of the City Police caught a few minutes sleep at City of London Police Headquarters. He might be ill, but he could do his bit. Sir Charles also did his, jolting through the streets in his police carriage, issuing suggestions right, left, willy, nilly and, given his lack of police training, sometimes silly. Word of his coming preceded him wherever he went, so each post or patrolling policeman was ready and alert when he appeared, although a few ducked into a doorway to hide and take a pull from a flask warmed next to a street lamp until he passed.

Coulls changed and made for his new assignment. Once at his destination, neither the satins and delicate patterns of the upper-class lady nor the poplins and silks of the respectable middle-class matron were anywhere to be seen. Here were the heavy checks and printed imitations, the shawls and tatters of the working and non-working poor. Even the frock coats of the gentlemen were gone, just the endless procession of everyday utilitarian working wear. The conveyances also reflected the East End image. Occasionally a landau or single-horsed brougham rushed through the streets as if to pause would mean instant contamination and a fall from grace. Here were only the modest traps and the tradesmen's dog- and push-carts.

Coulls stared at the building before him, a monolith of stone and brick, cratered by dozens of caverns that seemed more like animal burrows than places of human habitation. Oh well, he conceded, might as well get started. Interviewing was new for London's correspondents, but it gave him the opportunity to show himself a better reporter than many of the older hands who had been raised on the Old Journalism. He would prove that he had learned the New Journalism, with interviews and more entertaining stories. He found the first doorway unbarred by lock or chain. The vibration from his knock caused the rickety door to creak inward on its rusted hinges and remain half ajar. Coulls' sojourn into the abyss had begun.

The evening dragged on. Everyone who moved in the area was stopped by the police and questioned, newsmen and vigilantes included. The latter roved in threes and fours, usually talking up a storm, rousting cats, dogs and drunks from their resting places. Time after time the police stopped a lurking suspect, only to find he worked for *The Telegraph, The Gazette* or some other newspaper. Police stopped Coulls thrice in four blocks before he ducked into a pub to avoid being questioned yet again. The alienist Forbes Winslow walked the streets, as did George Lusk and his men, joined by merchant Tod Lachen, a recent recruit to the Mile End Vigilance Committee. The East End was a kicked hornet's nest; the buzz of activity everywhere. As the hours passed, more than one inspector said, "So far so good" and sighed in relief. Even *The Star*, one of the most vocal critics of the police, acknowledged that the Met were doing all they could to find the killer. George Lusk had let Lusky out when he left for his patrolling duties and his cat now slipped along a damp alley, well-hidden in shadow in his quest for prey.

Chapter Thirteen

Sunday, 30 September

Midnight turned Saturday into Sunday. A weeping rain that had been soaking down finally stopped. The night would be described by those still alive in the morning as "chilly." The thermometer fell to 43 degrees. Even though it was a wet, dismal night, the citizenry still went about their nightly ways; no one believed that God in his infinite wisdom would deem that their life should be cut short this night by the phantom murderer.

The man with the black bag strode along, hunting. He was gaining skill and confidence and it showed in his easy flowing stride. As he turned a corner, a grey cat froze in his path. Lusky stared up at the man for an instant—he had seen him before—and then, sensing something threatening in the man's eyes, darted for safety behind a row of dustbins. The man smiled at the memory of a childhood adventure when he had caught a kitten; such fun he had had with it, at least until it had spoiled his fun by expiring. He strode on in search of more suitable prey. Boys played with kittens; men played with women.

At 12:30 a.m., Joseph Lave, a printer and photographer visiting England from the United States and staying at the International Working Men's Educational Club, left the club and walked through the yard to Berner Street for fresh air— or as fresh as London's soot-filled atmosphere could provide. In the parish of St. George-in-the-East, Berner Street ran south from dug-up, congested Commercial Road. It was lined by two-story tenements with broken windows patched with brown paper, smoking chimneys and bare wood floors that housed Poles and Germans who toiled as shoemakers, tailors and cigarette makers. Even with so many living so near, Lave saw no one as he left the club or when he returned from his airing 10 minutes later.

After a long tiring day writing articles, proofing copy, including a Catherine McLean story, and setting type, Philip Kranz, editor of a Yiddish radical weekly, *Der Arbeter Fraint* (*The Worker's Friend*), was reading a novel in his room beside the printing office at the rear of the yard beside the club.

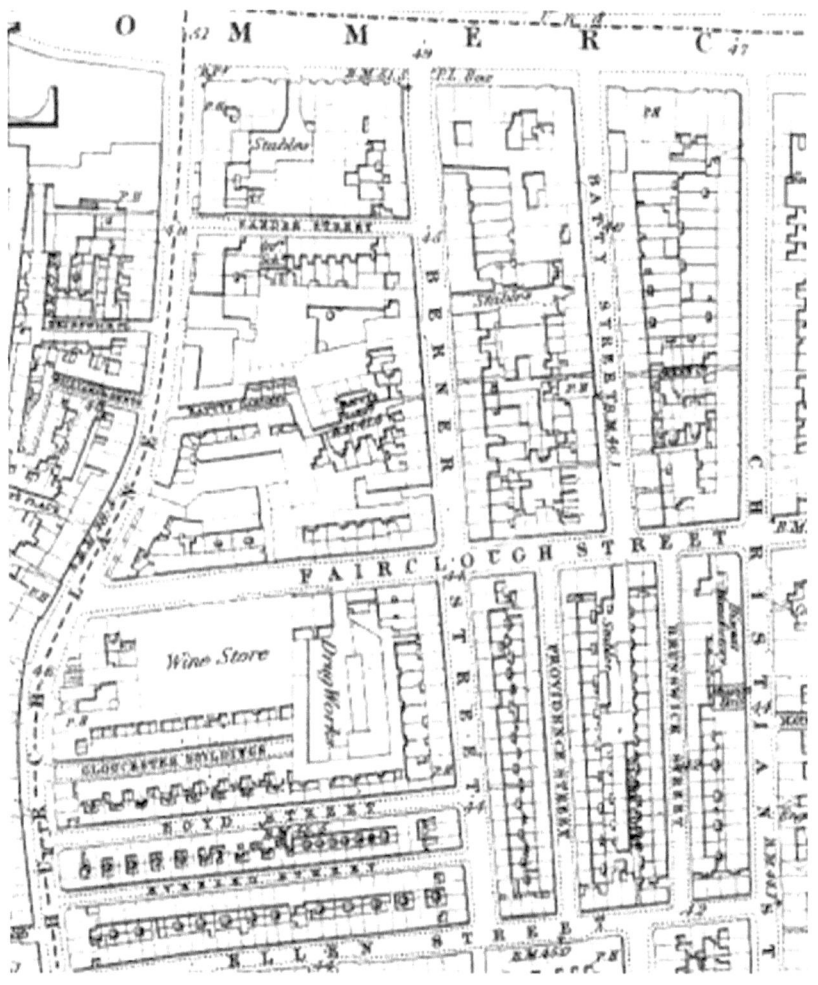

1873 map showing Berner Street. Commercial Road is at top of map.

At 1 a.m. Louis or Lewis Diemshitz or Diemschutz blinked to stay awake as he used his whip to prod his pony to continue pulling his two-wheeled barrow along Berner Street. Diemshitz had been on the road peddling his cheap jewelry at the market near Crystal Palace since eleven Saturday morn. His costermonger's cart creaked and groaned, grumbling and grating horribly on its mushy, rusty springs and dry bearings. He was almost home. Berner Street yawned ahead of him; a dark chasm in a dimly lit world. It was completely dark for about

18 feet from the street into the yard, between Nos. 40 and 42. It was more familiarity than present perception that guided his pony toward Number 40. Since Diemshitz was steward of the International Working Men's Educational Club, he and his wife lived on the club's premises.

Diemshitz's pony shied to the left. The wood gates at the narrow nine-foot entry to the club's backyard stood open. He could see that the club's front door on Berner Street was closed, but a side door into the yard was partly open and noises drifted to him from within.

The pony shied farther away from the kerb. Diemshitz leaned over and peered into the blackness below. Must be something down there. Ah, some damn bundle; maybe a discarded tarpaulin. Might be worth something. He used his whip to prod the bundle. He still could not tell what it was. He climbed down. Light spilled out of two-thirds of the windows in the club and tenements that lined the yard, as well as from the club's kitchen and the printer's office at the back of the yard. Even with all the slivers of light, however, where he stood near the bundle, he couldn't even see his holed shoes. Diemshitz rummaged through his pockets, produced a match box and tried to strike a match. It took several scratches on the worn box before the match flared into usefulness. The light only whitened the blackness for a few seconds, but it was enough.

A woman's body. Another murder!

The discovery of the body in Dutfield's Yard, from "The Pictorial News," 6 October 1888

Stark fear rushed through Diemshitz. It tore away any vestige of rationality, leaving him an agent of his nerves, a being without deliberate thought. Gawd! Was the bloodied blob before him his wife? Migawd. He could have struck a second match and easily found out, but there was a part of him that did not want to find out, at least not in such a first-hand manner. Perhaps because it is better to have companions in a crisis, Diemshitz ran full bore into the club through the side door from the yard.

"Where's my wife?! Have you seen her?!" he screamed as he ran headlong past the few mostly Russian and Polish Jewish members still in the club. Then he bumped headlong into his wife. He fell into her, hugging her hard and not letting her go. "You're alive!"

"Course I'm alive. Have yah bin at the drink agin, Louis?"

Diemshitz sobbed. Then he blurted, "There's a woman lying in the yard, but I cannot say whether she's drunk or dead."

With a lit candle in hand and a companion in the person of Isaac Kozebrodski, a young tailor machinist from the club, Diemshitz led the way back into the yard. The flickering candlelight lit the pathetic, prone figure of the woman. From the door, as soon as Diemshitz's wife spotted a stream of blood trickling down the yard terminating in a pool, she screamed.

Too frightened to touch the body, Diemshitz and Kozebrodski, now joined by another club member, Morris Eagle, set off to find help. They ran past the Beehive Public House on the corner of Christian and Fairclough Streets, where Edward Spooner and his girlfriend stood staring into each other's eyes. As they ran, the three men from the club yelled, "Murder! Police! Murder! Police!" At Grove Street, out of breath, they stopped.

It was strange. There seemed to be no police anywhere. Where had the police gone? Diemshitz, Kozebrodski and Eagle returned to where Spooner and his girl were still standing and blurted out the story about the Berner Street discovery. Spooner ran to the scene, passing others running in the opposite direction looking for the police. A crowd had already formed around the gateway when Spooner arrived. More adventuresome than most, Spooner approached the body, bent down and stuck his hand under the victim's chin; only slightly warm. He pulled his hand away and stared. Blood pumped in spurts from her neck. She was still alive! No one had tried to stop the bleeding. Spooner fumbled in his pockets for a handkerchief, but even as he did, the pulsing spray of blood stopped.

It was just after 1 a.m. when PC 252H (Whitechapel division) Henry Lamb and a brother constable became the first police presence on the scene. Lamb knelt beside the body and checked to see if she was dead. She was, although her face was slightly warm. Distaining Victorian convention, Lamb took hold of the hem of her skirt and yanked it up.

A bystander in the crowd demanded, "What's 'e about?"

"Checking to see if she's mutilated like the others."

She was not. She looked as if she had been reverentially laid down to rest.

Lamb had last passed Berner Street only six or seven minutes before. He leaned back on his haunches, the hem of his long blue swallow-tail coat scraping the pavement, and surveyed the body. Her face was turned away from the street and was only a few inches from the grime-covered brick wall that formed one side of the club. Some of her blood was still in a liquid state. Lamb knew it took from five to ten minutes for blood to coagulate. There were no signs of a struggle. He sent his fellow constable for the nearest doctor and sent Eagle, who had since returned, to the Leman Street station for help.

In minutes the constable reached 100 Commercial Road, the residence of Dr. Frederick William Blackwell. The constable had the 37-year-old doctor awoken and while he dressed, his assistant, Edward Johnston, accompanied the constable back to Berner Street.

At 1:12 a.m., Johnson reached the death spot. By the light of Lamb's lantern, he made a cursory examination. A stream of clotted blood trailed away from the lifeless body. He unfastened the woman's dress at the throat to see if her chest was still warm. It was. Only her hands were corpse cold. The wound in her neck had stopped bleeding and the blood below it had clotted.

Nearby Lamb questioned Diemshitz and wondered.

"Why didn't that little socialist sod see the bastard?" Lamb muttered to another constable. "Is he shielding one of his pals?"

At 1:16 a.m. the long-bearded and mustached Dr. Blackwell reached the scene. With the aid of a policeman's lantern, he noted that the corpse's legs were drawn up and that her dress was unfastened at the neck. The rain was coming down harder now and a rill of rain rolled down Blackwell's cheek and dripped onto the corpse. Her face appeared placid. The killer had not disturbed the woman's clothing.

Dr. Blackwell found the neck and chest quite warm, the hands cold, the legs and face slightly warm. The de-life process was taking its relentless course. He noted that the victim's right hand was open while the left clutched a packet. He bent the lifeless, supple—rigor mortis would not set in for about four hours—fingers open. They held cachous, small aromatic sweetmeats, sucked to sweeten the breath, wrapped in tissue paper.

A check silk scarf circled tightly and cruelly around the woman's neck, the bow pulled noose-tight. On careful examination Blackwell noted that a long, barely visible incision sliced right along the bottom border of the scarf. The head had tilted slightly forward pushing the top part of the cut throat over the bottom segment. The scarf was frayed in places where the knife had cut through into the flesh beneath. The incision—no, heavens, no—there were two incisions. They ran from the left side two and a half inches below the angle of the jaw, nearly severing every vessel on the left side, but not nearly so deep on the right. The wind pipe was asunder. What God had put together, the Whitechapel beast had cut asunder.

The newly arrived Inspector Marcus West interrupted Blackwell's examination, "Anything you can tell us now, Doctor?"

Blackwell shrugged. "The murderer may not have got much blood on him. Depends on what angle her body was when he slit her throat. I can't exactly tell."

Dr. Bagster Phillips arrived and asked Blackwell, "Mind if I take a look?"

Dr. Frederick William Blackwell

The medics examined the corpse as Lamb held a lantern for them.

Blackwell said, "Killer probably grabbed her scarf and pulled her backwards to the ground before cutting her throat. But that doesn't explain the placid look on her face or the cachous in her left hand. Wouldn't it have flown out of her hand as she was whipped back? Or would she have grasped it even more tightly? In either case, the strangling effect of the scarf would guarantee there would be little or no noise."

Phillips said, "Her throat was not cut while she was standing." He carefully undid the buttons nearest her neck and peered underneath. "Discolouration on the chest and both shoulders." He redid up the buttons. "She was probably thrown to the ground and held down by pressure on her chest while her throat was cut."

"Agreed, or blood would have spurted onto the front of her clothes."

"Her clothes aren't wet from the rain, so she has not been here long. Must have been in dire straits to be out and about looking for trade on such a cold wet night."

"She would have lost body heat slowly, since she would have bled out over quite some time. The carotid artery on the left isn't completely severed and only the vessels on the left side are cut. She died slowly. Probably not dead more than 20 minutes, so 12:46 to 12:56 a.m."

"I would say about an hour ago, in my opinion."

While the doctors examined the body and debated, Lamb had a constable close the yard gates to keep the rapidly gathering crowd out. Arthur Dutfield had moved his business to Pinchin Street, but the wood gates were still emblazoned in white with "W. Hindley, Sack Manufacturer, and A. Dutfield, Van and Cart Builder." Remembering Sir Charles' orders, Lamb advanced on the semi-circle of gawkers and demanded, "Let's see your hands."

"Wot for?"

"I've got orders and orders is orders. Got to check everyone's hands and clothes."

"Christ! If you think it's one of us did it, you're bloody barkin'."

"Hell, Constable, the murderer's miles away by now. He wouldn't stand round here waitin' to be pinched."

"Just the same, I've got to check everyone at the scene."

"Here, you can check me, dearie."

"Just the men, ma'am."

"Why's they so favoured? Wouldn't think a cute 'un like you would just like the lads, would yah?"

Lamb, joined by Dr. Phillips, proceeded to examine the hands and cuffs of the men in the crowd. Compliance was accompanied by grumbling and heckling, but every man was checked. No blood was found.

Lamb then looked carefully around Dutfield's Yard. It stood on the west side of Berner Street, directly across from the new London School Board building. In the yard on the right at No. 40 stood the club. A row of cottages lined the yard beyond the club. At the top of the yard teetered a workshop belonging to Hindley's sack manufacturing concern and a disused stable. Lamb decided to start with a search of the club's premises. He found no blood or suspicious stains anywhere inside. Then he searched the cottages across the yard. He found the tenants in various states of undress and all frightened, but again found no sign of blood anywhere. Next were Hindley's store and two privies in the yard. He found no blood stains, let alone a concealed Phantom.

Sergeant Charles Pinhorn, Superintendent Thomas Arnold (H Division), who had rushed over from his home at the Arbour Square station, and DI Reid joined Inspector West at the scene. They conferred and decided to interrogate everyone in the surrounding crowd, to re-check everyone's hands for blood stains, and to ask everyone to turn out their pockets for any sign of a blood-stained knife. Lamb, still a junior man even if he was in his late thirties, had only inspected their hands. Most of the 28 persons now gathered at the scene objected to this exercise in sheer stupidity, but all acquiesced; everyone wanted Jack the Ripper found. The search discovered nothing incriminating.

The doctors finished their initial examination and the body was moved to St. George Mortuary, Cable Street. The local area canvass commenced. Rooms were searched, loft doors kicked in, dozens of people questioned, many questioned a second time, some even grilled a third time. The police were dealing with socialists. To many Peelers, the Whitechapel murderer had finally struck close to home, right outside one of his workingman's clubs. The police worked with renewed zeal, but found nothing of significance.

Local police stations were notified by telegraph. Policemen on horse and velocipede rushed from post to post yelling to the men on the beat to be on the alert, but there was no organized intelligence behind this ant-like activity. There was only fluster, fervor and good intention. What exactly were they supposed to be alert for? What did the murderer look like? Although it was supposed to be the Whitechapel murderer who was mentally disorganized and frenzied, a casual onlooker would have concluded that the opposite was true. It was the police who appeared to be the muddle-brained emotionalists.

The noise and excitement was disastrous for Lusky's hunting plans. He scurried along the kerbside, his paws whisking him away from the running men behind him. He had twice been almost at the end of a stalk when some fool human burst onto the scene and sent his prey racing for their life—and for cover. Now he had just been forced to drop a dying young rat he had managed to grab when a huge dog leading a fat man on the end of a leash had charged toward him. Lusky ran for the sanctuary of home. It was quieter there, and safer.

It was 1 a.m. when the sobering female prisoner in the Bishopsgate gaol gave her name as Mary Jane Kelly of 6 Fashion Street, Spitalfields, and was released. She announced, "I shall get a damned fine hiding when I get home."

"And serve you right," PC George Hutt said. "You had no right to get drunk."

Hutt held the door for her. Kelly laughed and said, "All right. Good night, old cock."

Hutt watched her meander off towards Houndsditch and Mitre Square, a close about 400 yards away. Standard policy was being observed; release anyone brought in drunk and disorderly as soon as he or she could look after him or herself. If such individuals were not released, the tombs at each station would soon be more packed than the District Railway at rush hour. A special order to follow every woman released after midnight issued by Acting City Commissioner Major Henry Smith was never relayed to the night staff at Bishopsgate gaol. This sin of omission left Mary Jane Kelly alone on the street in the middle of a Whitechapel night.

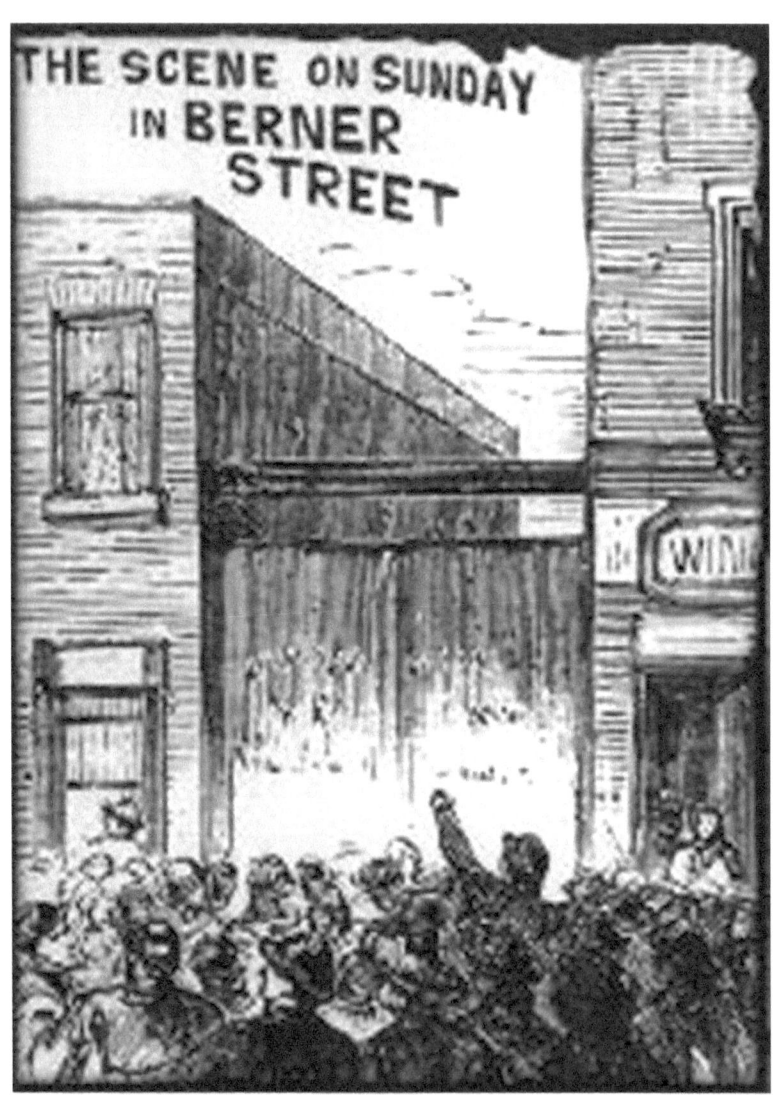

Berner Street, Dutfield's Yard, 1888, from "The Illustrated Police News" October 1888

Chapter Fourteen

By 1:30 a.m., the byways surrounding Berner Street swarmed with inspectors, constables, vigilance committee members, newspaper correspondents, and, of course, the curious. But across the nearby civic boundary in the City of London normality prevailed in what had once been the entire Roman City and was now just over a square mile of Victorian metropolis. The murders had all occurred on the Metropolitan side of the line and this night it was as if Metropolitan London, the vast district that encircled the City, was as distant as Mars. The frenzy of activity did not touch the City. Here was quiet, if not peace.

Mitre Square is off of Mitre Street, about ten buildings up from Aldgate. About 24 yards square, a respectable place with mostly business premises, the square was busy during business hours but almost deserted at night given its few residential inhabitants. Tall warehouses crowded in on every side with just a few derelict and even fewer occupied houses amongst them. Several of the houses appeared to be still standing only through the power of their owners' prayers. A *Daily News* journalist later wrote, "This particular square is as dull and lonely a spot as can be found anywhere in London."

The only residents were a City policeman, PC 922 Richard Pierce, and his family, who lived at No. 3, one of two tenements in the western corner of the square between the four-story warehouses of Walter Williams & Co. and Kearley & Tonge. The adjacent abandoned house was crumbling with broken windows and warped walls. Pierce's was the only dwelling that faced the square. On the south side of the square four houses faced Mitre Street. Three, with windows that overlooked the square, were empty. Only one was occupied, but served as Mr. Taylor's shop, a picture-frame maker. It was locked and empty at night. George Clapp, a resident caretaker of a private yard owned by Messrs. Heydemann & Co., general merchants of 5 Mitre Street, lived with his invalid wife and her nurse in rooms with second- and third-floor windows overlooking the square.

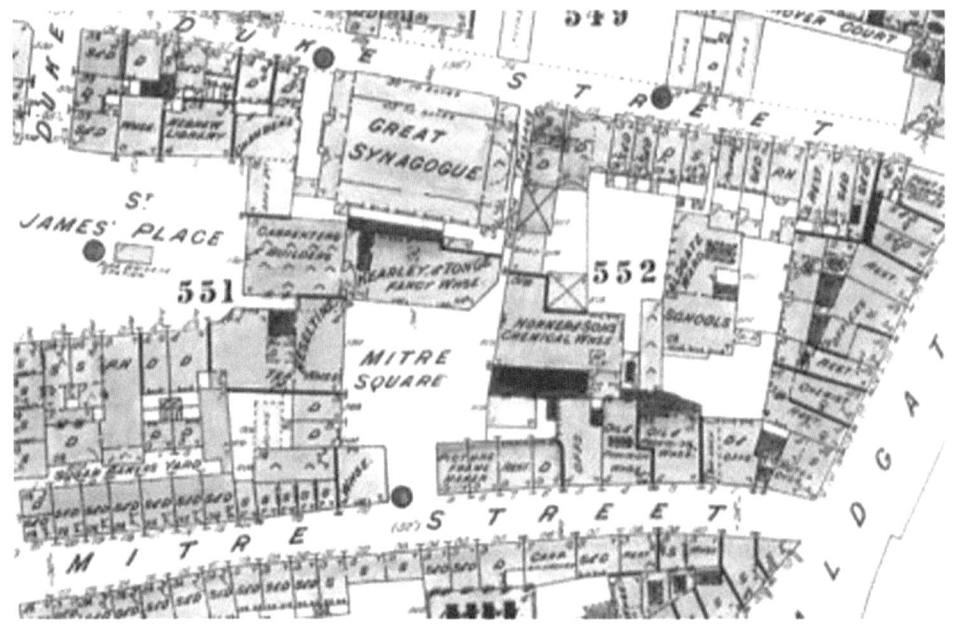

Mitre Square map

Mitre Square could be reached from three directions. On the south, an eight-yard long carriageway entered the square from Mitre Street. At this point of entry, the square widened by seven or eight yards on either side, providing secluded corners to the left and right. The northwest corner included a narrow covered passage that led via Creechurch Lane to St. James' Place, locally known as the Orange Market. It was here at the market that three Metropolitan Fire Brigade men served on night duty until daybreak relieved them of a night's invariably dull work. Duke Street connected to Mitre Square through covered Church Passage from the northeast past the Great Synagogue, which completed the three-way entry system. It was a secluded, almost secret back-place created by a jumble of planning designs and errors over the centuries. Mitre Square should never have been. Its closet-like configuration suggested where 17th Century roads had collided with 18th Century thoroughfares. This womb in the chaotic cluster of city streets attracted the only man who could profit this night from its existence.

At 1: 30 a.m. bearded PC 881 Edward Watkins trudged his bore-some City beat. Weary of carrying his lantern, Watkins had attached the light to his leather belt.

He circled his arms in ever increasing arcs in an attempt to remove the stiffness and dampness that seeped into his bones. God, how quiet it was. Having entered the square from Mitre Street, he paused to scan the almost enclosed courtyard, a pocket of urban emptiness. The sky was clear. The thermometer was down to the mid-40s. Thank goodness the rain had stopped. Watkins left the empty square to continue walking his beat of boredom. In 12 to 14 minutes he would complete his circuit and be back in Mitre Square, again.

Commercial traveler Joseph Lawende left his club at 1:30 a.m. He wasn't concerned about venturing into the streets at such a late hour. Men were less vulnerable to attack than women and despite the frequent commission of crime in London, mostly theft, most citizens never had any direct experience of it. Victims were many in number, but few in proportion to the almost five million who inhabited greater London.

Lawende noticed a man and woman standing together at the edge of Church Passage in Duke Street. The man was taller than the woman. The woman, whose back was to Lawende, wore a black jacket and bonnet. Her hand was on the man's chest. The man was clothed in a Navy serge coat and a peaked grey cloth deerstalker cap. As to the man's facial appearance, Lawende paid little attention. He did see the man as being young and of medium height, but all he saw of the man's face was a small, fair mustache. Lawende passed the pair and was alone again, plodding his way home. Focused on aspects of his own business of importance only to himself, he thought nothing of the incident, if it even qualified as an incident.

Across in the Metropolitan part of greater London, the police, vigilantes and press continued to cascade from street to street in search of the Berner Street slayer. The fact that time, the silent accompaniment to all human endeavor, most often slips by unnoticed, unheeded and un-estimated, was quickly apparent to interrogating officers. What time was it when such-and-such happened just couldn't be remembered by witnesses and, even when it was, the degree of certainty was far from precise.

A Mrs. Mortimer of 36 Berner Street claimed to have stood in her doorway nearly the entire time between 12:30 and 1 a.m. as she listened to some club members sing and not to have noticed a thing. She gave up her vigil, went back inside, changed into her nightdress, flopped into bed, and found her mind was flush with emotion and still very, very wide awake. When the sound of a ruckus at the socialists' club erased any feeling of tiredness from her brain and body, she got up, re-dressed and rushed into the street. She found a coming together of East Enders. The police were cordoning off part of Berner Street. Ever curious, Mrs. Mortimer waded into the crowd of her neighbours, both known and unknown. To her, excitement like this was happiness. It wasn't long before a tall, rather handsome young policeman was interviewing her. He was even polite enough not to inquire as to why she was out of her abode at such an hour. Mrs. Mortimer was emphatic about the time she had been standing in her doorway.

The constable completed his interview and, flipping his notepad to a new page, moved on to the next potential witness. He knew that Mrs. Mortimer had the time wrong, but there was no point in arguing with the woman. All the hubbub following Diemshitz's discovery of the body occurred at approximately 1 a.m. Morris Eagle went through the yard at 12:40 and saw no body. So, if Mrs. Mortimer was correct in her times, she must have been standing in the street during the murder, unless she went inside for a moment—the moment when the murderer struck.

At 1:41 a.m. City PC 964 James Harvey passed the Mitre Square entrance from Duke Street and Church Passage as he trudged along his beat. Hearing and seeing nothing to attract his notice, he did not enter the square.

At 1:44 PC Watkins again turned into Mitre Square. He had lost count of the number of times he had entered the almost enclosed pocket this night; not that he ever counted such things, since it would merely quantify his boredom. This time, however, it was different.

Discovery of the body in Mitre Square from "The Pictorial News" November 1888

In his lantern's light, the body lay in the square's southwest corner flat on its back. The arms seemed to have fallen beside the torso as if they were independent of any attachment. A thimble lay near a finger on the right side. The face, turned to the left, was dreadfully disfigured—the eyelids, nose, jaws, cheeks, lips and mouth were all slashed—the raw underside of the skin and flesh was exposed in sticky, gooey prominence, and the haunting whiteness of bone, striates of muscle, yellows of fat and streaky reds of blood made a grotesque mask of what once had been a human face. The throat was separated by a seven-inch trough of blood and spittle that transformed the neck into a savage mulch. Her clothes were pulled above her waist. A twist of torn apron was flung around to the side of the shoulder and neck. The abdomen was slashed completely open. A clinging, awful smell assaulted Watkin's nose like a physical presence. The rubbery, semi-solid, liquid-looking strands of intestine were drawn out and thrown over the right shoulder like some giant skein of grayish-red sausage. One piece of intestine was completely divorced from the cadaver. It lay between the left arm and the body, a forlorn sac, as if it had been misplaced on the paving stones. Puffs of vapor rose in white-gray wisps from the hollowed out cavern of the abdominal cavity. The entire apparition was ringed by darkening, clotting blood. The ears had been slashed and almost dismembered. Watkins thought, as he later told *The Star,* "She was ripped up like a pig in the market."

This was the horror that would give the 17-year veteran insomnia for years to come. Watkins stopped three steps into Mitre Square and stared at the document of death before him. Judas Priest! The Ripper had struck again. He felt an upwelling of nausea. Goddamn. He must get hold of himself.

He pulled his lantern from his belt and pointed it in an arc around the square. Empty. Wait! The door to a tea merchant, Kearley & Tonge's, was ajar. Was the Phantom hiding in there? If so, Watkins had him. He clutched his truncheon and inched forward. If the sick sot was in there, he'd have a knife for damn sure. Watkins fought back his fear and, tightening his hold on his wooden weapon, wrenched the door open.

A short, pudgy man was sweeping the stairs. The two men stared at each other for a second before Watkins, his last reserves of courage exhausted, blurted out, "For God's sake, mate, come to my assistance." It was a strange idiom to use, but the circumstances were of an alien nature and Watkins was overcome with nervous exhaustion. The stocky man, George Morris, a Metropolitan Police pensioner, paused in his sweeping. Apparently thinking the shaking pale constable before him must be either sick or hurt, he asked, "What's the matter?"

"There's another woman cut up to pieces!"

"Blimey!" Morris had been working with the door ajar, mere feet from the square. He had heard nothing. He had also, not two minutes before Watkins roused him about the murder, looked out into the yard and saw nothing. He usually heard even the footsteps of the patrolling policeman as he came past every quarter hour, so, he later said, the woman could not have uttered any sort of cry without him hearing it.

Watkins dispatched Morris for help, while he guarded the mutilated body. Morris yelled as he ran out onto Mitre Street and then into Aldgate. PCs James Harvey and James Thomas Holland heard him and rushed to the scene of the murder.

After the Tabram and Nichols murders, Acting City of London Police Commissioner Major Smith sent more plainclothes men into the area to patrol, watch prostitutes and account for every man and woman out at night. A third of his force was detailed to such duty. By chance, Detective Sergeant Robert Outram and Detective Constables Daniel Halse and Edward Marriott were patrolling the passages only a few streets away from Mitre Square when they heard of the murder. They arrived at Mitre Square at 1:58 a.m. and immediately spread out in three different directions searching for the murderer. Halse went by Middlesex Street into Wentworth Street, where he stopped two men, who gave satisfactory accounts of themselves. At 2:20 a.m. he went down Goulston Street and then returned to Mitre Square.

Dr. Frederick Gordon Brown

At 1:55 a.m. news of the murder reached Inspector Edward Collard at Bishopsgate station. He telegraphed City Police headquarters and sent a constable for Dr. Frederick Gordon Brown, the City Police Surgeon, at fashionable 17 Finsbury Circus, half a mile from Mitre Square. Collard then set out for the scene of the crime. When the 42-year-old Collard arrived minutes after 2 a.m., he found Dr. George William Sequeira of 34 Jewry Street, Aldgate, already on the scene. The doctor had been called out by PC Holland at 1:55 a.m., arriving before Dr. Brown.

Sequeira said, "Death occurred no more than 15 minutes before I arrived."

No one, not even Sequeira, touched the body until the more senior Dr. Brown arrived. Collard noted that the body lay 18 inches from the wall and railings that enclosed the yard of Heydemann's premises. Her feet pointed toward the carriageway that led to Mitre Street. Near her head, a filthy metal plate covered the entrance to a coal chute. An arched grating next to her left leg admitted light to the cellar of an empty house next to Mr. Taylor's frame shop. Glancing around, Collard saw that the body was in the darkest corner of the square. He knew it was a favoured location for prostitutes and their clients to consummate their transactions. The nearest lamp post was 65 feet away, while the corner of Mr. Taylor's shop blocked light from the only lamp on the wall in the square, so the body was in darkness even when the gas light was lit. As Collard made notes and sketched a map, Dr. Brown arrived and he and Dr. Sequeira began to perform the initial examination.

At 2:05 a.m. a hansom stopped beside PC 101H Robert Clifford Spicer. A detective in the hansom warned Spicer that the Whitechapel fiend had struck twice already this night. "Keep a keen eye out. He's got to be making his getaway right now. God knows which way he'll be going."

The words echoed in Spicer's thoughts. He was walking his beat backwards and had been varying his pace. The feeling among his fellow beat patrolmen was that the Whitechapel murderer knew every back alley and side street in the East End and was well aware of every Peeler's beat from beginning to end, as well as the timing of each and every constable. As a result, many, like Spicer, had on their own initiative started to vary their routine. To hell with Sir Charles' patterned intricacies that made it all predictable clockwork. Any fool could soon fathom a constable's beat and waylay his prey at will. Their initiative was commendable, but it caused an unforeseen problem. The latest routes had been mapped by Abberline for the Met police and by Smith for the City Police. These staggered times crisscrossed each other and guaranteed a maximum of coverage, but when patrolmen ignored the latest duty grid and went their own way at their own time, the result was the occasional gap in time and space that left a few streets, back alleys and closes uncovered for varying periods of time—in the case of Mitre Square for 10 or 15 minutes.

Spicer trekked along Brick Lane and cut into Heneage Street. It was strange how quiet the area was. He entered a narrow black alley called Heneage Court.

Dark as a closed coffin. He moved his bull's eye lantern around. A pair of men's legs moved down by a dustbin. Drawing his truncheon, Spicer crept up to the bin and barked, "Hallo! Hallo!"

His light shafted onto a man and woman sitting on a ledge beside the bin. Spicer recognized the woman as Rosy. He didn't know her last name; never had. She probably changed it every court appearance anyway. She was jiggling a pair of shillings in her hand; a fortune for an unfortunate. Even so, it was the man that drew Spicer's attention. His shirt cuffs were stained with blood and he had a brown bag with him.

"May I ask what you two are doing here?" Spicer asked.

Rosy giggled. The man remained silent and sullen, his features etched in a shadowy sandstone colour from the tawny beam of Spicer's lamp. The light sparkled off a gold watch and chain hanging from his vest. No poor man this.

"How did you get those stains on your cuffs?"

"That is none of your damn business," the man said.

Spicer's face hardened. "Oh, isn't it? Come along with me."

The man shrugged, drew himself to his feet, picked up his bag and walked out of Heneage Court a step ahead of Rosy and Spicer. The constable caught up and studied the man closely. He appeared completely unconcerned. He wore a high hat and a black suit complete with silk facings. Spicer assessed him as being five-eight and 12 stone (170 pounds). He had a small fair moustache. His cheeks were rosy and his forehead high. It was, Spicer realized, a description that came close to many he had heard concerning the Whitechapel murderer.

The trio was soon walking up the block toward the Commercial Street station. Some fool woman stuck her head out of an upstairs window and yelled, "They've got 'im! The Phantom's bin caught!"

Christ, Spicer swore at his luck. He quickened his pace. The man still seemed unconcerned. Faithless Rosy trailed faithfully behind. She jingled the shillings in her hands, as if preparing to throw them as dice. Heads popped out of windows and doorways left, center and right. The trio was drawing a crowd. Fortunately, the people who followed along seemed more concerned with herding the man along than interfering. With considerable relief Spicer marched the suspect into the station where Station Inspector Walter Beck eyed them with considered interest.

"I found him in Heneage Court with Rosy here," the twenty-year-old Spicer said, not hiding his enthusiasm. This could make his career.

The 17-year veteran Beck looked unimpressed.

Spicer whispered to Beck, "For God's sake man, he's got blood on his cuffs and he's carrying a bag big enough to contain a knife and the devil knows what else."

"Do you have any complaint against this man?" Beck asked Rosy, who giggled amid coin jingles and shook her head as she smiled.

Beck turned to the man and asked, "Your name and address, sir? Just for the record."

The iron-eyed man sullenly took out his wallet, glanced disdainfully at Spicer, and said that he was a doctor and that he lived in Brixton. Beck turned stone-faced toward Spicer and said, "You have no evidence against this gentleman. You should be reprimanded for bringing him in. He is a respectable doctor and can establish his identity. You should know better than to do such a thing."

Filled with fury, Spicer asked, "Sir, what is a respectable doctor doing sitting by a dustbin on a rainy night in a dark, dirty alley at two o'clock in the morning with a common prostitute? It doesn't make sense. At least look in his bag."

"Hold your tongue, constable," Inspector Beck ordered. He turned to the man, apologized for Spicer's lack of discretion and escorted the man and Rosy to the door. Spicer stood quivering as rage coursed through him at Beck's stupidity. Beck returned and told Spicer to get back on his beat.

"You're bloody lucky he didn't lodge a complaint," Beck growled. Then, in a more friendly tone, added, "I've been reprimanded twice myself for questioning such respectable persons. Leave them alone. The man was just up the alley for a little bit of the new."

Spicer returned to his beat, a sadder but not wiser young man. The only consolation was that the murderer was probably heading west into the City or north toward Finsbury. The Brixton doctor could just be another of Rosy's customers and the blood on his cuffs could have come from examining an injured patient. Still, Spicer thought, Beck should have asked the doctor to at least open his bag. Would an innocent man object to such a benign request?

A knocking at his door roused City PC Richard Pearse. Although it was annoying to be woken from the peaceful oblivion of a deep sleep and wonderfully warm bed, there was something wickedly exhilarating about being called to duty at such a time. It might only be a neighbour's boy trapped in a closet or a cat up a pole, but it thrust you into the lime-lit center. It was better to be bothered than bored.

"The Whitechapel murderer! Lord alive!" Pearse muttered upon being told what had happened. Utterly amazing. The bastard had struck in Mitre Square. Jesus. Pearse's bedroom window overlooked the murder spot. He cursed his missed opportunity, fully knowing that only the slightest of chances would have ever led him to look out the window at precisely the right time. It was a dark, dungeon-like close at best and lit only by the feeblest of lights. Cunning and chance favoured the Phantom. If they hadn't, there would, of course, have been no Phantom. He would, Pearse knew, have been caught after his first murder, tried, hung and rightfully forgotten. As it was, the killer was the one murderer among many who had the right combination of intelligence and luck to stay free and make himself nationally and internationally notorious.

The bed in the Cloak Lane Police Station was decidedly uncomfortable. Major Smith, acting Commissioner of the City of London Police while the soon-to-retire Commissioner James Fraser was on vacation, twisted, tossed and rolled beneath the rough blankets. After the Chapman murder, he had taken to sleeping at one station or another most nights after checking on various beats and constables. This station was particularly trying. A railway goods depot fronted the station, while a furrier's took up the backside. The stench of skins being treated permeated every room and every object in them, including the thin rough blanket Smith attempted to use to stay warm. The bell rang. Smith rolled into a sitting position and stared vaguely into space.

"Another murder, sir!" a constable announced. "In the City."

After donning his suit jacket, Smith jumped into a hansom. He would have preferred almost any other transport. He believed a hansom was "a detestable vehicle" and an "invention of the devil." Worse, designed for two people, Smith was far from alone in the conveyance. He shared the interior with a 15-stone superintendent, while three detectives hung on the back like limpets on an especially choice rock. None of the additional weight added to the hansom's safety or comfort. As Smith later recalled, "We rolled along like a seventy-four in a gale."

When the overburdened hansom arrived at the scene at 2:18 a.m., Smith found that Dr. Brown had completed his examination of the earthly remains in Mitre Square.

"She's a horrible mess, sir," he told Smith in the light of several constables' lanterns. "Mutilated beyond belief. Throat cut across. No one disturbed him this time. Intestines cut out and thrown over her right shoulder; some smeared with feculent material. A piece about two feet long detached and placed between the body and the left arm, apparently by design. Part of the right ear has been cut through. The uterus and the left kidney are missing. Probably did not take the intestine with the faecal matter, given the stench. He would not want to carry that around with him. The fellow must have a leather bag or something to carry organs like that in. He couldn't carry such things away in a coat pocket. The blood would seep through clothes in too short a time for him to make a safe getaway."

Smith asked, "Anything further?"

"No superficial bruises, no blood on the abdomen, no secretions on her thighs, and no spurting of blood on the pavement. Actually no signs of blood below the middle of the body and no blood on the front of the clothes; probably slashed her throat when she was prone."

Smith looked down at the body, wishing he could not smell it, and saw several buttons resting in the clotted blood.

Dr. Brown continued, "He's no stranger to dissection, I would venture. He had to have a good deal of knowledge to know exactly where the organs were and how to remove them. The way the kidney was dissected especially suggests it was done by someone who knew what he was about. The kidney could easily be overlooked by an amateur. It's covered by a membrane. See? There's the membrane over the other kidney. Medical students often have a devil of a time finding it, but this blighter located it quite easily in a dark alley with the chance of a constable happening upon him at any moment. Takes a steady hand and considerable skill."

Smith hid the grimace he felt behind a stern countenance. "A doctor then?"

"Not necessarily; someone accustomed to cutting up animals would have the same knowledge. He wasn't in a hurry; notice how he nicked the lower eyelids. That took precision. No frenzied rush. No shaky hand."

"How long do you think it took him?"

"Five minutes at the most."

Smith was amazed at how much damage could be done to a human body in less time than a pint lasted. "How long has she been dead?"

"No more than thirty or forty minutes; about 1:30 a.m."

"Could she have cried out?"

"Her throat was instantaneously severed. No chance of her making a sound. Then she was mutilated, after death, so not much blood."

Thinking of any way to identify the murderer, Smith asked, "Any idea what weapon we should look for?"

"A sharp, pointed knife, at least six inches long."

"Any evidence of a struggle at all?"

"None. He struck like lightning. And he follows a pattern. Notice how the intestines are drawn out and placed over the shoulder? Just like the Chapman woman."

Dr. Brown sent the body to the City Mortuary on Golden Lane for a later, more thorough post-mortem examination. When the body arrived at the mortuary, part of an ear dropped from her clothing. The murderer had cut her right ear clean through.

When Detective Inspector James McWilliam, head of the City Detective Department, heard of the Mitre Square murder, he rushed to the City Detective Office at 26 Old Jewry, near the Bank of England. When he arrived at 3:45 a.m., he wired Scotland Yard the news and then hurried to Mitre Square. When he arrived, he met Smith, with whom he would head the investigation, and ordered a search of the area. Several men were stopped and searched, but none were blood stained and none carried a sharp, pointed knife at least six inches long.

Ex-baker, ex-9th Lancer and current Metropolitan PC 254A (Whitehall) Alfred Long hurried along Goulston Street, playing the light of his lamp from sidewalk to gutter, doorway to window sill. Long had been seconded from Whitehall to supplement H Division, so he was unfamiliar with his Whitechapel beat. He had been a constable for only four years, far shorter than his twelve-year Lancer career.

At 2:55 a.m. and unaware of the Mitre Square murder, Long stopped. His light spotlighted a piece of cloth. The material—an apron—appeared to have bloodstains on it. He lifted his lamp and noted the address: numbers 108 to 119 Wentworth Model Dwellings. His light caught something written on the wall in chalk. He looked closer and read on the black fascia of the lower part of the wall: "The Jewes are / The men that / Will not / be Blamed / for nothing."

Who wrote that? Was it connected to the bloodied cloth? Odd way to spell Jews.

Thinking the bloodied apron might be from a rape, Long searched several staircases nearby but found them empty and devoid of any blood stains or bodies—living or dead. He hadn't seen the apron or the writing twenty minutes ago when he last went by on his beat. He picked up the cloth and hailed a constable from farther up the street. He told the other man to guard the writing, then ran for help, reaching the Commercial Street station at about 3:05 a.m.

Detective Constables Halse and Baxter Hunt soon returned with Long, whom they had told about the Mitre Square murder. The three Bobbies surveyed the words on the wall.

"Is that a 'u' or an 'e' after the J in Juwes?" Halse asked.

"An 'e,'" Long said with great certainty.

"No, it's a 'u,' clearly," Halse disagreed.

Hunt rushed to Mitre Square to report and ask for instructions, while Halse stood guard and, even with the spelling disagreement, congratulated Long on noticing the writing and leaving a guard on the graffito.

Hunt found Chief McWilliam in Mitre Square, who listened to Hunt's report and ordered Hunt to arrange to have the words photographed. He also ordered Hunt and Halse to search the tenements in Wentworth Model Dwellings for the Whitechapel murderer. Hunt returned to Goulston Street and he and Halse searched every tenement in the immediate area, but found them Phantom-less.

News from Berner Street brought Sir Charles to the Leman Street station early that 30 September morning, although his early rising was nothing unusual for him—murder or no murder. He arrived at the Leman Street station shortly before 5, where 53-year-old Superintendent Thomas Arnold, a Crimean War veteran and the new head of H Division, briefed him on the murders: the Met was investigating the Berner Street murder, while the City Police were focused on the Mitre Square case. Arnold also briefed the Met Commissioner on the scribbled words on Goulston Street.

Arnold said, "I fear for public order if those words are left on the wall in that district, sir."

Both men knew that anti-Semitic feelings were growing, fueled by press coverage of Leather Apron/Pizer as a suspect.

"It is a predominantly Jewish area," Arnold added. "I suggest we have the words removed immediately."

Superintendent Thomas Arnold

Sir Charles snuffed and ran his fingers over the ends of his long moustache.

"I have already sent an inspector to Goulston Street with a sponge and bucket and instructions to await my orders, sir," Arnold said. "I can have the words removed within the briefest of times."

"Yes, well, that is the question, wot? Ah, well, I believe that I should decide the matter myself, as it is one involving so great a responsibility whether action should be taken or no," Commissioner Warren said, pursing his lips and standing at attention before his subordinate. "I intend to stop at Goulston Street to inspect the words on my way to the Berner Street murder scene and then make my decision regarding the graffito."

Dr. Phillips, who had been given charge of the blood-spotted cloth from Goulston Street, arrived at the Golden Lane Mortuary to compare it to the apron found around the Mitre Square victim's neck. As Dr. Brown and DI McWilliam looked on, Phillips matched the torn edges of the cloth to the corresponding torn side of the apron encircling the dead woman's severed neck.

"It fits," Phillips said. "Neat as a dye."

Seemingly oblivious to the icy sanctum and its ghoulish contents, McWilliam laid out a street map on an empty dissecting table across from the corpse. He studied the map and said, "The shortest route between Berner Street and Mitre Square is left along Commercial Road, left along Aldgate, right on Duke or Mitre Street and straight into Mitre Square. But the cloth was found on Goulston Street. Here. It means the blighter was doubling back after the second murder.

He probably took the apron to wipe off his hands and knife. He keeps to the backstreets by the look of it. The question is: where in hell was he headed when he went back toward Goulston?"

It began to pour around 3:30 a.m. Normally rain would not have bothered anyone overly much, but coming during a pair of investigations, its effect was negative beyond belief. Water splashed along the sidewalks and soaked into the narrow edges of bordering dirt creating a soft mush that became footprints when a constable stepped by. Then the mark would be found and a debate would ensue. Was the footprint there before? Was it a Phantom footprint? Memories were stretched. Questions were counter-questioned; answers contradicted. The rain was now the murderer's ally. It became another hated thing in cruel, cursed Whitechapel.

It was in another blind cul-de-sac that the full arrogance of the Whitechapel murderer came home to DI McWilliam. A constable found a bloodied pool of water sitting in a public sink in the center of a dead-end close off Dorset Street and summoned McWilliam.

"God! He walked in here," the constable guessed. "Right up a dead end. We could have trapped him if we'd been lucky. He must have washed his hands off and walked right out as calm as could be. Either he didn't know it was a dead end or—"

"Unlikely he blundered up this little alley," McWilliam said. "The entranceway even suggests a blind end, but you're right constable; if it was him, he's got no fear in him at all." Not wanting to dampen the constable's excitement, he didn't mention that there was no way to link the blood to the murders. It could have come from anyone, especially in a neighbourhood with dozens of slaughterhouses.

They watched the bloodied water, spotted by rain drops, ever so slowly draining away in the un-stoppered sink.

"Couldn't have been too long ago; maybe ten minutes, maybe a half hour ago. Some of the blood is caked on the side of the bowl," McWilliam said, deciding they better act as if the murderer had washed up here. It was their best potential lead yet. "Well, in any event, the bounder's human; he gets blood on his hands, probably his cuffs, and we can be certain he knows Whitechapel. If it was him, this blood suggests he was heading north. Canvass the area and see if anyone saw him entering or leaving this close, and we'll widen our search to the north of this point."

The teams of searchers spread out. The hunt continued but no one had been seen near the close all night. No suspicious people were reported north of Dorset Street. The investigation was grinding to a stand-still. Then a pair of pawnbroker's tickets and later a knife was found. The tickets were quickly traced not to a possible suspect, but to the Mitre Square victim. The knife, found in

Whitechapel Road, proved more interesting. Possibly discarded by the murderer right after the Berner Street killing, it was a black-handled, ten-inch, razor-keen pointed blade.

"No one would throw away a knife like that in a district as poor as this. We'll have to check if that's blood," Abberline said, who had rushed to the scene with Helson as soon as he was informed. "The question is; why would the Ripper—if it's his—throw it away?"

"Perhaps he saw someone coming and had to get it out of sight in a hurry," Helson suggested.

Abberline shook his head. "Throwing it away would have attracted more attention than just hiding it in his coat."

City Detective Constables Halse and Hunt stared at the writing on the wall in Goulston Street. A half-circle of eager, excited Metropolitan Police ringed them, as if the detectives were buskers on the Blackpool pier.

"Christ, it'll start a riot if someone sees this," a huge Met constable said. "They'll think the murderer's carrying out ritual Jewish mutilation-murders against Gentiles, just like the papers say."

"Let's rub it off," another said.

"Wait," Halse ordered. Then he added, "Please." They *were* Met and he *was* City.

Sir Charles arrived in his shining chauffeured coach just as the sun tinted the eastern horizon. As he descended, he spoke briskly and authoritatively, "I've heard you found some writing."

Halse nodded and indicated the graffito. Sir Charles strode over to peer at the words. He sniffed and ran a hand along one wing of his mustache.

"In an hour, the streets will be shoulder-to-shoulder with people," Sir Charles said. "Cause a riot, private property damaged, lives lost, disorder on every block and in every lane, I dare say."

"It's in good schoolboy hand," a Met constable said. "Maybe some urchin wrote it."

"Probably has nothing to do with the murders," another constable said.

"Nothing whatsoever," Sir Charles agreed.

"The writing should at least be matched against the letters," Halse suggested.

"The letters are most likely hoaxes," Sir Charles said. "Make a copy and then rub it off. People are coming into the street. Petticoat Market is opening and soon everyone in the East End will know what it says."

"Can't we just cover it with something, at least until Major Smith or McWilliam arrive?" Halse asked, imposing his lean body in front of the writing.

His patience gone, Sir Charles snapped, "Rub it off."

"Maybe just rub off the first line?" Halse offered in compromise. Where the hell was McWilliam, Smith or Hunt?

"Rub the bloody thing off, man," Sir Charles said. "That's an order."

"I've sent word to City Chief of Detectives McWilliam," Halse said to no effect. "A photographer couldn't take longer than an hour to arrive." Even as he said it, he was swept back from the wall by several beefy Met constables, including one holding a sponge and a bucket of water. By the time he regained his position, the writing was gone. It was 5:30 a.m. Whether it matched the handwriting in the Ripper letters was now a matter for memory since no one had photographed it.

McWilliam arrived to find the writing obliterated. Halse overheard McWilliam disagreeing strongly with Sir Charles' decision. Soon after, Major Smith arrived. As the three senior men conferred, Halse loitered nearby and overheard Smith use the words, "unpardonable blunder" and "fatal mistake." Halse sighed. Sir Charles would not be the one to pay for the fatal mistake; that bill in all likelihood would be paid by yet another unfortunate.

It has been a hectic night for Lusky. He had been doubling back and forth all evening. He was now in a particularly dangerous street. Urchins peeped menacingly out from basement windows, their ashy faces catching the morning sun in a strange hideous manner that made them appear more like albino moles than members of the human species. These little paupers would snatch at a passing cat, their mothers urging them on. Cat pie was acceptable on a plate long devoid of meat, although Lusky would have much preferred the humans stick to bow-wow meat instead. Lusky kept out from the building's edge. When a little grasping hand lunged his way, he sprinted away from this valley of potential death. It was time to go to ground.

At 5:30 a.m., PC Albert Collins was charged with washing the last vestiges of gore left uncleansed by the rain from the Berner Street yard, leaving it as clean as it ever was.

It was 6 a.m. when George Clapp of 5 Mitre Street woke up. He stared, not first comprehending, as his wife yattered something at him. Finally he growled, "What are you on about now, woman?"

"There was a murder in the square last night. Police are at the door. They want to know if we heard anything."

"Not a bleedin' thing," Clapp replied from beneath long-unwashed covers and greasy hair.

God, George thought, the Knife was out there last night. Their bedroom overlooked Mitre Square. He felt a cold spasm pulse down his back. Even so, he fell back asleep.

In Mitre Square, Major Smith and DI McWilliam reviewed the movements of the murderer. Smith was in a foul mood.

"In less than 15 minutes," he told McWilliam, "the murderer lured the victim into the square, killed her, mutilated her and made his escape, taking the woman's left kidney and womb with him, virtually under the noses of four serving or ex- policemen."

"He's a lucky one, sir."

"Well, let's make certain his luck runs out, James. What do we know?"

"At 2:20 a.m., PC Long patrolled along Goulston Street and didn't see the apron. Halse went past at about the same time and also did not see it. So the apron was dropped between 2:20 and 2:55; between 36 and 71 minutes after Watkins discovered the body in Mitre Square. You can reach Goulston Street in five minutes from Mitre Square, so what in the name of Hades was the killer doing the rest of that time?"

Smith stalked back and forth as his mind worked on what little they knew.

McWilliam said, "The killer slipped out of the City when the police were already alerted and into Whitechapel, which was also already alerted because of the first murder, but paused on Goulston Street to leave the apron and write something?"

"What fool fleeing a murder stops to write on a wall?"

"Our fool, sir," McWilliam said, managing the hint of a sardonic smile.

"If he did write it. In either case, let's figure out if there's anything else we can do to find our fool." Smith feared the murderer was far from a fool and that he had already gone to ground somewhere safe, quiet and secluded, and without a description, what could they do?

With action assignments reviewed, inspectors canvassing the area and dawn long past, Major Smith finally found a bed at 6 a.m., at which time, he later admitted, he was "completely defeated."

"God, is she mutilated!" the police photographer exclaimed, looking at the fleshy lump of the Mitre Square victim in the mortuary shell. "You can fix her up now and then I'll take another flock of pictures so we can circulate 'em to find out who she was."

Drs. Brown and Sequeira nodded. With two other doctors, theirs was the terrible task of reconstructing the distorted mulch that had once been a human face.

Behind them and well out of the pictures the photographer had taken lay the nude body of a hump-back child who yesterday had been a chimney sweep, complete with bent leg from a fall, an underdeveloped torso from chronic respiratory disease and the ugly lesions of cancer of the testicles. For once, in death, he was washed and scrubbed clean of soot and tar. His sightless eyes reflected the gas light, spitting back flecks of white. He had died from neglect and malnutrition. The gashed-up body of the woman was tragic news, the chimney sweep's body was simple all-to-common tragedy.

The Mitre Square victim was the first to be identified. A policeman from Bishopsgate station recognized her as the drunk released as sober in the early hours of the morning, Mary Ann Kelly. A burst of investigative activity ascertained her true name as Catherine Eddowes, also known as Kate Conway and Kate Kelly.

"Age 43. Hazel eyes. Dark auburn hair. 'T. C.' tattooed on left forearm. T. C. is or was probably her man, at least at some time," McWilliam reported to Smith, who had managed to catch a brief nap before returning to duty. "She was certainly living on the streets. Look at what was in her pockets: five pieces of soap, small tin box with tea and sugar in it, a ball of worsted, two clay pipes, and a blunt table knife. Nothing romantic about her. She was even wearing a man's boots. An utterly unattractive drunken old drab who'd revolt any normal man, but that's the bloody problem, this murderous bloke isn't normal."

Catherine Eddowes

John Kelly—no "T" or "C" in sight in his name—the man Eddowes had been living with, confirmed the corpse's identity. A half century of life in the slums had encased his inner self in a beetle-stiff outer shell to protect him against the buffets and knocks of poverty, unemployment and the absence of hope. His face remained expressionless chiseled stone as he stared at the body in the mortuary. "We got throwed together in a lodgin' house quite a bit. Struck up a bargain. Lived there together, except for the hop season. She'd get the odd job charring and I'd do most anything. Kate'd drink but she never was troublesome. We went hop picking again this year, but warn't a great deal of money in it, so we hoofed it home. We was so broke I had to sell a pair of boots so's we'd get a bite to eat."

"When was the last time you saw her?" McWilliam asked.

"Oh, 'bout two Saturday afternoon. Said she was goin' to see if she could find her daughter Annie in Bermondsey. Said she'd be back by four. I heard from a woman that she'd seen Kate in Houndsditch with a pair of constables and that she'd been taken to the station. I figured she'd been drinking, would sober up and be back Sunday morn."

McWilliam nodded. He did not ask if it even entered John Kelly's mind to have come and met or even inquire further about his Kate at the station. Such ideas were not the stuff of such a man's thoughts.

The police net brought in for questioning almost every pervert known to every policeman in Greater London. There was Gilbert, a young man who specialized in caressing his naked penis in front of little girls and who had chased a trio of six year olds, his organ spitting semen after them as he climaxed during the chase. There was Anthony, a 30 year old, who first came to police attention when a constable came upon him standing in a public bird bath clutching a goose to his crotch. When the constable discovered that the goose and Anthony were attached, Anthony, the zoophiliac, was arrested for indecent exposure, cruelty to dumb animals and creating a public nuisance. There was Thomas, a quiet, timid little fellow who kept creeping around the foliage outside neighbourhood bedrooms, excitedly trampling flowerbeds into patches of unsightly undergrowth whenever he spotted a female in the act of undressing. There was George, who wanted women to jump on him, pee in his face and lash his backside with a barber's strop. There was Henry, who liked older women, and Dennis, who liked even older ones. Both liked to undress them, fondle their ancient parts and masturbate in their wrinkled faces. There were many, many more. After their alleged whereabouts on key dates were ascertained, checked and rechecked, their innocence of, at least, the Whitechapel murders was definitely determined. Their peculiarities were diagnosed as indications of madness and they were untreated accordingly.

Ordinary Whitechapel awoke to a bustle of blue. To many an East Ender, it seemed the police were everywhere. By dawn, just hours after the two victims were found it seemed that everyone in Whitechapel was out in the streets.

Curiosity, the evolutionary byproduct of several million years of humanness, asserted itself with a vengeance. Crowds encircled the two locations now notorious for their geographic association with grisly, instant death. Windows overlooking the sites were sold for viewing, eagerly sought. Costermongers sold fruit, sweets and nuts. Newsvendors did a spectacular trade. Many could not read or could not read English, so the literate few read the latest extra news stories out to the crowds. Perhaps it was the need to review and remember the primitiveness of the past, to realize that man was only a few facades removed from the carnal kill that brought droves of people out. Or maybe it was a deep unrecognized desire to gloat over the dead, to flaunt being alive, to reassure oneself that a certain invulnerability still separated one's self from the dead. Whatever it was, the streets were packed. The police sealed the entrances to Mitre Square with blue-coated constables. The situation at Berner Street was no less of a commotion and extra constables were assigned to keep order. Both sites attracted crowds for several days. Elsewhere, Lusky trotted past the Buck's Row site on his way home with nary a person in sight, while a young tabby tried to ambush a bird in the empty backyard of 29 Hanbury.

Members of the Workingmen's Club protested the intensive interrogations and searches that continued in the vicinity of the club's Berner Street location. The club was a rendezvous for Russians, Poles and Continental Jews all tainted by socialist ideas and foreign blood; all the target of suspicion by legions of good and true Englishmen and women based on the reigning wisdom of the Victorian day. One of them was obviously a good bet to be the Whitechapel fiend. Inspector Chandler observed, "By God, some of them barely speak the Queen's English. Unfathomable."

On a second interrogation, Mrs. Mortimer remembered seeing a man walk by her doorway in Berner Street just after 1 a.m. The man was young, in a hurry and carrying the oft-mentioned black bag.

When he heard of her latest interview as he stood in Dutfield's Yard, Abberline said, "Since she never seems able to get her times straight, her testimony is of rather dubious value."

Helson stood and patiently waited for Abberline, who was doing what appeared to be nothing, but was actually hard work: thinking. Although nothing much appeared to be happening when one thought, it was what had led to every advance in human history and every apprehended murderer.

Abberline thought the killer could not escape from the yard through the Working Men's Club because the front doors were locked by 12:40 a.m., so he must have left through the main gate. Mrs. Mortimer stood at the door of No. 36 for most of the time between 12:30 and 1, yet saw no one leave the yard by the gates. Diemschitz approached the yard at 1 a.m. and saw no one running away. Abberline scratched his receding hair and made a shocking realization.

"Helson, the killer probably was in the yard, waited for Diemschitz to find the body and run into the club, and then made his escape. Otherwise, if Mrs. Mortimer is anywhere close on her times, there was no way to get out of the yard after the murder without being seen."

Helson stared at his chief. "Fear must be foreign to him."

At a less luxurious level of police business, the slow accumulation of details continued to mount. Inspector Collard located the witness Lawende during house-to-house inquiries. The visiting Lawende changed his recalled memory from seeing a man with Eddowes in a dark Navy serge overcoat to seeing a sailor in a pepper-and-salt jacket and reddish neck handkerchief. The validity of the description remained in doubt, although the suspect's estimated height of five-seven or five-eight, fair complexion, age 30 or so, and medium build was consistent with the description of the man Liz Long had seen with Annie Chapman.

"The bastard sure has nerve," Jennings said back at their office after he and Old Boy returned from the scenes of mayhem in Berner Street and Mitre Square. "Anyone could have come along Berner Street or popped out of the Workingman's Club. What a risk. He was more secure at the second spot. Mitre Square is as dark as the inside of a camel's ass."

"Someone could have strolled into it from any of three different directions at any time; that's taking a risk," Old Boy said. "A market opens good and early every Sunday morning in Middlesex Street right close by, so there'd be plenty of people about."

"So our killer likes to play long shots of at least 50 to one."

"I did get something else, Aaron, maybe worth a few inches. A guy named Albert Backert was asked some suspicious questions by a bloke in the Three Nuns Hotel. This bloke wanted to know when the loose women in the pub left and where they usually went. Backert left with the crowd at midnight and walked along with this stranger as far as Aldgate station. That isn't far from the scene of one of the murders."

"Get a description of the bloke?"

"Sure, what kind of reporter do you think I am? He was a shabby genteel sort of man, dressed in black clothes, black felt hat, and he was carrying a black bag."

"Probably worth a few inches."

The Berner Street victim, still unidentified, was put on display for public view. It might be macabre, but the police were desperate. Without an identification, their investigation was at a stand-still. Hundreds of London's East End citizenry filed by the coffined body. Constables watched to see if anyone looked overtly excited. Excited or not, no one recognized the victim.

That afternoon, the Mile End Vigilance Committee held an outdoor meeting in Victoria Park which unanimously passed a resolution demanding that Home Secretary Matthews and Commissioner Warren resign. Four other meetings were held in other parks and passed similar resolutions. Police informants reported the Committee's activities. Matthews concluded George Lusk, a vigilante leader, was a radical while Sir Charles decided the man was a socialist. Both made moves to have the man watched.

Londoners still proposed means of nabbing the Whitechapel menace. A Surrey resident argued for a force of bicycle-riding constables who could noiselessly and swiftly patrol the streets. He must be deaf, someone concluded. The advocacy of using bloodhounds to track the culprit continued. The Queen asked what was being done about searching the barges and ships that came and went with the tides, apparently based on the wide-spread belief that no Englishman could possibly commit such horrific murders and that the killer must have come from across the sea, as had the Vikings, William the Conqueror and the Plague.

Inspector Reid tunneled his way like a mole through the crowd—he wished his theatrical performances drew such crowds—to reach the St. George-in-the-East Mortuary so he could examine the body from Berner Street. Finally inside, he saw that she looked about 42 and was 5 foot 2 inches tall with dark brown, curly hair. She had a pale complexion and light gray eyes. Her upper front teeth were missing, which, he hoped, she had lost fighting the Ripper, although from past experience of the way Jack attacked, Reid, sadly, doubted it.

He found where the victim's clothes were piled: a long black jacket trimmed with black fur, a worn black skirt, a dark-brown velvet bodice, two light serge petticoats, a white chemise, pair of white stockings, side-spring boots and a black crepe bonnet. He thoroughly searched each item, but found nothing to identify her.

Upon returning to his office in the Arbor Square station in Stepney, Reid sent her description by wire to all Met police stations. Normally her identification would help find her killer, but with Tabram, Nichols and Chapman it had done little good, since they appeared to have been murdered by a stranger. With such murders, all ordinary means of detection had thus far failed.

Later that day, the accumulation of people outside St. George-in-the-East Mortuary overflowed into the street. The paling light of early autumn afternoon glinted through the mortuary's grime-layered windows. The continual shuffle of East End feet mingled with the occasional certain step of a West Sider as hundreds filed by the Berner Street body.

"That's Liz, that's my Long Liz." The man quivered, his hands shaking. He sank almost to his knees, cursing not in anger but in bitter frustration, "Damn, damn, damn."

He clutched the side of the coffin, dropping his hat. He did not sob. He only swore in terse-lipped rebellious profanity that condemned senseless death. A constable helped the man to a chair.

"You say she's Long Liz?" the constable asked.

"Yes, Elizabeth Stride. Everyone who knows 'er, calls 'er Long Liz."

"How do you come to know her?"

"She's bin livin' wid me for on three year now. Off and on, that is. Sometimes she'd go away for a while, but she always returned. Christ. I cautioned 'er the same as I would a wife. It was drink that always made 'er go. She couldn't stop."

"You cautioned her?"

"About takin' up wid other men—for money, with this murderin' bastard around 'un all."

"Your name?"

"Michael Kidney, sir. I'm a waterside labourer." Kidney buried his head in his hands.

Once Kidney's identification of Elizabeth "Long Liz" Stride was made known, a stampede of former acquaintances came forth to view the body. Sven Olssen, a clerk of the Swedish Church in Princes Street, said he had known her for 17 years. "Her real name was Elizabeth Gustafsdotter. She was born at Torlanda in the old country. It's near Gottenberg. Her birthday was the same day as my wife's, 27 November 1843, except my wife was born in '33. I can remember the year, because the difference was exactly 10 years. We used to get together for a little party, nothing extravagant, every birthday. She was poor. Not in good circumstances."

Another witness supplied Long Liz's most recent address as 32 Flower and Dean Street, reputed to be the most decadent thoroughfare in all Spitalfields. The witness acknowledged, "She walked the streets in the general Whitechapel/Spitalfields area, like all the rest of us."

Old Boy also recognized Stride, but he knew her as Annie Fitzgerald, who had been charged and convicted on countless occasions for drunkenness at the Thames Police court. With some digging, he found that Stride was a casual prostitute. Although Swedish, she spoke perfect English, as well as Yiddish and often worked as a char for Jews in the area. She had moved from Gustafsdotter to Gothenburg as a domestic, but in March 1865 the police registered her as a prostitute. She was just 21 and was treated twice that year for venereal disease at a special hospital, Kurhuset. In 1869 she married John Thomas Stride, a carpenter. She claimed to have nine children, but Old Boy was far from certain about the figure. In talking with her friends and acquaintances, he found she was not known for her honesty in relating the finer details of her life.

More clues continued to turn up. Helpful citizens showed Sergeant Kevin Dudman a series of blotches on the doorway and window sill of a house at 36 Mike Street. The stains in various graying and darkening colours were suspiciously blood-like. The general consensus was that someone had rubbed his hands and drawn a knife along the doorway and sill in an attempt to clean up. Daniel Hurtig, a resident of 36 Mike Street, had not noticed the stains before. Since the address was a short distance from Mitre Square, an inspector was sent for.

Dudman's attention was also drawn to blood-like blotches on the windows of a building adjacent to Mitre Square, but this particular discovery faded from significance when the occupant pointed out that the windows were shuttered at night.

The finding of things suspicious or things made suspicious was not left just to residents of the Whitechapel area. The proprietor of the Nelson Tavern in Kentish Town, northwest London, discovered a parcel in his convenience, kicked it into the street and only remembered it when he heard the news of more slayings in Whitechapel. He retraced his steps, examined the package's contents and summoned a constable. The parcel contained a pair of dark blood-stained trousers. The paper was also blood-marked. The discovery led nowhere.

Albert Backert, who had earlier told Pierce and the police about a man asking him about the habits of loose women in the Three Nuns Hotel, went back to the police with an expanded story. He now remembered the man had asked him how old the unfortunates were and had asked whether he thought a woman would go with him down Northumberland Alley, a lonely court off Fenchurch Street. Backert also recalled seeing the suspect go out and talk to a woman who was selling matches and give her something. The story would have ended there, but Fenchurch Street abutted Mitre Street. Backert's description of the man was again taken. This time he was dark, about 38, five-seven or five-eight, dressed in a black felt hat, dark morning coat, black tie, and was carrying a shiny black bag. The police routinely inquired further into Backert's story. Pierce dutifully reported it. Subscribers gleefully read it. Almost no one believed it.

The horror of the double slaughter stirred police units into frenzied activity Sunday evening. Abberline and Smith assigned every man they could find to the East End. They patrolled vigorously. Even so, confident the Whitechapel murderer wouldn't strike since Monday was a working day and, having done all that could be done, an exhausted Abberline went home early at 10 p.m. It had been a sleepless weekend. He leaned back and let the bath water seep up around his barrel chest, its warm liquid touch creating an incredible soothing effect, especially on his painful varicose vein. He stared down the rounded expanse of his body. Damn, how he hated being fat and old. We live in the wrong direction, he thought. We don't improve. We grow towards death, not birth. It wasn't even comforting to realize that everyone, including Jack the Ripper, was in the same hot water. If he didn't fear getting caught in a dark close, Jack would certainly never fear growing old.

After dark, Coulls, on his undercover investigation, noticed a reduction in the number of prostitutes in the East End. By evening, the streets were deserted, except for the best lit ones. In a first, some lodging house managers let women stay even if they could not pay, although many women were, as usual, turned out if they lacked their doss money. Some went west to better lit streets. Coulls still found many on darkened streets the evening after what was being called the Double Event or the Double Murder. He asked one unfortunate if she was afraid.

"Afraid? No," she said, whipping a knife from her pocket. "I'm not the only one armed. There's plenty more carry knives now."

The average Brit did what anyone else on earth would do under a similar circumstance. Helpless to do anything about this atrocious intrusion on their feelings of security, they went about their business with faint regard for anything outside of immediate personal concern with the universal human conceit: the Ripper might get you, but never me.

Chapter Fifteen

Monday, 1 October

As Abberline had guessed, the Ripper, Phantom, Knife or Red Fiend, as various newspapers called the murderer, did not resurface on Sunday night into Monday. It was a cold crisp day. The temperature barely touched 50 degrees. The sky arched blue, bright and frosty over the city. The birds circled in their feathered finery and the air sparkled. Autumn was falling. Life went on in a thousand little ways. For some it went to its end. Four men were killed when a steam boiler in Birmingham exploded. In Gloucestershire, Mr. T. Gambier-Perry died of a heart attack. For Mr. Gambier-Perry, a Justice of the Peace, it was an important and significant event. For the vast majority of Brits, the life or death of Gambier-Perry was singularly unimportant.

"Blimey, look at that!"

A crowd encircled the message being posted in the window of the White Hart pub. Similar notices were put up in other public places and delivered to all residences throughout Whitechapel, Spitalfields and the neighbouring parishes. It read:

POLICE NOTICE

To the Occupier

On the mornings of Friday, 31st August, Saturday, 8th and
Sunday, 30th September, 1888, women were murdered in or
near Whitechapel, supposed by some one residing in the
immediate neighbourhood. Should you know of any person
to whom suspicion is attached, you are earnestly requested
to communicate at once with the nearest Police Station.

Metropolitan Police
30 September 1888

It meant: Help! But its arrogance did not go unnoticed by the people of Whitechapel.

"'Supposed by some one residing in the immediate neighbourhood.' How do they know that?"

"What cheek. The descriptions of 'im by those that's seen 'im is that of a swell and no swell lives 'ere."

One of the many recent immigrants who did not read English asked, "Wot's it say?"

The Star reported that at 1:30 a.m. a man was seen wiping his hands in Church Lane between Berner Street and Mitre Square on the night of the Double Murder. No one seemed to follow up this report, not even the newspaper-addicted Helson, although hundreds of other reports were pursued with great thoroughness.

A *Times'* editorial reminded readers that in 1876 the murderer William Fish had been detected with the help of bloodhounds, implying that the same four-footed friends might be used to apprehend the fiend behind the current murders.

Elizabeth Stride

Coroner Baxter opened the first day of the Elizabeth Stride inquest in the confines of the two-story, Doric-columned Vestry Hall in Cable Street, St. George-in-the-East. Given the notoriety of the case, the swollen jury consisted of 24 men, good and true, while the gallery was as full as the rail at Royal Ascot, all listening transfixed to the proceedings, which included the questioning of 76 butchers and slaughterers about their whereabouts during the times of the murders. Inspector Reid attended the inquest for the police on the off chance that something new would be revealed, even if such an occurrence was as unlikely as the Prince of Wales marrying a divorcee or, God forbid, an American.

William West or Wess, overseer of the printing office attached to the Working Men's Club on Berner Street, testified first. At 12:10 a.m. he said he walked out of the club's side door to take some literature to the printing office across the way. Returning, he saw that the yard gates were still open, but that the yard was empty.

Then a discussion of the lighting or lack of it on Berner Street included varying opinions as to the general visibility in the area. No one suggested going out and actually testing the area's luminosity after dark.

Next to testify were Morris Eagle and Louis Diemschitz, who described their finding of the body on Berner Street. Reid yawned and ran over some lines in his head that he was trying to learn for a production he was opening in two weeks.

Eagle, a Russian Jewish traveling trader in jewelry and a club member, said he chaired the meeting at the club that night, which attracted about 100 people in the first-floor of the club to debate, "Why Jews should be Socialists."

"As much right to be as anyone else, I suppose," a burly man next to Reid muttered.

Reid was glad that at least someone still upheld the right of an Englishman to speak any nonsense they wished, even outside Speaker's Corner.

After the club's discussion ended at about 11:30 p.m., Eagle said, most of the people left and Eagle took his young lady home at 11:45. He returned at 12:40 a.m. He entered by the back door through the yard since the front door was locked by then, but he noticed nothing untoward in the yard at that time. Twenty minutes later a member called Gilleman came in and told everyone that a woman's body had been found in the yard. She was lying across the pathway, her feet 6 or 7 feet inside the gate, so if the body had been there at 12:40 a.m., Eagle, with the eyes of his namesake or not, would have tripped over her.

After Baxter finished with Diemschitz, the coroner announced that the body had not been identified as yet.

The jury foreman frowned and said, "I thought it was the body of Elizabeth Stride."

"It was a mistake," Baxter said. "It would be best to say that the woman is unknown."

As murmurs of excitement rose from the gallery at the possibility of a continuing mystery centered on the victim's identity, Reid rose with the rest of the crowd and realized he had just wasted a small, but at least to him, significant part of his life. The police were confident the victim was Elizabeth Stride, but there was still a possibility that Mary Malcolm, who claimed the body as her sister's, was correct. Reid didn't think so, but time would sort it and, in any case, he didn't have time to listen to baseless bicerking about a name—he had lines to learn.

Given all the grief Sir Charles had been given over obliterating the graffito on Goulston Street, he decided he should mount a stout defense. Dictating to his personal secretary a memo to the Home Office, he explained that the writing was in clear view to any passerby and that the street was beginning to fill with Jewish vendors and Christian buyers. Unfortunately, he said, nothing could have been put up to cover the graffito that would not be in danger of being torn down. He also claimed that it would have been hours before a photograph could have been taken.

Sir Charles paused and considered whether a cordon of police could have guaranteed that any covering would have stayed put until a photograph was taken. Possibly, he thought, but the risk of the words being seen and passed on was high, risking public disorder, damaged property and even deaths. Given that the writing was undoubtedly unrelated to the murders, just like the letters, why even consider running such a risk?

A stout defense if ever there was one. However, Sir Charles had learned at Sandhurst that the best defense was a vigorous offense, so if he could somehow turn the words into a valuable clue, his eradication of them would be forgotten

Clearing his voice, he began to dictate his offensive, "The idiom does not appear to me to be either English, French or German but it might possibly be that of an Irishman speaking a foreign language. It seems to be the idiom of Spain or Italy. The spelling of Jews is curious." Very well done, he thought. That should keep the Home Office at bay. Perhaps Sir Charles was not without talent after all, for the prerequisite of any administrative post is the ability to turn alibi to advantage, falsehood to truth and failure to fortune.

Sir Charles then met in emergency session with the top Met officers investigating the murders, including Abberline, Helson, Chandler, Andrews and Moore. After making their reports, Sir Charles rose from the table and strode over to his window to peer down at Scotland Yard below. "With few clues and every suspect cleared, what are we left with, gentlemen?"

Abberline didn't know if it was a rhetorical question, but from the smirk on Helson's face, he guessed his colleague was thinking 'Sod all.'

"I am investigating the possible use of bloodhounds," Sir Charles announced.

Abberline was amazed, but remained silent. Maybe the dogs might work, but he hoped the use of canines was not the be all and end all of Sir Charles' plans to catch the killer.

"It has been suggested that we conduct a house-to-house search of a major section of Whitechapel for any clues related to the murders," the Commissioner said, turning back to his men. "I hesitate to order such a search for obvious reasons."

Abberline recalled the battle in Trafalgar Square on Bloody Sunday between the Met backed by soldiers against social democrats, Irish nationalists and the unemployed. The public reaction had been far from positive, at least in the poverty stricken and unemployed East End. The West End had supported Sir Charles' stance for law and order, but Sir Charles wasn't considering a house-to-house search of the West End. Take for bloody ever to search some of those mansions, Abberline thought.

"The public has been pressing for action," Sir Charles said. "A reward has been proposed."

Abberline had heard reports of at least five public meetings in the East End calling for the removal of Sir Charles. Public anger against him was focused in large part on a reward. At the request of Sir James Fraser, the City Police Commissioner, the Lord Mayor had authorized a £500 reward for anyone who provided information leading to the discovery and conviction of the Mitre Square murderer. The reward only increased criticism of Sir Charles and the Met for not offering a reward for information pertaining to the other murders.

"I favour the provision of a reward," Sir Charles said, "but given the state of current policy guidelines, that avenue is most unfortunately and definitely closed to us. Therefore, gentlemen, we find ourselves in need of some other means to identify and capture this wanton murderer."

Abberline had heard via the Met's gossip network that Home Secretary Matthews had refused Sir Charles' request to reverse the policy of his predecessor barring such rewards.

"We are left with one sole avenue open to us: a search," Sir Charles said. "Even given the potential difficulties, not to say challenges, of a thorough search of the East End, we are faced with the fact that we must do something to apprehend this monstrous villain and do it forthwith."

Abberline realized that, like the press and public, Sir Charles had had enough. Used to success in almost everything he had done, the soldier of action had decided to act decisively to at least do something to try to catch Jack the Ripper. The East End would be searched.

Seeing confirmation of his Double-Murder vision in the press, Robert Lees fainted. When he recovered, he rushed to Scotland Yard. He forced himself through the public entry into the oddly designed building, which featured two floors of austere granite topped with red and white brickwork, ornate casements and Flemish style tourelles. Inside, Lees managed to convince the desk sergeant to let him speak to an inspector. He need not have bothered. With his story of a vision of two victims and bleeding ears, the inspector strongly implied he was a lunatic. The news about the Double Event was known to all; who in their right mind would believe Lees had seen his vision before the murders? The Continent was looking better and better.

The murders were already being turned into fiction. The short gothic novel, *The Curse Upon Mitre Square* by John Francis Brewer, focusing on the murder of Catherine Eddowes in Mitre Square, appeared in bookshops and newsstands.

The speed at which news now spread complicated the police investigation.

"Look what the Central News Agency got in the mail," a junior constable waved a postcard above his head as he ran into Abberline's office that afternoon. Abberline, Chandler and Helson were discussing how to implement Sir Charles' massive search plan. Abberline took the postcard and read,

> September 30
>
> I was not codding dear old Boss when I gave you the tip, you'll hear about Saucy Jacky's work tomorrow double event this time number one squealed a bit couldn't finish straight off. ha not time to get ears for police. thanks for keeping last letter back till I got to work again.
>
> Jack the Ripper

"This must be authentic," Chandler said. "It was written and mailed before the papers were out."

"He also refers to the earlier letter," Helson said.

Abberline was far from certain. "News of the Double Murder spread throughout the East End within hours. Reporters were asking everyone they could find whether they had seen anything." Abberline peered at the card. "It's franked OC1, not SP30, so it was posted today and by today every newspaper had stories about the Double Event, not to mention all the extra editions that sold out last night."

"He might still have written it yesterday," Helson said. "Could have placed it in a post box, been collected late Sunday after the last pickup and then franked and delivered today."

"Probably was written and posted on Sunday—given the wording," Chandler said. "'You'll hear about Saucy Jacky's work tomorrow,' today, in Monday morning's papers."

"And the Mitre Square victim did have one ear lobe cut off," Helson said.

"That's far from an entirely missing ear, let alone both ears," Abberline said. "And her face was mutilated anyway, while the Berner Street victim had no injuries to her ears."

"Didn't she have a tear in the lower lobe of her left ear?" Chandler asked.

"Dr. Phillips said it was an old wound," Abberline said, "caused by forcible removal of an ear-ring, now healed."

"So God only knows if the postcard's authentic or a hoax," Helson said, shaking his head in frustration.

"If it is authentic," Abberline said, "we'll need to consult a graphologist or an alienist to see if there's anything in it that might help us find the writer."

The Double Murders brought a deluge of mail to the police and newspapers naming suspects by the dozen, with many names plucked from the newspapers, such as Dr. Forbes Winslow, a self-appointed Ripper hunter, and Richard

Mansfield, the star of the stage production of *Dr. Jekyll and Mr. Hyde*, who worked himself into such a frenzy on stage that some thought he did so off stage as well. Other suspects were far more plausible. Several cabmen were talking in a shelter about the recent murders when a stranger claimed he was the murderer. Abberline read the report and dispatched detectives to investigate. They tracked down one John Davidson and like so many before him, cleared him. Abberline continued sending out inspectors to track down leads and chase down possible suspects. Sooner rather than later, he prayed a lead would actually lead them to the murderer.

Gossip galloped back and forth across the City and Metropolitan area all day so that by the time the evening papers hit the streets, people were buying every sheet in sight to confirm or disconfirm the latest they had heard from their neighbours, co-workers or pub-mates. The papers fueled the conversational conflagration. As evening came, more and more Londoners had more and more time to talk and speculate about the crimes. People chattered, yattered and nattered as rumour rolled over rumour in endless waves.

"They say the first woman's body was found in total darkness. He's a demon, able to see in the dark."

"Found her right next to the Socialist International Club. I wouldn't put it past the Peelers trying to pin it on one of those working stiffs."

"They say the socialists are connected with the killings."

"Who the 'ell says?"

"The police."

"You gonna believe them?"

Housewives, fishwives, mothers, grandmothers, maids, butlers, lords and ladies talked about the killings.

"They say she wandered the streets all night. I shouldn't wonder she got herself killed."

"I heard she was strangled with her own intestines."

"They was wrapped around her neck."

"A mad doctor, that's what he is."

"Mad! Mad! Mad!"

Husbands threatened wives with "I'll Whitechapel you!" Parents threatened their children with "Look out for Leather Apron!" John Pizer was forced back into hiding, innocence no defense in such times. A series of sinister and sinister-appearing human beings were arrested on suspicion of being the murderer and either quickly released or gaoled to await trial for lunacy. Abberline was beginning to wonder if insanity wasn't catching as London appeared to be in the throes of a mindless epidemic.

Colonel Sir Alfred Kirby, Commander of the Tower Hamlets Battalion, Royal Engineers, volunteered a £100 reward on behalf of his officers and the services of 50 of his men to protect citizens or search for the murderer. With an eye on the English distrust of standing armies in their midst who might threaten their hard-won liberty, he emphasized that his volunteers would be acting as private citizens, not soldiers.

East End merchants expressed considerable economic concern. Evening business had plummeted dramatically. Respectable women had disappeared from the streets, which took the contents of their purses out of circulation. Only a very brave or very foolish few ventured forth under escort. Merchants made motions at a District Board of Works meeting for better street lighting. The laxity of officialdom in servicing East End utilities was well documented; a Whitechapel courtyard that was without lighting repairs for a week was a striking example of civic indifference despite the Ripper outrages.

With his sermon delivered yesterday, the Reverend Barnett was already at work on his next oration. Given the distant deadline he had more than enough time to rant to his wife, Henrietta, about the Whitechapel murders in their snug quarters in Toynbee Hall, their pioneering university settlement established to better the lives of the poor.

"A creature of unimagined cruelty and depravity stalks London's East End at a time when our city is the center of the human universe," the reverend said, striding the five steps from one end of his sitting room to the other. "We are on the cusp of the 20th Century, certain to be a century of peace, prosperity and unrivalled English achievement. The sun never sets on the British Empire. Britannia rules a major share of the earth's waves and a quarter of its land mass. London is the largest city in the world, the most cultured, the wealthiest, the center of the world. God's city. How dare this phantom entity of the night so arrogantly seek to impose his satanic self on the hopes and glory of this blessed plot, this earth, this realm, this England? It is an affront so offensive that such a beast could only originate from Hell itself."

Henrietta nodded as she paused in her perusal of a proposal to the Whitechapel Gallery to loan fine art to Toynbee Hall for the education and enlightenment of the poor. The East End might be Hell, but even Hell could be educated and enlightened.

As night descended, PC Joseph Lee patrolled Whitechapel with his truncheon on his belt and bullseye lantern in hand. As he trudged along he spotted a masculine, tall woman in ill-fitting clothing. Something was far from right.

"You there, stop," Lee yelled, his suspicion mounting. Then he realized the source of the problem. "You're a man, aren't you? No denying it, mate. I can see what you are."

"I am," the figure replied evenly in a resonant baritone.

"Are you a detective?" Lee had heard that some detectives were dressing as women to try to decoy and trap the murderer.

"No, sir."

"Then kindly tell me who you are."

"A reporter; thought I'd dress as a prostitute to better root out some copy about the murders."

"Lucky for your neck you didn't root out the Ripper."

Tuesday, 2 October

Bright sunshine brought Londoners a magnificent blue sky and a most pleasant autumn day. John Brown, a 45-year-old labourer, was charged at Westminster with murdering his wife by slitting her throat, while at Dalston, Frederick Lawrence attempted to stab his spouse. Neither Brown nor Lawrence garnered much press or public attention. The name of Jack the Ripper had caught on now in the public domain, at least in Britain. On the continent, the down-to-earth French were calling him 'Jack the Stomach Opener,' although the exact translation was open to debate.

The effect of the publication of the Ripper letters was anything but pleasant for the police. More than one insightful observer noted that Mitre Square was only a few hundred yards across Fenchurch Street and along Mitre Street from Minories Street. Why hadn't the police warned the public about the Ripper's threat to kill again in the Minories?

Abberline, Chandler and Helson met in Abberline's office for a working lunch.

"The woman found in Berner Street, Elizabeth Stride, fits the general description of all the rest," Abberline said. "A poorly dressed middle-aged prostitute addicted to alcohol. Only difference is that she was fairly tall: five-foot-five."

"She was an unfortunate in more ways than one," Helson noted. "She lost her husband and children when the *Princess Alice* sank in the Thames."

"Rubbish; her husband died of heart disease in '84," Chandler said as he munched on a ham sandwich. "The usual sympathy-seeking saga of woe these women can pour out with a second's notice. Most of them have an actress's grasp of the dramatic. She may have been a passenger on that steamer when it went down, but that's as close as she came to that tragedy."

Abberline eyed Chandler and said gently, "I know we're all exhausted and frustrated, but we must never allow our frustration to deflect onto this lunatic's victims."

Chandler nodded, sighed and said, "Sorry, sir."

Helson peered down at yet another report. "Evidently the Mitre Square murder was committed while our plainclothes men were watching several premises in Windsor Street. That's why the patrols near the City boundary were thinned out."

"Who ordered that pack of men on Windsor Street?" Abberline asked, reaching for the duty assignments past his untouched meal of cold bacon on bread.

"Sir Charles put on a special surveillance; one of his last-minute edicts. You know, watch the anarchists, the social disruptors, and hang the Ripper."

Helson finished his sheep's trotters lunch and hurried back to Bethnal Green station. Chandler set out to investigate yet another lunatic who had been released just before the first murder. Abberline read reports, ordered investigations into still more suspects and ensured all information reached Swanson for his review.

Several hours later Chandler returned; another lunatic cleared. Helson returned and reported, "We may have caught a break. One of our patrolmen may have seen the Ripper with Long Liz Stride in Berner Street before the murder."

"Did he get a name?" Abberline asked.

"No, sir."

"Did he at least question the man?"

"Afraid not."

"It'll be a break in both our necks if the press finds out we were that close and didn't pinch him. Why didn't the constable follow orders and at least talk to the man?"

"I guess the man didn't look the least bit suspicious."

"I'll go talk to him and see if I can get anything of importance out of him. Name?"

"PC William Smith. He's in H; beat covers Berner Street. He'll be checking in for the afternoon shift about now."

It was mid-afternoon when Abberline met with 26-year-old PC Smith. Abberline eyed a man with a youthful face but a full, black mustache. His hair was thinning atop a soft, pudgy face. His small, dark eyes were alert and Abberline prayed they had been wide open the night of the murder.

Smith said, "I go by that spot on Berner Street where I saw that man and woman about every 25 minutes, maybe every half hour at the worst if I get delayed."

"When did you see them?" Abberline asked as he settled into a wood chair in a borrowed office at the Commercial Street station. He had faced a monstrous muddle of traffic to reach the station and had exited his official growler three blocks short of the station to hobble with his cane the rest of the way to catch Smith before he went out on his beat.

"About half past 12; no, maybe as late as 20 minutes to one. They were talking. I'm pretty certain the woman was the deceased, but I can't be dead sure."

"What about the man?" Abberline asked, taking out his pad and stub of a pencil.

"He held a parcel wrapped in newspaper. It was about 18-inches long and six or eight inches wide."

"What did he look like?"

Smith paused, frowning as he struggled to remember. "Five foot seven. Dark, hard felt deerstalker's hat. Dark clothes. Maybe 28 years old. I didn't see him all that well. A small, dark moustache. A black, diagonal cutaway coat. Respectable appearing chap; white collar and tie. I couldn't hear what they were saying."

"Where precisely did you see these two?"

"Right across the street from where the woman's body was found. Oh, the woman had an embroidered flower on her breast. When I saw the body at the mortuary, I recognized that flower right away. There could be another woman with her general facial appearance and size, but I doubt it and the flower made me pretty certain. I guess I should have at least spoken to them; got his name."

"Your orders were to stop and question any suspicious-looking person," Abberline said evenly. "Especially anyone talking to a woman in the streets. And especially someone carrying a package. Didn't you realize he might have had a knife in that parcel? Where was your brain, lad?"

"I dunno. If I stopped and questioned every couple on my beat, I'd take all night just to make a single round. But I should have stopped that pair."

Abberline held his frustration deep inside and said, "You didn't know and as you say, you can't question all of them."

Sir Charles twirled the tip of his military mustache. His brow and cheek tightened as he said, "I don't really know where to begin."

Major Henry Smith, ex-Suffolk Artillery Militiaman and current Chief Superintendent of the City of London Police, wondered what could be troubling the Met's Police Commissioner. Colonel Sir James Fraser, the City of London Police Commissioner, simply waited for his counterpart to speak. Fraser looked sick, but the Ripper was now operating on his territory. He had to find the killer.

"There's a rather delicate matter that concerns both your department and mine," Sir Charles said. "I've been to the Palace. . .and. . .er. . .there's considerable concern about the Duke of Clarence."

Ah, Smith thought, that was it; Prince Albert Victor, Duke of Clarence, eldest son of the next man in line to be king. It was rumoured that the Duke's personal equerry, and possibly the Duke, had patronized a male brothel in Cleveland Street for several years now. Homosexuality was a crime and a trigger for social ostracism. Smith found discretion paramount to detection when a case was coloured with royal purple. He knew that the law reserved for royalty was in a court of its own in terms of leniency. He also knew that this was not due to any heart-felt mercy for the deviant, but because of a genuine need to insure that the concept of royalty kept its place in the hearts and minds of the throng. True or false, the public must never know about Clarence's rumoured proclivity for male company.

"Of course," Sir Charles continued, "the Duke has sown a few wild oats, but he's still. . .the Duke. There is an ugly rumour about that—it's hard to imagine where these sordid and unfounded allegations find even a modicum of verdant soil to take root—but some people have had the audacity, nay, the effrontery to suggest that the Duke may be responsible for this horrid business in Whitechapel. The Queen wants us to clear Clarence's name, but at the same time not to make any of this public. Well, there you have it, gentlemen."

"How do we clear the Duke's name if we don't make the investigation at least somewhat public?" Smith asked.

"Well, I. . ."

"I think," Colonel Fraser suggested, "by finding the person who is responsible."

Smith asked, "What has led to the Duke being a suspect?"

"A number of people have reported seeing the Duke in Whitechapel," Fraser said.

"It's preposterous. Absolutely preposterous, a tissue of lies and innuendo," Sir Charles said, before adding, "We did keep it out of our written reports."

"As preposterous as it may be, what if the Duke is guilty?" Fraser asked. "He would never be legally guilty, of course. The Ripper is insane, you agree?"

"Yes, definitely," Sir Charles said. "Most definitely."

Smith nodded and studied his sly superior, Fraser, who went on, "If the Duke were found to be ill, he could be quietly edged out of the limelight and sent away for an extended rest somewhere comfortable and discrete. But, of course, he isn't guilty anyway, so we have nothing to worry about."

"Nothing to worry about, nothing at all," a clearly worried Sir Charles said.

"Our job," Fraser continued, "is to check the Duke's movements for the past month in a most discreet manner and to see to it that he doesn't get in any mischief from now on. We'll have to assign our best, most loyal and most trusted men to this. You'll head the investigation for the City, Major, and, I understand, Sir Charles, that your Assistant Commissioner, Sir Robert Anderson, has been assigned the task for the Met."

"Unfortunately, Sir Robert couldn't attend us today. He's still ill and on the Continent, but will return on the 10th. I've already named a good man in his stead in the interim. Fellow I met during my tours through Whitechapel. Damn good man, quite sound."

"Have I heard of him?"

"Probably not; a youngster named Enright."

"What about Fred Abberline?" Smith suggested. "He's my peer over there, a most sound detective."

Sir Charles shook his head. "The Queen and her advisors have specifically said they do not want Mr. Abberline or any of his immediate assistants to have anything to do with this part of the Whitechapel business. In fact, he is not even to know it's on."

Major Henry Smith, Chief Superintendent of the City of London Police

Prince Albert Victor, Duke of Clarence

The Lord Mayor, solidly attuned to public pressure, asked that an additional £500 from the city coffers be added to the mounting reward, which private donors had increased to £1,200 at a time when £2 bought a decent Sunday suit. The

Lord Mayor left his own money safely deposited in his friendly neighbourhood bank. The request seemed politically and financially reasonable. The Council would have to act on it Thursday. If they turned it down, the public heat would flame their way. If they agreed, he would get credit for instigating the offer. And if the money was actually spent, then the Ripper would have been caught and he again, as Lord Mayor, could claim a titbit of glory. If not, the money would remain unspent and no one could blame him for not trying. That was *realpolitik*. He rubbed his hands together and thanked his lucky stars for a no-lose situation. Murder was not all bad.

In the Vestry Hall in Cable Street, St. George-in-the-East, Coroner Baxter presided over the second day of the inquest into the Berner Street death of Elizabeth Stride. Once again, the overworked police department sent only DI Reid to report on the inquiry. The strain on manpower was wearing the police down both individually and én masse.

Much of the early part of the inquest focused on the membership of the Workingmen's Club, the nationalities of its members being of primary concern. Another line of inquiry targeted a nearby beer dispensary. What any of this had to do with the murder went unquestioned, except by a few people in the audience, including Reid, who had almost learned all of his lines for his upcoming theatrical production by reciting them in his head as the inanities continued.

Baxter examined PC 252H Henry Lamb, the first policeman on the scene, with microscopic care. Lamb noted that fixed-point men ceased duty at 1 a.m., peace and order being left to the beat men thereafter. The fixed-point man nearest the Berner Street murder was rooted to the end of Grove Street. Drawn from his theatrical lines, Reid idly wondered why, if the fixed-point system was so superior, it was abandoned an hour past midnight.

Baxter questioned Lamb's every wink and blink, and criticized him for not posting men at various exits from the club's yard to possibly prevent the murderer from escaping. The 37-year-old constable could only say, "I believed the murderer had escaped before I arrived."

The slayer not being on hand to validate the belief didn't help the sacrificial Lamb.

Baxter then called Edward Spooner, a horse keeper with Messrs. Meredith, biscuit makers. Spooner described how two Jews ran up to Grove Street looking for a policeman but failed to find one.

Where the hell was the point man? Reid wondered, jotting down a note to pass along to Abberline. Probably slipped into a pub for a pint before closing time and never returned. Once Abberline found out who it was, that man would have plenty of time for pints, if not the shillings to pay for them.

Baxter next called Mary Malcolm, a tailor's wife, who introduced a surprise into the proceedings. She said the body she had viewed yesterday at the mortuary was not Elizabeth Stride, but that of her sister Elizabeth Watts.

Reid was one of the few in the hall not surprised. Abberline had told him that when Mrs. Malcolm first viewed the body on Sunday, she could not identify it. When she returned to the mortuary on Monday, twice, she finally identified the body based not on her face, but on a small dark mark on one leg, which Mary said was from an old adder bite. Mary explained that she had not recognized her sister the day before because she saw the body in gaslight at 10 at night.

When Baxter pressed her, Mrs. Malcolm proceeded to evoke the supernatural to aid her claim. She explained how she woke the night of the murder, sensed a pressure on her breast, felt kisses on her cheek, and was certain her sister needed her.

With a smirk, Reid wondered whether she was sleeping alone.

Mrs. Malcolm stated that when she later read the Sunday paper the premonition returned.

"The curse of the Phantom," a man beside Reid proclaimed. "You can feel it in the air."

"Curse, my arse," his mate retorted. "All she felt was the draft from an open window."

Laughter turned to sympathy when the verbose Mrs. Malcolm explained between sobs that the news of her sister's death and the public exposure of her sister's way of life would kill her other remaining sister. Her sisterly concern melted instantly away, however, when she described how she was glad to get rid of the deceased anytime the victim visited her. The deceased had once left a naked baby at her door. Reid sensed that after that story the audience felt that if the victim were sister Watts, she got what she deserved. Sympathy was fine, but it was wasted on the sinful. When Mary recounted that the suspected father of the abandoned babe turned out to be a policeman, eyebrows were lifted. One young wag near Reid said, "Well at least the police are capable of doing something."

When Baxter pressed her on the identification, Mary said, "I have no shadow of a doubt about the identity of the body."

Reid jotted down notes; was the body that of Elizabeth Stride or Elizabeth Watts? Or had they been one and the same person? Many of these women changed names more often than Reid changed suits. Reid doubted Mary's testimony, but the possibility of an error in identification had to be investigated; in fact, it was already under investigation.

Dr. Blackwell followed. A stir of horror ran through the onlookers when he said the deceased had probably taken a minute and a half to bleed to death, since her neck had been cut only on one side and not completely severed. Some imaginative souls wondered whether she was awake but unable to call out due to her severed throat during those horrible 90 seconds.

A reporter, Jennings, whom Reid knew and sat near, whispered, "Some French savants believe a thought or two still passes through a severed head as it rolls down the ramp into the basket after the guillotine blade falls."

"Isn't a victim with a slit throat in the same situation?" Pierce whispered back. "After all, there's still blood in the brain."

The inquest ended on such shudder-inducing thoughts.

Crime continued. Many people tried to do or did bodily harm to sundry others, but the shocker came at 3:20 p.m. when Fred Wilborn, a carpenter, working for Grover and Sons on the foundation of the new Metropolitan Police Headquarters on the Thames Embankment, unearthed a neatly done up parcel in one of the cellars. Although hoping for buried treasure, to Wilborn's shock and horror, the package instead contained a woman's badly decomposed upper torso.

"Under our very noses?" Abberline asked on viewing the grisly hulk of decaying human. It was simply a trunk; no arms, no legs and no head.

Investigation found that a woman's arm found on 1 October in Lambeth seemed to match the torso. Another arm found several weeks before in the Thames matched up fairly well on the other side of the trunk. Since the limbs had been detached in an extremely unskilled manner, the examining doctors concluded this butchery was not connected with the Ripper murders. Abberline and the investigating inspectors agreed.

It was evening when Abberline, Helson, Chandler, Swanson, Major Smith and McWilliam, head of the City detectives, gathered at CID headquarters to compare notes over a dinner of roast pork with specialty rose potatoes, carrots, cauliflower, fricassee with rice, and dinner rolls with various jams and jellies, all well irrigated with tea, coffee and tankards of English, Irish and Scottish beer.

"We're investigating a doctor out in Brixton," Abberline said, eyeing the meal that attracted his gaze, moistened his mouth and filled his nose with wonderful scents. "Constable Spicer found him in a dark alley off Heneage Street with a local tart. Someone on the desk at Spicer's station house didn't even look into a bag the doctor was toting. I'll drop around after we eat and give that desk man a piece of my mind, since he appears in desperate need of it. The doctor himself seems to be harmless enough. Immoral as all get out, but harmless." Gesturing at the meal, he said, "Helson and I usually survive on pub grub. Who do we have to thank for laying on this most appetizing table?"

"My treat from Dick's," Major Smith said. "In the interest of inter-departmental cooperation."

"Hear, hear," the other men said as they began to eat.

Spreading a map on the only space left at the table, Abberline said, "The cloth from Eddowes' apron was left in Goulston Street, here. She was last seen after leaving Bishopsgate station heading down Houndsditch. That means she probably met the Ripper around the corner of Aldgate and Houndsditch. They could have walked along Duke to where they were seen about to go into Mitre Square."

A long discussion followed about possible routes the Ripper could have taken. Unfortunately, there were too many possible routes in the maze-like area to be of much use to the investigation.

"Eddowes's heart was missing," Major Smith announced as he finished a cauliflower bathed in cream sauce. "Contrary to press reports, her head was not severed and placed beneath one of her arms, although her ears and nose were cut off, her body disemboweled and the flesh torn from the forehead and cheeks."

The men, hardened by the past few weeks, continued to eat.

"The severing of Eddowes' nose may have been the murderer's way of branding her rightly or wrongly a syphilitic," Abberline said, gesturing with his fork, which was laden with tender pork glistening under a honey glaze. In its final stage, tertiary syphilis ate away the nose bone, leaving a hole in the patient's face.

"Might the killer have syphilis?" Chandler asked as he drained his Rogers' ale.

Swanson said, "Given how common syphilis is, I doubt it would help us find a suspect anyway." Syphilis was the scourge of the Victorian Age. It was so prevalent that artificial noses of sterling silver were on display and for sale at the Great Exhibition in 1851.

The detectives continued their discussion and their meal and, by the end, they were full and some distance from sober, but no closer to finding the Ripper. At that very moment, however, across East London the cases looked like they might be solved.

The young man tottered into Bishopsgate Street Police Station somewhat like a squirrel crossing a busy road. He would start left, stop, evidently undecided whether to go in that direction, suddenly lurch right, take a step or two…or three, then go wobbling to the left. Inspector George Izzard, working the night desk, smiled. In past days it had been cheap rum, now it was the low price of gin. Rum, gin, whiskey, whatever, the effect was the same.

Finally reaching the front desk, the young man introduced himself, "I am Will…William Bull. I wish to give myself up for the murder in Aldgate on Saturday night or, if you wish, Sunday morning."

Trying to ignore the wafting whiffs of alcohol from the man before him, Izzard placed his pipe on the edge of his residue-ridden ashtray and said, "Well, we'll need a few details. You don't mind if Constable Melton takes notes?"

Bull didn't mind. Melton, eagerness almost exploding from his youthful frame, jumped to the job. This would be something to tell his grandchildren, when he had some; the night he arrested Jack the Ripper.

"Tell me now," Izzard said, "in your own words, what you did Sunday morning."

"I'm a medical student at London Hospital. About two in the morning, I think it was, I met a woman in Aldgate. I went with her up a narrow street, not a main road. I gave her a half-crown. While walking together a second man came up and he took the half-crown from her."

"And you did nothing?"

Bull grasped his head, saying, "My poor head. I shall go mad. I have it. I must put up with it."

Izzard picked up his pipe and asked, "What did you do with the clothing you had on after you committed the murder?"

"I threw them and the knife in the Lea, near where it flows into the Thames."

Izzard nodded, filling his pipe with tobacco and glancing over at the immensely involved Melton, who was writing furiously, getting every vital word. "I think you better take Mr. Bull down to the cells, Melton. You go with the constable, Mr. Bull."

Melton escorted Bull away. Izzard sent a runner around to London Hospital. Melton was hardly back from the tombs, glowing and crowing about the lucky break they had caught, when the runner returned from the hospital. There was no such medical student as William Bull.

"I think we'll find most of what that poor fellow said to be nonsense. Too bad," Izzard said. "When he sobers up, he'll probably deny knowing or having anything to do with the murder."

Melton looked crestfallen.

"Fifth confession I've heard in two weeks," Izzard went on as he lit his horn pipe. "Why anyone feels so terrible about himself that he has to own up to a piece of butchery like that Mitre Square slaughter, I'll never know. Although this fellow did complain about his head. Maybe his brain's addled or injured in some way."

"What do I do with these notes?" Melton asked, holding a wad of papers curled from all his writing.

"File them."

The dejected Melton couldn't bring himself to call it a confession, so he filed the incident under the heading, Bull: Story.

As the day waned, PC 101H Robert Spicer looked over his evening assignment. Christ! He had been switched to a far less desirable beat. Accosting that Brixton doctor had led to its rapid repercussions. The doctor was perhaps a harmless man whose sexual tastes ran to the disrespectable, but like most sinners, sexual or otherwise, he was not a forgiving man. Humiliated and angered by the incident, he had extracted his vengeance. A word to the right official and Spicer was relegated to London's least of beats. He was so far out in the sticks he wondered if his left elbow would brush the remains of Hadrian's Wall. He had been ordered to keep an eye out for any damp linens left out to dry, for fear they might be stolen. He fumed; reduced to guarding wet laundry. Spicer stomped along wondering where to look for another job; maybe he'd stop at a pub, if they had them this far out, and consider the matter. Yes, he would do just that.

Wednesday, 3 October

Unsettled weather held sway as a succession of clouds brought a steady drizzle to the metropolis. Police made facsimiles of the Ripper letter and card and turned them into posters with which to plaster the East End. The posters asked that if anyone recognized the handwriting to contact the police immediately. Assisting the police as well as their circulation numbers, several newspapers published them the next day. Even if they appeared to be helping the police, *The Star* damned the Met as "rotten to the core," while the *East London Advertiser* said there was "no detective force in the proper sense of the word in London at all." While the press brutally criticized the Metropolitan Police, most newspapers praised the City of London Police, who were only dealing with one murder, for their courtesy and cooperation. Worse, a semi-starved William Waddle, the Durham mutilator and murderer, had been captured near Newcastle, not by the police, but by a civilian, which only worsened the Met's reputation.

Crime continued its violent career in the East End. Mary M'Carthy jabbed a knife into Ann Mason's face during a spat in a Spitalfields lodging house. George Nicholson, a journeyman baker, was remanded for the axe murder of his wife. Charles Ludwig, who had chased Alexander Finlay round and round his coffee stall, was found to have threatened to stab Elizabeth Burns of 53 Flower and Dean Street. Since Ludwig had been in custody during the latest Ripper rampage, he was exonerated from any connection with the hideous mutilation murders and released. Threatening a person or persons with a knife was evidently not a punishable offense in Whitechapel. The police were well aware that Ludwig had a 'double' who could have been the culprit, which would make proving the case against Charles in court extremely difficult, if not impossible.

Jennings spent the afternoon in *The Empire* newsroom reading letters from readers obsessed with penning their views on the identity of the Ripper and how he might be apprehended.

"This idiot suggests we send woman decoys all over Whitechapel with a steel collar attached to a storage battery around their necks," he told Pierce, who was intermittently writing a story. "If the Ripper grabs one of them he gets a shock. I'm not sure how they're supposed to lug a big battery about except perhaps hide it in an enormous bustle. Another guy wants women to carry a piece of paper covered with bird lime so when the Ripper strikes, the victim can slap him on the back with the lime paper, thereby identifying him for all to see."

"What happens to the woman?"

"Why, she gets killed, Old Boy."

The short dumpy woman with the over-jowled face would have been unnoticed on the streets of Spitalfields or Whitechapel if not for an accident of birth and a peculiar social propensity for people to elevate certain of their equals to an existence of elegance. The woman was Victoria, Queen of the United Kingdom of Great Britain and Ireland, Empress of India and ruler of an empire that covered far more than its fair share of the globe. Her austere expression and plain black garments belied the opulence and wealth her position represented. Like anyone hoisted to social prominence by conditions of attitude, her exalted personage was perched on a pedestal of precarious opinion. This led her to naturally and firmly believe she deserved all the respect, honours and rewards heaped upon her. What was perhaps more amazing was that even the starving minions over whom she reigned also firmly believed she deserved her power and position.

Queen Victoria's brow creased in serious thought as her private secretary read her a petition that had been signed by 5,000 of the most humble labouring women of the East End. The instigators of the petition were the far less humble leaders of several religious agencies and educational services. Victoria was a sincerely kind person and despite her insular position, she felt a certain compassion for the drabs of the East End. The Queen was still a mortal woman despite all the tuneful entreaties to God to single her out for 'eternal' salvation.

"This we shall have to act upon," she announced.

Her secretary was soon reading the petition aloud to several advisors who had been hurriedly summoned. The petitioners mentioned feeling horror at the dreadful sins that had been committed in their midst because of the shame that had fallen on their neighbourhood; "We have learnt much of the lives of those of our sisters who have lost a firm hold on goodness and who are leading sad and degraded lives." It was not long before an expertly worded reply was drafted. The working poor could be pacified with the fact Her Majesty had been graciously pleased to receive their petition. The Secretary of State wrote that he hoped the influence for good that the petitioners could exercise and the pressures the police could bring to bear would mitigate the evils of whoredom.

Such replies were as writing on the wind in the world of diplomacy, their true importance signified by the fact it took three weeks before the reply reached the instigators; the same day the petition and answer were printed in the popular press.

Jennings stared at the petition and said, "This bloody thing isn't condemning the Whitechapel murderer. It's arguing prostitution is a greater sin than homicide."

Pierce looked up from a letter he was reading and said, "Some would argue those women don't have to prostitute themselves. It's their choice."

"Then murder is the Ripper's choice."

As he tossed the latest letter onto his desk, Pierce said, "Some bugger thinks the killer's an American Indian."

"Probably is," Old Boy said. "But certainly not a Mohican."

"Why not?"

"None left, at least according to Cooper."

One man penning a letter this Wednesday evening may have made all the other letters tolerable. He was Fred W. P. Jago of Plymouth, who wrote to the Editor of *The Times*:

"The [Jack the Ripper] letter is said to be smeared with blood, and there is on it the print of the corrugated surface of the thumb." Jago paused to dip his nib. "The surface of a thumb so printed is as clearly indicated as are the printed letters formed by any kind of type. Thus there is a possibility of identifying the blood print on the letter with the thumb that made it, because the surface markings on no two thumbs are alike, and this a low power used in a microscope could reveal." Jago suggested the thumb print be compared with the thumb print of each major suspect.

When someone mentioned the gist of the letter to him, Sir Charles had a man check on Jago's background. When the report on Jago reached his desk, he saw that Jago was, of all things, the author of an English-Cornish dictionary and another book on the ancient dialect of Cornwall.

"What in the name of all that's holy would such a man know about criminal investigations," Sir Charles demanded, "let alone such a bizarre and I suspect completely unfounded subject as finger marks?"

"He does hold a bachelor's of medicine from the University of London," his secretary pointed out.

"Lacked the proper sort of family for Oxford or Cambridge, did he?"

The third day of the Stride inquest opened at 1 p.m. at the classically elegant St. George-in-the-East Vestry. Elizabeth Tanner, deputy of a common lodging house, Catherine Lane, a charwoman living at Tanner's lodging house, Charles Preston, a barber, and Michael Kidney, a waterside labourer, all identified the victim as Elizabeth Stride. Mary Malcolm's testimony was outnumbered and outdone.

The identity of the victim apparently finally unequivocally settled, Coroner Baxter asked Edward Johnson, who assisted Dr. Blackwell, to describe his examination of the body. Johnson provided no new revelations, at least for Reid, who attended.

Thomas Coram, who worked for a cocoanut dealer, described finding a knife on Whitechapel Road opposite No. 253, a laundry, on a doorstep the morning of the murder. The production of the knife created a whispering sensation in the packed room, its discovery not having been generally known. It was a knife such as would be used by a baker in his trade; flat on the top and not pointed, as a butcher's knife would be. The blade, which was discoloured with something resembling blood, was a foot long and an inch broad. The black handle was six inches in length and strongly riveted in three places.

"Not exactly a knife for dismembering someone," Pierce muttered to a *Star* correspondent beside him.

Coram said, "There was a handkerchief round the handle of the knife; the handkerchief having been first folded and then twisted round the blade. A policeman coming towards me, I called his attention to the knife, which I did not touch."

The policeman Coram summoned, PC 282H Joseph Drage was next on the stand. He was on fixed-point duty in Whitechapel Street opposite Great Garden Street the night of the Double Murder. He said he questioned Coram closely as to what he was doing out so late, searched him, took the knife and then made Coram accompany him to the Leman Street station.

"Christ, is paranoia a prerequisite for joining the police force?" *The Star* reporter asked Pierce.

"Certainly helps, especially paranoia about foreigners, the Irish, socialists, anarchists and trade unionists."

The coroner concluded by asking Constable Drage if Coram was sober at the time.

"And they bitch about a lack of cooperation on the part of the East Enders," Pierce muttered, shaking his head.

Baxter then called Dr. Phillips, who described his examination of the body, which revealed little new beyond what was already known by Reid or Pierce, who had gathered most of the details from mortuary attendants who favoured a free pint over the police policy of secrecy. Baxter adjourned the inquest for the day.

A quiet-spoken wisp of a man held an emotion-charged interview with Abberline at his CID office in Met Headquarters. It was one of hundreds of such interviews and whether it was of significance was as much Abberline's as anyone's guess. The visitor finally left, head bowed, body bent forward, face deeply troubled. Abberline thoughtfully tapped ash from his pipe as he rubbed the back of his left knee. He just didn't know. He just didn't know.

"You look troubled," Helson said as he strode in for yet another meeting with Abberline to discuss next action steps for the investigation. "Anything to do with the chap who just stepped out?"

"Yes," Abberline said, checking the time on his hunting watch. The others should be here soon. "He thinks his brother is the Ripper."

"Been 30 people in here accusing one relative or another. I'd put my brother-in-law's name in, but he has an alibi for one of the murders."

"I know, I know, but this fellow's story had a different feel to it."

"Who's the unlucky relation?"

"Chap named Montague John Druitt. The brother called him 'sexually insane,' whatever that means. Montague's a cricketer. Trained as a barrister-at-law and is an assistant master at a school in Blackheath."

Montague John Druitt

"Blackheath; not too far away. He'd be busy during the week. Fits in with the weekend and holiday murders, and he'd probably be off at the end of August for summer recess when Tabram was murdered."

"Respectable family background. Went to Winchester and Oxford on scholarships, so he's clever enough. Born 1857—makes him about 31—on the young side for the estimates of the Ripper's age, but who knows? The family's prominent in Dorset. Father was an M.D."

"Where's Druitt's law practice?"

"That's the intriguing part; Number 9, Kings Bench Walk. Brother says

Druitt never really practices."

"Can't blame him; too many solicitors and barristers for more than one in four to make a living."

"Compared to his father, sounds as if Montague's what that socialist writer Shaw calls a 'downstart.'"

"A what?"

"An 'upstart' starts low in life and goes up, making something of himself. A 'downstart' starts high and plunges thereafter. So if your son becomes Met Commissioner, he'd be a grand upstart."

"Beyond measure."

"We better find out all we can about Druitt. Kings Bench Walk is only a few minutes from the scenes of the murders. Set a couple of men to watching him, and increase our efforts on finding those bloody lunatic Russians."

Helson nodded, scribbling notes. "The others should be here in a few minutes." He consulted his notes and said, "Our men rescued John Lock, a seaman, from a crowd in the vicinity of Ratcliffe Highway. The crowd chased him shouting 'Leather Apron' and 'Jack the Ripper.'"

"His crime?" Abberline asked, rubbing his eyes with the palms of his hands. He could use a nice long ten-minute nap, but even that was a dream at this stage of the investigation.

"His light plaid suit had paint stains on it, which the crowd took for blood."

"I won't paint my study anytime soon then."

"At least not red."

"Next?" In this investigation, there was always a next.

"An immigrant Hungarian Jew, Israel Schwartz, who came into Leman Street station on the 30th in the evening."

"We're just hearing about it now?"

"Statements cross many desks before they even reach mine. Schwartz said he witnessed an attack on a woman he identified as Elizabeth Stride at 12:45 a.m. at the entrance to Dutfield's Yard the morning of the Berner Street murder."

Abberline opened his eyes wide and stared at Helson; maybe, just maybe an authentic witness.

"The man tried to pull the woman into the street, turned her round and threw her down on the footway. She screamed three times, but not loudly. Schwartz, to avoid the confrontation, crossed the street and saw another man, lighting a pipe. Schwartz walked away, but the second man followed him. Frightened, Schwartz ran as far as the railway arch, but the man didn't follow."

"Please tell me he was able to provide a description."

"He did indeed; the man with the pipe was aged 35, 5 feet 11 inches with a fresh complexion and light brown hair. He was dressed in a dark overcoat, an old black hard felt hat with a wide brim and had a clay pipe."

"A little tall for our man, but he may have seemed taller to Schwartz if he was coming after him. Send out a description and let's chase him down."

"Got a man who can identify the Ripper, sir," a constable said as he stuck his head through Abberline's doorway.

"Send him in," Abberline said, hope springing eternal.

"Didn't want to waste your time, sir," the constable said with a smirk. "Some medium called Lees; says he had a vision of the killer. Sent him packing back to whatever asylum he escaped from. Sergeant McPherson called him a madman and a fool, which probably helped him on his way."

Night came. The tall, well-dressed man emerged like an apparition from the shadows. The woman gasped and threw her hand over her breast, her lower lip flickering in fearful anticipation. The high black walls of Cable Street, just south of Commercial Road, enclosed the avenue in a trench of darkness. Where once men had twisted hemp ropes into ships' cables, faraway street lamps cast a ghost-like luminescence on face and figure on the empty road.

"Come with me, lady," the man commanded. "Come! Or I'll rip you up." His voice was as steely as a blade. "I'll rip you," he repeated, tugging at the woman's arm.

She screamed again—a terrified, primitive screech that echoed and re-echoed across the chasm of brick and cobblestone. It was a scream of pure terror.

And it worked!

The man bolted. A policeman, approaching from a block away, gave chase. The policeman soon overtook and, with a little assistance from his 17-inch truncheon, overpowered the man. The suspect was hustled to the Leman Street station before the gathering crowd could do him much lasting damage. A couple of enthusiastic onlookers did get in a punch or three, but the blows rained down on the man's shoulders and arms as he cowered in police custody, missing his cranium. At the station he asked the startled inspector in charge, "Are you the boss?"

Despite the Americanism, within the hour the man was cleared of any Ripper connections.

Abberline, Swanson and Smith compared notes, discussed strategy and shared an evening meal at Abberline's club.

"This Jewish thing on the wall," Smith asked, as he sliced his mutton, "do you think it's anything more than a tissue of lies?"

"Four feet off the ground, written in chalk," Abberline said, sipping his ale. "Children practice their letters that way in the East End."

Smith said, "Wish my children's writing was as well-formed. Sure it was a child?"

Abberline shrugged.

Swanson said as he speared a carrot with his fork, "I was told the writing was blurred, so it might have been old. Smith said Halse thought it looked recent."

"Walter Drew wonders why the killer would delay his escape by writing on a wall, although he admits murderers do foolish things," Abberline said. "In any case, in a Jewish section, such anti-Jewish graffito would not last long, so it was probably recent."

"And the apron?" Smith asked chewing on a fatty piece of mutton.

"Might have dropped it near the graffito to mislead or by chance, unrelated to the murder. If he dropped it 20 feet farther on, it would have been near a completely different set of graffito—it's all over the East End." Abberline frowned. "The Ripper may be a Jew-baiter, but that doesn't help much. There's no shortage of anti-Semites in London."

"The writing was on a building in which many Jews live," Swanson said. "It's clearly intended to point blame at them."

Smith nodded. "There's a rumour that Jack is a Jew. That double-negative phrase—'the Juwes are not the ones to be blamed for nothing'—could be an attempt to divert suspicion from the Jews; at least in Jack's warped mind."

"The Jews are also among the leaders of these vigilance committees," Swanson said.

"Doesn't say, of course, that Jack isn't a Jew." Smith shook his head. "Regardless of its provenance, I can't believe Sir Charles ordered it rubbed out."

Abberline asked, "You know what that little bit of stupidity has led to?"

Smith smiled. "Some East Enders, the more suspicious ones, and most West Siders think we're covering up for the Jews. The very thing Sir Charles wanted to avoid—hatred of the Jews—has increased. You can't win. Oh, by the way, I did find out one intriguing thing. The Russians often use the double negative in their native language. It may not mean anything, but it could mean Jack was saying the Jews are not blamed without good reason—that is, if he's Russian."

"Helson told me the *Pall Mall Gazette* said Jews in the area speak a hybrid of Yiddish in which Jews is spelt 'J-u-w-e-s,'" Abberline said. "But Sir Charles told me Acting Chief Rabbi Hermann Adler told him that in Yiddish, Jews is written 'Y-i-d-d-e-n' and that he doesn't know of any dialect or language in which 'Jews' is spelt 'J-u-w-e-s.' Sir Charles is still concerned about possible anti-Semitic riots, so he's issuing a statement to the press making it clear that 'J-u-w-e-s' is not the spelling of Jews in Yiddish. Even so, he believes the writing was written with the intention of inflaming the public mind against the Jews."

"I agree," Major Smith said. "I've heard we have multiple spellings of the graffito anyway, since several constables copied it down, each in a different way. City D.C. Halse reported it as 'J-u-w-e-s.'"

"Met constable Long reported it as 'J-e-w-e-s,'" Abberline countered.

Smith grinned. "And the City force backs Halse's spelling, while the Met backs their man, Long."

"Constables aren't known for their spelling ability," Abberline said. "I have suspects with at least four spellings of their names in my files."

"Whatever the spelling, you can twist that writing six ways 'til breakfast and still not get any definite sense out of it," Swanson said, cutting up a boiled potato into consumable sections. "This ale is rather fine, by the way. My father would have savored every sip, even if it isn't his brew."

Abberline said, "The real trouble is that we've got no certain means of identifying people. Oh, Bertillon's method of measuring this or that limb is fine if you've already caught the bloke, but the Frenchman's system is of no use with the criminal who's still on the loose or has never been caught."

"Lombroso, the Italian alienist, has done some work on trying to identify a criminal head shape," Smith said. "Trouble is, it seems to me, it's what's in the head, not outside it, that counts."

Abberline rubbed his forehead and said, "Most of the Yard believes the graffito is a red herring but, gentlemen, even if the graffito was written by the murderer, how does it help us identify our killer?"

Chapter Sixteen

Thursday, 4 October

F. S. Langham, coroner for the City of London, opened the first day of the inquest at the Coroner's Court, Golden Lane into the death in Mitre Square of Catherine Eddowes. Major Smith and City Superintendent Alfred Lawrence Foster attended for the police. A large crowd filled the court, while those who could not fit inside gathered outside, hearing snippets of testimony as it was passed person to person from inside the court.

The inquiry started with Eliza Gold, Catherine Eddowes' sister, identifying the body, as did John Kelly, an amply muscled labourer who had lived with Catherine for seven years, but had known her as Catherine Conway. Frederick William Wilkinson, deputy in Eddowes' lodging house at Flower and Dean Street, had little to add, nor did PC Watkin, City Police, who described his actions the morning of the murder. Baxter called Frederick William Foster, an architect, who provided a plan of the square where Eddowes' body was found. When asked, Foster said it took 12 minutes to walk from Berner Street to Mitre Square—about three-quarters of a mile.

Baxter next called Inspector Collard, who testified that he found no sign of a struggle and no evidence to indicate that Eddowes had been murdered somewhere else and moved. Dr. Brown then testified about his examination of the body. The crowd appeared somewhat disappointed when Brown said that Stride's body had no mutilation beyond the death-inducing damage to her neck. The day ended with the announcement, with the jury's hearty approval, of the Lord Mayor's £500 reward.

A few new street lamps were installed and a few more were ordered for Whitechapel and Spitalfields. Mary Malcolm's sister, Elizabeth Watts, turned up alive, thereby confirming Stride as the official Berner Street victim. Many preachers prepared speeches and Sunday sermons on the futility of the desolate way-of-life and the wastefulness of the Whitechapel/Spitalfields way-of-death. Suspects Severin Klosowski, Michael Ostrog and Nicholai Vasiliev were still lost in the labyrinth of East End common lodging houses and tenements, if they had ever even been in London in the first place. The fiery-eyed bald man who had caught Abberline's eye had not been seen anywhere in Stepney and the detectives detailed to watch the new suspect, Druitt, were unable to find him at his listed residence in Blackheath, the school or at his office in King's Bench Walk.

The air was ocean blue in Abberline's office. The paint was blistered and Abberline ended with a sore throat, shaky hands and a terrible giddy feeling in his head on top of the numbing heaviness behind his left knee. It was not in his nature to reprimand anyone. Such confrontations always left him in a whirlpool of emotional stress, but this had been necessary. He had put it off as long as he dared.

The object of Abberline's assault was Desk Sergeant Beck. The objective was to ensure that Beck, or anyone else—news of the dressing-down would leak its way through the force faster than any order—never let a suspect like the Brixton doctor go unsearched ever again.

When the portly policeman's harangue was finally over, Beck left grateful that he was still a sergeant; losing the desk for a time didn't matter. He would go on night patrol with a grim determination. From now on the Met would treat toffs far less tenderly.

Abberline leaned back, closed his eyes for a moment to regain his composure and opened them to stare at the pile of letters that publication of the Ripper letter and card had evoked. Thinking that Swanson was supposed to be handling the paperwork for the case, Abberline sighed, but realized that he was the one who wanted to see everything first. You never knew what might trigger a new avenue of investigation, an avenue that just might lead to Jack.

"A Mr. Lees to see you, sir," a constable said.

Abberline tried to recall the name, but could not. A tall man with a moustache and a well-trimmed, pointed beard walked in, hesitating at the door and then again a step inside. His eyes were large and his receding hairline gave his face an open appearance that encouraged trust.

Abberline asked him to sit down, glad to avoid more paperwork, at least for a time. Abberline listened while the medium explained who he was and then told his tale in a well-modulated, soothing voice. Abberline thought about bloodhounds and photographs of victims' eyes—and wondered about clairvoyance. Many a famous and not-so-famous personage believed with all their heart and mind in such visions, including, it was said, the Queen. Abberline did not know what to believe and if the press heard the police had turned away anyone willing to help, there would be headlines galore castigating that officer by name and undoubtedly former rank.

"Contact me if you have another vision," Abberline said as they shook hands.

"Thank you so very much," Lees said, holding onto Abberline's hand longer than was usual. "You won't believe the reception I received when I came before to offer my services."

"I can well imagine," Abberline said with a knowing smile. "Most of our constables are ex-labourers and have rather an aptitude for full-flavoured speech."

When Lees had departed, Inspector Reid arrived to fill Abberline in on the latest details of yesterday's Stride inquest. "Phillips mentioned finding a bluish discolouration on the chest, shoulders and under the collar bone, just like the other two."

"I've seen those bruises and discolouration before, usually with a peaceful look," Abberline said. "It's always been on a strangled corpse. That's why they can't cry out. If I'm right, he's a powerful blighter."

"There is one other bit. Some people feel Stride may not have been a Ripper victim. Her body wasn't mutilated and her throat was cut from left to right. All the others were slashed from right to left."

"Nichols might have been from left to right, and Diemschitz might have interrupted the Ripper before he could carve up Stride. The left-to-right business could just mean he grabbed Nichols from a different angle, perhaps from behind, or that he's ambidextrous. Given that the strangulations were committed with bare hands, the more pertinent question is; who's likely to have strong forearms and wrists?"

"A labourer."

"Descriptions of him don't fit a labourer—but maybe a gentleman athlete. I wonder if he's left- or right-handed—or ambidextrous."

"Who's that?"

"Fellow named Montague Druitt."

Helson flopped into a chair in Abberline's office, tossed his hat on the desk, sneezed and sighed, before saying, "We can cover this island in railway lines, control cholera and rule the waves, but we can't conquer a bloody cold." He blew his nose. He looked like a re-warmed corpse. "I found out a few things about that Blackheath teacher, Druitt. He's had some trouble at his school, George Valentine's school, but no one will say exactly what. All very mysterious."

"Could be trouble with the students." Abberline cut into a thick slab of roast beef a constable had brought for dinner from a nearby pub. He was saving the gravy soaked Yorkshire pudding for last.

"Could be, but could be fiddling the books, missing lectures or cheering too loudly for a rival school." Helson sneezed again, rubbing his red nose with a blue handkerchief. "He was in Greater London the morning of Chapman's murder. She was killed about 5:30 and he played cricket for the Blackheath Cricket Club against the Brothers Christopherson on the Rectory Field at Blackheath at 11:30 that morning."

"Only a half dozen miles away. We live in a mobile society, even working stiffs take a holiday train down to Margate for a rare day off. The East End to Blackheath is as easy as walking across Commercial Street; probably easier now with the tram construction."

"Druitt was playing in Dorset for Canford against Wimbourne the morning of Nichol's death."

"Commit the murder, back to his chambers for a clean up, grab his cricket kit and catch the first train to Dorset in what, three hours?"

"Hard to believe anyone could wander around Whitechapel half the night, carve a woman up, then calmly go off and put on their best whites to play a cricket match," Helson said, consulting his notes. "Tabram died on Tuesday, 7 August. The Friday and Saturday before, Druitt played cricket for Bournemouth against the touring Parsees at Dean Park, Bournemouth, and on the following Friday and Saturday, he played at Dean Park again for the Gentlemen of Dorset in a match against Bournemouth. Don't know where he was during the week in between."

"Is he right or left handed?" Abberline took his first bite of pudding; crisp exterior and fluffy interior—excellent.

"Take your pick. He's ambidextrous and bull strong. He was a gifted Fives player at Winchester College. Won the School Singles title." Helson snuffled, burying his reddened nose in his handkerchief. When it reemerged, he said, "Druitt's brother lied to you, sir. He said there was only their mother and him left in the family. There's another brother: Edward. He's 29, a cricketer like Montague, and unlike Montague, a Royal Engineer."

"Which regiment?" Abberline stopped, pudding-laden fork half way between plate and mouth.

"My source wasn't certain. Godley's chasing it down."

"If it's the Royal Sussex Regiment, the 'M' on that envelope could be the start of Montague, not Mister, and it may not have been the envelope scrap Annie Chapman picked up."

"Why would the brother lie to you?"

"To protect baby brother's good name, perhaps."

"The family is scalpel deep in doctors; the father, a cousin and some others, I think. Montague's the only one who hasn't been a success. Oh, I've got a picture of him. Here. Who do you think he looks like?"

Abberline took the photograph and stopped short. "Jesus, he's the spitting image of the Duke of Clarence. The Duke's been reported in Whitechapel, but they could be seeing Druitt, not Clarence."

A constable brought in a tray.

Abberline said, "I ordered you chicken soup and a hot totty. Any progress on that headless, limbless thing someone dumped on the site of our new home on the Embankment?"

"The medics think the torso is six weeks old and it doesn't seem Ripper connected." Helson sipped his steaming totty.

"I agree. It isn't his style. He dismembers; he doesn't amputate. And if that torso is that old, he'd have mentioned it in his note. He's proud of his work."

Helson started eating his soup slowly and methodically, as if willing his body to consume the food.

"Did you forward the letter threatening murders in Dublin to the authorities there?"

Helson nodded, finished a spoonful of soup and said, "The Garda are alerted. I also tracked down one Matthew Packer, a 58-year-old greengrocer who trades from his front window at 44 Berner Street. He told the police he neither saw nor heard anything the night of the Stride murder. Said he closed shop at 12:30 a.m. because of the rain. Then two days ago two private detectives employed by the Mile End Vigilance Committee, LeGrand and Batchelor, interviewed Packer. He told them he sold grapes to a man at about 11:45 the night of the murder who was with a woman fitting Stride's description."

"I heard rumours about grapes, but I didn't see any at the scene," Abberline said, cutting farther into his gravy covered Yorkshire pudding. He eyed the cauliflower on his plate and decided to leave it for last; some gravy might mask their taste admirably.

"Two sisters told a newspaper they saw a blood-stained grape stalk in the yard near where the body had lain. The private detectives claim they found the grape stalk in the yard."

"God save us from correspondents and private sodding detectives."

"They even got Packer to say the police hadn't questioned him. Here's his statement. We talked to him."

Abberline swallowed another mouthful of succulent pudding and said, "Pick him up and question him again."

"He may not like it."

"He bloody well better not like it; lying to the police. Cheek of the man. What does he think he's playing at?"

"I looked into the supposed private detectives."

"Let me guess, not the empire's most upstanding citizens," Abberline said, knowing notorious crimes often attracted the worst sorts of characters looking to turn a profit in various unsavory fashions.

"LeGrand has a long history of villainy dating back to 1877 when he was convicted of larceny and served eight years in prison. He has more aliases than our Russians. Batchelor's not much better."

Abberline sliced some boiled cauliflower and dragged it through the remaining gravy on his plate. "We were talking about Stride possibly not being a Ripper victim," he said. "I spoke with Dr. Phillips. He said Stride's neck cut had a 'very great dissimilarity' with Annie Chapman's cut. It was a deep cut to the spinal vertebrae in Chapman, but not in Stride. A 6- to 8-inch knife was used on Chapman, but Phillips thinks a short-bladed knife was used on Stride, such as those used by shoemakers."

Abberline chewed on the piece of cauliflower, wishing his plate held more gravy, even as he wondered for a moment what his Emma was having for dinner. He missed her and her cooking. "The murderer was probably scared off before he could mutilate Stride's body or cut her neck as deeply, and the same killer could easily have used different knives. Dr. Llewellyn thought Nichols was killed with a short-bladed knife, too." He chewed a little more and said, "This business will never be as neat and orderly as clockwork, will it?"

Friday, 5 October

William Bull—he of the aching head—was formally charged with the murder of Catherine Eddowes. It was quickly shown that Bull's confession was false. The presiding magistrate regretted not being able to charge Bull and hoped the sot would take the abstinence pledge. Elsewhere, the Clerkenwell murder trial of Henry Glennie had gone before the courts, but the Ripper's monopoly of the public's attention continued and Glennie's possible gory transgression of murdering a woman, Frances Maria Wright, received little attention. At another time it would have made headlines.

The fourth day of the Stride inquest at the Vestry Hall found Inspector Reid once again in attendance. He listened as Dr. Phillips testified, "The Coroner desired me to examine the two handkerchiefs which were found on the deceased. I did not discover any blood on them, and I believe that the stains on the larger handkerchief are those of fruit. Neither on the hands nor about the body of the deceased did I find grapes. I am convinced that the deceased had not swallowed either the skin or seed of a grape within many hours of her death."

Reid hoped the grape fiction would finally find its final resting place and be forever forgotten.

Turning to the knife that had been found, Dr. Phillips said, "The knife produced on the last occasion was delivered to me, properly secured, by a constable, and on examination I found it to be such a knife as is used in a chandler's shop and is called a slicing knife. It has blood upon it, which has characteristics similar to the blood of a human being."

Reid frowned. He thought experts could not distinguish between human and animal blood.

"It has been recently blunted," Phillips continued, "and its edge apparently turned by rubbing on a stone such as a kerbstone. It evidently was before a very sharp knife."

As the packed gallery listened intently, Phillips described the murder. He believed the murderer seized Stride by the shoulders and forced her to the ground. "From a position on her right side, he then cut her throat from left to right. The wound would have taken two seconds to inflict. The stream of blood would have been directed away from him into the gutter, so no blood would necessarily be on the killer." Phillips said he thought the killer had some anatomical knowledge, but did not elaborate.

Dr. Blackwell then testified largely in agreement with Dr. Phillips' conclusions, followed by Sven Ollsen, who was active in a Swedish Church in St. George-in-the-East, and who identified the victim, yet again, as Elizabeth Stride.

William Marshall, a labourer, testified that he recognized Stride's body as that of a woman he had seen with a man at about a quarter to 12 the night of the murder. Reid knew that Abberline and Swanson already had his statement, somewhere.

Marshall said, "The man had on a black coat and dark trousers. He seemed to me to be a middle-aged man. He had a round cap with a small peak, something like what a sailor would wear. He was about five-foot-six and rather stout. I'd say he was decently dressed. He had more the appearance of a clerk than anything else. I didn't see his face. I don't think he had whiskers, but I can't be sure."

"Did you hear him say anything?" Coroner Baxter asked.

"He was kissing her for some time. I heard him say, 'You would say anything but your prayers.' That's all."

A few in the crowd hoped she had.

Marshall added, "He was mild speaking. Appeared to be an educated man. They went down Berner Street."

"Which way?"

"Toward Number 40."

Copies of Marshall's description of the suspect had already been circulated to every police station in London. It was opposed by other descriptions including that of James Brown of 35 Fairclough, who was next to testify and had seen Stride with a man in a long dark overcoat. Did he see Stride or someone else? Reid had noticed a red rose set against a maidenhair fern on the breast of Stride's coat, which Brown did not mention. Did he forget or just not notice it? Unfortunately, Brown's possible Stride suspect had been in the shadows.

PC Smith testified next about his actions that night, followed by Stride's ex-bedmate Michael Kidney, who identified some of her effects. Philip Krantz, who worked in the printer's shop next to the working men's club, said he heard and saw nothing that night. Baxter next called Constable Albert Collins, who said he washed away the blood at 5:30 a.m. Last to testify was Reid, explaining the state of the investigation even as he wished he had far more to impart. With further investigation warranted, Baxter adjourned the inquest for a fortnight.

Robert Anderson, the new Assistant Police Commissioner called back from the continent, was summoned to Matthew's lair in the Home Office to join Sir Charles, Abberline, Swanson and Major Smith, who had also been ordered to the Home Secretary's side.

Matthews spoke directly to Anderson, "I can speak for Her Majesty's Government. We hold you responsible for finding the murderer."

A frown flitted across Anderson's face. "If I may be blunt, sir, I don't want the job. I'm ill, as I told you before I departed for the continent. Can't you find someone more suitable and in better health for the responsibility?"

Matthews shook his head. "No, I cannot. It is a matter I cannot and will not discuss. We have only just appointed you. We cannot keep shuffling administrators like a deck of cards before a game of bridge. The Prime Minister. . ."

Abberline watched Anderson and saw a look of acceptance on his face as the Home Secretary made his points in favour of Anderson being the only man for the job.

After Matthews finished, the devoutly religious Anderson said, "With all due respect to Sir Charles, the methods we're using are in my opinion, indefensible—scandalous. These women prostitute themselves in full sight of the law. We know what they are doing. We should arrest and lock every one of them up or tell them the truth: we can't protect them from this murderer."

"Don't be patently ridiculous," Sir Charles said.

"Oh, be quiet, Sir Charles, the government is considering your position," Matthews said, his flint-gray eyes as cold as a slug's.

Sir Charles sat frozen, stunned.

"We haven't the ability to lock them all up," Smith said, voicing Abberline's own thought. "There are 62 brothels in the Whitechapel division alone, with another 233 common lodging houses and, I would hazard, 1,200 prostitutes. We don't have enough constables to arrest them, let alone enough gaol cells to hold them."

"If they wished, such women could at least be off the streets at night," Anderson said.

"Most of them are on the streets because they're trying to earn the money to pay for a doss house for the night, so they can get off the streets," Abberline said.

Matthews said, "If we tell them we cannot protect them, the press will hear of it and roast us alive like effigies on Guy Fawkes Night."

He had made his point. Ignoring Sir Charles, Matthews began to interrogate

Abberline, Swanson and Smith about police procedure and the state of the investigation.

By the end of the meeting Anderson was left with a bureaucratic gun to his head, but Sir Charles had felt Matthew's cold, lawyerly tones tear into him like lead pellets. The erasure of the writing on the wall was a particular sore point.

"Why not cover the graffito until a photographer arrived? What could you possibly have been thinking of?" Matthews asked, his arrogant tone suggesting there could be no sensible answer.

There probably wasn't.

At the Commercial Street station, Chandler was dismayed as he ran his gaze down the latest list of Ripper confessors. "They seem to come out of the brickwork like so much loose mortar. Why would anyone even want to pretend to be that monster?"

"Never underestimate a person's, that is, a little insignificant person's burning desire to be significant," Abberline said, perusing a stack of reports on Chandler's desk from inspectors who had interviewed potential witnesses. "Just like any one of us gets a feeling of importance when we boast how well we've done at the track or at billiards, these fellows want attention. Bloody lucky none of them have garnered enough attention to get themselves lynched."

"More bad press for the Met." Chandler handed Abberline the *East End News* report on a Whitechapel District Board of Works meeting about "The Mysterious Atrocities." Abberline wondered if Helson and Chandler spent their lives reading newspapers, as so many appeared to do these days. Relieved to avoid the reports for a moment, Abberline read, "The marvelous inefficiency of the police in the detection of crime was forcibly shown in the fact that in the very same block containing Mitre Square...and at a moment when the whole area was full of police just after the murder, the Aldgate Post Office was entered and ransacked, and property to the value of hundreds of pounds taken clear away under the very noses of the 'guardians of peace and order.'" Abberline stopped reading and muttered a curse. "At least no one was murdered in the burglary."

He skimmed the rest of the article, which recounted the common criticism of Sir Charles that the police were too militarized to be an effective detection force, although the reporter at least pointed out that having a constable on every corner to deter crime would be far too costly for the public purse to bear. Even so, the Board agreed to petition Sir Charles to increase the number of police in Whitechapel to prevent a repetition of the murders.

"If we transfer any more constables to Whitechapel," Abberline muttered, "the rest of London will be patrolled by three constables and a dog."

Jennings and Pierce were busy in the newsroom wading through the latest batch of letters from the public. Coulls was still absent; rumoured to be out on some secret assignment.

Jennings mused, "Here's one of the silliest yet. Some ass has concocted the ultimate double-reverse theory. Read this. . ."

Pierce read: "Perhaps you will allow me to suggest that the murderer's object may be—first, by his crimes to cause a reward to be offered, and then by the accusation of an innocent man, and by the manufacture of apparent tokens of guilt against him (as by staining his clothes with blood), to win that reward."

Old Boy said, "No one seems able to conceive of the Ripper being a lunatic with lunatic urges."

"The sane man gives a sane reason for the murders. When will the public learn insane people have insane motives? The Ripper must be all twisted up inside. I imagine he's terribly alone. He can't divulge the wishes he has to anyone. Maybe he's had them for years. Keeping them to himself, there's no correcting force to bring his crazy ideas back in line. He just gets crazier and crazier."

"He's certainly ripping his victims apart more and more. I'd hate to find his next victim, especially if I'd just eaten a proper kitchen physic."

Sir Charles Warren's life was going to the dogs. On 2 October Percy Lindley, a bloodhound breeder at York Hill, Loughton, Essex, wrote a letter to the press extolling the virtues of his breed. "I have little doubt that, had a hound been put upon the scent of the murderer while fresh, it might have done what the police have failed in." He suggested keeping two bloodhounds at a police station in the area ready for immediate use when Jack the Ripper next struck to track him to his lair and end his bloody reign of terror.

The Home Office dutifully sent the letter along to Sir Charles, in part because other bloodhound breeders soon wrote in to support Lindley's suggestion, in part to avoid having to make a decision themselves. Decisions led to effects and effects just might be negative. Sir Charles glared down at the letter. His wounds from the Transkei War were causing him pain as usual but, in truth, at the moment the bloodhound business caused him greater grief. From his own fox hunting experience, he wondered how a bloodhound could track the killer without any of his clothing or blood? How would the hound know who to track? But, even so, given the tenor of the press and public these days, he certainly could not reject the proposal out of hand. In any event, what could a few canines hurt? Hang it all.

Some days ago Sir Charles had been told that a bloodhound breeder, Edwin Brough, had offered to loan two dogs to the Met for free as part of his civic duty, but it had quickly became apparent that Brough expected to be paid for the purchase or lease of the dogs. Sir Charles smiled as he decided to let Matthews put the Home Office's funds where its canines were. He dictated a note asking the Home Office for funds to go to the dogs—or at least to Bough; £50 this year and £100 pounds thereafter to keep the bloodhounds in top lunatic-tracking form.

Dogs were far from the only issue souring the relationship between Sir Charles and Secretary Matthews. On 3 October, Sir Charles had agreed with Matthews that it was best not to offer a reward. Matthews argued a reward would produce a plethora of false leads, while Sir Charles argued that the City authority had already offered a £500 reward, so why duplicate efforts and waste public funds?

But now, two days later, Sir Charles changed his mind. The City reward, evidently, wasn't large enough to produce results. Besides, what was a few hundred pounds to the Home Office? Even so, he decided to give it one more day to see if the City reward led to a productive lead and, if nothing materialized, then he would apprise Matthews of his change in views on the reward issue.

It had been a challenging week for Coulls. Dressed in the oldest rags he could find, he had entered the East End world of the 4p dosshouse, the begged meal and the street poor. Carrying almost no money—or at 'low tide' as the locals called it—Coulls begged his way back and forth across Whitechapel. He learned that the best name for a dosshouse would be louse house. The little blighters loved him, perhaps because he had fresh succulent meat on his bones. Every time he bedded down on the straw the poor slept on, he missed his mattress and found himself bitten on every square inch of his body by morning. His scratching had inflamed some of the bites, turning them into painful red, open sores. He began to wonder if he would survive this assignment. He was always damp and cold. His choices always boiled down to sleeping in cellars that leaked from below or garrets that leaked from above. He also discovered that he was a lousy beggar. Every occupation has its skills. Begging and scavenging have theirs. For a time Coulls thought he was not going to make it and would shrivel away somewhere along Whitechapel High Street, probably in sight of London Hospital. But as he tried to avoid the Salvation Army saviors out looking to save his soul, he made friends of other poverty stricken East Enders and, driven by hunger, learned.

His inexperience and "fine" clothes—"Christ, guv, that's hardly worn"—made some East Enders suspect he was a police spy. To save himself from their muscular wrath, he confessed he was a newsman working undercover. They didn't seem to mind newspaper spies. In fact, Coulls was bombarded by information and encircled by genuine friendship.

He was sore and hurt everywhere from his louse-inhabited scalp to his fetid feet. Not having a bath for so long had irritated his skin in several thousand places. His inadequate diet had cost him almost half a stone in weight and where his bones stuck out, his clothes rubbed his skin raw. This led to his clothes hanging from his sparse frame in a most convincing pauperly style. As one companion in cups said, spitting a stream of laughter-launched gin on him,

"We'll make a Cockney outa you yet, guv."

Coulls could only laugh back. He ached too much to do anything else. The gin, which he had avoided at first, was a most welcome painkiller. It dulled the mind and senses.

Lusky watched the street people from his perch on the roof. He didn't come up here often, but it did have its advantage. The birds roosted along these ledges and occasionally one could be ambushed. The secret was to keep changing your places of attack and to be patient. Lusky settled down to wait, his grey coat blending in almost perfectly with the unwashed sideboards of a dormer. Birds circled above, oblivious to the hungry menace on the ledge several hundred feet below. Patience.

"A future king, the Ripper?" Abberline asked. He stood, stretching his legs as he looked out into the gathering gloom on the public entrance to the Met below off the street called Scotland Yard. "I think you'll find the Duke has been at one or other of the Royal residences or Army barracks at the time of each murder."

"You've already checked on the Duke?" Helson appeared astonished.

"Discretely, very discretely."

Helson blew his nose. "Sir Charles has drafted a few of our men for special duty concerning the Duke. You aren't supposed to know."

"Sir Charles picked Enright to head up the investigation. How wasn't I supposed to know? Enright began by accidentally sending me a list of people picked for 'Clarence duty.' It'll keep Enright and his bunch busy for months. We can concentrate on catching the Ripper. Putting Enright on special assignment, although he doesn't know it, may be the cleverest thing Sir Charles has ever done."

Helson rasped through his cold-wracked throat, "We've learned that Druitt is well connected. He's a member of the masons."

"Did you track down his latest residence? He never seems to be home in Blackheath."

"We can probably talk to him tomorrow afternoon—should be home on a Saturday afternoon with school closed—too late today."

Abberline nodded. "Let's finish this duty roster. Do you think we need tighter time schedules on our beats?" Abberline stared at a multi-hatched hunk of cardboard lying on a long table. Constable's numbers were slotted into appropriate spaces indicating times and streets patrolled.

"I dunno," Helson muttered. "PC Smith takes 25 to 30 minutes to walk his beat and the Ripper got Stride right in the middle of it. The fellow can kill in seconds. He can pick when he strikes, right after a constable passes from sight. We'd have to put a man every 20 feet to even come close to covering the area effectively."

"I hope the Home Secretary approves the use of those Tower Guards. We could at least use them to escort women home." Abberline sighed. "I fear that this will have to do."

"We got a report concerning that postcard Jack sent us. The experts think it was written by a person accustomed to writing a round hand, the kind of writing done by an office clerk. The writer spelt kidney 'k-i-d-n-e' suggesting he was uneducated, but his calligraphy is excellent and both margins were immaculate, so he knew how to use a pen properly."

"I thought the note was stained."

"Deliberately, to make it look like the work of an uneducated or clumsy man with a dip pen. The experts feel it had the look of a clerk or bookkeeper."

"Or a school teacher or solicitor—always writing wills: Druitt?"

Helson shrugged. "The letters and postcard pose quite a puzzle apparently. If the writer is English, he's most likely of the middle or upper class since most lower-class Englishmen are illiterate. The foreigners are far better educated— better spellers—even the ones in Whitechapel. That suggests Jack's a foreigner, but the grammar suggests he's an Englishman."

"A mystery for the ages, it appears, although it fits Druitt and who knows who else." Abberline rose. "Well, it's time for station rounds. Shall we be off?"

Abberline left the postcard behind in the files. On one side of it was a tolerably clear imprint of a bloody thumb or finger mark. The mark meant nothing to Abberline or Helson.

The *Evening Post* reported that "a few minutes before midnight a cab containing two men and a woman was seen to pass along Brick Lane, not one of the best thoroughfares in Spitalfields, and stop in a dark portion of the lane. The two men bore the body of the 'unconscious' woman from the cab and deposited it on the pavement, afterwards re-entering the vehicle and driving away." The Ripper? Another victim? The police investigated and found it was the result of a drunken brawl, which had become garbled in the telling and countless re-telling.

Saturday, 6 October

A pavement artist attracted huge crowds in Whitechapel Road when he drew a graphic delineation of the murders. Swordsticks were selling well to gentlemen who wished to be better prepared to defend themselves and their ladies. In the East London Cemetery the remains of Elizabeth Stride, nee Long Liz, nee Gustafsdotter, were laid to rest. In the East End, any criticism of the victims for their lifestyles was quickly and resolutely squashed. Almost everyone expressed the greatest sympathy for the victims.

With still no productive leads arising from the City of London's offer, Sir Charles raised the stakes in the reward game by writing Secretary Matthews requesting that a free pardon be offered to any of the killer's accomplices who provided information about the murderer and suggesting that the government offer a reward in the princely sum of £5,000. To the average lower-middle class worker who made £20 a year, it was a dream-inducing amount.

"What in the bloody name of all that's holy does he think he's playing at?" Matthews demanded when he received Sir Charles' note. Fearing a change in policy would batter his image since he had publicly stated his position opposing a reward, a furious Matthews ranted at an assistant, "Anybody can offer a reward and it is the first idea of ignorant people."

Matthews, however, had not risen to be Home Secretary by not being adept at bureaucratic infighting. With a sly glint in his eye, he dictated a note back to Sir Charles stating that he would be more than happy to offer such a reward, if Sir Charles would just take a few moments to dictate a letter stating he had exhausted all other means to find the killer and needed a reward to make any further progress.

With a frugal Scottish eye on the bottom line, based on Sir Charles' earlier note, Mathews also approved only the £50 payment for two bloodhounds for one year and nothing thereafter. Who knew? Bloodhounds made more than most workers. Besides, there was no need for dog funds for next year. The Ripper would be apprehended long before the year was out, reward or no, wouldn't he?

As the medium Lees stood on an omnibus from Shepherd's Bush, which had stopped at Notting Hill, he glanced back. There he was! The man in the vision, standing only a few feet away, waiting to board the back of the very vehicle Lees was in. Excitement exited from Lees in a chaotic collage of widening pupils, shaking hands, flailing arms and sweat-filmed skin. Lee pointed and screamed, "There he is! There he is!"

"Who?" his wife demanded, the irritation at his outburst clear in her words and face. "What *are* you going on about Robert?"

"That's the murderer! Get a policeman."

"Don't be ridiculous. You're making an absolute fool of yourself, Robert."

The two-story horse-drawn omnibus stopped at Oxford Street.

"He's exiting! Come on!" Lees yelled at his wife.

Lees bolted off the ad-festooned, yellow omnibus in hot pursuit of his prey. He ran toward a constable on Park Lane who was standing unconcernedly at his fixed point of duty. Pointing back at the blur of now agitated onlookers around the omnibus, Lees yelled, "That's the Whitechapel murderer! I saw him in my vision. I'm Robert Lees, the medium…"

Amused, bemused or, perhaps, feeling a bit abused, the constable gave Lees a patronizing pat on the shoulder, "Just take it easy, sir."

"You don't understand. The man who butchered that woman in Buck's

Row is over there," Lees screamed, waving his arm even more vigorously in the general direction of the now startled swarm of citizens gathered by the omnibus.

Mrs. Lees continued pleading for her husband to quit being so foolish, while the constable continued trying to placate the agitated medium. "Calm yourself, sir! Calm yourself," he implored, his patience waning. "I wouldn't want you to do yourself a mischief."

"A mischief! A mischief!" Lees screamed, tearing himself away from the clutches of both legal and marital restraint to run towards a cab into which the man he believed to be the Ripper was now climbing. The cab started to pull away.

"Stop! Stop!" Lees screamed. But the driver, seeing a dash of disheveled citizenry, an angry Peeler and a fattish female running hell bent for his hansom, panicked. He snapped his whip at his horse and was off, far faster than even the agitated Lees could follow.

Finally out of breath, Lees crumpled to the pavement, exhausted and disheveled. Drained of energy and élan, a repentant medium sat with tears of despair streaming from his eyes. He had seen the Buck's Row murderer and had let him get away. The long-ago learned reality that there were very few men of vision like himself and even fewer men who believed anything they said crashed in upon him once again.

"We better go home, Robert," his wife said, eyeing the constable, who was eyeing her husband. She sounded concerned, but Lees knew from years of experience and from her tone that she was furious with him. "You're still ill, dear."

"Ill is right," the constable concluded as Lees and his lady walked away.

But Lees did not go home. He rushed to Scotland Yard. In Abberline's CID office, Lees related the details of his vision, including mention of the killer cutting off his victim's ears, and told Abberline about seeing the man from his dream on the omnibus. Concluding it would do no harm and just might lead to the killer, Abberline took down the description and sent it for distribution.

"I thought it might be the Ripper, since I hadn't seen the man on my beat before," a young constable reported to Inspector Dew at the Commercial Street station. "When questioned, he proved to be a member of the patrols set up by the Mile End Vigilance Committee."

The Committee was composed mostly of small tradesmen—a builder, cigar manufacturer, tailor, picture-frame maker, victualler, merchant, and an actor. They were joined by men from the Working Men's Vigilance Committee, composed mostly of burly waterfront workers. They claimed they were organizing 57 patrols a night on the streets of the East End.

Dew muttered an oath. "We spend more time checking on vigilance committee members than watching for the bloody Ripper, and Sir Charles encourages the sodding vigilantes."

"Worse than that, sir," the constable said. "The plainclothes detectives watch the vigilance men, who watch the detectives—most are strangers to the area—and one thing leads to another and some rather heated exchanges have brewed up into fights between the vigilantes and our men. Lucky we don't have more men ending up in a surgery."

The torso murder at Westminster took a further bizarre turn when a woman's leg was found to add to the mounting pile of arms and legs at the current police headquarters. Levi Richard Bartlett, who had beat his wife Elizabeth to death on 28 September with a hammer and slit her throat, was charged with willful murder.

Abberline and Helson rode southeast to Blackheath, just south of Greenwich, to talk to Montague Druitt, cricketer, problematic school master and brother-anointed murder suspect.

"Damn," Abberline said as they approached Druitt's door. "Another beautiful sunny day. Where's our famous London fog?"

Montague John Druitt was a calm, quiet spoken, tidy man. He didn't seem ruffled by the presence of the police at his door. Could he be acting? Abberline couldn't help remembering something he had read while searching Druitt's antecedents. Montague had been in a school production of *Twelfth Night*. A critic had written, "Of the inadequacy of Druitt as Sir Toby Belch what are we to say? It can better be imagined than described." Apparently Druitt's calmness couldn't be attributed to any acting ability.

The interview went leisurely along. Druitt mentioned his trouble at Blackheath before the detectives could bring it up. He didn't say much about it, but they could hardly expect a man to admit the homosexual molestation of a boy, if that was in fact what happened. The issue remained opaquely vague.

Abberline asked, "Where were you on the weekend of 31 August/1 September?"

"It's difficult to remember. May I consult my cricket schedule?" Druitt took a diary from a roll-top desk and sat back down in the small drawing room. "I was in London. Alone. I went to a play."

"Which play?"

"*Dr. Jekyll and Mr. Hyde.*"

Druitt's revelation of being at the most controversial play in London on the night of Polly Nichol's murder neither supported nor destroyed his role as a suspect. He could have seen the play at any time, keeping the ticket stub for just such a moment as this. Richard Mansfield's melodrama based on Robert Louis Stevenson's classic novella had been running for weeks. The American actor-producer was making a mint and maybe, Abberline thought, a convenient alibi for Druitt. The play was drawing SRO crowds to both the Lyceum and the Opera Comique. Critics argued over which company gave the better performance, parrying periods and commas in the local papers, but the ultimate critics, the paying customers, seemed to favour Mansfield's acting efforts at the Lyceum. Pound for pound it was the winner.

Montague John Druitt

Abberline asked, "You went alone?"

"Yes, I went to Mansfield's version. I like the American style of producing plays. Oh, I usually go on my own. Some of the chaps on the cricket team often pal around together, but I guess I'm pretty well a loner. Oh, I do take the occasional lady out, but not lately; can't afford it."

Abberline wondered about the heterosexual reference; was it truth or window dressing? "What about the weekend of 7-8 September?"

"I don't really remember. Most likely London. Usually go down on a weekend on my own. I'm afraid I don't keep an extensive diary."

"Last weekend?"

"Again—in London. That I can remember. Went to my office. Cleaned up some work. Visited my brother. Went out for a drink at night."

"You went to a pub with your brother?"

"No, heavens, no. I went alone. My dear brother is a teetotaler. Lips that touch alcohol will never be his."

"Can you remember where you went?"

"Some pub. I can't remember which one. Wait. Probably the Blue Anchor. It's in Aldgate, near Minories. Actually I don't drink that much, but I don't mind the occasional pint of bitters, especially in the evening, kind of relaxing, especially with a game of darts. I like to see that sharp, steel point zip into the cork. It's kind of artistic in a way. Don't you think?"

"I suppose. By the way, would you mind writing out these lines for us? Just a matter of routine."

Druitt took the printed sheet from Abberline. His hands were icy cold, but steady. He said. "Oh, those Ripper letters. They've been in all the papers. That's what this is all about. I'm a suspect, am I?"

Druitt sat down at his desk and took up a fountain pen in his left hand. He wrote slowly and deliberately in an easy, round flowing hand. When finished, he handed Abberline the paper.

The Inspector took the sheet and studied it. He took a facsimile of the Ripper letters from his pocket and—watching Druitt the entire time—put the facsimile down beside Druitt's writing on the desk. There was some similarity, but Abberline was no graphologist.

Druitt asked, "Is there anything else? Unfortunately, I must be off. Cricket practice. I love all kinds of little games. Don't you?"

"Oh, most. Ah. . .do you mind if we look over your place here and your offices in town?"

"No. You've got your job to do. You'll need a key for my office. Here's a spare. Could you post it back? It's really more my brother's office than mine."

"Thank you," Abberline said and smiled. "This is all just routine, you know."

"I know," Druitt said and smiled back.

Abberline stared for a moment at the man. He seemed to be only smiling with the bottom part of his face. His eyes stared back in a cold, passionless fashion. Abberline wondered if he was only imaging these things.

They did not find anything of significance at Druitt's residence or office.

As they rode back to headquarters, Helson said, "If he's the Whitechapel murderer, he's got iced arteries."

"I knew his place and office wouldn't be worth searching," Abberline said. "He didn't hesitate a second in letting us search them. If they hadn't been clean, he'd have us filling out the papers to do a search. We best keep watch on him. He could be as innocent as he seems or he could be our cold-blooded killer. Who knows?"

"Get 'im, 'es the Ripper!"

The yell was like the wail of some avenging biblical assassin of ancient times. The little man jumped. His eyes dilated, his mouth flared open, his body surged with fright. They were running right toward him; a gang of burly bully boys. The oft-chased Isaac Jacobs turned and fled.

"After 'im!"

"Don't let 'im get outa sight!"

Jacobs ran. He was no longer a youth and he had never been an athlete, but he was scared. It was enough for his quads and hams to hurl him along like a West Bromwich forward on a breakaway. He turned into a side street. It was Crispin. He ran, his mind racing ahead to how he might elude his tormenters.

"We're gainin' on you, Ripper!'"

They were. He turned left into Brushfield and quickened his pace. He couldn't keep this up much longer. Many of them were taller and leaner, their young hearts driving their young legs ever so fast. He swept into Commercial Street, angling across it, past a mass of carts and stalls, gaining precious time and even more precious distance. The gang had stopped at the corner of Brushfield and Commercial as they tried to pick out his running figure in the ever-shifting crowd. He walked now, gaining life-sustaining breath. Mustn't arouse the attention of any bystander or they'd get him for sure. He cut up Fashion Street, walking at a subdued pace. When he reached Brick Lane he had to duck back. The gang had circled around to the north. They must have cut across Hanbury to Brick. He reversed course on Fashion and wondered what to do. He'd better go south to Commercial and get lost in the crowds.

His heart still pounded. He could almost cry. This was the fourth time he had been chased in the past two weeks. He had taken to avoiding the area around Backchurch and Providence because they always chased him there. But now it wasn't safe here either. He decided to try down toward Mansell and the Minories. Maybe he could cadge a dinner at the Sally Ann Mission and, better yet, get some different clothes. He didn't know why they always thought he was that dreadful Ripper person.

He checked Wentworth Street to make certain the gang of bullies hadn't decided to come down it. They were nowhere in sight. He scurried on down across Whitechapel Road and crossed into Leman Street. A man standing on the corner watched Jacobs scoot by and muttered, "Suspicious-looking bloke."

Sir Charles was presenting his yearly report to the press at Scotland Yard.

"We hear often enough of the faults and failures of the police and of every undiscovered crime, and every crime that has been committed with special daring," he said, his voice defensive.

Old Boy, scanning his transcript of the speech, which had been distributed beforehand, underlined a few cogent words for the story he would soon write: "Of the injuries sustained by the police in the discharge of their duties there are less than usual." Beside this in the margin, Old Boy scribbled, "The Commissioner, perhaps, as an old soldier, thinks less of these than would a civilian." He smiled and lapsed into reverie. Ah, how cute that little tart at the theatre in Haymarket had been last night. Too bad he was so afraid of picking something up. When it came to whether gonorrhea, syphilis, venereal warts or Victorian morality governed a man's sexual proprieties, Old Boy was a firm believer that the last ran a poor fourth.

Pulled back to his job by an increase in the volume of Sir Charles' words, Old Boy consulted *The Chief Surgeon's Report* to see how the police had fared: 847 traumatic injuries in the past year. Most common problems: diseases of exposure—rheumatism, phthisis and lung disorders. Out in all weather, no bloody wonder.

Old Boy flipped through the commissioner's report. As of 31 December 1887, the Met force included 14,081 persons; 8,773 being available for street duty—one for every 624 citizens. He made a marginal note that 5,308—more than a third—weren't employed on the streets; administrators of one bloody sort or another. Sir Charles had even added five chief constables to the Met hierarchy between the superintendents and the assistant commissioners. More bureaucracy; such institutions never shrank—until they collapsed. Reflecting on the streets and alleys to be covered, Old Boy marveled that 1,833 miles of new streets had been added to the district since 1849. That represented a lot of shoe leather.

Sir Charles mentioned the introduction of a new truncheon and the approval of a new pattern of boot. The new truncheon symbolized Sir Charles' thrust to progress. Made of hard coccus wood, it combined weight and strength and, as reporters from the radical papers were want to point out, did not take a gram of intelligence to wield.

Chapter Seventeen

Sunday, 7 October

Throughout the night Whitechapel/Spitalfields was flooded with constables and inspectors, vigilance committee members and newspaper reporters. Lusky even curtailed a foray and returned to the house early because of the overabundance of humans in his hunting grounds. The night also passed without the Ripper coming out to kill.

The sun dominated the day's sky, although temperatures only reached the low 40s. The sun might be out, but the aura of fall was everywhere.

The ritual of religion held its Sunday sway as usual with the unfortunates of Whitechapel being alluded to in church after church. The rhetoric ranged from talk of their sad calling to condemnation of the midnight seeker of the harlot's hire. More than one male parishioner with something to hide stared sheepishly at the floor. Others stared at the floor, but it was only out of boredom. The Ripper had stirred deeply into the public psyche and had awakened more of a dislike for monetary sexual exchanges than any deep distaste for murder by mutilation. Sex, not sadism, was under general sermonic attack.

One preacher did talk of the wasted bodies packed in parish coffins, of scant human shells which lately contained immortal souls. Another offered a crumb of comfort, arguing that the outcasts had died quickly with scant bodily suffering. Another dwelt on the terror, the utter terror that must have flooded through each victim's mind as the blade approached the blood-letting. This fellow was later cautioned by a collared colleague to perhaps tone down the vividness of his sermons a touch. But the vast majority talked of poverty, prostitution and debasement. The agents of God were taking on the whores of Whitechapel. Their Christian zest may have stemmed from less uplifting motives than one could imagine. A recent survey by some enterprising savant showed that 98 percent of the lower classes did not attend church. Some clerics saw the Ripper's onslaught as a judgment for such universal truancy: a plague on whores.

Monday, 8 October

Reporters, artists and policemen waited in Regent's Park for Sir Charles to commence his much-discussed and already much-maligned bloodhound tracking trials. Abberline, a cold-ridden Helson and Major Smith had declined to attend. Instead they sent out further memos to their street patrols to be on the lookout for Klosowski, Ostrog, Vasiliev and the dark-eyed bald man. Druitt and Eddy continued to be watched.

An hour past daybreak, the sun cast an ever-lightening greyish sheen over the greens and emeralds of the park. The assembled host was now half frozen; mostly the extremities. A proud Edwin Brough, bloodhound breeder and owner of two magnificent hounds, finally led his two prizes out onto the field. On his left walked Burgho, possessor of an exceedingly well-formed body and head. He strutted in utter distain of the lesser beings who viewed him. His specialty since puppyhood had been tracking "the clean shoe," that peculiarly difficult task whereby a hound must track footwear treated with blood or aniseed. The handsome beast beside Burgho was Barnaby, a champion at gaining bench points in prize shows, but he too was a master tracker.

"Ah, the first trial," Jennings noted as a burly constable trotted off leaving a trail of trampled green-white blades through the hoar frost that any creature with even one good eye could have followed. The two hounds sat calmly amid the shifting, drifting wisps of ground fog that streaked the field in whitish bands. Sir Charles puffed unconcernedly on a cigarette. His aide glanced anxiously at his pocket watch. Time dragged by. The overweight constable was now only a slight blue ball in the distance and then he was gone, lost in the trees. Perhaps forever, Lusky, who believed cats far superior to canines, would have quipped. Fifteen minutes elapsed. Then the hounds were released.

"On Burgho. . .On Barnaby!" Brough shouted.

"There they go!"

"Run! Run!"

Off across the park went the bloodhounds, behind them charged a flock of police, a gaggle of press and a murder of curious passersby. A partridge that had been nestling in the grass flew into the air. The hunt was on. Through the trees, the underbrush, past thicket and thorn, Burgho and Barnaby led the hunt. Finally—huffing and panting—the pod of police, press and passersby were brought by the sniffing and snorting pair of pooches to the crouching constable, who had hidden behind a well-trunked tree.

"They found him! They found him!"

The cheers of success sent a flurry of birds scattering for aerial ascendancy.

"I knew they could do it," Brough said.

Sir Charles said, "We'll have to recheck their abilities in another park and at night."

Jennings frowned and muttered, "Not many a park in Whitechapel."

The Harbour Police extracted the body of a middle-aged woman from the Thames near Pimlico Pier. Her demise was quickly ascertained to be unrelated to the Ripper's activities. Someone else, just as unknown, was deemed responsible. The police also dealt with a possible homicide when a man died of carbolic poisoning, a suicide when a woman stabbed herself to death, and an accidental death when a man's artificial tooth slid down his gullet and death followed a surgical attempt to extract it. A murder at Westminster widened in interest as parts of a woman's anatomy were discovered in a trunk. The upshot of attempts to identify the remains brought to police attention the remarkable number of missing women in London.

Several politicians deplored the continuing migration of Russian revolutionaries into the East End and, over a substantial eight-course lunch, discussed how the flow might be stemmed. Reverend Barnett began work on his next sermon, roughing it out over several cups of tea. He was annoyed.

"Imagine," he said to Henrietta in their parlour, "that cretin they have for a Vicar at St. James the Great is marrying parishioners for seven pence. Seven pence! And what's worse, he has them lie. Lie!"

"How is that, dear?" she asked. "Do they have to claim they haven't been living together when they have?"

"No, nothing so innocuous. They have to swear before God—swear before God—that they live in his red Church's parish when they obviously do not live there. It's a disgrace. It makes a mockery of matrimony."

"I suppose so, dear."

The funeral of Catherine Eddowes, the Mitre Square victim, was held in the afternoon. The body had been preserved on ice as the police waited to match the missing internal organs, if they were found, with the frayed ends left in the corpse. The grim legacy of the Ripper was finally released for internment as decomposition became advanced and room in the sawdust-and-ice enclosure was needed for new lifeless arrivals of far less public notoriety. The key parts were kept on ice in case the missing organs were ever found.

Crowds five deep, swelled by workers taking their lunch break, filled the sidewalk, leaned from windows and perched on roofs along the route between the mortuary in Golden Lane and the cemetery at Ilford. Sympathy ran through the crowd. Rough-looking labourers removed their hats as the hearse passed.

The crowd was so thick at some corners that policemen were rushed in to reinforce the many already directing traffic. Lusky wondered what all the fuss was about and quickly reversed his course. No use getting trampled in that sea of senseless curiosity. He'd never understood why humans were so compulsive about burying their carrion.

Behind him, the body went by in an open hearse, simple wreathes leaning against either side of the elm coffin. Two coaches crowded with mourners followed, including a black-suited John Kelly and four of Catherine's sisters, also in mourning black. Behind this the procession was completed by a wagon load of women attired in gaudy styles totally unbefitting a proper Victorian funeral.

"Gawd, look at that outfit. You would think she would wear something more dignified," a haughty, middle-aged matron scoffed.

Ensnared by the crush of the crowd, tired, louse-ridden and hungry, Coulls glared at the matron and asked, "Ever think that may be all the clothes those ladies own?"

"Well, you can call them ladies, but that's hardly the right name for them."

Coulls ignored the rejoinder and noticed the sad man on the wagon. Coulls guessed that Kelly, who had lived with the deceased for seven years, only thought that it was kind of the ladies, however dressed, to come.

Coulls turned away when he spotted a brougham bringing up the rear squeaking on its springs under the weight of a packet of correspondents. Coulls didn't wish to be recognized, although such an identification was unlikely given his current sorry appearance.

After hundreds of mourners gathered at the City of London Cemetery, the Reverend T. Dunscombe performed the service at 3:30 in the chapel and at graveside. The City authorities, who owned the cemetery, remitted the usual fees and George Hawkes, vestryman and undertaker of St. Luke's, paid the funeral expenses.

Coulls strolled away from the funeral. He had a meeting to attend. A fine, gray cat sat watching him.

"Hi there, puss." Coulls stopped and stroked the big, satin-soft beast. Lusky purred. Coulls scooped up the friendly feline and walked down Union to a meeting of the Central Vigilance Society which met irregularly at various clubs and pubs.

"We've got to put some pressure on those damn two-faced politicians," a huge tower of a man exhorted. "They let those bawdy houses run wide open."

Carrying the sleek gray cat, Coulls ordered a pint and "Some milk for this fine fellow," before slipping into a back seat.

A shorter, stockier sort of citizen was now speaking. "Fine, we write the papers, plead to the public to elect more responsible politicians. What the hell good does that do? The bloody public can't tell one lying politician from an honest one, if such a creature exists. They can't get to know them all personally. They never could and they never will."

"We need to take more vigorous action and push the whole bloody rotten structure over."

"The sooner the better," a third man said in glassy-eyed lack of sobriety.

The talk went on from there, calling for social and political change, but with little direction or real plans.

The Central Vigilance Society continued its class-conscious considerations of conditions in Whitechapel. The group was joined by the dark-eyed bald man, who quickly asserted his ability to out-talk anyone in the group. It was strange, Coulls noted, that he did not seem to win many of the Vigilance men over to his views. Perhaps it was the clash of backgrounds. They were labourers. He seemed a once well-to-do man who had experienced a personal economic decline. Deciding he had heard enough socialism for the day, Coulls finished his pint and left. Lusky lapped up his milk.

"No one has recognized the writing on that letter or postcard," Helson reported, as he finished going through the latest batch of reports. He worked at a table squeezed into the corner of Abberline's CID office.

"Relatively easy to disguise your writing, I imagine," Abberline said.

Helson snuffled, nodded and said, "I had a man further investigate the carman Cross who found the body in Buck's Row. It appears that Charles Allen Cross may really be a Charles Lechmere. Cross is his stepfather's name."

"No crime in using your stepfather's surname."

"Whatever his name, he's a carman working for Messrs. Pickford and Company delivering meat to butchers, so being covered in blood wouldn't cause anyone to give him a second look. He lives about five minutes' walk from Buck's Row and it's on his way to work. He usually leaves at 3:15 a.m., but the morning of the Nichols murder he claims he was 'behind time' and left home at 3:30. He found the body at 3:35, only a few minutes before the other carman, Paul, happened along. But he could have been there 20 minutes if he left home on time."

"Is 20 minutes long enough to chat up Nichols, settle on a transaction and price, walk into the row, strangle her, slit her throat, and then hide the knife and clean off any blood?"

"Maybe."

"He also had to have used part of that 20 minutes to walk to Buck's Row from his house—five or ten minutes?—it'd be tight, unless he left even earlier than his regular time. Does his wife back-up the time he left?"

"Who would want a wife who wouldn't?"

"Would he leave early on the off chance of meeting a potential victim?"

"Not as if you make an appointment with that sort of unfortunate."

"Find out more about him, but do it quietly. I don't want potential witnesses thinking if they cooperate they're going to be hounded by a dozen detectives, let alone the press."

"Most of 'em like being hounded by the press, but we don't want a repeat of that bloody Packer business with his baseless claim he sold grapes to Elizabeth Stride and a mystery man the night of her murder."

In one of his few early evenings home, Helson sat at dinner with his wife, Mary, and their four children. Helson glanced at the mantle clock; he and Mary were expected at a colleague's for a charades party in just over an hour. Even with his lingering cold, he was looking forward to spending an evening out with his wife. Abberline had sent him home early, given Abberline's belief that weeknights were far less likely to produce a Ripper murder than weekends. Based on that belief, Abberline had developed a rotation plan to give the lead investigators a night off once a fortnight.

Despite Helson's best efforts to steer the conversation to school, apprenticeships, football or even possible Christmas presents, the conversation at table soon focused—as it did in so many homes—on the Whitechapel murders.

"I just don't understand how anyone would ever go anywhere near such a monster, let alone walk out with him," Mary said as she sliced into her shepherd's pie.

"Maybe we should talk about something else," Helson suggested, eyeing his wife with what he hoped would be a strongly suggestive look as he sipped his glass of Bow Brewery India Pale Ale, which he was sampling for the first time.

"I'd never walk out with someone like the Ripper," 11-year-old Florence announced.

Helson frowned. Mary's attempt to persuade the children to read more had unintentionally led to the elder ones reading newspapers, which were full of Ripper reports. Such a topic was far from what he wanted on his young daughter's mind. He asked, "How is your new Snakes and Ladders game?" The game was just appearing in stores from India and his father was lucky to have found one for his granddaughter.

"It's fun," Florence said. "Like Mother, I wonder why anyone would ever go with him."

"You are never going to be the sort of woman who parades about Whitechapel with anyone," Mary told her daughter absent any trace of uncertainty.

Abandoning his attempt to change the topic of conversation, Helson asked his precocious daughter, "How would you know he was the Ripper?"

"He'd look like a monster, wouldn't he, Father?" she asked, as if no one stupid enough not to realize such a fact could even manage to breathe.

"Far from it, Florence."

"Monsters don't really exist, do they Father?" 10-year-old Albert asked, his eyes wide.

"I fear they do. They're rare and you know what my job is?"

"What?" Albert asked, focusing all his attention on his father.

"To catch 'em and see them hanged by the neck until dead."

"Now that is a topic we can do without at table," Mary said, tilting her head and meeting Helson's gaze with an unwavering one of her own. He wanted to tell her that she had started the conversation down this sordid path, but thought better of it before the children.

"I'd never step out with any murderous lunatic who looked ghastly," Florence announced with utmost confidence.

Staring at his daughter, Helson asked, "What if he was handsome?"

That night, the bloodhounds were put through their paces again, this time in Hyde Park. It was dark, so the dogs were kept on a leash, but they succeeded in tracking a man for more than a mile.

"No wonder the Ripper hasn't struck again," a constable told Jennings as they trudged back through the park to the nearest street to find a cab.

"Why?"

"With the bloodhounds close to hand, he'd have to be a lunatic to risk another murder."

Jennings thought that was exactly what the police thought he was: a lunatic.

Tuesday, 9 October

The bloodhounds were hard at work once again, running six more trials, with Sir Charles himself the target twice. The hounds found their man each time, even when the trails were deliberately crossed.

"They track on grass in fresh air," Jennings said as he rode back to *The Empire's* offices with Pierce, "but how will they do in paved, reeking Whitechapel?"

"Can't do worse than the police have done."

A Member of Parliament suggested cordoning off all of Whitechapel and conducting a house-to-house search. The idea was forwarded to Sir Charles, who, although his more limited search was already being planned for a section of Whitechapel, sent the proposal back with the statement that he was quite willing to take the responsibility for such drastic and arbitrary measures, "however illegal they may be." However, since the Home Secretary could not order him to do an illegal act, the responsibility would be his. Therefore, Sir Charles requested a guarantee of immunity from the government for any such illegal actions. The government, of course, refused to issue such immunity and the suggestion died. Every liberty loving British citizen breathed a sigh of relief.

Detective Sergeant Robinson of G Division went to Phoenix Place, St. Pancras, with another detective sergeant to check on a possible suspect. Robinson was dressed as a decoy for the Ripper: as an unfortunate.

As the detectives made their way along the street, two cab washers, William Jarvis and James Phillips, started watching the oddly dressed Robinson closely. Jarvis approached and demanded to know what Robinson was doing.

"I am a police officer," Robinson declared, betraying his gender and destroying any effectiveness of his disguise.

Jarvis and Phillips, who did not like strangers in their neighbourhood and far from believing Robinson's response, told him to leave the area. Push led to shove, a fist was thrown and a fight erupted. Robinson hit Jarvis over head with his truncheon, which he had hid in his skirts.

Dressing as a decoy proved to have its downsides. Although Robinson and his colleague managed to arrest Jarvis and Phillips, Robinson was stabbed over the left eye and on the bridge of his nose, while another man, who tried to help the police, was stabbed in the face and suffered a dislocated jaw. None of it got the police any closer to apprehending the Ripper.

Cold shafts of autumn night iced their way on wisps of wind through the streets and back alleys of Stepney. It was 1 a.m. as Elizabeth Jennings hurried along on an errand. It had been nine nights since the twin killings had riven London with tumult. The feelings of fright had subsided within days and were now replaced by more muted emotions. Elizabeth scurried along, furtively glancing from side to side. The bravado that had sent her out on the errand was waning with frightening alacrity. She sighed as she saw a well-dressed gentleman appear from a side street, but relief turned to terror as the man grabbed her arm and said, "Come with me."

She screamed.

People burst out of unlit buildings, shadowed doorways and darkened alleys. Men emerged from corner pubs and common lodging houses. The street seemed to fill in an instant.

"Jack the Ripper! Jack the Ripper!" It came from everyone in general and yet no one in particular. Screams tore like spasms of terror through the night air. Knights clad in cloth aprons and drab working clothes charged to rescue the damsel in distress. The well-dressed molester released Elizabeth and stood befuddled. He was about to run when the brawny arms of several muscular workmen encircled him and held him fast.

"Don't move an arm or leg, you murderin' bastard."

"They've got the Ripper. They've got him, this time."

The message travelled in a torrent of emotion throughout the district. Coulls was roused from a dosshouse bunk he shared with a stranger; pigging together, as it was called. He followed the procession of the penniless out into the street. The police took the molester into custody and began the mundane business of sorting out this latest commotion as the crowd dispersed. Coulls and his cohorts returned to the dosshouse and, after an argument over whether they would have to pay again for a bed for the night, persuaded the dosshouse deputy to let them bed down without repaying. It was better to let a clutch of cranky, tired men lie down than risk bodily ruin.

While CID was dispensing with this latest pseudo-Ripper, a young man staggered up to a constable (PC 200 of J Division, Bethnal Green), who was standing point duty in Essex Road. The young fellow shakily announced he wanted to be taken to the nearest police station.

"If you don't take me I shall murder someone tonight," the young man threatened. Then staggering into the constable for support, the young man whispered, his breath reeking of gin, "I am Jack the Ripper."

At this revelation, he pulled a rather chipped and rusted pocket knife from inside his coat and tried unsuccessfully to open it. The constable, disgusted with this bumbling, bogus, drunken Ripper, said, "Go home. Just go home and sleep it off."

The young man reeled off and disappeared into a pub. All would have ended there but a few minutes later he wandered out and, navigating even more randomly than before, bounced off a lamp post and crashed into the street. The constable shrugged, pulled the young man to his feet and with the aid of a passerby, dragged the latest pretender to the Ripper's throne to an eventual choice between a £5 fine or 21 days in prison. The young man decided to pay the fine and spend the next 21 days drinking.

The Pall Mall Gazette ran a series of articles criticizing the police with headlines proclaiming, "The Headless C.I.D." and "Why Detectives Don't Detect." Sir Charles complained in a letter to Sir James Fraser, "We are inundated with suggestions and names of suspects!" Abberline knew it only too well, as he, Helson and Chandler worked late into the night assigning detectives to chase down dozens of leads and suspects the next day. Swanson had sent back a dozen possible suspects from the piles of reports he had been reading. Chandler went home to tend to an ill wife and child, while Helson, as the other senior detectives had taken to doing on many a night, bedded down at the station; on this night Helson collapsed onto a cot in the hall just outside Abberline's office. It was cold in the hall, but Helson, utterly exhausted, didn't seem to mind.

"God, the night isn't half bloody over and we've got our third Ripper report," Abberline said sometime later as he worked through sleep-starved eyes reviewing the night's reports. "The latest involves an Elizabeth Jennings. A toff, who turns out to be a harmless drunk out for some primal intimacies, grabbed her. Claims he thought she was an unfortunate. She screams 'bloody murder' and before he can explain that his intentions, although not honourable, are economic, not murderous, half of Whitechapel is screaming 'Ripper.' Good Christ."

Helson mumbled something before dozing off again.

An hour later, Abberline cursed as he read the latest order from the Met Commissioner. He called to the slumbering Helson, "Sir Charles has ordered us not to tamper with any new Ripper victim. We're to wait for him to arrive and personally direct the investigation, and to send for those bloody hounds. They're going to track the bastard."

Helson muttered something, his words thick with sleep.

Abberline read the next report on his desk. He threw up his arms in mock despair, "Now there's some crackpot accusing Sergeant Thick of being the Ripper."

"Johnny Upright?" Helson asked in disbelief as he sat up, abandoning his attempt to sleep.

"Pretty hard for an on-duty policeman like Thick to be the Ripper, unless Johnny Upright has figured out a way to kill without getting the least bit of blood on his uniform and to carry kidneys around in his back pocket."

Common logic used illogically was casting suspicion this way and that. For every person even remotely associated with the murders, there was someone in the city who suspected that he was the killer. Paranoia had entered the public domain.

Wednesday, 10 October

Abberline attended yet another meeting at the Home Office. At least he was able to commiserate about the wasted time with Swanson on the walk back along Whitehall to the Yard past the government ministries that ran the empire from Egypt to Burma, Cape Town to Singapore.

"Now we've got the top brass wanting us to investigate a scheme whereby some unscrupulous manufacturer is distributing inferior cigars wrapped in counterfeit bands," Abberline told Swanson. "Give the bastards at HQ their due; they sure know what's important."

The pair strolled along and Abberline said, "Helson read in a newspaper that a man whose West End home had been broken into and ransacked accused the police of devoting too much attention to the Whitechapel murderer and not enough to protecting proper people's property."

Swanson frowned. "Haven't patrols in the West End been doubled since 9 September?"

Abberline nodded. "Sir Charles fears the Whitechapel murderer just might move west."

"About as likely as me moving into St. James's Palace."

Thursday, 11 October

Mist, the harbinger of night fog, drifted in and out of the East End streets all day long, sometimes lying in white wispy pockets, at other times floating across stretches of thoroughfares, engulfing everyone and everything that happened by.

Lord Mayor-elect Whitehead and a posse of ex-sheriffs toured Brussels in grand style, happily oblivious to the problems of the East or West End. Reverend Barnett continued his campaign for philanthropic purchase of tenements by his East End Dwelling Company to be turned into low-cost homes for Whitechapel unfortunates. His pleas went both heard and unheeded. Sir Charles produced yet another public statement, pointing out that as long as the public couldn't see any detectives, then they must be hard at work. Evidently, what you couldn't see could help you. East Enders had a more empirical view of a detective's function. Catch the bleedin' Ripper and you had done your job. Fail to catch him and you had not.

The morning saw the continuance of the Eddowes inquest at the City Coroner's Court, Golden Lane, with Major Smith and Superintendent Foster attending. Police ineptitude and helplessness were accentuated when testimony revealed that PC Watkins was not the only constable patrolling Mitre Square. City Constable 964 James Harvey regularly crossed into the square from his beat coming from a different direction. Evidently the boundaries of jurisdiction between the Met and the City police were as obscure as the Ripper's identity. Harvey was the officer who probably came closest to catching the Ripper bloody handed, since he entered Mitre Square at 1:40 a.m. Sunday, 30 September, just minutes before the body was found. The image of the phantom, immune from capture, flitting leisurely between the endless clockwork spins of the police on their beats cast a grim hopelessness over the proceedings. It was as if an invisible enemy was able to meander through a great, teeming ant heap undetected despite the constant patrolling of thousands of guard ants. Of course, the Phantom might just look like any other ant.

Dr. Sequeira testified about his examination of the body in Mitre Square. He was followed by William Sedgwick Saunders, Medical Officer for Health for the City, who had examined Eddowes' stomach for poisons. He found none.

"Poison?" Pierce whispered as he sat with Jennings in the back of the crowded courtroom. "They don't think nearly cutting her head off was enough to kill her, the murderer needed to poison her, too?"

"Might think she was drugged and then taken to Mitre Square," Jennings whispered.

"Attract a bloody lot less attention walking with a live prostitute than dragging an unconscious unfortunate into a dark square."

Annie Phillips, Catherine Eddowes' daughter, testified next. She provided some background on Catherine and Catherine's father, who had been in the 18th Royal Irish or the Connaught Rangers, or maybe both. Annie had two brothers but apparently had lost track of them, as well as her father and mother. Detective Sergeant John Mitchell, City Police, testified that he had tried to find the father and brothers, but without success.

Dr. Brown testified that there was no basis to the theory that the body had been moved after death. Catherine Eddowes, like the other victims, was murdered where she was found.

City Constable Lewis Robinson explained how he took Eddowes to Bishopsgate Police Station when he found her drunk and smelling "strongly of drink" in the middle of a crowd on the night of Saturday, 29 September. Sergeant Byfield remembered her from that night at the station. He said she was "very drunk" and gave her name as Mary Ann Kelly. Next called was Constable Hutt, the Bishopsgate goaler, who testified about his brief conversation with Catherine/Mary that night, ending with her saying, "I shall get a bloody fine hiding when I get home" and his parting remark, "Serve you right; you have no right to get drunk."

George James Morris, the night watchman at the tea warehouse on Mitre Square, had nothing new to add, nor did George Clapp, caretaker at No. 5 Mitre Square, Constable Pierce, who lived on the square, Constable Long or Detective Halse. No one had seen the murderer or heard the murder.

Next into the witness box was Joseph Lawende, who was about to describe the man he had seen on the street with the victim, when Henry Crawford, City Solicitor, appearing on behalf of the City Police, shot to his feet and said, "Unless the jury wish it, I do not think further particulars should be given as to the appearance of this man."

Crawford had already spoken with the jury off the record, so the foreman dutifully said, "The jury do not desire it."

"But he's probably seen the sodding murderer," Pierce muttered.

Crawford asked Lawende, "You have given a description of the man to the police?"

"Yes."

The City Coroner, Samuel Frederick Langham, asked, "Would you know him again?"

"I doubt it. The man and woman were about nine or ten feet away from me."

"When was this?"

"I have no doubt it was half-past one o'clock when we rose to leave the club, so it would be twenty-five minutes to two when we passed the man and woman."

"Did you overhear anything either said?"

"No."

"That isn't what he told Collard during the house-to-house," Jennings overheard Major Smith in the police box before him whisper to Superintendent Foster. "Might be better to let the public know a description of the killer, even if it violates police policy."

Description or not, the jury returned a verdict of willful murder against a person or persons unknown.

It was late in the day when a startling revelation ran its worded way across the various police divisions in particular and the East End in total. It concerned the capabilities—or was it incapabilities?—of the bloodhound. A canine expert had pointed out that the animals stopped pursuit once they came across a streak of blood. In a local Whitechapel pub, a table of labourers discussed the newest information about man's best friend.

"Where the 'ell do you think they got their name? They are bloodhounds, ya know."

"My uncle raises hounds. The word 'blood' in their name is about recording their ancestry or bloodlines."

"Why would any fool do that?"

"First bloodhound came over from France with William the Conqueror; toffs want one descended from the original."

"Bullocks."

"Sod off. My uncle told me that when I was a lad."

"Their name must refer to tracking blood."

"Judas Priest! So they'll stop at the scene when they smell blood and won't set a paw farther?"

"Hell, old lags used to cut themselves and drip a spot of blood on a post or log to throw them off the scent."

"I'll be damned."

"More likely a dog would lose the scent with all the other scents of people and blood from slaughterhouses in Whitechapel."

"It'll be a helluva Tuesday in November if those hounds end up standing around, whimpering over some corpse."

The last was said more as a joke than a prophecy.

"They accepted our offer of a £100 reward, but not of our men's help," Colonel Sir Alfred Kirby of the Tower Hamlets Engineers told his officers in the unit's mess in Victoria Park Square. "Well, if they do not desire our assistance, there's nothing to be done for it."

Captain Sharpe asked, "Did they provide any reason for the refusal, sir?"

"Just that there would be a problem of compensation if an injury occurred."

"Compensation? The truth is, they'd rather have a battalion of Rippers on the streets than a squad of volunteer engineers," Major Rogers said. "I doubt we'd pose much threat to the average citizen's liberty, sir."

"Couldn't we take it up with the Home Secretary, sir?" the Colonel's aide asked.

"From what I understand it was as much the Home Secretary's idea to reject our offer as it was the decision of Sir Charles."

"We could have done something safe," the aide said. "Directed traffic to free a few Peelers to hunt the bloke if they're afraid of our getting injured."

"We are soldiers, sir," Major Rogers said, "even if volunteers. What good is our training if they never allow us in harm's way?"

"Enough, Major," Kirby said. "Ours not to reason why."

"Just to do nothing and let those poor women die," Major Rogers muttered.

Friday, 12 October

The long dry week continued with the sun ducking behind one rainless cloud then another. Even though he was starting firmly to believe that the Ripper only struck on weekends, with the worrying Nichols' Thursday summer night exception, there was no way Abberline was going to be caught at home if the Ripper changed his pattern. He spent the night that turned Thursday into Friday visiting police stations, constables on the beat, detectives in plainclothes, unfortunates on the streets and locals at doss houses until 5 a.m., when he finally returned home for a nap.

"Anything?" Emma asked, her eyes still closed as he slid into bed beside her.

"Nothing," he said, the word brimming with good news—no murders— and bad tidings—no Ripper apprehended and the threat of still more murders looming. He closed his eyes.

Sleep was already surging in from all sides as her hand reached out to squeeze his. "You'll find him. If anyone can, you will, Fred."

At 7:54 a.m. a telegram arrived via a messenger boy who used the front-door knocker like a snare drum. Another important witness or suspect demanded Abberline's personal attention. As he downed a cuppa and munched on a fried slice Emma had made him while he dressed, he couldn't remember which it was and, given the number of false leads in the case, it probably really didn't matter.

The Home Secretary's aide perused an urgent dispatch from the Foreign Office headed, "Pressing and Secret." Matthews had already scanned it, but only briefly as he prepared an answer on capital punishment for Parliament's Question Time on Monday. Given the issue's recent notoriety, some MP was certain to ask about it.

During a pause in drafting his answer, Matthews said, "Well, the fact the Marquis of Salisbury has the F.O. send us a dispatch from our Ambassador in Vienna means he thinks it has merit. The F.O. guards its domain with absolute and complete jealousy."

His aide nodded. The dispatch was from Sir Augustus Paget, the British Ambassador in Vienna, who had been approached by a man claiming that he could produce the Whitechapel murderer. There was one catch; he wanted the British government to foot his bill to journey to London where he would finger the Whitechapel slayer.

"What do we know about this informant?" Matthews asked, half his legally trained mind refocusing on his Question Time answer. Capital punishment was a difficult issue for him; personally he opposed it, but it was government policy and therefore his to defend. He would never repeat the flippant answer he had made the year before about a Miss Cass, incorrectly accused of prostitution. The furor in Parliament and the press still echoed painfully in his memory.

His aide scanned the rest of the dispatch. "The informant's been seen by the Ambassador and the Consul General in Vienna. Both think he is acting in good faith. He's an Austrian subject, born in Poland, has an English grandmother."

Matthews nodded approval. "Not a complete foreigner, then."

"Lives near Vienna and has a manufacture of drugs. Dispatch claims he is well dressed and of respectable appearance."

"A sound gentleman then; could afford the trip himself. Go on."

"He doesn't want his name disclosed because he's the chief of a socialist society, which he manages in Austria and Hungary. The party split some time past into two factions: his is a passive group; the other is a terrorist organization. He fears for his life. He won't name the killer without receiving a guaranteed reward."

"These socialists are suspicious fellows. All cloak and dagger; probably fears he'll trip on his cloak and fall on his dagger."

"They've communicated with the socialist leader in London, but the London leader couldn't match the suspected man's handwriting with the Ripper letters."

"Anderson says the letters are probably the work of some damn journalist. The Central News Agency distributes more false news than real, and the press has published enough details so anyone could forge a convincing letter."

"The man in Vienna showed Sir Augustus the coded communique from the London leader."

"Coded?"

"I imagine the socialists don't want anyone to read their mail; cloak and dagger again."

"If it was in code, the contents could have been pure gibberish for all Sir Augustus would have known." In his answer supporting the execution of criminals and felons, Matthews crossed off one phrase and inserted another, better phrase.

"The socialist in Vienna has ordered the London leader to keep the suspect under surveillance and to prevent his escape."

"Why couldn't the man have ordered the London leader to point the man out to the police and get his reward without ever setting foot outside Vienna?"

The aide shrugged. "In any case, the men on the ground in Vienna believe the informer has no personal gain in mind, except the glory of furthering the socialist cause. He wants the reward to go to the Society."

"Odd."

"Oh, the informer also wants to bring a colleague with him from Paris to London."

"Nothing wrong with that, I hazard to guess, if he proves able to identify the killer," Matthews said. "Although I would be far more comfortable if he would just tell us the suspect's name."

"He's afraid he will not receive the reward if he does. Sir Augustus had the Vienna police look into the man's background. He is a known socialist. Other than that, Sir Augustus feels he is quite respectable and of good character. He emphasizes again that he was well dressed."

Matthews nodded. "Sounds worth pursuing, but with the utmost caution. The sum involved is far from negligible. Let us ensure we are not throwing good money after a phantom."

A tip came in suggesting that Charles Ludwig's double, Schloski, was working for a barber in West Green Road, Tottenham. Abberline and Helson rushed to the shop only to find the man was gone once again.

"But his name's not Schloski, Mr. Abberline," the owner said. "It's Klosowski and his first name's Severin."

Severin Klosowski. The name rang out like a firearm discharge. They had been looking for Klosowski for two months. Good God, they might be onto the Ripper at last.

The owner continued on about Ludwig's double, a man who had an alibi walking around Whitechapel in his look-a-like, "He's a Pole, not a Russian. Came here last summer. He was some sort of a barber-surgeon in the Tsarist Army."

It was the Severin Klosowski they had been looking for, no doubt about it.

"I don't know where he's at now. Quit a couple of days ago. Odd thing about him. . ."

"What was that?" Abberline asked.

"As I said, he's a Pole, but he talks like an American."

Elsewhere, a hand penned a poetic note: "I'm not a butcher, / I'm not a Yid, / Nor yet a foreign skipper, / But I'm your own light-hearted friend, / Yours truly, Jack the Ripper."

A wry smirk of evil endeavour crossed the man's grim face as his pen finished his note.

Abberline and Smith brought their men to a heightened state of watchfulness.

Maximum Met and City patrols went out for Friday night. The Ripper had not struck in two weeks. The dry weather continued and it would be a moonlit night. The streets would be crowded with vagrants and n'er-do-wells, unfortunates and their customers—and the Ripper?

"The papers are still roasting us alive for rubbing out that writing," Helson moaned, reaching for his handkerchief as he and Abberline prepared in the latter's office to head out once again to tour the Ripper's realm. "My cold just might outlast the Ripper. Luckily the children haven't caught it; they always seem to, sooner or later."

Helson told Abberline about a statement from Sir Charles in *The Times* in which the Commissioner stated that he was decreasing the shortest permissible height for members of the Metropolitan Police from 5 foot 8.5 inches to 5 foot 7 inches. The age limit was still 35, but as a rule a recruit had to be under 27 so he could put in sufficient service years to entitle him to a full pension. An accompanying story argued that detectives should not necessarily be chosen from the patrolman ranks where qualities needed for detective work might not be in abundance. It asked, "What really intelligent person wants to spend two or three years trudging a beat in the backstreets of Stepney before being considered for better things?"

"Or kowtowing to dull authority," Abberline said. "The copper who makes waves is demoted and the one who would like to make waves eventually quits."

"At least Sir Charles said it was not true that a constable had to serve two or three years in division before joining CID."

"I am more than certain that two years will still be the norm in practice, unless a man's smarter than that detective of yours, Sherlock Holmes."

"Probably have to be smarter than Sherlock's smarter brother, Mycroft."

Chapter Eighteen

Saturday, 13 October

The night passed quietly; very quietly for the headless body of a well-dressed man found on the railway tracks in Kensington. Police and volunteers searched for the missing head so that proper identification could be made. It was not found. The search continued.

The operation Sir Charles had authorized on the 1ˢᵗ was finally ready. Hundreds of detectives gathered to search some of the sorriest slums of Whitechapel and Spitalfields. The designated search area was bounded by Lamb Street, Commercial Street, the Great Eastern Railway and Buxton Street on the north, Whitechapel Road on the south, the City Boundary to the west, and Albert Street, Dunk Street, Chicksand Street and Great Garden Street on the east. Plainclothes detectives went from house to house, searching every room, looking under beds, in cupboards, inspecting knives, and interviewing every single person they found in every home, business or on the street. Sir Charles' fear of widespread obstruction failed to materialize. The press reported, "The greatest good feeling prevails towards the police, and noticeably in the most squalid dwellings the police had no difficulty in getting information."

After consulting Sir Charles and Secretary Matthews, Major Smith, Acting Commissioner of the City of London Police, sent a memorandum to the Foreign Office in Vienna advising them that the informer might be allowed to come over if he agreed to name the murderer upon arrival. Matthews had argued that the man should be asked to give definite details and then, and only then, if an arrest were made, the 2,000-florin reward would be paid. Matthews' memo had sufficient lawyerly ifs, buts and perhaps's in it to guarantee that he had enough leeway to find a course to the leeside if the whole affair turned from tempest to storm. As a Queen's Counsel, MP and finally a cabinet member, Matthews had well learned how to negotiate the rough seas of politics and diplomacy, always keeping his stern well protected.

Elsewhere in London, Margaret Knight was charged with assaulting a 10-year-old girl with a broken piece of glass. Mary Hawkes and James Fordham came before a magistrate for stealing a man's money and trousers after he was accosted in a lodging house bedroom in Flower and Dean Street. These were three among many offenders of the day.

"See," a West Side citizen commented, "the police are cracking down on those criminals in the East End. It's about time."

Jack the Ripper became a pretense for mischief of many kinds. He was now a household name like Guy Fawkes and Dick Turpin. Young toughs used the pretense of searching for Jack the Ripper to harass lone working men and toffs found about at night in the East End, asking for coins. If not paid off, the toughs threatened to haul the victim to the nearest police station claiming he was Jack the Ripper.

A young girl might accept the shelter of a gentleman's umbrella only to walk along asking if it were true that the Ripper was "a-cutting down the feminine seek in London?" Realizing "seek" meant "sex," the stranger would say, "Yes," and follow with a discourse on how the number of murders was increasing. The wonder of it all was why the frail slip of a thing had voluntarily walked alongside the man alone in the first place. The woman would shake with fear, look apprehensively about and continue to walk towards home or work, shop or croft with a total stranger. But after all he was well-dressed; a gentleman.

Sunday, 14 October

The Ripper remained inactive as the Met continued their extensive search through Whitechapel and Spitalfields. After church with Emma, Abberline took time to consult his friend, the Professor.

"A rather hazy series of accusations hint the Masonic Lodge is somehow implicated in the Whitechapel murders," Abberline said. He uncorked a salt-glazed stoneware he had procured at a nearby public house and poured himself a full measure. It was not a very good wine, but then again, he was not a very good connoisseur. "Evidently the Master Mason draws his right thumb across his throat in some ritual threatening a throat-cutting for anyone revealing the society's secrets."

"You might have something there, Frederick. In Masonic tradition, the word 'Juwes' is supposed to refer to the three men who murdered the Masonic Grand Master and builder of Solomon's Temple, Hiram Abiff. The murderers were Jubela, Jubelo and Jubelum. The word 'Juwes' supposedly comes from their names. The murderers were found lamenting what they had done. Jubela was supposed to have said, 'Oh that my throat is cut across, my tongue torn out, my body buried in sand.' Jubelo said, 'Oh that my left breast be torn open, my heart and vital organs torn out and thrown over my left shoulder.' Jubelum said, 'Let my body be severed in two and my bowels burnt to ashes.' A significant story, perhaps, if we guess that the murderer is a Mason and, most importantly, barking mad."

It was like viewing a web spun by a drunken spider. The Professor went on to argue that the murderer lived in a world of disconnected strands, asymmetrical patterns and unfinished webs: a mad, distorted world, so anything was possible.

"The story itself is a great humbug, of course," the Professor said, "but the Ripper may believe it. He could easily incorporate it into his abnormal way of thinking. This would be more likely if being a Mason were, say, the only achievement in his life."

"One of our suspects is a Mason and he hasn't had too many achievements, but all this could be mere coincidence, Professor. After all, Eddowes' intestines were over her right shoulder, not her left."

The Professor nodded.

"Sir Charles is a mason," Abberline said, "and a fairly senior one. He may have rubbed that writing off the wall not because of any fear of an uprising against the East End Jews at all. He may have simply wanted anything even remotely related to the Masons kept out of the case."

The two men refilled their cups.

The Professor laughed. "There's always the possibility that the Ripper is simply a lousy speller."

"Or that someone in no way connected to the murders wrote the words on the wall. He'd never come forward now and admit he wrote that drivel, not after all the publicity about it."

"Precisely what Sir Charles said he wanted to avoid by expunging the message from that wall."

"He certainly failed to expunge it from the public mind."

"The writing certainly looks alike," the River Tyne Police Superintendent concluded in his office overlooking the broad river in Newcastle upon Tyne in northeast England. He held up two pieces of paper: one a facsimile of the Ripper postcard, the other articles signed by an Austrian seaman who had joined the crew of a Faversham vessel Saturday, 13 October, in the Tyne. The ship had sailed for France.

"We'll notify the French police and have the Frenchies look into it," the Super told his subordinate. "Probably only coincidental. With hundreds of thousands of people trying to match someone else's writing to these Ripper samples from the newspapers, there's bound to be a few people whose handwriting will be similar to Jack's. The man will probably prove to be innocent."

The police arrested a man in Liverpool trying to hang himself. When he confessed to murdering a woman by throwing her over a bridge parapet in London on the night of Tuesday, 9 October, their interest rose. When he mentioned he had recently been discharged from the *National Eagle*, an American ship, their interest soared. But when it was found he was at sea at the time of the Nichols and Chapman murders, their interest evaporated. Since every policeman wanted to solve the Ripper murders, every criminal's worth was assessed according to his chances of being the Whitechapel murderer. On the scales of importance, Liverpool's suspect sailor came off weighing less than sea foam. The state could hang him for pitching some unknown female over a bridge and onto an embankment, but the police would condemn him for not having anything to do with the Ripper murders.

"Major Smith's been rather busy the past few nights keeping an eye on Eddy for us," Abberline said as he helped Helson fold street maps from the house-to-house search.

Helson smiled. The secret patrol was public knowledge. Several thousand Metropolitan District policemen each with ears and eyes, each on alert for anything suspicious, couldn't help but see a little of this and a lot of that. Abberline often got a report on His Royalness before Major Smith did.

"Poor Major Smith," Abberline said, "Has to keep all this quiet. Well, he's doing a fairly good job; couldn't help it that Sir Charles chose Enright to head our side of things. I'll give the Major credit; he hasn't said a thing to me about it. But I don't hold it against him. I'd do the same if I were in his size 9s."

Monday, 15 October

Light wispy sprays of whitish cloud tinted a pale blue sky that deepened into a fine azure as the day passed. The second weekend without any stirrings from the Ripper left Abberline and his colleagues puzzled, but relieved. Unfortunately Swanson's list of possible suspects he had sent Abberline led only to cleared suspects.

The crackdown on crime in the East End continued as did the house-to-house search.

"Albert Bentley, Florence Bentley and William Shepherd, you are charged with being in the company of prostitutes in a common lodging house at 8 White's Row, Spitalfields. How do you plead?"

It was the beginning of a brief trial. Albert was 11; Florence, five; William, eight. The house they had been found in had 102 persons registered in 51 double beds. The children were sent to an appropriate poorhouse.

The volume of mail concerning the Whitechapel murderer was extreme in both amount and rationality. Letters pointed poisoning pens at this and that person. Among the accused were a lunatic living in Fulham who recited tragic stories while wielding an ivory handled knife taken from an ever-present shiny black leather bag; two Germans who worked in the Hanbury Street Sugar House; William Onion, recently released from a lunatic asylum; a watchman in Mitre Square who had been seen peeping out a warehouse door and laughing at the police (this revelation being seen in a dream); and a German who skinned people and used these second skins as disguises which he pasted on his face with American glue.

There were letters from ladies of great respectability offering to take the place of prostitutes to act as decoys and from fetish seekers wanting locks of this or that victim's hair so they could divine the murderer by touching such objects. Letters suggested that female dummies be placed in dark corners which would entrap anyone touching them in an octopodial embrace of steel-springed arms. There were letters urging that women wear spike collars and letters advocating the five hundred odd detectives on the case be augmented by borrowing a thousand policemen from Berlin. The young Emperor of Germany, being fond of his Royal English grandmother, would no doubt willingly lend such a force. Felons in Berlin applauded the idea, but cooler heads containing English-speaking tongues commented on the language barrier. Logic, let alone practicalities did not deter the letter writers. One suggested that since the Ripper was stunning his victims with a chloroform-soaked handkerchief, the police should arrest anyone who came near a woman and tried to blow his nose. Helson, still suffering from his cold, thought this a singularly nonsensical idea. Still another letter suggested that newsagents write "horrible" beside the names of clients who read the newspaper accounts of the latest atrocity too eagerly. Given record newspaper sales, everyone in London would probably be labelled "horrible." Another missive proposed the police hold a public meeting to discuss how to catch the murderer. Since he was bound to attend they could lock him up once the meeting had started. Why he should so surely attend and, more importantly, how he was to be identified in the mob wasn't specified. The writer merely proposed the theory; implementation was left to the police.

Pierce had a solution. "They'll be fed dozens of cups of tea. No one will be allowed to exit until the Ripper confesses. He shouldn't be able to hold it any longer than anyone else. No one pees until we get a confession."

Jennings shook his head as he looked up from the weather report he was composing and wondered if half the people in London, including his colleague, had gone looney.

"That rabble-rousing dramatic critic over at *The Star* has found an ally," Pierce said over the rim of his cup of tea.

"An ally?" Jennings asked amid charts and maps, temperature lists and barometric readings. It was all meteorology to him.

"That young Welshman, Lloyd George, is going after the police for harassing dockworkers, denying strikers their rights and failing to catch the Ripper. He and his radical friends made an excursion into the back alleys of Whitechapel a few nights ago. It wasn't in any of the papers, which is an oddity in itself. A pack of politicians ploughing their way through Whitechapel and the press not getting wind of it, or more exactly, their not making sure the press got wind of it—amazing."

"Wind? Prevailing winds were—"

Pierce, oblivious to his colleague's attempts to concentrate, went on, "They describe the appalling conditions in Whitechapel in speech after speech. Old Tories are being roasted alive."

Jennings focused on the cloud cover over Western Scotland and the increasing rain squalls in the Highlands. Tomorrow should bring some clouds and. . .

Old Boy went on, "I figure Sir Charles' biggest blunder was the Cass case, that respectable young woman who was wrongly arrested for soliciting in Regent Street last year; caused Matthews no end of bother for his flippant statement about it in Parliament. Bad enough Sir Charles sent his constables in like troops—with troops—against the workers, the unemployed and the Irish in Trafalgar Square on Bloody Sunday last November; that only made him against Labour. But when he didn't apologize for the Cass foul-up, he went against Respectable Womanhood."

"Who isn't?" Jennings asked, his mind and his heart straying from the Highlands.

"Who isn't what?"

"Against respectable womanhood; can't get anywhere with them, Old Boy," Jennings said and returned to the weather. Unlike everyone else, he had to do something about it.

The package moved through Her Majesty's Mail with speed and ease. Postal workers were proud of their swift, efficient service. The package was addressed to Mr. George Lusk of the Mile End Vigilance Committee.

Tuesday, 16 October

At 11:30 a.m. the new General Gordon monument was uncovered in Trafalgar Square. The Ripper was defenseless against British reverence for dead heroes as the press covered the event with vigor and dispatch. Just to the east, the police search of Whitechapel and Spitalfields continued for the fourth day.

The man appeared out of nowhere. The sergeant on desk duty at Kings Street Police Station in Westminster looked up and there he was, like a phantom materializing.

The man said, "I've lost a black bag."

The sergeant reached for the appropriate form and a dip pen.

"Sir, where did you lose the bag?"

"Cut 'er wide open I did. Wide open."

"Sir, I—"

"Oh, shuuush or I'll cut off your head."

The sergeant stared at the man, pen dipped in India ink poised above the form. It sounded as if he might need another form.

"I could you know. I'm an engineer, but I studied medicine for some years. Yes, I could very easily cut off your fine round head."

The sergeant gestured to a nearby constable who pinned the man's arms. Another constable went for the divisional surgeon. It was not long before the man had been examined, declared a lunatic with homicidal tendencies and placed in a cell. A passing constable recognized him. "Don't know his name, but he's been over at Lambeth Infirmary for weeks. Nutty as a Christmas pud, he is."

The man's writing somewhat resembled the Ripper facsimiles, but there was little else to link him to the Whitechapel crimes. He was held for further investigation before being committed to an asylum and forgotten by the Ripper investigators and the world.

The package arrived at George Lusk's residence in the late mail. Lusky sniffed at the package and did not display his usual air of indifference to the post. He pawed at the string and the cover, but finding no way to tear it open, he tired of the enterprise and padded off to laze on the front room rug as near to the coal fire as he could without risking immolation. It was a chilly day.

One serious semi-savant at a City Mission meeting, possibly influenced by stories from the Levant and the Near East about Sharia law's stringent punishments, argued for the painful mutilation of criminals. His thesis was that a felon would repent and change his lifestyle rather than face further painful punishment of a fierce nature. The threat of having a finger lopped off would surely deter a thief from further larceny. Unfortunately, this advocate noted, people were too kind and preferred to mete out painless and therefore useless punishment. His argument floundered when someone noted, "The threat of being mutilated by the Ripper hasn't led any whores in Whitechapel to renounce their calling."

Lusky sprawled on the rug by the fire. He had ventured out to hunt, but his stalking had led to nothing. Sometimes hunting went that way. His human, George Lusk would be home soon and that often meant a treat. Perhaps there was one in that package that had come in the post.

The Vienna socialist and his possible lead continued to occupy Secretary Matthew's time and to whet his more than ample ambition, even though he had thought the matter settled. The informant was confident he could persuade his fellow travelers in London to point out the Ripper within 24 hours of his arriving from Vienna, but now he needed 2,000 florins before he could journey to London.

Matthews reread the dispatch. The latter part of the note troubled him. Sir Augustus Paget, the F.O.'s man in Vienna, had advanced the man 2,000 florins on his own responsibility while telling him the 2,000 florins would, of course, come out of the reward when it was paid. Frowning, Matthews asked his assistant, "Was not the reward 2,000 florins in total?"

His assistant nodded.

In any case, the man was supposedly on his way. There was also a request for a letter from Sir Charles stipulating that the informant's name would never be divulged.

Matthews was pleased. The man was coming without Matthews having to commit himself. Sir Augustus had advanced the money. Sir Charles would be responsible for the informant's secrecy of name. Matthews could step in and claim credit if the man did identify the Ripper and if he didn't, Matthews was free of any responsibility, let alone blame. Matthews smiled with the contented cunning of the bureaucrat about to reap the rewards of a decision not made.

George Lusk arrived home at 1 Alderney Road, late, tired, hungry and frustrated. The Mile End builder was discouraged with the way the press was still portraying Whitechapel. There seemed no end to their insults, both veiled and unveiled.

Hallo! What's this? A package in the evening post; postmarked the 15th. As he set it on his desk in the study, Lusky reached up and pawed at the box with both gray forepaws.

"Down, Lusky."

Puzzled, Lusk snapped the string and tore away the wrapping. He lifted the top of the box and gasped. His heart seemed to rattle, beating in agitated discord. The box contained a blood-striped whitish blob in the shape of half a human kidney and a note. Lusk gulped down the searing bile of revulsion in his throat and, gingerly picking up the note to avoid any contact with the kidney, read:

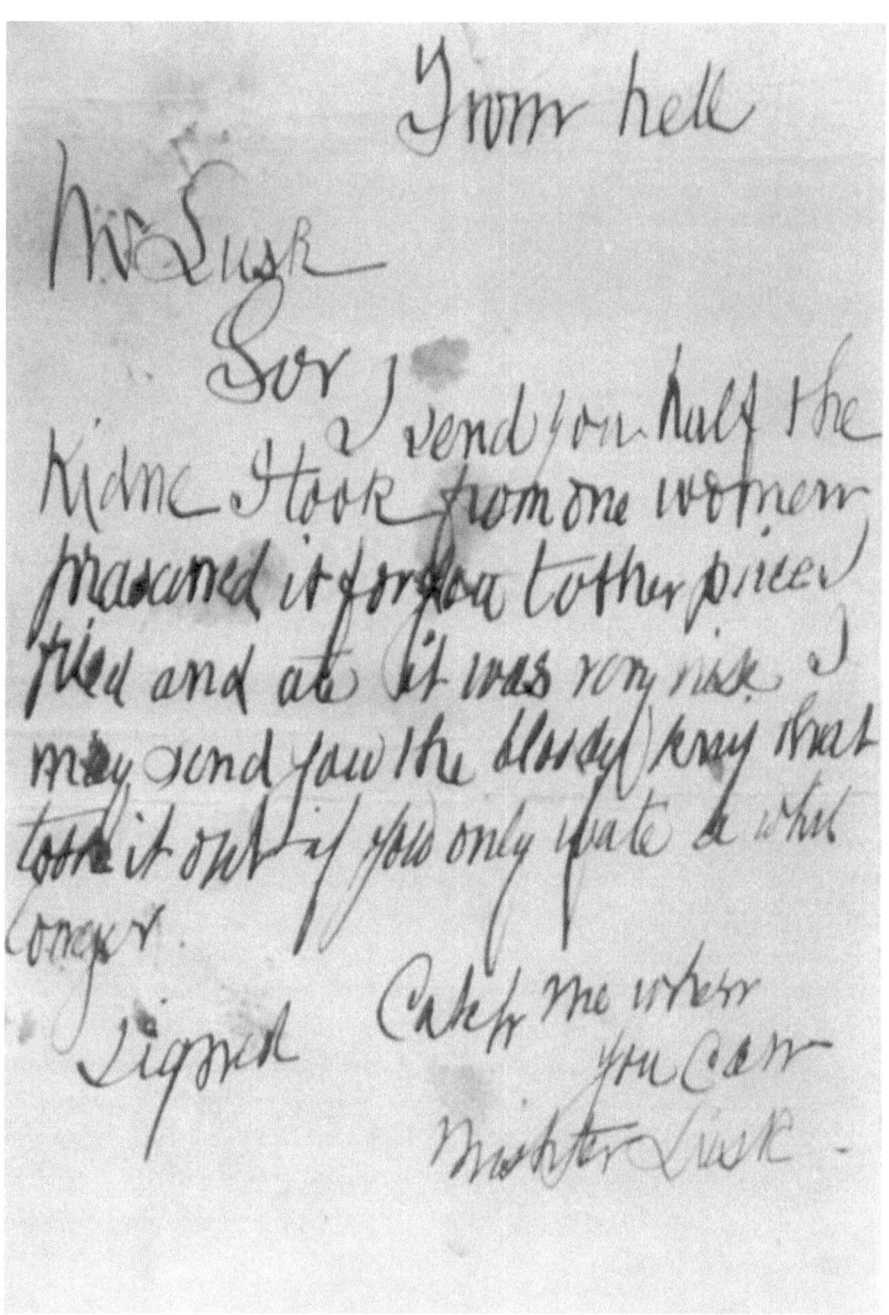

From Hell letter sent to George Lusk

From hell

Mr Lusk
Sor

I send you half the Kidne I took from one woman
prasarved it for you tother piece I fried and ate it was very nise.
I may send you the bloody knif that took it out if you only wate
a whil longer.

Signed
Catch me if you can Mishter Lusk

Brushing aside his curious cat, Lusk thrust the note back into the box and
slammed on the cover to hide the hideous sight.

What to do, what to do? Lusk wondered. The papers were full of reports
of letters supposedly from the Ripper, yet the police appeared to believe them
all hoaxes. Lusk had no desire to appear in the newspapers as the purveyor of
a hoax. He had a hard- and long-earned reputation to preserve. Even so, the
note had been sent with what appeared to be a kidney. Did it really come from
a victim?

If he hadn't lost his dear Susannah last February, he would have consulted
her. She always knew just what to do in the stickiest of situations. He considered
asking one of his grown sons, Albert or Walter, but quickly rejected the idea.
They were busy with their own lives and why involve them in something that
must be a prank? Someone was playing a joke on him and wanted him to take
the "kidne" to the police or the papers. He finally made his decision; he would
not be the butt of their joke.

Seven-year-old Lillian, the youngest of his seven children, scampered into
his study with a wild scream of abandon. Lusk thrust the parcel into a desk
drawer just in time to catch Lillian as she launched herself at him.

"You're getting too big to be hurling yourself like a rugby forward into me,"
Lusk said, but smiled broadly all the same. "You'll break my back before long."

"Never, Daddy," Lilly said, nestling into his arms like a baby robin into a
nest. "You're too big and strong to ever break, not ever."

Wednesday, 17 October

While the pauper residents of Whitechapel and Spitalfields cast solemn eyes
into the foggy, dull weather and half-expected Jack the Ripper to materialize
from behind the nearest lamp post, a menace of an even more fundamental
nature threatened the equally poor peasants of Welikogub, a forest district 100
miles from St. Petersburg. Here the natives were besieged by hungry bears who
killed and mauled in as brutish a fashion as the monster of London's East End.
The bears actually claimed more victims. But bears being bears and the victims

being Russian, neither the bruins nor the bitten received much press attention in London.

"Matthews wants me to state in writing—would you believe it?—that we have expended all means to find the Ripper and that our only recourse is to offer a reward," Sir Charles ranted to his private secretary in the privacy of his Met office. "Does he think me daft?"

No stranger to bureaucratic wars in and out of the army, Sir Charles declined to say any such a thing, let alone in writing. He dictated his reply, "To this I have to reply, NO. I think we have hardly begun: it often takes many months to discover a criminal."

With that the reward matter reached a bureaucratic impasse and, the issue apparently fading publicly, the Home Office let the matter die a quiet death.

As the Met search of Whitechapel and Spitalfields continued, Abberline took afternoon tea with the Professor, who noted as he played mother, "After some research at King's College library I found a case similar to this Ripper style of mutilation-murder. Sugar? Cream? No, that's grand then. In the 15th Century a French aristocrat, Gilles de Rais, one of the richest men in France, had his servant bring him peasant youngsters, whom he abused sexually before murdering the child or watching them be murdered. He enjoyed it, from all available reports. He often caressed, had sex with or dismembered the corpse while it was still warm."

"Did no one stop him when they noticed children going missing?" Abberline asked, sipping his Darjeeling tea as he eased onto a well-used sofa. His varicose vein ached, but the tea sometimes helped.

"Not until he ran afoul of a political rival, the Bishop of Nantes, who brought him to trial in 1440 for heresy, sodomy and murdering 140 children—apparently in that order."

"Good God; that many?"

"The death toll may have been higher. He was executed, so we shall never know with any certainty."

"He must have been a rare case," Abberline said, as visions of pursuing the Ripper through the murder of 140 unfortunates cascaded through his exhausted mind.

"Far from rare, in fact; the Beane family in the 1430s, who lived east of Edinburgh, were known cannibals and practiced incest. There were also a series of similar such killings as we have experienced that occurred between 1861 and '65 in France. A servant, Joseph Philippe, murdered and mutilated a number of prostitutes. He strangled at least two women before slitting their throats. The face of one of his victims—his eighth—turned black from strangulation before her throat was cut."

"He might be our Ripper."

"I doubt it; Phillipe was guillotined in 1866, unless his ghost is skulking about Whitechapel."

"Probably is; applauding the Ripper."

"In 1867, Frederick Baker abducted and dismembered a seven-year-old girl in Hampshire. He carved the child to pieces in a barbaric frenzy."

"So much for all that rubbish that an Englishman couldn't do such horrific acts."

"A mad mind has no nationality. Eight years ago in Paris, Louis Menesclou strangled a little girl—three or four years old—slept with her body under his bed, then chopped her into pieces."

"Was he caught?" Another potential suspect?

"Yes. Lost his head."

"Not a viable suspect then," Abberline said with pursed lips. "I thought this kind of butchery was something new, but apparently I was wrong."

"Probably as old as man; as long as there was a brain to go berserk, there was a chance for it to go the way of the Ripper. Just today we have the press to spread tales of their atrocities far and wide. A hundred or more years ago, the news wouldn't have spread beyond the village it occurred in, save for tales of werewolves, ghouls, vampires and bloodsuckers tearing their victims apart. Tales used to frighten children or make daughters stay a little closer to home when young men came calling."

"More deranged minds out there than your average John Bull could ever imagine."

"Not really deranged minds," the Professor said, frowning as he considered the idea and sipped his tea. "More of a cold, calculating rationality to carry out their crimes, often without being caught for quite some time, combined with a chilling inability to see or treat others as thinking, feeling human beings."

"So they know what they are doing is wrong, criminally and morally?"

"Beyond any doubt; they just don't care or even have the ability to care."

That evening at a meeting of the Mile End Vigilance Committee, George Lusk hesitated, uncertain whether to mention the alleged Ripper note and the "kidne." After a discussion about plans to increase patrols in the area, he waited for a pause in the conversation and blurted out, "I received a letter from the Ripper and half a kidney."

Joseph Aarons, the treasurer, laughed but stopped when Lusk grumbled, "It is no laughing matter to me."

After Lusk described what had arrived in the post, the committee discussed the matter at length. Finally, Aarons said, consulting the silver time piece attached to his suit vest with a matching chain, "It's late. Why don't we wait until tomorrow and go see someone about it?"

Thursday, 18 October

During the night on Tooting common, a sheep was killed. The inspector summoned to the scene thought it might be a case for the bloodhounds. He requested the canines be brought, but Burgho had already returned home to Scarborough and Barnaby was out training.

Early in the morning, Aarons and the Mile End Vigilance Committee's secretary, Mr. B. Harris, and members Messrs. Reeves and Lawton called on George Lusk at his home to see the supposed Ripper note and kidney. In his study, Lusk, his face set in a grimace, took the 3.5-inch square box from his desk drawer.

"Throw it away," Lusk said as he set it down on his desk. "I hate the sight of it." He had slept only intermittently the night before and his head was engulfed by a dull ache.

After no one moved to do the honours, Aarons reached forth and with great care opened the box. Inside, nestled against the note, sat what did indeed appear to be a kidney cut in half diagonally. The men wrinkled their noses and backed away. The organ stank.

"Doesn't look like a sheep kidney," Aarons said, frowning down at the contents of the box.

One of the others carefully took the note, read it and passed it around. Lusk wished they would just tell him it was a hoax and throw it all in a dustbin for disposal far, far away from him.

"Why don't we take it over to Dr. Frederick Wiles?" Aarons suggested. "He can tell us if it's really a human kidney or just a hoax."

The five men trooped over to 56 Mile End Road. The doctor was out but his assistant, Mr. F. S. Reed, agreed to inspect the contents of the box. After peering down at the organ, he said, "It appears to be a human kidney, probably belonging to a female."

His five guests fell silent. Lusk swallowed hard. Why would the killer send him part of a victim's kidney? True, he was well known and had been mentioned in the newspapers as a leading proponent of the vigilance committee, but why wouldn't the killer send the kidney to one of the policemen investigating the case? Was he safe from the lunatic? Were his children safe? He decided to ensure they did not venture forth alone and certainly not out at night, at least until the murderer was apprehended and hung.

Reed said, "It's part of the left kidney and I suggest that the woman had been in the habit of drinking or the kidney has been preserved in wine."

Having thanked Reed, the five men and their kidney stood on the stoop at 56 Mile End Road and debated how to proceed. They agreed that if Dr. Wiles had identified the organ as a woman's kidney, they would have gone straight to the police, but Reed was a just an assistant. Although no one said so, Lusk felt that no one wanted to deliver what might well turn out to be a hoax to the police.

"Why don't we try an expert?"

"Where?"

The five men and their kidney now trooped over to London Hospital in Whitechapel, where they convinced Dr. Thomas Horrocks Openshaw, Curator of the Pathological Museum, to examine it under a microscope.

Openshaw reported, "It is from someone who died about the same time as the Mitre Square woman, and I agree with Reed, it is a ginny kidney, belonging to someone who drank far more than was wise."

"Can you tell anything else?" Lusk asked.

"It's probably from a woman of about 45 years of age, and the organ was taken from the body within the past three weeks."

On the steps of London Hospital, the committee members reconvened. After a brief discussion, they agreed. With such eminent professional analysis, a hoax was ruled out and Lusk's party took the parcel and its macabre contents to Leman Street Police Station.

"A letter from the Ripper, you say," the desk sergeant said.

"And a kidney," Aarons added.

"Part of a kidney," Lusk corrected his colleague. He wanted to stick to the truth as precisely as possible.

"Part of a kidney, it is then," the sergeant said, scribbling a note with a dip pen. "Had an arm last week and an ear the week afore that. Soon we should have an entire corpse, whole and complete, just like Dr. Frankenstein."

The sergeant chuckled, but Lusk and his colleagues just stared at him.

"Where are this note and kidney—sorry, part of a kidney?" the sergeant asked peering over his prominent mustache at Lusk.

Lusk had declined to be the bearer, so Aarons handed over the box with its gruesome contents. The sergeant accepted the gift, set it on his desk and finished filling out the appropriate form. When he was done, he looked up to see that the five men were still standing before his desk like choir boys before an altar waiting for absolution.

"Thank you, gentlemen."

Lusk wondered what happened next, but was uncertain whether civilians were allowed to ask after the intricacies of such police business. With a nod to the sergeant, Lusk led his committeemen out of the station, their civic duty done.

Although Robert Anderson thought a journalist had written the 1 October postcard and Sir Charles agreed, on 10 October Sir Charles told Geoffrey Lushington, Permanent Undersecretary at the Home Office, "At present, I think the whole thing is a hoax, but we are bound to try and ascertain the writer in this case." Therefore, Chief Inspector Henry Moore had been assigned to compare the handwriting in the various Ripper letters received to date.

Having not yet heard of Lusk's kidney and note, Moore sat at his desk in Scotland Yard across from Abberline and Helson, and reported, "Having carefully perused all the 'Jack the Ripper' letters, I failed to find any similarity of handwriting in any of them, with the exception of the two well remembered communications which were sent to the Central News office; one a letter, dated 25 September 1888, and the other a postcard, bearing the postmark 1 October 1888."

"So they're a hoax?" Helson asked, snuffling his runny nose.

"I believe so; at least no single person wrote them all, save for those two."

Abberline said, "Many appear to have been written by an educated man trying to appear less so."

"A journalist?" Helson suggested.

"The ones that were sent to the Central News office don't have any spelling mistakes and are neatly written," Moore said.

"And they weren't sent to Scotland Yard," Helson said, "so the writer knew just where to send them for maximum publicity—as a journalist would."

Moore said, "One of the letters sent to the Central News was posted in the East Central District, where Fleet Street is; home of most of the city's newspapers."

"But the press delayed publishing them," Abberline said. "If a journalist wrote them, wouldn't at least their own paper have published them immediately for what they call a scoop?"

"So are they a hoax or not?" Helson asked, desperation and frustration in his voice.

Abberline and Moore shrugged in unison.

The police turned a suspicious eye on any case of a male brutally assaulting a female. Santiago Dias, a Frenchman and cabinet maker, fell into this category when he beat up a woman in Cleveland Street at 1 a.m. His past behavior came under careful examination, but his activities showed no links to the Whitechapel murders. He left court that day 40 shillings poorer—enough to pay for basic groceries for a year—getting off with a warning and the fine. It was all the punishment beating up a woman deserved. After all, she was an unfortunate.

The massive Met search of Whitechapel and Spitalfields was finally completed after six intensive days. Despite the effort, the Ripper was not found.

"Of course," Abberline said as he rode in a hansom to CID headquarters with Helson after the long final day of searching, "We know so little about the Ripper, we could have interviewed him a dozen times and not known it."

Although his varicose vein throbbed with a pain that he feared might fell him, Abberline did not go home that night in what was becoming his normal routine. His usual 10-hour-day, six-day-a-week schedule, like all the inspectors working the case, had only increased with each murder. As the sun set he watched the last of its light filter through his office window, glinting off the coal dust in the air. In the summer, with the window open, everything in his office was coated with a fine coal-dust layer despite the best efforts of the charwoman. In the winter, with the window closed, his office's location next to a coal storage room from whence came constables and inspectors carrying scuttles of coal to their offices and billets, combined with the coal heater in his office did nothing to improve the cleanliness of his work space.

Whatever the state of his office, wiping his hat off with the back of his suit jacket sleeve, Abberline hobbled out, walking stick in hand. After a grueling night on the streets, at 5:30 a.m., exhausted, Abberline reached home and bed. He had begun to have trouble concentrating and when he tried to sleep, he invariably failed to find any deep reinvigorating sleep. His mind ran this way and that thinking about this suspect and that. Was one of their suspects the Ripper or was the Ripper still unknown to them? Helson had told him that the *Atlanta Constitution* had pondered whether there was a tie between a series of brutal murders of Negro women that remained unsolved from three years ago, which had abruptly stopped. Had the killer moved to England? As he tossed and turned, Abberline's active mind wondered, considered and pondered. He finally fell asleep, but even in sleep, his mind pursued suspects. Awake and asleep, the Ripper dogged his every thought.

Friday, 19 October

Deciding to feed a cold, Helson sat down to a breakfast of tea, fried slice, fried eggs and a fried slice of ham as he read a newspaper story, which said, "It is stated that Sir Charles Warren's bloodhounds were out for practice at Tooting yesterday morning and were lost. Telegrams have been dispatched to all Metropolitan Police stations stating that, if seen anywhere, information is to be immediately sent to Scotland Yard."

Helson frowned, shook his head and told Mary, "Press got it wrong again. Turned a dead sheep into a trial for the bloodhounds; the dogs weren't even there."

"Maybe Albert could become a correspondent," Mary said, mentioning their ten-year-old son with a motherly smile. "He has only a passing familiarity with the truth."

"God forbid he ever becomes a newspaperman; better a police surgeon than a bloody newspaperman."

That morning Chief Inspector Donald Sutherland Swanson, in charge of coordinating inquiries and long buried in reports, witness statements and all manner of paperwork pertaining to the investigations, sought to summarize police activity in a report for the Home Office. He wrote that the police had distributed 80,000 handbills requesting information about suspicious people, conducted an extensive house-to-house search throughout Whitechapel/ Spitalfields, questioned more than 2,000 lodgers, made inquiries of Asiatics in various opium dens in London, and had the Thames Police question sailors aboard a fleet's worth of ships in the docks and on the river.

Puffing on his pipe, Swanson paused, consulted his voluminous notes on the investigations and continued his report. The police had questioned more than 300 people as a result of communications from the public including 76 butchers and slaughterers, a troupe of Greek gypsies in the area, and "three of the persons calling themselves Cowboys who belonged to the American Exhibition" who "were traced and satisfactorily accounted for themselves." Swanson did not bother to explain that the cowboys arrived in London as part of Buffalo Bill Cody's Wild West Show to perform at Queen Victoria's Golden Jubilee celebration. The show sailed back to the New World in the spring of 1888, but some members of the troupe liked England well enough to stay on in the Old World. Swanson smiled; let the Home Office mandarins ponder the mystery of what American cowboys were doing camped out in the East End.

Swanson paused, puffed on his pipe, and continued. The police had detained 80 people. Abberline and his detectives had produced some 1,600 sets of papers related to the murders. Swanson had 994 dockets besides police reports. All of the paperwork was the result of long hours of duty and nights devoid of sleep. Swanson himself put in extraordinarily long hours. Even when he decided to steal a nap, let alone a full night's sleep, having read the gory reports and seen the vivid photographs of the victims, he rarely slept. He had even heard that many a detective who had seen the mutilated bodies of the victims now complained of loss of appetite and nausea at the mere sight of red meat, let alone of a butcher shop. Swanson did not include the latter information in his report, although, he realized, he hadn't touched his cold roast beef at breakfast—he had noticed a drop of blood in it.

Down the hall from Swanson at CID headquarters, Abberline pondered the significance of the dull, but warm weather. In one way he hoped the Ripper had gone to ground, but in another he wondered how they would ever catch him if he didn't surface again. It was a dilemma that cut deep into his conscience. He felt guilty to even think about another murder, although such thinking only reflected his fervent desire to catch the monster. Justice must be done.

Abberline flipped a page over and read yet another report. The body of an old woman had been reported stolen from a grave at Finchley Cemetery. Perhaps the Ripper was turning to carrion. Abberline had ordered his men to look closely into this ghoulish endeavour, but nothing of significance had surfaced.

Helson strolled in, looking far fresher than Abberline felt, even if he was still red-nosed and snuffling. Maybe having children at home provided Helson with a welcome distraction from what had become an all-encompassing investigation for Abberline.

As usual Helson carried several newspapers under his arm. "More letters in the press blaming the newspapers for their morbid coverage of the Whitechapel crimes."

"People buy the extras about the murders faster than the presses can print them," Abberline said.

"The letter writers fear that such sensationalism may stir the public imagination to unimaginable deeds."

"When I started as a constable, many a veteran regaled me with stories of unimaginable deeds that happened long before newspapers were so common or as sensational. I'm surprised the editors publish letters criticizing their own coverage."

"Never fear, they also publish plenty of letters blaming us for not catching the Ripper and many that blame the whores of Whitechapel for the murders."

"Does anyone blame the Ripper?"

"Not that I've ever read."

It was mid-afternoon. A quiet, seemingly empty street in Islington. A man stopped along the street and began to write something in chalk on a brick wall. Another man coming out of a recessed doorway paused and noticed what the first fellow was writing. "I am JACK THE RIPPER" stood out in white, calcifying relief.

"Hey," the newcomer yelled.

The chalker jumped at the sound of the voice and bolted.

"Hey, come back!"

The chase was on. Urchins and costermongers, passing workmen and trampers, even a puffing policeman joined in, but the writer-turned-runner outdistanced all pursuers and after several blocks of frantic sprinting got away. A puffing, groaning gaggle of men were left gasping in the street.

"Probably just a prankster," an air-gulping pursuer said.

Whether the chalker was Prankster or Phantom was irrelevant. He was gone.

The gnawing suspicion that Dr. Pedachenko, one of the many Russian Ripper suspects, was another alias for the elusive Severin Klosowski began to form in Abberline's sleep-deprived and over-stressed brain.

Abberline put on his coat. Time to make a final tour of the stations, talk to the men on the beats, see if he could help in any way, while trying to keep the men's spirits up. He would be up all night again. Even his new schedule with a night off every fortnight was draining his energy and destroying his ability to think clearly. Maybe they should add more inspectors to the rotation? The problem was that it had been difficult enough to convince Helson or anyone else to take a single night off. No officer wanted to be home asleep on the night when the police finally captured the Ripper—and it could be any night.

As he rode in an official four-wheeler to Bethnal Green Police Station, Abberline reviewed a file full of what the Met had learned about yet another suspect, Aaron Kosminski. The investigation into Kosminski had been hampered by various spellings of his last name when it was transliterated from the Russian Cyrillic alphabet into English, as well as the fact that he appeared to live with at least two siblings on an alternate basis: one at 3 Scion Square just off Whitechapel High Street (almost across the street from the Tabram murder site); and the other, a brother, Isaac, who lived in either Greenfield or at 76 Goulston Street, both right in the neighbourhood of the killings. So far the murders, Abberline thought as he pictured a map of the area in his mind, had been moving away from Kosminski's supposed lodgings. The Goulston lodging, if the address was correct, would provide Kosminski with a place to clean up after a murder, except for the presence of his brother. Can a man who kills women on a semi-regular basis share a house with someone else and not be turned in, even if it is a brother? Abberline made a mental note to have a detective determine the correct address, even as he patted his pockets and regretted forgetting his pad and pencil. No, he had remembered them. He made a note as best he could in the bouncing, jarring four-wheeler.

Leaning the file toward the evening light coming in through the open window of the four-wheeler's door, he read that Kosminski was born in 1865, making him younger than witnesses claimed for the Ripper. Kosminski was said to have been hearing voices for the past six years and to be a paranoid schizophrenic. Was he violent? Some witnesses said yes, some said no. Abberline shook his head at the all-too-common lack of certainty.

A hairdresser, Kosminski was said to dress, not as a labourer, but decently and respectably in a manner that fit Ripper descriptions of "shabby genteel." Abberline dredged his memory and recalled that Mrs. Long and George Hutchinson said the suspect looked Jewish, which also fit Kosminski.

Helson had learned that Kosminski had witnessed violence and rapes during anti-Jewish pogroms in Poland as a child. Abberline knew from experience that violence hardened some men to it, but made others abhor it; again, information that could lead to opposite conclusions.

Helson had also discovered that Kosminski's father had just died in 1887. Had the removal of parental authority triggered the murder spree?

Abberline rubbed his varicose vein as he read on. One of Kosminski's voices, or "instincts" as Kosminski called them, told him he should not wash, accept food from others or work. Unwashed and lacking any money to maintain his clothes, Abberline found it hard to believe that Kosminski in such a state and with no money could lure anyone into a dark alley to commit murder.

Abberline read that Kosminski was reported to have gone insane due to 'solitary vices.' Abberline smiled. Masturbation was said to cause all manner of lunacy and adverse health conditions. The Professor had said that when his headmaster had regaled the students with the theory that "self-abuse" would lead to blindness, one young wag had asked, "Can I just do it until I'm short-sighted?"

The four-wheeler jolted to a stop at the Bethnal Green station. Abberline closed the Kosminski file and steeled himself for another night on the streets. The proliferation of suspects made the Ripper's capture more and more difficult. Each new suspect meant a diversion of effort, a possible turning away from the right man. But which was the right man? Only pursuing each and every suspect could determine the answer. Abberline muttered a curse, said a prayer when he thought of what Emma would think of his language, and climbed down out of the vehicle to search, once again, for the Ripper.

Saturday, 20 October

An obese constable breathed heavily in cardiac conflict as he made his way up the last flight of stairs to the exalted confines of the Assistant Commissioner's office. The portly policeman carried a package of bizarre content.

"Here it is, Major Smith," the portly one announced as he entered the Acting Commissioner's office. "There's a report as well from Doctors Openshaw and Reed. Neither of them think it's a hoax, sir."

Smith nodded. "We'll let Brown go over it just to get a third opinion."

And so the curious kidney once coveted by Lusky as a meal continued on its transported career. It was already being referred to as the department's 'floating kidney.'

Dr. Frederick Gordon Brown concluded that it was a human kidney that had not been charged with fluid, as it would have been if taken for purposes of dissection at a hospital. He also found that the kidney showed signs of advanced stages of Bright's Disease; the same as the kidney left in Catherine Eddowes' corpse.

Smith, Abberline and the other top police officers still believed the kidney and the accompanying note were probably a hoax, so the 'floating kidney' was take to Dr. Sutton, a senior surgeon at London Hospital and the greatest living authority on kidneys. Matching the mailed kidney half to the kidney left in the victim, he concluded that the kidney was from Eddowes. Sutton said that the kidney must have been removed by the killer, not by someone from the mortuary and had been put in spirits within a few hours of its removal from the body. Therefore, it was not a hoax, he concluded, since a murder victim was not taken direct to the dissecting room, but awaited an inquest, which was never held before the following day at the earliest.

Abberline discussed the reports with Swanson in the latter's Scotland Yard office.

Abberline said, "Someone said it was posted from the Central or East Central District, but packages going between districts are usually franked by both districts, and Lusk's package was only franked in the Eastern District."

"So it was mailed in the same district as it was received, the Eastern," Swanson agreed, nodding as he puffed on his pipe.

"It's too large to have been dropped into an ordinary post box, so it was probably posted at the Lombard or Gracechurch Street Post Office in the East Central District."

Swanson frowned and asked in his Scottish brogue, "Why those two?"

"I had men check. Those two have receptacles with unusually wide dimensions; wide enough so the sender wouldn't have to check the package at the counter with anyone who might later remember him."

Swanson tapped a newspaper on his desk with his pipe's stem and said, "I see Dr. Openshaw attempted to clarify his role in the kidney saga. He arranged to sit an interview with *The Star*."

Abberline looked over at Swanson past the piles of reports and statements on his desk and wondered when he had any time left over to read newspapers. He must read inhumanly fast.

"Openshaw told the correspondent that he knew the kidney was human," Swanson said, "but couldn't tell if it was from a woman, given the great similarity in size between a kidney from a man and a woman."

"So how did the other experts know it was from a woman? Did they just jump to that conclusion, given the suggestion it might be from a Ripper victim?"

Swanson shrugged. "He also clarified that he couldn't tell how long since it had been dissected, since it had been preserved in spirits."

"So much for the other surgeons' statements about how long the kidney had been out of the body."

"The only thing Openshaw was certain of is that it's part of a left human kidney."

A constable appeared with two cups of tea, one of which Abberline thankfully accepted. He stretched his sore leg, massaged the varicose vein, and sipped his black tea. His mind worked through what he knew about the kidney, what he thought he knew and what he did not know. "If the kidney was from a preserved body, it would have had preserving fluid in it, but Dr. Brown said the kidney had not been in spirits for more than a week. And Lusk received the kidney 16 days after Eddowes' murder; far longer than a week."

"So it wasn't Eddowes' kidney? But Dr. Brown said Eddowes had Bright's disease, just like Lusk's kidney."

"Most, if not all of the other letters have clearly been hoaxes, so maybe this one is, too."

"None were sent with a kidney."

"Makes it seem a damn sight more authentic, doesn't it?"

"But doesn't help us identify who actually sent the bloody thing."

Abberline nodded. "Did you read the report on Emily Marsh?"

Swanson grinned. "I read everything that comes across my desk; doesn't mean I remember more than half of it on a good day and such days are becoming fewer and farther between."

Abberline guessed that the number of reports the shrewd Scot remembered was closer to ninety percent, but said as he glanced at his notes, "A Miss Emily Marsh, whose father trades leather at 218 Jubilee Street, Mile End Road, said a tall man dressed in clerical costume came into their shop on 15 October and asked for Mr. Lusk's address. She said that he should go around the corner and see Mr. Aarons, who knows Mr. Lusk, but the man declined. She then showed the man a newspaper article that contained Lusk's address. He did not take the paper but asked her to read out the address as he wrote it down, keeping his head down."

"Description?"

"Forty-five, 6 foot, slim build, sallow face, dark beard and mustache. Spoke with an Irish accent."

"The 15th; the kidney was delivered the next day. Coincidence or was he the Ripper?"

"Or another prankster? We checked and the newspaper story did not have a house number for Lusk, just Alderney Road, and the address on the package also lacked a house number."

"Did you distribute the description?"

Abberline nodded. He took his Whitechapel hunting watch out of his vest pocket and checked the time. "Maybe we're focusing on the wrong thing." Returning his prized watch to his vest pocket, he picked up the note that had come with the kidney.

Swanson nodded toward the note and asked, "Were the injuries to Stride and Eddowes attempts to cut off their ears as was mentioned in the 25 September letter?"

Abberline shrugged. "I asked a professor friend about this most recent note that came with the kidney. He said it looked like it was written by someone semi-literate. Lots of ink blots, as if he barely knows how to use an ink pen."

"No punctuation and kidney is misspelled, as are a host of other words."

"I count one in seven misspelled, but the Professor noticed that not all of the misspellings are phonetic, such as 'knif' and 'whil,' so the writer knew about the silent 'k' and 'h.' He must have had some education; he could not have correctly spelled 'piece' phonetically."

"The letter is also formatted in a formal style, just as they teach at school."

"The Professor said the writer has a cramped style with some retracing of the vertical strokes. The letters are crowded together with little space between the words, and the ink is almost ground into the page, heavily, as if he was concentrating hard on making each letter and word."

"So semi-literate."

"Or an educated man trying to hide his education. Either way, the Professor thought he's probably British or of British origin. The abbreviation Mr. written with the 'r' above the line is peculiar to English writing, and 'tother' used instead of 'the other,' which is common to Scotland, Ireland, England and America. 'Prasarved' and 'mishter' may reflect a Cockney dialect or Irish."

"So he could be Scottish, Irish, English, American, or it's a hoax and he's none of the above, or, then again, he might be. A most useful analysis."

"This is serious business, Miss," the magistrate said. "You have created more than a public mischief."

"It was only a joke, your honour."

"A joke?"

"Yes, a joke."

"I'm afraid I don't appreciate your sense of humour."

The proceedings in Bradford Borough Court concerned two letters sent to the local newspaper and the Chief Constable by 21-year-old Maria Coroner. In the letters she mentioned paying a visit to Bradford. Such an intention would have gone unnoticed except she signed the letters "Jack the Ripper." The Bradford constabulary tracked her down and found further similar letters among her belongings. She was remanded and the Bench declined to accept bail.

"At least we haven't got the Ripper coming here to Yorkshire," a constable sighed. "Imagine, a Yorkshire Ripper."

A more serious copying of the Ripper occurred near Swansea.

"Why, oh why, do they have to do things like this?" Thick asked. He and Godley had been called down to view a body and determine if there were any connections between it and the Whitechapel murders. Before them lay the remains of a five-year-old boy. The tiny carcass had been split open from pubis to sternum and disemboweled. The deep red of the insides surrounded by the fish-white outside made the cadaver appear like a gutted Scottish salmon.

"Some 18-year-old half-wit did this," Thick said. "Luckily the local police caught the miscreant. The bugger's a butcher's helper. The only connection with the Ripper is up here." He tapped his head. "Or lack of what's up here."

Godley nodded.

Thick continued, "The killer—name's Thomas Lott—can't give any motive for doing this."

The two policemen and the morgue attendant stared at the three-stone waste before them.

"It's so damn senseless," Thick said. "I wonder if Lott would have killed this kid if there'd never been a Ripper."

"Only God knows," Godley replied.

"More likely it falls within the Devil's purview."

The creature eased the back window of the morgue open, checked the street, then slipped into the darkened recess of the carbon-black room. He moved along, bumped lightly into a trolley, and felt the top of it. The cold soft sponge-like sensation of death came back through his fingertips. Man or woman? He felt excitedly around. Small frame. Could be. Damn. A man. He released the lifeless penis he had held for a second through the covering sheet and slithered on.

His excitement was mounting. He could feel the rigidity spreading through his organ. A hard 'un! He was a man! A real man! He moved along. Ah, breasts. Big, beautiful breasts! He squeezed them. How heavy was she? Not too bad. He could carry this one on his cart. He could hardly contain his excitement. He ran his hand up the cold rigid leg and fondled the hairy cleft. Only gone a few hours—still rigid. If only he could get this one home. What fun. He pulled the trolley with one hand and felt ahead with the other in the blackness like a blind man. His cart was just outside the window. It shouldn't be too difficult. He'd hide the body under his tarp. He was breathing hard; more from sexual than nervous excitement, but there was that too. The danger coupled with the sheer anticipation of the delights to come stirred him tremendously. He could hardly keep his hands from shaking. He had almost reached the window. He hurried. But the trolley caught on something. He tugged. Crash!

Whatever it was, it fell over. He froze for a semi-second in utter terror.

"Wot's goin' on in there?" a voice demanded from somewhere.

He could hear feet tramping toward the door. He fled.

The tired morgue attendant wearily shone his taper around. Seeing little, but judging that something was amiss, he proceeded to light the gas lamps.

"Christ!"

Several trolleys were in disarray and a corpse had been knocked onto the floor. It sagged in a ghoulish crouch against the corner of a work bench. One of the morgue assistants joined the attendant and asked, "What's up, Paul?"

"I think we just had a visit from that damn necrophile. Crazy bugger tries to break in here or across the river every year or two; wants to steal a fresh one. We better notify the police after we straighten up here. He lives over on Back Church Lane, I think."

"Why don't they lock the nutter up?"

"They have, but what can they ever prove? Just breaking and entering. He used to assault the cadavers in here. Caught 'im once sprawled atop a three-day-old 'un. He was wanging away like all hell. I chased 'im, but he got away. Ran down the street with his prick sticking out like a cutlass. Never saw anything so silly. But he got away. Was his word agin' mine and he's a 'respectable businessman,' he is. But the police will go round and give 'im a good scare and he'll leave us alone for another year or so. Then he'll be back. At least he can't hurt anyone. These are beyond caring about his peculiarities. Come on, let's get this cadaver back on the table."

The morgue attendant looked out the open window. The light from the room sprayed into the empty street revealing an old wooden cart. "He was in such a hurry he forgot his cart, I don't wonder."

"The police should be able to buckle him with that as evidence."

"How? He can just pretend it was stole. Anyway, what crime is it to leave your cart under a morgue window? Can't prove he was in here, can we?"

"This corpse didn't get down off the bench by itself. It can't walk."

"Can't talk, either."

Sunday, 21 October

The 83rd anniversary of the Battle of Trafalgar was a quiet, Ripper-less day in London.

Monday, 22 October

On the day the Ussker Chronology said, based on the Old Testament, that the world was created in 4004 BC at approximately 6 p.m., the continual kaleidoscope of life cascaded by. Fire inspectors examined the effects of a great blaze on Friday that had eventually spread to 25 East End tenements. The displaced residents wearily moved on to even greater congestion in the surrounding lodging houses, lofts and converted cubbyholes. Abberline attended another daily Home Office meeting. No one present had found the Ripper.

Tuesday, 23 October

The fifth day of the inquiry into the death of Elizabeth Stride, the Berner Street victim, continued. Considerable time was spent clarifying the misidentification of Stride as Elizabeth Watts. Both had been courted by policemen, both had the same Christian name, both were born in 1843, both had lived with sailors, both had once kept coffee-houses in Poplar, both were nicknamed 'Long Liz,' both had children being raised by other people, both were alcoholics, both lived in

East End common lodging houses, both had been charged at the Thames Police Court, both had lost their front teeth, and both were unfortunates. At least 13 points of similarity linked them together. There was one difference. Stride had met Jack the Ripper. Watts had not.

The issue was settled once and for all when the real Elizabeth Watts turned up, alive and well. She said she hadn't seen her sister Mary in years, even if Mary had claimed her as a Ripper victim. Elizabeth said of her mistaken sister, "Her evidence was infamy and lies, and I am sorry that I have a sister who can tell such dreadful falsehoods."

At the inquest, various witnesses testified that Stride was in the company of a man for almost an hour before her demise. The unanswered question remained: Was the man Jack the Ripper? She had been overheard saying to the man, "Not tonight, but some other night." The public would construe what she was talking about in only one way even though there were hundreds of possible constructions. This proved either that the public had incredible insight or lacked imagination.

Detective Reid, stuck again with the job of attending the day's inquest, yawned almost continually. He had been rehearsing for his latest theatrical on top of long hours on the job and almost fell asleep as the same parade of fact and speculation slid by. The faces changed, but it was the same as the Nichols, Chapman and Eddowes' inquests. Anything could become old hat, even a gory murder inquest. Reid forced his eyes open and stared at the thinning rows of news correspondents. The similarity of the victim to the still-living Liz Watts would be their story. Other than that, the Ripper cases were losing their macabre appeal and their ability to sell newspapers.

Helson's cold worsened. Sniffling and feeling miserable, he stared at the work before him on his desk at the Bethnal Green station. The mad butcher of Swiss extraction named Joseph Isenschmid was cleared of any connection to the Ripper murders. He was in Grove Hall Lunatic Asylum on the night of the Double Event.

Even so, Isenschmid was far from the only lunatic on the police list of possible suspects. Helson glanced over a report on the chemist/surgeon named Puckridge or Puckeridge, who had been released from an asylum as healed on 4 August and was supposed to be in London. The police had still not found him, even though Sir Charles had mentioned him as a prime suspect in a report to the Home Office.

Turning to yet another file, Helson read that a man was reported to have come into a Whitechapel brothel after the 30 September murders with bloodstains on his clothes. The delicacy of the location may have accounted for the three-week delay. Helson sent a man to investigate.

Klosowski, Ostrog, Pedachenko and Vasiliev still remained out-of-sight if not out of Helson's mind and, he was certain, Abberline's mind. At least Druitt was still under surveillance. To the sniffling and aching Helson, there seemed to be an endless stream of suspects all of whom became instantly invisible once the police heard about them. He sighed and went back to work dispatching inspectors to try to find one suspect or another.

Sir Charles received a letter with the then common penchant for capital letters from the Traders of Whitechapel; "For some years past we have been painfully aware that the protection afforded by the Police has not kept pace with the increase of Population in Whitechapel. . .The universal feeling prevalent in our midst is that the Government no longer ensures the security of Life and Property in East London and that in consequence respectable people fear to go out shopping, thus depriving us of our means of livelihood. We confidently appeal to your sense of Justice that the Police in this district may be largely increased in order to remove the feeling of insecurity which is destroying the Trade of Whitechapel." More than 190 tradesmen signed the letter.

Sir Charles would have loved to have hired more constables and even more inspectors for the evidently ineffectual CID to further inundate the East End with police, but he could barely get the Home Office to fund two dogs, let alone two more constables. Negotiations with Brough were still ongoing. It had been more than two weeks since Sir Charles had changed his original bloodhound request to the Home Office to £100 to insure Barnaby against accident while the police were using him, pay for the use of Barnaby through the end of March 1889, and, with an eye on the future, to purchase a bloodhound puppy. Sir Charles only now learned of the belatedly approved £50 Home Office disbursement based on his original request. Unfortunately, Brough had given up on ever being paid and had taken Barnaby and Burgho home. His purebreds would not return to the capital to go a-hunting homicidal lunatics.

Wednesday, 24 October

A foggy, hazy day gripped London in gray fingers of gloomy mist. A general dampness slid into all and sundry corners as the temperature stayed in the mid-to-low 40s. Paris reported frost. Winter was working its way toward Europe's middle latitudes.

The letter accusing Sergeant Thick of being the Ripper was finally filed as acted upon. It had taken more than 800 man-hours and countless depositions from policemen, reporters, citizens, and even a few felons to clear Thick by putting him in other places when the Whitechapel murders occurred, but a good man had been cleared and one less Ripper suspect file cluttered Abberline's desk. Abberline scribbled the cryptic words "Not Substantiated" across the top of the Thick file and tossed it onto a pile of files that did not need to be moved to the new Met headquarters on the Embankment.

Surgeons finally concluded that the kidney sent to George Lusk had come from Catherine Eddowes' body. Like the kidney left in Eddowes' cadaver, the mailed specimen was in the advanced stage of Bright's disease. More importantly, the severed portions of the renal artery matched the section left in the body. Despite this evidence, which to Abberline seemed irrefutable, Sir Robert Anderson, Sir Charles and other administrators would not budge in their belief that the whole kidney episode was a journalist's hoax; just as the postcard and all the letters were hoaxes. Abberline heard that the consensus at the Yard was that the Dear Boss letter was created by Tom Bullen or Bulling of the Central News Agency or possibly his chief, Charles Moore. Abberline wondered whether any prankster would go to the trouble of finding a woman's kidney to mail, let alone one in the advanced stages of Bright's disease. And how could anyone but the killer or a morgue attendant find one that fit the renal artery left in Eddowes? Hoax or not, Abberline did not see how the kidney, postcard or the letter could help lead him to the killer.

Thursday, 25 October

Wet thick fog descended on the city and sent shivers through the police drafted in droves to patrol the anthracite-etched streets. Abberline complained to Helson in his Met office, "Another few days of this and our men will have grown as careless as ever. That's when he'll bloody well strike; this weekend or next. Our men can't stay at peak alertness forever and that bastard knows it. No matter how crazy he is, he knows it."

Helson blew his nose and moved his head over the steam from the hottest cup of tea he could brew. He was already far from peak alertness.

Chapter Nineteen

Friday, 26 October

"The fog's thicker than ever," Helson said, wiping his nose with a Macdonald tartan handkerchief. "I bumped into a newsstand coming into work; didn't even see the blasted thing."

Abberline nodded and peered even more intently from their hansom. They were riding through the East End, visiting each station house to get the latest news. They passed a slight commotion and Abberline ordered the driver to stop. He and Helson bolted from the hansom to find out what was going on. It turned out that several constables were trying to arrest a pair of men wrecking crockery in a common lodging house.

"This bloody Ripper business has got us all out of kilter," Abberline said when they were back on their way to the next station. "Two months ago we would never have stopped to see what that silliness was about. Now, we're afraid not to. I bet our men are doing the same thing—rushing to investigate every little thing and probably missing everything important."

In the Sheriff Court, Miss Maggie Lockhead pursued a breach of promise suit against Mr. William Kirkland. It seemed Miss Lockhead was intent on marrying a non-smoker and gave Mr. Kirkland the choice between "me and a cigar" as she put it. He chose the cigar. Many a married Londoner quietly envied the wisdom shown by the young man.

In another court, Mr. Alderman Renals released the hopeless, exasperated sigh of the totally frustrated. He glared at the prisoner before him and said, his voice low but laced with emotion, "You, Benjamin Graham have admitted to the murder of Martha Tabram, Mary Ann Nichols, Annie Chapman, Catherine

Eddowes and Elizabeth Stride. You have been found to be of sound mind. This may be so. I am no judge in such matters, but I am judge in this court and I regret the law does not allow me to send you—and people of similar sanity—to prison. You have displayed a mania that must be stopped. Even the most cursory investigation has revealed that you have no connection with these crimes. You are a fraud. You are a waste upon the public time and patience. Go—I can only discharge you."

And so Benjamin Graham became the 50th person to confess to the Whitechapel murders. Like the others, Graham soon disappeared into the anonymous oblivion that he and all the other confessors had wished so desperately to avoid.

Lady Mary J. Kinnaird, founder of the YWCA, chose this foggy day to initiate her Whitechapel Fund campaign; an extensive appeal to the "better off" to provide funds to bring Christianity to that dark corner of Whitechapel which, as the Dowager Lady said, "Was disgraced by the recent hideous crimes." She did not explain why those being victimized by the Ripper were so much more in need of enlightenment than the Ripper himself.

The Rector of Whitechapel, Arthur J. Robinson, pointed out that Lady Kinnaird's plans for the reformation of his parish were ill thought out since every single agency suggested by the good woman was already in existence, functioning and evidently still not turning the area into a Christian paradise. These objections did not deter Lady Kinnaird in the least. In bringing the gospel to the ungodly, she would do her damndest.

Police personnel poured into the Ripper's realm as another weekend began. Abberline had become certain, as had Helson, Swanson and several other top officers, that the Ripper struck on weekends or holidays, except for Nichols' summer Thursday night murder. Even so, the night passed without his murderous passions being activated or, if activated, at least not satisfied.

Saturday, 27 October

Angered by continuing criticism from the press and public, Sir Charles decided to counterattack. He put in a hard week preparing a carefully crafted rebuttal to all his critics for the November issue of *Murray's Magazine*. He pointed out that the police needed the cooperation of all London's citizens to do their job and warned of the dangers inherent in the upcoming Lord Mayor's Day when the people would be packed together ready to turn into a mob of miscreants at the slightest stimulus. Like Shakespeare's Caesarean soothsayer, he proclaimed, "Beware 9 November, the Lord Mayor's Day. Beware!"

More than 40,000 people gathered on the Greyhound Pleasure Gardens in the East End that afternoon to watch aeronaut George Higgins plummet from a balloon and then descend safely earthward in a parachute. Inspector

Reid wished he had been the aeronaut plummeting earthward. Despite what Sir Charles might have predicted, there was no disturbance, even when Higgins' descent was delayed for several hours due to unfavourable wind conditions. The multitude calmly accepted the inactivity, displaying a patience beyond anything Sir Charles could have imagined.

Having dispatched inspectors to lunatic asylums to search for anyone recently released, Abberline slipped out for a quick evening meal at his club. Emma was dining with relatives in Shoreditch. Startled mid-way through his repast, he looked up to see Lees, the medium, who seemed to have materialized out of the potted shrubbery.

"Sorry if I startled you, Chief Inspector, but they told me I could find you here."

"Sit down, Lees. Care for some tea, wine, whatever's your pleasure?"

Lees declined the liquid offer but sat opposite Abberline. From the lines of worry on his face and distraught expression, Abberline guessed the purpose of the unannounced visit. "You had another vision?"

"It's not...I don't want them. I don't want these horrible intrusions on my mind. I want to be me." He dropped his head in his hands. "God! It was the worst thing I ever saw."

Abberline stopped eating his mock-turtle soup with forcemeat balls of chopped meat and vegetables on top.

Lees looked up and grasped Abberline's arm across the table linen. "I saw a woman butchered to pieces, lying in a dirty, grimy little room," Lees whispered, his voice hoarse and barely audible but loaded to the brim with emotion. "You've got to stop him." Tears welled in Lees' eyes. His hand trembled.

"You have any idea where this room is?"

"Probably Whitechapel; it was a decrepit, poorly furnished affair."

Abberline gently detached his arm from Lees' grip and leaned back, considering how best to speak his thoughts. "Unfortunately that doesn't help us overly much."

If possible, Lees' face took on a look of even greater despair.

"When is this murder supposed to happen?"

"I don't know. I don't know."

Abberline nodded, glancing at the diners around him, some of whom were glancing at the distraught man and Abberline. "The Ripper hasn't killed anyone inside that we know of. All the murders have either been in a street or backyard." He thought for a moment before adding, "But as far as we know none of his victims had a private room of their own. How are you sure this will be one of Jack's jobs?"

"I just have a feeling; probably the sheer butchery."

"But no address, no date?"

"I do have a feeling that I might be able to track him—after one of his crimes."

"What gives you that idea?"

"I don't know. I just get the feeling. It has come on me recently. It's as if good and evil are at war out there and one or the other sends me glimpses of the future now and then."

"Well, we'll try the tracking bit, then. What about now?"

"No. There's no feeling. It'll have to be after…."

"Another murder."

It was relaxation time. The bottles were open. The smoke roiled in thick gray-white clouds across the ceiling. The billiard balls clicked and clacked and cracked as they caromed together. Jennings shot.

"Ha! That's that," he proclaimed as the last red ball dropped in their game of snooker.

"If you could write as well as you play this bloody fool game," Old Boy Pierce said, "you'd be another Mark Twain."

"Just call me John Roberts."

"Junior or Senior?"

"Doesn't matter; either. They're both great billiard players. The younger Roberts is probably better, but he's got better equipment and 20 years of the old man's instruction. Cook is damn good, too. Hey, I know, let's go over to the Prussian Eagle. That's where this whole Ripper thing started; might be worth a spot of background for a story."

"Better than you writing your groundless theory of the murders so Cartwright can write his own even more outlandish theory for the *Gazette,* and then it's your turn for *The Empire* again*,* and round and round you go feeding off each other for forever and a day."

"One must make use of what one has, which in the case of the Whitechapel murders is bloody well next to nil." Jennings bit the end off a new cigar and recited: "Up and down the City Road, / In and Out the Eagle, / That's the way the money goes, / Pop goes the weasel."

Old Boy followed the big man out the door. The pair was unable to find a cab that wasn't taken, so they commandeered one with another newsman already in residence. Since the vehicle was licensed to carry only two passengers, and physically capable of transporting little more than 600 pounds, it took an extra guinea to persuade the driver that the remote risk of a fine or more probable chance of a complete collapse was nicely balanced by the trip's increased income. The trio was soon grinding along in the hansom, its bearings groaning and moaning in a mechanical pitifulness befitting the torture its ancient parts were undergoing.

The Prussian Eagle Tavern in Wellclose Square, Limehouse, was a center of bawdy singing, Teutonic dancing by overweight *frauleins* or just as often *fraus,* sailor horn-piping and copious consumption of alcohol. The tavern was actually located in a more sober, law-abiding part of the East End that was rapidly becoming a tourist attraction for the slumming aristocracy simply because a sizable portion of London's small but exotic Chinese community had settled there.

To the unfortunates who plied the pavement in and around the Eagle, sailors were top prize. The occasional aristocrat was likely to run back to the high-class whores of the West End. Tommy Atkins, that stolid soldier for Queen and Empire, was most likely broke, but Jack Tar, just ashore, would have a fat wad and an appetite long-deprived to spend it. Some argued that the term "to shoot your wad" originated in the Eagle. Whether or not it did, the term's double meaning insured it was kept for conversational posterity.

The two reporters entered the Eagle in reasonable sobriety. They soon were lapping up the atmosphere—pint by pint. Research was research.

It was sometime later when Jennings observed, "Christ, look at those buggers rushing down drink after drink. The Refreshment Houses Act; what a bloody farce."

He was referring to a particularly sanctimonious piece of legislation that decreed all taverns must close by 1 a.m., which led to a stampede of customers bar-ward, who drank fast and furiously during the last hour before closing time. The clock striking midnight seemed a signal to unleash the thirstiest of instincts. It was also during this period that the lower-class whores descended on the taverns like vultures around a corpse. The more penny plentiful customers had been reaped off already by the prettier, younger prostitutes, but by closing time enough pints made even the ugliest of unfortunates a fortunate find to well-lubricated pub patrons.

"No wonder they call it the witching hour. Look at those hags. I like them younger," Jennings said. "Let's get the hell out of here."

They left the Eagle and proceeded to the Angel and Crown. This took them into the heart of Whitechapel. Closing time was later here or, if there was an official closing time, it was ignored. The noise was deafening as women, skirts flung high, kicked their way around the room to "Knees up, Mother Brown" accompanied by whoops and drunken cries. Singers appeared. Dancers disappeared. Drinkers went on forever. A man in a gaudy check suit sang. His song went on and on, but few listened. Drunken laughs punctuated the verses, but in the wrong places. Long garuffs of private conversation did the same. Whitechapel Saturday night!

"Martha Tabram visited here and the Eagle on the last night of her life," Old Boy said. "She was found in the wee hours of the morn on a staircase in George Yard Buildings stabbed nine times in the throat and a heck of a lot more times in the breast and abdomen."

"Shite," Jennings said, almost spilling his drink. "I remember now. Turner's throat was stabbed, not slashed, and no organs were taken from her body, unlike our Jack. Here we are and this bloody place probably has no connection with the Ripper at all."

Soon after, they left. The fresh night air seemed a gust of pleasantry despite its urinal reek. Half the lushingtons in town seemed to have used the nearby alley as a latrine, but booze and exposure dulled the senses and the smell soon went unnoticed by the correspondents. The pair walked deeper into the catacombs of the East End in a quest for a cab.

"Mister. . .Mister." The little girl tugged Jennings' sleeve.

The reporter stared down at the ragamuffin. "Christ," Jennings said, disgusted.

"You said you like them younger," Old Boy said, laughing.

Jennings tried to support himself against a not too steady brick wall. The damn thing kept drifting off into the night. He fumbled in his pocket and, producing a coin, pressed it into the girl's tiny hand. He was about to walk off and join Old Boy, but the girl tugged at his sleeve once more. It was obvious she expected to have to work for her money. She pulled, indicating that an adjacent alley would suffice. Jennings bent down somewhat unsteadily toward the girl and said, "Look, little Miss, go home."

"Can't."

"Why not?"

"Mum's got a friend in."

"A what?"

"A friend. You know they—"

"Fine, fine, dear. You don't have to tell me, but. . .ah. . .hell. . .forget it." Jennings pulled away and joined Pierce. "Let's get the hell out of here. I feel sick."

The little girl shrugged and went off toward another man emerging from the tavern.

"Christ," Jennings swore. "Must be a thousand of 'em. They're in Hackney, Whitechapel, Dalston. Hell, Mile End Road is a paedophile's paradise."

"It isn't pretty, is it? No research here. We can't write about it. We work for a family paper. Let's go home."

"Grand idea. I feel bloody awful. That goddamn gin never agrees with me." Jennings walked along shaking his head. He felt guilty. Maybe he should have given the girl more than a crown. When he told Pierce, Old Boy only shrugged and said, "I think the usual price is a haepenny. You could have bought her for a month for that much."

Jennings didn't answer. He threw up.

Sunday, 28 October

The Ripper remained in limbo. Even so, Sir Charles approved Abberline's request that one inspector, five sergeants and 50 constables be retained for duty in Whitechapel/Spitalfields to augment the standard police presence in the area.

One of the sergeants on special duty pulled yet another report across his desk in the seeming unending tidal wave of paperwork threatening to engulf him. He swore there were enough reports and statements to dam the Thames. He read that on Saturday, 25 February 1888, at 5 p.m. a soldier's widow, Annie Millwood, staggered into the Whitechapel Workhouse Infirmary with numerous stab wounds to her legs and lower body. Bloody hell. It was an old report, but—wot's this?—Annie was admitted from 8 White's Row, off Commercial Street, only a short stroll from George Yard Buildings, where Martha Tabram was found, and close to the other murder sites.

The sergeant repositioned his posterior on his high wood stool. The attack bore some resemblance to the Ripper murders, albeit far less brutal. The police at the time found no witnesses to the attack. The sergeant thought that Annie might have had a length of service pension from Chelsea Hospital based on her husband's army service or she might not. In either case, as a widow, she might have been supporting herself as an unfortunate, like the other Ripper victims. Was it an early case of the Ripper learning his trade?

The sergeant debated whether to forward the report up the police hierarchy. He sipped his tea and drummed his stubby fingers on the edge of his worn desk into which many a bored sergeant had carved their initials and someone had taken the time to craft an intricate coat of arms. The sergeant concluded that his superiors may as well see the file, even if Annie hadn't been murdered and the cuts sounded barely worth the name of an attack. It would be best to let them decide whether the attack was Ripper-related.

The sergeant was about to file the report with others to be forwarded to Abberline when he noticed that someone had penned a note on the bottom of the last page: on 31 March 1888 in the backyard of the South Grove Workhouse, Mile End Road, Annie Millwood had collapsed and died. The inquest led by Coroner Baxter determined that Annie had died of a "sudden effusion into the pericardium from the rupture of the left pulmonary artery through ulceration"—natural causes unrelated to her stab wounds of February 1888. The sergeant nodded to himself and changed his mind. He tossed the file onto a pile of cases unrelated to the Ripper to be sent to storage. Even if Inspector Abberline wanted to interview Annie, he couldn't now. Case closed, filed and forgotten.

Monday, 29 October

Morning came and at the daily Home Office meeting Abberline was able to report no word yet of any further Ripper ravage. Southwest sun-dried winds brought unseasonably hot temperatures as Londoners enjoyed a September-like day. Lady Kinnaird's campaign of belated benevolence was facing considerable competition. Messrs. Barclay, Ransom and Company had put together a fund-seeking effort of their own before the good lady could fully launch her soul-saving effort.

"Ah, good old Christian capitalism," Pierce said as the do-gooders fought it out to see who was going to spread salvation in the East End the fastest and the farthest.

The official police stance on any Ripper correspondence was now to refrain from submitting it to any handwriting expert based on the conclusion that all such missives were hoaxes by enterprising journalists. Even so, Abberline and Helson took the material received thus far to the Professor's townhouse. The rest of the police hierarchy might be afraid of being fooled by a "so-called" expert as had happened in several past cases or by some creative journalist, but Abberline was willing to risk ridicule for any potential lead. He knew that no journalist had gained a scoop from any of the letters and a London-based journalist would lack the time to wander all over Britain mailing crank letters. His superiors discounted these arguments. Their logic—or illogic—escaped Abberline's comprehension.

Abberline spread the facsimile letters out before the Professor in the latter's drawing room. Which were genuine? Which were hoaxes? There was a lot of correspondence. The volume had increased steadily ever since accounts of the first Ripper letter were published.

"The press has published enough about the letters and the murders, I could easily pen a letter that would be extremely challenging, if not impossible, to tell was a hoax," the Professor said, "at least from the content alone."

The trio scrutinized the letters. After eliminating a pile they unanimously agreed contained information that contradicted what they knew of the murders, they studied the remaining letters like misers inspecting possibly counterfeit gold sovereigns.

"Given the nature of the attacks, so sudden and fast, and the frenzied mutilations," the Professor said, "it all suggests someone mentally disturbed with great rage against women; probably someone personally and socially inadequate. I should think someone unable to converse with a woman for long, hence the sudden, vicious attacks."

"You sound like a psychic with visions," Abberline said with a smile, thinking of Lees.

"Some psychics may turn out to be right; relying at some level on logical thinking to present an image of the murderer."

"What if the Ripper is someone personally and socially inadequate?" Helson asked. "How does that help us?"

"If true, then such a personality doesn't fit someone who writes clever letters to taunt the police," the Professor said. "But he must be charming at times, such as when he is about to attack, to be able to lure these women into closes and alleys with him, and none of them have had defensive wounds. He's probably a quiet loner, not a masculine butcher type."

"Unfortunates have to be adept at assessing men or they won't be in the business long," Helson said. "End up pummeled or worse."

"The Ripper's victims have all been on the older side, so they must have known their trade and how to read men," Abberline agreed.

"Yet, they went with him," the Professor said. "So he must have some degree of charm, at least when he feels he's in control of the situation. Tea?"

The tea poured and adulterated with cream and/or sugar, Helson said, "This one's rather interesting."

It read: "I've no time to tell you how / I came to be a killer. / But you should know, as time will show, / That I'm society's pillar."

Helson said, "Suggests he's a toff, maybe a surgeon."

"Perhaps," Abberline said. "Certainly if it was written by the Ripper, he's quite literate, a poet."

"And he expects to be caught," the Professor said. "Note, he writes, 'as time will show,' intriguing, wot?"

Nodding as he noticed another letter, Helson said, "And this one also makes him a poet of sorts." It read: "Up and down the goddam town / Policemen try to find me. / But I ain't a chap yet to drown / in drink, or Thames or sea."

The Professor said, "One part of his mind may be considering suicide. Why 'yet' to drown? Is his demented mind looking for a way out? Suicide would be an escape from the torment he must be feeling."

"Torment?"

"Yes, Frederick. He's at war with himself. One side is fighting for stability and sanity; the other, raging in utter madness and chaos. His is a mind torn by savage impulses. On the outside, he'd probably be rock-rigid in deportment—a real stickler for neatness—his bearing arrogant, but refined. He'd appear as sane and sensible as a saint, but on the inside—ah, the rage, the turmoil, the unrest is boiling and churning like a North Atlantic gale."

"Here's another poem, Professor," Helson said. "He seems quite rational in this one, if it was written by the murderer."

The Professor read the poem: "Eight little whores, with no hope of heaven, / Gladstone may save one, then there'll be seven. / Seven little whores begging for a shilling, / One stays in Heneage Court, then there's a killing. / Six little whores, glad to be alive. / One sidles up to Jack, then there are five. / Four and whore rhyme aright, / So do three and me, / I'll set the town alight / Ere there are two. / Two little whores, shivering with fright, / Seek a cozy doorway in the middle of the night. / Jack's knife flashes, then there's but one, / And the last one's the ripest for Jack's idea of fun."

"This is extremely interesting," the Professor said. "Parts of this are written as if he were outside himself looking in: 'One sidles up to Jack'; 'Jack's knife flashes.' Other parts are written from Jack's point of view, in the first person."

"A different writer?" Abberline asked, frowning.

"Not necessarily." The aged savant shook his head. "It could be written by a different state of mind. It's rare, but it occurs. Two different persons in the same body. In a sense, they take turns using the body."

"Like Dr. Jekyll and Mr. Hyde?" Helson ventured.

"Well, they don't drink any potion to transform themselves. Just sort of switch on and off inside the mind, but the idea is essentially the same. You've likely read in the papers in the past year or so talk about double consciousness, dual personality or split personality; probably where Stevenson got the idea for his story."

Helson said, "I thought it was just some alienist hoax."

"Far from it."

"Do they know they're the other person?"

"Sometimes, Frederick, but not always."

"You mean in everyday life Jack could be totally unaware of his murderous activities?" Abberline asked, shocked.

"It's possible. There are a few cases on record; not criminal, you understand."

"That'd make him damn near undetectable. He'd be as cool as November's rain," Abberline said.

"If he isn't a double person, he could also be just as cool for other reasons. You know how callous some of our hardened criminals can be. Sometimes I think their central nervous systems don't fire the same way as normal people's do."

"He mentions Heneage Court in this letter," Abberline noted. "That was the place where one of our constables, a man named Spicer, found that Brixton doctor with an unfortunate."

"You're right," Helson said. "Is the Brixton doctor our man?"

"Perhaps," Abberline said. "But if he isn't, a newsman, a wag or the real Ripper could have easily heard about Spicer taking the fellow in. The story's all over Whitechapel, as is Spicer's relegation to some beat on the far distant outskirts of the city."

"Anyone could have written this drivel then," Helson said.

Abberline nodded. "Could be creative journalists, hence the poems; they love playing with words."

The Professor and Abberline sipped their tea.

"If they are one writer's letters, he certainly gets around," Helson said. "This one's from Liverpool and this one's from Glasgow."

The Professor studied the Liverpool letter with great care. It read:

Prince William Street, Liverpool

What fools the police are. I even give them the name
of the street where I am living. Prince William Street.
Yours,
Jack the Ripper

"It's the same sardonic humor; same arrogance. I assume you checked every Prince William Street address in Liverpool," the Professor asked.

Abberline nodded. "It's dozens of blocks long. He could have stayed at a hundred places. No one recognized pictures of our prime suspects at any of the places on Prince William Street."

The Professor turned to the Glasgow letter and read:

Think I'll quit using my nice sharp knife.
Too good for whores. Have come here to buy
a Scottish dirk. Ha! Ha! That will tickle
up their ovaries.

"If this is authentic," he paused to light his pipe, "then he's definitely an educated man. Aren't too many people in Whitechapel who could spell 'ovaries' or know to put an exclamation point after each 'Ha.'"

"That Blackheath school master is well educated," Abberline said, "but so are Dr. Michael Ostrog and Dr. Pedachenko, and Klosowski is depicted by some as educated, others as illiterate."

"Or it could be by a journalist," Helson said with a grin. "Even a few of them can manage to write grammatically now and then."

"Druitt wrote with his left hand," Abberline said, "but his writing doesn't match this, does it, Helson? At least we didn't think it did." He opened a file he had brought, extracted a folder and said, "Here's Druitt's handwriting."

"Not too similar," the Professor said, comparing the samples, "but what real evidence do we have that this mailed-in writing is left-handed? Lefties usually bend their wrist over when they write. Look at this. The letters slant forward here, back there and are mostly straight here. Who writes that way? Almost everyone learns to write with a steady slant—backward, upright or forward. We don't vary it every two or three words. He is clearly trying to disguise his penmanship. He could have produced this multi-slanted style by writing unsupported, with his arm up off the table, or with his non-dominant hand. Here he traces back over his own writing as if he's trying to hide how he forms a letter. Here, he forms an 'e' differently to here. He uses a continental seven, the downward stroke of the figure hatched by a horizontal stroke. Gentlemen," the Professor concluded with a sigh, "whether by design or by accident, we are confronted by a most intriguing puzzle. There are simply too many variations; too many clues in all these letters. It's like the old trick: where is the best place to hide a precious egg?"

"In a henhouse full of other eggs," Abberline replied.

"That's precisely what the rascal may have done. The Ripper alone, the Ripper abetted by a pack of journalists or a pack of journalists by themselves have given you a basket full of eggs. Look at this one; according to your police notation in the margin, sent to Dr. Openshaw the pathologist who was examining that kidney." It read:

> Old boss you was rite it was the left kidny i was
> goin to hoperate agin close to your ospitle just as
> i was going to dror mi nife along of er bloomin
> throte them cusses of coppers spoilt the game but i
> guess i wil be on the job soon and will send you
> another bit of innerds
>
> Jack the ripper
>
> O have you seen the delve
> with his mikerscope and scalpel
> a-lookin at a kidney with a slide cocked up.

The Professor shook his head. "He spells 'kidney' wrong in the first line and then in the last line correctly. 'Will' is correct here and wrong there. A devious person. At the end of this other letter—the Heneage Court poem—he describes the last proposed murder as the ripest for Jack's idea of fun. This is strange stuff about the devil with his microscope and scalpel. . .hmmm. . .Could it be? Could it be?"

"Could it be what?" Abberline asked.

"Could someone he hates, someone like his father or a brother, be a doctor or a surgeon? He equates the devil with being a doctor."

"At least one of our suspects has a father who's a doctor."

"It may not mean anything, but it may bear keeping in mind."

"What else can you deduce from these letters?" Abberline asked.

"Providing we've guessed correctly and all these letters here are authentic and none in that other pile are, he's well educated, neat, devilishly clever, and mad; but not mad in the usual sense. He wouldn't appear the least bit of a lunatic to the average person."

"He could carry on every day quite well, then?"

"There might be little slip ups. Problems in his life might also trigger the attacks. The killings can be seen as a sort of release."

Thoughts of Druitt's mysterious misadventures at the Blackheath school crossed Abberline's mind.

"I've been thinking," the Professor said. "It's rather complicated, but perhaps something I learned several years ago is of potential value." The Professor refilled his pipe. "When I was in Paris three years ago, I met a fascinating young man, a friend of a neurologist friend. This young man was working on a rather revolutionary idea concerning diseases of the mind. I've been thinking about what he talked about and its relevance to our present business."

As the Professor talked, he poured new tea for all and then lit his pipe. Abberline and Helson settled back into their chairs. The lecture was about to begin.

"The Ripper hates his mother; fears her," the Professor said.

"What makes you say that?" Helson asked, frowning.

"He attacks uteruses and the internal organs of reproduction."

"Why? I don't understand," Helson said.

"First let me backtrack. This Ripper fellow thinks he's a he-man, but he is probably impotent. That's why he attacks prostitutes with a knife. The knife is a symbol of masculinity. When he carves a woman up, he's symbolically having sexual relations with her and, at the same time, on a deeper psychic plane, he's killing his hated mother and on an even deeper psychological plane, killing himself, destroying his very birth."

"Jesus, Professor, you've finally flipped your wig. You sound crazier than he is."

"Let me finish, Frederick," the old man said, smiling. "You want my opinion, I give it. Listen, this man hates his mother for some reason. Maybe he found out she was immoral or at least immoral in his eyes. Who knows?"

"Is that why he kills unfortunates?"

"Perhaps, but not necessarily, Joseph. They are easy prey. But I'd guess he kills them because they are symbols. Symbols of the mother he hates."

"So we have a man who hates his mother, may or may not hate whores, and is probably impotent or thinks he is," Abberline said, staring at the edge of his tea cup. "Even if it's all true, and it's fantastic, how does it help us catch him?"

"Plenty," the Professor said. "This suspect Klosowski is automatically out. Your reports suggest he actively chases women and beds many a wench. But this schoolmaster, Druitt, is a real possibility; lives alone, well educated, clever. I can't tell if his handwriting matches the mailed-in material, but there are a few similarities. Who knows? Find out about his mother. Find out if he has any lady friends. He's a cricketer; seems to see himself as a he-man. Question is: Is he? This trouble at Blackheath suggests he isn't and that would provide him with even more motivation to prove he's a real man."

Abberline tried to think through all the Professor had said, even as he fought down embarrassment. Sex was far from a common Victorian conversational topic. "You know, the more I think of it, you may be right," Abberline said. "Klosowski has been described as dark and heavy-set, while descriptions of the Ripper have tended to suggest a blond or brown-haired man who's stout, but not heavy-set. Some witnesses have said Klosowski's almost illiterate. Druitt's definitely an educated man and he has a fairish complexion. He's had the time to wander all over England posting these letters. He's off weekends and would have been off the Thursday night in August when Nichols was murdered."

"The school term would not have started yet," Helson said, nodding.

"Druitt just could be the Ripper," Abberline said. "Most importantly, since we have had our men keeping an eye on him, there have been no more killings."

"That's right," Helson said.

"According to this impotent man-hates-mother idea, what will the Ripper do next? Can you tell?" Abberline asked the Professor.

"Keep killing and if he ever gets a chance. . ."

"Yes?"

"He'll rip a woman into a hundred thousand pieces."

"Why?"

"The European savant's theory would be that he wants to symbolically kill his mother forever and to make love to her at the same time. Remember, this European alienist believes acts like the ripping represent the normal sexual act to the killer."

The two detectives sat in stunned disbelief. Helson finally broke the silence, "He wants to make love to his mother? Good grief! Who is this friend of a friend you met in France? I want to avoid the crazy chap at all costs." Helson's voice was high and unnatural, filled with disgust and shock.

"I don't think anyone over here has ever heard of him."

"No wonder, with ideas like that," Helson said. "I'd guess, no one ever will."

"That may be, but it may not."

"Pray tell, what's his name?"

"Sigmund Freud."

Tuesday, 30 October

A dull sodden sky hung over London all day, cascading a continual curtain of rain on the metropolis and making citizens scurry from place to place like overly excited water beetles, each on a mission of frightful importance to him- or her-self, if not society. Mr. R. Rycroft told a meeting of the parish vestry of

St. Mary, Whitechapel that trade in the district had fallen off nearly 50 percent during the past month. He blamed the Ripper, or more accurately, the police for failing to catch the Ripper. Others argued that the middle of October had been foggy, covering the city in a dense smoke-laden fog, which kept people in and out of stores—and, apparently, the Ripper off the streets, too.

Vigilance committee members caught Isaac Jacobs sleeping atop a shed under the eaves of an overhang. Proclaiming him the Ripper, they sent him scurrying off the other side of the shed, fracturing his thumb in his desperate scramble. He managed to elude his pursuers in the black maze of narrow rain-slickened streets.

Newspapers enjoyed massive sales, and broadsheets, some in verse and sung by hawkers to popular tunes, appeared in almost every street for sale—and they sold. Omnibus and cab companies made money from the crowds going to see the murder sites, as did costermongers selling food and householders who rented seats at windows overlooking the sites. Even the International Working Men's Club charged a small admission to enter their premises. The club, even if socialist, could always use a few more shillings in its communal coffers. Pranksters brandished knives and yelled, "I'll cut you up" as they chased women down dark city streets. A few attracted mobs in hot pursuit of the faux Rippers, but the real Ripper remained dormant.

Wednesday, 31 October

It was a day of intermittent sun and rain storms, the periods of sun being shorter than the counter-posing periods of rain. The Gaiety bubbled with *Faust Up to Date*, a naughty burlesque that furthered the fortunes of the promoters, satisfied most of the gentlemen viewers and scandalized the souls suitably set to be scandalized. Lord Mayor-elect Whitehead reluctantly accepted the withdrawal of the Metropolitan Volunteers from the 9 November parade due to the citizen-soldiers lack of funds to keep their equipment in proper condition. Always a fighter, Whitehead issued an appeal for funds.

"We found out more about Klosowski," Helson told Abberline as they sat at table in the latter's CID office eating a pub lunch. "He fits the description of the Ripper in some ways, after all. It looks like he uses his double Ludwig to establish a false trail when he's off on a criminal enterprise."

Abberline listened over his light mid-day meal. At the suggestion of his physician, who believed that losing weight might ease some of the pain from his varicose vein, Abberline was making another attempt to diet. And failing. He envied Helson's fatless frame. Abberline walked daily from the Home Office meeting to the Yard, patrolled the streets at night for mile after mile and never lost a pound. Abberline took a small bite of his spotted dick while Helson, still feeding his cold, devoured his mutton curry.

Between mouthfuls, Helson continued over the tattoo of rain on the window, "Klosowski entered this country on 24 November '86, according to the border service. He's been here for almost two years, so if he killed some woman in Poland and if he is the Ripper, he certainly doesn't kill regularly."

"He may have been in goal somewhere." Abberline sipped lager from a tankard.

"We also found that a medical student, John Sanders, who was reported as a Ripper suspect, went abroad about two years ago with his mother."

"I assume she was still alive at the time?" Abberline asked with a wry smile.

"The future is being focused on the inanimate," the Professor told Abberline at the former's club. "Our enchantment with the locomotive, the six-story guildhall, the water-closet, Dalton's ceramics, and all the rest have turned our minds to seeking salvation in concrete things." He set down his pint glass and watched the last of the white foam slip to the empty bottom.

"I never thought I'd hear you speak of spirituality," Abberline said, sipping his ale. He had decided to take an evening off—a weekday evening. Helson, Chandler, Moore and Andrews had strict orders to contact him immediately if the Ripper struck again, although it seemed unlikely on a week night.

"I mean, well, it's like this new Savoy Hotel they're building: smoke room, Turkish bath, artesian well, pile carpets, brass bedsteads, inlaid cabinets, mahogany this, walnut that—comfort and convenience based on enameled ash, carved do-dads and Japanese wall hangings."

"Sounds nice."

"No. . .no soul to it, I fear. No real point."

"And my job?"

"No, different, Frederick. Super science will make catching crooks easier for a time, but somehow I think the villains will evolve and be even more difficult to bring to justice."

"Or the public's idea of what we should do with the caught and convicted will change," Abberline said. "When I hear some of the inspectors talk about morals, well, I wonder what the next generation is coming to. We're not talking about morals. We're talking about madness. When we catch this monster we won't execute him because of his being evil or his having done something bad; we'll execute him because he can't stop killing women. We execute murderers for our own protection and if we ever forget that we'll be in awful trouble. A society would have to be mad if it came to see evil as excusable."

"Shiny prisons and clean bedsheets will make the convicted healthier, but not one iota more honest. No, Frederick, my old friend, there's no future in this concrete-centered society."

The two fell deeper into a gloomy depression that reflected the end of a frustrating day. The Ripper was no nearer to being caught.

In the back of the Mitre restaurant in Fleet Street, Jennings smiled as he surveyed the new Lambeth Patent Pedestal combination water closet: slop sink and urinal united in a functional grandness that made his diarrhea almost bearable. He would have agreed with the Professor that an emphasis on material things was a false path to paradise, but since this world wasn't paradise, materialism was a sensible route to follow, especially when your arse hurt.

Part Six: Dorset Street

Chapter Twenty

Thursday, 1 November

Snug in his office at CID headquarters with coal glowing in the cast-iron stove, Abberline penned a report on Chief Inspector Donald Swanson's questioning of Israel Schwartz, a Hungarian. Schwartz had seen a man assault a woman, who he later identified as Elizabeth Stride, just after midnight on 30 September near Berner Street. The man then addressed another man as "Lipski." When the attacker started toward Schwartz, Schwartz ran away. Godfrey Lushington, Home Office Permanent Under-Secretary, had scribbled in the margin of the report that the use of the name Lipski suggested the Whitechapel killer was Jewish, a possibility that should be followed up since it "might lead to something of importance."

Abberline sipped his tea, rubbed the back of his knee and took up his fountain pen to discount the theory that two accomplices were behind the Ripper mutilation murders. Based on his experience in Whitechapel, Abberline wrote that a Jew named Lipski murdered a Jewess in 1887. Coroner Baxter, in fact, conducted the inquest. Since then 'Lipski' had become an insult to Jews. Schwartz looked Jewish, so the other man probably used Lipski as an insult to Schwartz, not as a name of his accomplice. Even so, Abberline reported that his detectives had searched the area for anyone named Lipski. None was found; yet another dead end. Abberline sent his report off to the Home Office and copied Swanson.

Abberline leaned back, stretched and massaged his varicose vein again. *Murray's Magazine* sat on his desk, containing the article by Sir Charles Warren. At Helson's suggestion, Abberline had read it early that morning. Sir Charles had supported the vigilante patrols that most constables on the beat detested, since it led to many a disturbance between vigilantes and men they believed to be the Ripper, who invariably turned out to be no such thing, leaving the police to sort it all out. Sir Charles defended the stringent measures taken against the Bloody Sunday riots of November 1887, and argued that questioning of the police and their administration threatened to bring the mob into power. He denied he had been trying to militarize the police at the expense of detective work, let alone as an attack on democracy as some in the press alleged. He referred to the people as "rabble" and would-be criminals; probably not the best public-relations approach. He also brought his long battle against Monro and the Home Office for control of the CID into public view. The Met Commissioner complained that Home Office clerks were sending orders to his men without even consulting him. Abberline glanced at Lushington's note on the Schwartz file as a case in point. Even so, Abberline knew the Home Office would loath having such internal disputes made public and feared that not only Sir Charles would be made to suffer; Matthews might punish the Met and, especially, CID.

Abberline rose to pour another cup of black tea. October had been foggy and quiet. The fog appeared to have accomplished what the Met could not; keep the unfortunates of Whitechapel fortunate and alive. Not even the Phantom wanted to bumble around the East End in a dense fog feeling about for victims like a child in a game of Blind Man's Bluff. Abberline hoped and prayed the fog would continue into November, but he feared that not every weekend night would be so protectively cloaked.

It was now two months since the Buck's Row murder of Polly Nichols. The public and press continued their anti-police agitation. The vigilance committees swarmed into the night streets with self-righteous zeal. The police continued to collar a covey of criminals on charges various if not vile. Two more men were arrested for prizefighting.

"Fighters are catchable, Rippers are not," Jennings noted as he turned to his day's work. Levity had prevailed in the day's court proceedings, which he had just covered. A dirty dustman had been arrested for kissing various female customers in Putney. It seemed the ladies felt that lips that touched dust should never touch theirs.

Lord Mayor-elect Whitehead hosted a banquet at the City of London Club as was his right and honourable duty. It was a stupendous repast, complete with salmon, turbot, lobster, boiled and roasted beef, grouse, mutton, chicken, duck, vegetables of all seasonal variations, puddings, tarts, pies, puffs of cream, and jellies, as well as red and white wine, port, sherry and liquors of many colors and bountiful flavors. Abberline would have put on two pounds just thinking about it. The guests, elegant in attire and meticulous in manner, added their own private observations on the mediocrity of the police and the malfunctioning of idle East End society.

Someone noted, "The dregs always sink to the bottom."

The patrol was growing monotonous. The hansom weaved its way through the cobbled streets, jerking and jolting Abberline's bottom, aching leg and back as the wheels clattered from uneven stone to uneven stone. Godley sat beside him as quiet and composed as a Buddhist statue.

Peering out into the gloom, Abberline said, "Let's walk for a while. Come on, Godley. Pick us up at the Commercial Street station in an hour, driver."

The two policemen were soon alone in the street. Cliffs of hewn stone and aging wood rose into clusters of darkened buildings all around them. They walked at the bottom of this citied canyon as if they were in the most remote spot of the Outer Hebrides.

"Amazing," Abberline said. "We've flooded these streets with men. The Vigilance Committees are out in force. Half the population down here lives in the streets and yet here we are able to walk along without seeing a bloody living soul."

"Gap between patrols, sir," Godley said.

"It explains how the Ripper can strike so effectively."

In the next half-hour, they passed three vagrants, who had no way of identifying themselves. Why should they? No one had ever cared about their name or place of residence before. The policemen also passed a drunk woman escorted by a constable. Then they came upon a fine Russian blue cat. This plump feline fellow sat Sphinx-like on the top edge of a dustbin, his green oval irises encircling the blackest possible of night-adapted pupils. Abberline stopped to try and pet the big gray fellow, who watched him warily and kept his distance.

"Clever chap, this one," Abberline said. "He's not going to be a bit of stew for anyone. Can't blame you, old chap."

Lusky stared down at the roly-poly human before him. The man looked kind enough, but he did not take any chances at night. In the daytime, maybe. . .

Suddenly the man and the blue-coated constable beside him spotted something up the street. Lusky stared. What could it be? No rats. No mice. No dog. What? Wait. Human beings would probably be interested in the couple by the lamp post. Lusky had noticed them five minutes ago.

The couple disappeared into a dark alley.

A shriek.

The two men bolted up the street. Lusky watched them run off. Maybe it was some kind of territorial dispute over the woman. Lusky didn't profess to understand the ways of humans.

Abberline and Godley charged. The Ripper perhaps!

They rushed into the alley to find the woman holding her skirts up to her knees, jumping around as if she was doing some kind of exuberant dance. The man was attacking a pile of crates. He shook them wildly, as if they meant him harm. Abberline and Godley immediately grabbed him.

"Hallo! Hallo!" Godley cried. "What do we have here?"

The woman ran.

"Come back, we won't hurt you," Abberline yelled. "We're the police." He gave chase, but the frightened woman scurried off into the blackness. Puffing and with an aching knee, Abberline returned to where Godley held the man.

"Well, what do you have to say for yourself, young man?" Abberline asked, shining his lamp in the man's face: blond, about five-eight.

"Nothing. I was just escorting the lady home because of how things are down here."

"And how are they down here?"

"Pretty rough."

"Why did the lady run off?"

"She's probably an unfortunate and thought you might arrest her. She did have liquor on her breath."

"And you were just being a Good Samaritan?"

"I guess you might say that."

"What made her scream then?"

"Oh, a big rat jumped off that dustbin."

"A big rat?" Godley asked, incredulous.

"I was rattling those crates to make sure it was scared off when you jumped me."

"What's your name?" Abberline asked.

"I'm not at liberty to disclose that. I'd have to get permission from my boss."

"Is that so? I think you better come along with us."

Friday, 2 November

Commercial fraud surfaced on this rainy autumn day. Several butchers were arrested for supplying unfit carcasses for sale. Lord Mayor-elect Whitehead announced his intention of providing roast beef—hopefully not from one of the aforementioned fraudulent butchers—and plum pudding feasts on the Lord Mayor's Day for all residents of the city's workhouses. The meals would fill more than 2,000 starving stomachs, at least for the afternoon of the day on which he became Lord Mayor. It was perhaps unintentional that Terry's Theatre chose this week to commence a farcical comedy called *The Policeman*. The owners may have felt the public were laughing at the real-life police so much they just might transfer their humor to make-believe lawmen on the stage.

"Druitt's missing!" Helson announced as he entered Abberline's office.

"I thought we had our men watching him," Abberline said as he hung his coat on a rack. He had just returned from his daily Home Office meeting

"We did, sir, but he's either given them the slip or they've slipped up. He disappeared during a shift change."

"Damn," Abberline muttered and fought to control his anger. He sat at his desk and said, "Well, eventually we were bound to lose him. Probably be alright. They'll most likely spot him again. Make sure they're watching his place in Blackheath and that place he's got access to in King's Bench, and have them check the cricket team he plays for and keep an eye on all his immediate relatives. With the mutilation aspect of the attacks escalating, if he is the Ripper, I want him found right away." He glanced at the calendar on his desk and added, "Before tonight—it's Friday."

"He certainly doesn't destroy beauty," Jennings said, reviewing pictures of the Ripper's victims. "Nichols was a fruzzy old frump. Chapman was a roly-poly, double-chinned blob of suet. Stride was a gawky, raw-boned witch. Why kill such ugly women?"

"Maybe he kills what he detests," Old Boy suggested as they sat at their adjacent desks in *The Empire's* over-crowded newsroom.

"A normal person would be attracted to someone good-looking. Maybe the Ripper couldn't mutilate a pretty woman, but he probably doesn't care. Who knows? The guy's mind is so chaotic probably anything is possible."

It was a hopelessly speculative conversation. Jennings turned to his next assignment. Not again; the weather story. Would anything save him from his daily meteorological purgatory?

A half-hour later a copyboy brought a telegram, which requested that Jennings or Old Boy, who had gone out to eat, come to the Commercial Street Police Station. Jennings finished the much-hated weather chart in less than five minutes—probably leaving a few patches of cloud cover in the wrong places and starting a new ice age in Birmingham—left a note for Old Boy, grabbed a cab and was on his way. He was puzzled. The telegram gave no clue as to what the summons was about. Images of a big story flitted through his head, but anything big wouldn't just involve him or Old Boy, and it certainly wouldn't come by way of a personal telegram.

"Sorry to bother you, Mr. Jennings, but you know how things are these days," the desk sergeant at the station said. "We've been drawing in more than our fair share of nutters. Got one down here we thought you'd better have a look at. It's about that Ripper business."

Visions of a scoop reformed in Jennings' mind. God, was he going to be lucky after all? He hurried after the desk sergeant, who turned him over to the gaoler, who led him into a dungeon-dim row of cells in the station's basement. The gaol was ancient stone and brick, and may have been built in Elizabethan times for all Jennings knew. He expected to see Falstaff banged up for some drunken bawdy business preparing his plea for a royal pardon from the young Prince Hal. The gaoler stopped before an end cell and pointed toward a derelict bag of rags encasing an unwashed, whiskered waif of Whitechapel waste. The creature was asleep, snoring and snorting like a grime-garbed country boar.

"Do you know this 'un?" the gaoler asked, gesturing with his truncheon at the sad bundle of what might be humanity.

Jennings shook his head. The sleeper's face was buried in unkempt hair, untrimmed beard and unwashed rags. Jennings tried to close his nostrils, but the putrid smell of the place found their way in nonetheless. "What's the bloke banged up for?"

"Suspicion of bein' the Ripper. But we think he's 'armless. Claims to know you."

"Me?" Jennings stared into the dim cell. The ragged figure rolled over on the scattering of straw and snorted a long growling series of snores.

The gaoler banged the bars with his truncheon. The creature woke and sat up.

"Coulls!" Jennings exclaimed, finally recognizing his colleague.

Abberline and Godley had taken him into custody during the night. Without identification and having given a silly story about defending an unfortunate against a rodent, it had taken considerable time to persuade the station officials to send a telegram to *The Empire*. The only reason they relented was that one of them mentioned there'd be hell to pay if the bloke really was a correspondent.

Later that day, the vagrancy case against Adrian Alexander Coulls was thrown out. The judge suggested he get a shave, a bath and new clothes, and that he dress and act like a proper newspaper correspondent in the future.

Grasping at the one thing they thought they knew about the Ripper, Abberline and Smith ensured that Met and City Police patrols once again went on special alert as another weekend began. With the whereabouts of Klosowski, Druitt and a portrait gallery's worth of other suspects' whereabouts unknown and a mounting undercurrent of fear flooding the minds of a number of administrators that the Duke of Clarence might be involved in the Whitechapel crimes, even more police bodies were poured into the cauldron. Several dozen additional men were switched from day to night duty and a few more were moved from West Side beats to areas in the East End that they should have been assigned to right after the Tabram or, at the latest, the Nichols murder. Still others had their single day off cancelled and many more were put on what amounted to overtime after their usual 10-hour shift. Although their pay rate did not increase, they did get the chance to work a few extra hours at regular rates. Some administrators suggested they should be put on half-rates since they would be getting more money than men working regular hours. Sir Charles took the suggestion under advisement, but decided to pay the men for their time at their regular rates. He had learned at Sandhurst that the first duty of an officer was to his men. Besides, if one of them caught the Ripper in the act, it would be well worth the additional expenditure.

Chapter Twenty-One

Saturday, 3 November

It was a quiet night. The Ripper remained unnoticed, unheard and undetected. As the day progressed, the municipal election returns took up the majority of West Side conversations; the Liberals garnering 60 seats, the Conservatives 58 and the Liberal Unionists four. The Ripper inspired considerable talk in the East End where electoral returns were of little interest and had even less effect. Parties right, left or center made no real impression on poverty, prostitution and the paucity of hope that prevailed throughout most, if not all, of Whitechapel and Spitalfields.

Sunday, 4 November

It dawned a pleasant Sunday morning. Emma took pity on Abberline and allowed him to sleep late and attend a later church service than their usual 7:30 a.m. observance. He remained in bed in blissful comfort for an hour after waking. Even his varicose vein seemed to be willing to give him a restful period free— well, almost free—from pain. He had heard of no attacks during his roving throughout Whitechapel last night and the morning brought no telegrams. As he lay in bed, he remembered he had to send an apology to that reporter fellow, Woulls or Coulls, that he and Godley had taken in under suspicion. After a hearty breakfast with Emma, he only dropped by headquarters for a half-hour to send the note and set up an extensive night watch before meeting his wife for the afternoon church service. Then, tomorrow being a special day, Abberline went out into the East End after dinner to ensure the police were alert and ready throughout the dark hours.

Monday, 5 November

The night passed quietly and Guy Fawkes Day arrived. Sir Charles ordered every available man into the streets, even if many had already been on patrol throughout the night. A fire at the Inner Temple of the Freemasons took up much of the London Fire Brigade's time, even though the dull rainy weather helped contain the blaze. The crowd kept a reasonable distance despite the tantalizing temptations of all going berserk at once. Sir Charles' theory of madness by mobbing together seemed to have been murdered by a gang of ruthless facts.

At CID headquarters, Abberline continued to find evidence of police inefficiency. He growled, "This business at Thames Police Court about a pot-man indecently assaulting a fourteen-year-old girl doesn't have any Ripper link. Why do we still get these funneled to us? I thought we set up a committee of constables to screen this chaff?"

"We did," Helson said. "That one just slipped through."

"It sure did. I got word to go to Thames Court this morning about it, as if the Ripper himself had been caught." He sighed. "I guess we police are for protection, not perfection."

There were the usual arrests. Just in the category of last name beginning with C: James Cosgrove for beating up his spouse, John William Cooper for cutting and wounding his wife, and Edward Connell for assaulting two police constables while in execution of their duty. All three assailants were the worse for drink at the time of their transgressions.

Matthews rubbed at the smooth skin just beneath his nose with his left hand, a little nervous ritual that belied mounting emotion. A telegram from the Foreign Office concerning the Vienna socialist had just been handed to him. It said that the Ripper had called himself Johann Stammer while in San Francisco and John Kelly while in London. He was described as of medium height, broad shouldered and between 35 and 38 years of age with brilliant and large white teeth, a scar from a stab wound under his left eye and the rolling gait of a sailor. He was now thought to be living in Liverpool.

The informant had given Sir Augustus the description and Sir Augustus had given the informant 2,000 florins. The Foreign Office was certain the informant was acting in good faith. However, the man had left Vienna for London via Paris but had never arrived in London nor had he returned to Vienna.

Matthews stared at the telegram. "Hasn't the Foreign Office ever dealt with the criminal class before?" the ex-attorney wondered, shaking his head. "What did they expect would happen to their witness after giving him 2,000 florins?"

Worse, Sir Augustus had submitted a claim to the Foreign Office for the 2,000 florins, calling it a legitimate expense. Matthews handed the telegram back to his personal secretary, who read it and summed up what Matthews was finding somewhat distasteful to conclude. "It appears the socialist and the florins are gone."

As a clever assistant was wont to do, his aide then offered Matthews a soothing solution, saying, "However, as it is plain to see and I am sure you have already concluded, sir, the Foreign Office is clearly responsible for the entire episode and the 2,000 florins. It is certainly not the responsibility of the Home Office, let alone you, sir."

"You are absolutely right," Matthews said. "Let the F.O. pay the 2,000 florins if they deem it a reasonable and prudent expenditure, not that I would ever consider it any such thing." His lack of action brought a smile. Doing absolutely nothing was often the best bureaucratic action.

Despite intermittent rain, celebrations consumed the pent-up passions of most citizens as bonfires highlighted parades throughout the country, lit by fireworks and the burning of the day's namesake in effigy. Whitechapel featured one of the most-novel processions as shabby effigies, most of them depicting not Guy Fawkes, but Jack the Ripper instead, were dragged through the rain-slickened streets. To add to the festive atmosphere celebrating the survival of the English Parliament, coloured fires flared from roof tops and public houses sported Venetian lamps and Chinese lanterns. A good, if wet, time was had by almost all.

Tuesday, 6 November

A constant rain soaked the city from dawn to dusk and continued on through a bleak night. While Abberline took the wet weather on a weekday as an opportunity to spend an evening at home with Emma, the heavy rains cost the life of a West Riding Police Force sergeant who was swept over a dam and drowned while searching for evidence pertaining to a minor theft. Elsewhere, great institutional happenings were transpiring. The House of Commons went back into session and the Americans elected Benjamin Harrison to the Presidency. British manufacturers defended themselves for their poor showing in terms of awards, sales and public acclaim at various foreign exhibitions during the year. They did not see the results as having any long-range implications for British industry. A British expert who predicted the United States would lead the world in steel production in two years was considered eccentric and more than a tad irrational, not to mention unpatriotic.

Wednesday, 7 November

Lord Mayor-elect Whitehead released his nominations of various worthies and unworthies for city lieutenancy. In Wapping and Shadwell, police patrolled in pairs and despite their supposed increased vigilance due to the Ripper still avoided a notorious area where rows of brothels cohabited with lawless immunity. Any policeman foolish enough to enter this valley of death could fear plenty of evil.

The East End door-side doxies had developed a fatalistic attitude to the Ripper. A "husband" would ask, "Any luck?"

The "wife" would reply most literally, "No fucking luck."

"At least you didn't meet Jack."

The woman would shrug and answer haughtily, "Let him come; the sooner the better for such as I."

The Ripper was now accepted as a sort of occupational hazard, a part of everyday life, like the rain, soot, inadequate meals and rheumatism.

It was also of interest that only a third of men now accompanied their women into the streets as protectors. It had been only a matter of time before fear diminished and the less fearful reverted to past patterns of behavior. As the Professor said, time was far from neutral; it was on the side of the Ripper.

Francis Tumblety

The police arrested a medical quack and eccentric self-promoter, Francis Tumblety, an Irish-born American, on charges of gross indecency; in his case, a homosexual act. Bail was set at £300. The police found that Tumblety had been living in a boarding house in Whitechapel during the time of the murders. He also made a pretense of some medical knowledge, was reputedly a misogynist, and collected the wombs of different classes of women as anatomical specimens.

"Chase his background down," Abberline ordered Helson. "He might have the makings of a passable suspect."

Thursday, 8 November

Cold, a most prominent notice of the coming winter, came in on north-northeast winds that blew unabated from the surging sea-ice floes of the Arctic. Temperatures plummeted into the thirties and stayed there all day and all night. Things important and unimportant contributed to the day's mosaic. Anne M'Donald was charged with breaking a window. A well-dressed chap was arrested for obtaining money by false pretense. A costermonger came before the courts on charges of reckless but, at least, wreckless driving. His wild, drunken cart ride through the stall-lined East End streets had left a path of terrified pedestrians, cursing fellow drivers and miraculously little serious damage.

From their unheated conveyance, Abberline cast a solemn stare at the rampaging clouds that poured rain down on the metropolis off and on throughout the night. Carriages of the wealthy were home to coal-heated foot-warmers, but police carriages were home only to frigid inspectors. Exhausted and near the end of his mental capacity, Abberline fretted as he rode with Helson on a tour of the East End police stations. The cold coupled with Lees' vision of an inside murder had a double chilling effect. A woman was more likely to take a man inside in weather like this, and it was the verge of a major holiday weekend. Damn!

Friday, 9 November

It passed dawn and all seemed well. Abberline, Smith, Helson, Chandler, Swanson, and thousands of others sighed a breath of relief. James Whitehead beamed. This was his day. The Lord Mayor's Pageant and Parade was today. Whitehead had loved this pageant since he had come to London from Yorkshire as a spectator and now he was its epicenter. It was the culmination of his devotion to civic duty that he had embarked upon in his late forties after making his fortune in business. This was his day. Carriages decorated in the most excellent of finery rolled along the crowded city streets. Banners streamed. People waved. Proud riders astride prancing steeds promenaded like erect beacons of stolidness in a sea of weaving, waving colour. It was a kaleidoscope of imperial pomp; a great rainbow of a day. Whitehead laughed, waved and luxuriated under the glow that came in such surging fullness. It was just delightful—nothing could spoil such a day, not even the heavy rain that was falling. Absolutely nothing.

As always, life began for some and ended for others. A son was born to the K. Colby Sharpins, the R. H. Seightmans and the John William Davys. A daughter blessed the George J. Mansfields. And while the little Sharpin, Seightman, Davy and Mansfield made their first earthly noises, other people ceased to exist. Little five-month-old George Ernest Leverson died as did 49-year-old Dr. W. C. John Chalmers, Vice President of the British Gynaecological Society, and 79-year-old William Orlando Johnson, whose demise came just three months after his golden wedding anniversary. Four other men were killed when a house they were repairing collapsed. It was simply a matter of the great majority relentlessly increasing. But all these deaths were destined for obscurity—another was not.

John McCarthy, landlord and shop owner, glanced at the wall clock in his shop.

"Quarter to 11," he told his assistant John Bowyer. "I had hoped we might sneak away to see some of the festivities. Maybe we can make the end of the Lord Mayor's parade if you go collect the rent on the Miller's Court room. She's behind eight weeks."

1873 map of Dorset Street; Miller's Court is between the words Dorset and Street, north side

Bowyer nodded and stepped outside. The rain had turned to showers as he strolled along Dorset Street, which had an occasional stable or chandler's shop but was almost entirely occupied by 13 decrepit common lodging houses, home to about 1,500 people paying four- or six-pence a night. Prostitutes used the narrow courts that led off the 150-yard long street for their brief, but intense business transactions. At night, many a constable avoided patrolling the street alone between the two pubs that bookended it, but Bowyer felt at home on the narrow cobblestoned road with decrepit three-story brick buildings lining either side like exhausted sentinels. He ducked under a clothesline someone had rigged to dry clothes across the street; a common practice on the narrower East End roads.

The room was in one of the courts off Dorset, called Miller's Court, which could only be reached through a three-foot wide arched passage. The passage was semi-black on a cloudy day and tomb-dark at night. Miller's Court was no more than a 10-by-30 foot irregularly shaped clearing in a towering clump of houses, shops and squalid rooms. The renter at Number 13, Mary Kelly, owed more than 30 shillings on a one-room flat that was almost barren of furniture and completely bereft of beauty. Mary's house fronted on Dorset Street, but the only entrance was from the court. She rented the room for 4s. 6d. a week.

13 Miller's Court from "The Illustrated Police News" November 1888

A gray Russian blue cat flitted out of the square as Bowyer sauntered across the courtyard. Stopping before the second door on the right just inside the square, Number 13, he knocked. No answer. The bitch was most likely lying in. He knocked louder. Still no answer; probably sleeping off a gallon of gin. Bowyer was about to give up and return to the shop when he noticed that one of the two windows on the left side of the door was broken. The hole in the window, like hundreds in Whitechapel, had been stuffed with rags; this particular aperture being filled with a man's old coat. A cheap muslin curtain covered the rest of the window.

A LOST WOMAN
MARY KELLY
IN MILLER'S COURT

Mary Kelly

Bowyer, well-disciplined after 20 years of army service in India, decided it was his duty to make the extreme-most attempt to return with all or part of the back rent. To avoid cutting himself, he carefully removed the old coat from the window. A good shout and he would be able to wake the dead—and collect the rent.

He looked in. His mouth opened to yell but nothing came from his throat;

nothing but a terrible gurgling loss of air as his mind reeled at the scene before him. What was left of the Kelly woman was lying like a piece of slashed, serrated meat on a blood-bathed bed. Her body was little more than a skeleton encased in blood-drenched pieces of flesh. The corpse was not even recognizably human. Lumps of tissue clung to the walls where they had been plunked onto nails meant for pictures. Other clumps of raw human meat were piled on a table beside the bed. Splatters and sprinkles of blood were everywhere as if there had been an explosion in a morgue. It was carnage beyond descriptive perception.

Bowyer withdrew his head from the window, gulped fresh air and felt an involuntary surge of vomit rushing up his gullet and filling his mouth. He staggered away, retching. Then, all control gone, he ran in shrieking horror back to McCarthy's shop. He shook. He stammered. He felt that terrible wet reflex of diarrheal impulse. God! How else would a man react when he had just looked into the bowels of hell?

The mutilated victim in Miller's Court

"Christ, John, that Kelly woman's been butchered," Bowyer managed to say when he burst into the shop. "Cut to pieces. You never saw anythin' like it. It's horrible."

Bowyer's words spurted forth. McCarthy's brow furrowed. For a split second he thought Bowyer had gone mad. Then he realized that it was not madness that tore at Bowyer. It was sheer revulsion. Reason not always being paramount in human affairs, McCarthy hurried down Dorset and into Miller's Court to see for himself the cause of Bowyer's distress. Perhaps something told him that Bowyer had to be exaggerating or perhaps there was a morbid neurotic need deep in McCarthy's psyche that demanded he see such a horror for himself. He would wish for the rest of his life that he had been far less curious.

As Bowyer hung back, McCarthy looked through the window, gaped, gasped, withdrew his head and promptly threw up. He had looked into a nightmare.

"Get the police," McCarthy gasped between retches. Bowyer nodded and ran for the nearest station.

The police were quick to gather, but they did nothing. McCarthy sat on the cobblestones dumbfounded at what he had seen. Bowyer was shaking and now that the police had arrived, he couldn't stop talking. "Dorset Street is well lit. The lodging house across the way is open all night. People pass in and out of it all hours," he rambled on and on.

"The murderer had to have been cocky as hell," a constable noted. "Anyone could have seen him enter this court. It's a trap. Only one entrance and that's as narrow as a sentry box."

Several of the other policemen nodded. Telegrams were en route to Abberline, Sir Charles, Smith, Anderson, Moore, Andrews, and every other senior police official.

Soon a host of milling policemen was congregated before 13 Miller's Court. At 11:30 a.m. Abberline stepped down wearily from the hansom he had hurried over in. His back, bottom, head and knee ached. He had stayed up all night supervising patrols, walking the occasional beat to get the feel of things, conferring with constables and citizens in doss houses and on the streets, completely tiring himself out. It seemed he had just got home and into bed, intent on catching a few more than 40 winks after reassuring Emma that he was well, when the summoning telegram arrived.

Abberline surveyed the situation. As per the latest orders, the first officers on the scene had sent for Sir Charles and the hounds. Since neither hounds nor commissioner had arrived, the police could only stand in idle disarray amidst the puddles. At least the cold showers had finally moved on out of the East End. The gathering citizenry nodded to each other. Abberline feared that the police's inactivity just confirmed their deepest suspicions about the ineptitude of the constabulary.

Dr. Phillips emerged from the crowd of constables, saying, "From what I can see through the window, she's been completely butchered, like a steer. I do not believe we should force the door until Sir Charles or the dogs arrive."

"Isn't there a key to the place anywhere about?" Abberline asked.

"Not that anyone can find."

Abberline shrugged in resignation. "Let's leave it closed then. Sir Charles should be here soon and those bloody hounds can't take forever to get here. Orders are orders."

Crowd at Dorset Street, from "The Pictorial News," 17 November 1888

At 12:30 p.m. the Lord Mayor's procession of important persons, horse-mounted and socially exulted, started marching through the City's crowded core. The heavy rain had cleared by 11 a.m. and the flags, banners and floral streamers adorning streets for the event fluttered in a dry breeze, save for a sparse shower or three. Under a gloomy sky, the gala parade moved along in imperial splendor escorted by police and a troop of the 19th Hussars, with 40 mounted police nearby, armed and ready if a riot broke out. The worst that broke out were some scattered jeers. At the center of it all the new Lord Mayor, James Whitehead, beamed like a new star. Then the piercing cries of the newsboys on the edge of the crowd began to be heard.

"Another 'orrible murder! Extra! Extra! 'nother murder!"

"The Ripper strikes again!"

"Another Whitechapel killing!"

"Victim 'orribly mutilated! Worst yet!"

"Police do nothing!"

The words echoed and re-echoed in the streets. Whitehead gasped. His greatest day was ruined. That bloody, murdering bastard of a maniac had ruined everything. The crowd was already disintegrating into trios and quartets, pairs and quintets, discussing the latest Ripper ravage. Lady Godiva could have ridden by unnoticed. Whitehead cursed and cried in helpless rage and frustration.

As 1:30 approached, Abberline paced in anxious agitation before 13 Miller's Court. Helson had arrived bearing Abberline's walking stick which Abberline had forgotten at his office at some point. Most of the policemen had looked in through the broken window. No one wanted to talk about what they had seen.

"I've sent constables to canvass the immediate neighbourhood to see what they can learn," Abberline told Helson.

"Maybe, unlike the other murders, someone saw something," Helson hoped.

"I ordered the court cordoned off and now all we can do is wait for Sir Charles and the bloodhounds."

"And listen to water drip off the roofs," Helson said with a forced grin.

Abberline glanced at a large placard rippled from the rain and pasted on the wall of the decrepit house adjoining Number 13. It offered a £100 reward for the discovery of the person or persons who had murdered the woman in Hanbury Street. He pursed his lips in disgust. In little more than a month, Annie Chapman, murdered only about 300 yards distant, had become "the woman."

Superintendent Arnold strode through the narrow archway from Dorset Street. "Hello, Abberline. Have all the photographs been taken and the medical exam completed?"

Puzzled, Abberline said, "No. Sir Charles' standing orders are to wait 'til he arrives to personally supervise and the dogs arrive. We haven't even opened the place up. Door's locked and there doesn't seem to be a key anywhere about."

Arnold swore. "Sir Charles just resigned. That order was cancelled hours ago. Get the bloody door open, now."

Two constables forced the door. Dr. Phillips entered the room first, followed by Abberline, Arnold and the landlord, John McCarthy. The smell of the dismembered body assaulted their noses with enough force to make Abberline see things. The room was a carnal chaos. The body lay on the bed, naked. She had been completely disemboweled and her entrails removed and placed on a table. Her nose had been cut off and her face gashed and mutilated so as to be beyond recognition. Her breasts had been cut off and placed beside her liver and other entrails on the table. The body and bed were covered with blood. Abberline pursed his lips to keep the bile from rising too far up his throat. He felt ill for a moment, but it passed. A wave of nervous heat swept over him, but he waited a moment and it too passed.

McCarthy later said, "The sight we saw, I cannot drive away from my mind. It looked more like the work of a devil than of a man."

"Please let us get to work, Mr. McCarthy," Abberline said, ushering the green-faced landlord out of the room as a photographer began to take photographs.

"At least we'll have photos of the body at the scene this time," Abberline said.

"Too bad we didn't have photos taken of the other victims," Helson said.

"New technology always takes time to become routine."

One set of pictures brought out frowns on almost everyone.

"Sounds crazy to me," Major Smith, who had just arrived, said. Miller's Court wasn't in his jurisdiction, but Abberline welcomed Smith and his City men. The yard was being searched and the door-to-door canvass, on Abberline's orders, was expanding outward from the murder site as more constables and inspectors arrived.

Arnold shook his head as the photographer worked with his box camera and flash powder in the carnal room. "I think it's a waste of time, but we'll be damned if we don't try it. Any method we fail to employ leaves us wide open to criticism because the press can always say 'It might have worked.' That's just how it is."

"I agree, I agree," Abberline said. "It sounds crazy, but we venture little in taking the time."

And so the deceased's staring eyes were photographed on the basis of an obscure and unfounded theory that the image of what the deceased had been looking at just before death was retained on the retina of each eye.

"Keep it quiet," Abberline suggested to Arnold and Smith. "No need for the press to learn we're trying anything and everything—unless it works."

Trying to ignore this photographic esoterica, Abberline and Smith looked around the tiny room slowly and carefully, while Arnold checked on the progress of the canvass. There had been a large hot fire in the grate, so hot and long burning that the spout and handle of a metal kettle had melted away. Stirring the ashes ever so cautiously with a stick from the yard, Abberline found the charred remains of a straw hat and women's clothing. A few articles of women's clothing were folded neatly on a chair at the foot of the bed.

"The door was jammed, so did he escape out the larger of the two windows?" Smith asked, looking at the windows, one with 24 small panes of glass, the other, slightly lower, with four panes—one broken. "Must have had a devil of a time of it when he realized he was stuck in the room with the body."

"Maybe he jammed the door as he left," Abberline suggested.

"Why the fire?"

"Probably to see what he was doing; be black as tar in here in the middle of the night. There's only one stub of candle left on top of that wine bottle and there don't seem to be any candles in that little cupboard. I imagine the candle was getting low so he burned anything at hand in the fire to get sufficient light. The kettle spout probably melted because he just left the fire roaring away when he escaped."

"First one we've found inside," Smith said glancing over at the mutilated victim.

"Commercial Street is all dug up with the work for the new tram, so many unfortunates who worked it are taking men to their own rooms to conduct business."

"Improve public transport, kill a prostitute," Smith said, his lips a bleak narrow line. "The rain and cold also probably made a room more appealing than against a wall, too."

They looked solemnly at the corpse. The coroner for the northeast part of East Middlesex, Dr. Roderick Macdonald, a crofter's son from Skye who had risen to become MP for Ross and Cromarty, as well as coroner, had arrived to confer with Dr. Phillips. The photographer was busy taking photographs by the window. It was a crowded, congested scene.

After Macdonald examined the corpse, Abberline asked, "Anything for us, Dr. Macdonald?"

"She was killed while facing the wall. Had her right carotid artery slashed clean through; couldn't have cried out. There are a couple of quarts of blood under the bedstead. The paillasse, pillow and sheet in the upper corner are saturated with blood, like sponges. She obviously thought she was going to have normal intercourse on her side with penetration from the rear. It pretty well clinches the idea that Jack is left-handed or ambidextrous; awkward as the devil to slice her throat with the right hand if she's facing the wall."

"But if he strangled the other victims, laid them down and then crouched at their head facing their feet to slit their throats, a left-to-right cut would indicate a right-handed murderer," Abberline said.

"That may be true, but in this case, he certainly didn't kneel by her head."

As Macdonald spoke, Dr. Thomas Bond (A Division, Westminster), Coroner Baxter (Whitechapel), Dr. Gordon Brown (City police surgeon) and Dr. William P. Dukes (H Division, Whitechapel) arrived in rapid succession to join Dr. Macdonald and Dr. Phillips.

Macdonald continued his clinical assessment. "He then dragged her body across the bed and proceeded to carve her to pieces. He must have been at it for hours."

After Abberline thanked Dr. Macdonald, Baxter and Macdonald fell into a discussion of jurisdiction over the body. As Baxter began to make his argument, Abberline decided he did not care which coroner conducted the post mortem and the inquest, just as long as he got a report. He decided to move outside to give the medics more space to argue, and to avoid having to see and smell the mutilated corpse any longer than he already had, although he knew the smell would cling to his nostrils for days.

As they stepped out into the court, Smith said, "Well, that's that. Dr. Phillips wants to shift through the refuse in the grate more thoroughly after they finish with the body. See if anything flesh-like turns up."

"That'll be a horrid mess to reconstruct," Abberline said. "Has to be done. Take all the doctors in there hours to figure out that mad puzzle and make sure the monster hasn't carted anything off, like another kidney."

It had been a harrowing experience. The two veteran policemen stared into the gloom-laden, overcast sky, breathing evenly.

"How the hell are we going to catch this bloke?" Abberline finally asked, his nose still reeking of the slaughterhouse smell of the disemboweled corpse.

"I don't know. If he didn't leave any clues in there and if no one outside saw anything significant, we're no further ahead than we were when the murders began."

"At least this murder eliminates some suspects."

"Such as?"

"Francis Tumblety, an Irish-born American who collects uteruses."

"Why?"

"We're holding him on charges of gross indecency."

"One down, how many dozen to go?"

The routine interrogation of every person in the vicinity of Miller's Court eventually brought the police to Mrs. Caroline "Carrie" Maxwell. Abberline studied the fattish, middle-aged woman as they stood in the court that afternoon.

"I came out of my lodging house between 8 and 8:30 this morning, went across the court into the street and Mary Kelly was standing opposite me in Dorset Street."

"You are certain it was 8 or 8:30 this morning?" Abberline asked.

"Yes. I fixed the time by my husband finishing work."

"You're sure it was Mary Kelly?"

"Yes. I spoke to her. It was unusual to see her up then. She never associated much with anyone. I said, 'What brings you up so early, Mary?' and she said, 'Oh, Carrie, I do feel so bad.' Just looked dreadful, she did."

"She called you by name?"

"Yes."

"How well did you know Mary Kelly?"

"I've spoken to her a couple of times."

"Did she say anything else?"

"She said she had a glass of beer and brought it up again. I figure she had been in the Britannia beer shop on the corner. I went on to Bishopsgate, got my hubby's breakfast and saw her talking to a man outside the Britannia on the way back."

"What time was that?"

"About a quarter to nine."

"What did this man she was talking to look like?"

"I couldn't say. Too far away. He was taller than me and stout."

"What was he wearing?"

"Dark outfit; looked like a plaid coat. I can't remember anything else."

"What was she wearing?"

"Dark skirt, velvet bodice, maroon shawl, no hat."

"You are certain she called you by name?"

"Yes, she said, 'Carrie' quite clearly."

Abberline paused and said gently, "When you saw her the doctors believe she had been dead for five or six hours. Could this have been yesterday morning that you saw her and not this morning?"

"No, definitely not. It was this morning. The doctors must be wrong."

Abberline took his notes and wondered.

The interrogations continued. Bearing wads of constable reports and witness statements—mostly wit-nothing statements—Helson reported hourly to Abberline.

Helson said. "A Mrs. Cox saw her at about 11:45 p.m. Kelly was drunk and with a man. She wore a red knit crossover and a linsey frock. They went into Kelly's room together. Mrs. Cox wished her good night."

"His description?"

"Right here; 36 years old, 5 foot 5 inches, blotches on his face, small side whiskers, thick carroty mustache, short, stout, shabbily dressed. Had a pot of ale in his hand. Longish coat, dark colour, and a round billycock hat."

"Doesn't fit any of our other descriptions of the Ripper."

"Cox heard her singing as late as 1 a.m. She, that is Cox, had gone out and returned at 1 to warm her hands. It was raining, hard. Cold. She went out again. When she returned at 3 a.m. the light in Kelly's room was out. Even with the noise of the rain, Cox heard the tread of men coming and leaving the court, but she said she heard nothing alarming during the night," Helson said. "A flower seller living at Miller's Court, Cahterine Pickett, also heard the deceased singing, 'A Violet from Mother's Grave' of all things at 12:30 a.m."

"That puts the murder between 1 and 3, or most likely after 3. Mrs. Cox should have seen reflections of that fire in the grate flaring up through the window if she was out when she claims to have been."

"We also tracked down an Elizabeth Prater. She also lives at 13 Miller's Court, but in the other side of the house. She returned home at 1 a.m. Stood on the corner there until 1:20. You can imagine what all these women do for a living."

Abberline nodded, not having to use his imagination at all.

"Anyway, she went right by Kelly's room, saw no light and heard nothing. Claims she could hear Kelly move in her room through the thin partition that passes for a wall. Prater went to bed. Her kitten woke her at half past three or quarter to four. Claims she heard a faint voice cry 'Murder' and claims it came from the court. Such cries are so common roundabout here she took little notice and went back to sleep."

"She could have imagined she heard it after she heard Kelly had been killed. These women have a flair for the dramatic."

"Prater said she rose at 5:30 and went over to the Ten Bells for a tot of rum. She saw no one in Miller's Court when she went out or when she returned."

Helson paused to flip through the wad of reports and statements in his hand. "Kelly's been living with a man named Joseph Barnett; lived with her up 'til last Tuesday week. He gave the victim's full name as Marie Jeanette Kelly, born in Limerick. Said she was married at 16 to a collier who was killed in a mine explosion; had a spot of trouble with the company over paying compensation. Supposed to have lived in the West End and in Paris. On returning to London she lived with a man named Morganstone. Haven't located him yet. Barnett and Kelly quarreled when they drank. He lost his job at a fish market a few months back and left when she brought some whore friend of hers to live with them. We're trying to track down the woman. Three in a bed apparently doesn't leave much room at 13 Miller's Court."

"Better three than sharing it alone with Jack the Ripper." Abberline found an old wood crate to sit on, stretching his aching leg out before him.

"Another possible witness: Sarah Lewis," Helson reported. "The evening of the 7th she said she was walking along Bethnal Green Road with a female friend when a man who had passed them turned back to speak to them. He wanted one of the women, didn't care which, to follow him. Both refused. He went away but came back. Offering a treat, he tried to get them to come down a passage. 'What are you frightened of?' he asked and put his bag down. The women ran away."

"Description?"

"About 40, short, pale faced and sported a black moustache. He wore a short black coat, pepper-and-salt trousers, and a long brown overcoat. Had a high round hat and a 9- to 12-inch black bag."

Wrong night, but Abberline knew Helson would get to the point, soon.

"After a quarrel last night with her husband between 2 and 3 a.m., Sarah went to stay with her friends the Keylers at No. 2 Miller's Court. At 2:30 a.m. in Commercial Street near the Britannia she saw the man who had accosted her on the 7th. In Dorset Street, in front of a lodging house across from Miller's Court, she noticed another man. Not tall, but stout, with a black hat. The man was watching the court, as if waiting for someone to come out. She barely slept at the Keylers' and like Prater she heard the cry of murder just before 4 a.m.; 3:30 probably. Sounded like a young woman not far away, but Sarah didn't even look out the window."

"If you looked out the window at every yell and scream in this neighbourhood, you'd never get any sleep."

At 2 p.m. Dr. Thomas Bond finished a preliminary examination assisted by Drs. Phillips, Brown and Dukes. They agreed that Bond would be their messenger; a compromise between Coroners Baxter and Macdonald, since Bond was from Westminster, not Whitechapel (Baxter's domain) or East Middlesex

(Macdonald's realm).

"Rigor mortis is setting in," Bond told Abberline, who knew it usually started roughly 6 to 12 hours after death. Therefore, Mary died between 2 and 8 a.m.

"The body was fairly cold," Bond said, "so she probably died between 1 and 2 a.m."

"It was a cold night," Dr. Phillips added as he joined the conversation in the court, "so I believe she was murdered later than 2 a.m. With the body cut to pieces and no clothes, the body would cool more quickly. The room was also cold, with the window broken. I put the time of death at 5 or 6 a.m."

"Possible," Bond admitted.

"What about the fire?" Abberline asked.

"Could move the time of death somewhat earlier," Phillips conceded.

Abberline nodded and told Helson, "Prater and Lewis' testimony match the medical evidence, while Caroline Maxwell's does not. Lewis and Prater may have heard Mary's final scream."

Bond, who had said Mary would not have had time to cry out, said, "It's possible. I did find a small incision in her right thumb and abrasions on the back of her hand and forearm."

"From fighting back?"

"Let's hope she castrated the bastard," Bond said.

As Abberline and the physicians discussed the corpse, Mrs. Prater took the excuse of getting some water from a pump in the square to peep in the window of Mary's room. "I could bear to look at it only for a second," she later said, "but I can never forget the sight of it if I live to be a hundred."

The pictures taken of the deceased's eyes came to naught, the entire episode kept from the public and press. The careful sifting of all the material in the grate turned up little more than fragments of a woman's clothes and ashes, as well as soot-stained fingers for Dr. Phillips, the sifter. Kelly's ex-mate, Morganstone, was located, but he added nothing new. A thorough examination of the room failed to uncover the door key.

"The Ripper may have left with Kelly's lone key," Abberline said. "Something to look for among any suspect's possessions."

Helson gestured for Abberline to come watch him. Helson closed the door to Mary's room and then, reaching his arm through the broken window, he reached over and flicked up the latch. "Easy as reaching for a pint at your local."

"So he could leave and lock the door on his way out, with or without the key," Abberline said. "Stuffing the rag in the broken window for good measure."

"Found this," Helson said, holding up a man's clay pipe.

"The Ripper's?" Abberline asked, praying the murderer had finally left something of his own behind.

It was not to be.

Dr. Thomas Bond

An inspector brought Kelly's former 'husband,' Joseph Barnett, to speak with Abberline in the court late that afternoon. Barnett was a dapper looking man with a waistcoat and cravat, neatly combed hair and moustache. A top hat would have suited him well. Barnett identified the pipe as his property. He said he visited Kelly between 7 and 8 the previous night.

Did Barnett murder Kelly? Abberline wondered. Helson had reported that they had quarreled. "How was she when you left her?"

"Well as I found her," Barnett said.

Abberline continued his questioning but the timing was wrong for Barnett to be the Ripper. Abberline finally accepted the conclusion that, although gathering information on the victim usually helped find a murderer, it was becoming apparent after the fifth victim that this was not the case with Jack the Ripper, who murdered strangers.

It was 3:50 p.m. when *Old Catchall* crunched and creaked to a stop on Dorset Street at the narrow entrance to Miller's Court. The driver and his assistant flipped back the tarp, removed a dirty, scratched and scraped shell, and lugged the much-used coffin into the courtyard.

Whitechapel's word-by-mouth telegraph system alerted all those near and far that the Miller's Court body was at last going to be moved. People, mostly paupers, emerged from side courts, alleys, streets, pubs, shops and doss houses. Under the press of onlookers, the police cordon all but collapsed. Crowds surged forward and encircled the cart.

The two men, aided by a pair of constables and led by an inspector, carried the shell out toward the cart. Abberline was about to order constables to clear a path to *Old Catchall*, but the men in the crowd slowly doffed their ragged caps and stood aside solemnly as the cold wind stirred and ruffled their greasy uncombed hair. Old crones wept as the crowd parted, as if for royalty. It was spontaneous sorrow. Even the most insensitive seemed to be aware that something terribly pitiful had occurred here. The constables loaded the coffin into the cart. The usually noisy street fell into silence as the cart and its sad cargo creaked away in the late afternoon stillness. A shiny black crow cawed. What remained of Mary Kelly was taken to Shoreditch mortuary.

It was about five in the afternoon and almost dark when an apprehensive Robert Lees walked around Miller's Court and said, "You'll have to stay back. I can't concentrate with a mob of people about me. I just have to go where it feels right."

And so Lees, followed by Abberline, Helson, Godley and Reid at a discrete distance so as not to interfere with any astral stirrings, set out across Whitechapel.

"Christ! You realize, gentlemen, we're four grown men following a human divining rod and we've been bitching about Sir Charles wanting to use bloodhounds," Abberline said. "Luckily Lees hasn't sought any publicity about this or the press would have made us the laughing stock of all England by now."

"Many believe in the occult," Helson said. "Papers are full of such stories: visions, apparitions, séances and such. My wife's sister's cousin once awoke and—"

"He's turning again."

"He's been gradually heading out of the East End."

Lees led the quartet along street by street.

"Good grief. He's getting into a cab. Quick grab that one."

"This is more like it," a tiring Godley said. "The Ripper couldn't have gone all this way without hiring a cab."

Almost an hour after sunset, they trundled through the darkened, cold streets, peering ahead to keep the lights of Lees' cab in view. It wasn't easy. The jolting, jarring, copper-carrying carriage bounded from paving stone to paving stone with unpredictable vehemence. Godley bumped his chin twice on the window frame as he leaned street-ward trying to keep Lees' carriage in sight. Godley spit blood from his mouth after the second bump.

"All well, Godley?" Abberline asked.

"Nothing save a cut lip, sir. Had far worse on duty many a night."

"I was luckier," Reid said, watching from the other side of the carriage. "Only cracked the top of my head near open. It's so hard, damaged the carriage more than me."

"Thank, God. He's stopping at last."

They alighted and stood in a spacious West End square with mature plane trees in a garden in the center. Lees gestured toward a magnificent house and said, "He's in there."

"There?" Reid asked, frowning.

"Who lives there?" Abberline asked. "Anyone know?"

"I'll go ask a neighbour," Helson volunteered. "Don't worry. I'll tell 'em I'm looking for my wayward sister."

It took Helson a long five minutes to return. When he did, he told Abberline what he had discovered. Abberline said, "Christ! He's one of the most prominent surgeons in London."

"Pillar of society. Highest in the land," Helson said.

"We haven't got any legal reason for busting in. What the hell are we going to say? This nice gentleman here has visions of you being Jack the Ripper, mind if we search the place?"

"Then why have we followed Lees all over London in the first place for?" Reid asked.

Abberline felt a fool.

"Look, he's the man," Lees pleaded. "I'll describe the inside of that house. I can see the whole scene when he came home from the murder."

"If you can describe the inside of that house," Abberline said, "I'll arrest him myself at the risk of losing my positon, pension and what little reputation I have remaining."

Lees closed his eyes, his face reflecting a certain inner serenity. He spoke softly, "There's a hall. A high porter's chair of black oak sits on the right side. At the end of the hall, at the extreme end, is a stained-glass window. A large mastiff is asleep at the bottom of the staircase."

Abberline bit hard on his pipe. "Alright, let's see whether there is any truth to any of this."

The group trooped to the door and without hesitation, Abberline knocked. A kindly, round-faced woman answered. All eyes went past her and stared in silence down the hall at the high porter's chair of black oak on the right and the stained-glass window at the hall's end. There was no mastiff.

"I'm Chief Inspector Frederick Abberline of CID and these are Inspectors Helson and Reid, and Sergeant Godley. And this is Mr. Robert Lees. We'd like to see the master of the house, if it wouldn't be too great an imposition."

"By the way, Miss, do you own a mastiff?" Helson asked, peering around Abberline's shoulder into the hall.

"Yes, I just now let him out. He's been asleep on the rug by the stair. I don't think he would harm anyone. He's in the back yard. Do you wish to see him?"

"No, no," Abberline said. "Just the master of the house, if you please."

"He's upstairs. I'll send Nellie to fetch him. If I may ask, what is it you wish to see him regarding?"

"There have been a series of murders in Whitechapel—"

The woman blanched. "Merciful God! No!" She stifled a sob. "My poor husband hasn't been of sound mind for some time. I caught him torturing our cat only last week and..." She broke down.

Abberline nodded, his excitement rising; had they at last found the Ripper?

The lady recovered enough to say, "He's threatened me and our children, but I don't think he's the Whitechapel…"

"Perhaps not," Abberline agreed, praying he was, but knowing the odds of a psychic leading them to the Ripper seemed far from likely. "But, all the same, we would like to speak with him."

The routine of "arresting" the prominent doctor followed. He was taken to a West Side station house. Major Smith and other prominent police officials were called in. The doctor was soon explaining that he had on several occasions found himself sitting in his room with blood on his shirt, unable to remember where he had been. On another occasion, he noticed scratches on his face. The episode ended with the doctor being removed to a private asylum in Islington.

"We've finally got the Ripper," Helson exclaimed as the policemen rode back to Scotland Yard in an official four-wheeler.

"I'm far from sure," Abberline said, trying to make his exhausted mind focus. "His wife can't document all his movements, but vouches for him on the night of the Chapman murder. Who knows where he was on the nights of the other murders. He doesn't fit any description of the Ripper we have and we didn't find anything of significance at his house or office."

"But Lees led us right to him," Helson said, "and described the interior of the house exactly."

"He could have seen the house before and known the doctor was as mad as a hatter," Abberline said. "He wouldn't even have to be deliberately deceiving us. Lees could be as befuddled as half our suspects."

"We have to assume this deranged fellow isn't the Ripper," Inspector Reid said. "If he is, the killings will end. If he isn't, well…We'd be fools to relax our vigilance."

When reporters learned of Kelly's murder, the press bemoaned the lack of bloodhounds in the city. *The Telegraph* reported, "Amongst the populace, there was very widespread disappointment that bloodhounds had not been at once employed in the effort to track the criminal."

Abberline had heard many express the belief that the Ripper had not struck in a month because of fear of being tracked by the bloodhounds.

"Maybe he heard the bloodhounds were back in their kennel in Wyndgate," Helson said, "and felt it was safe to venture forth again."

"Given his audacious attacks, I doubt he fears a dog, let alone a dog's nose."

Ripper accusations continued to flood in to the police. The Ripper was the illegitimate son of British Royalty. The Ripper was George Gissing, the novelist. Hadn't he stolen from fellow students at Owens College, and just read what he's written and you'll see. The Ripper was the painter, Walter Sickert. Didn't he paint a picture of a nude woman on a bed in a dingy bedroom? Wasn't that Kelly? Well? The Ripper was Dr. Barnardo, founder of the East End Juvenile Mission. Didn't he spend all his time drifting through the back alleys of Whitechapel? Wasn't he devoted to waifs? Didn't he open a home for unfortunates, perfect for getting to know future victims? Weren't most of the unwanted street urchins the produce of prostitutes? Wouldn't he secretly harbor a hatred for these unfortunates who left their kids to forage for themselves? No one could be as kind and generous as Dr. Barnardo appeared to be, anyway. He must be up to no good.

Abberline shook his head at the wild accusations. No one prayed more than him that one of them would prove correct, but he could not justify wasting valuable detectives' time chasing down ludicrous leads. No evidence at all linked Barnardo to the murders, not to mention that Barnardo was 43 and only 5 foot 3 inches tall; far from fitting the descriptions of the murderer. He was also married with three children, unlikely to have the opportunity to disappear for long periods in the middle of the night to murder prostitutes. He was also well known in the East End, making it unlikely no one would have recognized him if he had embarked on a murder spree in the area.

Even so, Helson made some discreet inquiries and learned that Barnardo did visit No. 32 Flower and Dean Street the day Elizabeth Stride was murdered. Barnardo spoke to lodgers in the kitchen, and later viewed the body and recognized Elizabeth Stride as one of the women who listened to his plans to save children from the streets.

"Apart from that," Helson told Abberline in the latter's office at the Yard, "Barnardo appears to have been named as a suspect because he was in the newspapers and works in the East End."

"If we arrested every man doing good works in the East End," Abberline said, "we'd have to arrest several hundred missionaries and Salvation Army members. Not to mention Reverend Barnett's undergraduate volunteers from Oxford; half of them are from wealthy, upper-middle class families."

"Matthews would hate to be asked about that during Question Time."

Landlords told of lodgers who kept to themselves, stayed out all hours of the night, snuck in on cat's paw feet in the wee hours of the morning, rushed out to buy the latest edition of the morning paper, and could be heard stoking the fireplace late at night, no doubt to burn evidence. Panic and paranoia prevailed.

The day finally passed. Lord Mayor Whitehead could neither eat nor sleep, his perfect day perfectly ruined. Abberline had a fierce pain behind his left knee and visions of blood and gore that invaded his dreams like vengeful spirits. His tossing and turning kept Emma awake, too. Major Smith needed a stiff drink to sooth himself to sleep. Helson and his wife did not make love. The four doctors who had tried all day to reassemble Kelly's corpse didn't sleep, nor did they make sexual overtures to their respective wives. Two constables stood guard over 13 Miller's Court all dark long, even though the windows had been boarded up and the door padlocked. Although many passed by to see the site of the latest murder, there was little to see and the constables sent them on their way with alacrity. A dustbin full of burning debris provided little warmth and less comfort, but plenty of eerie, flickering shadows on the brick walls of the court. It was the longest night London had experienced in decades.

Chapter Twenty-Two

Saturday, 10 November

A *Boston Daily Globe* headline screamed, "Baffled. London Detectives at Their Wits' End. Whitechapel Fiend Still at Large" in black font large enough to read from across a parlour. Closer to home, the London press blamed the police for concentrating their forces in the West End for the Lord Mayor's procession, instead of the East End where the Ripper struck. Alongside the front-page Ripper stories, the London Necropolis advertised a special on funerals as the metropolis reeled under the news of the most horrific, heinous butchery in British criminal history. The athletic world, oblivious to all things outside its professionalized sand pile, continued in accordance with its pre-set schedule. West Bromwich Albion suffered a 2-nil upset at the feet of Burnley, while Wolverhampton edged Bolton 3-2.

The Cabinet Council met and agreed that Mr. Matthews should stand firm against offering a reward. Under constant and increasing press and public pressure to do something, they did agree to offer a pardon to any accomplice of the murderer of Mary Kelly who could assist the police in apprehending the killer.

It now appeared as if the police were in as much of a frenzy as the Ripper must have been as they made arrest after arrest. Crowds gathered outside district police stations. Agitation and excitement mounted as each suspect was escorted in. Many a supposed Jack the Ripper breathed relief on making it to the sanctuary of the cells beneath a station. Innocent men inquiring about the case were tried and convicted by angry mobs and chased at full sprint through the streets. The papers ran warnings for men not to wander through Whitechapel carrying anything from knives to black bags that might cast suspicion on them.

Hysteria ran high.

"Remember the Maxwell woman, the one who saw Kelly alive at 8 or 9 the morning of the murder?" Helson asked Abberline. They stood outside Mary's room as a pale sun crested the buildings surrounding the court.

Abberline nodded; conflicting and confounding testimony was not soon forgotten.

"I found someone," Helson said, "actually several someones, who saw Kelly in front of and in the Britannia at about 8 or 9 on the morning of 8 November, the day before the murder. I confronted Mrs. Maxwell with this news, gently suggested she might have mixed up the days, but she insisted she did not. Claimed all the people in the Britannia must be wrong."

"Her name and story are in every newspaper in London. She'd look a prize pickle if she changed her story now after all the attention she's received. She probably truly believes by now that she did see Kelly yesterday morning."

"I chased down a little more on Charles Cross or Lechmere," Helson said, consulting his notes. "The one who found Nichols' body in Baker's Row. He's married to Elizabeth and has seven kids. I have four children and couldn't find time for a pint at the pub; doubt he'd have time to commit five murders with such a large family."

"Probably not, and if the Professor is right, Jack's probably a loner and unmarried. Cross's wife and children make poor witnesses either way, but unless he left home much earlier than he claimed, I doubt he had time to meet Nichols, negotiate a price, enter Buck's Row, murder her and clean himself up before that other carman, Paul, arrived."

"Even so, Cross lived close to his mother until a few months before the murders started, when he moved a short distance to 22 Doveton Street. The Hanbury, Mitre Square and Dorset Street murder sites are on routes between his home and place of work at Pickford and Co."

"And Berner Street?"

"His mother lives on Berner Street."

"Might be a shadow of a suspect, although thousands of men live and work near all the murder sites; they're all so close together." Abberline mulled over the information. "Rare for a killer to act like they 'found' the body, except in penny dreadfuls; rare, but not unknown."

That afternoon, the overwhelmed Abberline consented to see Francis Galton. Where mysticism failed, Abberline prayed science might succeed. Galton had coined the name 'eugenics,' in part based on his half-cousin Charles Darwin's work on evolution and in part on his own research into heredity, but Galton was far more than just a eugenicist. He was a tropical explorer, statistician, progressive, sociologist, alienist, anthropologist, geographer, inventor, meteorologist, geneticist, and psychometrician. Arriving from his lab in the science galleries of the South Kensington Museum, the balding, 66-year-old polymath entered Abberline's office.

After the usual pleasantries, Galton explained identification by finger impressions. "Back in 1823 one of the finest scientists of the time, the Czech anatomist and physiologist Jan Purkyně, discovered that fingermarks have certain basic patterns: spirals, circles, ellipses, double whorls."

"So you want to match the fingermarks of our more promising suspects with any fingermark that might be found at the scene of one of the murders or on any correspondence?"

Galton nodded.

"Sounds like the idea may have merit. If it works. . ."

"If I may be so bold to suggest, it's most unfortunate that we did not apply this idea sooner," Galton said. "William Herschel has been using the inked impressions of fingermarks of the two forefingers to identify people in India since 1860. He even wrote to the authorities in London concerning the validity of such hand marks. Unfortunately, they just thought he had got too much sun out in India; didn't even bother to look into it.

"Henry Faulds didn't have any success either. He wrote an article in *Nature* in 1880 on how the Japanese have been using fingermarks for identification for years. He wrote the Home Secretary, the Police Commissioner in London, and my half-cousin, Charles; not one of them even answered. The officials at Scotland Yard thought Faulds was a swindler. A few days ago, a Jew named Jago or Bago had a bit on fingermark identification in the Letters to the Editor in *The Times*, but I fear no one paid it the least bit of attention either."

Abberline guessed that Helson had probably read about it and, given time, would mention it. He took a card out of a file on his desk. "Well, we've only got one good impression, probably of a thumb, on this postcard. Open question whether it's from the Ripper or not. I think it is, but that's no matter. You can compare our best suspect's fingermarks to it."

"You have one?"

"A doctor—a man named Lees helped us find him—who we just committed to a lunatic asylum. You can fiddle around with his fingermarks. When we find any of the other suspects, you can compare their fingermarks to the mark on the postcard. It won't be usable in court, but it may shake loose a confession." Abberline was desperate, dog-tired and willing to try anything—even science.

Also giving science a go was Dr. Thomas Bond, Fellow of the Royal College of Surgeons and police surgeon for A Division (Westminster). After much thought and many cups of tea and cocoa, he wrote the Home Office about the murders from a medical perspective. Maybe it would help identify the murderer. He wrote, "All five murders were committed by the same hand, with throats cut from left to right, except in the last case, which was so brutal, it was impossible to determine which way the cut was made. In every case the woman was found lying down and her throat was cut first. In the first four cases, the murderer attacked from the right side of the victim. In the Dorset Street case, he must have attacked from in front or from the left, as there would be no room for him between the wall and the part of the bed on which the woman was lying. The murderer would not have necessarily been splashed or deluged with blood, but his hands and arms would have been covered and parts of his clothing must certainly have been smeared with blood."

Bond paused to dip his pen and consult his notes. "In each case, the mutilation was inflicted by a person who had no scientific or anatomical knowledge. In my opinion he does not even possess the technical knowledge of a butcher or horse slaughterer or any person accustomed to cutting up dead animals. He used a knife at least six inches long, pointed and about an inch thick; may have been a clasp knife, a butcher's knife or a surgeon's knife. He was a man of physical strength and of great coolness and daring."

Bond recalled that he had heard the Cabinet was considering offering amnesty to any accomplice of the killer. He wrote, "There is no evidence he had an accomplice. He may be in a condition sexually" that is called "satyriasis:" an uncontrollable or excessive sexual desire in a man. "The homicidal impulse might have developed from a revengeful or brooding condition of the mind. A religious mania may have been the original disease, but I do not think either hypothesis is likely."

Bond considered for a moment. "He may quite likely be a quiet inoffensive-looking man, probably middle aged and neatly and respectably dressed. He must be in the habit of wearing a cloak or overcoat or he could hardly have escaped notice in the streets if the blood on his hands or clothes were visible. He is probably solitary and eccentric in his habits, and likely to be a man without a regular occupation, but with some small income or pension. He is possibly living among respectable persons who have some knowledge of his character and habits and who may have grounds for suspicion that he is not quite right in his mind at times. Such persons would probably be unwilling to communicate suspicions to the police for fear of trouble or notoriety, whereas if there were a prospect of reward it might overcome their scruples."

Early that evening, just as Abberline was about to leave for a tour of the stations, Coulls was admitted to his office overlooking Scotland Yard. Abberline was about to ask how a correspondent had winkled his way past the desk sergeant, when Coulls politely apologized for the intrusion and asked for a comment on Sir Charles' resignation. The resignation had not surprised Abberline, who had heard rumblings of his imminent departure for months. Matthews was appalled by Sir Charles' article in *Murray's Magazine* and finally, after being offered the Commissioner's resignation in March and again in early summer, accepted it.

Even so, the timing could not be worse: the Whitechapel murderer was still free. Normally Abberline would have had the reporter tossed out on one of his ears, but Abberline's anger at what had been said about Sir Charles in the press caused him to change his mind. Maybe he could help, at least a tad, to set the record straight, or at least make it somewhat less crooked. It went against policy, but he would not be speaking directly about the cases themselves.

"Sir Charles is a good man," Abberline began, choosing his words with great care. "Honourable, diligent, brave, a hard worker, early riser, a good sense of humour."

"But was he an effective Commissioner?" Coulls asked, sitting on the edge of the wood chair across from Abberline, who sat back down behind his desk. "The rank and file criticized him for failing to provide pensions for men injured on duty and for increasing penalties for being drunk on duty."

"Sir Charles requested the pensions, but the Home Office refused, and the Home Office wanted the punishments for being drunk on duty stiffened." Abberline offered Coulls tea, which was declined. "Sir Charles was appointed when morale at the Met was at its lowest point in our brief history in the years after the 1877 Turf Scandal."

"A pair of confidence tricksters were bribing officers to tip them off when they were about to be arrested, right?"

Abberline nodded. "Sir Charles was appointed in '86 to restore discipline and raise the morale and reputation of the force. He reorganized the Detective Force into the CID, improved discipline and did raise morale. He was popular with the men."

"Less so with CID."

"He did hire more constables to deter crime."

"What about inspectors to solve it?"

"It is true that London has fewer investigating detectives than any comparable city in Britain. In the Met, the percentage of men engaged in detective work compared to those in other duties is 2.42, in Manchester it is 2.7, in Liverpool and Glasgow 3.5, in Dublin 3.6, and in Birmingham 4.5," Abberline rattled off the figures from memory. "But resources are limited and choices must be made." Abberline paused. "You are no doubt aware, Sir Charles and Monro did not see eye to eye about CID, but every possible measure has been taken to solve the Whitechapel murders."

"What about charges that Sir Charles was seeking to militarize the police; turn them into a political police force to spy on Irish nationalists, labour unionists and anarchists?"

"Sir Charles certainly adores his dress uniforms, but the Met Police Commissioner, by statute, can only have 500 Army reserve men in the police ranks." Abberline recalled something and chuckled. "When I joined the force, all the men drilled in public to ensure discipline, which included training with the cutlass. I never liked such training, but with Fenians, anarchists and labour unionists always threatening to unseat the government, some such training is clearly warranted. But militarizing the police? No, the Met were trained in basic military drill long before Sir Charles was appointed, even if it had lapsed before his appointment. In truth, we spend little time on Fenians, anarchists and labour unionists, at least at the divisional level. That's more in Sir Robert Anderson's line."

"Radicals and many in the press castigated Sir Charles for what some would call his military response to the events of Bloody Sunday against those very groups."

"And conservatives and the Conservative press supported him; evidence of a healthy democracy, I would say. Whatever the case, Sir Charles' defense of the police after that day greatly improved morale and made him far more popular with the rank and file."

"But not with the people of the East End."

"Met relations with the people of the East End have improved markedly since those sad events in November. Look at the cooperation we received in searching large sections of Whitechapel for the Ripper."

Abberline spotted Helson loitering just outside the open doorway.

Coulls said, "I have learned Sir Charles required long reports on such things as truncheons and boots, when many would say police time would have been better employed searching for the Ripper."

"Do you know how far an average constable walks on his beat each and every day?"

Coulls shook his head.

"Twenty miles; a good pair of boots is an essential piece of equipment. Sir Charles has always shown the greatest concern for the welfare of his men." Abberline shuffled some papers on his desk, rose and nodded at Helson that he was coming. "I must be off, but I will say that Sir Charles Warren was suited for his job as commissioner. He exercised authority, organized the disorganized and turned the Met into a confident organization, although he had limited police experience. He's an administrator, the much-maligned fellow who can get a mish-mash of individuals to put their personal goals on hold long enough and often enough to achieve a common goal, particularly where too many individuals believe they are, as the Americans say, the boss."

Helson said, "*The Times* said of Sir Charles; 'He has been saddled with all the responsibility, he has had no freedom of action, and in consequence his position has become daily more unbearable.'"

"So, a good man in a difficult position?" Coulls asked, rising as Abberline headed out the door.

"You could say that," Abberline said. "Matthews is the first Roman Catholic minister to hold Cabinet rank in 300 years. The PM wants to keep him. Sir Charles had a better chance of finding the Ark of the Covenant on his archeological digs in Palestine than he did of besting Matthews in their battle for control of the Met." As Abberline and Helson walked down the hall, Abberline called back to Coulls, "Besides all that, anyone hunting Jack the Ripper is in a damnably difficult position."

As they began to tour Whitechapel that cold night, Helson asked Abberline, "Why tell the press a thing?"

"Better they get at least a glimmer of CID's perspective than be imprisoned by their wrong view forever."

"I didn't think you thought highly of Sir Charles anyway."

"Focusing on his shortcomings just encourages the belief that we've made a hash of finding the Whitechapel murderer. Sir Charles may not have been the finest Met Commissioner, but I doubt even the finest could have caught Jack the Ripper."

Sunday, 11 November

A quiet night passed by.

After church service with Emma, Abberline went to his office to read through the doctors' report on Mary Kelly. She had been found on her back entirely naked. Throat cut from ear to ear. The cut had penetrated clean through to her spinal column. Face slashed beyond recognition. Abberline took a sip of tea and continued reading. Ears, nose and breasts cut off. The latter placed in two lumps on a bedside table. Stomach and abdomen ripped wide open. Kidneys and heart removed; also placed on bedside table. Liver removed. Where in that bloody Hell of a room did he put that? Part on her right thigh, part on the table. The thighs were stripped in places to the bone, the meat and muscle scraped away. Pieces of flesh had been stuck on nails on the wall replacing several cheap prints as wall hangings. The prints apparently had been burnt.

Abberline took a bite of buttered toast he had made over the coal fire, which was just now finally beginning to warm his office. He was regularly eating at work now. As he pulled his coat tighter around his throat to fend off the lingering cold, he read on. Furniture in room: old bedstead, two tables, one chair. No organs missing. No knife found. Another bite of toast. Her clothes were laid out on the floor beside the bed. Abberline finished his toast. The unfortunate, Harvey, who had shared the room, said she took all her clothes with her when she left and that Mary Kelly had very little wearing apparel. The clothes burnt in the grate were most likely Kelly's.

No sign of a struggle. So, Abberline thought, the Ripper was so unthreatening that Kelly got undressed, climbed into bed and never once anticipated what was coming. To say, 'Maybe it was better that way' was trite, but possibly true.

The murderous carnage was forever seared into Abberline's memory, especially the image of a dark clotting pool of blood on a piece of bone. There was something incongruous and spine-squeakingly squeamish about that dark, dark blood surrounded by the white, white bone. All this slaughter while flames crackled and spit in the hearth and fantastic grotesque shadows danced on the wall. An inferno of heat and perverted passion. Hell in the heart of Whitechapel.

Monday, 12 November

A gloomy semi-darkness pervaded the day while a thick swampy fog wrapped London in a damp vale of mist. Figures loomed up at each other out of the fog, both oncomers wide-eyed with fearful anticipation that the other might be the awesome Jack the Ripper. Fear clutched many a heart—both male and female—this day. Many people forsook errands that took them away from home and safe shelter. Men escorted ladies more often than ever. Even in Whitechapel and Spitalfields, toughs escorted aging drabs from lodging house to market with a kindness and care often found only among the gentlest of folk.

With the press breathing fire over police ineptitude and continually pointing to the immoral mix of citizenry that inhabited the East End, it was no accident that the major thrust of police endeavor fell on bawdy houses. It seemed the more streetwalkers the Ripper disemboweled, the more the police pursued prostitutes. Albert and Amelia Becker of 35 Berners Street were charged with knowingly permitting their house to be used for immoral purposes. It seemed Albert threatened to stab his wife if she did not earn money for him by leading a dissolute life. It was a clever plea. Women, considered simple and child-like, were their husband's responsibility, so women were often found not guilty of crimes in which they probably corroborated with their husband. The husband would be found guilty; the wife set free, regardless of their true involvement. No one asked why Amelia didn't just flit off and never return instead of coming back regularly with copulative customers. He got a month's hard labour and she got a fine of £4 20s, a sum she could probably earn in the coming month before Albert returned. No one asked: if she was really threatened, why should she be fined at all? The public was apparently appeased. The police had shut down one wee whorehouse: a sort of mom-and-pop operation, like the corner sweet shop. Only a few people noted that the closure would only be for a day and no one stressed that some 8,000 prostitutes didn't miss a trick during this token gesture to the district's moral adjustment. If the law were an ass, then the public most certainly was its rider.

A telegram from Francis Galton arrived that morning telling Abberline that the doctor to whom Lees had led them was most likely not the Ripper. The man's thumbprints did not match those on the postcard.

An inspector found a witness, George Hutchinson, who saw Kelly entering her room with a man at about the right time. Abberline interviewed Hutchinson in his office.

"I walked back from Romford early Friday morning," Hutchinson, an alert-looking labourer, said. "Been out in Essex looking for work. When I passed Thrawl Street I saw a man on the corner. I didn't pay too much attention to him then. I went on towards Flower and Dean Street where I bumped into Mary Kelly. I've known her for quite some time. She asked me for sixpence which I didn't have. She went off then; said she must go and look for some money. This fellow on the corner of Thrawl Street comes up to her, puts his hand on her shoulder and says something. I didn't hear what it was, but they both bust out laughing. He puts his hand on her shoulder again and they both walk towards me, slow-like."

"Did you get a good look at him?" Abberline asked. In a corner of the office, a constable with a dip pen was filling in a witness statement and, frozen in suspense, waited for the crucial information.

"He was wearing a soft felt hat which was drawn down over his eyes. I put my head down to look him in the face. Strange thing, he turns and glares at me. Then they walked off down Dorset Street. I don't know why, Inspector, but I followed them. They stood at the corner of Miller's Court for two or three minutes. That's when I heard Mary say that she'd lost her handkerchief; said it in a loud voice. He pulled out a red handkerchief and gave it to her, and then they went into Miller's Court."

"And?"

"I went up to the entrance of Miller's Court—see if I could spot them, but I couldn't. I waited around for near an hour. I don't know why, probably hoped he'd come out, go away and maybe Mary'd take pity on me. Can't blame a bloke for trying."

"What did the man look like?"

"About five-foot-eight. Dark complexion. Dark moustache turned up at the ends, not as severely as that German Kaiser fellow's that you see in the papers, but turned up just a bit."

"How old?"

"About 35. He was wearing a dark coat, long thing, trimmed with astrakhan."

"With what?"

"Fur of young lambs." Hutchinson must have a relative who was a tailor. "He had a black necktie with a horseshoe pin in it. White collar, of course."

"Anything else?"

"Hmmm. Dark spats with light buttons over his button boots. He wasn't no regular bloke that lives here. Had a massive gold chain on his waistcoat and the chain had a big seal with a red stone hanging on it."

Abberline leaned back in alarm. The description fit Pedachenko, the elusive Russian doctor who was described by some witnesses as wearing spats and a heavy chain with an unusual seal. Trouble was CID had never been able to locate this doctor of mystery.

Hutchinson went on, "He had dark eyes, bushy eyebrows."

This fitted Klosowski, not Pedachenko. Recalling Pedachenko's description, Abberline asked, "Side whiskers?"

"No, his chin was clean shaved. Looked like a foreigner."

Again the man was described as looking like a foreigner. But what kind of foreigner? Truly foreign or just a well-dressed man foreign to the East End?

"Any guess as to nationality?"

"No. There was just somethin' about him that made him look like a foreigner, not an Englishman."

Abberline tended to believe Hutchinson, in part because his testimony placed him near the murder site. He did not have to come forward. Why incriminate himself if he wasn't certain—and innocent? "Was he carrying anything?"

"Small packet 'bout eight inches long. Had a strap around it. He was holding it pretty tight, in his left hand, I believe."

"What was the packet made of?"

"Looked like that new linoleum stuff. But it was dark coloured. Hard to tell. I do distinctly remember that he had a pair of brown kid gloves in his hand."

And so another description of the Whitechapel murderer was added to the list.

"It's not unlike the others," Abberline told Helson after the constable had Hutchinson sign his statement before ushering him out. "Fits Pedachenko, the mad Russian, best, but it could fit Klosowski, that barber surgeon who seems to flit around the East End at will." He paused. "When I think of it, the description almost fits Eddy, the Duke of Clarence to a T. He looks foreign and, damn— who looks like Eddy?—that barrister Druitt. And he's missing. You check to see if he's off playing cricket somewhere, Joseph?"

"Couldn't track him through his cricket club. Whatever he's doing, it isn't cricket."

At 11 a.m., as a Salvation Army parade led by a bass drum, a major, two lieutenants and a dozen black-clad female saviors marched up Whitechapel Road, the inquest into the Kelly murder opened at Shoreditch Town Hall under the direction of Dr. Macdonald, coroner for the North-Eastern District of Middlesex. Abberline reluctantly attended to give evidence; he had far more pressing matters to attend to than listen to testimony in all likelihood he already knew. Large numbers of the public had to be shut out of the packed hall. Correspondents filled every chair in the reporters' section.

The jurors were sworn in and Abberline conducted them to the mortuary to view the body. Mary's corpse had been stitched together and coffined. Abberline had seen to it that her mutilated body was concealed under a grey cloth. Only her face was visible. Then he took the jury to Miller's Court to view the tiny murder room before returning to the hall for the inquest.

Even before Macdonald began, a juror rose to question why he had to serve on an inquest in Shoreditch for a body discovered in Whitechapel. Macdonald explained that it was where the body was taken, not where it was found that determined jurisdiction. Annie Chapman had been murdered in Spitalfields, his jurisdiction, but since the body had been taken to the Whitechapel mortuary, Coroner Baxter had presided over the inquest. This time the reverse had happened, so Macdonald would conduct the inquest with jurors from Shoreditch.

The sullen juror dealt with, if not appeased, Dr. Phillips testified briefly about the medical aspects of the case. He said death occurred by the severing of the right carotid artery; other than that, he told the jury nothing. Abberline waited, but no jury members asked anything about mutilation or if any organs were missing. Did none of them read the newspapers? A juryman rose to say they had no further questions on the understanding that more detailed information about the medical examination would be provided at a later date.

Nine local residents, including the key witnesses, gave evidence based on statements from 9 November, which Abberline himself had taken, and had nothing new to add. Maria Harvey, a laundress, testified that she was one of Mary Kelly's closest friends and had lived with Kelly. She said that on 8 November she was with Mary at No. 13 when Joe Barnett arrived. Maria then left, at which time, 6:55 p.m., she said, "They seemed to be on the best of terms."

Barnett then testified that he arrived between 7:30 and 7:45. Abberline noted the time discrepancy, but put it down to failings of memory. Barnett said he stayed about 15 minutes and that Mary was sober. Mary Ann Cox testified that four hours later she saw the victim on Dorset Street and Mary Kelly was drunk and with a stranger. Cox, a 31-year-old widow and prostitute, described by *The Star* as "a wretched specimen of East London womanhood," lived at 5 Miller's Court. She had been working on Commercial Street amidst all the tram construction, but it was cold so she returned home to warm up at 11:45, but noticed nothing of note. Abberline recalled she had told Helson she returned at 1 a.m., saw nothing, went out and returned again at 3, when Mary's room was dark. Abberline sighed; witness stories changed every time they were retold.

Abberline rose to give a deposition about his activities the morning the body had been discovered and then the day's proceedings ended in what had become routine for the Ripper murders. The jury returned a verdict of willful murder against some person or persons unknown.

When Abberline arrived at the Bethnal Green station to go over the evening's duty assignments, he told Helson, "Our latest victim was pregnant, about three months. Came out at the inquest."

"Anything else of note?"

"Dr. Bond, based on food in her stomach, thinks she was killed at about 1 or 2 in the morning."

Helson nodded, jotting down yet another new possible time of death.

Abberline said, "Mary Jane Kelly didn't have syphilis."

"Then, based on the post mortems, none of the victims had it. We tracked down the woman that Kelly brought to live with her; name's Harvey."

"She was at the inquest."

"She last saw Kelly Thursday night. She moved over to a room in New-court Friday. We also found out a little more about Kelly. She was 22. When drunk, she was noisy and given to singing Irish songs. She was fined in Thames Magistrate Court on 19 September for drunkenness. Tall and pretty, 'as fair as a lily,' a fellow lodger said, although another said she was stout. At the mortuary, her ex-husband, Barnett, identified Kelly only by her eyes and hair."

Abberline swallowed hard at the thought of Mary's mutilated body.

That night Abberline sent the labourer Hutchinson into the East End with two detectives in hopes of spotting the man Hutchinson had seen with Mary Kelly. They were out until 3 a.m. but failed to spot him.

Tuesday, 13 November

No sign of sunshine pierced the fog and low cloud that continued to smother London. The eerie quiet of some streets sent shivers of terror along spines as visions of the Ripper continued to cloud people's minds like a miasma of evil. Despite this, business continued and life, albeit somewhat shakier, went on. Piggott Brothers featured a line of boxing equipment at their commercial establishment and the police sought out illegal prizefighters.

Abberline sent Hutchinson out again with two detectives in search of the man Hutchinson had seen the night of the murder.

"Hutchinson's story is in several evening papers," Helson reported to Abberline at the Yard.

"The description too?" Abberline asked, hoping against logic that it might have been omitted.

"Every detail."

"How did they get the story?"

"A correspondent interviewed Hutchinson this morning."

"Blast. I asked him not to speak to the press."

"Hard to resist when they come at you like a Tartar horde."

Abberline fumed. "They may have just alerted the killer that we know what he looks like."

"Who knows how he'll react."

"He'll either go to ground or alter his appearance and strike again. No point sending Hutchinson out again tomorrow. I'll ask that 100 officers be retained for extra duty in Whitechapel, especially this weekend."

Hutchinson returned to report that he saw no one to fit the image in his mind of the man he had seen. Abberline thanked him for his efforts and did not mention the story in the press. What would be the point?

Wednesday, 14 November

Londoners took some solace in the sight of the sun seeping through a patch of blue-gray in what otherwise was a dull overcast sky. Old Sol standing sentinel in the sky for at least an hour suggested that there was a silver lining to those fleecy folds of white way up upon high; that there was hope and peace and goodness. The idea was quite irrational, but it was comforting all the same. It was also comforting to see justice prevail at Newgate as Levi Richard Bartlett, convicted of murdering his wife, plunged through the trap, reached the end of his rope and entered eternity.

In Parliament, Sir Charles' resignation was announced. Members cheered. The vast majority of Met constables, sergeants, inspectors and administrators had a far different view of the matter. A deputation of superintendents representing the entire force expressed to Sir Charles their profound regret at his resignation.

In Lambeth, Detectives Michael Leek and Donald Reed raced toward the sound of a ruckus. They soon came upon a crowd encircling a man, obviously the worse for drink. The surrounded one was yelling, "I'm Jack the Ripper. Got a nice sharp present for you ladies."

He grabbed the nearest woman and wrestled with her, clutching one of her breasts with one hand while waving a leather bag with the other. Leek and Reed had trouble breaking through the crowd to the would-be Ripper. No one realized they were policemen nor wished to give up a prime viewing position in the assembled ring of spectators.

"Here! Watch who you're pushin', mate!"

"Police," Reed said, flashing his badge into an indignant pair of eyes.

The more forceful Leek reached the drunk first.

"Come on, now, just calm down," Leek said. "We're police."

That statement produced a roundhouse swing of the leather bag which missed Leek and hit a lamp post. Reed grabbed the man's right arm and Leek latched onto his left, but the man disagreed with these attachments and being of considerable strength hurled the detectives street-ward. The crowd cheered.

Reed and Leek fought back and finally wrestled their man to the ground, the effort being aided by a wayward knee catching the man in the groin. Again the crowd cheered.

"Let's get him to the station before this lot turn ugly," Reed whispered. Then leaning close to the man's ear said, "You better come quietly. This mob just might decide to lynch you."

"Piss on you," the drunk roared and almost threw Reed off, but the plucky detective hung on and this time delivered a deliberate boot to the man's area of maximal masculinity. The drunk roared and lifted the two detectives skyward in a towering rage. Three more constables arrived just in time to help wrestle the drunk to the stone street. Finally in control of their man, the five policemen hurried him through the mob, who had cheered police and prisoner alike during the see-saw battle. Now they seemed to favour the law, but some suggested they mete justice out themselves. Amid calls of "Hang 'im! Hang 'im!," the police quintet rushed the man to the Brixton Police Station. Once inside he was placed in a cell to sober up while the police examined the contents of his leather bag.

"Good God!" Leek exclaimed as he extracted from its innards two pairs of scissors, a dagger and sheath, and, of all things, a life preserver.

Identification of the prisoner came rapidly. He was well known to many in the crowd.

"Yea, I know 'im. He's a hairdresser. Lives in Peckham. Everyone calls 'im the 'Mad Barber of Peckham,' but his real name is Perriman."

"John Benjamin Perriman," Leek headed his report, telling Reed, "Probably just another lunatic. We'll have to notify CID and track down his movements at the times of the murders."

In his heart, Leek hoped Perriman was the Ripper, but in his mind, he was certain Perriman wasn't. The sly and resourceful Jack the Ripper wasn't likely to give himself away in a drunken bout of bravado. But you never knew. It was that sliver of doubt that extended each investigation to its final cul-de-sac in a rush of hope that it would lead to the Ripper. Within an hour it was found that Perriman had been in gaol from mid-August to mid-September. He was not the Ripper.

Thursday, 15 November

In things almost as mad, Parliament, the huge edifice of empire, sat late. The Secretary of State gave vent to considerable criticism of police operations. Most importantly, he accused the recently resigned Sir Charles of contesting the Commons' right to control the police. Editors put it on their front pages with enthusiasm. Mr. Douglas Stuart, a worthy and thrifty Scot, followed, repeating his demands for a financial statement on police affairs. Editors put Stuart's remarks on page 10. The debate thundered on with flashes of spoken lightning ripping forth from this or that orator, with speech rolling like thunder off the paneled walls, with criticism crashing against criticism. All members survived the battle, the only casualty being a sore throat suffered by one of the more outspoken orators. He lived to talk about it.

On Commercial Street, a week after Kelly's murder, the tramway finally opened as brown horse trams began running between Bloomsbury and Polar for 3d a ride. The congestion soon lessened somewhat, although Commercial Street was still a Gordian knot of traffic on a daily basis.

Friday, 16 November

"Another weekend and Jack the Ripper still at large." It was a pronouncement on a thousand lips, a thought on a million minds. All of London now realized the Whitechapel murderer always struck at week's end. It took great courage to face the fact that the police were still no closer to catching the monster than they had been two-and-a-half months ago. Most of the public continued to blame the East End for its ills. The sins of the Ripper were again visited on the very people he was victimizing. Victorians, like most humans throughout history, were steadfast in their belief that a certain powerful right always prevailed in the universe. The Ripper killed unfortunates; if they hadn't been unfortunates, they wouldn't have been murdered. It was therefore their own fault. Any fool could see the logic of that. Which was true—any fool could.

Reverend Barnett, Whitechapel's crusading man of the cloth, publicly admitted being more appalled by the disorderly and depraved lives of his neighbours than by the actual murders. To him, commercial sexual encounters and alcoholic consumption were sins of a superior order. Murder was, after all, only inevitable death, something all must succumb to under God's great plan.

"The acts of a madman are not matters for horror, and his escape is not sufficient reason for wholesale condemnation of the police," Barnett sermonized from his pulpit at a morning service. "A series of courts, such as Miller's Court, where rooms unfit for stables are let at 4s a week, where cries of murder are too common to arouse anything more than passing notice, where vice is the staple trade and drunkenness the chief resource—this fact should arouse horror."

He suggested that the wealthy owners could police their own establishments by hiring agents to act on their behalf. The rooms could be made fit for habitation and provided with locks for privacy. Night watchmen could prevent rows and insure the inhabitants led respectable lives.

"Reverend Barnett's faith in his fellow man is only exceeded by his naïveté," Coulls noted over a whisky and shepherd's pie lunch after overhearing another pub patron report on the sermon to a pal. Coulls had felt like a change from beer. He certainly wasn't going to drink water with the attendant risk of cholera or some such nefarious disease lurking in its murky contents. His lunch was superb, even if Catherine McLean had begged off again due to the demands of work. Instead, Jennings met him for lunch.

"Barnett always appeals to their Christian charity," Jennings observed as he finished his pint of bitters and haddock before the pair headed back to the office. "If they had any of that, they wouldn't own all those places in the first place."

John Perriman, the "Mad Barber of Peckham," who had so rashly claimed to be the Ripper, came before the courts. Treating the entire episode as if it were some colossal joke, Perriman quipped and taunted, smirked and smiled his way through the few minutes of proceedings. It was decided to hold him without bail pending psychiatric examination.

Another weekend came. Abberline ordered the Friday night police shifts doubled and re-doubled as had become standard in the East End.

Saturday, 17 November

A fair fine day gave a mixture of clear sky, warm temperatures and more fear-filled thoughts about the Ripper. Two keepers of an East End bawdy house were brought into court and duly punished for the evil of their ways. Some constables nailed strips of rubber to their clunky regulation boots in a bid to patrol silently if not awkwardly, hoping to surprise the Ripper at his work. The University of London awarded degrees for the first time to women. Saturday night came and went with no Ripper attack and no sleep for Abberline, Helson, Chandler or any of the other senior inspectors, who spent the night on the streets—as did hundreds of their men.

Sunday, 18 November

Isaac Jacobs, the one-time slaughterhouse worker who had been chased repeatedly by mobs of avenging, if mistaken, Ripper-hunters, was found babbling incoherently to himself. Certified as a lunatic at large, he was committed to an asylum.

"Well, he might have cracked up anyway," a doctor concluded, "but these continual Ripper accusations couldn't have helped."

"Maybe he'll respond to rest and quiet," his colleague suggested.

"At an asylum?"

Monday, 19 November

As news of the latest murder made headlines around the world, a large number of people accumulated into a crowd before Shoreditch Mortuary, which was behind St. Leonard's Church, despite a constant drizzle that misted the air and soaked through wool, tweed and linen. The grotesque grisliness of the latest murder overcame all repressions, releasing a torrent of sympathy for Mary Jane Kelly.

At half-past 12, a coterie of men, solemn of face and slow of pace, carried a simple common coffin from the church to a waiting carriage. Three large wreaths adorned the casket. The hearse was followed by two coaches of black-clad mourners as it trundled off into the mists along Hackney Road towards St. Patrick's Catholic Cemetery in Leytonstone.

At the service, Reverend H. Wilson Robinson commented that Mr. Henry Wilson, clerk of St. Leonard's for 50 years, was bearing the cost of internment. If anyone wished to contribute and a surplus realized, a headstone would be erected. What remained of the latest Ripper victim soon descended into an unmarked muddy grave and another life of suffering reached its inevitable end. The few wet mourners departed, leaving two sodden workers to fill in the grave. The stony-faced pair shoveled in unbroken rhythm, motivated as much by a desire to get out of the rain as anything else.

"I hope they catch that murderin' bastard," one muttered, "before he fills up the whole sodding cemetery."

Tuesday, 20 November

Mr. Henry Wilson shook his head in solemn disbelief. On paying Kelly's funeral expenses, Wilson came upon one of those little details that made cynicism a more exacting statement of the human condition than most people wished to admit. Kelly had told her friends that she left Cardiff for London's West End and had lived the life of a high-class, but fortunate unfortunate—a "daughter of joy" as some sillier citizens called upper-class whores. This excursion was pure fantasy. Kelly had not gone to the fashionable side of town but had set up a tiny shop in Commercial Street from the paltry proceeds paid her by the mine owners after her husband's untimely subterranean demise. She had been kept waiting for the money a year and a half.

"She may not have become a whore if she'd gotten even a reasonable amount of money in a reasonable time," a Vestryman at St. Leonard's commented to Wilson in the church as rain pattered down on the slate roof.

"God knows," Wilson said. "It might not have made any difference."

"No, probably not," the Vestryman, an ex-labourer who had risen far in the world, replied, "but it's damn certain the petty sum withheld didn't make any difference to those mine owners either."

The uterus collector, Francis Tumblety, jumped bail and fled to France under the alias Frank Townsend.

"No great loss to the Empire," Abberline said when he heard. "He's too tall, almost 6 feet, and too old, 56, to be the Ripper according to Mrs. Long's testimony or Joseph Levy's, who saw a man talking with Kate Eddowes. Both said the man was not much taller than the women, who were both about 5 feet."

As he tried to increase the temperature to a bearable level in Abberline's frigid office by stoking the fire, Helson said, "They could have been mistaken."

"True, but the goaler wasn't; Tumblety was in goal when Kelly was murdered."

Wednesday, 21 November

It happened with incredible abruptness. Shouts suddenly flared in a dark hall. Seconds later, Annie Farmer staggered into the communal room, her throat streaming blood. Clutching her bleeding neck, she toppled into the main eating table. Thick red blood poured from between her whitened fingers and ran in spurting cascades of crimson over the backs of her hands. The iron odour of blood filled the room. A woman ran to Annie's assistance, wrapping the speech-deprived woman's neck in a scarf. Another woman summoned a patrolling constable by yelling from one of the house's first-story windows. The scarf stemmed the flow of blood, but, even so, Annie passed out. The constable joined the throng who had gathered to see and, maybe, offer assistance. A man was sent on the run for the divisional police surgeon. Dr. Bagster Phillips was soon beside his newest patient—this one still alive.

"Not too bad, my dear," Phillips said. "The cut is not that deep and it does not appear to have severed an artery." He glanced at the two women who helped hold Annie upright as she sat at the long wood table in the communal room. "Just turn her head a slight bit there. What, pray tell, is this?"

Annie's mouth popped open as they turned her head and a stream of coins poured out. Most onlookers were astonished, but several more alert souls plunged floor-ward to retrieve the unexpected manna from mouth.

"Did anyone see who she was arguing with?" the constable asked.

No one had seen Annie's assailant. Whether the man had been Jack the Ripper had yet to be ascertained. Arriving at the scene, Abberline ordered inspectors and constables to scour the building, alleys and adjoining buildings. They found nothing.

A constable standing off to one side said, "There's something funny here. Amelia or Annie Farmer; where have I seen her before?"

"Christ," another constable exclaimed. "She was Annie Chapman's friend, but her name wasn't Farmer then. It was Palmer. These women change names as often as we change shifts."

"God, you're right. Now the Ripper has gone after her friend."

Abberline frowned as he took in the news. Chance meeting seemed to be the way the Ripper chose his victims, not by stalking specific individuals across Whitechapel. Abberline had found no link between the victims, let alone a common male friend, client or acquaintance. And did someone targeting particular individuals mutilate his victims with increasing ferocity?

"They've got that Ripper letter in Portsmouth. Here's a telegram with what he's written," Helson, the divisional mail-, report- and cold-carrier sniffled. "They're sending a facsimile copy for comparison purposes. It'll arrive in the next post."

Sitting behind his desk in his office at Scotland Yard, Abberline asked, "Another cold?"

Helson shook his head. "Same blasted one."

Abberline studied the telegram. It read:

Dear BOSS,

It is no use for you to look for me in London because I'm not there. Don't trouble yourself about me until I return, which will not be very long. I like the work too well to leave it alone. Oh, it was a jolly job the last one. I had plenty of time to do it properly in. Ha, Ha, Ha! The next lot I mean to do with Vengeance, cut off their head and arms. You think it is a man with a black moustache. Ha, ha, ha! When I have done another one you can try and catch me again. So goodbye dear BOSS, till I return.

Yours,
Jack the Ripper

"This could be genuine; sounds the same arrogant laughing bastard," Abberline said. "He's playing a macabre bloody game; catch me if you can."

"The Portsmouth police are on high alert."

"Still, it may be the work of a prankster, but who can tell? Send them everything we have; descriptions of all suspects."

It was all CID could do and it was very little, although Abberline once again asked his superiors to maintain the increased number of police in the East End. With the Kelly murder fresh in their minds, the request was approved.

Thursday, 22 November

"What's the latest on this Amelia or Annie Farmer case?" Abberline asked a tired, croupy, tea-sipping Helson. Abberline hung up his coat and hat after returning from his daily Home Office meeting. The coal in the stove was heaped and glowing, but all the heat seemed to go up the chimney, almost none deigning to invade the confines of his office, even if it was the approximate size of a fingernail. Cold air seeped in around the window frame assaulting his neck with its frigid fingers. It felt as if he was embarked on an Arctic expedition with Franklin, Back or Dease. He leaned his walking stick in a corner out of sight behind the door; no one liked to see symbols of their own failing health and mortality.

"I don't—cough—think the bastard's going after a little circle of harlots who know each other," Helson said. "It looks as if Farmer was trying to jack-roll a customer, hence the mouthful of coins, probably stolen."

"So he gave her a slash on the throat and would have got his money back if she hadn't yelled 'Ripper!'"

"That's it, but she isn't going to admit any damn such thing."

Friday, 23 November

Crime and consequent police work continued. Five girls, ages 15 and 16, were charged with stealing a loaf of bread. The cutting of Annie Farmer's throat finally proved to be the gashly end of a domestic quarrel with her common-law husband. He was still at large.

Saturday, 24 November

"This should kill any rumours left about the Ripper being Eddy, our illustrious Duke of Clarence," Helson reported as he and Abberline met at the Professor's townhouse. "Careful checking has verified that the royal personage was still in Sandringham on 9 November. It was Daddy's birthday celebration."

Abberline nodded. "Well, we can be certain he's not the Ripper."

"The power elite will always sacrifice the person for the concept," the Professor observed. "No royal family worth its throne would willingly let any one family member sacrifice centuries of future privilege because of some personal indiscretion. They keep a pretty close watch on that decadent little son-of-the-rich."

"There's talk they're shipping Eddy off to Denmark as Daddy's personal representative," Helson said as the Professor played mother.

"If he were, or if they really thought he was the Ripper, they'd have him secured in some posh asylum by now," the Professor said.

"You know there's another rumour surfacing," Abberline said. "One of our superiors has suggested that Sir William Gull, the Queen's physician, is our Whitechapel culprit."

"Christ, he's at least 70," Helson said. "Had a stroke last year, didn't he?"

"Yes, he's half paralyzed," Abberline said, accepting a cup of tea from the Professor. "Remember when we had to consult palace security? He could hardly move."

"While you're talking about rumours, Eddy's former tutor at Cambridge has been suggested as a suspect," Helson said, wiping his nose with his handkerchief as he sat on a book-littered divan. "Fellow's name is James Stephen, a poet and son of Sir James Stephen."

"The High Court judge?"

"That's probably where fuel for the rumour comes from."

"And the fact that Stephen is a poet, like Jack."

"Stephen suffered a serious brain injury last year. He's reputed to be rather eccentric, actually quite mad."

"It appears," the Professor said, "that anyone in a position of public prominence is a candidate for suspicion; comes with the panic. Can't really blame them. People are scared. Unless you can catch Jack, it'll only get worse. What else can they think? They don't know Timothy Nobody who lives in Spitalfields, but they've heard of Stephen, Gull and the Duke of Clarence. It may not be totally logical but it's got a certain degree of silly sense to it."

"Do you know anything about colds, Professor?" Helson asked. "Ones that last an eon?"

"No, other than illness can be brought on or prolonged by life's little headaches and challenges."

"So we can blame the Ripper for Helson's cold?" Abberline asked.

"Should hang and quarter 'im just for that," Helson said and sneezed loud enough to be heard in Greenwich.

Mrs. Maxwell's testimony that Mary Kelly was alive hours after the medical examiners claimed she must have been dead led to even further distrust of the police and allowed another surge of rumour to run rife.

"Maybe the Ripper ain't a bloke after all, maybe he's a she."

"Maybe she's a midwife or an abortionist who botched an abortion or two and sliced those women up to hide what she'd done."

"Don't be bloody daft, except for Kelly, those old drabs were closer to the change of life than your grandmother."

"But you gotta admit a woman could wander around without arousing suspicion."

"So could a Skye Terrier."

Such banter crossed a hundred fences, a thousand pub tables and a myriad of other conversational partitions.

"Better check back in the files," Abberline ordered Helson when he heard the latest rumour. "There was one of those Russkies who went around disguised as a woman."

"Konovalov, I believe," Helson said making a note as they sat in Abberline's office in the Yard. "I'll check, but no one's seen hide or hair of him."

"Konovalov? Don't remember him. Christ, there's no end to them." Abberline closed his eyes and in an instant realized he better open them again or he would fall asleep. He felt for the cold reassurance of his hunting watch. "Circulate his description anyway and leave me a copy. Wait a minute, I remember now. Konovalov was one of the many names used by Pedachenko. Re-question the Russian immigrant crowd. I wonder how our undercover man is doing. We'll also have to make sure everyone is on their toes again tonight; it's Saturday."

Sunday, 25 November

The propensity for various persons to claim to be Jack the Ripper continued to astound the police, press and public. The latest pretender to Satan's throne was Harry Humphreys, a man who had spent his 36-odd years (and they were odd) chasing various schemes incorrectly calculated to increase his wealth with little to no expenditure of labour. It was thus that his listed occupation on lodging house rolls was that of billiards player, a euphemism for other less legal occupations. Sunday was waning when Humphreys stepped from obscurity into a moment's limelight. His stage was a street corner where Annie Vaughan waited for a friend to join her. The general area was cluttered with people, reasonably sufficient for an audience. All would have been disinterested if Humphreys had only been seeking the coital companionship of Miss Vaughan, who most likely would have complied for a sum less than the price of a game of billiards. But Harry had other designs. Something within him desired attention, notoriety or fame at almost any cost. He grabbed Annie by the arm and snarled, "This will do for you."

What followed was an almost comic charade, the least sinister aspects being a torrent of severe cussing, the most sinister being the brandishing of a fancy dagger, carefully selected to glint in the gaslight. Annie screamed, jerked free of Harry's hold and fled. The crowd reacted and Harry was soon in police custody. The moment of glory for this poor player had flitted past. The final curtain concluded in court with it being found that Harry knew Annie, had tossed ammonia on her the night before and since this had not attracted the least public interest, he resorted to the curse-and-carve extravaganza. Annie refused to prosecute, but the judge, no lover of amateur theatrics, imposed a £500 fine or a month in gaol. The fine being more money than he had ever seen, let alone earned in a lifetime, hapless Harry disappeared from public scrutiny for the rest of his unnatural life, the first 30 days being spent at public expense. Few thought he was worth the price of containment.

Part Seven: Newlane and the Thames

Chapter Twenty-Three

In London, squalls of rain chilled anyone venturing out. Constables thanked their lucky stars that Monro, the new Police Commissioner, had abolished the fixed-point system. They could keep moving and at least try to keep warm.

Things were drier and warmer in Havant, 60 miles south of London and 11 miles northeast of Portsmouth. On his way home from an errand, diminutive, eight-year-old Percy Searle walked from a shop along North Street and turned into a dark, narrow alley called Newlane, which shrouded away into shadow before him. He had not disappeared into the blackness long before screams of "Murder! Murder!" shattered the silence. A lad named Bobby Husband burst into a run from the darkened street. He enlisted the aid of an adult friend, dairyman John Platt. Man and boy rushed back and entered the dark, dingy alley. Platt could hardly see a thing. He moved cautiously.

"Blimey! He's been attacked," Husband cried.

Platt peered, saw nothing. He feared for his safety. His heart pounded. "Where?"

"Straight ahead. Can't you see him?"

Platt moved farther along keeping close to the brick wall. Seeing nothing, he bumped into something. He struck a match. The flaring match illuminated a disheveled bundle of boyhood propped grotesquely against a soot-blackened wall of brick in a pool of blood and mud, yet still clutching the bundle of fabric he had been sent to procure. Platt looked closely and said, "His throat's been slashed from ear to ear. It's the Ripper!"

Platt cast his eyes around almost in anticipation of seeing the murderer coming toward him, then stared back in Husband's direction. Almost hidden in the dark, the boy was cowering several feet away from the body. He moaned at the sight of his young friend. Then, at Platt's bidding, Husband ran for a constable.

Lighting a twist of rag he had in his pocket, Platt found a piece of wood in the alley's surfeit of debris and soon had a makeshift torch. He leaned over the tiny body before him. He thought he heard something. God, the lad wasn't dead. The dying child was mumbling through bubbles of blood. Platt leaned over to try and hear what Percy was struggling to say, but he couldn't make any sense of the boy's gurgling. He wrapped a scarf around the lad's wee neck. Where the hell was help?

The child died before the first constable arrived. Platt, his senses stunned, sat beside the little body.

The police searched the district. The Ripper letter mailed from Portsmouth six days ago was paramount in every mind. Every full, half-full and empty building and outhouse, and every possible hiding place was searched. Hundreds of people were questioned. By nine o'clock, a common jack-knife had been found. Its smaller blade was clasped closed and broken, but its bigger blade was open and clotted with thick, wet clumps of blood.

A man with a few facial scratches and a furtive manner was soon in custody. The fellow, complete with a bundle under his arm, fitted earlier descriptions of the Ripper. His suspicious attempt to hurriedly board a train for Portsmouth soon after the murder brought the police down upon him.

The divisional police surgeon, Dr. F. St. Quintin Bond's examination of the murdered boy cast considerable doubt on whether the Ripper was really in custody. The boy's throat was lacerated by four clumsy, careless gashes. The Ripper's work had, up to now, been of a quick, decisive nature. His victims had been women, all unfortunates and all but one had been severely mutilated. But one never knew when dealing with a maniac. The investigation proceeded.

The police questioned Platt at a local station. He sat shaking his head. He ran his large, work-worn hands through his thinning hair, sighed and, looking up at the bulbous-faced Sergeant Knapton, said, "I'm worried about the boy."

"Oh, don't you mind, sir. He's where there'll be no more worrying."

"I don't mean 'im. I mean young Husband."

"Husband, sir? Whose husband?"

"No, no. The boy who showed me where to find the body. His name's Husband."

Knapton learned that Platt had sent Husband for help, but the boy never returned.

"I'm worried," Platt said, "the young fellow must have had quite a shock. Wonder if I could, at least, go over and see how he's making out?"

"Certainly, sir, certainly. I'll come along with you. I'd like to congratulate the youngster."

They found young Husband at home and well. The boy was wiping his hands on a towel when his father, who didn't seem overly friendly, answered the door. Sergeant Knapton put it down to the poor's chronic aversion to authority, which also might explain why the boy didn't fetch the police after finding the body. After introductions, Knapton asked young Husband if he had seen anything.

"Yes," the boy replied. "I saw a tall man. He ran across towards Fairfield."

The interrogation did not last long. Platt, satisfied the boy wasn't overly upset by his friend's death, and Knapton, armed with the description of the tall man, soon left.

"You know," Platt said, "I don't know how to say this, but maybe the boy saw something he's afraid to tell you."

Knapton stopped mid-step.

"Well, sir," Platt said, "when we discovered the body, the boy spotted his friend long before I did. He's got good eyesight; much better than a man my age. He may have seen someone he recognized."

"How far would you say the boy was away when he spotted the body?"

"Oh, a good 10 yards."

"That's 30 feet. That boy does have exceptional eyesight. Yes, he just might have seen something. How old is he?"

"Eleven."

Tuesday, 27 November

It was early morning when Dr. Bond's examination at the station found blood on the cuffs of Husband's shirt.

"Did you touch the body, my boy?" Sergeant Knapton asked Husband after the examination of his clothes. Dr. Bond stood against the wall in the cramped interview room.

"No, sir."

"How then did you get this blood on your shirt cuffs?"

"I cut my arm," Husband said, rolling his sleeve back to reveal a bandage. Husband peeled the dressing back to reveal a vicious gash. Dr. Bond stared thoughtfully at the wound.

The Havant police were having the same kind of luck as the London police. The man who had been apprehended rushing to catch a train to Portsmouth and who had been their prime Ripper suspect turned out to have acted suspiciously only due to being deaf and late for his train. His movements checked out witness by witness and eliminated him as either the Whitechapel maniac or Searle's slayer.

A railway man named Lester Steele became the next candidate for suspicion. His nomination for Ripperhood came from the simple fact he was seen running to catch a train shortly after the Searle murder. Steele's candidacy lasted less than

24 hours as his whereabouts easily checked out as innocent.

Chief Inspector Daniel Hood and Sergeant Knapton checked the scene that evening at the time the murder had occurred.

"Rather dark, isn't it, sir?" Knapton asked.

Hood nodded. "Too dark. Let's talk to this fellow Platt again; this friend of little boys."

Lusky spent the day indoors. The weather was getting too chilly for his liking. Although his distant ancestors may have carried his genes through the snow of Tsardom, he was one Russian Blue feline who preferred temperate climes. Perhaps his forebears had stalked prey in the Tsars' domains that touched on the Black Sea. Warm or cold, hunting was getting harder. The flood of humankind and not-so-kind that kept filling up the streets every night now was keeping the rats and mice cellar-bound. Lusky only slipped out to do his biological business and then flitted back in to sleep by the fire.

"Only got a few routine questions for you, Mr. Platt," C.I. Hood said in his gentle way. "Try to answer as carefully as you can. I'm not trying to trick you or anything like that, but I do want to get some precise answers. Ready?"

Puzzled, Platt could only nod as he sat in an interview room at a Havant police station.

"You were the only person who went near the body before our men arrived; is that true?"

"Yes, but the boy, Bobby Husband, might have gone near it when he first discovered it."

"True, but he said he didn't because he was afraid. The dying boy was a rather grotesque sight."

The match-lit image of the gored youngster flamed across Platt's memory like a day-mare as he nodded.

Hood went on, "Husband stood quite a ways back while you examined the body. In fact, you sent him off for the police before you started to examine the body, isn't that so?"

"Yes."

"And it was your scarf we found around Searle's neck."

"Yes, I was trying to stop the bleeding, but I couldn't."

Hood nodded, deciding to bring the Husband boy in to continue the questioning in Platt's presence the following day.

"Just to confirm Platt's story," he assured Knapton, who was to persuade the boy and his father to cooperate. The pair discussed the entire case.

Hood concluded, "Not a pretty line of thought we're pursuing."

Knapton said, "Life often is far from pretty, sir."

Wednesday, 28 November

Jagged streaks of lightning bolted across the southern sky at irregular intervals, their sudden violence seeming to symbolize how easily the Ripper could strike and be gone without a trace, leaving only the rumblings of thunderous calamity behind.

Hood and Knapton met with Platt, Bobby Husband and his father.

"That's a horrible thing you're saying," Platt said. The old dairyman was visibly shaken. Behind him, Knapton moved closer. Husband and his father sat in shocked silence.

"We have the evidence, Platt. Here, a blood-stained knife identified as belonging to Robert Husband's brother by four witnesses, including Robert's brother, George. Here, a deposition by our police surgeon verifying the knife as most likely being the murder weapon. Here, a sworn statement by Thomas Stevens, an errand boy, identifying the killer as having tried to sell him the knife in the afternoon, only a few hours before the murder. You knew all these boys, didn't you, Platt? Even the victim?"

Platt nodded, holding his head in his hands. Sparse tufts of whitish hair spilled out in ruffled disarray over his shaking fingers. "God, how. . .I don't. . ."

"I'm sorry," Hood said. "It's a dastardly crime. I'm going to have to arrest you, Robert Husband, for the willful murder of Percy Knight Searle."

And so the Ripper files closed forever on the Havant case.

Thursday, 29 November

"Fred, Fred."

Abberline heard the voice with only a sliver of his brain; the rest remained deeply asleep.

"Fred." The voice again.

Someone touched his shoulder. The touch became a gentle push.

"Fred, a telegram arrived."

Abberline kept his eyes closed for a whole second, savoring the warmth of the bed, the feel of Emma's soft hand on his shoulder, and the fragment of a second before the vein in the back of his left knee announced its presence like a bayonet pricking his skin.

"I sent the boy away, but I think you'll want to read it," Emma said, her voice low, yet filled with urgency.

Abberline opened his eyes and saw in the paraffin lamp light Emma framed by her long brown hair staring down at him. He closed his eyes again. "I can't do this," he announced.

"Are you ill?"

Abberline managed a smile. He would welcome a flu or cold just bad enough to justify staying in bed for a few days; anything for rest. "No, no, just tired." He let his body go limp with the last word, as if it was almost too much to even say the word, let alone contemplate getting out of bed. He opened his eyes the narrowest of slits.

Emma frowned for just a moment. "They need you, Fred."

Abberline managed the suggestion of a nod. She believed in him, always had, but he knew Helson or Reid could handle the day's work, unless. . .unless the Ripper had struck again.

"Message?" he muttered.

Emma handed him the telegram slip.

He forced his eyes to open and move, left to right, to read, to understand and to force his exhausted mind to process the words. He was needed to interview yet another suspect. Helson could handle that. He closed his eyes again.

"Freddy?" she asked, rubbing his shoulder.

"Can I just have an hour, a few minutes, a second? My leg's trying to kill me one throb at a time, I fall asleep daily at my desk and Helson has to remind me of the simplest details of the cases. Not sure whether it's worth working today; doubt I'm adding much, if anything, of value to the investigation. In any case, we aren't any closer to catching the Ripper now than three months ago."

"You have suspects."

"Oh, we have enough suspects to fill Newgate Prison a dozen times over. What we lack is a suspect who actually committed the murders."

Emma reached under the covers and gently massaged his leg above and below his varicose vein, which bulged from behind his knee like an engorged snake.

"They need you, Fred. You know Whitechapel better than any man alive. If anyone can catch the Ripper, you can."

He reveled in the easing of the pain in his leg as she massaged it. He knew it would not last, it never did, yet he savored it all the same.

"Have a lay-in for a good long time and then when you're more yourself, get up and have at the day. If the man they want you to interview is the Ripper, there's no rush. He's not going anywhere. Helson will make sure he's kept locked up tight in the tombs."

"And if he isn't?" Abberline asked, eyes closed.

"Even less reason to rush."

Friday, 30 November

PC Spicer walked along a lonely beat far from Whitechapel. He still cursed the system that prevented his following up the discovery of the Brixton doctor with Rosy. Abberline had come around and told him witnesses cleared the doctor during the crucial times of the murders. It was nice of the Chief Inspector to let him know, but Abberline had been unable to get Spicer off his isolated beat. Oh well, Spicer philosophized, he was young, other job opportunities might soon open up. He was certainly looking.

Saturday, 1 December

Another Ripperless night passed.

Just after Abberline returned from his daily Home Office meeting, Helson rushed into his office with news and a hacking cough. "Druitt's been dismissed from the Blackheath School."

"What for?" Abberline asked as he cleared his desk for the pub lunch a constable had just brought in. The Home Office meeting had run long, very long.

"That's what makes things interesting. Reason they gave was vague and I asked every which way I could, but they gave me next to nothing. He's evidently not much of a teacher. They may have used some incident as an excuse to sack him."

Sunday, 2 December

It rained. The search for the Ripper continued as did Helson's never-ending cold. Maybe it was bronchitis and sinusitis? Lusky stayed in. Abberline went to church with Emma and spent the sermon wondering about the Ripper, his motivations and how best to find him. A part of his mind also wondered if a telegram would arrive announcing another murder; it didn't.

Monday, 3 December

Passing showers swept across the capital on south-west to south winds, beating out a steady pitter-patter of moist monotony punctuated by occasional glimpses of sunshine.

In Parliament, Mr. Hanbury asked whether it was a fact that four redundant Supreme Court clerks, who had never gone near their offices for four years at last count, nevertheless received the triennial rise in salary given those who did frequent their offices. Mr. Jackson answered that the four were paid, would continue to be paid and would receive their pensions in two or three months upon their retirement. This revealing piece of information did not raise any great stir among the honourable members. Rank had its immunities. Corruption was not confined to Whitechapel, although it was far more profitable in Whitehall than Whitechapel.

The biggest event of the day was a 1-all football sensation between

Cambridge and West Bromwich Albion. Inspector Chandler was stunned.

Lusky ran his raspy tongue down a silvery foreleg. The evening dampness brought the soot and ash down and nasty particles accumulated in his fine fur. Between showers, he had come down to snoop along the waterside. A figure emerged from the shadows, startling Lusky, who bounded away to a safe crevice behind a boulder. Lusky watched as a man, his pockets swinging with some sort of heavy objects, hesitated just a moment and stepped off the breakwater into the Thames. Lusky stared as the river washed the man away into the night. Odd. He seemed familiar. Very odd, but no threat to him. With all quiet once again, Lusky returned to his spit bath.

Chapter Twenty-Four

Tuesday, 4 December

Labour unrest led to 3,000 men being locked out at the Barrow Hematite Iron and Steel Company yard. Police were dispatched to maintain order. When he read of it, the unemployed Sir Charles managed a bittersweet smile as he prepared for his departure to Singapore, where he would command the garrison, including siting the guns to defend the Gibraltar of the East. The jungle would protect the landward approaches far better than any guns ever could, so he need worry only about the seaward approaches.

Wednesday, 5 December

A dull, deceptively warm late autumn day was concluded by a duller, deceptively august annual dinner of the Police Committee. Dignitaries from the most important portions of the City and district's social strata attended. Perhaps the most important guest was Sir Robert Peel, son of the man whose work had led to the founding of the London Police in 1829, even lending his name as a nickname to all police: Peelers. The chairman, Alderman Cotton, noted that the younger Peel's appearance at the dinner was of prime significance (but not as prime as the beef). Cotton praised the City's investigative and law enforcement units, mouthing tributes of Olympian proportion. The evening underlined the ever present capability of those in power to keep their self-coveted positions, to support one another in mutual security and to jealously guard against any threat to their self-contained comfortable empires.

The self-aggrandizement complete, the dinner and alcohol consumed, the cigars smoked, the affair ended with a toast to the ultimate authority that guaranteed them position and property. Raising their glasses high, the gathering responded to the simple words that symbolized their right to the best England and her Empire had to offer, "Gentlemen, the Queen."

A police band struck up that strangely British anthem that implored a deity to save a human being from the consequences of being mortal. In the streets of Whitechapel, it was devil take the hindmost. While at Havant, Robert Husband was committed for trial for the brutal murder of Percy Searle.

Thursday, 6 December

"Probably doesn't mean a thing, but the name Kelly is rather prominent in this Ripper business," Abberline said as he strolled along the Embankment with Major Smith. They had decided to couple their strategy session with a brisk walk. Abberline hoped it would help ease the pain behind his knee. "Mary Kelly was butchered in Miller's Court. The Mitre Square victim, Catherine Eddowes, gave her name as Mary Ann Kelly at the Bishopsgate station and also went by the name Kate Kelly. She had lived for some time with a John Kelly. And I think a Kelly figures in the background of one of the other victims. But the important thing is that some people feel the Ripper may be after a specific Mary Kelly."

"A rather far-fetched idea," Smith said. "Bumbling about in the dark back alleys of Whitechapel after one particular woman and apparently getting it wrong not once, not twice, but multiple times. He must be the most incompetent murderer I've ever heard of. No." Smith shook his head. "If he had known Eddowes was in gaol, he would have been waiting for her, not off killing that Stride woman in Berner Street."

"That's what I feel."

"These women change their names every time they're in court, and there must be a couple of thousand Kellys within two minutes walking distance of us right now. The Irish have poured into this capital cauldron by the shipload."

"There is another common thread," Abberline said, looking out across the Thames at the barge and ship traffic that made London one of the busiest ports in the world. "Four of the last five victims attended the pauper's clinic south of the river."

"Odd, but you might expect that. They would have to go to a pauper's clinic and it may be the most convenient one for a north-of-the-river unfortunate."

"There's some suspicion that one of our Russian suspects, Pedachenko or Ostrog, worked at the clinic. Anyway, if he was there, he isn't there now."

"Kelly was pregnant—was she? I don't recall for certain—and the others were sick. Eddowes had Bright's Disease. Chapman was consumptive. Maybe nothing more than coincidence. I gather your men have chased it down."

Abberline nodded.

Smith continued, "I think we'll find there's no connection between this rascal and his victims. He kills whoever's available."

"I agree. Druitt's still missing. He's a fairly good suspect, but we have no idea where he is, and the Russian with the big watch fob, Pedachenko, is nowhere to be found either."

"The Ripper seems to flit all over the country. He could be in Scotland or in a warehouse down there in East India Docks this instant for all we know. How close are we to catching him? Is he one of our suspects or haven't we the faintest glimmer who he is?"

The detectives continued their dismal, dejected stroll along the river. The Thames swept leisurely along the Embankment. It was silent except for the occasional squeal of a seabird and toot of a ship's horn warning of danger or the passing thereof.

Chief Inspector Donald Swanson, the quiet man behind the investigation that produced enough paperwork to rebuild Hadrian's Wall with a pyramid on either end for good measure, perused the file of Aaron Cohen as he sat in his paper-filled office in Scotland Yard. A violently disturbed man who associated with unfortunates, Cohen had been present in the area of the killings when they were committed. Swanson read more closely, but other than that point of possible guilt, there was no evidence linking him to the murders.

Several reports later Swanson read of Jewish bootmaker Nathan Kaminski. Born in 1865, he resided at 15 Black Lion Yard between Old Montague Street and Whitechapel Road. Diagnosed with syphilis, he was treated at the Whitechapel workhouse infirmary and discharged as "cured" six weeks later. Swanson frowned. He glanced back at the Cohen file. Both men were the same age, race and shared the same occupation. Their description also matched that of John Pizer, Leather Apron. Descriptions of males in London's East End overlapped enough that a hundred men might share the same age, complexion, general appearance, ethnicity and job. Even just collecting all the lunatics in the area would yield enough characters who appeared similar to fool even their closest relatives into thinking they were someone else, especially on a dark London street at 2 in the morning. For a moment, Swanson wished he had remained a teacher, but then he thought of the challenge he faced and the stakes; such stakes gave meaning to life. He opened the next file on the next possible Ripper suspect.

Friday, 7 December

"The financial figures are in," Helson said, setting down a wad of papers on what had become his desk in the corner of Abberline's Scotland Yard office. "The Commissioner will get £2,000 per year; a Chief Superintendent £615; the receiver £350; divisional surgeons £300." Helson went on listing the pay of various and sundry sergeants, constables and other near paupers.

Abberline smiled. "That's life. The few at the top take no risk, plot unrealistic, unworkable schemes and get exceptionally high financial returns. Those at the bottom take all the risks, devise some bumbling way of getting the job done and receive even more exceptional financial returns, but theirs are exceptionally small. At least we can thank God we are above those bottom tiers of financial tragedy, let alone any lower."

Perusing the rows of numbers in the report, Helson said, "The new Met Commissioner, James Monro, reported to the Home Office that after the Chapman murder in September, 27 extra plainclothes officers were sent into Whitechapel and Spitalfields. In October after the Double Event, the number rose to 89, and now after the Kelly murder an extra 143 officers patrol the area, not to mention the increased uniformed presence."

"For what good it's done," Abberline said, stretching his back, his chair squeaking in protest. Maybe he would get a new chair at the new headquarters. "Inspector Henry Moore told me you could put two regiments of police in the half-mile of the district and half of them would be as completely out of sight and hearing of the others as though they were in separate cells of a goal, and I believe him. He had his men form a cordon around the spot where one of the murders took place, guarding, they thought, every entrance and approach. Within a few minutes they found 50 people inside the lines. They had come in through two passageways his men hadn't found."

"To make matters worse, East Enders never lock their doors. To escape, the murderer has only to lift the latch of the nearest house and walk through it and out the back."

"And people wonder why we've never caught him in the act."

Inspector Walter Andrews, who had been on the periphery of the Ripper cases, was sent to escort Roland Gideon, who was wanted in the Dominion of Canada for financial crimes, to Toronto. While he was in the New World, Andrews stopped in New York with an extradition request for Francis Tumblety, collector of uteruses, one-time Ripper suspect, and committer of indecent acts. The Americans concluded there was no evidence to link Tumblety to the Ripper murders and his having jumped bail for the indecency charge in London was not enough to bother extraditing him back to the old world, so Tumblety remained in the New World—and remained a Ripper suspect to some.

Saturday, 8 December

"Little more than two weeks 'til Christmas," Abberline said as he, Helson and Chandler sat around a table at the Commercial Street station plotting patrol assignments for the holidays. "It'll be worse than Hell ascending if the Ripper strikes on the holiday. He's been quiet as a dormouse for a month now. We can't figure him to hibernate much longer. He must be seething to kill again. A murder around Christmas would fit his warped sense of humour."

The patrols set, Abberline rode in an official growler the short distance back to Scotland Yard; thank God the Commercial Street tramway was finally finished and traffic wasn't quite so snarled. As he rode, Abberline read official statistics in *The Times* released by those concerned with tabulating such impersonally personal things, which showed that there were 1,461 deaths and 2,644 births in London during the past week. Glancing at these figures of sadness and happiness, Abberline wondered if any of those births and deaths meant anything. Nature seemed to have to produce an awful flock of people to get a Dickens or a Da Vinci, the whole effect seeming almost purposeless; or if not purposeless, at least, wasteful. And how many people did nature have to produce to get a Jack the Ripper?

Sunday, 9 December

Another weekend passed. The Ripper remained in limbo. The Professor argued the British needed to employ new methods. He told Abberline and Helson about scientists on the Continent who were opening the skulls of fresh corpses, scooping out the brains and observing what happened to the throat when an assistant choked, strangled or cut the neck of the remains.

"Seems too improper for England," Helson said.

"Damn it," the Professor said, "maybe that's what's wrong."

The well-endowed and well-used Isabelle smiled as the Londoner entered the establishment.

"Hello, you haven't been around for quite a while," she teased.

"I've been busy; quite busy."

"Do you want to be busy tonight?"

"Yes, I think you and I can be quite busy," he said, smiling and running his hand teasingly along the top of her gown where it rose to follow the rise of her paper-white breasts.

They laughed. He continued to smile, but his thoughts were as dark as he knew the hair between her legs was. She'd spread those long white legs of hers for a crown and a half for anyone. How he despised this brown-eyed bitch and her flaring, throbbing cunt. He'd love to ram a knife up her hole and really give her what for. He smiled almost genuinely. Yes, that'd be his secret fantasy for tonight. He liked his little games.

Monday, 10 December

Sir Charles was elected a life member of the Council of Cheltenham College, which he had attended for a term before he moved onto the Royal Military Academy, Sandhurst. East Enders heard the news and some commented, "Well, the toffs have to look after their own" and "I've always said those college clots don't know their arse from a hedgehog's orifice." By focusing on his failure to apprehend Jack the Ripper, such critics appeared to have forgotten or to have never known that Sir Charles was a Royal Engineer who had created two highly accurate models of Gibraltar, conducted the first excavations at Jerusalem's Temple Mount, ushering in a new age of Biblical archeology, and led the Warren Expedition to Bechuanaland, which was the first British Army in the field to use observation balloons. It just went to prove that accomplishments and failures, like love, were in the eye of the beholder.

"God, another throat slitting," Abberline told Helson as he read a report in his office. "Some bloke named William Atkins, known as Silly Billy to his friends and acquaintances, slit a young girl's throat in a shop in Bermondsey. She's in critical condition at Guy's Hospital. Lyle Bardford, the D.S. over at M Division, said she probably won't live through the night, but that she named Atkins as her attacker. He seems to be a simpleton who was merely copying the Ripper."

It was becoming clear that fools rushed in where Rippers tread.

Tuesday, 11 December

Accidently meeting Abberline on the Chief Inspector's way to lunch, Reverend Barnett joined the portly detective and outlined his latest plan to pry money from the rich, who had proved exceedingly capable of accumulating and keeping it, and giving it to the poor, who seemed singularly incapable of getting or keeping much of it. This new enterprise was, as always, based on the generosity of the "haves" who had no particularly good reason to reduce their amount of "having" by giving their monies to the "not-haves." The good Reverend's tirade ruined lunch about as effectively as the Ripper had ruined many a previous meal for Abberline.

A letter from a young man in Dresden claimed to know the identity of the Ripper; a Polish Jew named Julius Wirtkofsky. The police investigated and concluded the young writer was just seeking a journey to the big city of London, gratis.

Wednesday, 12 December

It being less than two weeks until Christmas, Parkins and Grottos toy department featured a fine line of exquisite dolls, mechanical figures, model engines, steam cranes, rocking horses, and musical and clock-work toys. Parents were encouraged to browse at their leisure.

Thursday, 13 December

The continuing inquest into the murder of Percy Searle brought home the terrible influence Jack the Ripper was having. A boy named Charles Clark took the oath as a witness and calmly explained he saw the accused lad, Robert Husband, shortly before the murder. Husband had said, "Here comes Jack the Ripper!" as he waved what would be the instrument of murder at Clark. By proxy, Jack the Ripper had claimed another two victims: the dead Searle and the deluded Husband.

Friday, 14 December

Abberline met with the department's undercover Russian-speaking constable in a secluded booth in the rear of the East End's George Tavern.

"Cross one of those mad Russians off your list, Mr. Abberline," the undercover man said. "You remember the balding, fierce-eyed radical that upset a speech by the Secretary of State for India by continually interrupting with a stream of silly questions? Quite some time back."

"I remember. I spotted a hard-eyed bald man at one of the inquests. We've called him Baldy in our files since we didn't know his name."

"That's the bloke. Well, he's clean. I've been able at last to get absolute proof where he was at the time of each murder. I've got it all here. Reputable witnesses and all."

Abberline took the envelope his agent was tapping and asked, "What was Baldy's real name?"

"He has a long unpronounceable Russian name. It's in the file. He's no threat. Nothing but talk, talk, talk."

"Most of those anarchists and socialists are harmless. Making any progress on the other suspects: Ostrog, Pedachencko, Vasiliev—I'd almost forgotten him—or Klosowski? I'm particularly interested in Klosowski."

"I should have something definite on Klosowski in a few days. As for the others, I doubt if they were ever in England, let alone London."

Abberline nodded. He glanced through the papers. His agent smiled, pointing to a picture of Baldy he had been able to obtain. "He isn't much of a threat, but he has been distributing articles by some lawyer in Russia who seems full of revolutionary ideas. Now, he has been attracting some attention."

"As long as he stays in Russia, he'll be no bother to us." Abberline gathered the papers and as he rose to leave, asked, "Just curious, what's the Russian lawyer's name?"

"Vladimir Ilyich Ulyanov."

"That's more than a mouthful."

"He took another name, too."

"Which is?"

"Lenin."

Saturday, 15 December

A dense fog gripped the city, giving total cover to anyone lurking in wait for the wary, let alone the unwary. Of course, the lurker would be no more able to see his prey than the prey would be able to see the lurker.

The horrendous task of sorting out the letters to the editor fell this day to Coulls, who rejected most, only picking the ones he thought had broad reader appeal. A West Ender asked if "nothing" could be done to prevent a stream of urchins from showing up in the West End suburban squares yelling at the peak of their voices about "Another 'orrible murder in Whitechapel" as they hawked newspapers. It seemed worth printing. After all, Coulls thought, the privileged prick objects because some kid trying to make a living upsets his serene evening. What the bloody hell about the poor old whore who got cut to pieces? No compassion for her.

Another letter was from the landlord of a Whitechapel pub who'd gone bankrupt because of the drop in foot traffic caused by fear of the Ripper. Coulls tossed it into the "to print" pile. The Ripper murdered not only women, but other's livelihoods as well.

Abberline did not take Friday or Saturday night off and the usual multitude of patrolmen surged into Whitechapel and Spitalfields for special Saturday night surveillance, but the Ripper stayed silent and unseen.

Sunday, 16 December

"We've tried everything conceivable and we still couldn't catch the fellow," Smith said after he arrived home from church with his wife. He stared morosely down at the carpet in his spacious drawing room. "We tripled patrols. We had dozens of men sprayed all over the City's East End in plainclothes as early as September. We interviewed thousands of people. Offered rewards. We've ignored the stupidity our so-called superiors have saddled us with, from photos of the victims' eyes to bloodhounds, bicycles and barmy foreigners as suspects who have never even set foot in London. When they said don't bother examining the correspondence, we examined it; when they said don't check too closely into this or that toff's background, we checked. What else can we do?"

His wife shrugged. The strain of the past few months was taking its toll on the Major and their marriage. By way of distraction, his wife asked, "Did you read that the Boers, someplace in Africa, have declared their independence?"

Smith just frowned and asked, "Who's boring whom? Where?"

Monday, 17 December

The ancient highland capital of Inverness, 444 miles from London's East End, reeled under the news that a woman had been beaten, stabbed and slit through the throat over the weekend. Although the local police found no connection between her slaying and the East London murders, the fear that the English murderer had come to Scotland spread like an auld raising of the clans. The Scots went on alert from Glasgow to Edinburgh, from the Marches to the Northern Isles. The letter that mentioned coming to Scotland to buy a dirk was remembered and treated seriously. Transplanted Englishmen whispered about Jock the Ripper.

To the south, the London Metropolitan Police continued to stumble from calamity to calamity. The latest bad news was the wounding by shooting of PC Walter Whittemore of X Division (Willesden) by a pair of burglars.

"Bastards are probably Americans," another constable said. "They're always shooting someone."

His comrade asked, "Weren't there American cowboys somewhere about in London?"

Tuesday, 18 December

In *The Empire* newsroom Jennings tossed the last of a pile of peelings from a precious orange into a dustbin and continued his reading, saying, "We should keep these bloody letters for some brain specialist to study. Every lunatic in London must have a compulsion to write something on the Ripper."

"Not just in London," Coulls said, flipping a letter across to his colleague. "Read this masterpiece."

Jennings gave Coulls a doleful look and read the letter which was from a woman on the Isle of Wight who was convinced the Whitechapel murderer was a large ape:

> The animal would be swift, cunning, noiseless and strong, standing over its work until a footstep was heard and then vaulting over a fence or wall, disappearing in a moment, hiding

its weapon high up in a tree or other safe place, and returning home to lock itself up in its cage.

"Christ!" Jennings shook his head. "She's read her Poe, at least. Must be *The Murders in the Rue Berner.*"

"This one thinks Jack leaves respectable people alone and can only hope his last sigh will be, 'Jesus, sweet Jesus'—can you imagine that?"

Several letter-writers believed the killer used London's sewers to escape. Frederick Allison of Gordon Street, Plaistow, wrote that the killer might be dressed in the "garb of a sewerman." Sewer theory or not, slaughtermen were common suspects, as were patent medicine doctors, surgeons and almost anyone in the public eye, as well as the ever popular foreigner.

"My God, this one—Mrs. S. Luckett of 10 Somerford Grove—writes," Coulls read, "'Who is the author of *Dr. Jekyll & Mr. Hyde*? Is he a capable and likely individual to be the perpetrator of dire offenses?'"

"She's accusing Robert Louis Stevenson? She's barking."

The two journalists continued to wade through the mail. They took delight in classifying the letters into various categories according to what the writer attributed the Ripper to be: Totally Insane, Sexually Diseased, Foreigner, Simian.

Some still held to the theory that the Ripper was badly disfigured by venereal disease, possibly that his privy member had been lost, and that he was avenging himself on the sick unfortunates who brought this plague upon him.

"So check everywhere for penis-less men?" Coulls asked.

"Hate to be in on that search," Jennings said.

"Don't worry, the idea's only half-cocked anyway."

A sub-thesis suggested that a syphilitic Ripper was using parts cut from his victims as poultices to drain the virus from his ulcerated genitals. Since man can be eternally creative and infernally stupid at the same time, variations on this thesis abounded. One writer suggested the Ripper was a Hill tribesman well versed in dangling such organs around his neck as amulets. This creative moron suggested the murder would be a sacred action. He went on to consider the most horrible of all possibilities—that the Ripper was a white man who had adopted these barbaric practices while on a military or civic visit to alien lands. He noted that the white's transformation would be a result of sunstroke (a sort of tanning of the brain).

Coulls muttered, "Bloody writer's the one with the tanned brain."

William Waddell, who had been arrested for the mutilation and murder of Jane Beetmoor in Birtley Fell, County Durham, was swiftly convicted of the 22 September murder. Less than 90 days after the murder, he was hanged at Durham prison. He was 22 years old.

Wednesday, 19 December

It was a grim day. Dull cloudy weather whipped in on winds from the south. Much of England experienced showers. Robert Husband, the 11 year old suspected of mimicking Jack the Ripper, was charged with the willful murder of eight-year-old Percy Searle, and Thomas Lott, the 18-year-old half-wit mimic, was charged with killing four-year-old John Harper.

"Murder must be the ultimate bloody crime," Helson said as he stoked the coal stove in Abberline's office. It never seemed to heat the room beyond a suggestion of warmth.

"It sure as hell deprives the person of the only thing we are certain of—our existence," Abberline said.

"What do you think they should do with this Husband kid down at Havant?"

"I don't know. I imagine it doesn't really matter very much whether they put him in prison, an asylum or hang 'im in the long run."

"You mean that?" Helson asked, looking over at Abberline in surprise.

"Whatever they do, I doubt he'll be the next Dickens, Disraeli or Pasteur."

Helson nodded. There was a point where a policeman reached but one belief: punishment should, at least, be swift, certain and sanitary. All other distinctions were superfluous.

Thursday, 20 December

It was about 4:15 a.m. when Sergeant Robert Golding and Constable Thomas Costella of K Division (West Ham) found the body of a woman lying in Clarke's Yard in High Street, Poplar, just east of Whitechapel/Spitalfields in the Borough of Tower Hamlets. The routine ritual of a police investigation followed.

The body was that of yet another unfortunate, but the body was unmutilated. Dr. Matthew Brownfield, divisional surgeon, wondered, if the Ripper strangled and then mutilated his victims, whether this time he was possibly interrupted, leaving "his work half finished."

Back from the scene, Abberline told Swanson in the latter's Scotland Yard office, "We only found a faint mark on the throat, so probably not strangulation. Dr. Bond said there were no signs of strangulation or even any marks on the neck. What mark anyone could find only went a quarter of the way around the neck. It's probably not even a case of murder."

"Inquest?" Swanson asked in his Scots brogue as he perused the file.

"Starts tomorrow; Baxter said it might go three days."

"Three days? What in heaven's name for? I don't think we should spend any time investigating what appears to be a case of death by natural causes."

"Anderson agrees with you. File it with all the other non-Ripper cases."

Swanson dropped the file onto the floor beside his desk on an uneven tower of files, the bottom of which had already collected a discernable amount of dust. Even in death some people were less equal than others.

Swanson said, "Here's another: Elizabeth Crowe, lone resident of a small farmhouse on the Isle of Man, was discovered terribly mutilated about the head. Her body was found in a pathway, her bonnet and milk pail nearby. The ground bore indications of a furious struggle. The body had 13 wounds, any three of which could have caused death. A stick studded with nails and a sharp-edged stone, both matted with hair and blood, were found close by. No link has been found between her brutal extinction and the Ripper's activities."

"Let the locals handle it?"

"Aye. The press has barely noticed it, so I doubt even they will try to tie it to the Ripper."

His Lordship informed the jury in the Havant murder trial that, "No act done by any person over seven and under 14 is a crime, unless it be shown affirmatively that such person had sufficient capacity to know that the act was wrong." He noted that the boy, Husband, must conceive beforehand of the awful wickedness and consequences of the murder before they could convict him.

The jury returned a verdict of "Not guilty" and Robert Husband was released. Back home his playmates congratulated him on his good fortune. The conqueror had returned. None of the boys mentioned Percy Knight Searle. Husband had gotten away with murder—and got a job to boot: serving pints at the Newtown Tavern, which advertised its now famous new bartender to attract customers.

Friday, 21 December

The pace of police life continued. William Onions was convicted for the 61st time of being in a drunken condition and causing a public mischief. Coulls wondered why they just didn't lock the drunken sot up and throw away the bottle. Isaac Mitcham was charged with felonious assault on a woman. The delicacies of social decorum kept the trial lawyers from mentioning what was soon apparent—a case of common rape with threat. Since everyone knew what it was all about, the woman was dishonoured for all Victorian time.

Another woman's body—complete with skull broken in two spots— was found near Ramsey on the Isle of Man. The possibilities of any Ripper connection were considered, but no linkage seemed possible. A tie-in with the clobbering of Elizabeth Crowe, which also occurred on the Isle, was also discounted. The inquest into Crowe's murder began, but no police or press attempt was made to draw any similarities between the farmyard homicide and the urban Whitechapel murders.

The inquest into the death at Poplar commenced. Coulls covered the inquest and reported to his editor, Cox, in *The Empire's* rapidly emptying newsroom as reporters escaped early for a Friday night out. "Has some similarities to the Ripper slayings: the woman's body was found in a dark, neglected byway, the area was surrounded by small workshops and trading establishments, and no cry of distress was heard."

"Anything else?" Cox muttered as he edited a headline on another story, shortening it with brutal efficiency.

"Not that I could find."

"Maybe an inch or two on the back page if there's space."

"The police aren't investigating, since Assistant Commissioner CID, Dr. Robert Anderson, and his detectives believe the case was suicide or death by natural causes."

"Then no story at all."

At lunch with Abberline at the Chain and Anchor, the Professor noted, "The ways of men are often strange. The Crowe murder has as many points of similarity with the Ripper murder as this homicide in Poplar, but the former's similarities are of a psychological nature, therefore no one says much about them."

"And the Poplar murder?"

"It just occurred in the general Whitechapel/Spitalfields area, which is probably the reason for any supposed similarities being seen."

Helson wiped his narrow nose. He was reporting their undercover agent's latest findings on Severin Klosowski to Abberline in the latter's office. This time, at least, Abberline had succeeded by the afternoon in stoking his fire into enough life to actually make Helson remove his overcoat as he sat down.

George Chapman with one of his wives, Maud Marsh

"Klosowski, who appears to also go by the name George Chapman, has left England, hopefully for good," Helson said. "He's gone to the United States. Some Polish woman, a Lucy Baderski, went with him. The pair was married on forged certificates. Evidently he attracts women like Don Juan."

"If there are no more Ripper murders here and if they start in the States, then Klosowski could be our man, although I don't see why a man like that would bother slicing up women. He gets them without using a knife. In any case, we better alert the Americans."

"Consider it done."

"Did you revise the duty roster so married men can be home Christmas morning?"

"Done, although a few requested duty that morning; can't stand the in-laws or the children home from school or apprenticeships."

Saturday, 22 December

A quiet, cold day with no new Ripper victims and no sign of Druitt.

Sunday, 23 December

In other news related to prostitutes and knives, the Dutch painter Vincent Van Gogh cut his ear off with a razor and delivered it to a prostitute for safe keeping. Of more immediate concern to the Met, Abberline was relieved there had been no new unfortunate murders in East London over the weekend. He lit his pipe in Major Smith's office in the City Police headquarters on Wood Street. "Well, Major, do you think this mess in Poplar is Ripper connected?"

Major Smith toyed with his cigar for a moment, then admitted, "I don't know, but I doubt it. Look at the key facts. There was no mutilation, no slashed throat. Just because this maniac Jack the Ripper is loose, doesn't mean other murders won't keep occurring. The fellow doesn't have a monopoly on murder."

"I've been wondering about the handedness of our killer," Abberline said. "Nichols had the left side—her left—of the neck sliced down to the vertebrae. Chapman, Stride and Eddowes were all cut from left to right."

"So he's right handed."

"All depends on where he stood and how the victims were positioned when he slit their throats; probably knelt at their head facing their feet after strangling them and laying the victim down. That way, no blood would get on him. If that's true, then he's probably right handed, but Kelly clouds the issue, with the bed and the wall blocking any attack with a right hand if she was facing the wall."

"So right for most of them, left for Kelly," Smith said, frowning. "Ambidextrous?"

"Or someone familiar with using both hands, such as an athlete."

Monday, 24 December

With Christmas only a few hours away, Abberline strengthened the police patrols in the East End. Progress was made on the Poplar murder. An unfortunate named Alice Graves recalled seeing the deceased, now identified as Alice Downey, Fair Alice, Lizzie or Drunken Liz, with two men outside the George about an hour and 45 minutes before her body was discovered. The composite picture that emerged from the collage of information, misinformation and rumour from a parade of prostitutes, pimps and public nuisances was that the victim was a perpetual drunk, who was seen walking along East India Dock Road after passing a Mrs. Hill before she turned onto Commercial Road. The fact that she had entered Whitechapel/Spitalfields and then returned to die in Poplar led many to speculate that she may have met the Ripper.

"There are certainly some people who just ask to be murdered," Abberline said, staring out his office window east toward darkening Whitechapel/Spitalfields. "Imagine wandering through that labyrinth for an hour and a half. She was eventually bound to get robbed, beaten, ravaged or murdered."

"True, but it doesn't excuse the culprit," Helson said.

"Some cretans will think it does."

Tuesday, 25 December

"Merry Christmas!" While most of London shouted this refrain, a few people retorted, "Humbug." With her German-born husband, Queen Victoria had only relatively recently helped make Christmas a major holiday, as it long had been in Germany. Abberline could remember working as a clockmaker's apprentice on Christmas as a boy, barely noticing its passing.

A man was arrested for stealing a quantity of manure. Many privately felt his detainment was the grossest injustice of the year.

The Ripper remained inactive.

The identity of the murder victim in Clarke's Yard, High Street, Poplar, continued to change. New evidence suggested her name was Rose Millett or Mylett. Abberline was prone to think that Rose by any name was still dead. Her slayer or slayers were free and clues were non-existent; if she had, in fact, been murdered. It was a bleak Christmas for the stout detective. Abberline gave Helson the day off to spend with his wife and children, while he checked in at various stations. Then, with Emma, he went to his sister's for a dinner of oysters on a plate, turkey with chestnut stuffing, ham, goose and quail, brandy punch, mashed potatoes with onions, mince pies, shortbread, crackers to pull, gifts to exchange, and spirits to consume. Through it all, Abberline tried to forget this autumn of agony.

Wednesday, 26 December

"Thank God, we're past Christmas Day and no further word of the Ripper," Helson said in the Professor's parlour.

"I can't understand it," Abberline said, having just left Emma and a stack of boxes they had filled to give to the charwoman and various tradesmen as gifts for Boxing Day. "It just doesn't make sense."

"Perhaps he has gone to America or the Continent, or he's in goal for some other crime."

"I don't know. I just don't know, Joseph." Abberline finished making tea and handed Helson, Smith, Chandler and the Professor cups.

"Sexual," the Professor announced.

Everyone else froze as if the Professor had passed wind.

"Yes, these murders are sexual. Oh, they're perverted and they're terribly abnormal acts, but they are still sexual. The motivation is not blood. It's sex."

The four policemen remained silent.

"The Ripper wants to prove he's superior to mere mortals. He wants to flaunt the moral code and get away with it and, like the man who goes to a brothel, he's excited by the lure of the forbidden. But to him, the forbidden isn't a glimpse of a woman's leg or her nudity or the thrill of illicit intercourse, no, it's something grotesque. It's violating the inner sanctum of her body, getting at and into the womb and then possessing it."

"Preposterous," a red-faced Chandler sputtered, jumping to his feet. "I'll not sit here and listen to this…this…sick…silly…balderdash, poppycock and piffle."

"Oh, sit down, Joseph," Abberline said. "The Professor means no harm."

Chandler was adamant. "No," he proclaimed. "I'm leaving."

The Professor shrugged, politely showed the offended officer out after wishing him a fine Boxing Day, returned and, smiling, said, "I think I said the ideas of this European savant were controversial. Joseph will get over it, no doubt."

"No doubt," Abberline agreed.

"Is all this sex stuff so hard to believe?" the Professor asked, still smiling. "We have well-to-do men who go to the butcher shop, buy a tasty roast, take it home, ream a hole in it with a knife and masturbate into it. We have men who seek to penetrate the anal cavity whether the anus is part of a man or woman— or have a man or a woman stimulate their penis orally. We have men who want to copulate with other men, with animals, even with corpses and, finally, we have the Saucy Jacks. And that should be his name: Saucy Jack. Not Jack the Ripper. This is a laughing madman. He's having fun. He wants to dismantle the object of his desire, to assert his ultimate dominance by boring into the very core of the sexual object, by eating it and such."

The speech left his remaining audience stunned. The Professor plied them with brandy and talked of other things, but he knew they would wrestle with what he had said and do with it what suited their minds best. The self-absent Chandler would reject the entire idea as poppycock. Helson would consider it possible and have trouble making love to his wife tonight. Major Smith would think it over with great care. He might question parts of it, but he would at least see the general logic. Abberline would wonder about his own sexuality, especially given his lack of children, as would all the others except Chandler, but Abberline would, like Smith, see the sense in it. All would be bothered by what the Professor had said. Why shouldn't they be, thought the Professor, it bothered him at times.

Thursday, 27 December

Dinner brought Abberline back to the Professor's town house. Emma was dining with her parents and Abberline had begged off. The Professor eyed Abberline closely as they sat at table.

"Don't let the criticism of the police in the press dampen your holiday cheer, Frederick," the Professor said. "Any large organization suffers such attacks on almost any given day. Put humans together in a bureaucracy and you will have some bungling."

"Have we bungled?" Abberline asked with a wan grin.

The Professor poured a Spanish wine for them both and said, "Not egregiously. But I hope you will take no offense when I say that since half of humans are below average in intelligence, the police force must have its fair share of such individuals to muck up the works."

"More than our fair share, I'd say," Abberline said as he sipped his savory turtle soup.

"To begin with, we tend to blame the foreigner, as if an Englishman could never be the Ripper."

"We do have a long list of Russian suspects. Are we blind to home-grown suspects?"

"Perhaps a touch myopic. It's not just the English; if the murderer was in America, they would think he was an Englishman. If the victims were African, many would think the killer Caucasian, and vice versa."

The Professor's cook brought them roast turkey with chestnut dressing and two vegetable side dishes.

The Professor said, "Leave room for the Citrus ice, it's excellent and next on the bill of fare."

The pair sat and ate for a time in companionable silence, save for the click of their silver utensils on the china plates.

"There's another theory worth considering concerning this Whitechapel business," the aged savant said. Evidently there was something he had left unfinished from last night's evening of shock.

Ah, Abberline thought, the Professor has decided to mix business with pleasure as usual. Abberline would nod, listen and eat a great deal; there were probably another five courses in the offing, if past experience was any guide. The thin Professor would bob, talk and eat little; too fascinated by ideas to eat.

"A German named Richard Krafft-Ebing, actually Baron von Krafft-Ebing to be exact, has written extensively on sexual aberrations," the Professor said. "He completed a masterpiece, *Psychopathia Sexualis,* two years ago and I have just finished reading a copy I was fortunate to abscond with from a colleague."

"I'll let Helson know; have you nicked for theft."

"Wasn't in Bethnal Green; not his jurisdiction. In any case, the bookstores don't stock nearly as many German language books as they should; anti-foreign bias, again. Helson should arrest the booksellers for that grave offense."

"I'll see to it immediately after dessert."

"Krafft-Ebing is an expert on sex and crime and particularly the criminal mind. He's gathered, if not the first, at least the most comprehensive collection of case histories on sexual deviation ever. He cites several cases of interest. There's the girl-stabber of Bozen. He was 30, a soldier, went around stabbing girls in the abdomen or genitals. He preferred the latter. He was eventually caught. Evidently, he experienced a heightened sexual impulse and an increasing intensity of fury during these episodes and only found satisfaction in the thought and act of stabbing females. He'd get the impulse for a few days, enter a confused state which only went away after he'd stabbed some young girl."

Abberline sat in silence as he considered the Professor's words and ate the Professor's fine food.

"The stabbing gave him the same satisfaction as that produced by coitus."

Abberline stopped eating.

"And this was increased by the sight of blood dripping from his knife."

Abberline said nothing for a long silent seven seconds, finally blurting, "Blood lust."

"That was part of it."

"How'd he get that way? People just don't come packaged that way, do they?"

"Difficult to say. His sex drives—if you believe him and there's really no reason to doubt him but some people do—got the best of him at about 10 years of age. He went from masturbation, 'progressed' to violation of immature girls—making them masturbate him and engage in sodomy. Gradually, over the years, he came to think more and more about how pleasurable it would be to stab a pretty young girl in the genitals and take delight at the sight of her blood draining down his knife."

"An obsession?"

"Yes. The German Police found objects of a phallic cult and obscene pictures he had painted of Mary's conception. He was a very peculiar, irritable man. Shy. Fond of women. Moody. Glum. He had become impotent through early sexual excesses. The investigators concluded this predisposed him by continuance of his intense sexual desire and heredity to sexual perversion."

Abberline fell silent again and stopped eating. What the Professor had told him seemed fantastic, but he had seen more than his share of the fantastic in his decades on the streets of the East End.

"This Girl-Stabber of Bozen was caught in 1829, which means he predates our Butcher of Buck's Row by almost 60 years."

"So much for those who are calling our present killer a lone aberration in the history of crime."

"Far from it; even our Bozen stabber is not a lone case. In the 1860s, a sadist in Leipzig was going around stabbing young girls in the upper arm."

"That isn't sexual—the upper arm?" a confused Abberline asked. All this was new and humbling to him; he thought of himself as a man of the world.

"He had an ejaculation each time at the moment of stabbing the girl. A girl's arm was certainly sexual to our Leipzig Lothario."

"But these two didn't cut open or kill their victims?"

"That's true," the Professor noted as he played with the stuffing on his plate with his fork. "Maybe they were caught before their desires deepened and they killed someone, or maybe this kind of disorder is on a continuum. Some men have a mild case of whatever this really is, while others have a more severe form of the same disorder."

Abberline nodded, trying to take it all in as he resumed eating. The last thing he wanted to do was offend the Professor's cook; the man was far too gifted to ever risk losing.

"Perhaps I can sum up Krafft-Ebbing's psychiatric picture of this monster, Jack the Ripper. It would be better, of course, to use the other name this monster used in one of his letters. It's really the important one: Saucy Jack."

"Saucy Jack?"

"It's psychologically more descriptive. Krafft-Ebing would argue that such a sadist as the Whitechapel murderer doesn't get his fun, his sexual satisfaction, from just causing pain and death, like a cat playing with a mouse before killing it. The cat feels nothing for the mouse; the Ripper feels nothing for his victims. The real meaning of his assault is an act of defloration; symbolically, that is."

As the turkey was cleared and the citrus ice brought forth, Abberline was puzzled. "You mean this fiend thinks he's depriving an old whore of her virginity when he carves her up? It doesn't make sense."

"Not to a normal mind, but remember, we're not dealing with a normal mind. The chief wounds are always in the stomach region. Often the deepest cuts run from the vagina to the abdomen. In mutilating boys, these monsters—and there have been others, many others—will even create an artificial vagina with their knife."

"He could have molested a young boy or two then?"

"Quite possibly. And something else—the victim is often killed by means of strangulation. The genitals or sometimes some other parts of the victim are taken away and kept as a sort of trophy."

"It certainly fits everything we know about what the Ripper's done."

"Look for an impotent, quiet, neat, reserved character who may have a history of homosexuality, pedophilia and fetishism."

"God, it's all so close to one particular suspect, except the last three points and those would be kept quiet, very quiet. He did work at a school."

"The young make easy victims. Watch that one closely, ever so closely."

The dinner proceeded to jams, jellies and sweet pickles, followed by fancy cake and preserved fruit, and finally coffee and hot punch. Through it all Abberline was beset with but one name: Montague John Druitt. He would be Krafft-Ebing's candidate, and he would be the young mentalist, Freud's best bet, too. Trouble was; where the hell was Druitt?

Monday, 31 December

On the last day of the dread-filled year, a mist was falling all across the city, laying a carpet of dampness over every crevice and cranny, street and court, row and alley. The rain seemed to merge imperceptibly with the Thames. Out on its slip-slopping waters, just off the Thorneycroft torpedo work's wharf, a little steam launch yawed and pitched, bobbed and rolled its way against the wind-whipped waters and what seemed a stronger than usual current. Swirl after swirl of foam washed over the bow.

"Ain't much more'n a quarter mile now and we kin put in," Skipper Henry Winslade shouted down to his two crewmen.

A chilling breeze blew along the river. It would be good to get back to his warm home to see in the New Year. Winslade spotted a dark form in the water off the prow. He yelled, "There's something in the river."

His number one boatman ran along the side of the boat and prodded the murky waters with a harpoon-like pole.

"I think it's a body," the boatman yelled.

The river craft came to a shuddering halt, its screws twirling in defiance of the currents that threatened to twist the stubby little craft into a senseless whirl of directionlessness.

"Steady! Steady!"

The solemn ceremony of removing a human carcass from the river took time. The bloated, water-saturated, rotting remains were poled alongside the vessel.

"Blimey, 'e's 'eavy."

Amid grunts, groans and scattered curses, the body was hiked, piked, poled, rolled and, in general, wrestled on board.

"Jesus, weighs a bleedin' ton."

"No goddamn wonder. Lookatthis; pockets loaded wit' boulders. Look at the size of that sodding rock."

"Wonder who he was?"

"There's a train ticket here. Return half—bloody hard to read. What's that say?"

"Looks like Hammersmith to Charing Cross. The date's plain enough—December 1st."

"He's probably been in the river for quite a while, I dare say. Bloated enough. Christ, what a mess. The crabs have been at 'im. Any other stuff in his pockets? We'll have to tell the harbour police. They can tell his next a kin."

"Here's a card or somethin'. Maybe a cheque; here's another. Can you make out the name?"

"No, but my eyes ain't what they were. Damn 'em."

"Let me see. . .hm. . .looks like Monta. . .something. . .John. . .Druitt."

Later that day PC George Moulson of T Division (Hammersmith) continued his report to Abberline, Helson and Major Smith at Scotland Yard, "The body was discovered in the Thames near Chiswick. A body search revealed £2 and 10 shillings in gold, seven shillings in silver, 2d in bronze and two cheques drawn on the London and Provincial Bank: one £50, the other £16. Also a first-class season pass on the South Western Railway; Blackheath to London."

"That fits the body being Druitt," Abberline said.

"There was also a silver watch, gold chain with a big spade guinea on it—remember the description Hutchinson gave us, sir, of the man with Mary Kelly?" Moulson asked.

Abberline nodded.

"Also a pair of kid gloves and a white handkerchief. The body was fully clothed. No hat or collar. No papers or letters of any kind. Just four large stones in each pocket of the top coat. No marks of injury, other than crab bites, on the body, which was rather decomposed."

Abberline rose from his chair and said, "Let's contact his family and look over his rooms."

It continued to rain for the remainder of the day. The theatre crowd mourned the passing of comic vocalist H. G. Vance who had died while singing at the Sun Music Hall, Kingsbridge. A woman was found strangled in Poplar. The Royal

Society of British Artists held an exhibition of the best in British oils. Richard Roberts was charged with murder at Merthyr Tydfil. The Royal Theatre put on *The Babes in the Woods*. Henry Sumner, a 27-year-old groom, got a year's hard labour for indecently assaulting a pair of girls: one, 11; the other, eight. Life, good and bad, contented and discontented, continued. Abberline ordered heavy patrols in Whitechapel and Spitalfields for New Year's Eve, as Major Smith did for the City. Neither wanted the Ripper to kill again on the last day of 1888.

1889

Chapter Twenty-Five

Tuesday, 1 January

After a drunk-infested New Year's Eve, London was quiet. Abberline, Smith and Helson descended from a carriage at Druitt's last known address in Blackheath even as Abberline said a silent prayer of thanks that the Ripper had not struck on New Year's Eve. Even though they had searched the rooms before, this time Druitt would not know they were coming.

Using a master key from the building's owner, Smith opened the door to the dead man's flat. The detectives methodically began to search the deceased's rooms.

"When we finish here we'll go over to King's Bench Walk," Smith said as he started to look through a roll-top desk.

"Let's hope we don't have to," Abberline said, starting to inspect the clothes in a wardrobe.

Helson rummaged through a box he had found tucked away in a closet corner. Smith slowly sorted wads of paper onto the desk's fold-out leaf.

"We should also ask his brother if we can search his room in Bournemouth," Helson suggested. "Druitt seemed to stay with his brother down there in Dorset regularly."

As they worked, the morning winter sun glinted faintly through the windows. Abberline turned on the gaslights.

"I learned his estate is valued at £2,600," Smith said.

"A bloody fortune," Helson said as he sorted through a trunk full of summer clothing.

"He came from a well-off family," Abberline said.

It took several hours before the trio was satisfied.

"Well, what have we really got?" Smith asked.

"A great deal and yet not a great deal," Abberline said. "Clothes that could fit those worn by the Ripper as seen by witnesses of varying reliability. Paper that is like that of the Ripper notes, but paper that could be found in every second home in London. A few newspapers with stories about the Ripper, but you'd find the same papers lying around a thousand homes, I imagine. No sign of any red ink or dried blood. No bottles. No sign of any bloodied clothes, stains from bloodied organs or such. The place is remarkably clean and neat, for a bachelor."

"Let's try his office."

As they searched Druitt's chambers at King's Bench Walk, Helson said, "Jack's a crafty one. If Druitt was the Ripper, I doubt we're going to find enough to convict him."

"Maybe not in a court of law," Abberline said, "but we may find enough to know whether to keep the extra patrols in the East End."

Wednesday, 2 January

The inquest into the demise of Montague John Druitt was held as was common at the Lamb Tap public house in Chiswick on a clear, cold winter day. It was revealed that the deceased had left a letter addressed to Mr. Malcolm Valentine, a Blackheath School official, which alluded to taking his own life. The jury returned a verdict of suicide whilst of unsound mind.

Someone muttered, "Those whom the Gods will destroy, they first make mad."

Thursday, 3 January

"The deceased was a gentleman, well known and much respected. He was a barrister of bright talent, of promising future. We can only deplore his untimely end. His loss will be felt."

The coffin creaked against the straps as it sank deeper and deeper into the damp abyss.

"Ashes to ashes. Dust to dust. . ."

The words went on. The handful of soil sprayed in a grainy trickle over the casket. A few wetter grains stuck to the shiny lid standing out like pin-point warts in a field of varnished sheerness.

And then the funeral was over.

The few mourners were gone. Two lonely gravediggers shoveled dirt in steady paced rhythm over the casket until it disappeared beneath the growing, swelling lump of fill. Finally, the cut sods were fitted back over the loose, tamped down earth and only a patchwork plot of yellowing grass marked the spot. A stone would be added once the soil settled.

"I wonder if he really was the Ripper," Helson said as he and Abberline prepared duty rosters for the coming weekend in Abberline's office. The door was open to evict smoke from the coal fire, which had proved recalcitrant in being lit.

"Whether he was guilty or innocent, only God knows," Abberline said. "Maybe the Ripper is Pedachenko or—yes—maybe, Klosowski."

And with the last mentioned name being overheard by the passing desk constable who Coulls now regularly bought pints for, a legend—one of many—that Abberline had always thought Klosowski was the Ripper was born.

It was an austere meeting of top police officers.

"Discreet, the key is being discreet," Monro, Sir Charles' successor as Met Police Commissioner, said as he ran a long thin finger down the assignment lists. "If there are no more mutilation murders, we'll gradually reduce our extra patrols in the East End from 143 to 102 and, if all goes quietly, to 47 in February. First in the parishes outside Whitechapel and Spitalfields, then gradually in those two cesspools. Anyone leaking any of this to anyone—the press, vigilance committees, fellow inspectors, subordinates—will find himself walking nightshift in purgatory 'till Hell freezes solid. I've taken you into my confidence. I expect you to observe that privilege."

Monro paused to cast his large brown eyes around the room, fixating solemnly on each and every man assembled. Abberline stood and prayed he was correct that, with Klosowski or Chapman in America and Druitt dead, the murders would stop. He prayed with great fervor.

"And who knows," Monro went on, "we may even make a dent in the daily dole of theft and mayhem in the East End by keeping extra men on duty there for a time. The Ripper is only one of hundreds of miscreants and villains on those accursed streets."

While he spoke, not far away at Worship Street Court, Ellen Mahoney, 39, an unfortunate, living at a dosshouse in Flower and Dean Street, was charged with failing to provide necessary food and clothing for her infant child, and Henry Yutton and James Davis were convicted of stealing a silver chain from a woman's neck while she walked in High Street, Whitechapel.

Friday, 4 January

Abberline, Major Smith, Helson and the Professor gathered for dinner at Abberline's club.

"Druitt left a note for his brother," Smith said as he held up a copy of a letter. "The brother brought it over this morning. Letter says that 'since Friday,' Druitt felt he was going to be like his mother and the best thing for him was to die."

Abberline nodded. "Druitt's mother was in a private mental home, Brook Asylum, in Clapton, in July. In September she was moved to Brighton. Has melancholia. Sits around, does nothing, totally depressed, might have attempted suicide. Helson and I couldn't even interview her. She's unresponsive and, when she does respond, she's incoherent. Druitt visited her sometime around December 1st or 2nd. One of our men finally tracked her down—on the 4th. We've always been a step behind poor old Druitt."

"He could have hated his mother," the Professor said as he cut a piece off his roast beef. "Could have felt she was responsible for his oncoming madness. And he could have, symbolically, killed her again and again. When he became so afraid and so certain that he was going mad, some part of his mind, some decent sane part, may have decided to end the nightmare forever."

"Murders for months and he only worried 'since Friday'—whenever that was," Smith said as he set the letter on the table and then neatly sliced his baby potatoes into quarters.

"He lost both his parents, in a way, within the past short while," Abberline said. "That may have triggered it. Or it might be more related to dismissal from his job at the school on 30 November for 'serious trouble.' He covered night-time duties at the school, so he may have interfered with a student."

"He's been at the school eight years and trouble only now?" Helson asked.

"Might have been in trouble before, but it's a place for toffs," Abberline said. "Disraeli went there back in 1810. They'd be very hush, hush; wary of news leaking about any mischief that might damage their precious reputation."

Helson said, "He may have committed suicide the day after he was paid off from the job on the 30th, after seeing his mom one last time on the 1st or 2nd."

The Professor paused and shook his head. "In one way, it doesn't fit with my picture of the Ripper."

"In what way?" Abberline asked.

"I can't believe that such an egotistical, grandiose individual would ever commit suicide; no one like him ever would, I wouldn't think, and yet there must be some deep guilt in the Ripper, if there is any humanness in him at all. If there is, maybe he wanted to punish himself. There was that letter we analyzed that suggested suicide by drowning, if he in fact penned that note."

"Was that fellow Galton able to match Druitt's fingermarks with the mark on the postcard?" Smith asked.

"No," Abberline said. "The body was too decomposed. Skin all flayed off. Crabs and water. Maybe someday those science fellows will learn how to get fingermarks off a corpse. Right now they can't and that's that."

"So, what do we have?" Smith asked.

Consulting his notes beside his dinner plate, trying to avoid dripping gravy from the roast onto it, Abberline said, "Druitt was gaunt but had strong arms and wrists. On 9 March 1875, he placed third in a cricket ball throwing event at Winchester with a toss of more than 92 yards. His father, uncle and cousin were all doctors, so he was raised among medical men and medical books, and probably had some medical knowledge. His age fits almost all the descriptions, except Elizabeth Long, who thought the man talking to Annie Chapman was over 40. Long said she didn't see his face, though. Druitt would have been well-dressed, as most witnesses said. He was a bachelor. So he had the strength, confidence, knowledge and presence of mind to have committed the murders."

Consulting his notes, Helson said, "He lived at 9 Eliot Place, Blackheath, a resident master at Valentine's school. But it would be a challenge for him to operate from there since there's no overnight train service between London and Blackheath. The last train to Blackheath leaves London Bridge Station at 12:25 a.m. The earliest leaves Cannon Street Station at 5:10 a.m. The murders were at about 2:30, 3:40, 5:30, 1:00, 1:44, and just before 4 a.m. After the Tabram, Stride and Eddowes murders, he would have had a long wait for a train."

"Druitt's chambers were at 9 King's Bench Walk, near Victoria Embankment, within easy walking distance of the East End," Smith said.

"The killer's movements don't make sense for that address," Abberline said. "After killing Stride in Dutfield's Yard before 1 a.m.one, he walked west to Mitre Square in the City, where, between 1:30 and 1:45 he killed and mutilated Eddowes. If his base was in King's Bench Walk, he would then have continued west, away from police activity stirred up by his crimes and towards his chambers. Instead, he went the opposite direction, deeper into the East End, leaving the blood stained apron piece from Eddowes in Goulston Street to the northeast."

"After the Berner Street murder," Helson said, "he may have been walking in a great circle back towards Kings Bench Walk. Perhaps the City Police were thicker to the west so he decided to head east, then north."

"What bothers me the most is that we can't be sure," Abberline said. "We can't definitely prove that Druitt was the Ripper. Evidence and the Professor's alienist analysis points to him, but far from enough to have ever convicted him. Even if the murders stop, it could merely be coincidence that he died at roughly the same time. It could be him, any of the other suspects or, for that matter, someone we haven't even heard of, and probably never will."

"That's what life is," the Professor said. "No definite endings. Unless you know all the events, emotions and feelings that went into creating a Browning or a Jack the Ripper, a Newton or the Queen, you have no way of judging them and their behavior. We don't know how this or that event will turn out. A father or mother doesn't know what will become of their children. We all have old friends we haven't seen for years and will never see again. We know nothing about what happened to them. You and I don't even know when we are going to die. Life is simply a series of incompletions."

"Is this all there is to it then?" Abberline asked, feeling a great hollowness at what felt like the open-endedness of the investigation. "Will we just keep investigating until the Second Coming?"

"I suppose so," the Professor replied. "Life isn't a play that comes to a nice neat climax. It's more a series of almost unconnected scenes that could end any time or go on almost indefinitely. It's not like a novel or a play, with a definite beginning, middle and end, and there aren't any heroes or stars, or even villains."

"What about the Ripper?" Helson asked. "He's a villain if ever there was one."

"Not really," the Professor said. "Villains are hissed and booed and shooed off stages, but they're still larger than life, like the hero. But Saucy Jack is something smaller. Those who've met him would probably consider him insignificant. He probably appears glib and superficial, with an inability to feel empathy for anyone or anything, and therefore he never feels remorse or guilt. He may, at times, come across as egocentric and, to himself, grandiose; his letters suggest that. If a journalist wrote the letters, then he is a rather perceptive chap. I suspect Saucy Jack is probably impulsive at times, with violent outbursts, which he fights to control so as to appear normal. But his need for excitement will always, eventually, come through. Whatever his makeup, he's not the stuff that great drama is made of. Murderers like Macbeth would have his heart out in a second. No, I'm afraid the Ripper's legend will outshadow his reality, but what I'm most of afraid of is that he'll be followed by centuries of similar insignificant fellows committing horrible murders in a bid to bypass boredom and gain the all-coveted recognition."

"Recognition?" Smith asked, frowning.

"It's as good a term as any. Man has been striving to get ahead since Cain and Abel first set to farming. Some people just have to win."

"Win?" Abberline asked as liveried waiters cleared the dinner plates.

"Yes, win. These murders are motivated by a kind of drive for dominance. A need for mastery, so to speak. Oh, they're distorted and crazy and cruel, but they're still an attempt by one sick sot to assert his individuality, his immortality. Unfortunately, it's in a terrible, terrible way."

"At least he is unique," Helson said.

"I wonder, Joseph, I wonder."

"You mean there is more than one Ripper out there?"

"No, not now. But the conditions that culminated in this brute will combine again to produce more of his kind at some future time, and more investigations rife with mistakes and lost opportunities, a press that sensationalizes every aspect of the murders, and wild speculation about the identity of the killer but, worst of all, more horribly mutilated victims."

Silence descended on the men at mention of this unpleasant prediction.

Saturday, 5 January

The *Southern Guardian* suggested, "Suppose we catch the Whitechapel murderer, can we not, before handing him over to the executioner or the authorities at Broadmoor, make a really decent effort to discover his antecedents, and his parentage, to trace back every step of his career, every hereditary instinct, every acquired taste, every moral slip, every mental idiosyncrasy? Surely the time has come for such an effort as this. We are face to face with some mysterious and awful product of modern civilization."

How prescient the writer and the Professor were proven to be.

Epilogue

As the Professor predicted and *The Southern Guardian* warned, mutilation murder did not end after the Miller's Court horror. At 12:50 a.m. on 17 July 1889, the body of Alice McKenzie, a habitual drunkard and woman of the streets, was found in Castle Alley, Whitechapel. Her throat was severed and there were scratches on her abdomen. The murder had been preceded by a letter signed "Jack the Ripper," which suggested the fearsome siege of slaughter would begin anew. Dr. Bond thought the evidence revealed many similarities with the previous Ripper-discarded corpses. Dr. Phillips did not. There was one thing they both agreed on—McKenzie's throat had been severed by a single cut. This differed from the customary two deep cuts found on past Ripper victims. Phillips summed up the murder in what was, perhaps, a classic comment, "There was no particular skill about this crime except that it showed sufficient knowledge of how to deprive someone of life speedily." Commissioner Monro, fearing Jack the Ripper had returned to work, reinstated extra police in Whitechapel, sending an additional three sergeants and 39 constables into the area. The murder was never solved.

Two months later a woman's headless and legless torso was found under a railway arch in Pinchin Street, south of Commercial Road, Whitechapel. Dr. Phillips, Monro and Swanson did not think it was Jack's work, but Monro sent an extra 100 men into Whitechapel/Spitalfields anyways. The murder was never solved.

Five months later, on 13 February 1891, the body of a pretty young woman was found in Swallow Gardens, Whitechapel. The place was misnamed, being merely a squalid railway arch linking Royal Mint to Chambers Street. The woman was identified as Frances Coles, known locally as Carroty Nell. Her throat was severed and her lower abdomen mutilated. When he discovered Coles as she lay dying, PC Thompson saw a man hurrying away from the murder scene. For the rest of his life he wondered if he could have caught Jack the Ripper if he had chased the man. Regulations required him to summon assistance and then remain at the site of the crime, but he also could not bring himself to abandon the woman, who was still alive, if barely. Afterward, Thompson seemed to sense that the event presaged some evil for him; a premonition he often spoke of. Nine years later, when he intervened in a disturbance at a coffee stall in Commercial Road, he was stabbed to death.

At first James Thomas Sadler was suspected of murdering Coles, but further investigation proved him innocent. Sadler, like Isaac Jacobs before him, was hounded by citizens as interested in finding the Ripper as they were disinterested in justice. On 17 August 1888, Sadler had signed on at Gravesend for a voyage to the Mediterranean in the *Winestead*. He did not return until 1 October, so he was far away on the wine-dark sea when Nichols, Chapman, Stride and Eddowes were murdered. Coles' murder was never solved.

Other women might have been Ripper victims before and after the fall of 1888, including "Fairy Fay" (probably a hoax, since no police record of such a murder can be found), Ada Wilson, Emma Smith, Elizabeth Jackson, and Carrie Brown. Debates continue and probably will as long as the name Jack the Ripper is spoken. The historian and well respected Ripper expert Philip Sugden argued that Annie Millwood, stabbed in the attack on 25 February 1888 and who later died in March 1889, was the Ripper's first victim. The Ripper may have been learning his craft before he moved on to the ferocious but disorganized attack on Tabram in August and his full *modus operandi* in Buck's Row three weeks later.

How many did the Ripper kill? Inspector Reid believed he murdered nine women, Abberline thought the total six, and Superintendent Arnold counted four. Today, five is the most-accepted figure—Nichols, Chapman, Stride, Eddowes and Kelly—forming a canon of sorts, but only the Ripper and the Devil would know, and the Ripper is dead and the Devil never tells.

From the few witnesses, Jack the Ripper was a white male, average to below average in height for the time, in his twenties or thirties, who had a "shabby genteel" or respectable appearance. He may have been "foreign looking," whatever that meant in the East End in 1888. All of the murder sites were within a single square mile and he knew the area well enough to escape in each case, suggesting he was a local man either living or working in the area. Abberline thought the killer had a home, shop or office in the vicinity, since he would not want to be seen in a common lodging house washing blood off his hands. He was probably right handed or ambidextrous, with some anatomical knowledge or skill. He cut out organs quickly in poor light while the risk of detection was high. His motive was not sex in any normal sense, but sexual sadism. Psychologically, he was cool in dangerous situations, a sadist of women, but able to be charming enough to lure unfortunates into dark alleys even after every sane woman feared the Ripper. He probably displayed a diminished emotional response to people and was probably a social loner, quiet and obedient at work. It is unlikely he was married. He probably had a private income or a job with the summer, or at least the last week of August, and weekends off.

The police received more than 320 letters about the murders; 143 naming suspects, of whom 101 were British, 21 European, 6 American, 3 East Indian and 2 Malay. Forty-six percent accused a doctor or surgeon. The letters naming possible suspects and outlining potential theories kept arriving into the mid-1890s.

Suspects for the Ripper continue to be debated. He might have been a complete nobody, never interviewed by the police and never suspected by anyone, then or now. Many, however, have been named as suspects based on various theories. As Abberline said, "Theories! We were lost almost in theories; there were so many of them."

John Pizer, the "notorious" Leather Apron, successfully sued several newspapers for libel since they had erroneously named him as the Whitechapel murderer.

Aaron Kosminski, the lunatic who lived on the streets and heard voices, did not fit the image of the Ripper who could lure women into dark passageways. He attacked his sister with a knife in 1891 and was committed to an insane asylum, where he was a quiet, cooperative patient. Doctors believed him to be no threat to anyone. He died in 1919.

Severin Klosowski (Ludwig Zagowski, George Chapman or George Smith depending on which name he preferred) poisoned three wives and was in London at the time of the murders. Abberline later said of him, "If the theory be accepted that a man who takes life on a wholesale scale never ceases his accursed habit until he is either arrested or dies, there is much to be said for Chapman's consistency. You see, incentive changes; but the fiendishness is not eradicated. The victims, too, you will notice, continue to be women; but they are of different classes, and obviously call for different methods of dispatch." But Abberline was probably in error, his view reflecting the Victorian focus on class. Would the Ripper change from strangulation and dismemberment to poison? Most serial murderers, once they are mature, do not significantly change their method of murder. A sexual sadist would derive far less or at least a far different type of sadistic pleasure from poisoning a victim than by strangling and mutilating them.

The police never found Michael Ostrog, Dr. Pedachenko or Nicholai Vasiliev in London. Later reports suggest that Ostrog was in prison in France on petty charges during the time of the Whitechapel murders. Pedachenko may not have even existed. Later, it was suggested that the Russian secret police, the *Ochrana*, sent Pedachenko to London and that he worked with a woman who distracted the victims as Pedachenko attacked. A second man, Levitski, it was said, kept a lookout and wrote the letters to the press; a rather complicated conspiracy to involve not one, not two, but three people who remained at large throughout the investigations and forever after. *The Star* accused the source of the conspiracy story, a Russian anarchist named Nicholas Zverieff (or possibly he was a German-Swiss named Johann Nideroest) of being a complete fraud. At least he had a vivid imagination.

In February 1895, William Grant Grainger, a ship's fireman, was arrested for stabbing a woman in Spitalfields. The police established his whereabouts during the 1888 murders. He was at sea.

Dr. Neill Cream, found guilty of murdering four prostitutes in London in 1892, is supposed to have yelled, "I am Jack the. . ." as he plunged to extinction. The hangman swore these were Cream's last words. Major Smith, who was by then Commissioner of the City of London Police, still keen of hearing and present at the execution, never heard Cream say a thing. But a newsman in search of a story agreed with the hangman. Cream's claim actually suffered on several points. He killed with strychnine and not a knife. He also did not mutilate his victims. Most importantly, he was incarcerated in the Illinois State Penitentiary at Joliet in the United States between November 1881 and July 1891.

Frederick Bailey Deeming, who murdered two wives and four children in 1891-2, also boasted that he was the Ripper, creating a rumour sufficiently believable to get his death mask displayed as that of the Whitechapel murderer in the Black Museum (the Crime Museum of Scotland Yard). He was never on anyone's list of suspects, except his own. Deeming was executed 23 May 1892 at Swanston Jail, Melbourne, Australia.

Prince Albert Victor, Duke of Clarence, died of pneumonia on 14 January 1892 at the age of 28. He was proven to be outside London during several of the murders.

After the Kelly murder, social reformer Dr. Thomas John Bernardo suffered a swimming accident that left him almost completely deaf. Some believe the murders stopped because Bernardo feared he would not be able to hear anyone approaching if he committed another murder and, therefore, he would be caught. Apart from the complete lack of evidence against him and the difficulty of being Jack the Ripper with a large family and a well-known visage in the East End, given the increasing fury of the attacks, would turning deaf ears to the impulses behind them stop a sadistic serial murderer? What is known is that in 1866 Bernardo founded a charity, which today operates as Barnardo's and runs more than 900 centres for children and young people. Other social reformers also used the murders to lobby for and achieve a number of changes in the East End, including improved lighting, better housing for the poor, and more humane treatment of animals in the slaughterhouses.

The man with the clay pipe Israel Schwartz saw arguing with Elizabeth Stride before her murder was never found.

In July 1889, Abberline relinquished the Ripper case to Chief Inspector Henry Moore, who had no better success than Abberline solving the murders—not that anyone could have done better at the time. The murder investigations highlighted the state of forensic science and police investigation in 1888. Crime scene management was in its infancy. Fingerprinting, which might have helped solve the Ripper mystery, was finally adopted by the English police in 1892. Medicine was still evolving. In relation to the kidney sent to George Lusk, modern doctors know that Bright's disease is unrelated to drinking, and that it is extremely difficult to distinguish a kidney as being from a man or a woman.

The rampage in the autumn of 1888 remains the most profound mystery in the history of English criminal infamy. The murders ended abruptly, suggesting the Ripper died, moved far away, was incapacitated or sentenced to gaol and never released for whatever reason.

Master builder George Lusk, who at one time employed 20 men and specialized in music hall renovations, fell on hard times and declared bankruptcy in 1901. He recovered enough to continue as a builder into the 1910s and keep Lusky and a long line of feline companions in treats.

Colm Coulls never did connect with Catherine McLean. Coulls returned to Canada, only to return to England in 1914 as a war correspondent with Toronto's *The Globe*. He was killed in a bombardment during a battle with no name on the Western Front in 1916.

Aaron Jennings returned to America in 1904. He became a crime reporter with the Chicago *Tribune* and later wrote a column for a national wire service. He married, divorced and remarried. After retiring in 1932, he lived with his second wife in Florida. He died of lung cancer in 1938.

Old Boy Pierce became a prominent London editor in the 1910s. He married, had two children, and died in 1919 from the global influenza epidemic.

The Londoner continued to patronize the city's brothels. In his later years he suffered from locomotor ataxia, a disorder of the lower brain stem brought on by syphilis.

The money for a headstone for Mary Jeanette Kelly was never raised. Since the gravekeeper's records were lost during the World Wars, the exact spot where her last remains decayed into dust is unknown.

On several occasions after he was transferred back to Whitechapel, PC Robert Spicer saw the Brixton doctor accosting women. Each time Spicer sidled up to the doctor and said, "Hello, Jack. Still after them?" Each time the good doctor bolted. In April 1889, Spicer was dismissed for being drunk on duty and interfering with two private persons, probably the Brixton doctor and a prostitute friend—Rosy? One is left to wonder if Spicer drank because he believed he had been deprived of the chance to catch Jack the Ripper.

Inspector John Spratling, who investigated the Nichols murder, boasted that he collected his pension longer than he worked. He died in 1938 at the age of 98.

Detective Inspector Reid attained professional standards in acting, singing and sleight of hand. An aeronaut, a Druid and a detective, the *Weekly Dispatch* called him "one of the most remarkable men of the century." After retiring from the Met, he owned The Lower Red Lion pub in Herne, Kent, worked as a private detective, and led his neighbors in a fight against sea erosion of their properties. He eventually lost his home to the erosion, the last householder to leave the area, and remarried in 1917 at the age of 71, dying the same year.

Inspector Joseph Chandler was demoted to sergeant in 1892 for being drunk on duty. He retired in 1898 and in 1901 was living in Hackney and working for HM Customs. He died in 1923 in Hammersmith.

Major Henry Smith became Commissioner of the City of London Police in 1890, serving until 1901. He was knighted in 1910 and published his memoirs, *From Constable to Commissioner*. He died in 1920.

Frederick Abberline retired from the Metropolitan Police Force in 1892 with 82 commendations and awards, worked for the Pinkerton National Detective Agency and in 1904 retired to Bournemouth. He died in 1929 just three months before his beloved wife of 50 years, Emma.

In April 1890 the last plainclothes officers were finally withdrawn from extra duty in Whitechapel.

Officially Saucy Jack's murders were never solved.

Notes

The preceding manuscript was discovered among the papers of Tod Lachen, a multilingual Scottish merchant trader who lived in London in the 1880s before immigrating to Vancouver, Canada. The original manuscript was written during and soon after 1888 predominantly in Lachen's native language, Gaelic. Lachen spent the rest of his life revising the manuscript as he gathered new information and theories about the Ripper murders.

Since he did not read or speak Gaelic, Lachen's grandson, Dr. David Stevenson Lachen of Calgary, had no idea of the contents of the yellowed, curled and much annotated manuscript he inherited until an elderly Irish-Canadian patient who read Gaelic spotted the manuscript on his office shelf. Dr. Lachen then approached me in 1979 to translate his grandfather's story of the events of autumn 1888, more for the family than anyone else.

The manuscript was far from a clean, typed copy. Handwritten, it bore copious and extensive notes on every available space of paper, as if penned by someone suffering from hypergraphia, as well as containing scraps of paper, envelopes and news clippings about this or that addition, deletion or revision that Lachen was considering when he died in 1938. Having read the manuscript, the Lachen family and I agreed that, given its historical value, the manuscript deserved a wider readership than just the immediate family.

Translation was a challenge given the combination of Gaelic, English (including Cockney and Victorian slang), French, Russian and German the multilingual Tod Lachen used to tell the story. In trying to be faithful to his particular viewpoint, I made few changes in the text except to translate the other languages into English and to "translate" certain colloquial Cockney and 19th Century British expressions that no longer have meaning in English today. I have left some of these quaint expressions in the narrative, particularly when it appeared that a change would result in a loss of the flavor of how Mr. Lachen and his fellow Victorians saw their world; prostitutes are left "unfortunates," an English word Lachen used repeatedly in the manuscript.

In translation, spelling is often an issue. In the case of the spellings of the names of some of the foreign suspects, disagreements have arisen from attempts to make the English translated name sound the same as the name in the native language rather than any disagreement over the identity of the individual, although there are enough of those disagreements as well. Since 1888, disputes have also arisen over the spellings of some place names, such as Buck's or Bucks Row, and even the Anglo-Saxon names, such as Polly Nichols or Nicholls. Spelling in the 1880s was far less standardized than in today's form-filled, computerized world, so different spellings of names are far from a surprise and, more importantly, do no harm to the basic truth of Tad Lachen's story.

I thank the Lachen family, particularly Dr. David Lachen and his sister, Mrs. Leah Gordon, for their trust in employing me as translator for this work. I became interested in Jack the Ripper as a boy, listening to stories about the murders from my grandmother, who lived in London in the 1880s.

Although the events in this story happened more than a century ago, what occurred could have easily transpired yesterday or today, for Mr. Lachen's chronicle concerns the cruelty and stupidity that has always characterized the human species. The story has neither heroes nor villains, just people making mistakes, some erring more than others. His is a story of ineptitude and insanity, error and evil. It is the story of a society attempting to cope with a phenomenon it did not understand, just as every society faces issues that are far from fully understood. It is a story that has resonated for more than a century because it is rife with universal elements and a mystery that will never be solved.

—Neil W. Macdonald

In March 2016, my beloved father, Neil W. Macdonald, died, leaving behind the preceding manuscript. He had been labouring over it for more than thirty years. Far from taking Tad Lachen's story at face value, my father, who had been a crime reporter and then a psychologist, thoroughly checked the vast majority of the facts, events and roles of each individual in the story. Even so, some aspects of the manuscript eluded even his rigorous attempts at verification. Tracking down the identity of the "Professor" proved impossible without a surname. At a time when newspaper stories often appeared without bylines, verifying the existence of several of the reporters proved impossible. The parts from the point of view of the Ripper are, of course, fictional, although based on the best available evidence. I found that in certain cases where a witness provided information to the police but no record existed for which officer took that information, Lachen or my father chose an officer working the case as the recipient. Even so, my father was able to ensure that the vast majority of the story was true or as truthful as human memory, press articles, court reports, psychological theories, and logic can make it.

Just like Tad Lachen before him, my father wanted to ensure that the manuscript included any new revelations or potentially valid theories about Jack the Ripper. Such dedication to accuracy and currency meant that my father never did consider the manuscript complete as he transitioned from being a translator to what amounted to being a co-author. I beg only one thing of the reader; grant my father leniency. If some fact, event or individual's role appears to deviate from what you believe to be true, it is only because he passed from this life before his work was done and his youngest son, with little knowledge of psychology, reporting, serial killers or Saucy Jack, was far from able to check facts as diligently or as well as he could have, and always intended. Just as many believe that death ended the Ripper's reign of terror, death ended my father's quest to tell the story of the murders that, unfortunately, mimicked a lengthening history of such crimes ever since. In fact, my father's extensive records on the manuscript show that he was considering adding footnotes to relate the similarities between the Ripper case and later serial murder cases. I lack the expertise to make such comparisons, but experts will surely note the similarities between Jack the Ripper and the all-too-common serial murderers who have haunted our cities since 1888—and probably long before.

I want to thank all those who went before in trying to identify Jack the Ripper and tell the story of the unfortunates he murdered, especially the authors Tom A. Cullen (*Autumn of Terror*), Donald Rumblebow (*The Complete Jack the Ripper*), Paul Begg (*Jack the Ripper: The Uncensored Facts*), Alexander Kelly (*Jack the Ripper*), and most of all, Philip Sugden (*The Complete History of Jack the Ripper*).

I hope you enjoyed my father's life's work. As badly as Abberline wanted to catch the Ripper, my father wanted this book to be perfect but, like Abberline and his quest for the Ripper, some goals are unachievable no matter how much effort and time are expended on them.

—K. Scot Macdonald

About the Authors

Neil W. Macdonald was a shortstop scouted by the Pittsburgh Pirates. After rheumatic fever ended his baseball dreams, he became a sports and crime reporter for *The* (Vancouver, BC) *Province,* (Eugene, OR) *Register-Guard,* and the (Blaine, WA) *Northern Light,* as well as a book reviewer for *The* (Vancouver, BC) *Sun.* He wrote *The League That Lasted* about the founding of the National Baseball League. With five degrees from the University of British Columbia (BA, MA, MPE), the University of Oregon (MA) and the University of Minnesota (PhD), he was a psychology professor for 30 years, specializing in serial murderers and human sexuality. He was married for more than 50 years and has three children and six grandchildren. For many years, he had a prized Russian blue cat, Amos.

K. Scot Macdonald is the author of five novels and four non-fiction books. Educated at the University of British Columbia (BA), University of Nevada, Reno (MA) and the University of Southern California (MA, PhD), he lives in Los Angeles with his wife, daughter and spoiled wheaten Scottish Terrier, Skye. You can learn more about him at kscotmacdonald.com.

About Kerrera House Press

Kerrera House Press is an independent press dedicated to producing the books you keep. For more information about our books, please visit Kerrera-HousePress.com.

Other Books by K. Scot Macdonald

Non-Fiction

Deadly Dance: The Chippendales Murders (with Patrick MontesDeOca): Tells the bizarre, fascinating story of the murder, attempted murders and arsons behind the Chippendales male exotic dance troupe and their founder, Somen "Steve" Banerjee.

Fictional Deceptions: Using Deception to Baffle, Surprise and Entertain Your Audience: The first book to outline, for writers, the seven principles and ten major techniques of deception with examples from every genre of movie, novel, play and short story, as well as from the realms of espionage, warfare, magic and con games.

Propaganda and Information Warfare in the Twenty-first Century: Altered Images and Deception Operations: Analyzes the use of altered images as propaganda and to support deception operations in politics, diplomacy and warfare. The book discusses the five ways that images can be manipulated, and explains why the United States is a prime target for propaganda and deception operations based on altered images.

Rolling the Iron Dice: Historical Analogies, Regional Contingencies and Anglo-American Decisions to Use Military Force: Shows how leaders use lessons from history to guide foreign policy decision making when the stakes are at their highest.

Fiction

A Plunge into Evil: Travel guide Race Traveler and his peppermint-popping boss, Scarlett Wynter are leading an excursion to Greece, but one of their excursionists dies even before they land in Athens. As Scarlett and Race investigate whether it's a case of death by natural causes or murder, a wallet goes missing and then an excursionist narrowly avoids plummeting from a castle to her death. Is it an accident or attempted murder?

The Shakespeare Drug: Neurosurgeon Julie Stein has discovered a drug that lets her write like Shakespeare, fulfilling her lifelong dream of becoming a writer. The only problem: the drug just might kill her. Will she risk her life for her dream? Her son, with dreams of the NFL, is a little too weak and little too small. What will he do to achieve his NFL dream?

In Justice Found: Los Angeles mediator Arden "Never-Fail" Jeffries seeks justice for the CEO who cost him his retirement and for the burglars who ransacked his home and knocked him unconscious. Will Arden find justice or only injustice?

Mouse's Dream: Commodity broker Anthony "Mouse" Maas is stuck in the Baby Boomer crunch with three free-spending daughters and financially strapped parents. A reunion with his high school sweetheart sparks a plan to bilk his bosses of enough money to settle all his problems and pursue a long-held dream—as long as nothing goes wrong.

The Grizzly Extinction Plot (writing as Liam Shay): Anti-technology revolutionaries are plotting to blow up the Vancouver Grizzlies basketball team, which in their new state-of-the-art arena is having the winningest season in NBA history. Only a romance-novel addicted, Romantic-poet quoting, community college English professor, Sebastian Gianninni, stands in the path of the ruthless New Luddites.

Other Books by Neil W. Macdonald

The League That Lasted: In the early 1870s, baseball was in chaos, mired in mismanagement and corruption. William Hulbert, the owner of Chicago's National Association team, believed that a league run efficiently with honest competition would survive and flourish. Hulbert, relying on his pragmatic philosophy of "molasses now, vinegar later" and working with his prize recruit Albert Spalding, overcame rivals, dissension and corruption to found the National League in 1876.

www.ingramcontent.com/pod-product-compliance
Lightning Source LLC
Chambersburg PA
CBHW020628020726
47494CB00001B/95